Thank you to my editor, friends, and family, to everyone who gives this book a read.
Thank you to all who believe in the magic authors create. You are the fairy dust that makes our imaginations fly.

The Book of Hook

of Hook

AMY COOK

Book cover design by *BespokeBookCovers.com*
Edits by *Jennifer Schultz*
Formatting by *The Nutty Formatter*

CHAPTER 1
EASTON

The air was heavy with the muggy sort of pretense that comes right before a storm. Easton huddled deeper into her soft black sweater. The season's change had been subtle, the brisk atmosphere descending slowly over the city. Tonight, however, left little doubt that fall was nearly upon them.

She was going to have to upgrade to thicker clothes on the next job; the holes in this one were letting in every wisp of chilled air. Sliding a pair of soft leather gloves over her fingers, Easton reveled in the warmth they provided. These gloves were the one splurge she had allowed herself. She spent a great deal of time wearing gloves, they were kind of a necessity in her line of work.

Over the years she had saved money, little bits here and there. She rarely dipped into those precious funds, and those rare occasions were usually for trading in the old rattier versions for new sleeker gloves. Her street family made fun of her for the sheer reverence she showed the things, but she easily traded their jibes for ones of her own.

Everyone had their weaknesses and secret pleasures. If you found those out, found out how to exploit them, you were set for life. Easton happened to be very good at that particular trait. Perhaps not something she should be proud of on the typical morality compass. But in E's world? You needed every advantage you could get, and she was rather fond of her particular arsenal of weapons.

"It's going to storm." Sad's warning cut through the air, the tone ever saturated in that quiet monotone way of hers.

"No it's not. " Noah argued, eyes fixed determinedly forward from where they crouched in the bushes.

"You always say that." Sad muttered.

"*You* always say that." Noah mocked in return.

"Because *I'm* always right!"

"No you aren't."

"Yes I am."

"No you aren't." E rubbed at her eyes. If she didn't step in this fight would continue all night long.

"She usually is right, Ark." Easton stated. "And she's going to be right again."

Noah frowned but didn't argue as he followed Easton's pointed look upward to the starless sky. E grinned and shook her head at the disgruntled look on his face as he scowled at the dark clouded night. It wasn't the first time this particular argument came up, and it wouldn't be the last. Noah had the uncanny tendency to choose the worst nights for a job.

"So what's the job? My legs are falling asleep waiting for your 'genius plan' to hatch." Easton poked his head playfully. Noah ignored the jab, eyes lighting with mischief.

"Trust me; it's going to be epic. All we have to do is get over that fence."

Easton eyed the huge metal fence up the hill from them. It was at least two stories high.

"Uh huh." Glancing at her friend out of the corner of her eye, she took in the full array of excited energy practically popping off of him. "Okay, I'm game. But that's a huge *electric* fence, Ark. Exactly how 'epic' is this plan?"

"*Epic* epic." Noah's assurances always came in levels; Epic, Awesome, Okay, and Lame. If he was adding on an extra epic, he must be pretty optimistic about their chances of success.

"Epic enough to climb into Jurassic Park? Because I am so not ready to be eaten by a raptor, Ark."

"E, you're such a nerd." Noah ruffled the hat on her head, making her bangs fall out over her eyes. Swatting his hand away, she shoved the rogue tresses back under the beanie.

"Don't worry, okay? The electricity will be turned off before we even touch it." He snorted, folding lean arms over his chest. "Raptors."

"Shut up, they're scary."

"Clever girl." Noah teased with a devilish gleam in his eye. Easton rolled her eyes.

A fear of raptors was one of Easton's unfortunate weaknesses. An unfortunate weakness made even more so by the fact that she had fallen asleep in the mess hall once, had a nightmare and screamed out about Raptors eating her. Thus alerting everyone to said weakness. The nice thing about this weakness was the fact that raptors were long ago extinct. Which meant her peers couldn't really use the weakness against her, aside from relentless teasing and lame pranks. But, provided scientists weren't really being all freaky-deeky like on those stupid movies, she was relatively safe. Shuddering E turned her attention back to the fence.

"How do we cut the power?"

"We don't. My connections do." Noah shrugged with a smug expression.

"Who is it this time?" Easton was always impressed by the long list of 'connections' Noah had amassed over the years. Unlike E, who intentionally made rare connections, there were very few people she'd come across who didn't at least hold a grudging respect for the guy.

"You know Joel?" Easton's nose scrunched slightly. Noah grinned deviously, already knowing her answer. "Of course you know Joel. Anyway, he works at that fancy shmancy power place. I made a deal with him."

"What kind of deal?" Her curiosity was piqued. E wasn't above making deals with people if it meant she'd come out on top in the end. Even sleazy people like Joel. That's what a life like theirs taught you. It all came down to how far you were willing to go and how well you played your cards.

"He takes down the electric fence for a few hours, and I promise to take his ugly sister on a date."

Sadie rolled her eyes at Easton, before her pale blue gaze turned glaringly toward Noah. Noah shrugged, not at all affected by Sadie's feminist ideals. Easton grinned at the play between her two best friends. Sadie was deep into women's rights and worth; and Noah was deep into antagonizing Sadie every chance he got.

Mostly the teasing came when the girl had gotten too quiet and was trying to pull one of her invisibility acts. The antagonizing was Ark's way of pulling her back out. It was a game he'd initiated in their youth and it still worked. Easton could never tell if Sadie actually knew that Noah did it out of good intentions, or if she thought he was just being a jerk.

Sadie was a serious one, and she very rarely said a happy word. Growing up she had earned the nickname 'Sad Sadie'. Now for time's sake they typically stuck with just plain 'Sad'. The girl didn't seem to mind overly much. They'd all garnered their own nicknames over the years. Some were just more poignant than others. Noah's nickname of 'Ark', for example, was rather obvious in its origins. Glancing back over Noah's smug face, a thought suddenly occurred to Easton.

"Wait. Ark, you already took Joel's sister out. I remember you took her to that masked kegger last Halloween." Noah's grin held a mischievous undercurrent.

"I know that and you know that. But Joel doesn't know that." Shifting a sly glance towards Sad, he added another barb. "Put a bag over her head and she's not that bad. Like most women." Sadie karate chopped Noah's neck, earning a choked laugh from her victim. E knew Noah hadn't really made that kind of deal with Joel; he just didn't want to share how he'd actually gotten Joel to do the job. He never did. It was one of his weapons in staying relevant to the group, and safe in their lifestyle. That didn't stop E from asking, and it didn't stop Ark from making up ridiculous answers that almost always made Sad angry.

Easton shook her head. She wished those two would just make out and get it over with. The way they picked at one another it was obvious they were crushing, though clearly neither one of them was willing to admit it. It was going on two years now since Easton first caught glimpses of their silent love/hate affair. In fact, E was pretty sure everyone but these two recognized their relationship for what it was. How clueless could two people get?

The wind picked up, tossing Sad's black hair about. Easton was always telling the girl she should tie it back on their little adventures, but Sad was entirely against the idea. Sad insisted that it made her neck too cold. E, however, was certain the girl simply wanted to look cute for Noah, who had a freely proclaimed love of long hair. For her own part, when on missions E always kept her trademark hair tucked under a dark cap. The fiery color tended to be a bit of a tip-off, especially in the dark.

Sad caught her knowing look and sent an ugly grimace in reply. Sticking her tongue out with a grin Easton returned her attention to the darkened landscape before them. A castle-like building rose from the vast expansion of lawn before them, reaching toward the sky like some cursed stone monster of the Dark Ages. If there was ever a candidate for haunted buildings, this would be it. As though accentuating that thought, lightning suddenly lit the sky with an eerily beautiful glow.

"Damn! It had to be lightning. I hate lightning." Noah grumbled.

"Told you." Sad stated.

"As if the place isn't creepy enough already, we're raiding it in the dark. You really picked a winner, Ark." E teased.

"Shut up, E. You'll be thanking me after the haul we get tonight. You'll see." Noah shuddered, looking up at the sky.

"So *you* say." Easton replied in a sing song tone.

"You sure no one's up there?" Sadie whimpered, gnawing at her lip.

"What? Why, you see something?" E asked, crouching lower in the bushes, eyes hunting the darkness.

"No. I just… I can't explain it. I feel like we're being watched."

"No one's there." Noah rolled his eyes, relaxing.

"Sure?"

"Of course I'm sure, Sad. This is hardly my first time in the theft rodeo, you know. My guy over at Delbro's Insurance said this place, and everything in it, is going up for auction tomorrow. They said no one's been living here for months."

"Know the story?" E asked.

"My Delbro guy said the owner was always on time with bills, but about eight months ago the money stopped coming in. Apparently he had a lot of bills. Guy was pretty old so eventually they sent someone over to check if he died. Apparently no one was there. Said the dude just disappeared."

"Disappeared?" Sad asked in a small voice.

"Yep. No one ever answered the door or phone calls, so they hunted down his old staff for clues, but they weren't much help. About nine months ago the old duffer went nutty, just up and fired them all. Booted them out immediately, no explanations or warnings. Apparently they weren't too upset about leaving though. They said he'd been acting more and more wacko over the last few months; hearing voices and seeing things that weren't there." Noah shrugged.

"Think someone offed him for his stuff?" E reasoned.

"That's another weird thing. Delbro's went through the whole place last week. Dude was an OCD freak about cataloguing all of his stuff. They went through his lists, and none of his crap is missing. So, either whoever killed him is really good at covering their tracks, or the dude just went crazy and wandered off somewhere."

"This whole thing is creepy to me." Sad muttered.

"Yeah." Ark shrugged. "Anyway, the banks want to sell it off to help pay his debts. Joel said that's the only reason the fence is even active again; banks activated it to protect the stuff inside until auction day." He shook his head. "Wait till you see what's inside, E! My guy couldn't give all the details of the items, but the way they're protecting it, it's got to be big. Just wait. You're gonna faint." East-on's face lit up, feigning the most dramatic swoon she could conjure.

"Oh so much old guy stuff! I can't wait to get more denture cream!" Giggling, she ducked out of the way as Noah sent a kick in her direction.

"Knock it off you two." Sad grumbled, rubbing at her arms. "When's this going down Noah, I'm getting cold." Noah gave up his playful attack and glanced at his watch.

"Any minute now, we're just waiting on Wiley. He's at the fence line testing for charge. He's supposed to signal when it's clear."

Wiley made up the fourth and final member of their little motley crew. The four of them had been best of buds for most of their childhood. They knew each other inside and out, making them one of the best crews on the streets. As if on cue, a faint glow stick suddenly bloomed to life on the hilltop, waving in the air to signal. Noah grinned like the Mad Hatter.

"Right on time. Come on!"

Shoving through the bushes he yanked his mask down, grabbed his empty duffle and slunk along the well-manicured lawns. Easton scrunched her nose at Sad before pulling the beany down into its full length ski mask and quickly followed Noah up the hill. Wiley's bulky form came into view, lounging lazily in front of the fence, glow stick still in hand.

"It worked?" Noah whispered, as though he needed a verbal acknowledgment to his plan's actual success. Not that he would get one, not from Wiley.

As far as they could tell, Wiley was mute. He'd shown up at the orphanage at nine years old, bruises all over his neck. They'd never heard him say a word. Wiley got his name from the cartoon character Wiley Coyote.

When he first moved in, Wiley spoke through little notes that he scribbled down and showed you. He wouldn't tell anyone his real name. Eventually he learned sign language, but since most of the foster kids weren't around long enough to bother learning, he still had to use notes with them and the nickname stuck. Probably because of his condition, Wiley was the only one that hadn't been constantly in and out of foster homes. No one wanted to take on the extra work or stigma of learning how to communicate with a mute kid.

Wiley shrugged with a bored nod, showing Noah the readings on the instruments in his hands. Noah waved them away, staring up at the fence with a dopey grin.

"You know I can't read that mumbo jumbo, Wi."

Rubbing his hands together Noah held his palms just over the fence, hesitating, weighing his fear of electrocution with his faith in the 'epic' plan. Wiley sighed, sending Easton a knowing look. E grinned devilishly before giving Noah a shove. The guy squeaked out an exclamation of fear as he stumbled full-bodied into the fence.

"What the hell was that E? What if that fence was still on?" Noah stumbled away from the metal barrier, face pale from the scare. Easton smirked, pointing at Wiley, who had been leaning against the fence since their approach. Ark's brow scrunched.

"Oh. Right." He cleared his throat, blushing slightly at his behavior. "Still, wasn't nice." He mumbled. Shaking out his shoulders Noah grabbed the fence, wedging his tennis-shoe-clad toes into the chain link and starting his way upward.

"Loot winner doesn't have to find lunch for a week. Don't bother trying to keep up guys, because I'm gonna win." Ark challenged, scaling the fence quickly. Sadie grumbled about getting blisters and started her slow climb.

Wiley motioned toward E, his hands gesturing his plan. E eagerly rubbed her hands together. Wiley answered with his own broad grin stretching the fabric of his mask. Crouching and linking his large fingers together, he nodded. Easton strode a few yards away, digging in for a good sprint. Pushing off the ground she sped across the ground, leaping to press her right foot into Wiley's palms. She reveled in the rush sent to the pit of her stomach as Wiley expelled a silent grunt of air, tossing her upward. She soared past Ark, grabbing ahold of the fence and scaling the last few feet like a spider.

Throwing a leg over the top of the fence she quickly descended, Ark's grumbles sweet music to her ears as he moved faster to catch up. She leapt the last four feet, immediately racing onward the moment her shoes touched grass. Reaching the walls, Easton pressed against them, slipping along the smooth surfaces until she hit the main door. Noah was only moments behind her.

"Cheater," he whispered, twisting the top of her hat so the whole mask went askew.

E swatted his hands away, shuffling the eye and mouth holes back in their rightful place. Her hair was going to be a brutal rat's nest by the time she got home. Wiley came trotting up next, lithely sliding into their hidden corner. He destroyed every myth about big men and their inability to move gracefully. Wi was easily one of the stealthiest members of their team. He may as well have been a shadow.

"*Should have tossed Sad up, too*" Wiley signed in exasperation.

"Tossing Sad? When hell freezes over, maybe." Noah snorted.

Sad would rather choke than have any guy do something for her that she could do herself. It took her five minutes, but she finally caught up, out of breath and in a bad mood.

"Should have just cut the stupid fence open." Lock picks in hand the girl sulked toward the doors.

"You know the rules; in and out with as little evidence as possible." Ark smirked at her back as she huffed in response.

Within seconds Sad had the door open and was moving on toward the alarm system on the wall. Even with the power off, the alarm had a silent back-up to worry about. But soon that was also dismantled, and the bundle of picks and tools carefully stowed away in the pouch at her side, a small secret smile on her lips.

Easton was always in awe at how swiftly Sadie handled security. She'd had a knack for B&E from day one at the orphanage, which for Sad, was about the age of eleven.

She hadn't talked about her past much, but Easton and Noah had eavesdropped on the orphanages manager once, overhearing his conversation with one of the live-in attendants that made it pretty obvious Sad's past hadn't been fun and games. He had made it clear that they needed to keep an extra eye on Sad because she'd been living alone on the streets for years. Stealing whatever she needed or wanted was as natural as breathing for Sad. They hadn't wanted her disappearing off the grid again, or ending up back in juvie.

Picking locks and dismantling alarms was about the only time E ever saw Sadie with a smile on her face, despite all the years they'd known each other. It transformed the girl's features, and in that split second Sad always looked like the version of beauty she could be, if she were a happier person. But growing up with their particular brand of lives had a way of sapping all those illusions of happiness from a person.

"Everyone sync your watches." Noah pressed the fabric back off his face and the others followed suit as they ensured their watches all matched timing.

"We have exactly one hour to sack this mansion and be out. Split up, we'll meet back here at 11:45. Remember, anything we take we have to be able to get up and over that fence again. And we have to be on the other side before midnight."

Everyone nodded and silently split off into their different directions, Easton taking the third floor. She clicked on her flashlight, yanked the black duffle around from back to front for ease of stashing, and started perusing the layout.

Lightning flashed through the massive windows of the mansion, lending eerie details to the majestic setting. Noah hadn't been joking when he said the old guy had expensive taste. Everywhere she looked there were fancy knickknacks, china vases, crystal candlesticks, gold gilded paintings, expensive tapestries. E liked to case out her area before deciding on which items would get her the most payout for the work put into carrying it out.

She shivered as the glow of her flashlight shifted across a huge marble bust of some dude with a crazy mustache. She cautiously walked closer, leaning toward the face to get a better look. Whoever made this thing had a lot of skill at realism; too much skill for her comfort. The statue's eyes looked so realistic it felt like they would follow her throughout the house.

"*Eaaaaston.*" A whisper floated to her ears on a chilled breeze, and Easton's heart lodged in her throat. Spinning around she shone the light in every direction, waiting.

"Real funny, Ark. But Raptors don't talk!" Easton called out in a hushed shout. She waited for several agonizing minutes, yet no reply came. Swallowing hard E scowled at the bust to her side, annoyed that it had spooked her into imagining things. E was big on not being afraid of the things that go bump in the night. She prided herself on her nerves of steel. Yet something about this house felt off, felt wrong in such a way that she couldn't ignore the constant creep of goose bumps skating along her flesh. The sensation that someone was watching her.

"*Eaaaaston.*"

"Holy freaking crap on a stick!" Easton gasped, swinging the light back across the hallway. The hushed whisper came from all around, no particular source making itself known. It was like the voice came out of thin air. And something else had been very apparent this time. The whisper was distinctly female.

"Sad?"

Easton whispered, instincts warring with the word the moment it left her lips. Sad was not a pranker. No matter how mad she got at someone, she never stooped to pranks. It just wasn't her thing. Yet, aside from Easton, Sadie was the only other girl in the house. A creak from down the hall to her right startled an embarrassing squeak from E. The flashlight swung to land on a doorway, the huge wooden portal slightly ajar.

Easton swallowed hard. That door hadn't been open a minute ago. She knew it hadn't been. Easton also prided herself on being aware of everything around her, their position and layout, at all times. Especially doors. Open doors creeped the hell out of her. Anybody or anything could walk through without any warning. And she *knew* this door hadn't been open when she first walked down the hall.

Easton bit her lip, staring hard at the door, waiting. An internal voice of warning kept screaming at her to leave, to back away and find everyone else. To get out of this friggin' zoo while she still could. Going against every survival instinct in her body, E did something she rarely had. She ignored the internal warning. Ungluing one foot, E took a step forward, the light still firmly pointed at the offending doorway. A second foot followed. With each step, her temper rose.

Easton James didn't back away from anyone. Had it been a crazed animal, or the building threatening to fall in on her head, she would be halfway down the stairs by now. Crap like that wasn't worth the risk. But people? Easton didn't fall prey to the pranks of others. She didn't show fear or weakness to anyone.

Clearly this was someone who knew her, someone who wanted to make a fool of her. For all she knew, it was a competing band of thieves that was trying to steal the loot from under them. The place was big. They could have climbed the fence at the back of the property and snuck in just like Noah's group had. Joel had a big mouth. Who's to say he didn't share out the info on their target with a competing guild?

Anger overwhelming any fear she'd felt moments ago, Easton moved swiftly toward the door. Shoving it open, she swung the light around with an angry shout.

"Who are you?" Her voice echoed in the vast room, the only reply she was to receive. She was very much alone, in a room packed to the gills with books.

"*Who are you?*"

The whisper came at E's back, from the blackened hallway. E spun to an empty, oppressing darkness. Thousands of tiny goose bumps erupted across her skin, carrying a sickening feeling of knowledge with its passing. This wasn't right; in fact, it felt entirely unnatural. E swung about to slam the door shut. Breathing hard she grabbed a nearby arm chair and shoved it in front of the door, quickly backing a safe distance away.

"What the hell, what the hell, what the hell?" E whispered over and over to herself. The light stayed fixed on the knob as she continued her retreat, watching for the telltale jiggle of someone following. Bumping into a table, she grabbed hold of a lamp as it wobbled from the force of impact. Hefting it in the air like a makeshift weapon Easton stood frozen in place, eyes never leaving that knob.

Nothing happened. Eventually her arm began to ache from the weight and awkward grip on the lamp currently held over her head. She wasn't sure how long she'd stood in one place, but it felt like an eternity. Risking a glance at her watch, E bit her lip in frustration. Sometime during her freak out, the face of the watch cracked, breaking it. Mumbling a curse to herself E watched the door for a moment longer before sweeping with the light. A grandfather clock to the far right read 11:00 pm. E swallowed in relief. At least that thing worked. Her gaze snapped back to the door, waiting.

Nothing came through, and with each shallow breath, E felt embarrassing reality seep back into her brain. Throw in a couple of creepy statues and whispers, and Easton James turned into one big baby. Whoever had been playing games with her head had obviously gotten the reaction they wanted and then left. Likely with a video of her that was about to be posted on YouTube, white-faced and shaky as she slammed the door against a whisper.

With a frustrated growl Easton placed the lamp back on the table, squared her shoulders, and refused to look at that stupid door until she was done getting some goods. As she pulled her hand away from the cool metal lamp, her fingers trailed across an oddly textured item. Shining the light across its surface, Easton found her attention riveted to a new source of interest.

"Peter Pan, the Boy Who Wouldn't Grow Up." She whispered, fingers slipping across the indented title on the worn book.

Thunder rumbled through the marbled floor at her feet and her eyes quickly shifted to glance at the door once more. Gritting her teeth at her reaction, E carefully picked up the large leather-bound book and cradled it to her. She couldn't help it. Drawn to the book like a moth to the flame, E held the book in one arm, the light falling across the pages as she opened the cover.

So enamored by the treasure she held, E ignored the cool breeze that flitted across her skin, raising a shiver in its passing. Beautifully ornate paintings met her gaze from the open cover, the colors popping with a nearly metallic sheen as the light fell across it. Easton's lips parted in wonder as the painting seemed to shift on the page the harder she stared at the details.

"You walk the plank of death!"

The harsh whisper sounded just at Easton's ear, the breeze again shifting across her skin, much like breath. She gasped, swinging about in panic. Someone was there; she couldn't see them, but there was no denying it this time. And whoever it was, they were dangerous. She could feel it in her bones. This time, Easton didn't wait for a confrontation; she didn't set about hunting down the source. Stuffing the book in her duffle she sprinted for the door, shoved the chair out of the way, and yanked at the knob.

The door moved slowly, suddenly ten times heavier than it had been when she first shut it, as though she were pulling against an unseen force. Finally fighting it open enough to squeeze through, she ran down the hallway at top speed, not stopping even when she hit the foyer. Noah, Sad and Wiley looked up at her in surprise as she stampeded past them.

"About time!" Noah laughed. "I just made my last trip over the fence. We were about to call out a search party." Easton didn't stop to explain, didn't stop long enough to think of the fact that her team was preparing to leave, that an hour had somehow flown by in what should have only been 15 minutes. She didn't even stop to think about how close she had come to being trapped in that place, locked up behind an electric fence powerful enough to kill with a single touch.

All she could think about was the voice's warning, the way she could have sworn she felt very real lips brush her skin as it hissed in her ear. Scrambling over the fence, she kept running until she reached the safety of the bushes they had hidden in earlier. Yet even there, she still felt the foreboding presence of eyes watching her from the darkened windows in the building. Unable to sit still, E paced back and forth, wishing her friends would run faster.

"Hot damn, what got into you?" Noah snickered as he got near. "I know that fence gave you the Jurassic creeps, but we still had fifteen back-up minutes to get over it before power went back on. We could have grabbed a couple more things even and been fine."

Wiley hit Noah in the arm, silencing him. Easton's gaze shied away from her friends, knowing that piercing brown-eyed expression all too well. Wiley was onto her.

"*What happened to you in there?*" He signed. Suddenly Noah and Sad's attention honed in on her too.

"Yeah, you're right Wi. She's really pale. More pale than usual, anyway. What happened in there, E?" Noah pressed.

Easton pulled off her gloves, tossing them in the duffle before shifting it behind her. She pulled her sleeve back to show them the broken watch, hoping that would explain her panic to get out of there. Dizziness washed over her like a wave. The watch was fine. Not a single crack in the glass, the hands happily ticking away fifteen minutes from midnight. Was she going crazy?

"E?"

"Nothing happened, I'm fine. Drop it." She yanked her sleeve back down.

"Like you just dropped your glove?" Sad's brow rose, pointedly staring at her. Easton looked at the ground, swiping up the glove in a panic. She would have very nearly cried if she lost that thing.

"Something *definitely* happened. She dropped her precious glove and didn't even notice. She's falling apart." The girl stated factually.

"No I'm not."

"Something spooked you." Sad reiterated.

"Shut up, Sad, I'm fine!" E growled, still feeling antsy and more than eager to get away from the place. "I just didn't want to get barbequed is all. Now, let's get out of here. I'm hungry."

"No wonder she's angsty. We all know how E gets when the blood sugar drops." Noah shook his head, a self-satisfied smirk on his face as he turned back to the mansion. "But man, what a heist! This one'll go down in the guild record books."

Wiley still stared at her with that look in his eyes, and she offered him a negligent shrug. His frown deepened and E knew he'd be watching her carefully for a while. Suddenly lightning flashed, and Noah jerked back in shock.

"Whoa, what the…" Noah muttered shakily. "Was someone else in there with you, E?" E froze, attention snapping to him.

"Why?"

"Your low blood sugar must be contagious. I swear I just saw some lady up there in that window." What little blood that was left in Easton's head dropped to her feet, leaving her light-headed.

"Where?"

"Up there, in that window on the third floor. You had the third floor right?" He didn't wait for Easton to confirm or deny. "It's probably just my imagination. Place creeped the hell out of me. But, there was a flash of lightning and *boom*, there she was." Easton chilled to the marrow, looking at the window that she imagined to be exactly where the library was.

"Weirdest thing; I swear she was dressed like one of those elves in Lord of the Rings." Immediately E's companion's relaxed, the frightening moment debunked in their minds by Noah's statement. Sad rolled her eyes.

"Oh hell, save us from your elven fantasies!" A new set of lights caught their attention. Red and blue flashes revolved in the night, ascending the hill towards the mansion, signaling the arrival of a very real threat.

"Cops! Go!" Noah hissed, crouching low to the ground as they scurried for the shadows. They watched for a few minutes as flashlights swept over the expanse of lawn, before moving into the building.

"I think we're good." Noah sighed in relief. "Damn Joel must not have covered his tracks good enough. He said no one would even know the power was down. Good thing E booked it out of there so fast, or we'd be screwed. Joel's gonna get a visit from me tomorrow."

Noah swore darkly. Ark could be pretty scary when he wanted to be, though it was a rare thing to see. His eyes shifted toward Sad, the frown of his lips lifting to mischief, the dark moment passed.

"I swear I really saw an elf, though."

Sad groaned and turned on her heel striding down the street. Noah quickly followed to explain in further detail what he loved so much about the elves, just to tick her off. Easton's attention shifted from the cop cars, toward the third floor. She stared up at it with a sick sort of fascination, willing the storm to give her just a glance at the apparition. If nothing else it would give her the proof that she wasn't simply crazy, or a total wimp. Wiley nudged her with his elbow, eyes concerned. She waved him away.

"I'm fine, it's nothing. Let's get some food." Wiley shook his head but didn't press the matter. It wasn't until they were on the subway, safely traveling the opposite direction of the mansion, that Easton finally started to feel some relief from the woman's gaze.

CHAPTER 2
EASTON

"You're seriously going to wear those huge fake elf ears?" Sad chuckled.

"It's cosplay, Sad. You gotta look the part."

"Whatever. If you're going to waste your hard stolen money on a ticket for that convention, you might as well splurge some of it on ears that actually look somewhat realistic. That's all I'm saying."

Forming the tail end of their group as they walked down the abandoned, dimly lit subway corridor, E listened to her friend's conversation with only distant attention. Stealing another glance at her wristwatch, E frowned in annoyance. It had been dark, she was spooked; she supposed it was altogether possible to have mistaken the watch being broken. Maybe she'd gotten spider webs on it and confused that for cracks in the darkness. And the grandfather clock in the library…it may have been ticking, but that didn't mean it was actually functioning properly. But was it really possible for her to have passed all of that time, in the matter of what felt to be only a few minutes? Forty-five minutes in that house gone, just like that?

"We should go through our stuff before we get inside. I want to see what we got so I can decide what I want to petition for." Noah's voice filtered through her ears. E's attention snapped back to the conversation, and for what felt the hundredth time that night, she felt dizzy. Biting her lip, E shifter her duffle to the front and dipped her hand inside. The leather cover of her one and *only* conquest met her fingertips.

What would they say when they realized she'd only grabbed a stupid book? What would she say when they asked what she'd been doing for 45 minutes, besides wasting valuable snatch and grab time by reading a kid's book? Her fingers smoothed across the cover again. As much as she wanted to hate the thing for her stupid mistake, she couldn't. It was too precious.

Which is why E secretly tucked the book into a broken part of the wall while her companions continued down the corridor, oblivious to her betrayal. She stepped back to ensure the book was safely obscured from view, so no one would swipe it before she could return for it. It was precious to her. So precious she would rather her team members thought she brought nothing back, than hand the book over to the guild.

"E, what are you doing?" Ark's voice echoed over the concrete walls, jerking her attention away from the broken wall she was absentmindedly caressing just now. E took several hasty steps away from the wall, trying to not look guilty, trying to play off another moment of stupidity. They stared at her when she reached their sides, no one saying a word.

"What?" She frowned grumpily.

"I said we need to compare what we each got. It's my turn to petition and I want to see what we got."

"Right, got it."

"Then stop groping the walls and dump out your bag. We're late enough as it is, they've already started." Only then did the noise and ruckus of the guild register in E's ears. Noah hated being late. It was one of the little quirks that made him who he was. Of course, being late for the Gathering made him twice as nervous as being late for everything else.

"It's not a big deal, Ark. We'll just slip in the back and act like we've been here the whole time. No one will notice." Easton smiled with a false bravado she didn't feel, patting his shoulder. Inside she felt anything but confident.

"Fine whatever, just hand over your bag so we aren't any later."

E bit her lip as she hesitated. No point in delaying the inevitable. E pulled the strap over her head and silently handed it to Ark. Ark blinked at the weight of the bag. Unzipping it, he stared inside for a long moment. His eyes rose to meet hers, understanding passing between them.

"It's empty."

"Yeah."

"We don't have time for games, E."

"No joke."

"You were in there for 45 minutes. Nearly an entire hour, but you didn't grab anything? What'd you do, fall asleep?" Noah blinked owlishly, anxiety splashing across his face.

"Not exactly…" E swallowed, mind rushing. The words came without her thinking them. "I passed out."

"*Passed out as in literally passed out?*" Wiley signed in concern.

"Yeah. I guess my blood sugar issue got a little out of hand this time. That's why I ran out of there so fast. When I woke up, I was disoriented, didn't know what time it was and panicked."

Ark stared hard at her for a long moment, and E fought to keep her expression focused. He gave a simple nod, and then without skipping a beat, all three of her friends dove into their own bags and divvied out enough items to make up for her lack. Easton bit her lip, guilt eating away at her stomach.

Her friends always had one another's backs; it was how they had survived so long. The fact that Easton hadn't gotten her fair share of the loot would put them all at a disadvantage, the amount being lower than what was demanded of their high-specialty team. Yet here they were, eagerly dividing out what they had to cover for her lack, not even the slightest hesitation on their part. Easton hoped the sheer value of what they had gathered would be enough to make up for the lack of numbers. Items divided equally, they cracked open the door and slipped into the back of the gathering room.

"Compass team! You're late!"

The shout rang out over the din of chatter, and suddenly the room fell silent. Noah cringed, and Easton sent him a wince of apology. They'd chosen their team name when they first joined Jag's thieves. They picked 'Compass', because the first initials of each of their names formed the four points of a compass. It also kept their group nice and small, just how they liked it. A small black compass adorned the inner wrist of each Compass member, visually linking them together. Every team had some sort of marker like that; it let other street rats know where and who they belonged to.

Slowly they lined up to face the imposing figure that strode toward them. Nearly the same hulking size as Wiley, calling Jag imposing was about the only way to put it. Also like Wiley, no one knew Jag's real name.

He had a self-appointed nickname they were all supposed to call him. 'Jaguar'. Because he thought he was a freakin' wild cat or something. Easton just thought it was a cheesy self-posturing effort to a claim of power. Words were powerful, but only if you knew how to use them properly. And Jag was anything but smart in the literary department; smart like a shark maybe, but not smart in any of the ways that would impress E.

Motioning them to move forward, he waited as they deposited their individual bags of loot on the floor. Jag sauntered toward the pile, crouching to dig through it himself.

"They're from the Wisner mansion. All high quality stuff." Noah stated a bit shaky in the delivery. Noah was not a huge fan of being in Jag's presence. "Fine china, gold, silver, crystal and all that good stuff."

"The Wisner mansion?" Jag looked up at Noah, no less imposing for his lowered physical position. "That's supposed to be impossible to get into. A team tried it six months ago and had two members end up in the hospital."

"It was pretty easy actually. Cake walk." Noah preened.

Jag stared at him for a long moment, before turning back to the pile. He frowned at it, clearly disliking something about it.

"Not much here. But if they're all tagged as high as you say, the price alone will cover for the small amount; this time."

"Wait, there's one more thing!" A small voice called out from behind them. Easton felt a very real shiver skate through her body when she saw Alan running toward them with her book in hand. She fought the urge to yank the book from his scrawny arms when he scuttled past her.

"I saw her hide it in one of the broken walls outside. She was trying to keep it for herself."

E glared the sneaky creep down. He was always lurking in the shadows and following people around, eager to tattle on them to Jag for his own gain. Alan grinned back at her, though she noticed he edged a little further back behind the protection of Jag's body.

Jag grabbed the book, and holding it by both covers shook it upside down. E winced at the rough handling. When nothing fell out, his dark eyes pinned her in place.

"What the hell's this?"

"A book." She stated.

"No kidding, dipshit. Why were you hiding it?"

"Because I wanted it."

Her friends stiffened, Noah's lips moving in a silent prayer, a plea for her to shut up. Easton ignored him, standing her ground and hoping she wasn't digging her grave. Jag's eyes shifted towards her, narrowing with suspicion.

"You know the rules. Everything gathered is brought to the guild. One member of your team gets to petition for something to take as bounty, the rest of it goes to the guild." Jag's attention shifted to the rest of the team. "Whose turn is it to choose?" E could feel Ark's hesitation, before clearing his throat.

"Mine."

"Did you know she hid this?" Again Ark hesitated.

"No."

Jag's inscrutable gaze shifted from E to Noah and back, gathering the discord and filing it away.

"Alright, E. What's so special about this thing that you tried to steal it, not just from the guild but your own team?"

"Nothing. It's just a book."

"Why would you grab a book unless it meant something? You

realize I could punish your whole team for this, right? I could with-hold the right to petition for bounty. As it is, your team's going to have to be on lockdown for three or four days. Maybe even a week, whatever it takes until I've decided you've been punished enough." He drank in the dismayed expressions of her teammates.

"Your team's going to be awful hungry for a while, because of your choice. So, why risk your team members, if it's just a stupid book?" He looked at the book, hefting it in his hands to test the weight. "Thing is so massive it probably took up most of the room in your bag. Huge waste of space that could have been used toward other things, E. Bet the rest of the team had to make up for you, too." She frowned at him, hating his full attention on her, hating how right he was.

"I like to read. There isn't enough crap around here to read. No biggy."

"Maybe." His tone was reasonable, but Easton wasn't the slightest bit fooled. She knew he'd found a nitch in her armor and he was going to dig until she bled. "Of course, I hear there's this place, great big huge building full of books called a library. And they just let you read them…for free and shit." E clenched her jaw, refusing to rise to his bait.

"So maybe this book is worth more than you're letting on. Maybe it's a collectible. An old fart like the Wisner mansion prick had to have a whole stash of dusty expensive books lying around. This thing could be worth thousands. I think it would be best for us all if we added it to the guild's collection. Don't you?"

She grit her teeth in an effort to hold the words back. The smart thing to do here was allow Jag to have the book, to pretend like it never came into her possession. She was smart, she knew this. Yet somehow she couldn't let him take it. Whether it was from the ordeal of her ghostly encounter, or from her own personal connection to the book, E couldn't give it up. Besides that, E had never been one for backing down.

"It's mine. I earned it."

"You earned it. You *earned* it." Jag mocked her angrily, voice growing with each word so that everyone in the room could hear.

"You *stole* it. And you stabbed your team in the back to do it, too." E kept her eyes averted from her team, refused to see the expressions of betrayal and anger she knew would be waiting there.

"So, what's the big deal E? Like you said, it's just a book." He roughly opened the cover, thumbing through the pages. "Peter Pan, the boy who wouldn't grow up." His voice was raised in a high pitched syrupy octave as he circled her, reading from the pages. E cast her eyes downward in anger when the rest of the people in the room giggled.

"It's a kiddie book." He laughed, earning the chorus of laughs from the rest of the thief's guild around them. "So what's the issue E, having bad dreams? Need a beddy-bye story to help you sleep?" He paused, leaning in to leer over her shoulder, goosing her in the process. "I have some better solutions than a book for that problem!"

The room burst into another round of jeers. Easton's chin rose in defiance, refusing to give him any sort of reaction that might encourage his playing to the crowd. When she didn't so much as flinch at another pinch to her backside, Jag straightened, face hardening once more.

"Fine. I'll make you a deal." He leaned closer, speaking for her ears alone. "I'll give you the book if you give me what I want in return." Easton's eyes flew to his. "Yeah, you know what I want. It's just that simple."

"No."

Jag hissed a curse, like the word was poison to his ears and backed several steps away. The skin of his face heated, and she knew that she was fanning some dangerous flames. Jag had anger management issues.

"What's the matter E, I thought this book was so important to you. You *earned* it after all. You think you're better than all of us, more deserving than the rest of your family. So do what you gotta do to take it!" Jag stalked around the circle of guild members formed around the compass team, looking to the crowd for a boost to his declaration. They didn't disappoint, jeering at her and egging him on.

"Forget it. I don't want it anymore."

"What?" Jag's voice dropped low with deeper rage as he turned toward her. "Why not?" When she didn't reply Jag got up in her face, eyes burning. "Why not!"

"Nothing is worth making a deal with you."

Her quiet spoken reply was like a slap to his face. He pulled back sharply, one hand rising to grip the fleshy lobe on his ear, tugging it repeatedly. This time Easton did flinch. She knew that reaction well. It was the precursor to one of his temperamental tantrums, the warning sign that the dude was off his rocker and just about to show you how far gone he was.

Gripping the book he stared down at it. His hands clenched, the leather binding creaking under the pressure. The atmosphere of the room was tense, every person in the room holding their breath, leaning forward in anticipation of what would happen next. Would he destroy the book, rip its pages to shreds right in front of her? Would he slam it across her face?

And then just like that, he pulled away from the brink, face breaking out in a forced, eerie grin.

"Good. I'll sell it, then. Now let's eat, I'm starved!" He turned and walked into the crowd that quickly enveloped him in cheers and sickening adoration. Easton released the baited breath trapped in her chest, muscles loosening.

"One day he's gonna bust you in the nose." Noah muttered and Wiley grunted his agreement as they brushed past her. Noah paused at her side. "Next time you decide you need a book, go to the library. Save the starvation and heart attacks for another time." She watched their forms retreating toward the dining hall. Noah was right. That had been a close call. But then, they all were, weren't they?

One day Jag would lay into her like he did to almost everyone else in this place. She'd have black eyes and a bloodied nose to show for her rebellions. In truth she was surprised it hadn't happened yet. In a small sick way she almost felt the need to push the envelope every time, like she wanted him to snap and finally hit her. At least then she would know what to expect from him. At least then, maybe she would have the guts to leave for good.

She knew that wasn't healthy thinking. She'd been through enough abusive foster homes and foster therapist offices to know that it wasn't. She'd considered leaving and striking out on her own thousands of times. And yet she was still here.

Because at the end of the day the guild was her home, her saving grace. The guild had pulled her off the streets, offered a safe haven for her shattered soul. And at the end of the day, it was still Jag that had found her, rescued her. No matter how much abuse was thrown your way, how could you turn against the person who had saved your life, and likely what was left of your soul?

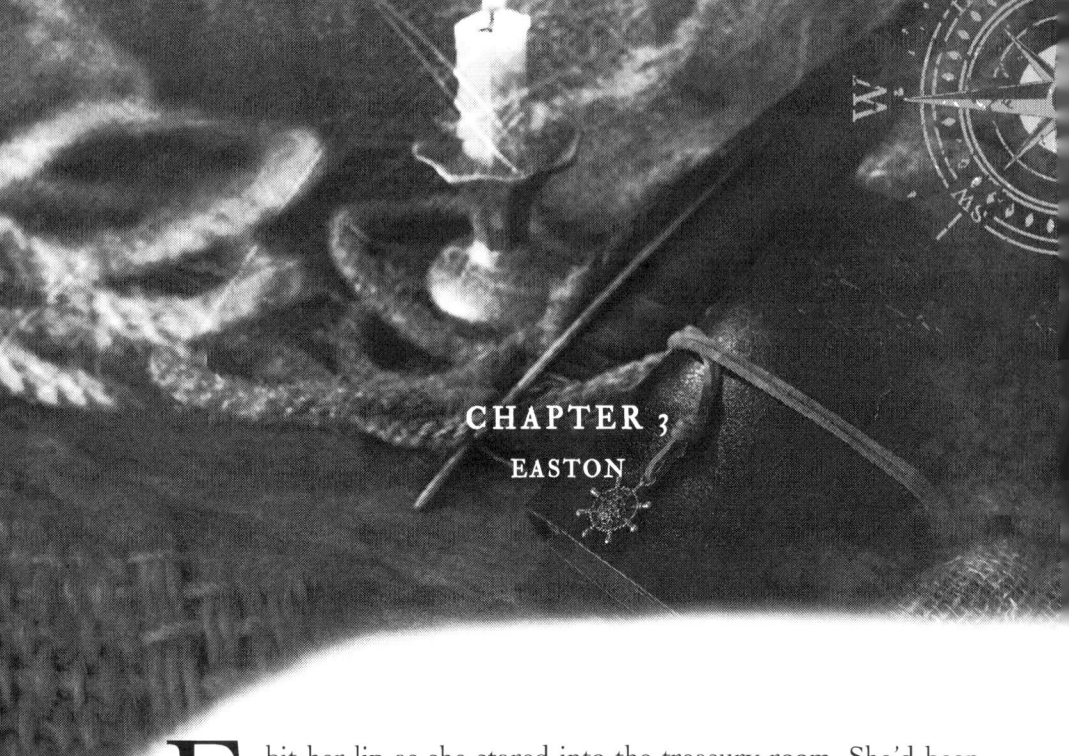

EASTON

E bit her lip as she stared into the treasury room. She'd been standing in much the same place, same position for the last twenty minutes. Entering the treasury room was forbidden, aside from the Sellers. Sellers were those of Jag's trusted allegiance that he sent out on the streets to bargain and sell the items his thieves stole.

E and the Compass gang, along with the other teams, were mere thieves not worthy of entering the room beyond; they stole the stuff, then handed it off never to see it again. In return they got their choice of what to keep from their offerings, and the protection of the guild. A cushy enough arrangement most thought. But suddenly it simply wasn't enough for Easton, not anymore. Maybe it never had been.

As she stared into the barred windows of the treasury room, she knew nothing the guild did would ever be enough for her again, not without that book. It was a stupid, childish thought. Yet it was one she couldn't shake. She'd been staring into these windows for three days with these same thoughts.

Easton had been distant, avoiding her teammates since the night she'd basically stabbed them in the back. She didn't know what they thought of her, and honestly she wasn't ready to find out. Thankfully her team seemed to have the same mindset, as they'd mostly left her alone. Though Wiley watched her carefully from a distance, even he didn't approach her.

During the daylight hours when most of them slept, she would secret her way to the treasure room: a small concrete room with one barred window and a locked metal door. It used to be where the ticket collectors would be, back when this part of the subway was still functional.

E would come to stare through the bars for what felt like hours, the book prominently staged on top of the stolen pile of items. Inevitably leaving empty handed, her mind would race the rest of the day as she lay in bed, thinking about the book and what it would take to get her hands on it again.

E knew how to pick basic locks, but didn't have much practice with the complex version Jag had outfitted the door with years ago. Even if she could pick the lock, going inside the treasury would be the equivalent of suicide. A stupid, quiet voice in her mind said that maybe it would be worth it.

Frustrated and restless, E turned her back and fled through the corridors. Slipping through the sleeping bodies on the floors and around the sheets marking off 'rooms', she finally collapsed on her rag-stuffed makeshift mattress. Her stomach rumbled and twisted in a hard cramp, protesting the three day fast. Staring accusingly at the brick ceiling, the telltale sting of tears threatened. She angrily rubbed them away before they could fully form. Easton James didn't cry. She hadn't shed a single tear since she was seven, and she was determined to never do it again.

Her mind drifted back to those younger years, the years she had first formed her attachment to the very book that called to her now. It had been a much simpler book, bound in paper rather than leather, as the one in the Treasury was. E suspected that might be the original version, or at least one of the very first copies.

A small smile graced her lips as she thought of how her childhood heart had lifted, soared with the characters in the story. How she had dreamed of adventures, wished for such tales of her own. E wasn't entirely sure if it was good, or just plain sad, that her heart still yearned for such childish things.

"Do you seek adventure, or does adventure seek you, Easton James?"

E sat up with a gasp, her heart lurching at the familiar, skin-crawling voice. It was the voice of the apparition in the mansion. Easton's eyes were drawn to the entry curtain that seemed to blow in a nonexistent wind, slipper-covered toes just barely visible beneath the hem. Leaping to her feet, she raced across the small space and ripped back the fabric. Empty space met her desperate glare. There wasn't a single soul to be seen, and no sounds aside from the mumbled snores often accompanying deep slumber.

Sweat broke out across Easton's face as her gaze swept back and forth, ears straining for sound. Distantly a wicked chuckle carried on the still air, and E spun about. She caught the tail end of a misty blue dress as the owner disappeared behind the corner of a sheeted off section. Without another thought, E dashed after it. Corner after corner, E chased along the apparition's trail, paying no attention at all as to where she was being led. Somehow, it came as little surprise when she had followed the trail directly back to the barred window of the treasury. The air stirred across E's ear as the apparition whispered to her again.

"It seeks only the price of your life." E froze as another wicked cackle washed over her from behind. She fought the urge to spin about, to face what waited behind her. She knew the ghost would disappear if she did, and so would her answers.

"What… what do you mean?" She asked hesitantly.

"Adventure, Easton James. It calls to you. Answer; abandon your life to it, if you dare. Or die alone and bare, child of vermillion hair. Both ends approach sooner than you expect, so choose wisely the path that will lead to the destination you most desire."

E could stand that chilled feeling no longer, spinning and pressing her back to the wall. As she suspected, the specter was gone…and she was grateful for it. How creepy could you get? As though by magic, her eyes were drawn once more to the book lying so innocently amongst the pilfered wares. The specter's cryptic warnings clattered about in her brain. Abandon her life to adventure, or die alone and bare? E valued life, perhaps more than most. However, breathing wasn't the same as living. The idea of dying alone and empty terrified her more than any ghost ever could.

If she was going to steal the book, it would mean leaving the guild. She'd have to run far and fast after that. She couldn't stay anywhere near Jag, he'd kill her for sure. Betrayal on that level would mean death, and any member of the guild would be more than happy to be her executioner at that point.

E snuck back through the sleeping members of the guild until she found the one she searched for. Carefully tipping up the corner of the sheet door, Easton watched Sad carefully for movement. If it was one thing E was good at, it was snatch and grab. She'd mastered the art of grabbing items from people without them ever being aware. She had just never done it to one of her own before.

For a moment she considered waking Sad, asking for her willing help. She bit her lip. She was taking a big risk here. On one end she would have a life of running ahead of her. On the other, if she was caught before even escaping, it would be the end in every way.

E wished she could ask for her help now. Yet if she did, Sad would be obligated to turn E into the guild, to inform the guild of E's efforts of sabotage. Or if she helped E in any way, Sad would be exiled, guildless...which might as well be a death sentence if she stayed in this town.

E shook her head. If she was going down, she was going down alone. She wouldn't pull the closest thing to a family she had down with her. Besides, after the stunt E had pulled with the book, she doubted Sad would have helped her anyway.

"What am I doing?" She whispered to herself, wiping a hand over her face. With a sigh, E turned away from Sad's room, walking away before she put herself in more betrayal than she already had.

This book seemed to have stirred up a whole crap load of stupid in her. Stupid, stupid, stupid. Glancing down at quivering hands, E shook her head. What the hell was she doing? Had she actually been considering taking those lock picks from her friend, and trying to break into the treasury room of all things? Had she finally gone off the deep end? She was hanging in the balance as it was, without being outright suicidal. E stumbled down the empty subway, fighting to pull air into lungs that felt like they were drowning.

She moved down the dark corridors, easily slipping by the guards Jag had in place to ensure Compass team didn't break their parole. She was really good at becoming a shadow when she didn't want people to see her.

Finally hitting the end of the corridor, E leaned back against the broken wall, letting the sounds of distant humanity lull her. Beyond the hole in the wall, beyond the large advertisement poster that covered the entry, people moved about their lives like normal human beings should. They swiftly moved from one area of life to the other: work, home, family, friends.

They flowed from one area of adult responsibility to another with a grace and ease of confidence that Easton desperately wished she could find within herself. There had been times in life when she'd envied those people out there who seemed to have been born into a better form of reality than she had. There had been times she hated them for it.

Right now, E just wanted to be part of it all. Wanted to melt into the busy crowd, meld into the flow of their purpose and become one of them. She'd tried before. She'd failed. A lot. Eventually life would rip at her shredded soul one time too many, and she would find herself begging for another chance at failure. Apparently today was one of those tipping moments. E felt the air closing off in her throat, the panic inside rising to suffocate her. She had to get out! This couldn't be her only lot in life, it couldn't be!

E pushed through the hole, carefully slipped behind the advertisement board so as not to draw attention to her movements or sounds. Not that anyone would notice. They were glued to their phones, or eyes locked on their destinations. No one noticed when she slipped into the crowd. No one noticed the shadow that brushed by near enough to steal a few bucks out of their pockets. No one noticed her at all.

Moving to the surface, E ducked her head against the persistent fall of rain and let her eyes slip over the dense traffic, along the large metal and glass buildings. What now? She glanced down at the money in her hand. She could pay a cab to drive her away, far away from here. But what good would that do? She had nowhere to go, and she'd just be left with a long cold walk back to the guild.

No. She should use it to grab food to share with her team members, since they were blocked from leaving the guild, even for food. Her stomach growled in agreement. Her own mind would certainly work better with some food in it. And maybe it would help soften the blow of betrayal to her friends if she brought them the life-sustaining thing they'd been denied because of her. E shivered against the moisture quickly soaking her sweater as she debated.

"Well, looks like the rain is flushing all kinds of rats out of the sewers today." E groaned, muscles tensing in preparation to run though she knew it was pointless. She knew it was too late to run even before his heavy hand latched onto her shoulder. Squaring her back, E turned to the man in uniform with a bright smile.

"Officer Baker."

"Where are you headed, carrot top?"

"I have somewhere important to be, actually."

"That's right you do," his fingers tightened, "at police headquarters for a chat with Officer Baker.'"

"You read my mind, I guess." E sighed. That was the last place she wanted to be, but it wasn't like she had a choice in the matter. Baker smiled and led her to the patrol car, making an exaggerated show of pushing her head down into the back seat, despite her lack of handcuffs.

"Thanks." She muttered.

"My pleasure." She had no doubt about that.

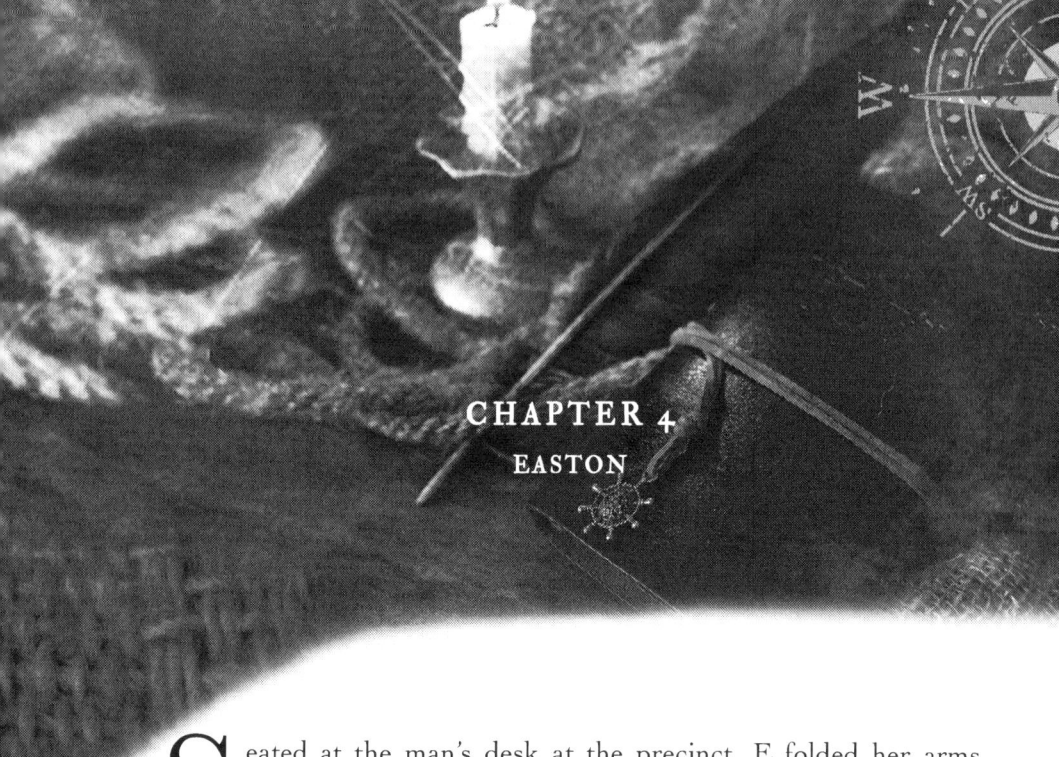

Seated at the man's desk at the precinct, E folded her arms across her chest, nervously avoiding looking at the huge number of cops that surrounded her. And half of the people in cuffs that were people she knew from the streets; some friendly, most not.

"So. Why don't you tell me what you've been up to lately, E?"

"I was going to go job hunting, actually."

"Job hunting. That's a good name for it. Very disarming. Much less ugly than, oh let's say... burglary, or aggravated theft, maybe?"

"That'd be a really stupid thing to list as skills on a resume. I don't think any employer would want to hire someone with that sort of skill set."

"You're probably right. But you're such an eloquent little thing I doubt you ever use words like that... right E?"

"Well, you know. I like to read. Can't read and not pick up some good language skills. You should give it a try some time."

"Cute. You know, it's funny you should mention reading. We actually just had a B&E go down a few days ago. Owner barely had time to get cold in the grave before they made their move." E fought the urge to lift a brow in surprise. Sounds like the old dude wasn't missing anymore. "And in addition to a bunch of rare and priceless item stolen from this poor old guy's house, they stole a book, too. A children's book, oddly enough."

"Odd, indeed. But, not my circus, not my monkeys."

"If I recall from all your stints in juvie, you enjoyed reading. Lots of fairy tales and crap like that. According to the will records, the missing book was Peter Pan, so this should be right up your alley. As a book expert of sorts, you got any idea why someone would steal a children's book with so much priceless crap laying around?"

"No clue. Maybe try asking the people who did it. I assume you caught them."

"Not yet." His lips pulled tight over coffee stained teeth in a grimace of a grin.

"So it's still an open case?"

"For now."

"Then maybe you shouldn't be discussing the details with a kid."

"Kid?" Office Baker looked at her with a sneer of barely disguised disgust. "We've known each other for quite some time now, E. We've gone through all the years of juvie and late night foster calls." He held up a thick folder with the name 'Easton Howe' stamped on it. Her record was a little more padded than most teens, she suspected. Baker grinned as though reliving sweet memories. "Ah, those were the days, eh? But it just occurred to me; you had a birthday not too long ago. Am I right?"

"Nine months ago. You never even sent me a card." E replied dully.

"You're right. But if I had a current address for you, maybe I would have." E merely hummed in reply. He'd like nothing more than to find the guild's hidey hole. "Let's see. So the birthday you just had, you know what that means don't you?"

"That I'm old enough I should be looking for a job?"

"That you're eighteen!" He threw his hands wide as though in celebration. "It means you're considered an adult in the real world now. That opens a whole new horizon for you. You can have adult conversations, hold adult jobs, go to college if you wanted to." His forced grin took a threatening hue. "Or, even be tried as an adult in a court of law."

"Well, that's one way to look at it." E slapped her hands down on her thighs and sat straight in the chair. With obvious desire to be on her way, E glanced at her watch. "Are we almost done here, Officer? As pleasant as this conversation has been, I really should get back to…" She gasped as the man reached out and grabbed hold of her hand, examining it.

"You've got pretty small hands, did you know that?"

"Let go." She spoke between clenched teeth, fighting the urge to slap away his grip, to claw away at the skin he'd touched.

"Sure, no problem." He held up his hands in mock surrender, leaning back in his chair. "I only mentioned it because I happened to find this the other night." E stilled as Baker pulled a bag out of the drawer in his desk, and inside that bag was a very familiar-looking glove.

"See, I was at the Wisner mansion on that B&E call, and I just happened across this glove lying on the ground. It's so small I figured it must belong to some kid. Which I couldn't figure out. I mean, what was a little kid doing at that big old house? But looking at your hands now, I'm wondering if I wasn't wrong about that. Maybe it wasn't a kid at all."

E swallowed in frustration. She'd picked that glove up! Had she dropped both gloves and not noticed? Was there a hole in her bag? It certainly looked like one of her gloves, and she'd been so wrapped up in the book situation that E hadn't even looked inside the duffel for her gloves since that night. It was entirely possible this glove was hers. She ratcheted up her bravado.

"There you go talking about your cases again, Office Baker."

"Oh, I trust you E. You're not the type that goes around telling secrets." He watched her with the expression of a shark, finger pointing in her face. "We're old friends you and I. So I figured what the hell, while you're here for a visit I might as well ask for your help. And you *will* help me, right E? Because that's what good friends do; they help each other."

"Technically you're too old and in too high a position of authority to be considered my friend, Officer Baker." He ignored her, moving on.

"I pulled the camera footage from the mansion that night. The thieves arranged for the power to go down, so they must have thought they were safe from the cameras too." E's heart stilled. "Unfortunately they were right about the cameras, *on property*. However they didn't take into account the street cameras. See it's a bit of an upper crust community over there, and every street light has a small security camera on it." E tried to quell the hint of panic growing in her gut as he turned the computer screen towards her.

"Three little dark windows, that's all it takes to give away a person's identity. I like to think of them as the windows to the soul; black and white in their undeniably obvious facts, just like the felons caught red-handed on tape." E's eyes glued to the three windows open on the computer screen, the figures of four people captured in each frame.

"Since you're from the younger crowd, and since I know you know a lot of people with mischievous backgrounds, maybe you could recognize these people?"

The figures in the boxes began to move and E watched with frozen interest as she saw herself and her teammates scale the fence. She saw her three friends, unrecognizable in their masks, come out and climb the fence once to drop off their extra bags, then return inside.

Then she watched as one dark figure darted out of the building, scaled the fence and flew across the ground as though the devil were on their heels. Several more frames ran across the screen, all giving images of what clearly were two females and two males, based on body proportions, but no distinguishable features beyond that. And since the images were even in black and white, no obviously distinguishable colors gave away important clues to identity, such as hair color for example.

The only troubling fact was just how close E *had* come to being caught. She'd never pulled the mask back down over her face when she left the mansion. Had she turned her face in the slightest toward that camera, they would have had a clear-cut case against her. As it was, there was just enough of a hint that Baker, who was obsessed with landing her in jail, had snagged it. Obviously he didn't have enough to go on, or he wouldn't be fishing for her reactions the way he was. E sat back with slight relief, though she hoped she kept it from her expression.

"Not sure what you expect me to get from that, except that maybe whoever the runner is should be in the Olympics with that kind of speed. However, I think I've been far more than patient here, Officer Baker. I have to go, and unless you have some reason to keep me here, you have no right to stop me."

"Listen you little..." Baker snarled, leaning closer into her personal space.

'Baker!" E couldn't help the smile that caught her lips when she heard Officer Lee's voice. Baker, on the other hand, looked like he wanted to spit nails as he moved out of his close proximity to her. Lee spoke low and firm, "Stop harassing the kid and let her leave."

"Stay out of it, Lee,"

"Let her leave." Lee cut him off. "You've got nothing to ride on. The footage isn't clear, the glove was long ago cleaned of any DNA evidence by this damned rain, and you're fishing for something that isn't there. There's no evidence, and no reason for you to have brought her in. Chain of command already told you to leave it alone. If she wanted to, she could bring you up on harassment charges, and she'd win." Lee turned to Easton and motioned for her to stand.

"Come on, Miss Howe, I'll walk you to the door."

"Don't think just because you're sleeping with the right ass, that you'll be able to get away next time, E!" Baker growled one last biting retort.

E stiffened, but Lee gently propelled her forward, ushering her to the door before she could give Baker exactly what he was pushing for: a black eye, and a reason to arrest her.

"Let it go, Easton." Lee muttered in a low voice.

"You can't let him get away with saying something as screwed up as that, Lee! You of all people don't deserve that!" E replied in anger.

Lee had to be the most decent cop she'd ever met. Lee had

always looked out for her. She'd given him plenty of reason to give up on her, but he never had. Hearing Baker drag his name through the sludge by saying he was sleeping with someone like her was so beyond wrong that she wanted to ram her fist through the guy's coffee-stained teeth. It'd almost be worth the jail time. Lee stayed silent as he walked her to the door. Only then did he turn and address her.

"Listen to me, Easton," he sighed tiredly, "I've watched your back for a long time now, plenty of times when I shouldn't have. I did it out of respect for your old man. I did it because I hate that we weren't there for your family when he needed us, and because I believe you never got a fair deal out of life from that moment on. I did it because I have always felt deep down in that troubled head of yours you have what it takes to become a good and decent person. Someone that has the strength and determination to make a real change in life, if channeled correctly. I've been waiting to see that day. But that change hasn't happened over all these years, and I'm getting old."

She felt her heart sadden a little as she took in the worry-deep-ened creases about his eyes and forehead, the way the color of white had somehow managed to win the battle on his black hair and beard over the years she'd known him. E knew a good deal of those changes were her fault. She looked at his brown leather shoes, the guilt too heavy for her to hold his gaze any longer.

"I'm old, I'm weary, and I'm retiring."

"What?" She gasped with a sudden surge of panic.

"Next Friday's my last day as a police officer. I'm not going to be around to get you out of trouble anymore. Don't count on anyone here to step up and fill my shoes. Most of the guys here are good and decent people just doing their jobs. I'm not going to ask them to break the laws they risk their lives to uphold, especially for someone that seemingly takes that help for granted." That stung, more so for the fact that it was more or less true.

"And you? You're eighteen now. With me gone and your record, Baker'll have you in lockdown by the end of the month." He was right, they both knew it. E's panic grew.

37

"I... what do I do?"

"Change." Lee stated firmly and simply. "Change is all you can do." Lee gently grasped her shoulders, making her look up into the kind green eyes that contrasted so nicely against his weathered mocha skin.

"Listen to me Easton. You've seen the ugliest there is to see in this life. But that isn't the only thing out there. There's a whole universe of beauty and adventure that doesn't involve theft and ankle trackers. Go out there and find the good things in life before the bad ones drown you. Cause you're the only one that can save you now."

With that, Lee opened the door and waited for her to leave. E blinked up at him, mouth wide open like a shocked fish. She wished she had words to say to him, wished she could beg him to fix her in the way she couldn't seem to figure out herself. Instead, she closed her mouth, averted her gaze, and walked through the doors with nothing but a tired nod.

Change.

E watched the traffic come and go, people rushing about to their different jobs and lifestyles. Everything in the world around her seemed to be in a constant state of change. Returning to the guild, E watched everyone around her, *really* watched. And felt like she was suffocating. While the outside felt alive and in constant forward motion, the guild and everyone around her felt stagnant. Like they were stuck to fly paper, flapping their wings, but never escaping or making progress.

Change.

E knew what Lee wanted her to do. He wanted her to go find an honest job, stop stealing, stop hanging out with the lowlifes of the guild world. But that kind of change wasn't easy. It was near impossible. To do that kind of change her entire life would have to shift in a big way. For the good, yes, eventually, but she would see a lot more of the bad first.

She couldn't stay in this city. Dirty, jaded cops like Baker would see to it she rotted in jail before she made an honest buck. The guild would see her dead before she had time to rot, simply for what they saw as the betrayal of purposely leaving them. Jag especially would see her dead. She carefully avoided looking his way. She'd felt the heat of his glare the moment she sat down. Did he know she'd been above ground, that she'd left when their team was on lockdown? He always knew when she'd done something he didn't want her to. It was almost unnerving how well he knew her moves, whether from Alan's tattling or simply from his constant watching.

She'd have to run pretty far away, several cities away. Maybe even a new state. Jag had a lot of connections. She had a little bit of money stashed away, but would it be enough? Even if she got away, where would she stay until she got an honest job? And once she got that job, how long would it take to earn up money for a new place to sleep on fast food wages? Because fast food was about the only thing she could land, given her lack of experience, education and past record.

Easton's wandering gaze snagged on Wiley across the room. He sat with Ark and Sad, the other two munching on a shared bag of chips. She wondered how much food like that they had left in their private stashes. She wondered if they would accept the couple of bags of food she'd gotten with the stolen money on the way home, in hopes of making amends. Would they accept it, or toss it even in the face of their empty stomachs?

At this moment, Wi didn't seem overly concerned about eating. Unlike Jag's heavy stare, Wiley's was made up of concern and confusion both aimed at her. Ark followed Wiley's focus, and seemed to freeze for a moment as he met her gaze for the first time in days. With a slow, forgiving smile, he raised a hand and waved. E felt her heart crunch. Even after everything, Ark was forgiving, inviting her back. Sad raised her brow as though challenging her to continue moping. Wiley's brown eyes gently beckoned her to join them. How easily they forgave her.

E offered a wave of apology, stood and walked away. She wasn't ready to forgive herself. She'd been a fool. How could she have been so stupid? Why did she get so caught up, risk everything just to grab a stupid picture book? What was wrong with her? She'd never risked so much in her life. She had never been so foolish and selfish; stealing from her friends, taking their guild rights and leaving them hungry, even sneaking behind the guild's back by going out onto the streets against orders.

Change.

Could she do it? Was she brave enough to do it? Was she even capable of it? Not just dip her toe in the water then come right back, but really truly leave and never return. And was she lucky enough to actually be able to pull it off without finding an early grave, or worse? Because yes, there were definitely things worse than death.

Over the next three days, Easton thought and planned. She walked aimlessly around the guild, mind deep in plans and doubts. Each day she waited for Jag's temper to come down on her. Each day she managed to escape it. Each day she found her wandering leading her back to the stupid treasury. She'd only snap out of her wandering thoughts when she realized she was staring at the book through the bars. She'd quickly turn and put as much distance between herself and that cursed book as possible.

But on the third day, drawn once more to the book, Easton found the book missing. Ridiculous panic choked her, a fear that the book had been sold.

"Back again?" Alan shifted out of the shadows to her right, smirk plastered on his scrawny snaggletoothed face. "Don't even try to deny it. Jag knows."

"Of course he does, little troll. You just can't help selling everyone around you out, can you?"

"Like you can talk." He chuckled. E hated that for once, he was right. Sneering, E turned to leave.

"He didn't sell it." Despite herself, she froze. Alan chuckled to himself again, clearly satisfied that he found Easton James' new weakness.

"Thought that would catch your attention. You know, I don't get it. You've been best friends with those three idiots for as long as anyone's known you. And then this book comes along and you toss the friendships out the window and follow after the book like a drug. So, what's so special about it, E?" he walked around her in a circle, emulating Jag's behavior towards her. The little creep didn't come close to the intimidation level of Jag.

"Obviously it's gotta be something big. Jag thinks so too. It's why he stashed the book in his room," He leaned closer, stale breath filling her nostrils, "under his mattress."

She could feel Alan watching her closely, waiting to glean any amount of info her face and body language gave away. Hoping she would take the bait of his information and do something even more stupid. E gave him nothing. Body relaxed, face smooth, voice even, she met his too big eyes.

"Stop following me, or I'll break your face worse than it already is."

Alan glared, annoyed by her lack of response. E walked away, headed straight for her friends. It was better that the book was gone, in a place she couldn't reach even if she wanted to. If anything, Alan's words had freed her from the haze she'd been trapped in for so long. Now, everything was clear.

She didn't want to see the cursed thing again. Besides, she had bigger problems. If Alan knew she was there so often, Jag knew. Why he hadn't acted on that knowledge yet was uncertain. But one thing was plain as day. E had to leave, now, because once Jag called down judgement, she'd never leave anything or anyone again.

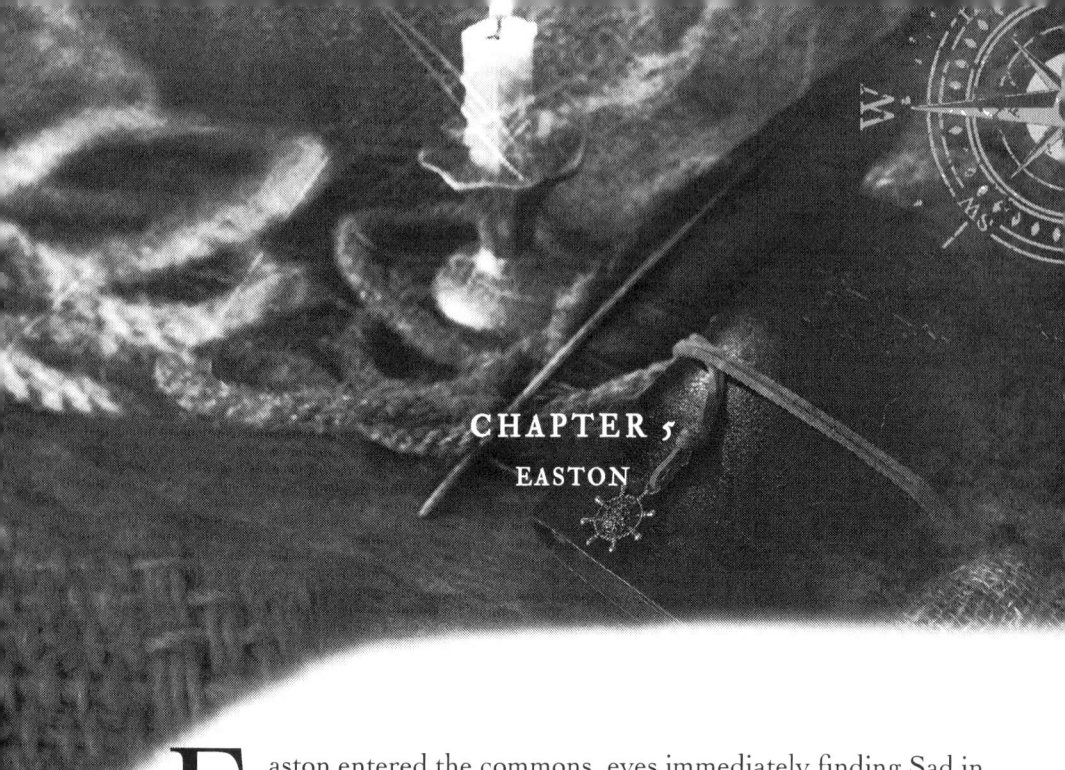

CHAPTER 5
EASTON

Easton entered the commons, eyes immediately finding Sad in the far corner. It was the usual haunt when her other three companions weren't with her. When in her corner, everyone left Sad alone; if they were smart. E wasn't sure if she was glad the others had left so she could face them one by one, or if it would have been better to get all of her apologies out at once. Either way, she'd had her chance earlier and she'd walked away from it. So, one on one it was.

E nibbled her lip, bolstering her courage. She wasn't sure who she had been, while in that fog hazed state of greed and lying. She liked to believe that it wasn't who she really was inside, that some spell had been cast over her. After all these years of trying to stay true to a mild oath of personal lines never to cross, E had jumped those lines without a single shred of doubt. Whether there was a spell or not, E had become that. She'd become a lot of things over the years, little by little. But she wasn't about to let that be who she stayed. Lee was right. She needed change.

Easton James didn't run from anyone, even herself. Easton James didn't let fear rule her for long, and Easton James was loyal. That was the core of who she had always felt she was, or who she

42

hoped to be, at any rate. Maybe it was a long road that she hadn't quite reached the end of, a road she had clearly deviated from for a time, but she was determined to get back on the right track this time. And part of doing that meant setting wrongs right. Nodding to herself in determination, E approached her friend. Sad didn't look up as Easton neared, but then she rarely did. Sad was not someone eager for company or conversation even amongst friends.

"I should have stolen more things. I shouldn't have freaked about the book and gotten you all in trouble. And... I shouldn't have thought about stealing your tools the other day while you were sleeping." Easton stated.

"You're stupid if you think I didn't already know about that last one." Sad stated just as factually, attention focused on solving the puzzle of a small combination lock in her hands. Easton should have guessed. Those lock pics were like an extra limb for the girl.

"Right." She sighed. "I'm sorry Sadie. It was underhanded and stupid. I never should have gone behind your backs that way." Sad shrugged.

"If you wanted to sneak into the treasury, all you had to do was ask. I've wanted to break in there for years." E's brow rose in shock. Quickly glancing around to ensure no listening ears, E moved to sit next to her teammate so they could speak more privately.

"I'm not going to risk getting you guys into more trouble over that thing."

"If you got caught using my tools, who do you think they'd drag into the blame right with you? You think they would've believed you stole them from me? At least if I went with you, I'd have gotten to actually enjoy it before getting booted."

It was true. No one would have believed E would stoop so low as to steal from a friend and guild member. Too bad they would have been wrong. Her shoulders slumped, and she bit down on the bitter taste of truth.

"But you didn't do it, so it's a moot point. At least you didn't stoop that low." Sad finally looked up, eyes narrowing like E was just another combination lock she was trying to open.

"Why's that dumb book so important to you, anyway?" The one

question everyone wanted the answer to, yet the one answer she didn't have.

"I don't know. Just reminds me of better days, I guess." She shook her head. She wasn't going to make excuses. "It was stupid, and I'm sorry I ever laid eyes on the thing." She pulled a gift out of her pocket. "Maybe this will help make up for it?"

For Sad, she'd gotten a particular bag of gooey cinnabun goodness that the girl quietly lusted over every time they walked by the vendor stalls. Used to people trying to swipe their items, the vendors had the sale items locked up behind thick plastic cases making it impossible to swipe something without being noticed. It was money or nothing there, which usually meant nothing for them. Sad's eyes rounded out as she reverently snatched it from E's hand and immediately ripped it open to eat, lock forgotten in her lap.

"There's no way you stole this." Her eyes turned suspicious. "Who'd you bargain for it with?"

"I bought it. I borrowed a little on the streets, and dipped into some of my stash too."

"You broke code." There wasn't accusation in the girl's tone, only mild interest. This was hardly the first time E had gone against Jag's wishes.

"Guess I'll always be a little stupid." E offered with a shrug.

"Better than bartering for it." Sad said, eyes drifting shut in ecstasy as she savored her new acquisition.

E smiled to herself, taking the obvious dismal and standing. If Sad was still suspicious of what would make E so hell-bent on the book, she didn't bother to give it credence. For now, E was forgiven. Though E knew all too well that trust wasn't something so easily mended. Forgiven or not, Sad's trust would only extend so far. But for now, it was enough. E moved toward begging forgiveness from her next obstacle.

Wiley sat in the abandoned subway car, open pocket watch in his hands, tinkering with the inner workings. Wiley had a thing for pocket watches. He collected them, fixed them. Sometimes he sold them, others he kept. She would often find him holding one to his ear when he thought no one was watching, eyes closed in a silent rapture to the calming ticking sounds. Everyone needed a coping method, and clocks were his. Helped drown out the sound of his demons, he told her once. Wiley set the watch aside at her approach, hands rising in greeting.

"I'm sorry for how I've been acting lately." She said, slumping onto the seat next to him, shoulder pressed to his. His eyes fell to hers, the brown depths capturing her in their intensity. Not being able to speak had a way of making his gaze a hundred times more intense than the average person. He observed everything around him, collected every detail. He spoke through his gaze as much as his hands. And right now, his eyes were asking if she was okay. She nodded.

"I'm fine, just a case of momentary insanity. No big." She offered a disarming smile that she knew he wouldn't buy. "I'm sorry Wi. I... well, I'm just sorry." His hands slowly rose to sign, needing no more clarification of apology.

"We're all broken E. I'm not going to be mad at you just because you're broken in different ways than me."

Smiling widely, E wrapped her arms around his thick neck and gave him a squeeze. He exhaled in a silent equivalent of a grunt, and then lightly patted her arm. E was closest to Wiley out of all their number. They'd formed a bond that was considered rare in their underground world. They relied on one another, trusted one another, and always had each other's backs.

To an extent, everyone lived that way here; you had to in their lifestyle. However you always held a healthy dose of distrust as well. Friends were just one decision away from enemies. You always had to watch your own back and make sure no one was slipping into position to shove a knife between your ribs. Easton had proved that much by hiding the book.

Down here, it was a matter of forming the alliances that were least likely to get a knife to the back. That was Compass Team. Amongst the thieves, they were the most trusting of one another. Or at least, they had been before E's destructive moves. Even they were not immune to the full effects of distrust.

Still, that wasn't how it was with Wiley and Easton. They trusted one another like a brother and sister. When Wiley showed up at the orphanage, everyone had been afraid of him. Mostly because of the ugly bruised appearance of his neck and the dark glittering of hate in his eyes.

Easton hadn't been. She'd walked right up to him, sat beside him without a word, and punched the first kid in the face that made fun of him. They'd been instant friends from that moment on.

She'd been at his side throughout the time it took him to learn sign language, learning right along with him. In between short stints for E in fosters, that is. It was never a doubt that E would end up back at the orphanage, rather only a matter of time before fosters got sick of her or they did something that had the police pulling her for safety. And every time she left to go to a new home, she knew Wi would still be there waiting for her when she came back. No one wanted the mute kid with demons in his eyes.

In a way, Wiley became her kind of home. The darkness in his eyes never fazed her. Her faults had never bothered him. She liked to think her own darkness had recognized his in that first moment they met; recognized it and bonded with it.

She'd been a fearless child then, cold and immune to much of the things that brought fear in others. Blame it on the way she'd ended up in the orphanage in the first place, but it had served her purposes well through the years. Fears had eked their way into her life as she aged, yet she was still considered somewhat of an anomaly in the guild. Truth was she was afraid more often than she let on, she simply didn't show it.

Easton pulled away from her personal reflections and slipped out of the subway car he'd claimed for his own, before he could notice the silver watch chain she'd left for him in his pocket. He never would accept it if she outright gave it to him. He'd know she would have dipped into her stash to make true amends. Nothing said I'm sorry than for a thief to use hard stolen money to buy a gift, rather than just swipe it from someone. And as such he would have marched her right back to get her money returned, Jag's grounding rules be screwed. He knew how hard she'd been trying to save money, and he wouldn't want that spent on him.

Noah made things more difficult. When he saw her coming, he'd turn and walk the other way. When she caught him unawares, and tried to strike up a conversation, he'd quickly turn to the nearest person and chat with them instead, completely ignoring her. She didn't buy for one minute that he was still mad at her. Hurt a little, maybe, but not mad.

This was Noah's way of teaching her a lesson. He'd offered her a chance out of the awkwardness back at the table, and she'd walked away from it. Now she was going to have to work for it. They had played this game for years, and somehow E's stubborn ass was always refusing to take the easy path to redemption when offered.

However, she didn't have time to woo him back to friendship for days on end. She was leaving tonight, and she needed to fix things fast. She couldn't bear the thought of leaving them behind, hating her. Luckily, through the years of this game, she'd gotten pretty good at maneuvering her way out of the self-imposed traps.

She lurked in a hall, waiting to catch his approach, weapon of choice in hand. She opened it wide before her face and leaned against the wall to wait. Out of the corner of her eye she saw his approach, but did not acknowledge it. Instead, she flipped another page in the calendar that would prove to be Noah's downfall. Noah slowed, moving only a few steps past her before his feet, visible below her view of the calendar, stopped altogether.

"That was fast. Crap finally hit the fan?" He asked, quietly. Translation: was she going to make a run for it?

"Like an asteroid to the moon." Ark stilled, catching her meaning. Tonight was the night.

"We'll be ready."

Suddenly the pinup calendar was yanked from her hands, and he strode down the hall, nose deep in the pages. Noah was all about vintage stuff; throw in a vintage style pinup calendar and you might as well be gold in his eyes.

She swallowed back the nervous smile, his words bringing her deeper relief than she would have liked to admit. Her friends would help her leave unnoticed, maybe even come with her?

They all had stashes, varying in size. And leaving was something

47

they'd occasionally discussed, when away from the guild's ears. They'd been ready for something like this for a long time. You never knew when things were going to head south fast, and you had to get out quick. E thought they'd all hoped their situations would miraculously fix themselves, without having to take that big step into the unknown. They all knew better than to believe it.

If her friends were with her, E had far better hopes for her future. They'd made it through tough situations far more times than she could count. Together, pooling their resources and skills, E felt they really could make it to a new life. Still, Easton couldn't help feeling a weight looming over her head. There was a storm on the horizon, and it was coming right for her.

She stared at the can in the middle of her small cubby room that night, the fire burning in it meant to heat the small space. Living in an abandoned underground subway meant a lot of cramped rooms with only ratty sheets as room partitions and cold drafts that stayed in your bones year-round. That and no privacy. A lot of the newbies didn't even get a private room; they just had to sleep on the floors and hope they didn't get stepped on.

Being some of the top ranking thieves in the guild, the Compass team was afforded their share of small rooms. A fact E was grateful for. The walls may be made of fabric, but even the illusion of privacy beat sleeping on the floor with fifty others.

Wiley was the exception to the room rules. He had claimed the small abandoned subway car for his own, and as pretty much everyone in the guild was as afraid of him as everyone in the orphanage had been, no one bothered fighting him for it.

E's mind drifted once more to the book that she now knew resided under Jag's mattress. Had that been a lie? No, E was certain Jag still had it. And that he'd sent Alan to see just how deep E's desire for the book ran. He wanted her to sneak into his room; he wanted her to show just how far she was willing to go to get it back. The question was, now that E knew she was leaving… would she try to take the book with her? Would she risk everything again, just for that book?

Sighing, Easton stood and stared at the pictures taped to her makeshift walls, trying to not think about the answer that had formed of its own volition. Her fingers rose to slip along the edges of the post cards. They all featured faraway places; places she dreamed of visiting, places she knew she never would.

A small smile lifted her lips. Or maybe, she could. She was starting a new life, one that promised the chance of freedom. In half an hour she'd be making a run for it, moving on to what could be a better life for her and her team if they chose to come along. And all she had to do was leave the book behind. It was too much of a risk to bother trying to take it, and the risk was not hers alone. She was done putting her team at risk for selfish reasons. A smile quirked the edges of her lips as a feeling of peace washed over her. This was the right move to make.

She stilled as goose bumps crawled the back of her neck. She wasn't alone anymore. The feeling of peace crumbled as though it never existed. Every muscle in her body froze, her senses honing in on finding the source.

"A life for a life." The ghost whispered in E's ear, a mad sort of humor evident in her voice. E winced, that heavy feeling that had been looming overhead for so long pressing down on her fully. The storm was no longer on the horizon, it was here.

"What kind of spell did you put me under, ghost?" E whispered quietly. "I didn't ask for this. I don't want the book." The ghostly woman laughed at this.

"Deny it as you will, child of vermillion hair, yet you still feel its call. It is a living desire that grows larger within you no matter how you try to run from it. You need the book as much as it needs you."

E wanted to shout that she didn't want it, that she didn't want anything to do with it. But her traitorous heart obviously couldn't hide its true desires, not from this ghostly creature. Maybe the book had drawn her in, but in the end she'd been given a choice that day she'd hidden the book away. And she'd clearly chosen badly, because the book seemed tied to her very soul now.

"What do you want from me? Why won't you leave me alone?" Even E could hear how her voice trembled over the words she wished sounded braver.

"I want only what you desire, as well. Freedom." The words hung heavily in the air, an odd sense of ghostly anticipation in the air.

"Freedom?"

"Yes. Your soul understands the yearning for it all too well, does it not, child of vermillion?"

"Yes."

"Tell me true. If given escape, would you take it without looking back? Would you change your entire world, sacrifice all that you know, for freedom from this life you now lead, Easton James?" Wasn't that what she was planning to do, by taking the risk of running from the guild?

"Yes." E whispered, her throat constricting. She could almost feel the pleasure that rippled through the air at her answer.

"The bargain has been formed; there will be no return until destiny is fulfilled."

"Bargain? Wait, I didn't…" E argued, feeling an invisible noose slipping over her neck.

"Know this, child of vermillion. There was no spell that drew you to the book. It is the adventure in your soul that drew you in. It is destiny born to your blood that calls you."

"Wait!"

"A life for a life, a bargain to fulfill."

A sudden thud on the ground behind her caused E to jolt, breath catching on a gasp. She spun about, eyes searching for the source of the noise. The ghost was gone and at her feet lay the heavy novel of Peter Pan. It had appeared out of nowhere as though by magic. Drawn to it, E crouched and reached out to touch it. Had the ghost been responsible for its appearance?

She glanced up, staring at the sheet that separated her room from the others. Eyes narrowing, she squinted. A pair of shadows were barely visible beneath the sheet; feet. No, the book hadn't appeared out of thin air or been summoned by a ghostly apparition. Eyes narrowed in fury E scooped up the book and marched to the curtain. The book called to her, sang happily in her arms the moment her skin touched it, demanded she open it. She ignored it. Flinging the sheet back E thrust the book under Jag's nose.

"You dropped something."

He pushed his way into her area, the sheet falling at his back to close them in. Suddenly her room felt impossibly small.

"Yeah well, I figured I'd save you the trouble of breaking into my room to steal it."

Her face stayed calm, but her heart skipped a beat. This was it. Jag was here for her comeuppance. But it was too soon. She was planning to leave, had actually worked up the courage to act! He'd waited days, drawn out the torment of not knowing when the ax would drop on her neck, and he chose now to do it, when freedom had been so close. She should have gone sooner, found a way to sneak out earlier. She should have left right after her conversation with Lee, never even stepped foot in this place again.

Now it was too late. E frowned. Why did part of her feel relief at being caught before leaving? She was screwed up in the head, that's why. She could have left sooner, but she had procrastinated, let her doubts keep her longer than she should have stayed. She could have left years ago, yet she'd stayed. Because deep down, she had been terrified to take the leap. It made her feel dirty to her very core, knowing that is who she had become over the years.

"What is it about that book, E? Betraying your team, haunting the treasury? If I didn't know better, I'd think you were just looking for an excuse to see me, to catch my attention." He leaned in close, lips stretched wide in a grimace that did a terrible job pretending to be a smile.

"So, here I am. You've got my attention. Whatcha gonna do with it?" E backed away, still holding the book out in front of her.

"Not interested. Take the book back."

"You make me crazy as hell, you know that?" Jag growled, mood swinging violently as he ran a hand over his buzzed head. Striding across the small space, he looked at the pictures taped to her sheet walls, a meaty finger running over the edges of the magazine clippings. It left her feeling violated, him touching her treasured dreams that way.

"We're never enough for you." The statement came out of nowhere, his mood once again shifting, becoming somber and leaving E grasping for what to say in return.

"The guild is my home." She replied carefully.

The phrase had become a sort of dutiful trademark reply for everyone in the guild. When you were taken into the guild, it became your life, your whole world. And in return it looked out for you. As long as you did your part, stayed loyal and didn't get caught, it had your back forever. Any of the politics that went on within the guild didn't matter against the overall picture of what the guild did for you. Or that is what you were meant to feel.

"It's not enough." He stated firmly, accusingly.

It wasn't. No matter what they had done for her, she still felt hollow. And that hollowness had only grown since the book appeared in her life. Maybe it was because the book was the one link to a normal time in her youth, a time she had felt safe and loved. Maybe it was a reflection of what she wished her life could still be like. Maybe Lee's words had been the final trigger point to feelings she had been trying to deny for a long time. Whatever the reasoning, the feelings were there, and they clouded her world here in the guild.

The guild was pushed deep into all the thieves' bones, and before the book came into her life, E hadn't had it in her to leave it behind. She wanted freedom, yet it had felt wrong to leave. But was it loyalty that kept her here? Or was it something darker? Darker: it was fear. She'd been on her own before, she'd been in that dark place. Her loyalty had been geared more toward self-preservation, than to the guild. Once she would have outright denied that. But now? She just didn't know anymore. And this is where her conflict lay.

She had two conflicting secret yearnings of her heart, two different directions. But which spoke louder? She had always thought herself brave and loyal. Wiley held her full loyalty. Noah and Sad held a portion. Jag held the tiniest portion, for having done his part to help her in her past. It was a loyalty given grudgingly, because of his more abundant unpleasant attributes, but it was there. In the end, she had to admit, most of her loyalty was that born of selfish self-preservation.

"I'm sorry." She murmured, not knowing what else to say.

"From that day I found you in the alley, getting the crap beat out of you, I knew you were meant to be with us. I knew you were something special." She startled slightly as his confession, the guilt of her secret yearnings and thoughts rising to the surface under the quiet sadness of his tone. "I thought you would be happy here."

"I am." The words hung hollow in the air.

"No you're not." He shook his head. "You're planning to leave." E parted her lips to argue, but the sudden way her heart stopped at the thought of staying, kept even breath from leaving her mouth. Jag offered a sarcastic smirk.

"You can't even deny it." The smirk turned grim. "But you won't leave E, I won't let you."

"You've been listening to Alan too much." The words rose, strangled, but spoken.

"I don't need Alan sneaking around to know this." He poked at one of the pictures on the wall. "You're not happy. You never have been. But I could make you happy, if you let me. I know I could." His fists clenched at his sides. "I look after my people. I make sure they are taken care of, have what they want. I want you to have what you want, E." Jag whispered, head down. "All you have to do is what I want you to do, first. Once you stop being so stubborn, everything else will fall into place. I know it will."

"No." She stated flatly. His head lifted, one hand rising toward his ear. Instead he reached toward the buzzed hair, rubbing it in an obvious attempt to contain his fury.

"I protected you, you know. I could have kicked you out onto the streets a long time ago. I could have let those thugs finish what they started in that alleyway. I could still let it happen." He threatened menacingly. "But I'm trying to protect you. All you gotta do is give me what I want, E." She swallowed, but held her chin high.

"No."

"It's a name, E! It's even an easy name!" A wild sort of desperation rose in eyes usually dark and stormy with secret fury, "All you have to do is say my name. What's so hard about that? Why can't you say it, just once?"

It would be easier if she gave in, if she just said it finally. It might even satisfy him enough that he would let down his guard and she could still sneak away. But she couldn't. She pulled her gaze away from the crazy depths of his and stared at the floor. Growling, he suddenly stepped forward, yanked the book from her hands and tossed it to the floor behind him. Her heart ached as the pages flopped open, baring their beautiful artwork.

"You can love this stupid kiddie book enough to betray the guild and your team! You can love it enough to sneak into my room and steal it before running away! You would have done it, I know you would have! But you can't say my damned name? What the hell is wrong with you? You're a broken and cold hearted witch!" She kept her eyes trained on the book at her feet, not meeting his gaze.

"If you want someone to fawn over you, there's a subway full of groupies out there just waiting to lick your shoes."

Stars floated in her vision, a ringing in her ears, and dully she realized she'd finally pushed him to the brink. He'd hit her, outright punched her in the eye and laid her out flat. An odd thought floated through her mind then. She had thought when he finally hit her that she would know where she stood with the guy. Only now that it had happened, she still had no idea what to expect from him.

His hands found their way to her throat, wrapped about it, squeezed. Years of her uncollected punishments had amounted to this one moment in time that would be the end of her life.

A life for a life.

The ghost's words filtered to her ears through their ringing, jolting her. Her feet kicked out in sudden panic as he lifted her from the ground, instinctual need for survival rising within. No! This couldn't be it, she wasn't ready!

"Just say my damned name!" He growled, shaking her. "Open your mouth, use that snarky tongue and say it! Say it!"

Eyes shifting to meet his, she was met with the unyielding force of his demand for obedience reflected there. She saw the gleam of power in his eyes, the joy he got from submitting others to his will. And with that glance, the panic instantly seeped from her bones.

Whether it was because she was losing consciousness, or because what she saw in his eyes sparked that stupid stubbornness within, it had the same reaction. If she were going to go out like this, it wouldn't be in a state of panic, it wouldn't be in a way that would simply fuel his craziness.

She stared him down defiantly, eyes burning with rebellious promises she couldn't speak. Even as the world began to swirl together, as her lungs screamed for breath, limbs twitching with the need to fight for life, E stared him down. And as though in a chain reaction, the fuel to his fury melted away. His hands loosened and E collapsed to the floor, dragging in ragged gasps of air.

"Why? Why can't you just say it?" The words held depths of lost confusion as he stared down at her, like a little boy who couldn't understand why his toy stopped working. "I've given you everything. I ask for so little in return." Wiley's words came back to her then. He had been entirely right.

"We're all broken. Just in different ways." She gasped drags of breath through a raw throat. "I think you're broken the worst of all."

The raw nature of those words seemed to only add to the vehemence with which their meaning struck the guild leader. He jerked back slightly, eyes gaining a haunted nature as his gaze dropped to her throat. For one split second, horror at his action echoed in his hollow gaze. Then, the angry shields slammed down once more, covering that moment of weakness within.

"Go ahead and leave the guild. We're better off without you. And keep your damned book. It's probably as worthless as you are!"

He turned toward the curtained doorway to leave. Yet when the sheet was pulled back, Jag came face to face with Wiley. A gleam of silver caught her eye, and she realized it was the silver chain she'd given him, hanging from the watch in his pocket. Likely he'd just discovered it and had come to thank her in their unspoken way, or maybe make her return it. But that wouldn't happen now. Wiley's eyes tracked toward where Easton slumped on the floor.

"What's going on?"

Wiley signed, looking back and forth between them. Then his gaze snagged on Easton's purpled eye. And when he zeroed in on her neck his eyes ignited with fury. His fist shot out putting Jag on the floor before the man even had a moment to register what happened.

Wiley leapt on top of their guild leader, and they rolled across the floor, barely missing Easton's legs in the process.

She quickly scrambled away from the brawl, still gasping in pained breaths, watching in mute horror. She knew better than to try and get between the two giants. Would Wiley win? And if he did, what did that mean for the leadership of the guild? What would it mean for all of them? What would it mean if he lost?

Breath whooshed out of her lungs, as though an invisible hand reached down her throat and ripped it free. Her feet slid along the floor, body pulled backward by an unseen force. A cry of panic and confusion issued from her lips, and Wiley stopped pummeling Jag long enough to look in her direction.

Whatever he saw made his eyes bug out in shock, and he reached toward her with a lunge, his hand grasping a handful of her baggy shirt. The unseen force wasn't the least bit phased, now pulling Wiley along with her. Jag slid along the floor behind them, his grip shooting out to grab hold of Wiley's ankle. Easton wondered in the panicked recesses of her mind if he did it out of an effort to help, or simply to continue the battle.

She had little time to consider that as the world around her began to constrict, her intestines crushing inward, clutched by a giant invisible fist. Her feet left the ground as she was lifted, the unsettling feeling of shrinking in on herself growing with each second. Her mouth opened in a silent scream of agony, the world around her flashing in a kaleidoscope of swirling colors that seemed to swallow her whole. She had the errant thought then; it was an odd sensation, drowning in beauty. And then everything went black.

It wasn't that she had passed out; E had done that often enough in her life to know what that felt like. Instead it was as though the world simply ceased to exist around her. The sensation of being crushed was replaced with the feeling of utter nothingness.

This is to say that Easton felt like the most wretched, broken creature in existence, her very essence saturated with such feelings of despair and hopelessness that it was more crippling than the physical sensation of being crushed had been. She found herself wishing that she could quite simply stop existing, if it meant ending the terrifying and debilitating torture.

And then as suddenly as it had begun, it stopped and a new sensation entered the fray. It was similar to the crushing, yet only in reverse, her insides expanding until she thought she would explode. If there was a hell, surely she had just found herself sucked into it.

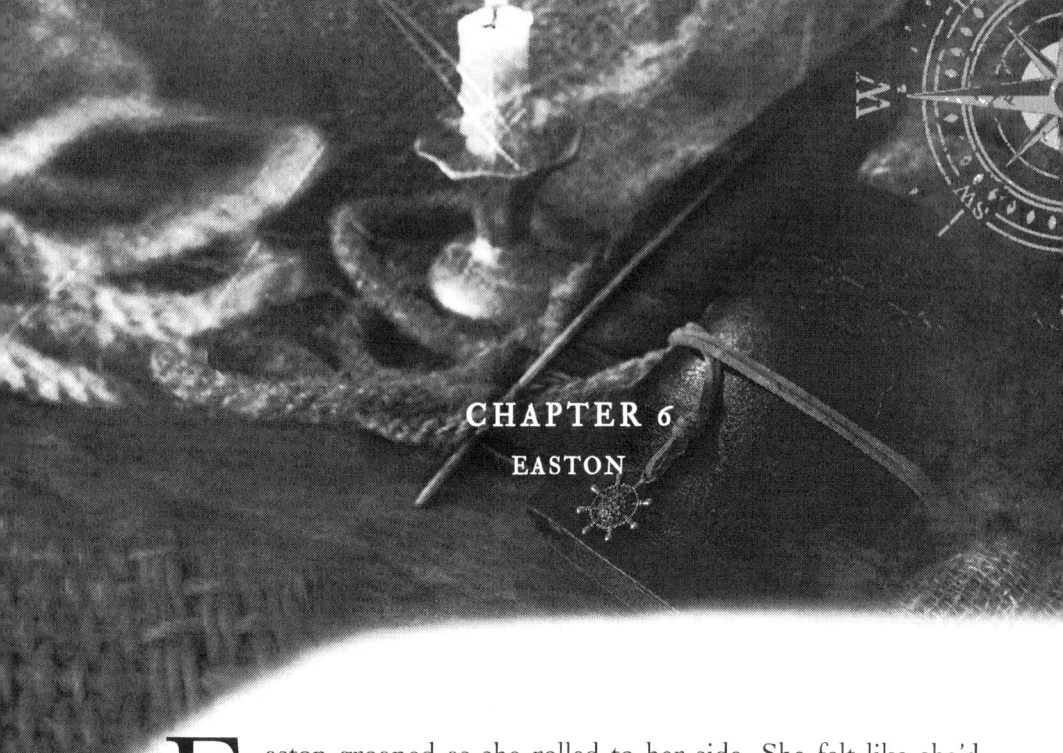

CHAPTER 6
EASTON

Easton groaned as she rolled to her side. She felt like she'd been through a blender. A distant roaring sound drew her attention, focusing her muddled brain. It sounded like a freight train. No, that wasn't right. Water?

Blinking open her lids, E released a strangled gasp. Half of her body was hanging over the edge of a cliff. Hundreds of feet below tumbled white rapids of water rushing down a river from the roaring waterfall nearby. If there was one thing Easton feared more than raptors, it was heights.

Gulping, she pushed in the opposite direction, rolling away from the cliff. She didn't make it far. Jag 'umphed' when her body collided with his, jerking him awake. His unfocused eyes found hers, and he stared at her for a long moment of frozen silence. She watched as his clearly visible thought process tumbled about in his eyes. She easily saw when the memories etched across his last encounter with her, before whatever happened to bring them here. The anger still simmered within, the unrequited demand for her obedience, and need to bend her to his will.

E felt trapped, her back to the wall of an easily fatal fall, her front facing a danger that could easily push her to that same death. She scrambled over him, on her feet and running in seconds. Her heart leapt into her throat when she heard him growl her name, jumping to his feet to follow after.

She didn't stop, didn't dare to even glance back. She leapt over fallen logs, slammed her way through tangling vines that angled across the nonexistent path she made. Branches and sharp rocks gashed through her sock-covered feet, but adrenaline overcame the pain.

"E! Where are you? Slow down! We have to stay together!" Jag shouted.

She didn't answer, trying to keep her trajectory as inconspicuous as possible. She was sure he could follow her elephant stampede of a trail, but if she could get far enough ahead she could pick her way through more carefully and try to lose him.

He didn't give her the chance, plowing into her from behind. Their momentum sent them rolling down a steep hill, slamming into trees and vines and rocks as they went. Reaching the bottom, Jag stopped in a lump, Easton rolling a few more feet away. Painfully climbing to her feet once more, she ran, moving as quickly as the limp she'd gained on the way down would allow.

"E, stop!" Jag cursed. The shift of anger to alarm in his tone was her only warning. She turned to look forward and collided into a human wall. She ducked, agilely managing to slip under the bear arms of the man that tried to wrap around her. He cursed as she began running once more. A rope lasso dropped over her neck, jerking her off her feet with a painful yank.

"On yer feet!" A gruff voice boomed, the man on the other end of the rope yanking, dragging her a good yard over the rough ground before she finally scrambled to her feet. Once standing, the rope loosened just enough she could pull in a breath. Her fingers rose to grip the scratchy fibers, but he jerked tighter. This time he didn't stop pulling until she was right in front of him.

"Douse it!" He growled. One of his men came forward and threw a bucket full of icy water on her. She gasped and spluttered, fingers giving up their efforts at the attempted hangman's rope, to wipe the hair and water from her face. Her captors scowled down at her, some with surprise or confusion, most with anger.

"Nothin' happened?" A small weasel faced man grunted, as though accusing her of failing to do her part of something. "What now?"

"We'll let him decide."

Turning her roughly, the hangman caught her arms behind her back and used the rest of the rope to bind them. Now, if she moved in the slightest direction, the rope tightened and cut off her air supply. Jag stumbled toward her, hands tied and two swords pressed to his back by his own captors. A rough bag of brown fabric was over his head. The world around her disappeared as another scratchy bag was dropped over her own head. She could catch tiny glimpses of images through the mesh of the woven bag, but it effectively kept her from knowing where she was going.

The man yanked her off her feet, easily tucking her under one arm. She quickly found that if her body sagged from its rigid position at all, the rope immediately cut off her life source of breath.

"Let's go." The gruff man holding her shouted to the others. Instantly they were on the move, making their way down hills, the men silent and sure-footed as dangerous mountain cats. Easton's body ached as the minutes stretched into what had to be hours, her muscles protesting under the strain of maintaining her stiff pose to ensure oxygen flow.

Several times they were stopped by what had to be wild animals, the skin-crawling sound of their odd screams in the forest around them. The swish of swords drawn was followed by men grunting and cursing, animal growls and hisses. Always it ended the same; a final death cry from the animal as swords sunk home, and then more walking until the next encounter. Sometimes those screams and death gurgles sounded all too human.

Despite the harrowing circumstances, E found comfort in her precarious situation at the hands of her kidnapper. At least she was safe from whatever was in the forest around them. She shuddered to think of what would have happened if she happened across one of those creatures in the forest in her earlier flight from Jag. She hadn't given any thought then to the dangers around her, only the one that pursued. Now, she found that she had time for thought and thought alone.

Her mind shifted to the events that led them here. The thoughts that tumbled about in her mind made absolutely no sense. Because in her head, she remembered Jag and Wiley fighting; she remembered being grabbed by an unseen force and dragged into a children's book that lay discarded on the floor. She remembered the disembodied wicked cackle of a ghost, demanding her life for a life, a bargain to be paid in full.

Though she remembered it all, the idea of being pulled into the deep recesses of a paper-bound book was ridiculous. Yet, what other plausible answer could there be? As the hours stretched onward, she found herself caught up in one speculation after another which always led her right back to the first. Somehow, some way, she'd been dragged into a story land; and dragged Jag and Wiley along with her.

Her mind would often freeze at that point in her thought process. Wiley, where was Wiley? Jag had been at her side. But Wiley? Wiley was nowhere in sight. Either Wiley had somehow managed to escape the book's pull, or maybe he was still lost in the woods some-where. Or...she swallowed against the tears that threatened. Or he had fallen off the edge of that cliff.

Given how close she and Jag had been to the falls, it seemed a far more likely outcome. No matter how positive she tried to remain, dark thoughts of Wiley's body tumbling lifelessly through the relent-less currents of that river kept flickering through her mind.

Easton's captor deposited her on the ground without the slightest warning. Her unsteady legs gave way and she fell right on the edge of a small rock that numbed her left butt cheek. She didn't have time to bemoan the bruise or her luck, as she was gripped at the back of her neck and hoisted onto her feet with as much ease as someone grabbing up a kitten. She forced her legs to remain firm beneath her this time, not looking for a second bruise. Squinting through the small spaces in the bag's weave, E took in her surroundings.

They were in a small clearing, surrounded by forest, forest, and still more forest. This whole world was one giant humid forest, and she was already getting sick of it. A small fire burned in the middle of what was clearly going to be their campsite, several men already cooking raw meat over the flames. Spotted and striped skins of animals were being scraped clean by other men nearby, and E realized the meat had probably come from the animals that attacked them along the way.

That was one thing about traveling around here, she supposed. You'd never be without meals, provided you survived the initial attack. The leader of the group shoved her toward a tree and tied her to the trunk where Jag already sat trussed; though she noticed they were nice enough to tie his hands in front, not behind like they had her. And they'd even removed the scratchy, hot bag from his head. Jerks.

"You just had to run, didn't you?" Jag sneered when the men stepped far enough away to not overhear. "I tried to warn you to be quiet and careful, but you just had to run off like a damned fool!"

"I was running from you!" She hissed back. "If you remember correctly, the last time I saw you, you were trying to kill me!"

"I wouldn't..!" He stopped short, blinking and looking away. "I wouldn't have killed you. I lost my temper, that's all."

"Yeah, a real Prince Charming." E retorted bitterly. They sat in a long heavy silence, before E spoke again. "We have to get out of here."

"You think?" Jag scoffed, "One problem; where's here, exactly? I have no freaking clue where we are or how we got here. Details like that are kind of important if you wanna escape, don't you think?" She ignored his tone, glancing around uncomfortably.

"I can't exactly explain the 'how' of how we got here, but I think I know the 'where'." E went for simple. The situation was already too difficult to believe without adding in the supernatural element of the ghost. "Somehow, we got sucked into that book, the Peter Pan story. That has to mean that this is Neverland."

The woods around them went oddly still, an uncomfortable silence in the air. The men near the fire looked up, eyes nervous as they surveyed their surroundings, hands on swords. Ever so slowly, the sounds of wildlife returned, the suffocating air of tension eased, and the kidnappers cautiously returned to their tasks.

"Did you feel that?" Jag whispered, sweat beading across his upper lip.

"Yeah. It's like the world reacted to my saying the name of this place." Jag blinked, anger returning to his features.

"Damn it! You've got *me* freaking out now." Jag hissed. "You're insane, and all that superstitious crap you just said doesn't mean a thing."

"And I suppose you have a better idea?" She growled back. Jag yanked on his ear with one bound hand.

"I don't know. Maybe one of the other guilds jumped us, sold us off to pay off some drug debts to freaking Cambodia or something." E scoffed, and Jag glared. "It's a hell of a lot more likely to happen than being sucked into some stupid bedtime story. Shut up and let me think."

Easton shut her mouth, not because Jag had ordered it, but because she was smart enough to know when she was pressing her limits, and right now she needed an ally, not another person to stab her in the back. She didn't trust Jag for a moment, but they were both in a bad situation, and if they wanted to escape they'd have to work together.

So, for now, Jag would serve the purpose of ally. She'd deal with the after-effects of that later. E began tugging the ropes at her back, shifting her wrists up and down in an effort to gain even the smallest amount of leeway. She only succeeded in choking herself. Jag elbowed her, glaring.

The men around the fire were watching the two of them like hawks. Occasionally the big man that hauled E around all day would lean over and whisper in the ear of one of his companions. They would nod or shake their heads, but those eyes always stayed glued to them. E felt an unnerving certainty that they stared at her more than Jag.

Eventually one of them brought over a hunk of meat to Jag. Jag tore into it, ignoring Easton's quiet imploring that he lift the bag on her head and share. Apparently the men approved of his snubbing, because they brought him another helping, and chuckled at her as they walked away. So much for working together.

Finally E gave up begging food from her companion. She pulled within herself, put up her mental barriers of protection. That was yet another skill one learned when living her style of life. If you let everything tear you down, you'd be shredded in days. You had to be strong, block everything out, pretend that nothing affected you, or gave you pain. Because otherwise, people would use that pain against you and they'd never stop kicking you.

Besides, hunger was nothing new to Easton. She'd gone days without a scrap to eat on more occasions than she cared to count. So let them try to break her down.

Resolved, E stared solidly into the dark forest around them. She didn't blink when the men came to untie Jag and lead him toward the fire. She didn't blink when the men jeered at her. And she flinched only a little when the animals of the dark let out yips and calls in the night at her back.

Eventually, she must have nodded off, because Easton woke to water being poured over her head and an incredibly sore neck from sleeping with it flopped backward all night to keep from suffocating on the rope. Now with the water soaking the bag to her face, it added a whole new level of torment by suffocation. She shook her head around to remove the water, gasping. The bag was pulled away and the man squinted down at her.

"Nope. Still didn't do a thing." Weaselface grumbled, stomping away in disappointment. Exactly what did he expect to happen? Flowers to pop out of her head?

The leader, who seemed to have appointed himself as her personal tormenter, yanked her to her feet and untied her hands. The pain of returning blood supply to the limbs was fierce, but nothing compared to the pain in her feet. Running through a forest with only socks was a horrible, horrible idea. The pain was enough to nearly bring her to her knees once more. She clenched her jaw and held her head high.

"Attend your business!" The man ordered, pointing behind the tree. It took a moment for E to catch onto what he meant.

"Do you plan to watch?" His eyes narrowed at her snarky reply, but he didn't bother to deny it, nor to release his grip on the noose around her neck. Apparently he had every intention of watching. Her eyes searched out everyone else in the camp, found them all to be staring at her. Jag stood with them, hands bound once more, but still included apparently. Seeing there would be no hope for support on propriety, E clenched her jaw and shrugged.

"Suit yourself." She couldn't, wouldn't show them weakness.

Limping behind the tree, she took a deep breath, yanked down her pants and squatted. She hoped the dude would have the decency to look away, but he didn't take his eyes off her once. It was some consolation that he didn't have an ounce of perv in his gaze while he stared, though. Just annoyance and that same sour gruffness he had always expressed. Finished, E grabbed a leaf, and then paused.

"This isn't going to make me break out in a rash and itch like crazy or anything is it?" He just stared at her. "Because if it does and you didn't warn me, I'll complain the whole way to wherever we're going." She threatened.

Still he said nothing, though she took the annoyed twitch in his eyes as the go-ahead sign. She doubted he wanted to hear her talk more than she already did. Of course, he could always gag her... taking a deep breath Easton pushed away the dizzying whirl of doubts and used the leaf. She cringed at the rough texture, but there wasn't an immediate reaction to it. Now she would just have to wait and hope she didn't just use poison ivy as toilet paper. She was a city girl after all. She knew street survival, not woodsy survival.

Finished, she yanked her pants back up and tried to ignore the audience of her contribution to nature, fighting the blush that threatened her cheeks. *It was just pee, get ahold of yourself!* E mentally grumbled.

"Well, can I at least have some water to wash my hands? Or do you want to be touching my pee hands when you tie me back up?" The man grimaced down at her, but obliged in pouring some water from his hip canteen on her palms before yanking the rope about them once more and plopped the wet bag back on her head.

She got the pleasure of riding underneath his sweaty armpit again for a few hours, before they finally reached a dirt road. Had anyone told her she would be relieved to be in that position, she wouldn't have believed them. But given the state of her feet, E was grateful for the lessened pain.

Unfortunately, it didn't last as long as she hoped. Plopping her on her feet, he ignored her wince of pain and roughly pulled the rope noose from around her neck and cut the rope short so that only her hands remained bound behind her back. He left the scratchy bag in place, but pulled it forward; creating enough space to safely cut away a small opening that only showed her eyes . The final touch was tossing a heavy, long poncho over her shoulders, leaving her to look like a scarecrow-headed nun in a convent. Leaning close, his foul breath assailed her.

"Don't bother calling for help, no one will care. Try to run and I cut your throat." E's brow rose.

"Straightforward and to the point. Got it." Glowering, he shoved her forward and their endless march renewed. Between her new outfit and the pain in her feet, E was soon as drenched from sweat as the other men. Her mind wandered, focusing on anything and everything but the pain. Over time it consumed her thoughts despite her efforts.

She barely noticed when the men spread out, opening the area around her enough to at least remove the claustrophobic sensation of the bodies invading her personal space. Jag took the moment to edge closer, apparently deciding he was finally ready to acknowledge her again. E frowned, staring straight ahead.

"You okay?"

"Have fun with your friends last night?" She replied instead, refusing to give him the satisfaction of her admittance to pain.

"They're pirates." E glanced sharply at his grudging reply. "I think you might be right. I don't know if it's a book or some other country, but it's definitely not home." He paused. "They have started to accept me. I've been working on smoothing my way into their number." He glanced her way, "They don't seem too fond of women. I told them that you're my slave that was trying to escape me."

"Well, at least you were honest." E snorted, knowing all too well how much Jag was likely enjoying playing up that role. He didn't seem to appreciate her humor. She ignored his dark glare. "So why aren't you the one yanking me around by a rope then?" He hesitated.

"I may have traded you to them in return for a place in their crew, if their Captain allows it."

"What!" E's brow rose in challenge, and Jag immediately shushed her.

"Shut up! Get too feisty and I'll have to put you in your place like the slave they think you are. They'll expect it."

"I'm sure that would just break your heart." The pain in her hands and feet added a sharp vehemence to her words, and he actually flinched. He refused to look at her sneer, staring straight ahead.

"Look, it's not permanent okay? I'm just trying to learn as much as I can, and when the coast is clear, I'll free you and we'll make a run for it."

"Right." Her tone made it clear just how much she trusted him. His eyes narrowed.

"I will. I told you I look out for my people."

"I'm not your people anymore." She reminded him archly. He ignored her.

"For now, they're taking us to their Captain. They have to do some sort of ceremony before I can join up. After, if he accepts me, I'll be golden as part of the crew. Then we'll figure out where we are and work on a plan from there." E's interest perked up.

"That's the second time you've mentioned their Captain."

"Yeah." Jag shook his head. "They said he'd be interested in you. Something about your hair."

"My hair?" She asked, incredulous. That was just weird. He sent a nervous glance her way.

"They don't like it. Something about the color makes them angry."

"I guess that explains the scarecrow hat." E replied snippily.

"Just keep your mouth shut and I might be able to get us out of this."

He grumbled, before walking ahead, and striking up a conversation with the men. E wished she could believe that, but her eyes were telling her he was merely positioning himself for saving, and using her as his stepping stone.

The men marched them along the road that seemed to only lead deeper into the forest until they stepped into a small clearing. Straw huts formed a village of sorts, under the protective canopy of huge leafy branches above. People in the village stopped to gawk at them as they walked down the streets. The air was oppressively silent; no children ran in the village, no laughter filled the air. In fact, only men wandered the streets. Easton offered a few nods to the villagers they passed, though she received only blank gazes of bored, empty despair.

It would have been easier if they met her with anger. Anger she understood, she knew how to guard herself against it. Yet that despair? She'd seen it on plenty of the homeless in the streets back home. It was an outward emotion that so reflected the blackness resonating within her own soul it was eerie. She never wanted to end up with that expression. She shuddered, choosing to keep her eyes forward from that moment on. Big and broody was right; no one would care here if she begged for help.

Bawdy cheers and rowdy laughter ahead lifted her spirits some, pressing through the gloomy surroundings of the village and the people. The sounds emanated from a large building at the heart of the village, the crisp scent of wood smoke rising from the chimney.

A wooden sign swung precariously on a hook over the doorway. At one point the place had been named "Goldenheart Inn." Those more cheerful words had been gouged out with a knife and replaced above with "Blackheart Inn." E's brow rose. Well, it was certainly more fitting for the feeling of the village...fitting and entirely ominous.

"Get movin'!" Her jailor jabbed her in the back, pushing her towards the door. She spared the sign one last glance before moving as he ordered. Stumbling over the threshold of the inn, E's eyes swept over the occupants. There were probably twenty men in the building, though the inn was easily large enough to accommodate three times that number.

Villagers sat huddled in the middle of the room, sprawling over each other and the tables, one or two sang terrible off-pitch songs that her ears could make no sense of. She wondered if they would make more sense to her if she could understand the language they were sung in, or if they would have been just as garbled then. Given the inebriated state of the villagers, she was more inclined to believe the latter.

E hissed in pain as her fat-head jailor grabbed her arm and escorted her quickly to the back of the tavern, her feet screaming. She actually sighed in relief when he tersely pressed her down onto a rough-hewn wooden bench.

"Stay there." E looked up at him, offering an innocent expression of obedience, voice demure.

"Yes sir."

The man stared at her for a long moment of confusion, before the soured expression of disgust returned to his face. Immediately he turned his back on her and headed for the bar, attention shifting to the drink and the fellow pirates at his sides. E glanced at the plate on the table near her. The place setting was dirty and covered in food from the last person to sit there. A goblet lay on its side, half its contents spilled over the spoon, a two-tined pitchfork thing, and knife. A knife!

Glancing back and forth between the men and the plate, she slowly inched towards the knife, eyes never leaving the men across the room. Her arms screamed in protest when she forced them to lift high enough behind her back to reach the potential weapon.

She quickly moved back to her previous position, not a moment too soon. Her jailor glanced over at her with his customary glare, staring her down. All the while, E stealthily made short work of the ropes that restrained her. The moment the rope slackened, E's shoulders sagged in relief. Even though they burned with the return of circulation, it felt amazing. It felt like victory. She wished she could do something for her feet, too.

E huddled down, instantly feeling safer as she pressed her back into the shadowed corner she'd been relegated to, knife in hand. She carefully kept her arms in a position that would maintain her appearance of being tied up, just in case. She wished she could risk touching her neck, to feel the extent of damage done to her skin from the harsh fibers of the pirate's rope collar he'd made her wear for so long. Or survey what she was certain were the mutilated bottoms of her feet. But she didn't dare move and give away her freedom, not until her arms had had a few moments to regain their strength.

Her eyes shifted back to the men, digesting what she saw. Jag stood amongst their kidnappers, while they all laughed along with the big jerk. They toasted him and drank with him as though he were a long lost pal. She told herself it was because they recognized a fellow slime ball when they saw one, and that was why he'd so easily joined their ranks. Yet she couldn't help feeling an air of jealousy as she watched how easily they interacted.

All accounts considered, she *was* a thief and just as much a 'bad guy' as Jag was. But they didn't know that. And even if they did, would they accept her? According to Jag, women weren't high on their lists of respect. She sighed, feeling a confusing storm within; the same storm that had always kept her from feeling completely at home in the Guild.

Did she really want to be considered 'bad' enough to join? She was supposed to be moving in the direction of change, after all. Maybe she did things that weren't strictly legal, and her moral compass was a bit skewed. That proved she wasn't all good. But she wasn't all bad either. She had lines drawn in the sand that didn't move, and weren't crossed. She gnawed on her lip as she thought back to breaking the Guild rules.

Jag's eyes momentarily shifted to catch hers, and she felt an uncomfortable itch of understanding in her stomach. She couldn't blame Jag for doing what he had to do to survive. Lines in the sand could be wiped away with the slightest puff of wind, especially when your own survival was on the line. Life as a foster child, and then a street thief, taught you that. Was she willing to so quickly abandon her choice to change if it meant her survival?

They accepted Jag because they felt he would be a worthy member to add to their slimy crew. They thought her to be a slave, some gift to give to their Captain. And since they hated her hair so much, maybe they simply planned to give her away as target practice for a bored man in power. Just how far would she have to go to achieve Jag's status with them? What would she have to do, what left of her already tainted soul would she have to give up in order to save her life? Was selling out to them even an option?

She couldn't change her gender, but maybe she could dye her hair. Yet, if they disliked her so much already, would they even give her the opportunity to wheedle her way into their good graces long enough to plan escape? Or should she even try, when that option might lay before her now?

One thing was obvious. Despite her earlier attempt at escape, they clearly didn't consider her too much of a threat in this tavern. You didn't turn your back on someone you felt was a threat. And you certainly didn't leave them near a weapon. Why were they suddenly so disinterested in her, when they'd been breathing down her neck since her arrival?

Something was fishy and she didn't like it. Her fingers convulsed around the handle of the knife at her back. The feeling was slowly returning, and she felt confident that soon she would be able to use it if she had to.

But should she risk it? Should she try to escape? When her jailor came back, she could stab him and make a run for it...but, what good would that do her? Her feet were crap. She could hardly limp across a room without nearly crying out in pain. Even if she managed to escape the men, she was trapped in a world that she had a deep suspicion resided within a book.

She had no idea how to get out of it, no idea who to trust or where to go. She had no map, no food, water or weapons, aside from this small knife. What would she do if she were free? Even more, did she really want to go back to her old way of life? Hadn't she been just as much a prisoner there as she was now? At least here it was just a physical prison. Easton sighed.

Whether she stayed or found a way to leave, only one thing was certain. She needed to look for Wiley; at least try to be certain he wasn't dead in the falls, or lost somewhere in the woods. To do that, she would need to find a guide. Navigating through the dangerous streets of a city was a lot different than navigating through a danger-filled jungle.

For one, while the streets were dangerous, at least they had signs to tell you where you were. And a lot of the things lurking in the dark had been on *her* side, back home. Or at least she knew how to fight the ones who weren't on her side. Now, the things lurking in the darkness of vines and leaves would be more than happy to outright eat her.

Easton jerked in her seat as an unseen heated intensity crawled across her skin. Someone was watching her. None of the men at the bar paid her any further attention, not even her jailor. None of the drunks seemed to even notice her arrival, much less find her of interest to stare at with such intensity. Her eyes shifted around the room, sifting through the shadows around the edges of the inn.

Her search halted, focusing on a small gleam she saw in the shadows along the opposite wall. Immediately the gleam disappeared, replaced with the emerging form of a man as he stood from his seat. His head turned to watch the men at the bar as his feet carried him in her direction. He was tall, swathed head to toe in the darkness of shadows and cloak, which made it difficult to discern anything about him. Yet the shadows couldn't hide the sensation of danger that oozed from the man.

She stilled as her eyes tracked his progress, all the way until he planted himself on the seat beside her, closing her off from the rest of the room with his body. He sat without a word, kicking his legs up to rest on the table, dinner plate resting atop his left hand, mug of ale in his right. Her body tensed, shifting in instinctual ways that life with the guild had taught her. The muscles in her body followed every move of his, reflected it. It allowed her body to sense his next move before her mind did, let her react without slower thought leading the way.

He thumped the mug down on the bench between their bodies without so much as a glance her way. Right hand now free, it rose to grasp the two-tined fork on his plate, shoveling the food into his mouth. No, shoveling wasn't the way to describe it. He moved with

73

an air of grace and fluidity, the kind that spoke of his abilities as a fighter.

Usually when you ran into someone like that on the street, it was best to give them a wide berth out of respect and fear alike. The possibilities of doing just that had disappeared the moment he'd singled her out. She'd learned to listen to her instincts, and those instincts warned that any efforts of escape on her part now would be futile. It was best to hear the man out, see what he wanted, and then work from there.

"Why do you stare?"

She fought the reaction of her muscles, fought the jerk of surprise instigated by his voice. It was low, throaty and rough; in complete contrast to the fluid grace of his body. She also thought it may hold the smallest edge of an accent; something aristocratic that had been rubbed raw and sparse over time.

"Sorry, I tend to stare at shady men who randomly sit by me in dark corners."

She retorted, forcing some backbone into her words. Something about this guy's presence was numbing, like the effects of a poisoned bite. It made him even more dangerous. He offered a light, short chuckle, showing his approval of her response and finding slight humor in it as well. She didn't let her guard down.

"I don't think you're too worried about me. You've got that knife to protect you after all." Easton's skin itched as goosebumps erupted across her skin. How long had this guy been watching her from the shadows? And why?

"Interesting company you keep. Are you their slave, or their whore?" Her chin rose slightly at the searching accusation in his tone, yet she remained quiet. "What? No reply?"

He actually sounded surprised by her silence. The man shifted so that he was angled slightly toward her, his posture opening just the barest amount. The action offered a small withdrawal from the formidable promise of danger, an offering of momentary truce. Still she kept her mouth shut.

"I've never known a woman to stay so silent. I've heard you speak; therefore I know you have the ability. So I can only ascertain that this silence is out of a pigheaded sort of rebellion. Or perhaps, fear," he taunted, popping another bite of meat into his mouth as he watched her from the hooded depths of his cloak. She offered only a slight, wry grin in response, one he couldn't see through the rough fabric of her hood. The dim lighting reflected off of white teeth as his lips stretched to the side in an answering devilish smirk. One eye glittered at her from within the cloak, though the other caught no light.

"I can respect a woman who knows when to use her tongue." Something about the way he said it had her shifting in her seat.

He was a sly man, trying every tactic in his book until he found the one that got under her skin; the bold approach, the antagonizing approach, the flirty approach. Which approach would he try next, the first three having failed? No matter, he would find her to be a formidable opponent. Until he made an offer worthy of reciprocation, she wasn't giving him a word.

"A guessing game then?" The hood nodded, and turned toward the men at the bar. "I venture to guess that you are not willingly with this lively bunch." He didn't bother waiting for a reply, smart enough to catch onto her game the moment she devised it.

"I would guess that you are a prisoner, more than a slave." Her brow creased slightly, wondering what the difference was. The fork disappeared into the hood with more food, and Easton's stomach gave an uncomfortable twist of hunger. The man didn't so much as glance her way, though his hand, still holding the fork, lifted to signal the bartender. The man quickly shuffled to their table.

"Bring some meat and ale for my friend before he bites off my hand." Easton watched the man move away, ignoring the speculative gaze of the stranger seated next to her.

'He'? Obviously the guy knew she was a woman, he'd referred to her as one several times. So why talk to the barkeep as though she were a guy? Did this go back to the women hating thing? Did that weird fact go outside of the band of kidnappers? E filed the curiosity away, trying to remain focused on the man that could still easily be a threat to her.

If he had hoped she would act in outrage or deny his statement, he was wrong again; that food called to her stomach like a long-lost lover, and she wasn't about to act on some foolishly perceived insult and chance losing her upcoming dinner.

"Yet I find it interesting that as a prisoner, they keep so lax a guard on you. If you were a slave, I could understand. Slaves have typically lost their will to fight. But a prisoner? That is a very different story."

So that is what he meant by the differences in slaves and prisoners? She rewarded him a hum of agreement. His white teeth flashed into a grin once more, clearly pleased that he'd garnered some amount of response.

"I find it most interesting that you do not take this moment to flee. If you are a prisoner, you have had ample opportunity to escape. Perhaps you are more slave than I thought." His shadowy intimidating gaze swept back toward her, pinning her in place.

"Yet I sense a fiery strength in you that denies the possibility of slavery. So what is it that keeps you here, little dove? There are no tethers or clippings that hold you in place, now. Why do you not escape?" She could feel herself standing at an invisible crossroads. One that made it clear silence was no longer wise to maintain.

"Maybe it's smarter to stay where I am."

"She speaks." He nodded in approval, though that air of intensity hadn't lowered. "What could possibly make you feel safer in staying with a rowdy bunch of pirates, than being free? *What holds you*?" His voice had darkened, turned demanding and entrancing at once. She swallowed, fighting against the pull of it.

"How do you know they're pirates?"

"Everyone knows the men of Captain Hook."

"Easton's throat closed off. Hook?" The man sat impassively as he regarded her.

"You seem surprised. Has the knowledge of these men's identities changed your decision to stay?" Easton rolled that question around in her mind. Had it? Captain Hook. Her heart did an unhealthy leap of excitement. It couldn't be a coincidence, this was the final bit of evidence her mind needed to accept it. She *had* to be in the book.

Easton swallowed hard, pushing down on the reaction, and gave a resolute shake of the head.

"No."

"Then you must be a fool. Nothing should cause you more fear than choosing to stay prisoner to such a man." The stranger slowly turned back to his food.

"Wild animals in the jungle that want to eat a lost girl for lunch seem to be a more pressing fear in this moment." Her voice didn't hold as much witty sarcasm as she had hoped it would.

"You suggest fear of animals to be more terrible than that of the dreaded Captain Hook?" His tone made it clear he didn't believe her.

"I'm new here. I would need a guide and better weapons than a small meat knife to safely make my way in that mess out there. It doesn't do a person much good to escape one danger, just to toss herself into another. Stick with the enemy you know." He regarded her silently for a long moment, digesting her words.

"What if I were to offer my services as a guide. Would you flee then?"

"Take a stranger up on an offer to make me disappear, when he can't even show me his face? Yeah, I'm not that dumb. I learned not to take candy from strangers when I was old enough to speak. Not happening."

"Candy from a stranger." He mused quietly. "An interesting turn of phrase, but I think I understand your reasoning."

The food arrived, and instantly her mouth pooled with saliva. She glanced toward the men, uncertain. What would happen if they saw her hands free, stuffing food in her mouth? She bit her lip for a moment, before giving a mental 'screw it'. They would find out she was free eventually anyways, and she was starving. She might as well stuff her face while she could.

"I wouldn't, if I were you." The man cautioned, stopping her in her shift to remove the bag atop her head. "Showing your face in such a place is not wise. There are those who would... find disagreement with it."

"I'm not wearing this because I'm disfigured or something."

"All the more reason to keep it in place." He replied firmly. She sighed, but didn't further argue. She knew nothing of this place, and there weren't any major reasons she should fight him. She'd settle for lifting the bag high enough to push food in her mouth for bites.

Grabbing up the weird fork and her knife, she began hacking away at the meat. She didn't bother worrying about poison or anything being wrong with the feast before her. She doubted the innkeeper would poison her food but if he did, at least she would go out happy. This stuff tasted amazing!

The stranger watched her with rapt attention, and she in turn ignored him. If he wanted to watch her get food all over herself while she stuffed cow, or whatever it was, down her throat, more power to him. She'd already peed in front of a dozen men, what was eating in front of one?

"You said you are new here. How new?"

"Brand new."

"Where are you from?"

"You wouldn't believe me if I told you."

"I see…" He was quiet for a long moment. "If I were a reputable man in this village offering to guide you, would you take the opportunity to flee then?" She paused to think as she chomped her way through a huge hunk of meat in her mouth.

"How would I know you were reputable? I'm new here, remember? Besides, you make it sound like any smart person would be afraid of this Hook guy. So, any *reputable* man wouldn't be risking his neck sitting over here, without fear of what those men over there would do to you for it, much less take me sightseeing. So that rules you out as reputable, obviously." She pointed at where he sat so casually. "And that also means I couldn't get near enough a reputable man to help me escape. Besides that, I have no money to pay a guide. I don't care what kind of place this is, no one works without money."

"There is a bounty on Hook. Perhaps you wish to stay so that you may spy on his men. Or perhaps do worse." Easton showed no reaction to the surprising accusation, continuing to gracelessly shove the juicy meat in her mouth.

"What would make them special enough to spy on? I've lived

with men my whole life. Trust me, there's nothing exciting enough about them to spy on."

"You have many brothers?"

"Something like that." The grumbled reply only spurred him to dig deeper.

"Lovers?"

"Yeah, right." Easton snorted, annoyed that she felt the need to blush under such an accusation. What should she care what this man thought of her lifestyle, or lack thereof?

"Perhaps then, you spy because you have little choice. Perhaps your real fears lie not with the animals of the forest, but with the other inhabitants of it." Her mind shifted back to the all too human screams she'd heard in the forest, fighting the urge to shudder.

"If there are other things to fear in the forest besides animals, that's all the more reason to stick with the enemy I know."

"Perhaps you would not wish to escape without your friend over there, as well." The man tried a new tactic.

Easton's gaze tracked toward the direction of the men, eyes narrowing as Jag thrust his mug in the air. He laughed obnoxiously when the contents sloshed all over one of the poor villagers. The villager was so drunk he didn't even seem to notice, but Jag and his fellow thugs thought it was hilarious. He fit right in here. It was just like his little following back at the Guild. How sweet. Her mouth screwed up in annoyance.

"I hold no love for any of those men."

"Perhaps not." The stranger conceded. "But one in particular does hold your *loyalty*." Easton slowly turned to stoutly face the man beside her.

"What makes you say that?"

"I've seen the way you react in his presence. You fight to hold yourself separate, yet still your body reacts to his proximity. You stay close, yet shy away if he moves toward you."

"I do not!" She protested, annoyed that he was digging responses from her, yet angry and prideful enough to still give them. Besides, she hadn't been anywhere near Jag since they entered the Inn. He would have had to watch her long before the shadows of the inn to know any of her reactions toward Jag. Just how long had he been watching her? And why?

She grabbed up the cup of ale, hoping the liquid would wash down the meat that now sat like a lump of coal in her mouth. The man kept talking, though she wished he would shut up.

"It suggests a grudging, perhaps even fearful, loyalty born of something deeply ingrained. It is as though you are unconsciously waiting for his command." The hood shifted to the side as his head ticked to the right in thought. "Perhaps an abusive husband, based on the many bruises that cover what I can see of your face?"

Easton choked, ale gushing out of her nose, half-chewed lump of meat bouncing off the inside of the bag and plopping onto her lap as she spluttered and gagged. The whole establishment turned to regard her as she fought to not die from a lung full of food and drink. A tidy black fold of fabric was pressed into her hand.

Distantly she wondered what kind of man this stranger was, having such gentile mannerisms as carrying a freshly pressed hand-kerchief while stalking people. Shoving that thought aside she swiftly pressed the fabric to her face, wiping at her nose and mouth. Damn but ale burned your nose and lungs when it went the wrong direction!

"Are we ready to go, Capt'n? The villagers are…getting restless. Best to leave before their ale-fogged minds sharpen to a point of interest." Easton recognized the quiet spoken sour voice of the man who had put her in the corner, though her frazzled brain couldn't begin to comprehend what he was talking about. If he was upset about her freed hands, he didn't say a word about it. The man at her side answered.

"Gather the men and meet us outside, Smee." Smee. The name rang in her ears, foggy brain scrambling for understanding. She blinked the tears from her eyes, and immediately they honed in on the silver embroidered letter on the black handkerchief in her hand. One giant H was elegantly staring her in the face from the dark material. He leaned closer, husky voice melting through her hazed mind.

"We all have our secrets. Rest assured, I shall find yours and bare them to my eyes. Let us pray you are an innocent, and not the devil in disguise I fear you to be."

The dim light of the establishment shifted past the shadows in his hood and her watery gaze followed in shock. It revealed a devilish grin, and a black leather eye patch across one eye. Moving to stand, his right hand took the plate from his left, revealing not a hidden hand beneath, but a wicked silver hook. Plate safely pressed to the table, he offered a mocking bow, hook extended to the side.

"Shall we? And leave the knife there, like a good little spy."

E blinked in surprise. She'd forgotten about the knife, which now lay discarded on the table. Swallowing, Easton pushed upward on shaky legs, and limped toward the door without a word, handkerchief clutched tightly in her hand as though it were a lifeline. She had unwittingly found herself in the clutches of none other than the infamous James T. Hook. And that fact didn't scare her nearly as much as it should.

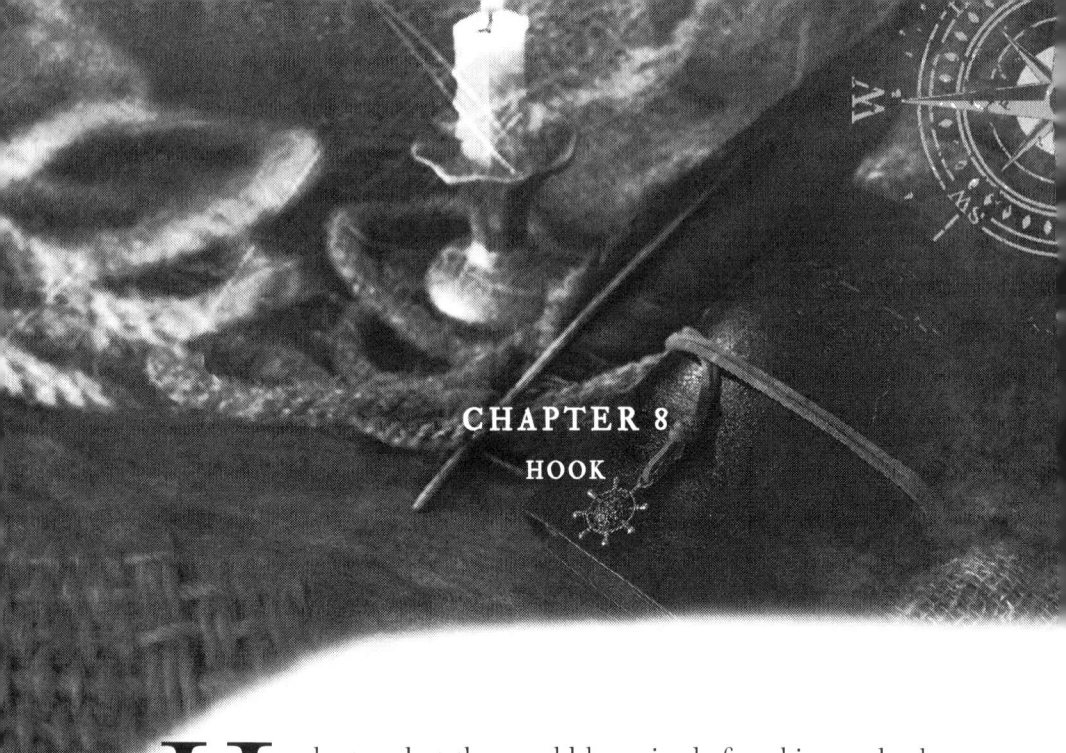

CHAPTER 8
HOOK

Hook stared at the would-be spies before him, and a bone weary sigh escaped him. He'd been at this business for far too long. If time were a constant thing, he may have been shocked at just *how* long. But in truth, time was never a constant here in Neverland. Aye, there were days and nights enough. But one never knew when to expect their coming and going. Days and nights could last interminably long; to the point you felt you'd never see darkness again, or feel the blessed kiss of warmth from the sun. Or they could be over in the blink of an eye. Yes, in truth, the only thing that was a constant in this hellish land, was age; age *never* changed.

His eyes refocused on their prisoners. Each Arrival was always the same. The skies would flash with purple lightning announcing the arrival of more 'answers' to their problems. Hook would send his men out to find them before his enemy did. Sometimes they were successful, more often than not they weren't. And those failures meant additions to his enemy's ever-growing army. Or dead bodies to bury. Even if Hook was successful at finding them first, at keeping them alive, his enemy easily swayed these would be 'saving graces' to his side before they could do Hook any good. The 'answers' to their problems seemed more often to be problems than answers.

Common Man was too easily corrupted by the fiend's pull. Now there was never a moment in Hook's life that he didn't feel as though he were fighting a losing battle; clawing his way upward through quicksand, only to be sinking all the faster for it. It was exhausting, down to the core of his soul. He wished to hell and back that he could be done with it. But there were loose ends in need of tying, and he was the only one capable of tying them.

The female prisoner stumbled, a low curse issuing from her lips. Straightening, she limped onward, fighting through the obvious pain that seemed to be growing with each step they took. There had never been more than one Arrival at a time. And it had always been men. This one confused them.

His men had seen her companion, thinking he was the Arrival. They'd captured the girl, thinking she was Pan's siren. Normally an Arrival would be welcomed with open arms. However, seeing the two behave as though they knew one another well, his men had erred on the side of caution and taken them both captive. The water test had failed, twice. He'd seen the second test fail with his own eyes, or he wouldn't have believed it. Either she had learned some new magic to fight the shift, or she was far too new to this life to have been corrupted.

A gleam of color from the edges of the female prisoner's covered head caught Hook's eye, a lock of her hair falling free of the hood in her struggles to walk. Full siren or not, that hair was condemning. Pulled from his thoughts, Hook called for a halt in their journey.

Smee tried to catch his eye, no doubt to silently reprimand him for wasting precious daylight. Hook ignored him, focused only on the girl ahead. He had to see the truth of it for himself. Smee had sent word ahead to him about their latest Arrivals. He hadn't believed the news and come to distantly watch their trek for himself. By then, Smee had covered any defining attributes, so details of her actual appearance were denied him. But her voice… there was no denying the feminine quality of that voice.

Grabbing the girl's arm he led her toward the forest. Hook carefully gauged reactions around him as they walked, though his eye never gave away those evaluations. The crew mostly ranged in degrees of curiosity. A few of them prodded one another with sly grins, clearly wondering if he was about to have his way with the girl. Several wore expressions of yearning, wishing they were in his position to do so, no doubt.

Smee's face was stormy with discontent, but it typically was. Most curious were the reactions of the girl herself, and the man she Arrived with. He expected the man to argue, stake claim to his woman. Yet he merely glanced their way with a conflicted air, before returning to rubbing his sore feet. Either he was too cowardly to take a stand, or he simply didn't care what Hook did to the girl.

The girl's reaction was most... interesting. She went along willingly, almost as though she were eager for him to get her alone. His gut instincts told him that the girl was no threat to him. Yet life-long experience taught him to be wary, especially of things that seemed too simple to be true. He'd been wrong over more certain things in the past. His hook itched, the way it always did when he felt threatened. It was always ready to protect its master. The girl stumbled, hissing in pain.

"What ails you?" He asked. She'd been limping for some time.

"My feet." The works were muffled by more than the bag, her teeth clenched with pain and an air of reluctance. She didn't want to reveal her weakness. But was it a trap to draw him in?

Hook cautiously reached out, carefully lifting the hem of Smee's large tunic above her feet. He muttered a curse of his own when nothing but ragged stocking-clad feet were revealed, soaked through with mud and blood alike. Gaze settling on a distant boulder, Hook swung her up into his arms. Immediately he regretted it. Her shrouded form became all too feminine in his arms, the curvy body melting into his grasp.

"I'm okay, you don't have to carry me. I can make..."

"Hush." Hook muttered and began what had seemed a short distance before, but now felt like an eternal walk.

Each step pressed her body more fully into his. While the position had to be uncomfortable with her arms tied behind her back, the girl still managed to melt into him, sighing with quiet relief. Hook shuddered, and the girl quickly looked his way.

84

"Are you cold? I'm sweating like a pig in this outfit." The statement caught him off guard, a welcome distraction.

"I was unaware that pigs sweat." Hook replied, curious despite himself. The girl frowned in consideration.

"Honestly, I have no idea why they say that. I don't know anything about pigs; never met one that wasn't on my plate. It's just a saying we have back home."

"I see. And where would home be, exactly?" he tried again to bring out information.

"...Far from here."

Her eyes instantly turned wary, and his instincts fired more warnings. She was hiding something to be sure, but it was a matter of whether that secret was a danger to their cause, or only to her. Finally reaching the boulder, Hook gently settled her on the moss-covered mound. Leaning close, his eye held hers.

"Do *not* try to attack me."

"Wouldn't dream of it." Hook frowned. Somehow, her words had rang oddly earnest in his ears. Ignoring the confusing sensation, Hook removed the crystalline sheath from his hook.

"Hold very still." He cautioned sternly, moving behind her to attend the ropes. He could use his dagger, should even; but this was an opportune time to test her reaction to the weapon. She didn't move an inch, her breath coming in smooth, calm draws. Her skin didn't redden or sizzle at its proximity. He frowned, assessing.

She didn't seem the slightest bit afraid of the weapon, or that he would cut her with it. He wished he held the same confidence. Clearing his throat, he sliced the rope and sheathed the hook.

"Thank you."

He hesitated, uncomfortable under the quiet gratitude in her voice, the way her eyes bored into him wide and clear. He lifted his chin, drawing on his air of authority.

"Please, remove your head wrap."

"Hallelujah!" She sighed in contentment, making quick work of the bag. The moment the rough fabric was gone, Hook took a step back. His heart clenched with a mixture of feelings he hadn't felt in a long time: awe and fear.

"Smee spoke true." He whispered, as much to himself as her. Her nose scrunched in confusion.

"Okay, I gotta ask. What is it with you people and my hair? You've all got a serious case of ginger phobia."

"What is ginger phobia?" He frowned.

"You know, gingers, you've got a thing against people with red hair."

"Vermillion is not a color looked upon kindly in this land." Hook replied carefully.

"Vermillion. You're the second person to refer to my hair that way. Makes it sound fancy. Or moldy. I haven't decided which." She swallowed, cheeks flushing slightly. "Sorry. I don't usually talk this much. Being kidnapped does that to me I guess." Hook rocked back half a step.

"Kidnapped?"

How Hook hated that word. It was the word whispered in the dark recesses of homes long since too barren and silent; homes once full of life, and now heavy with sorrow and hopeless devastation. It was a word that haunted Hook's every step, bearing guilt down upon his soul.

Was that what he was doing to this girl? Kidnapping her? Always in the past he'd considered the task as collecting prisoners, thought of it as a preventative measure. And in a way, rescuing them from a fate far worse than he and his men.

Yet now, looking down at the girl before him covered in bruises, wrists raw from being bound, he had to wonder if there was truly a difference. Was he any different than *him*? Clearing his throat, Hook shoved the thought aside. He couldn't afford weakness at this moment. Not now, not when their existence was so very near the end.

"Well, what would you call it, if not kidnapping?" The girl challenged, a spark of fire in her brown eyes that he found oddly intriguing. He pulled himself straighter.

"I call it being a prisoner of war."

"War?"

Her eyes rounded very slightly, giving away little of her inner emotions, though the surprise still shone through. Did she fight to hide her surprise, or was she artfully allowing the surprise to show in order to throw him off her scent as a spy? The girl before him was very good at crafting her reactions, hiding her truth within. A gift spies found very useful in their trade. Yet not a skill honed entirely to spies alone. A rough life often taught a person to be careful and guarded. Everyone in Neverland had a rough life. And he had no idea which life this girl came from.

He clenched his teeth. He needed answers one way or another, and somehow this girl was confounding him at every turn. Where he would normally see cut and dry lies or truth, she sent him on a path that could easily branch this way or that without any clues as to the right choice. And he certainly didn't like the uncomfortable feelings of guilt her presence stirred within him.

"Well, I don't know what war I've become a prisoner of, but I don't think I like it very much."

The girl shrugged uncomfortably, tugging at the neck of her shirt. Hook's eyes immediately fastened on the bruised and raw skin previously hidden beneath the wrap. He had seen the bruises near her eyes, the crest of her cheek... but he hadn't seen the ones on her neck. He felt a swell of guilt in his chest once more, and immediately moved to action. She startled slightly under his swift approach, though he noticed with some amount of approval that she didn't shy away in fear. Spy or not, she was a strong one, this brave little vermillion butterfly.

The snap on the pouch at his belt popped open, and he dug his finger into the salve within. The creamy slick yellow substance clung to his fingers, the medicinal properties instantly lending a tingling freshness to his skin. She flinched slightly as he pressed the cream to her pained skin, though it was hardly noticeable unless one was watching for it. Again, an admirable trait; and a trait that could easily single her out as a spy. He cleared his throat and concentrated on his task at hand.

"Wow. That stuff feels amazing. What is it?" Her shoulders sagged in relief as she tipped her head back a little to grant him further access, eyes sliding shut. He frowned as she released a low breathy sigh of pleasure.

"Byja root. It will refresh your skin and help it to heal more swiftly, keeps shallow wounds from festering." When her neck was sufficiently covered, Hook moved to her feet. As gently as he could with one hand, Hook pulled each stocking free. She jerked as fabric melded into wounds by dried blood and mud pulled at sensitive skin. Yet she did not cry out, merely uttered a quiet pained moan.

Propping each foot across his hooked arm, he poured the cool clear water of the Neverland rivers in his canteen over the wounds. Then, settling one heel at a time on his knee as he crouched, he swabbed on the medicinal cream. He felt the muscles in her calves loosening as though they were his own. He hadn't realized her pain was so raw it was almost a visceral thing, affecting him merely by his proximity. He also felt the weight of her gaze on him for far too long, and despite his years of layering on rough emotional armor, he still found her gaze unsettling. As he tended the second foot, she spoke, voice quiet, tentative.

"Why are you helping me?"

Truthfully? There were not many true women left in Neverland. They were a treasured rarity now, his enemy had seen to that. And whether this girl was an enemy spy or not, Hook couldn't ignore the discomfort he saw her in. He did ignore the fact that there may come a time down the road that they would be the ones causing her further pain, if it meant getting answers. So, he avoided the subject altogether.

"Where are your boots?" He wrapped long white bandages from another belt pouch around her feet, covering the worst of the wounds.

"Must have lost them on my way here."

"And where did you acquire the other wounds?"

"Around." She hedged. He leaned back, carefully assessing her. He knew for a fact that the rope burn was from Smee's favorite tool. Why would she lie about that? Why would she feel the need to protect the man that hurt her, to whom she held no loyalty? Confusion assailed him.

"I see." He replied slowly, standing. Again his gaze found its way to the hair, the dim sunlight sifting through the trees as though desiring to caress the gleaming vermillion tresses. Her eyes sharpened with questions of her own.

"Why does everyone hate my red hair? Just because it's not the norm? I don't buy that."

"As I said, vermillion is a rare color in our land. It is forsaken in all clothing, decoration, and in every aspect. Those with even a glint of it in their hair are banished for the land to claim, or worse. It is so rare in fact, that I know of only one other person who bears the same coloring." He watched her carefully. "It is the color of my enemy." Her eyes lit with understanding.

"Oh. You mean Pa..." His hand shot out, immediately covering her mouth. Her eyes widened, but again she didn't let the full range of her fear shine through, nor did she fight him.

"*Never* say that name!" He hissed. Immediately his eye surveyed their surroundings, listening, hoping that slightest lapse hadn't given them away to the land. The birds had quieted, but not entirely stopped in their singing, the wind still stirred around them in gentle puffs. They were safe, for now.

"You are clearly not from here, so I will give you the benefit of the doubt. I will imagine that you nearly said the devil's name out of ignorance, rather than an effort to see us dead."

She blinked up at him owlishly, and he quickly stepped away; stepped away from the silken texture of her skin. Away from the uncomfortable edge of the kind of caring that eyes such as hers could force upon a man. He'd ventured down that path once. He wouldn't do it again.

"The world reacts to his name." She stated in wonder. "I thought I felt something of that when I said it earlier, before we came to the Inn. Everything froze around us, like the whole world was holding its breath."

"It does." He nodded stiffly. "If you said the name, it is a wonder that you survived to reach the inn at all."

"Right; name equals death. I'll keep that in mind from now on."

She eyed him carefully. "So, my hair makes you think I'm somehow related to your enemy?"

"Related, or simply touched by the devil himself." Hook confirmed.

If even a hint of that color was seen in the sun's reflection on your head, you were deemed to be touched by the devil himself, the fiend of Neverland. People like that didn't last in civilization for long. None of the previous Arrivals had born hair color the least bit similar.

Hook was grateful Smee had had the foresight to toss a bag over the girl's head, or likely she never would have made it through the village. The villagers would have stoned her to death the moment she set foot within. Hook frowned at the errant thought that perhaps that may have been best for them all.

His thoughts had become a dark and foul place through the course of time. He fought the battle within daily, hourly. Despite his supposed immunity, Neverland had found her own way to begin tainting his soul. The girl's words suddenly pulled him away from the inner loathing.

"I promise, I have nothing to do with…" she paused, wisely remembering his warning and rephrasing, "with your enemy. I haven't laid eyes on him once." Hook eyed her steadily.

"We shall see. But we will not speak of this now. On your feet; they should feel numb enough to walk on. It is time we were back to our travels." She nodded, pushing to her feet before he had the fore-thought to help her. She smiled with relief when she found his word to be true, the weight on her wounds clearly not tormenting her as it once had. Grabbing up the bag, she pulled it back into place on her head. Then, hands extended behind, she turned and waited for him to bind them. Again his guilt flared. Annoyingly, some of that guilt must have shone through in his hesitance, because she glanced at him over her shoulder.

"Go ahead. I understand the need for it." Hook swallowed down the knot of emotion that rose within his throat, stomped it down with the anger that had served him well in times past. Somehow today it didn't serve him as well as before.

"Oh... I forgot. I will ask Smee to tie them. Sorry." Hook frowned, realizing she'd taken his hesitance for his lack of ability.

"Sit." He ordered gruffly. She did as he asked, watching with rapt attention as he pulled another length of fabric from his medicinal pouch. Jaw clenched, Hook pulled her hands around to the front of her. She needed bound, but it wasn't necessary to keep them bound from behind at all times. She seemed surprised by the boon, but didn't say a word, for which he was grateful.

He captured one end of the fabric between his knees, hand working at the other end to tie a small loop. The loop slipped over his sheathed hook, he set about wrapping the bandage around her wrists, then tying the ends, careful to ensure the loop didn't pull his sheath free in the process.

"You're very good at that." She offered.

"What some might see as a limitation is merely a challenge to overcome, for a wise man."

"I agree."

He glanced away at the bright smile that answered him, away from the admiration in her eyes. Bringing her once more to her feet, he carefully guided her toward the road with the others. Orders were quickly called and executed, everyone on their feet and marching within moments. Smooth workings, just as a captain demands it to be, the crew was a well-oiled machine on land or at sea. Smee stayed back with his Captain as the group moved forward.

"You should not be alone with her, Capt'n." He censured sternly.

"And you should not presume to tell me how to manage my affairs, Bo 'sun."

"You're paramount to the survival of our existence. I think it my duty to interject some intelligence when yours fails." Smee growled, moving to follow the other men. Hook's hook burned where it clung to his arm, demanding violence.

"Mr. Smee." His voice was quiet, smooth and dangerous. Smee paused, muscles tightening under the tone, but returned to his side. Ever the unwilling servant.

"Yes, Capt'n?"

"May I inquire as to where our guest received her wounds?" It sounded like a polite question, genial even. They both knew it was anything but. It was a demand, and one that was expected to be answered with the utmost truth. Smee's jaw clenched.

"The bruises were there before. We found her running away from the other with nothing but stockings on her feet. We had no boots; I carried her when I could. I assume the bruises were from him."

"I see. You assumed." Smee's jaw clenched under Hook's tone. "And the rope burns around her neck and wrists? Should I make my own assumptions?"

He'd seen the extent of damage done to both when administering the salve. The ropes were necessary. The wounds were not. Smee met Hook's gaze, muscles clenching as he fought to hold himself against the torrent of his Captain's dreaded stare. Again, they both knew where those wounds had come from. And they both knew Hook was fishing for a confession.

"I'm sure the wench has already whined to you for justice." He spat bitterly, a challenge embedded within.

"She did not utter a word of it." Hook nodded at Smee's look of confusion. "The girl, it would appear, has more courtesy and courage than my own crew." Smee's confusion shifted into a dark grimace.

"She tried to run!"

"A small girl tried to run from you. She must have frightened you terribly for you to tie her so brutally. How very… pathetic." Smee's face burned with fury. His voice fell low, gruff with emotion.

"You said we was to bring back every Arrival. You've never questioned my methods of bringing them in before!"

"I've never *had* to question your methods before, Mr. Smee." Smee leaned back, Hook's quietly spoken words a slap to the face. "I would like to think that your current treatment of the girl is not a reflection of her appearance nor gender."

"We've never had a female Arrival before. And hair like that ain't natural. It smacks of a trap, Capt'n!" Smee grunted.

"All true. But we are not like *him*, and your actions are putting us very near to becoming as such. We do not harm Arrivals. Must I remind you? They are not of this world nor familiar with our ways."

"She's not an Arrival, she can't be." Smee argued.

"And yet thus far our tests haven't been able to prove her to be one of his either. Until we have proof, she is to be treated as an Arrival. We detain them and question them if we feel they are a threat, but nothing beyond that until their innocence is proven otherwise." He stepped closer, hook moving to within an inch of the man's face.

"Mark my words, Mr. Smee." Smee's lip twitched, a trademark of rarely seen fear in a man such as him. "If one more bruise, one more ill word or mistreatment passes toward the girl of your accord, I will rend you into oblivion."

Perhaps it wasn't a wordy threat that would send most trembling in their boots. But it didn't need to be; not when it came to this particular threat. His hook was no laughing matter. The violence of his promise was reflected with violent vermillion burning in Hook's eye.

It was something he still never grew accustomed to, despite the seeming eternity of seeing it. The color alone was enough to unsettle any inhabitant of Neverland. It unsettled Hook himself. Smee's eyes shifted nervously away from his Captain's gaze, resting instead on the silver metal hook. And despite the fact that the hook was sheathed with a crystalline cap for protection against accidental death, the large man shied away.

"Understood, Capt'n."

"You are to be her personal guard until further notice, Mr. Smee. Keep her from harm. If she is found to be the devil's own, we will deal with her accordingly. Until then, treat her justly." Smee's hands clenched at his side, but he gave a stiff nod in acknowledgement.

"Aye, Capt'n."

Hook gave a sharp nod in the direction of the men, and Smee stomped off to do as his captain ordered. Slowly the violence drained from him, the vermillion leaving his gaze. Hook finally moved to follow, though his legs weren't as eager to do his bidding. He was tired, so very painfully tired. The Fiend of Neverland needed to die, so that Hook may finally die. He'd find no rest until then.

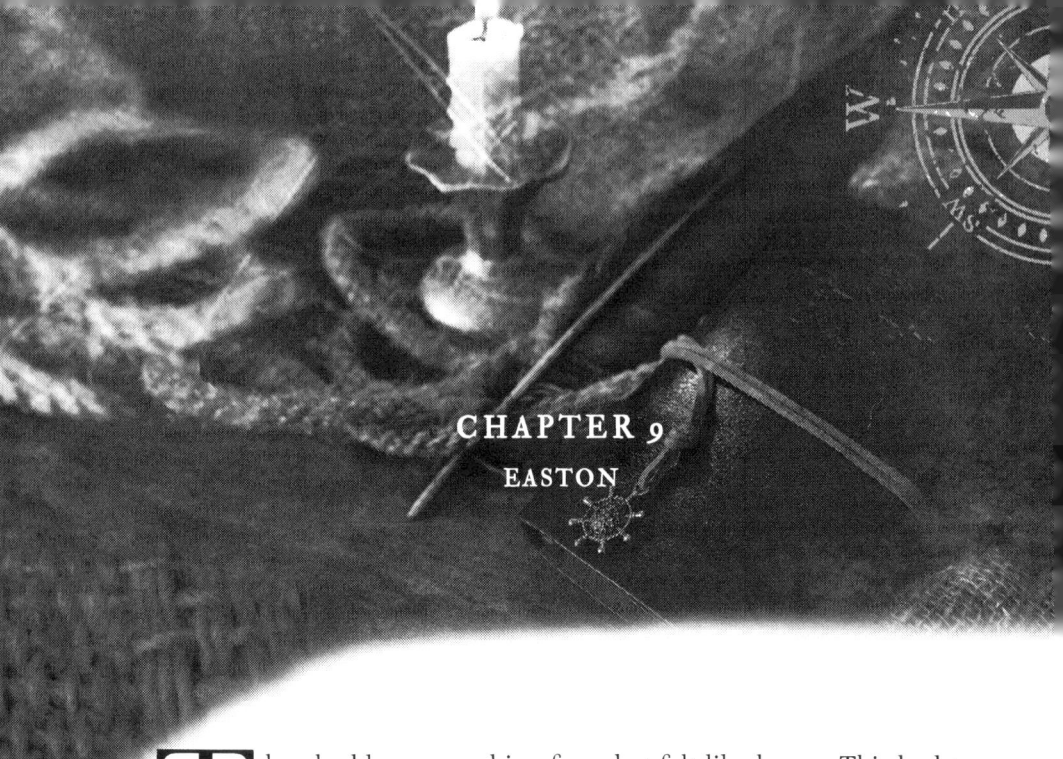

CHAPTER 9
EASTON

They had been marching for what felt like hours. This had to be the longest day in the world. The sun felt as though it should have set long ago and she should be curled up under a hedge sleeping somewhere. Yet it kept going on and on, just like this trek through endless jungle. It felt unnatural, being in this constant daylight.

Despite her exhaustion, E's eyes stayed riveted to Hook's back. James T freaking Hook! She couldn't believe it. The man that starred in much of her childhood fantasies was real and brooding only a few feet away from her. His cape flapped in the wind behind him, affording her eyes the perfect opportunity to slip along the lines of his body. Granted, the Hook in her childhood fantasies hadn't been this dreamy.

Not that she was going to complain about that. The loose-fitting black material of the clothing pressed against his form, accentuating the muscle beneath. The dude was a veritable rock, from what she could see. He wasn't a hulking giant of muscle like Smee, but he seemed to be covered top to bottom in lithe, firm muscle that any living, breathing, straight girl would drool over, kidnapped or not.

Having only one hand hadn't slowed him down on his exercise routine, that was for sure.

"What the hell, E?"

"What!" E squeaked, a guilty blush spreading to her cheeks as Jag popped up at her elbow, startling her from her lecherous staring of the captain's fine physic.

"What was that about, him pulling you off into the bushes like that?"

"Well, it's not like I asked him to do it." She glared. Jag scowled, but didn't argue that fact.

"What did he say to you?"

"None of your business or he would have dragged you along, too." E replied stiffly.

"Stop playing games!" Jag hissed quietly, leaning closer. "Our lives are on the line here, I deserve to know what's going on."

"Entitled much?"

"If you're trying to sell me out to save your own neck…"

"You'll what? Do the same thing? Oh wait, you already have!" E growled back. "You sold me out the minute we got here, after trying to choke me to death, I might add. Any loyalty I felt toward you in the Guild is gone. You look out for yourself, and I'll do the same."

"I saved your neck, I *own* your neck." Jag sent her a look of hostile superiority.

"What happened to you telling me to leave the Guild? That the guild would be better off without me?"

"Without me, you'd still be a little guttersnipe street whore. If I want to wring your neck, or sell you into slavery to save both our hides, I'll do it. That hasn't changed."

She sent out a fierce kick that connected painfully with Jag's shin. Not the smartest move, considering she was tied up and he wasn't. Not to mention the fresh wave of pain that shot up her leg. Hook's medicine had worked wonders numbing out the pain, so much so that she'd forgotten about the wounds until now. Exhausted, hot, thirsty and just plain tired of being the prisoner while he walked freely, she'd acted without thought. He didn't have the right to chew her out about loyalty, and he sure as hell didn't own any part of her.

"Damn it, E!" Jag howled, moving toward her with fury in his eyes.

"Is there a problem?" Smee towered over them both, glaring down his hooked nose. To her surprise, the glare was mostly centered on Jag. E smiled ruefully when Jag flinched. Were the tables starting to turn?

Smee was the same size as Jag, but he was the much more intimidating of the two. Smee left a person with the impression of being the kind of guy that would gut you first, and ask questions later. He had intimidation down to a T, and even Jag wasn't stupid enough to tempt the dark temperament of the man.

"No problem at all. Just making sure my *slave* remembers her place."

"She's no longer *your* slave; she's the Capt'ns. You'll do well to remember that and keep your distance." Smee glowered, muscles tensing. Jag swallowed.

"Sure, that's what I meant." With another covert warning glance her way, he quickly maneuvered his way somewhere else.

"Muckrat." Smee sneered at Jag's retreating back.

"You said it." She agreed with a grin. His pale blue eyes shifted to land on Easton's grin.

"Make no mistake, I hold no love for you either."

"Feeling's mutual, Hulk."

She grinned bigger at his expression of confusion as she picked up her pace. Despite the renewed throbbing in her foot, Easton found her step had more pep in it. Her eyes once again found their way toward Hook's back, drinking in every graceful stride. It was official, she had a severe case of the crush, and she couldn't even blame Stockholm for it.

She'd been holding onto that demented crush since her mother first read her the story of Peter Pan while tucking her in. She knew it wasn't normal to be crushing on the bad guy of the story, especially when she was only six. But then again, she hadn't exactly ever been a normal girl.

Without warning Hook dropped into a crouch before her. Watching him so closely, E instantly reacted in kind, moving to crouch only seconds before Hook's men also followed suit. Years of thieving on the streets taught you a thing or two about following the lead of those who knew what they were doing. If anyone had a reputation for knowing their stuff, it was James T. Hook.

Jag was the last to drop low, making E smirk. The guy might be a hard-core crazy leader, but it had been a long time since he'd been on the streets. He was rusty. E pulled her thoughts away from her internal gloating, focusing on what had set the pirate captain off. Her eyes scanned the trees ahead, ears filtering through the usual animal sounds in the woods.

The world around them began to darken, the wind swiftly picking up to such intensity it threatened to uproot the trees. E's eyes narrowed, wondering why they themselves weren't toppling over. If the wind could knock over trees, it could certainly knock over a few people. But while the wind ruffled their clothes and whipped their hair about, they mostly seemed untouched by the ferocity of the storm.

Easton turned to Hook, and felt her eyes widen in surprise. The wind whipped his shoulder length curled locks about his face, his features dark, fierce and deadly. A pleasant shiver raced her skin as she stared, enthralled by the imposing figure he made.

"They are upon us," his roughened voice warned with deadly calm, hook raised before him. Even with its crystalline covering still in place, the thing was intimidating. His one eye shifted toward her and her breath caught in her throat, frozen in wonder. Once sea green, now ruby red, his gaze almost seemed to challenge her for reaction.

Perhaps it was fear or horror he expected. She smiled instead. If this surprised him, she didn't have time to find out. The ground at their feet suddenly began to tremble, a small hill of dirt emerged, swiftly building upward.

"Move!" Hook shouted, shoving E backward with his hand a split-second before the ground erupted. Thousands of black wings spewed from the dirt, filling the air with an intensely loud thrumming sound. Smee's tree trunk arm wrapped around her waist, yanking her upward from the ground, depositing her behind him.

"Stay behind me!" He growled, turning back to the ominous humming fog of wings that surrounded them. Hook backed up until he too stood near her, the two men's bodies caging her in.

"Surround the other!" Hook shouted to his men, who quickly scrambled to surround Jag. Two more men moved to stand with Hook and Smee, further caging her in. The humming in the air melded into piercing shrieks. Easton's hands scrambled to cover her ears, but bound as they were she couldn't quite reach.

"What are those things!" She screamed over the sound. Hook's lips quirked upward in a devilish grin.

"Wings of black death, harbingers of our doom!" His red eye gleamed at her over his shoulder, devilish grin in place. "Let us meet it!"

A dark chuckled followed, raising E's brows. He seemed entirely too excited about their upcoming doom. And yet, despite the insanity of it all, his reaction tugged at her, drew her up into his mood. Her own laughter soon joined his.

"Bunch of mad loons!" Smee cursed under his breath.

She didn't have a chance to reflect on the absurdity of the moment, because the black fog descended to enfold them, and the sounds of battle ensued. The pirates slashed outward with skilled prowess, cutting down the fog, wave by endless wave.

E gasped, trying to keep her footing amidst the constant buffeting she received from the men that surrounded her. They were careful to stay in formation even as they fought, but that meant plenty of back and forth bouncing around for the girl caught in the middle. Memories of being the victim in that dumb 'monkey in the middle' game kids played came to mind.

Then one of the men to her left screamed out in pain. E turned, watching in horror as a black pixie-like creature embedded itself into the man's ear. Several others stole the opportunity to fly into his mouth as he screamed. His cries became garbled by their bodies clogging his throat, and he fell to the ground, twitching.

"Guard your orifices!" Hook shouted, then clamped his teeth

closed. Had the situation not been freaky as hell, E may have snorted over the awkward-sounding statement. Instead, she found herself suddenly grateful for the itchy bag covering her ears as an extra layer of protection. She stretched her hands to cover them the best she could while tied, and kept her own mouth tightly clamped. The buffeting of the men around her became more comfort than annoyance as her eyes frantically watched the cloud of wings around them. Funny how perspectives can change in only an instant.

A burning in her arm shifted her focus. One of the black winged creatures had made it through the fierce defense of her captors-turned-protectors. It looked like a huge deformed humanoid ant, and its mandibles were currently latched into the skin of her arm. Releasing a furious scream through tightly clenched teeth E scraped the winged ant from hell off her arm using Smee's back, much to his annoyance. Once it fell to the ground E stomped it under the heel of her foot. She really wished she had shoes on.

Hook glanced her way, clearly evaluating her level of distress. Everything slowed as she stared into his burning eye, time moving with each beat of her heart. Something in that wild gaze of his drew her in, like staring into the depths of an infinite universe. His eye widened slightly, as though he felt it too. A prickling sensation crawled up her spine and her eyes shifted slightly to the left. Moving fluidly, E grabbed one of the many daggers from Hook's belt, slashing wildly toward him.

Hook jumped to the side, face twisting with unforgiving fury. But when he grabbed her bound wrists in retribution, his gaze fastened to the ant creature impaled on the end of his dagger in her grip. The fury slowly melted into surprise, then apologetic understanding. She'd just saved him from having a nasty bug in his ear. With his left eye gone, he hadn't even seen it coming for him. E offered a wink and mischievous quirk to her lips he couldn't see. Hook blinked.

Without a word, he slashed through the bonds on her wrists. He pointed his dagger at her, eye narrowed in silent communication that he didn't want any funny business from her. She widened her own innocently at him and raised her hands in contrition. His expression turned droll, letting her know just how much he trusted her contrite promises.

Their momentary lapse of attention to the enemy took its toll, and Hook suddenly sneered in fury when several ants bit into him. He yanked two off his arm, while E grabbed the one from his thigh. Hook flinched as she pressed her back to his, but he didn't move away, taking her pledge of union for now. Smee backed up, moving closer.

It was just the three of them in this group now, the other man also having fallen at some point. They took turns saving each other from attack and bites alike, slashing little devils from the air at times, and yanking them from their limbs at others. The wind shifted to whip up around them, flinging many of the pixie ants away.

A trembling in the ground had the companions meeting one another's gazes in uncertainty. Were more ants coming to the surface? E frowned. This felt different, more rhythmic. E nudged Hook and Smee with her elbows, her attention drawn toward the sway of the trees to the right.

They, however, didn't seem to notice her efforts to warn them, probably thinking she was just bumping into them during her defense against the remaining ant creatures. She didn't dare open her mouth to shout out a warning, not with the psychotic bug cloud hovering around them. Hook turned and slashed another ant creature away from its course to attack her face just as a massive goat man broke through the tree line. That got their attention.

E stared as the monster barreled towards them, wondering if the ant bites carried hallucinogenic properties. The creature looked like the ones in fairy tales; the ones with the bottom half of a goat and the top half of a man. Horns grew from the long, stringy, hair-covered head, and an equally long tuft of hair grew from its chin. It towered nearly as high as the trees themselves, huge in proportion. Hook's eyes narrowed, and he quickly covered his mouth with the crook of his elbow, protecting it enough to shout out a warning to his fellow pirates.

"Satyr!"

All the pirates immediately turned, eyes wide. They no longer paid much attention to the pixie ants, shifting their full attention to the satyr coming to join the party. Translation? Goat dudes were even scarier than bug things that dug into your body and ate you from the inside out. Not good. E crouched low, following the behaviors of those around her. When the monster barreled into the group, everyone jumped this way and that, diving out of the way. The satyr was incredibly quick on its feet, for being so awkward and huge. It twisted about, kicking outward with its sharp hooves, taking out pirates left and right.

Hook tackled E to the ground, rolling with her for several feet as they dodged a swipe from the satyr. As though sensing their chance, the ant cloud returned in full force, dive-bombing them. Hook growled, rolling with E across the ground again as the whole cloud seemed to focus on them. E desperately did her part to bat the ants away mid-tumble, coming to her feet in tandem with Hook. They never saw it coming.

One moment they were rolling to their feet, and then next they were airborne. The satyr back-handed them, sending them sprawling. Hook bounced several feet away from her and was instantly set upon by another cloud of pixie ants. Then out of nowhere, dark, half-naked bodies joined in the fight. Forms that were covered in mud and twigs appeared out of the thick jungle area around them. They piled onto Hook, attacking him with branches and sharp rocks.

"Pigmites!" Hook gripped the crystalline cover on his hook and yanked it free. Turning a wild eye Easton's way, he shouted out a warning. "Beware the hook! Maintain your distance!"

E froze for a moment, caught up within the storm of that red eye and his dangerously violent face. Thus far she hadn't seen much of the dangerous man he'd warned her of in the Inn. Now, she could finally understand why some might find him fearsome enough to avoid. Yet his sudden darkness seemed to only work the small muddy figures around him into a darker frenzy. And there were far too many of them. He couldn't possibly fight them all off on his own.

E desperately looked around, searching for the dagger that was dropped when Hook tackled her. Chaos reigned as men ran about screaming, pixie ants, satyr and small mud men plaguing them in every direction. Her stomach churned as the goat man grabbed a pirate and bit him in half, dropping the rest of the body to the ground. A gleam in the grass nearby caught her eye and she dove for it, coming up from the roll with dagger in hand.

Racing back toward Hook she had nearly reached him, when a huge hand caught her around the stomach. Hook's eye met hers through the throng of creatures atop him as she was yanked upward. His wide-eyed look of panic was enough for her. This was bad, and very well could be the end of her. Time slowed; her heart beating at an agonizingly sluggish pace. Her mind flashed back to the pirate that just got chomped in half, and her heart stuttered. No way was she going to end up as goat chow!

She brought the dagger down hard on the hand wrapped around her midriff, yanking it back and forth as viciously as she could. A terrible screaming bleat issued from the goat man, and he shook her, hard. E felt every bone and muscle in her body protest, threatening to rip apart under the force.

The bag around her head went flying, her hair flaying about like a thousand whips. Her eyes blurred and the world swirled around her, noises muted for a time. The world felt upside down and wrong-side out, nothing made sense. But E was sure of one thing; with only a single shake, goat man had just about killed her. She was going to have to step up her game.

Gathering her faculties, she began twisting, turning about so she could see what she was doing. If she was going to die, she wanted to see it coming. If you saw it coming, you had a chance, a split second, to stop it. The satyr's mouth opened in a roar. But instead of shoving her directly into its mouth, it yanked her closer, eerie eyes with wide vertical slits for pupils staring her down. It brought her so close E could see her wild appearance reflected back through the glassy depths. Hot air shot across her legs as it blew out a great snorting breath from its nostrils, sniffing her. E struggled, her legs far too close to the blunt dangerous teeth that ripped people apart.

A large finger rose, jabbed her in the head, curiously prodding her. Easton was oddly reminded of the King Kong movie, when the giant gorilla kept poking at the girl in his hands as though she were a doll. Well, E wasn't anyone's doll; especially not a stinky-breathed goat man that would happily bite that doll in half.

Growling in what she felt would be her final war cry, E plunged the dagger deep into the satyr's freaky eye, pushing hard and yanking it side to side as she had in its hand only moments ago. The creature released a much louder scream this time, yanking her away. Though it nearly ripped her arms from their sockets, E held on to her grip of the dagger, wrist deep in the soggy orb. Goatman yanked E backward once more, and this time its eye came along for the ride.

The Satyr screamed, releasing her as it clawed at the empty socket left behind. If E's hands hadn't been lodged within the nasty, gelatinous mass, she would have fallen and splattered on the ground. As it was, she dangled near the creature's shoulder as it flung about wildly in the throes of pain and rage.

E pulled her hands and dagger free and began climbing the rope-like tether between the eye and its face. She tried not to think about what it was she was climbing, or what she was about to do. She focused on survival, and what had to be done to help the men on the ground; what had to be done to save herself. She was good at survival, always had been.

She ducked out of the way as a huge hand flew by, grasping to yank her free. She had no doubt she'd end up inside that mouth if it caught her this time. It may have been momentarily curious about her before, but now it wouldn't hesitate to have her for dinner.

She increased her pace until she reached the top. Then, steeling herself, E climbed inside the cavern that once housed an eye. As though coming to an understanding of what she was about to do, the Satyr howled, and a thick finger prodded its way into the hole in search of her. E flung herself to the side, dodging the finger. Instead of hitting its target, it gouged into the back of the socket, sharp nail tearing through the wall at the back. The finger knocked E to the side as it quickly retracted, the world rolling around her as Goatman screamed in self-inflicted agony. Taking a deep breath, E turned and scrambled inside the new hole.

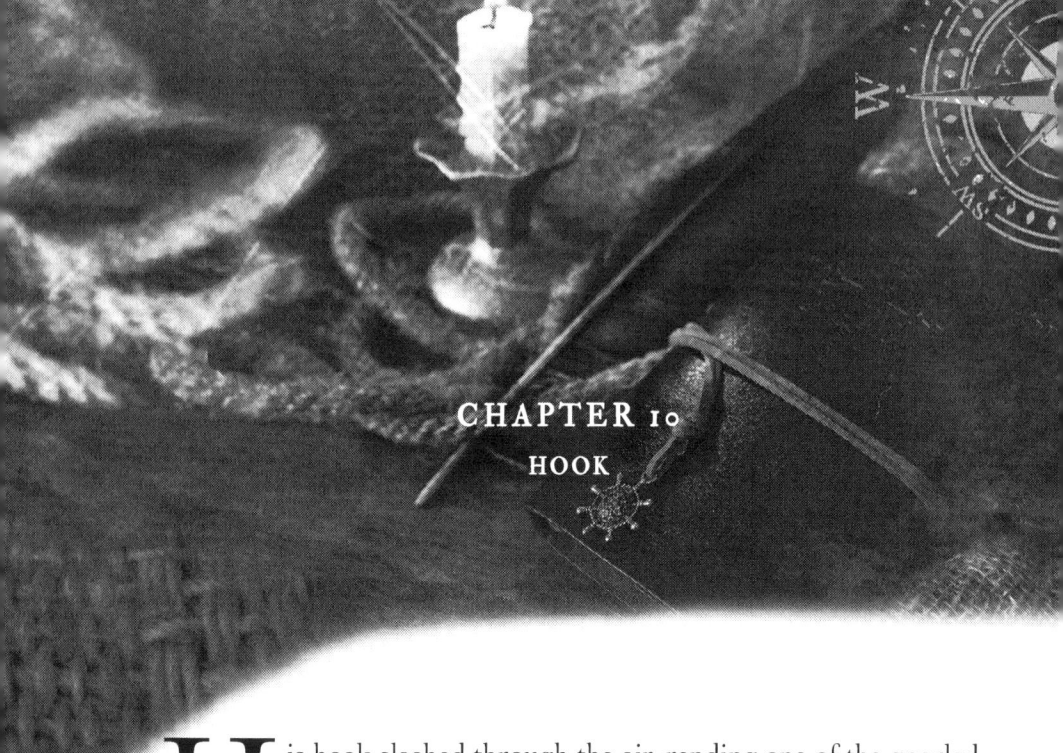

CHAPTER 10
HOOK

His hook slashed through the air, rending one of the gnarled bodies atop him. Instantly the Rift opened, swallowing the being whole, sucking it inward until nothing was left behind but the fading squeal not unlike something a gutted pig would issue. Fury coursed through his very bones as he sliced through his enemies, condemning them to their own personal Hells.

He focused on the task before him; his eternal duty. He tried to ignore the fact that the girl was likely dead by now, crushed on the ground or in the satyr's gut. He couldn't allow his focus to sway from his task. A second pigmite was swallowed in the Rift, followed soon by another. Hook's lips lifted in grim satisfaction. Their dreaded brothers in the Rift would have many new visitors today.

The satyr suddenly released a bone-chilling shriek, and the tiny figures atop Hook leapt away, gazes turning toward the monstrous fiend. An eye hung from a long ropey extension, wavering back and forth as the creature stumbled one way, then another. Its face bore the vacant expression of one near death. Hook had seen that look far too often to mistake it for anything else.

"Clear the way!" Hook shouted to the men below.

His fellow men quickly moved to obey his command, scattering the best they could, though some moved slowly due to their wounds. The Satyr hit the ground with such force that their feet were picked up beneath them, bouncing them upward. Hook maintained his balance as he met with the ground once more. Not as effortlessly as he could have, should he not have been so tired perhaps, but he kept his feet.

His gnarled attackers turned and fled into the forest, bleeding into the darkness as though they had never existed. What was left of the pixie cloud dissipated into the air.

Groans and muffled curses could be heard amongst his men in the stillness that was left to their little scene of carnage. Several of his men had been cut down. Though most were smart and swift enough to protect themselves from the carnage of the pixie's attacks, the satyr was an unforgiving foe. Hook had lost far too many men today. *Any* loss would have been too many in this never-ending war.

Clenching his teeth in age-old anger, Hook bent and dug through the carnage until he found his hook's crystal case. Carefully wiping the cruel metal across the grass to clean away the inky gore, he slipped the cover back over the weapon. He didn't breathe until it was safely locked away, his soul once more safe for the time being.

His eye searched the ground, dreading the sight of the girl's lifeless body. When he didn't immediately find it, he knew she had either been crushed under the giant, or resided within its belly. Either way, it was too late to save her. His eyes shifted across the men in the group, and found the girl's companion missing as well.

A familiar, cold realization settled across his weary shoulders. Now they would have to wait for more Arrivals and begin anew. How many more of his men would he lose in the meantime? Would there be any of them left by then? He closed his eye, teeth clenching as he fought the inward wail of desperation. He would never be free.

"What killed it, do ya suppose?" A whisper to the right registered in Hook's ears.

"Don't know. Even Capt'n's never slain one of them such as this." Another voice replied.

Hook forced his eye open, forced himself to focus on his crew, on the tasks they would still have to complete before he could be alone to reflect on their dire loss. Sheathing his dagger, Hook walked closer to the dead giant. Smee suddenly ambled to his side, covered in swollen ant bites and minor slice wounds on his face and arms. An unconscious form lay across one shoulder. Smee tossed it to the ground, and much to Hook's delight, he realized it was the girl's companion.

"Found that one running away, Capt'n. Caught up to him before he got too far." Hook didn't bother asking how the man became unconscious. In this instance, he truly hoped it had been from Smee. He didn't much care for the girl's companion before, but now knowing him to be a coward, Hook's esteem for the man lowered further. Still, it meant they may not have to wait for another Arrival before they could continue on with their task. And for that, Hook was glad to see him yet living.

He frowned down at the man's limp form. Part of Hook wished it were the girl who had survived; she held fire and life within her that was beautiful to behold, seen through the eyes of one such as he who had died long ago in so many ways. The hardened part of him was glad it was the man; if he had to put an end to one of them, it would be much easier to do to the man.

"Well enough done, Mr. Smee."

Smee nodded in acknowledgment of the compliment, though he was clearly distracted. Hook watched the man's eyes skitter over the dead on the ground, waiting for his Bo 'sun to come to the same conclusions he already had.

Smee may be a rough sort, and one not easy to command. But once he took a command to heart he carried it through, even if he hated every moment of it. To know he failed in his task to keep the girl from harm was likely gritting against his personal code of honor. That's not to say the man felt badly for the girl's death. Hook wouldn't venture to think so much of his Bo 'suns emotional depths. It was simply that he was frustrated over failing.

"How'd you kill it, Capt'n?" Smee asked, shifting the silent frustration to the giant on the ground.

"I didn't." Hook replied. Smee's brow rose, clearly disbelieving. His Bo 'sun had unsettling beliefs about Hook's abilities.

A strange sucking sound issued from within the giant. Everyone took quick steps back, hands falling to their weapons in fear that it was rising yet again. Liquid trickled from the empty eye socket, and something moved within the dark recesses.

Smee and Hook exchanged a quick glance, neither of them wanting to know what monster could possibly reside within the head of a dead Satyr. As no satyr had been killed by their hands, they had no idea what to expect of it. Was their battle not yet at an end?

Two arms extended from the cavernous socket, clasping the sides. Then, with one last loud slurping suction, a body tumbled out of the hole, washing toward their feet on a wave of slimy blue liquid. Hook's eye narrowed as he nudged the body over. A collective gasp came from the men nearby.

"It's the girl." Smee muttered in awe.

"How'd she get in there?" The men began whispering, awe mingling with their shock as they came to the conclusion in quick succession. The girl had been the one to kill the satyr.

Hook was already in motion, quickly wiping the mess from her eyes, nose and mouth with his handkerchief. Suddenly twisting to the side, she spit out a mouthful of gunk. Her body heaved in shuddering breaths and heaves of vomit for several long moments before flopping over on her back. None could form the words to speak, their shock was so great. So they watched her in silence; watched as her chest rose and fell with steady, albeit shallow, breaths. Watched as she lived through the impossible.

"Girl." Hook spoke gruffly, unsure how one went about rousing someone in this situation. He shook her shoulder, repeating himself louder when she didn't immediately reply. One eye cracked open, their brown depths taking him in. Hook felt his stomach bottom out in a strange way as a small smile cracked her lips.

"I knew you'd survive. You always do." She muttered. Hook's brow rose in surprise.

"More than we can say for you. You look like a drowned rat." Smee grumbled, bending to yank her upward to sprawl over his shoulder. "Still don't care for you, neither." He added as a side thought.

"Don't like you either." The girl grinned, tiredly flopping her head back against the Bo 'sun's back, coughing as the upside down position emptied more of the sludge from her lungs.

Smee grunted, turning to trudge into the forest. Issuing orders to his men to begin helping the wounded and accounting for the dead, Hook set off after Smee. He caught up easily, falling into step with the man, eye warily searching the jungle around them. He felt no danger nearby, but that didn't mean none would come. Venturing deeper into the jungle always brought its fair share of dangers.

"There's a small river up the way." Smee supplied an explanation of his current trajectory.

Hook nodded, eye still silently gauging their surroundings. They heard the water before they saw it, a cool burbling sound. It was music to Hook's ears. He missed the water when he was away from it. Even though the river was a far cry from the ocean, he reveled in it. The water came into view, and Hook drew in the deep musk of wet dirt and water. Smee stomped past him, directly into the river; and then he tossed the girl. Hook's eyes went wide.

"Have a care Bo 'sun!" He shouted, panic lodging in the gut. "That is our future you are tossing away!" The girl came up spluttering, the current thankfully not strong enough to carry her downstream far.

"She'll not be getting away again, Capt'n, I'll see to that." Smee promised darkly, before dunking the girl and swishing her around roughly in the water. Again she came up for air, and again he dunked and swished her.

"Mr. Smee." Hook growled quietly, stepping into the water. "If you damage the girl..." He reminded the man of his earlier promise.

"Don't plan on any such thing, Capt'n." Smee replied stiffly. Reaching down he yanked the girl up by the shoulders, carrying her to the shore. The girl coughed and spluttered, but still lived. The gore had been washed away, leaving her a sopping wet, but clean, mess.

"Can't know what the guts of a Satyr will do to a person. Best to be rid of it quickly." Smee added stiffly.

"I don't think I care for your way of taking baths." The girl gasped, pressing the dark red mess of hair away from her flushed face, teeth chattering.

"Didn't say you should." Smee replied.

Then without another word he grabbed the girl up, tossed her over his shoulder and headed back to where they left the crew. Hook followed behind, feeling oddly displaced. He had the strange feeling that he should be doing...something...more. Or perhaps, *feeling* something more. Though he hadn't the faintest idea what that would be. Feelings were a distant memory for Hook. They happened upon him rarely, and when they did, they left him confused. Feelings had no place in the life of one such as he.

Upon entering the clearing, Hook set about doing what he did understand. Soon the dead were wrapped up in large leaf wrappings that would serve as their funeral clothes. Smee plopped the girl on her feet at Hook's side before trudging off to add his efforts to Hook's orders. Hook steadied the girl with a hand on her arm, eyes never leaving the men.

Each crew member carried a fallen comrade over a shoulder. The girl's companion was still unconscious and, as he was too big to heft alone, two of his men had tasked themselves to the matter of carrying him. The few that didn't carry the fallen offered a shoulder to those who were injured.

"You're taking the dead with us?" A quiet voice asked at his side. Hook turned to the girl, her eyes watching the procession of men as they headed into the forest. Her small frame shook from the cold, and likely shock of what just happened. Yanking at the ties on his cloak, Hook smoothly transferred it to the girl's shoulders. She watched him silently as he secured it in place.

"Thank you," she whispered. He nodded, eyes shifting back to the men.

"They died honorably. Honorable men should be laid to rest in an honorable way. For a sailor, that is in the loving arms of the sea." His muscles flinched when her cold hand landed on his arm. Even through the fabric he could feel how the river water had chilled her. But it was from more than the cold that her touch caused him to react. Swallowing, he looked down into her eyes.

"I'm sorry for your losses. I know that saying never does much for comfort, when you've lost someone. But...I mean it still the same." Her tone assured him that she knew something of loss. He found himself swallowing hard, once again forcing emotion back. She elicited unsettling reactions within him, resurfaced dangerous humanity he had thought lost long ago. Hook swiftly looked away, his insides itching.

"You're different than I expected. And yet, not so different at all," the girl added, tone shifting to hold a curious depth. Hook continued to stare ahead, wondering if this would be her confession to a crime of spying.

"Oh?"

"Yep." The look in her eyes made him uncomfortable. Like she was unearthing his secrets rather than the other way around. He frowned, staring forward.

"And how would you know anything of me to make such a decision of character?" He felt on the precipice of answers, and yet annoyingly vulnerable.

"I've...heard stories." She hedged, once again denying him answers.

"I think it is time we discuss your being here, little Vermillion Butterfly. We are close to a place that we may speak openly of such things. Until then, we shall end this conversation." She blinked, shoulders shifting in a sign of discomfort.

"Right." Her spine straightened slightly, some of her spunk surfacing within her gaze. "And I do have a name, you know."

"It is better I don't know it." Hook walked away before she had the chance to say more. Still her voice followed him on the air.

"What about my hair? I lost the bag."

"It no longer matters." He grumbled. The pigmites had likely already seen her hair, and they wouldn't be crossing any more villages before their destination. There was no use in trying to hide it now.

"Aren't you going to tie me up again?" She called after him. Hook paused, turning slightly toward her.

"Do I need to?" She watched him carefully, gauging his question.

Slowly she shook her head. Hook nodded and continued on his way. Smee immediately stepped forward and tossed the girl over his shoulder.

"I have legs too!" She argued.

"Short, stubby, useless ones." Smee replied, stalking past Hook with long strides.

"Well that's not very nice." She muttered, but simply placed her chin in a hand propped against the Bo 'sun's back, giving up the fight this once.

Hook suspected the girl was more tired than she cared to admit. He lengthened his own stride, not liking the feeling of the girl's silent gaze upon him. The sooner they reached their refuge, the sooner he could unravel her secrets. Then he could be done with her and her searching eyes, one way or another.

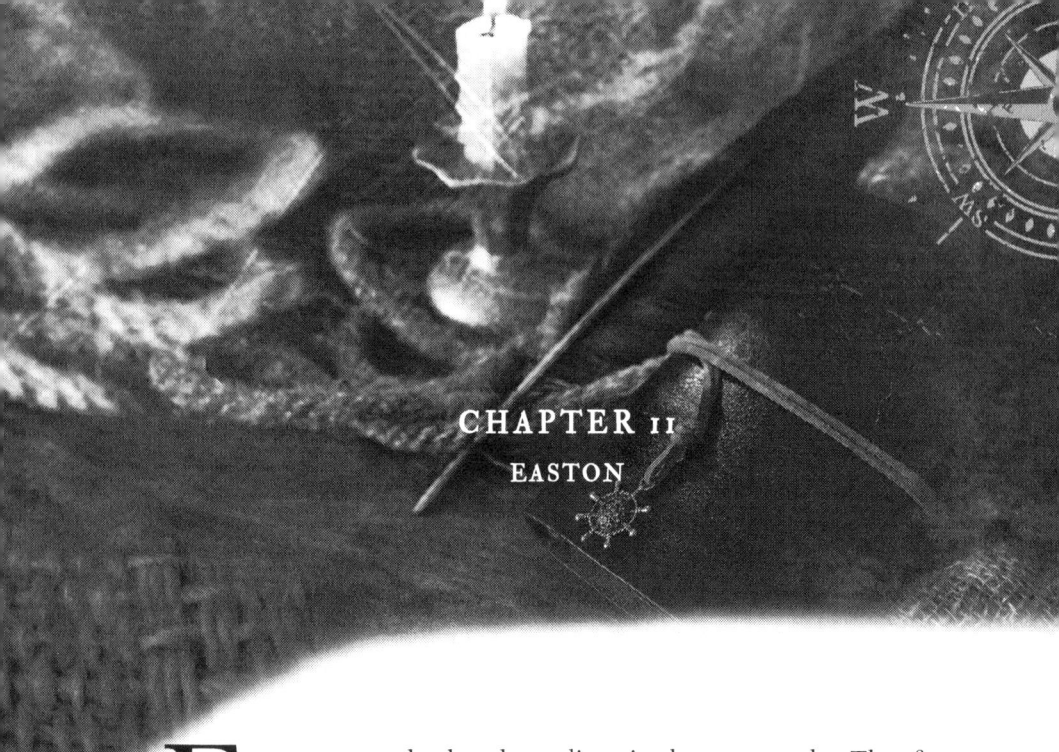

CHAPTER 11
EASTON

E aston gaped, dread pooling in her stomach. The forest opened, the oppressive dense greenness of it falling away as they stepped into a very small clearing. Overhead the trees still created a shadowy canopy that enclosed them, but the clearing gave some much needed room to breathe. The dread lay in what stood before them; massive sheer cliffs of black glassy-looking rock.

If she remembered back to her short time in school, the rock was something called obsidian. Or at least that was the closest thing she could compare the material to. And in the center of that mountainous rock was a tall, jagged crevasse. Something about it gave her the shivers, a sense of foreboding she couldn't shake. A tremor traveled the length of her spine when recognition clicked in her mind: it was the same disconcerting feeling that accompanied the specter from the creepy mansion back home.

Smee had relented and allowed her to walk some time before. She thought it had more to do with the fact that her elbows kept digging into his back than that he had a softening of heart for her complaints. As sore as her feet were, his shoulder in her gut had been worse. But as she stared up at the impressive black crevasse of doom before her, she almost wished he'd pick her up again.

Hook stood to the side of the cave, unraveling what appeared to be a thick-corded vine. The vine was wrapped around his waist and tied off, the rest of the length then passed down to each member of the crew. Everyone placed a hand on the vine and stood in line. Smee grabbed her hand and slapped it down on the vine.

"Hold tight, or you'll find yourself dead." He warned gruffly. E shivered.

"Good to know. I'd hate to find myself dead." Smee grunted as though in agreement. The vine slipped forward in E's hand, and she grasped it tightly. Smee might be a big-headed jerk, but she had no doubt that he was serious about the whole finding herself dead thing.

"We're going in there…aren't we?" E swallowed, mouth and throat dry. It was a stupid question, yet still it tumbled out of her mouth.

"The girl that climbs inside satyr heads is afraid of darkness?" Smee sneered, mocking her. E shrugged uncomfortably.

"I've realized a sudden dislike of being in dark enclosed spaces." Smee grunted a wry chuckle, which she chose to ignore. "What's in there?"

"You don't want to know." Smee returned ominously.

E felt little doubt that he was fueling her discomfort, and enjoying it. She didn't have time to offer a snarky reply, as the man before her disappeared into the crevasse. E gripped the vine tighter, using both hands as the line pulled her into the cave next. Shifting her shoulders slightly to slide through the rock, she was grateful that she wasn't as large as the men entering. The idea of being trapped in the rock became a very real possibility with such size. Her mind shut up, all thought fleeing the moment the shadowy interior swept over her.

The cave wasn't just dark, it was inky oppressiveness. The kind you couldn't see your own nose in. The kind of darkness that felt like an almost physical thing swallowing you up. Having already found herself in a similar position during her travels to this world, she wasn't eager for this new part of the journey. It had been a terrifying, gut-wrenching experience, one that E wasn't too keen on finding herself in again. Panic threatened to rise within but she shoved it down brutally. Easton James didn't show fear; she didn't back down to anything.

Gripping the vine tightly with one hand, E extended a shaky hand, intent on using the wall to give her some bearing. Instead of making contact with a solid surface, E's hand swiped unhindered through the air. Her heart sped up. Switching hands, she tried the other side. Again, she came up with nothing. If she thought being enclosed in the dark was bad, being wide open and exposed in the dark was worse. Anything could simply sneak up on them and... something cold landed on E's hand, and she let out a squeak.

"Sorry to frighten you, miss." A contrite whisper floated back to her a few feet away, hopefully from the man walking ahead of her, and not some other creepy thing in the dark.

"Um...no problem," she replied, trying to calm her speeding heart.

"I was just wonderin'. The lads and I were hopin' to hear the tale."

"Tale?" Her scattered mind tried desperately to grasp the meaning of the man's words.

"What with you slayin' the monster and all."

"Oh. I'm not much of a storyteller." E blinked into the darkness. Despite the fact that she knew it wouldn't change anything, she couldn't help the instinct to try and clear the darkness away with repeated blinking.

"We'd hear it still the same. If you don't mind, miss," the man added.

"Well." She began, not entirely sure where to start, and not entirely sure it was something she wanted to talk about in the confines of the dark. "He grabbed me and I stabbed him in the hand..."

"Louder!" Another voice demanded from somewhere behind.

"And more detail! Gives us a real story now, girl," a voice from in front added. Easton cleared her throat and started again.

"He grabbed me, and I stabbed him in the hand with a dagger, kind of jerked it around so it would hurt more."

"I saw her do that one! Savage brave she was, digging away at it like that! As high up as she was, she'd be a broken mess if it had dropped her," someone eagerly added. E stumbled slightly. She hadn't thought of that then but she was now.

"Where'd you get the dagger?" another questioned, saving her from too much contemplation on the matter. Others joined in, adding their suspicious curiosity to the first's.

"From the Capt'n, of course." Smee growled in reply. A chorus of understanding met her ears, echoing along the walls. Apparently if Hook had given it to her, they didn't find reason to be upset about it.

"Well, hurry up then!" Her skin crawled as the man's shout didn't so much as echo. Where were they that echoes didn't exist? She cleared her throat and focused.

"Right. Well, I stabbed him in the hand, but that just made him mad, and he shook me up like a can of spray paint…"

"What's that?" a disembodied voice interrupted again.

"Oh…um..where I came from, it's something you use to put color on things." Confused conversation was exchanged over that one. "Anyways, he shook me crazy hard. I twisted around in his hand so I could fight against it better. And then he started staring at me and poking me in the head, which totally sucked."

"His finger sucked? Like an octopus or somewhat?" Easton winced. Talking to pirates was harder than you'd imagine.

"No, it's… it's a phrase that means it was annoying."

"I bet it was the hair that drew it in," someone whispered. It was so quiet Easton wasn't sure if she was supposed to have heard that comment or not. She continued on as if she hadn't.

"He pulled me up really close to his face, and that's when I stabbed him in the eye."

Murmurs of approval filtered through the dark. Though the subject and memory were not something Easton enjoyed discussing, somehow she found herself getting wrapped up in it. Even more surprising was the fact that the dark didn't bother her so much anymore. The sounds of their voices in the dark took away some of the oppressive weight of the blackness, perhaps. Or, maybe the shock was simply setting in again.

"Keep goin', miss," the man in front of her urged.

"I dug the dagger in really deep until my hand got stuck. It kept yanking on me, but I didn't let go, and eventually the whole thing just sort of...popped out. That's about the time Goatman freaked out and let go of me. Thankfully I was still stuck in the eyeball, or I would have ended up a pancake for sure. I knew I had to try to find a way to finish it off or we'd all be dead, so I climbed the...well...the ropey, stringy thing that holds the eye in, I guess?" She shuddered at the memory of the gross-textured nastiness of everything to come.

"Then what?" The whisper held an air of suspense, and was echoed by many others.

"I climbed up inside the eye hole. It got mad and started jabbing around in there with its finger. But with those sharp claws, it ended up poking a hole in the back. I jumped inside and..." She shrugged. "I just started stabbing everything around me. I couldn't see anything, it was all liquidy and mushy and dark in there. Anyway... so yeah... I guess I ended up doing enough damage that it finally croaked."

"Croaked?"

"Died." They got that word. "It fell over, and the impact kind-of knocked me out for a while. I came to when I couldn't breathe and started fighting my way out. It was pretty lucky I actually found the hole and made my way out again, I guess."

Excited whispers bombarded her in the darkness, talking about which parts they had seen, which parts they wished they had seen, and all sorts of detailed questions about the ordeal. Some questions were downright gross.

"Curve your yaps! You sound like a bunch of gossiping women!" Smee growled, effectively silencing everyone. That cold hand was back, patting hers on the vine. She didn't squeak this time, but she did jump.

"Thanks for sharin', miss. A real delight, that."

"Yeah. Delight." E mumbled.

"Name's Muck, by the way."

"Hi. I'm..."

"Vermillion." Hook's unmistakable voice interjected from the front, cutting her off. Apparently when he said it was better that he didn't know her name, he meant it. She didn't realize he could even hear her from up there. Had he been listening to the whole story? Was his one of the excited whispers she'd heard? Somehow she doubted that.

They walked in silence until excited cheers from those near the front of the line filtered back to them. Soon she understood why. A warm brownish light was glowing in the distance, signaling an end to the suffocating tunnel. E almost felt like cheering herself.

Instead, she gasped in awe. Stepping out into the welcoming light, Easton saw a whole world opening before her. Everything was cast in an interesting shade of warm brown hues. Down below them was a brilliant blue expanse of water. A massive black ship bobbed up and down on the gentle waves. On each side of the huge river civilization abounded. An intricately carved obsidian bridge closed the distance between river banks, people walking its expanse.

The men behind E crowded past her, many hollering excitedly as they ran down the smooth carved pathway that led them to the banks. Looking upward Easton was surprised to see a dome of thick obsidian. With the sunlight shining through it, the rock was given a brownish hue, which lent to the odd warm coloration of light everywhere.

"Wow," she breathed, a small smile etching her lips.

"Welcome to our sanctuary, Vermillion." Hook's gruff voice washed over her from where he leaned against the side of the cave opening. She hadn't even noticed him there as she was caught up in the wonder of the secret world before her. He finished coiling up the vine and tossed it in a neat loop on the ground at the cave entrance.

"How did you lead us through that place without a light? I couldn't see or feel a thing in there." Hook shrugged, offering no answer. E sighed and turned to look back at the city below. She found herself grinning in appreciation of the natural beauty.

"This place is amazing."

"I am so glad you approve, as it will be your home for some time to come. The amount of time will depend solely on your innocence or guilt." E went still, noting the cold and hollow sound of Hook's reply. Smee moved forward to take her arm, but Hook waved him away.

"See the other to his quarters, and then take your leave, Mr. Smee. Go home to your family, care for your wounds. No need to worry for this one. She shall not stray from my side." Smee spared her another distrustful glance before turning away.

"I'll miss you too, darling." E called after the big man. Smee grumbled nearly inaudible curses, trudging away.

"Come along then, my little troublesome one. We have much to discuss, you and I." A chill slipped up her spine as Hook's voice shifted quietly across her ear. He'd moved much closer than she realized. The man was deadly silent on his feet. She turned, face only inches away from his as she looked into his eye.

"How are you so sure that I won't run the first chance I get?"

"Because you know that the slightest misstep can turn the tide between ally and foe. Running would only earn my distrust and anger. And because I feel that you have a keen understanding of survival." She blinked up at him, face passive in an effort to not give more of herself away. His hand slipped up the soft skin of her inner arm, goosebumps following its wake, ending as he firmly clasped her bicep.

"Given the circumstances, you will undoubtedly feel we are your best chances of survival, and your loyalty therefore lies in aligning yourself with us. That may change one day. But for now, we suit your purposes best." His brow rose, as though daring her to challenge his assumptions. E raised a brow in return, but remained silent. His assessment was far too close to defining her exactly. He grinned, the dark beauty of it breathtaking.

"Aside from that, I think you would find escaping me to be a more difficult task than you realize." E had no doubts of that. Not to mention if the cave was the only way in and out of this place, she'd die for sure. She lifted a hand, waving grandly before them.

"Lead the way, oh Captain."

Hook offered a stiff nod, before pressing her forward. His hand on her arm was gentle, but firm, letting her know she wasn't going anywhere he didn't want her to. Not that she planned to go anywhere. Only an idiot ran in a situation like this. She meant what she said in the tavern. Until she figured out her place in this world, and the amount of danger posed from her current company, she had no reason to run.

These men were gruff, sure. And yes, she was currently their prisoner. However, they had protected her and even allowed her to defend herself. They hadn't let her keep a weapon after the ordeal, but they did allow her to remain untied. An unsettled truce lay between them. Even enemies could easily get along, if it was beneficial to their mutual needs.

Maybe it was the close calls with her life today, or all the stress added up to this point. Maybe it was just because E tended to be feisty when she was in tense, unknown situations. Whatever the case, Easton couldn't help verbally poking the solemn man at her side, pressing her boundaries to feel out her footing.

"I see your eye is better." Hook looked at her sharply.

"I beg your pardon?"

"It was red earlier. I thought red was a big scary color around here." Hook looked forward, jaw clenching.

"Your concern is noted. I see that your mouth is just fine."

"Meaning?" Her brow rose in challenge, noting the way he evaded her accusation.

"It is still as sassy and heedless as ever, despite being stuffed with a giant's brain earlier."

"Touché. *Your* concern is noted as well." She grinned wryly. "This place really is amazing. Do I get a tour?"

"Perhaps. Later."

"After I've proven my innocence?" she surmised.

"Indeed." Hook's lips quirked upward on one side. "I do so hope that you are innocent, Vermillion. It would be disappointing if you were not." E stared at him for a long moment, perplexed. Though his tone obviously held an edge of dangerous warning, there was also something that hinted at true disappointment.

"Careful. I might start to think the fear-mongering Captain Hook cares about dangerous little me," E teased. Hook glanced at her from the corner of his eye.

"A ridiculous conclusion."

"Come on," she wheedled, enjoying this cat and mouse game.

"You can't tell me I didn't win any brownie points with that goat thing back there. Popping out eyeballs and mashing brains isn't exactly easy. Not to mention it's really, *really* gross." Hook hummed quietly.

"What are these brownie points?" She found herself having to explain an awful lot of what she took for granted as common knowledge. Either she needed to get used to explaining everything that came out of her mouth, or she needed to pick her wording more carefully.

"I guess…it's a way of saying you earned someone else's approval?"

"Am I to ascertain that you slew the giant only to win these so-called brownie points? Did saving your own life have nothing to do with the matter?"

"Fine, fine." E rolled her eyes. "Be picky about it."

Hook's lips quirked to the side once more, and this time, there was no mistaking the small glimmer of humor in the corners of those appealing lips. Somehow, the fact that she made James T. Hook grin sent girlish pleasure bouncing around in her gut. Hook's grin slipped back into its usual grimace as several people stopped to stare at them. She missed it immediately. Sighing, E turned her attention to the people. Their gazes were glued to her head. E rolled her eyes. There they go with the red hair hate again.

Blinding them with bright smiles, E met every single one of their stares. If she hoped to intimidate them right back with her blunt disregard for their grumpiness, her hopes failed miserably. Some stared back at her without the slightest emotion. Others grinned with devious smiles of their own, as if they knew something she didn't. It gave her the creeps. Still, she held her chin higher and her back straighter, refusing to show them weakness or doubt.

Concentrating so hard on the task of appearing strong and uncaring, E almost missed the bridge looming before them. Her eyes widened, lips parting as she lost herself in the admiration of its delicate beauty. Hook watched her curiously as one of her wrapped feet pressed lightly on the gleaming surface.

"It is quite safe, I assure you."

She nodded in acknowledgement of Hook's promise, but still held her breath as she pressed her full weight upon it. It was stupid really; people were coming and going over the bridge constantly. She'd even noticed an animal-drawn cart pass over it earlier. Still, the bridge looked so delicate, like blown glass. It seemed impossible that it was so strong. She reached out, lightly brushing her fingers across the dusky rock.

"It's warm!" E gasped in wonder. Hook surprised her then, releasing her so that she could explore the warm, smooth surface with both hands. He really *wasn't* overly concerned with her trying to escape. Of course, considering the black crevasse they had had to traverse to get in here, she wouldn't have been that concerned about her escape either.

"The sunlight passing through the rock warms it; warms the whole refuge, in fact. The rock holds the warmth throughout the night, and then gathers more during the days. Provided they are normal spans of day and night, that is."

E frowned. "Okay, explain that one. Because the days seem to last forever here."

"Sometimes they do." Hook agreed and left it at that. The man could be exasperating when it came to answers. Her attention shifted to the black ship in the water, diverting her need to press him for answers to a new topic.

"Is that your ship?" Hook nodded. "Can I go see it?"

"Perhaps. If…"

"I prove my innocence. I got it." She tiredly finished the sentence for him. "Does it have a name?"

"We call her The Hell-born Hag."

"Well that's…cheerful."

"You wished to know." Hook pointed out, his hand once again urging her onward. "That's enough touring for now. The time for truth and answers is long overdue."

"That goes both ways, I hope."

Hook sighed, that one sound conveying an endless exhaustion.

"Innocence first, answers second."

CHAPTER 12
EASTON

Hook led her through the town, ignoring the townspeople as they stared. For her part, E continued to grin at them like a complete freak. She wasn't sure it earned her anything besides sore cheeks. But she was too stubborn to stop. Aside from that, the constant wave of adrenaline she'd been riding up and down since her arrival in Neverland was ebbing. And with the ebb came the exhaustion.

She could feel the inevitable shaking of her body edging closer, carrying a load of hysterics buried within. E was tough, she had built her life around the need for strength. But eventually, everyone hit their breaking point, and E was toeing the line. Being petulant was her last defense in keeping herself pulled together for just a little longer.

Finally they stopped before a white dome-shaped building. Hook released her arm to speak with the guard at the door, leaving E to stare up at the wide expanse of the building. She couldn't tell what it was made of, but it appeared to be more of a taut stretched canvas than metal or wood. In fact, it looked like one of those giant green-houses back home, but with an X-files sort of twisted appeal to it. The thought made her grin.

The guard to the left of the door shifted, drawing her eye as he stood taller, arms crossed over his thick chest. Both guards had to be on some sort of Neverland steroid. Her exhaustion-fueled grin grew. Apparently the guard disapproved, sending her a significant look of warning. E ignored him, attention shifting back to the pirate captain. Hook looked over his shoulder at something beyond Easton's eyesight, nodding in agreement, hand gesturing.

Glare burning a hole in her, the guard never once looked away, eying her as though she were the devil himself, daring her to try something. Boldly meeting his glare, she screwed up her face and stuck her tongue out. She felt a perverse kind of need to test his limits and reactions. In her slightly crazed mind, the idea of irking the man seemed like the best sort of game. He stood straighter, hands dropping to land on the sword at his side. E choked, a giggle lodging in her throat as a hand closed around her upper arm; the second guard was gone, and Hook was back at her side, bland expression in his sea foam-colored eye. Obviously he wasn't overly impressed with her little display with the guard. For having only one eye, he sure could be expressive with it.

"You are a petulant wench."

Hook murmured in a gravely but quiet tone that might as well have been reserved for discussing the weather. E's grin reappeared. Call her crazy, but the word 'wench' was actually kind of cute. It didn't hurt that it came from the mouth of a particular pirate captain that she had obsessed over much of her life. Sad would be choking on indignation right now, if she could hear Easton's thoughts. The grin quirked her lips a little higher.

"I can be." She agreed all too willingly.

"Perhaps I should warn you, then. There are men in this world who eat tongue for dinner quite often. Especially those of young sassy wenches that don't know when to keep their mouths closed. You should keep yours safely hidden away."

E couldn't help the snorts that escaped. Even clasped hands over her lips couldn't hold them at bay. She understood that he had meant the statement to be intimidating. Being from her place and time however, Hook's threat had an entirely different meaning for E.

Hook had a way of living, breathing and walking with an air of menace. Yet in this instance, that statement coming from him was more comical than intimidating. Of course, she had a feeling her reaction had more to do with the fact that she was losing her battle with the impending mental breakdown. Hook frowned, calculating eye taking in her current composure, or lack thereof.

Hook spared E one last shrewd glance, before propelling her toward the door in the dome. E steadfastly ignored the grumpy guard as they passed. The door slipped open without a sound, closing just as silently behind them. Lighting in the room was dim, aside from a blinding white light in the center of the room. E blinked, squinting into the shadowy edges of the dome. Unease rose in her stomach as the shadows refused to reveal their nature. Again Hook urged her forward.

Stopping in the center of the room, he positioned her just so, eyes shifting over her in that calculated manner, as though measuring her place in the universe. He shifted her slightly to the left, then back to her original placement.

"I feel like a piece of furniture." E mumbled, eyes darting about the shadows.

"That will do." Hook nodded to himself before his voice rose in a clear baritone. "Bind!" Easton's muscles flinched with an instinctual effort to escape as she was suddenly encased in invisible concrete. Her breath drew inward, shaky and edged in the first blooms of panic.

"What did you do to me?" E gasped, fighting to move.

"Be calm, woman." Hook muttered, tone distractedly consoling as his eyes again measured her position. "We must test your place-ment before the Elders arrive. Tell me. What is your name?"

"Oh, now you want to know my name? Let me out of this voodoo crap and I'll give you my name. I'll stamp it across your butt with my shoe!" E promised darkly, though it was ruined by the very telling whimper of panic that escaped in its wake. Hook's brow rose.

"Tell me what your relationship is with the man that journeyed here with you."

"He's my granddaddy, obviously." The verbal quip wobbled out on breathless gasps as she redoubled her efforts to escape. "Please let me go!" she begged, all need for composure flown from her mind. Hook watched her carefully, intensity in his expression she couldn't begin to place.

"The binding disconcerts you." He surmised.

E choked, heart flying into her throat. With each passing moment in the grips of this invisible captor, her panic rose. Memories of being trapped in the goat's head rose, along with other darker memories she fought to ignore. Soon her mind was clouded with ugly panic, and all she could think of was the need to escape. Lightheadedness from a lack of breath made spots swim before her eyes. Raising his voice, Hook called out in a clear command.

"Dissipate!"

Instantly E felt the constriction disappear. Her muscles tensed, and then collapsed beneath her. She fell to her hands and knees, body shuddering as wave after wave of fear crashed into her. Hook approached and her eyes tracked his feet warily. Internally a battle waged. Hook was right when he said she had to trust him, had to see him as an ally, if she were to survive this ordeal. She had to get them to like her, to see her as an ally, rather than a foe. At least for now, until something else presented itself. But that concept had been a lot easier to accept before he went all voodoo on her.

"Do you fear confined spaces?"

Hook's voice was calm, so low she had to strain to hear it. Her body shuddered in silent reply. She *hated* confined spaces. Of course, up until now, she had always thought that simply pertained to dark, solid and enclosed spaces. Apparently she needed to add invisible enclosed spaces to the list of situations she avoided like the plague, now.

"What did you do to me?" she gasped, voice tinged with accusation.

"The process of judgement is not always easy, Vermillion." Hook explained cautiously. "Not all care for the binding. Yet it is an integral part of the process. If you fail this test, you'll not leave the building alive."

The world tilted as she stared up at him, tears of embarrassment, fear and rage gleaming in her eyes. He continued to watch her, suspicion and confusion warring in his expression. And then, a hint of grim understanding flitted across his sea foam gaze. That look sent a slap across Easton's brain; a slap that told her to pull up her big girl panties.

He didn't think she could handle it, and his disappointment in that fact was clearly defined in his eye. He expected more strength from the girl he had dragged through the forest, the girl who had single-handedly killed a satyr. No one respected a weak ally, and a weak enemy was easily discarded.

E pushed to her feet, thirst for survival forcing the wobbly limbs to hold firm beneath her weight. Easton James didn't back down to anyone or anything; she wasn't weak, and she didn't fold under pressure. Pressure formed her into a stronger person, made her tough when it would make others weak. It would do so again, now. She dashed the tears from her eyes, then shook out her hands, trying to dispel the pent up jitters in her system.

"Put me back in the stupid freezy thing." Hook's brow rose, silently doubting her fortitude. "That wasn't fear." E argued hotly, "That was exhaustion taking its toll. That's all. I'll prove it!"

Frustration threatened to choke her as he continued his silent staring contest. She'd revealed far too much just now. Her freak out had bared too much weakness, too early in this game they were playing. She had to take some of that power back. If she could prove to him that she could handle the situation without freaking, he'd lose that gambit of power she'd so stupidly handed him. He gave a stiff nod, the only warning of what was to come.

"Bind."

Instantly her muscles froze. Easton grit her teeth, fighting against the tide of panic that once more washed upward. Her heart rate rose, her teeth clenched to hold back the swift breaths. Though nothing could be seen, she could clearly feel the sensation of being closed in on all four sides, like being sealed away in an invisible coffin. Her heart sped, breath moving to match its speed. Sweat broke out across her brow.

"Dissipate." Hook ordered, folding his arms across his chest as he eyed her prone form, once again slumping to the ground.

"Again!"

She growled, pushing upward. She stumbled one step to the side, but somehow managed to maintain her standing position. Still he simply watched her. It was driving her mad with the need to prove herself.

"I can do it!" She promised fiercely. Finally Hook shook his head. Reaching down to the heavy laden belt about his hips, he untied a small flask. Without a word, he held the flask toward her.

"What's that for?" She demanded, tightly bound in angry survival mode.

"Take it."

"Why?"

"You are strong, little Vermillion. But we don't have time for you to overcome this fear of yours." She set her teeth on edge at the word, but didn't say anything. "One can only be pressed so far before they reach a breaking point. I think we both know you are very near the edge of such an event, and your trials are not yet at an end. The Elders are coming as we speak. They hold the final say over judgement and justice alike. One sip of this drink will help to calm you, to help you get through the process with a clearer mind. If you are to have any chance, this is it."

"So, if I win them over... I live?" Hook's eye narrowed at her question.

"You must speak honestly with them, they will know if you do not. It is the purpose of this room, the purpose of the binding. One misstep can change the tide..." E yanked the flask from his hand and drained a full gulp before he finished. Cursing to himself, Hook quickly retrieved it. She grinned at his wary expression.

"Wow. What they say about liquid courage is true!" She swayed, lightly flopping forward against Hook's chest. He shook the now empty bottle near his ear and heaved a slow hiss of frustration between tight lips.

"You drank too much, you daft wench. I said one sip." Hook muttered, trying to stand her upright. His words weren't harsh or biting. To her fuzzy ears, they even sounded oddly concerned. Confusion rose within.

"I don't get it, I'm your prisoner. Why would you want to help me?"

"Why indeed. I've clearly gone mad." Hook grumbled. An unplanned giggle bubbled from her lips. She was enjoying the uncomfortable confusion in his tone far too much.

"Oh Hooky pooh. You do care." She teased, pinching his cheek. Or at least, she tried to. Her hands and arms weren't exactly working correctly, and with her head once more flopped over on his chest, she couldn't see what she'd pinched.

"And you can't hold your ale, so to speak. Devus help us." Hook groaned, pushing her upright. E's eyes narrowed.

"Devus shmeevus. I don't need no Devus. I got this magic stuff."

Her argument was pretty lame; it came out muffled as her nose once again flattened on his chest, sliding downward against it. Her nose and lip plied upward, like someone running their face down a window. Hook propped her upward before she reached his belly button, thankfully. Clearly having given up on her upward mobility, he kept a firm grip on her shoulders this time.

"Watch your tongue, girl. Were we at sea I'd have to hang you over the edge of the boat by your toes to appease the guardian of the sea. Devus is easily offended." With a grimace, Hook shook his head. "Look at you. If you weren't going to make it before, you'll never make it now."

His lack of faith stirred her stubborn pride. Voices from outside of the door met their ears, and they stared at one another for a heart stopping second of indecision. Hook flew into action, with an arm looped about her waist, Hook dragged her to a single chair to the side, just outside of the light. He quickly pointed a gracefully long finger in her face. Those fingers were made to stroke the strings of an instrument, she thought distantly. Or things far more intimate.

"Do not move an inch, nor speak a word till I ask it of you. With any luck the brew will calm itself before it is your turn." He pulled away, mind clearly moving on already to the next task. Her lips parted, words forming without her consent.

"But what if..." Hook's finger pointed at her once more, a stern rebuke in his eye

"If you move I will be forced to kill you, as your actions will be seen as a threat to the Elders. And should your slurred words lead to discovery of my slipping you something to calm yourself, they will hang me and tack your skin to the walls. Now, shut your pretty little lips, and for Devus sake hold your tongue!"

He spun about just as the door slid open. She felt a smile stretch her lips. James T. Hook thought she had pretty lips. Slumping against the back of the chair, distantly wondering if he had been serious about the skin on the wall thing, E watched the procession of people entering the room.

They moved into the domed area, taking up a seat in a wide ring around the perimeter. Each wore a long white robe, hoods covering their features. There wasn't a single thing that differentiated them from one another, aside from size. Even that distinction was blurred by the odd shuffling and slumping of their stature. The outside light of the door cut off for a moment as the missing guard from earlier ducked through it. Walking before him was the very conscious and very smug Jag.

Jag's eyes sifted through the dim lighting until they found E. When he leered and winked, E wished she could punch him in that smug snoot. Instead, she wisely held her position and didn't offer an ounce of emotion. Punching him wasn't worth having her skin tacked to the wall. Jag's face darkened at her lack of reaction, but the grin didn't disappear as Hook beckoned him to stand in the light. He sauntered forward like he owned the place, like he was about to be crowned king. Apparently his brief stint into unconsciousness hadn't done his attitude any favors. Jag twisted to the side to grin at her once more, as though reading her thoughts. E rolled her eyes.

"Bind." Hook ordered stiffly, not bothering to position the man as precisely as he had Easton. Jag stiffened, hips and back frozen at an awkward, twisted angle. Jag cleared his throat, a nervous chuckle escaping his throat

"What is this? What's going on, Hook?" Hook ignored him, turning to face the judges.

"Bringers of Justice, Judges of the innocent and guilty; welcome."

The white cowls nodded in reply. Standing, they moved in unison; gracefully their arms drew to the sides, then rose to clap their hands together over their heads. The sound was uncomfortably empty without the echo that should have followed. Welcome to Neverland, the world outside of the laws of nature. What was it with this place and a lack of echoes?

"May the strength of honesty and goodness be with us as we meet this day, that we may discern ally from foe. May our hearts and minds be open to justice, in all of its forms," the cloaked figures intoned. A strange crackling sound fizzled in the air around E, tickling across her cheeks and down her spine. She fought the urge to giggle. As one the judges sat and waited silently. Hook turned to face Jag once more.

"In this sanctuary, we can speak anything without fear of repercussions from the land or the Fiend himself. We are protected. So, have no fear that your confessions may be overheard by his ears and spies."

"Okay, sure." Jag smirked. Hook stared long and hard at him, clearly not appreciating his attitude any more than Easton usually did.

"Before us today, Judges, is one who we assume to be of the latest Arrivals. We are here to judge the safety of allowing him to join our sanctuary and fight. Or uncover the depth of his treachery and put him to Judgment." A twitch took residence at the edge of Jag's eye, though the stupid grin was still there. "State your name."

"Jaguar." Hook's silent bland stare said what he thought of Jag's name. Again, E fought the urge to giggle. Jag didn't seem to share her amusement. He cleared his throat. "You know, like the big wild cat. You do have those here, right?" Hook didn't so much as bat an eye at Jag's snippy question.

"State your real name."

"That is my real name." Jag insisted. The bright light of the white dome flickered slightly. E wasn't sure if she'd actually witnessed it, or if it was a trick of her ale-skewed imagination. That was some strong stuff he'd given her. The ale in the tavern hadn't kicked this much!

"Let us begin, then." Hook straightened, hand and hook moving behind his back. "How did you come to be here?"

E saw the moment Jag's lie sprang to life in his eyes. He'd always been good at building and embellishing stories that held only a shadow of truth at the core. He liked to brag that he'd passed quite a few lie detection tests down at the police department that way.

"I was traveling. My group was attacked and much of our merchandise was stolen. I was hunting down one of my runaway slaves when I came across your men." Jag kept his gaze firmly on her. The light pulsed again, that same pinkish hue. E blinked, glancing upward, trying to figure out exactly what was causing the fluctuation in lighting. No one else seemed to notice it.

"And where are your traveling companions now?"

"I sent them ahead. I didn't want to risk any more damage to our goods. I planned to catch up with them again once I caught my slave." Another pink flash. "I told your men the same thing already."

"So you have." Hook agreed. "However, I find myself questioning your truthfulness. You certainly went out of your way to hunt down one woman. If she is so important, why then did you sell your slave to us, and volunteer to join our ranks? Are you not eager to return to your companions?"

"I'm always protective of my merchandise." Jag leered. "However, I like to think of life as an ever-revolving door of opportunities." E rolled her eyes. He liked to pull out that particular phrase. Months ago E had heard the same phrase being used on an episode of Jag's favorite tv show. There wasn't an original bone in that guy's body. "Survival means flexibility. I don't mind changing my plans if I have to."

The light flashed yellow. E's eyes narrowed. Interesting. She wondered if Jag had noticed the correlation of the light and his lies, or if he had even noticed the light at all. Yellow signified truth, or at least truth as Jag's mind saw it. Pink signified lies.

"Where is it that you traveled from?" Hook continued.

"Chicago. You've probably heard of it." The light flashed yellow.

Hook's brow rose. How anyone could look entirely bored and yet dangerous at the same time was amazing to E. Jag didn't seem to sense the danger, his face turned away from Hook as it was. Or maybe he just didn't care. Jag offered a snide grin, reading her thoughts.

"Don't worry about it. Not everyone can be in the elite groups of the world. If you were, you would have heard of it." Pink flash. Jag was an idiot; even he didn't believe that lie.

"You are a slaver?"

"I prefer to think of it as a business prospect. They help me, and I keep them safe. A fair trade really. They're better off with me, and they love me for it." Yellow; true? The idiot actually believed that. Clearly he was thinking about his band of underground thieves when referring to his so-called slaves. He would likely tell her that pirates would be more accepting of the whole slaver terminology. But Easton honestly figured he did think of them as his own personal slaves, who were all too happy to exchange their freedom for safety. And sadly, he wasn't wrong.

E's teeth clenched. Only she hadn't loved him for it. She'd hated him for his invisible shackles, no matter the benefits.

"I see. So you are a thief." Jag blinked, surprised by the twist in the question.

"Uh…no. I'm a businessman." Pink. He knew he was a thief just as much as everyone else, whether he admitted it or not. Sweat began to bead across his forehead.

"Are you aware that slavery is looked down upon amongst some in Neverland? That there are those who feel slavery is the act of stealing life itself?"

"A matter of opinion I guess." Jag replied stiffly.

"What is your relationship with the woman seated in the chair before you?"

"I told you, she's my slave." Pink flash. Easton frowned. He didn't believe that? He believed it about the others, why not her? Was the light broken? Jag's teeth clenched as though in pain.

"Try again with more detail." Hook spoke, voice growling through the air dangerously.

"She... I found her on the streets of Chicago and saved her." He gasped, breathing heavier as though he'd been running. Yellow flash.

"Saving someone and enslaving them aren't the same things."

"She needed help. I provided it. Nothing more." Pink. The light grew brighter still and Jag cried out.

Hook looked to the council, waiting for something. As one, they nodded. Hook continued, menace dripping from every word.

"I don't know if you are aware, but every lie that spews from your lips is recorded. If you are not completely honest, the council will know. And you will not walk away alive. The light does not look kindly on those who lie. With each lie your pain level will increase, until eventually you will quite simply die. Once the process begins, there can be no stopping it until the Light is satisfied with all answers."

"What is this? Do all of your men go through this?"

"This is about Judgment, Jaguar." Jag's name issued from Hook's lips with a sound of utter distain. "And if you think you are one of my men, you are sadly mistaken."

"Look, I was told..." Jag clenched his jaw. "I traveled with your men as one of them. They liked me. I'm basically one of you. I signed a contract. Can we drop this judge and jury crap now?"

"Enough, be silent!" Hook ordered. Immediately Jag's lips sealed shut, some invisible force keeping them silent. "You are a coward, a liar, and a thief."

E's jaw dropped. She'd never heard anyone talk to Jag that way. The pirate was rising higher yet in her books. She sat a little taller in interest, the effects of the drink beginning to sober in her body.

"As to the contract; you signed little more than a supply list of items needed to be brought back to our Sanctuary. But I suppose being from...Chicago, was it? You couldn't read the language of Neverland words as easily as you professed." Jag blinked owlishly, straining against the frozen state of his body to stare at Hook. Hook's eye narrowed.

"Do you suppose we so easily accept common criminals into our presence?" An audible swallow issued from Jag's throat, Adam's apple bobbing nervously. "We kept you in a manner that was best suited toward your imprisonment. Had we bound you, you would have found endless ways to make the journey more odious and tiresome than it was. We could not spend our entire time chasing you down, or lugging you along on our backs. Allowing you to feel as though you were amongst our number was easier, and had the added benefit of your loose tongue. Your constant boasting told us most everything we needed to know of your character, without so much as raising a hand to you."

Jag moaned a pitiful groan, finally realizing his actions hadn't helped but rather sealed his own fate.

"Furthermore, your conduct with your companion was most undesirable. To immediately sell her to us, for the promise of the safety of your own flesh? Such disloyalty could never be rewarded by the return of our approval. Further proof of this was made evident by the arrival of battle. Rather than fight at our side, you ran into the forest like a lily-livered lout. Again, how can we be expected to reward such outright deplorable acts of cowardice? My men all attest to these facts; their signatures are on this parchment, and they can be called upon for vocal testament as well should it be needed," Hook added, bowing slightly to the judges.

A guard came forward to retrieve the scroll from his hand, delivering it to the figures in the shadows. After the scroll had been passed to each judge, they nodded their heads in unanimous acknowledgment. Apparently that was good enough for them.

"Speak now. Are you, or have you ever been in any form, in league with the Fiend, Peter Pan, or his cohorts." Jag choked on a gasping laugh, mouth now freed, face red with anger, pain and fear alike. Had his hands been freed too, E knew he'd be yanking on his ear right about now. It must be driving him crazy, not being able to execute that nervous tick of his.

"Peter freaking Pan? I can't believe this." Jag snorted. "No, of course I haven't!" Yellow. Hook's jaw clenched, and E wondered if he had secretly hoped to reveal Jag as a spy for Pan after all. Jag's eyes jerked around, angrily trying to escape his confines.

"Let me go. I haven't done anything wrong! You're the ones who jumped me!" Jag shouted.

"The pain will remain until you answer all questions truthfully, so let us go back over your false answers. This is your last chance."

Jag gasped as though being crushed as his gaze frantically sought out her own. Easton frowned at the strange desperation he sent her way.

"What is your name?"

"Isen... Fermond." Yellow. Easton stiffened, the name ringing in her ears. Jag squeezed his eyes shut at her reaction. She watched in a daze as Hook continued.

"How did you come to be here?"

"We got sucked into some crazy book." Jag answered tiredly, as though resigned now that she would know his full truth. Yellow flashed.

"Where are your traveling companions?"

"One's here with us, the other... I don't know." Yellow.

"Are you a thief?"

"...Yes." Yellow.

"Why did you take that woman under your control?"

"Why do you care? You don't even like her!"

"Answer!" Hook commanded.

"I overheard a conversation I wasn't supposed to hear. About a man that was an undercover agent and double-crossed my dad. I told my father. He took me and his men to their house. I watched..." Jag sobbed. "I watched as my father's men broke into their house, dragged her parents out and lit them on fire. Then they set the house on fire. I didn't know... I didn't know she was inside." Yellow. Easton stared at the man before her as tears tracked down his face.

"I was only nine. I just wanted to make my dad proud. He was so difficult to please, he was always disappointed in me, told me I was worthless. I just wanted to make him love me." Yellow. Jag's eyes rose to hers, pleading in their depths. She stared back blankly, lost in a sea of shock.

"I didn't realize the consequences of my actions. Not until I saw what they did with my own eyes. We left once the house was on fire, but I snuck back, drawn to the sickening truth of what I'd done. The fire trucks were there, police and ambulances. A firefighter came out carrying a tiny bundle, blankets wrapped around a little girl. She looked at me as they strapped her to the gurney, just stared at me with those sad empty eyes, and I ran. But running didn't make it go away. Every time I closed my eyes she was there." Yellow.

"When my dad found out there was a survivor, he wanted to go finish the job. His men convinced him to keep an eye on her, and take her down if she looked like she would be acting as a witness. There was too much heat on them to act then. My dad's contacts in the legal department told us she hadn't seen anything, or didn't remember if she did. So they left her alone, but kept an eye on her." Yellow.

"Then the cops started sniffing around her. And my dad got nervous. The cop looking out for her wasn't on his payroll. His men jumped her in the street, tried to kill her. I stopped them, took her into the guild. I'd left my dad by then, separated myself from everything he did. He left me and my rats alone so long as I kept my nose dirty and out of his way, and paid him loyalty fees monthly. He let me keep her, so long as I kept her close, made her fear leaving, fear stepping out of line. So I did. I didn't want a repeat of what happened before…I was trying to fix what I broke. But I couldn't fix her. I couldn't fix her." Yellow.

His voice was a ragged whisper by the time he was done. The audience chamber was silent as a tomb. She felt Hook's gaze linger on her, but she couldn't tear her eyes away from Jag. He'd played a game he didn't understand and took away her one chance at normality. He'd taken away the people who loved her unflinchingly. And then he'd tried to fix her like some broken toy, slathering dirt into all the cracks in hopes it would work like glue. She wanted to be furious, to stride out there and take a note from the ghost's book. A life for a life.

Instead, she couldn't feel anything. She was empty, emotionless. Broken. And yet, in a really screwed up way, she felt whole. She finally had answers as to why her parents died the way they did. Answers to what her nightmares and triggers tried to explain.

"The light will judge you as it will. There is only one truth left to learn of you, *Jaguar*." Hook stepped closer, death in his gaze. "What did you hope to gain by stealing from me, and where have you hidden it?" E felt a shell of a smile cross her lips. Only Jag would be stupid enough to steal something from James T. Hook of all people. A tight grimace stretched Jag's features. E recognized it well. Hook continued on in his silence.

"It was a very small thing, something you likely thought I'd never miss. Perhaps a tidbit I took for myself from the spoils of pirating adventures?" Hook acknowledged lightly. The deathly calm of his tone sent shivers down E's back. "But, you see, it holds a great deal of importance to me, and I *will* have it back."

"Is there a witness of this theft, Hook? We have listened to your questioning ventures against this man, but you have reached the end of our patience. If there is no witness to the theft, there is no necessity to address this now. The light is not meant to be used for the sake of trinkets." One of the voices of a Judge at her back rang out of the darkness. E had almost forgotten they were there.

"No one knows of the theft but I. You have but my word to go on." Hook grimaced, an expression of frustration and anger reflected in its dark depths. Another burdened silence hung in the air, and E looked around, urging someone to speak up, to say that his word was enough. She stood.

"I can give witness. Check under his left armpit."

Every single head of the judges turned in unison to stare directly at her as the words left her lips. E swallowed hard, the weight of their unseen stares pressing down on her like an elephant. She hoped her voice remained steady, and she hoped Jag hadn't hidden it somewhere else; there was more than her life hanging in the balance.

She had sobered a good deal in the short time she'd been sitting here, listening to her destroyed life being laid out for all to hear. Now calm floated over her, a deceptive thing likely carried before the storm of rage to come. But for now it was useful. Would it be enough to mask the drink's effects? Hook's stern expression agreed with her internal concerns.

"He has this weird flap of skin under there…a birth defect of some kind. He doesn't like to talk about it, but he hides things in it.

Important things that he doesn't want anyone to know about. That's where he put it."

She lied. She hadn't seen him take the item, whatever it was. But something in her gut told her she was right. Jag's eyes burned through her, confirming her guess. Dark vengeance grew within her and she reveled in it. Whether she died for her outburst or not, she'd take Jag down with her. Hook watched her steadily, a debate clearly going on behind his eye. Swiftly he turned and moved toward his prisoner. Uttering a few quiet words, he was able to pry Jag's left arm upward in the invisible confines and ripped the left side of his shirt open.

Jag didn't bother to try arguing Hook's probing search. All the fight seemed to have gone out of him with his confession.

A look of disgust spread over the pirate captain's face as he ran a hand over the sweaty, hairy skin flap. Even from E's distance, she could see the noticeable bump under the skin. Hook quickly motioned to a guard at the door, who stepped forward to assume Hook's position. Hook turned his back on the men, addressing the judges.

"It is a rose gold ring, with a large pink ruby mounted at its center. Within the band can be found the inscription: 'Avida: my heart's eternity,' followed by the initials O.R.B."

E blinked in surprise as Hook's voice grew rougher than its usual coarse timbre. A new hush fell over the room, one of those awkward burdened silences. Hook steadfastly ignored E's gaze, fist clenched at his side. The guard stepped away, golden ring in his upraised hand.

"It is as described, Judges."

The guard bowed low. E noticed none of the judges wanted to hold the ring to see the evidence themselves. Not that she could blame them, considering where it had just been pulled from. Hook's fist loosened in relief. The guard produced a cloth from his pocket, wiping at his hands and the ring. The ring was respectfully handed off to the pirate captain, who held it carefully.

After a moment's pause, he tucked the ring away in one of the pouches on his belt. Wiping his fingers off on a handkerchief pulled from another pocket his gaze landed on her. Her eyes widened in surprise at the stiff nod of thanks that followed. Turning on his heel before she could react, he stalked back to Jag, whose arm was still ridiculously frozen over his head.

"I move for Judgment on the man in our midst." At Hook's proclamation, the Judges stood. Arms spreading wide once more, they spoke.

"We seek justice to be brought down upon the bound within our midst. The brand of his truth be marred upon his flesh until the day of his redemption, or even unto death."

At the clapping of their hands, the light pulsed around Jag, almost like flashes of lightning. Jag's head fell backward, mouth open wide in an eerily silent scream of pain. Smoke rose from his body, filling the air with an acrid scent of burning flesh. And then, as quickly as it began, it was over. Jag fell to his stomach, gasping and whimpering. The guard came forward once more, toeing Jag over onto his back. E's old guild leader lay on the ground before her, chest heaving for breath. Every inch of his neck was covered in dramatic black branding. Hook strode forward, standing over the crumpled man.

"You yet live. It would appear that you have been granted a chance at redemption, Isen. Despite your crimes it seems the Light finds some good within you. However, you have been branded with the marks of a coward, betrayer, thief, and liar. They shall pain you every day that you bear them. Each time you show attributes of these three brands, the marks will grow. Eventually they will cover your entire body. Should that happen, you had best pray, as your last breath will not be far behind. Should you, however, change your soul's darkness, the marks will slowly recede. Courage, honesty, loyalty and hard work will be your keys to salvation. The choice is yours."

Hook motioned to the guard, who quickly bent forward and grabbed Jag's hands, dragging him out of the domed room by his wrists. Silence followed the closing of the door, and E immediately felt the weight of every gaze in the room crushing down on her shoulders. She was next.

CHAPTER 13
EASTON

"What is your name?"

"Easton James. Er, Howe, technically. But I go by James."

Her voice seemed too loud in the oppressive silence of the room. She swallowed, and fought the edges of panic that threatened to crumble in on her. Hook had led her to the center of the room, and luckily her legs had been steady beneath her. Something Hook had been just as relieved to see, if the subtle twitch at the corner of his lips was any indication.

He'd placed her in the shield, eye silently warning her to stay calm. She returned a grim look of her own determination, hoping it was a promise she could keep. One question was out of the way now, and so far she'd managed to not pass out or go into full-on panic mode. One step at a time, she'd conquer this task.

"Where do you come from?" Hook intoned, stern gaze never leaving hers.

"I lived in Chicago."

E blinked in surprise. The words had been true, a fact supported by the yellow flash of light, so that was good. Yet it felt as though they had been plucked right from her tongue. It was as though the words *wanted* to be spoken. She wondered if this was part of the side effect of the binding. Or perhaps a side effect of the drink Hook offered. Both?

"How did you come to be here?" Once again Hook's words had her mouth opening without conscious approval.

"I think I came through a book." She winced, knowing how crazy it sounded. "Kind of like a portal from one world to another, maybe?"

The light flashed yellow. Internally E felt a mishmash of emotions swell at the affirmation of her speculations. Relief that she wasn't crazy, worry over the implications, confusion as to why the book pulled her in, the stirring of a forbidden excitement; and underneath it all the continual numb pain of her youth.

E forced herself to refocus on the trial that would determine whether she lived or died. She could sort through the emotions and implications after, if she were still alive. The light had confirmed her truth, but would they believe her? Or perhaps burn her for witch-craft? Did they do that sort of thing in Neverland? She didn't remember anything about witches in the book... Jag had mentioned the book too, and he didn't get burned for it... much, anyway.

"And this book was called what?"

Hook's tone gave away nothing as to his feelings on the matter, whether he believed her, nor whether she'd just signed a death warrant. Butterfly wings of panic fluttered in her belly. She ignored them.

"Peter Pan: The boy who wouldn't grow up."

"How did you come into possession of this book?"

"I stole it."

Quiet murmurs sifted toward her from the judges. The panic grew, renewed its efforts to swallow her, but she shoved it to the side. They already knew this much, she couldn't take back the words Jag had spoken. It was bad enough her tongue had a mind of its own; she didn't need the panic adding its own flavor of crazy right now. She focused on Hook, focused on the serious shadows cast on his face as he paced back and forth in front of her; anything to keep her mind off her very vulnerable and trapped position.

"When did you arrive in Neverland?"

"I...I don't know, the days and nights are weird here." She hesitated, trying to formulate a coherent answer in her hazy mind. "We passed through the book just moments before your men found us." Yellow.

"When my men found you, you were running from something. What was it?"

"Him. He was chasing me." Yellow.

"Who?"

"J..."Her throat froze. Even though the binding of the ceremony seemed to have a forcible way of making her speak truth, even it didn't seem to have the power to make her say the name. "One of the men I came here with. The one you just sent out." Hook stiffened, brow furrowing.

"*One* of the men? He mentioned another as well. Who was it?"

"My friend, Wiley."

"Where is this Wiley now?"

"I don't know. I can't be sure if he made it through the book or not, but I know he was pulled in. When I woke up, Wiley was gone. If he did make it through, I worry that he fell off the cliffs into the water when we landed." The words tasted bitter on her tongue.

"The man we just questioned prior to you, is it as he says? You are his slave?" She hesitated.

"I suppose I *was*, in a way. Where I come from...survival is difficult when you're alone. He offered a place of safety, if we did what he told us to do."

"This is why you played the part of thief? For survival at the hands of your slaver?"

"I needed help. I was living on the streets, and I had a record with the police,"

"A record with the police?"

"Um...police are kind of like soldiers, I guess?" Hook nodded, understanding that. "There were things I had done or was accused of doing, when I was young; more things I was forced to do to survive. The police wanted to punish me for it, and I was scared. *He* took me in off the streets. He protected me from jail, gave me a home, food, a family of sorts. And in return, I did what he said was my duty to help myself and everyone else in the family. I wanted to leave, to find a legitimate job, but my past made it difficult. And he knew it." Anger simmered in the pit of her stomach along with the panic now.

"I didn't know then what I know now… what he just told everyone. But maybe on a subconscious level, I somehow connected the two. Maybe that's why I couldn't ever bring myself to say his name when he wanted me to so badly. Either way, I was still going to go. I was sick of doing his dirty work. I wanted to be free. He stopped me before I could leave. Wiley tried to protect me. That was when the book pulled us in."

The light flickered yellow again. Tears welled in her eyes, and Hook's ever insightful gaze didn't miss it. Whether out of kind regard to her obvious feelings on the matter, or because he didn't need to know more, Hook didn't ask her to explain further.

"Have you stolen since you came to Neverland?"

"No."

"Would you?"

"If it came down to my safety, or the safety of someone I cared about, yes." Yellow. Once again that odd pause of silence descended on the room. She hated that weighted sensation of quiet.

"Do you hold any feelings of loyalty toward the man who calls himself Jaguar?"

"Any remaining loyalty I might have felt toward him was destroyed with his truth today." Yellow. She felt an odd sense of relief that the light agreed with her. That she didn't still have some sort of screwed up hidden allegiance to him.

"Have you ever had any contact with the fiend Peter Pan, or any of his cohorts?" Hook's eye scrutinized her, as though sifting through her heart's motives.

"No."

"Did you ever read the book that brought you here?"

"Many times. It was a favorite of mine."

"As such, do you find that you hold any sympathy for the Pan, or his cohorts?"

"No. Hook was always my cup of tea." Yellow. Her cup of tea? That came out weird.

"Hook?" His disbelieving tone left little doubt as to his surprise. "I would imagine Hook being cast as the villain, in such a story." The surprise narrowed to suspicion and challenge. "Perhaps you hold a soft spot for villains." She knew he was factoring in her distorted loyalty to Jag and life as a thief into that statement.

"My parents read me the story often, before they died. I used to refer to the story as the Book of Hook, because Hook was always the hero in my eyes. His character's strength bolstered mine when it was failing. When I ended up on the streets, I unofficially changed my last name to James, in his honor."

Hook's brow rose and her cheeks flushed. Okay, maybe having her skin tacked to the wall wouldn't be so horrible right about now. There was nothing quite like sounding like a complete stalker and freak to put awkwardness in the air. His surprise shifted into a frown, and then a blank slate. He turned and walked a few feet away. After what felt to be an eternity, he returned.

"A choice is placed before you. As you have seen where we reside, we can't release you to Neverland. The fiend would snatch you up and torture the information out of you, if it were not given freely. Until the threat of Pan is destroyed, you will have to stay within Sanctuary, though you would be free to choose what you would do within the confines of it."

"And my second choice?"

"Neverland is under the scourge of Pan and his minions. There are few left with the strength and will to fight him. I find in you the skills we require. You've proven yourself immeasurable in a battle. I would ask you to join our cause. But before I can extend such an invitation, I must know that your allegiance would be to your duty, to our efforts. So I ask you this," Hook stopped only a foot away, eye intently pinning her as surely as the shield. "Will you join my crew?"

E blinked in shock. She certainly hadn't expected something like this. To be tossed out, left to wander in the jungle and be eaten, maybe. But to be offered a place amongst them, let alone his crew? She shook her head, trying to clear the fog and put pieces together.

"Wait, what about the part of how I came to be here? That I came through a book? Doesn't that sound completely crazy to you? Or… like you maybe want to burn me at the stake as a witch or something?" Hook's brow rose and one corner of his lip twitched, fighting a smile.

"People often burn women where you come from?"

"If they thought they had magic, they used to burn people, yes." She replied stubbornly. Yellow. Hook's brow creased as he noted the color.

"Well, that doesn't happen here. No one thought you were a witch, Vermillion. There *was* a time my men thought you to be a siren of the fiend, but no siren has ever passed the water test."

"Is that why they kept throwing water on me? They were trying to turn me into a fish?" One of the council members coughed, and Hook's lips quirked.

"That aside, no one comes in or out of Neverland by conventional means, not anymore. That leaves but one option." His weight shifted, hand falling to rest comfortably atop the handle of his sword, the picture of ease. "In truth, we have known of the portal for a long time. We call those who travel through it 'Arrivals'."

"There have been other people like us here before?" She blinked in surprise, trying to grasp the concept.

"Countless." Hook held her gaze. "The only doubt lay in whether or not you were under the thrall of the fiend when we found you, whether his corruption had spread to you yet." He held up a hand, forestalling any further questioning on her part.

"All other questions on the matter can be answered at a later time. But for now, you have choices to make. I warn you, don't answer lightly. If you pledge yourself to our cause, know this; I do not suffer betrayal. The lives of many rest upon my shoulders, and should I for a moment think you are putting them in danger, I will not hesitate to end your life."

E stared at Hook, soaking in the sincerity of his dark promise, the strength that emanated from him. Her mind sifted through all of her memories of him, gained through the chapters of a book read by a mother to her small child. She took those memories, the strength she'd gained from an imaginary character, and compared it to the character of the real man she'd come to know so far on the trip here. Easton found that Hook was very much the same as her memories portrayed him.

He was a man who led from the heart and soul. He didn't fight for personal gain, he didn't fight for power; he fought for justice. He was a man who protected, who fought valiantly for what he believed in; fought to end horror, not create it. She had seen in battle that he truly cared about his men, not just about what he could use them for.

She didn't know everything about him, or his real story, that was true. Things had differed in Neverland than from what was written in the book. But one thing remained certain in E's eyes. He was a man she could respect. And until he gave her reason to believe otherwise, she believed him to be a man that would honor his promises, so long as their purposes aligned.

So she must decide; hide away in safety, or follow the man offering freedom of choice and adventure. She could stay in the city, she could be safe for once in life. Yet, the idea of wandering aimlessly in a city full of people who probably hated her for her hair color alone, leaving her fate for others to protect, it didn't sit well in her gut. As screwed up as it sounded the idea of endless safety was boring.

She'd lived a life of surviving one day to the next, unsure if it would be the day her luck ended, unsure what Jag would ask of her next and whether she could offer it without destroying the last pieces of her soul. Days of stealing to survive, knowing eventually she'd be caught out on evidence so compelling that Jag's presence couldn't save her from a new barred cage. Perhaps that life had ruined her to any hopes of being satisfied by a calm and serene lifestyle. Or maybe she was just tired of letting everyone else pave the path of her life.

If she were to join Hook, she would have a hand in forging the future, not just for herself but all of Neverland. The idea of putting her neck on the line for so many others was intimidating, and her survival instincts balked. However, it was also oddly liberating, enticing. She'd been afraid of the unknown for so much of her life, under Jag's thumb. Was it possible that Hook would teach her to understand the excitement that the unknown could offer? She frowned, saving that thought to ponder later.

Really, the choice was quite simple, from the overall vantage point of survival. There would be danger with Hook, yes. But based on the battles they had already faced, Hook was a man that would watch your back. He had protected her and treated her respectfully, despite being his prisoner. He offered adventure and freedom, a light at the end of her dismal tunnel of life. She could make a new life here, become the person she secretly hoped she was inside. If she were allowed to stay in Neverland, that is. Which left one line of questions.

"If I help you destroy Pan, will I be allowed to choose whether to leave or stay in Neverland? Will I be forced back to my world? And if I stay, will my place still be with your men, if I choose to be?"

"I can't attest to what the portal will do, should Pan be bested. We have no experience on the matter. Those who have Arrived have never left, save it be through death." Hook's eye held hers steadily, as though waiting for her flinch. When it didn't come, he nodded and continued.

"However once the fiend's disease is taken from the land, and should the portal allow you to stay, you are entirely free to do as you will. I do not hold with slavery, your freedom is yours. If you prove an asset to my men, you will be welcomed within our ranks for as long as you choose." Hook acknowledged. Steeling herself, E nodded resolutely.

"Then I will be loyal to Hook and Sanctuary alike. For as long as Hook and Sanctuary are loyal to their promises to me."

She added the last bit as a customary disclaimer. Adding a disclaimer was always smart. If you didn't watch your own back, you had no one to blame but yourself if things went south. Hook carefully watched the lights flickering for deception. A yellow flash brought his nod of approval. Taking a step back, hand and hook behind his back, he moved for the final step of her trail.

"There is one last matter to settle before this pact can be formed.

The Judges must extend a final judgement. If you are found to be loyal of heart and intention, you will become part of my crew. If you are found to be deceptive, if you are found to have been touched by the fiend as your hair suggests, fate shall be decided for you as it was for your companion. The Light always understands true intentions."

E swallowed, offering a stiff nod. She really hoped this voodoo crap agreed with what she felt inside. Either way, she was more than ready to be out of this shield. The drink had worn off a good five minutes ago, and it was getting difficult to control her fear. The judges swiftly stood, and E watched their actions play out as they had only a short time before with Jag.

"We seek justice to be brought down up the bound within our midst. The brand of her truth be reflected upon her flesh until the day of her deception, or even unto death."

Well, that didn't sound *quite* as ominous as it had for Jag…it was amazing what a difference a few changed words could make. She just hoped it was good enough to keep her alive and not smoking like a lump of charred wood.

At the clapping of their hands, the light pulsed around E, those familiar flashes of lightning encasing her. They flickered about her, licking their singeing touch across every ounce of her flesh. E clenched her jaw against the pain its touch elicited, but she refused to close her eyes, gaze locked on Hook.

He had been her strength while growing up; he'd instilled bravery in her when she had none. He'd be that same source of strength and bravery now, whether he chose to be or not. Her gaze seemed to disquiet him at first. Then, as though coming to some internal decision, Hook stood straight and offered a silent nod of support, granting her what strength she could take from him.

A small smile curved the corners of her lips; he was a true leader through and through, just as she always knew he would be. His eye showed that he knew this could be the end for her, but even though that would mean she hadn't passed judgement, he was still offering what he could. He was a leader she could have given her all to.

The pain lessened suddenly, shifting from a fierce burn to mellow warmth of welcome as it surged through her veins. It was invigorating, intensely powerful, as it embraced her like a lover. The weight, pain and frustrations of her world seemed to lessen, become distant memories. And then it was gone. E fell to the floor, shivering in a room that now felt freezing, for the absence of the fire in her veins. Firm hands gently rolled her to her back. She felt distant, oddly light and fluffy. Like a cloud. She smiled deliriously inside, though she couldn't say if the smile made it to the surface.

"Am I alive?" E blinked up at the stern face of Hook as he crouched at her side, conducting his exam of the judgement.

"Yes." Was that approval in his eye? Deft swordsman fingers slipped over the skin at her neck, leaving pleasant warmth in their wake. "No marks on the neck." His hands swept down her left arm, pushing the sleeve up from her wrist. He froze then, face a blank mask.

"What's the verdict, doc?" Easton asked. His reaction should worry her, yet she still floated on the high left from the fire's path, and no emotions warred within. It was kind of pleasant, not worrying for once.

"You bear the mark of the swallow and hook." His quiet voice carried a hint of something she couldn't place. She tore her gaze from his face to look at the wrist he still held in his hand. Sure enough, on the inside of her wrist were two brands. A hook curved gracefully toward her palm, as red in color as her hair. A matching black and red bird sat on the base of the hook, wings outstretched to the side as though flying.

"More red." She whispered, heart dropping. "What's that mean? Did I fail?" Hook stared down at her, his gaze a depthless expanse of sea.

"No, you didn't fail." He answered simply.

"Oh. Good." She blinked, eyelids growing heavy. "I didn't panic."

"Yes, you did well." He nodded, giving her hand a little squeeze.

"Can I get up, now?" Hook's lips lifted slightly, clasping her hand with his.

"You can certainly try, Vermillion." Her body swayed slightly as he pulled her upright and she clasped onto his arm, holding tight.

"Whoa. I feel...tipsy." She smiled a watery grin. "So. What's next, what do I do?" Her legs gave out from under her and she slumped against him for what felt like the hundredth time that day. She was too tired to be embarrassed though, sleep swiftly sucking her under. Her last conscious thoughts were of Hook lifting her into his arms, a smile in his low voice.

"Now you sleep, little butterfly."

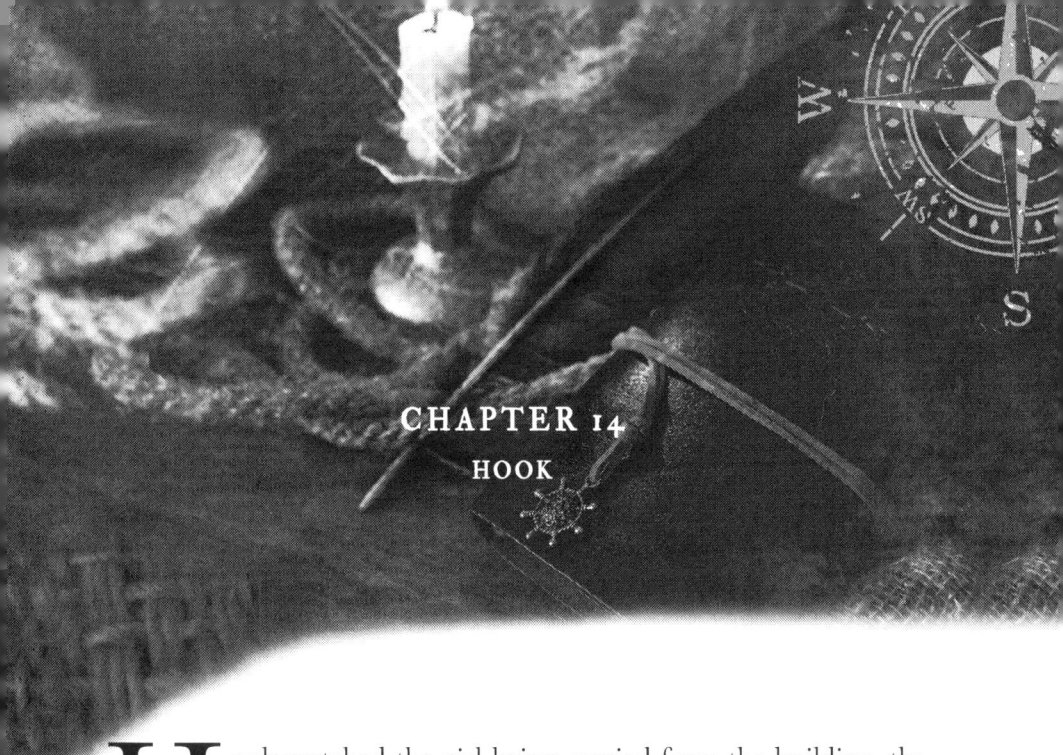

CHAPTER 14
HOOK

Hook watched the girl being carried from the building, the second guard taking her to the rooms that would now be hers. The first guard obviously held a vendetta against the girl, likely because of her hair, and couldn't be trusted to hold to the promises Hook made for her safety. He'd deal with that matter later, should problems arise. For now, he'd simply be mindful of who he assigned to be near her. The Elders strolled past him on their way out, all except for one.

"Her hair has become an even deeper vermillion than it was before the binding." Hook stated. The shadow at his back moved closer.

"The light serves to purify and bring to the surface that which is already there."

"The blood runs thick within her, then?"

"So it would seem."

"I don't trust her."

"Of course you don't." There was humor there, under that aged voice. "But one might wonder: if there is no trust, why then did you offer her a place within your ranks before consulting the elders of their opinions? Or waiting for the Light to guide you one way or another based on her markings, for that matter?"

"What *is* your opinion?"

"Why should my opinion on the matter hold sway now? The Light has spoken for her. Humor an old woman and answer my curiosity, Hook. Why did you offer her a place amongst you so prematurely? The Light compelled her to answer all matters truthfully. It was clear that her character and choices made before coming to Neverland were not entirely unselfish, nor trustworthy. And still, you offered her a place amongst your men. You didn't yet know what the Light would proclaim of her. So what could have been your motivation? Could it be you wanted her to go into the judgement with a sense of hope, and purpose? Something to ease the fears so obviously held within her shaking body?" Hook stiffened under the insinuation.

"I wanted it fresh on her mind when the light touched her."

"You wanted to ensure that there was no way the light could mistake her heart and its purpose, in choosing to join you. Of course that was the *only* reason," she surmised shrewdly, that taunting humor still in her voice, suggesting she knew that hadn't been his only motivation. Unfortunately it would seem the old crone knew he still carried a few soft spots under his self-made armor. And she wasn't happy to leave it rest as it was. He repressed a sigh as she pushed him for truth once more, for answers he didn't have to give, even for himself.

"Yet still you do not trust? One must wonder, is it the Light you do not trust, or the girl? Or perhaps it was that you did not trust yourself to make such a judgement, because she calls to you?" she cackled, walking around him towards the door.

"Wait! The brands: did you see them?" he called out. The old woman paused.

"Aye."

"And?" he ventured. The woman slowly shook her head, turning back to him with the tired resignation of a mother speaking to a child.

"As you will not admit it to yourself, I shall say it for you. The swallow signifies a long distance traveled, carrying the blood with it back to the land. The hook signifies her place amongst your men, the followers of the hook. The placement of the brands on the left arm shows that both matters align closely with her heart's desires or purpose. And the swallow's proximity to the hook? You heard from her own lips; the girl is tied to Hook, even from before the Arrival. Make of that what you will."

"Is she the one or not?" Hook growled in frustration. "Will she be the key to my release?" The woman continued her pathway out the door, wry chuckle drifting in her wake.

"How can I answer such a question? It is left to the two of you to forge your destinies, not I, nor even the Light. Not even for one as impetuous or dauntless as the infamous Captain Hook."

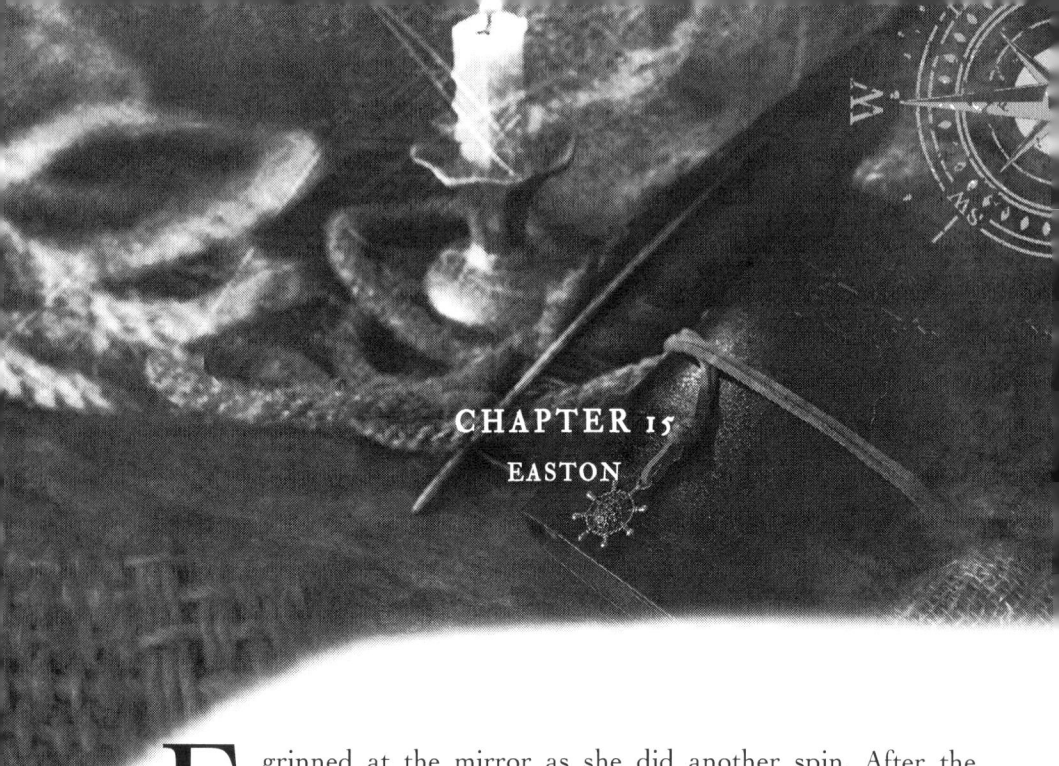

CHAPTER 15
EASTON

E grinned at the mirror as she did another spin. After the shock of waking in a completely unfamiliar room and finding a big weird guy standing guard by the door, memories came flooding back. She was in Neverland and now officially one of Hook's crew members. With the memories came excitement and a good dose of nerves. Life had never been easy in her old world, but she hadn't been in the position of needing to prove herself to anyone for quite some time.

When she first came to the guild, it was constant fights and clawing her way to a place of respectful distance from the others. Eventually it became well known that she was one of the best in her area of expertise and that was rarely questioned unless someone was looking for a fight. Most people learned to stay away from fights with E. She fought dirtier than most.

Now, standing before the mirror in full piratey garb, E's nerves were flopping around in her gut like fish. Hook was giving her a chance to prove herself. She had to prove herself not only to him, but his men. To all of Sanctuary, really. She'd made a few leaps and bounds on that front by killing the giant, sure. But at the end of the day, she still came to them as a prisoner with bright red hair.

E squinted into the mirror. Speaking of hair, maybe it was the lighting, but she could swear her hair had gotten redder, just to spite her. Nothing about E was easy, even her hair it would seem. With a sigh, she flipped the gently waving strands over her shoulder and readjusted the items of clothing on her frame for the hundredth time. While she was eating up the design of the clothes, she didn't love the way the shirt made her look like a furious ghost. White was not her friend, even less so now that her hair color seemed to have taken on a mind of its own.

The front of the shirt laced up with corded laces, the baggy sleeves coming to a tighter closure at the wrist, and the hem hung well past her thighs, as though it had been made for a much larger person. The pants were far longer than her legs, but at least they mostly stayed up on their own, which was good considering the belt was also too big. Luckily the boots fit perfectly. Clothing and jitters aside, she was still in love with Neverland's prospects for her.

Her fingers were drawn, for the millionth time, to the brands on her wrist. Her lips curled into a soft smile as she traced the lines of the hook. Flipping the hair back over her shoulder once more, she strode to the door and walked out with a bright grin.

"What's wrong with you, you look ill. Are you dying?" Smee stood outside the door, scowling down at her like she were a lump of earwax. She ignored his jab at the effects of the shirt on her skin color.

"Oh. It's you. Where'd the other guy go?"

"He chose latrine duty over guarding your door. Not that I can blame him."

"You know, you can pretend that you hate me, but everyone knows you are falling in love with me."

With a devious grin, E walked past him down the hallway of what she soon came to realize was an inn. She had expected the crew to all live in a military-style barracks, or on the ship. Living most of her life on crumby foster home stints, on the streets, or below them, E would have been up for any living arrangements Hook could throw at her. Finding out that they lived in a posh inn that was both clean and comfy was a shocker.

"In love. Pah! Disgust is more like it." Smee scowled, huge strides allowing him to easily catch up.

"Denial." She retorted.

"You look like a scrawny turnip drowning in a lake of milk."

"Charming."

"Hardly."

"Alright, where are we headed?" E cut off the conversation of insults.

"Now that you've slept the day away, you mean?" Her brow rose in challenge, though internally she was reeling. She must have been really wiped out after the judgement test if she slept that long. Of course, considering the days and nights seemed to be entirely unpredictable here, that didn't tell her much.

"The Captain wanted to speak with you when you woke. And since it's supper time, he'll be sitting down to eat with the others.

"And where exactly is that?"

"In a building across the street."

"Cool. See ya, Hulk." His heavy hand landed on her shoulder, stopping her short escape attempt.

"Unfortunately for the both of us, I'm under orders to escort you there."

"In that case, Hook must hate us."

"On that we can agree. And my name is Smee, not Hulk. Cease in referencing me as such."

E held back her snickers as she followed the grumpy giant down the stairs and outside. The restaurant of sorts was a matching set of the Inn, and she decided that both places must belong to the same people. The entry was covered with a set of those flappy style saloon doors you see in the old western movies on late night tv. E found herself grinning like a total geek as she pushed through them. The faces that looked her way were a mixture of interest, disgust, and humor. They continued to stare openly, not the least intimidated or embarrassed when she bluntly returned their gazes.

"Vermillion, back here."

E's eyes snapped to the back of the room, zeroing in on the figure of none other than Captain Hook. He cut an imposing figure, tall and regal, yet dangerous and stern. Immediately the eyes that had stared so hard at her shot down to the tables before them, their owners suddenly engrossed in the conversations and meals at hand. She smiled, feeling smug in the knowledge that, while they may not respect her, they certainly respected her position as their Captain's guest. Looking over her shoulder revealed the fact that Smee not only wasn't witnessing her minute triumph, but had disappeared altogether.

Putting confidence and a state of ease into her stride, E took the long walk back to Hook's table, doing her best to ignore both the covert glances of the other guests, and the burning gaze of the Captain. The man had that awe-inspiring gift of intimidation down to a T, and he didn't even have to show an ounce of expression on his face for someone to feel it.

He pulled out a chair, and it took her a moment to realize he wasn't changing seats, but was actually holding it for her. Clearing her throat, E moved to sit in the chair, praying she was doing it right. She'd never had the pleasure, or discomfort (take your pick), of accepting the gentlemanly prowess of a man. Chivalry was dead these days, at least it was back home. With the seat safely tucked beneath her and Hook once again seated across from her, Easton breathed a sigh of relief.

"Are you still ill? Has the binding taken such a toll on you?" Her lips immediately slipped from an expression of ease, into a self-conscious mutation of a smile.

"No, I'm fine thanks. It's the shirt. White isn't my best color and I think this outfit was made for someone twice my size." Hook's lips spread into a rakish grin so knee-wobbling she was momentarily stunned.

"I was actually referring to the fact that you slept for so long. But I will try to see to it that your clothing is adjusted to your prefer-ences. All of the clothing you wear was made for a man, so it is easy to understand the ill fit."

E blinked at the man before her. Something was different about him. While he still held that soul weary air about him that one would expect to see of someone in constant battle and leadership, he had gained a little something else. Sitting in this restaurant wearing fresh clothes and surrounded by warm lighting and laughter, Hook almost appeared…comfortable. Maybe that was a weird definition to label someone with, but the man she'd traveled with these past several days seemed so different from the one before her now. He lounged in his chair with a careful grace, well-mannered and seemingly at ease.

Growing up as she had, she could recognize the taut body language speaking of a man ready to fight at any moment. Yet, while she couldn't quite put her finger on the exact reasoning, he was different in this moment. Relaxed, mellow, perhaps even happy. She liked it. Though the fact that it was unexpected and a different level of character than she'd seen so far, put her on an uncertain level. How did one approach *this* Hook? His brow rose and she realized she was staring at him with her mouth wide open like an idiot.

"Oh, right, clothes that fit. Thank you. Though maybe I could borrow some old clothes from another woman in town who no longer needs them? No need to make me new clothes."

"I'm afraid that won't be possible." Hook responded sharply. The storm in his eye disappeared as quickly as it rose. "The few women in Sanctuary are not compatible with your stature. The tailor will make you suitable clothes. Now, back to your health. Are you certain you are well?" He changed the subject quickly.

"I'm fine, really. I think I was just tired."

"Of course. It has been a stressful week for you, I am certain."

"Yeah. Kinda has." She murmured, still not sure what to say. Hook motioned toward the bar keep, who swiftly disappeared into the backroom and reappeared with a plate heaping full of delicious smelling food.

"As you can't read the language of the menu, I took the liberty of ordering something for you to eat tonight. Later, when we have more time, I can read it out to you so that you may choose for yourself. And of course, if you are here for a long engagement, perhaps we can arrange for you to learn the language."

"Oh. Sure. That'd be great." She stuttered, mouth watering over the food before her. Like last time, she had no idea what the food was, but it looked and smelled amazing, so she dove right in. Eating on the streets taught you not to be too choosy with your meals, and to take your blessings where you could get them. This meal was definitely one of those blessing moments.

"The ink in the shape of a compass on your wrist; you did not acquire that during the binding."

"No." She blinked, curious as to where he was going with this.

"May I enquire after it? All compasses of my knowledge point North. Do they not do so in your world?"

"It was the mark of my team of thieves back in my world. Each letter of our first names corresponded with one of the points on the compass." She shrugged. "I'm the E."

She shifted uncertainly under the depthless expression he fixed her with. She wasn't entirely sure what to do with that look, or why it made her blush.

"You are the E." He murmured softly. E cleared her throat, pulling him from whatever thoughts swirled behind that eye.

"So, what is it you are going to need me to do, now that I'm part of your crew and all?"

"Let's save that discussion for tomorrow. It is late and such duties will not be required of you tonight. A fully recovered ally is better than an exhausted one. So for now, simply enjoy your food." She nodded her understanding, more than happy to simply enjoy her meal.

"I trust the accommodations are to your liking? You're comfortable? I tried to put you in a room further from the men, for your comfort and propriety's sake, but I am afraid there isn't much room left in the inn."

"What? Oh, no. It's amazing, really." She swallowed down the heavy load of food in her mouth, tried to act slightly more civilized. "I haven't had my own room since...well, since my parents." His gaze softened.

"That must have been quite a shock, hearing the truth that way." He paused. "I have questioned whether you would thank me for revealing such truths or not."

"Uh...." She paused, taking a moment to sift through her emotions again. She'd already done so many times since waking up.

"I don't know if it just hasn't hit me yet, or I'm too broken to feel it right. But honestly… I feel relieved. I know that makes me sound like a horrible person."

"Go on."

"It's just." She nibbled her lip, trying to find the right words. "It was screwed up and terrifying. Part of the reason I'm wigged out of the trapped enclosed spaces thing is because of the day my parents died. They hid me in a storage cubby under the stairs when the men started breaking in. It was dark and cramped, I couldn't move hardly at all much less get out. Luckily the firefighters heard me crying, or I would have burned along with the house." She chewed on a lump that tasted like a potato, giving herself time to think before continuing.

"I've had years to come to terms with the fact that life sucks and so do people. I've grown numb in many ways to how they behave."

"So you are numb to the truths you heard?" He asked curiously.

"In a way. Hearing why they actually died, it's kind of a relief to know the answers. It's been just another unanswered question in my world of unknowns. Knowing why and how… it's still screwed up but it brings me a little peace, too." She shrugged. "But it's more than that. I don't know how to describe it, but at the end… the light just kind of felt like it filled me with warmth and acceptance of all the crappy stuff that's happened to me in the past. Like I haven't forgotten about them, but I don't feel… crushed or defined by them anymore either."

"The light has a way of healing people, inside."

"And what exactly is the light?"

"It is Neverland." Hook scratched at his stubble-shadowed jaw. "What Neverland was once like, before the Fiend. When it was at its purest. Something about this place is sacred. It protects against the influence of the Fiend, and keeps all within safe. This is the last pure place of Neverland."

"Wow. Sounds like a lot of responsibility."

"It is. She maintains us, and we maintain her."

"Anyway, thanks for taking me under your wing and giving me a place to stay. Honestly, I was expecting a lot less, and would have been just fine with that. So, thanks."

"Less?" Hook mused. "I would hear more about where you come from, if you're open to sharing."

"Um…there isn't much to tell really. What do you want to know?" She shrugged, uncomfortable with sharing the less-than-appealing facts of her past.

"Where did this guild of yours live, and with whom did you share your life? Are there others waiting for you, back home? Friends, siblings, lovers?"

"Um…" The conversation slipped so easily from his lips, as though this were common small talk. Maybe it was, for most people. E was used to a close-lipped lifestyle. She paused at that thought. Maybe that was her old life, but did she really have to live like that now? She was away from the guild, sold off by the guild leader no less, yet here she was still living by their rules.

Neverland was her new home, at least for now, and Hook was her new leader. Was it asking so much to have a little small talk? Straightening her spine, E dove into as thorough an explanation of her lifestyle in the guild as she could. Hook listened attentively.

"You lived in open spaces with other men?"

"Yeah, sure, why not? Beggars can't be choosers, you know?" She grinned at her own joke. Hook seemed troubled, however, his easy-going manner evaporated.

"You have lived a difficult life, Vermillion."

"Oh," she stuttered, taken off guard. "Well. It hasn't been that bad, really. I'm alive, not in jail, and have all my limbs." She wiggled her fingers as proof, then winced. She'd been trying to lighten the mood, but that last bit probably wasn't too funny for a guy with a hook for a hand. Hook offered a distracted hmm of agreement, though he still seemed more uncomfortable with her past than her joke.

Honestly, E hadn't seen anything too gruesome about it. It sucked sometimes, sure, but it hadn't been all horrifying. Maybe that was because she had grown so accustomed to it, that kind of life becoming her new normal. But really, much worse things could have happened to her, and she'd been really lucky to escape as unscathed as she was. If she'd actually seen her parents burned alive, that probably would have screwed her up way worse, however.

Okay, so maybe things had been pretty bad. But he didn't need to hear all the details. The guild had actually been a much easier life than the one she knew before it. Maybe the real problem here was the fact that she wasn't used to people actually sympathizing with her, or seeing her life as so different from theirs. Back in the guild, on the streets, everyone had a sob story of their own, and a lot of them were worse than hers. If you started whining about your hard knocks, people would tell you to grow a pair and get over it. Biting her lip, E stared at the now empty plate in front of her.

"Can I ask you something?"

Hook pulled himself from his somber thoughts and nodded for her to continue.

"Why did you help me? I mean, I came to you as a prisoner, and someone you clearly thought was sent to kill you or something. Yet you helped me so many times along the way, treated me kindly. And whatever you had in that flask was a miracle worker. You were right, I never would have made it through the judgment process without your help. But, why are you helping me?"

"Kindness isn't something you are accustomed to." It was a statement of fact. E shifted in her seat.

"Yes, I guess, at least, not in this obvious way. I mean, I had friends. Three best friends, or at least as close to best friends as people like me get. Wiley was like a brother to me, and a real nice guy..." She paused, her stomach bottoming out. "Look, I know I'm new here, and haven't earned the right to ask for favors yet. But, I wanted to know what you plan to do about Wiley. Can we go look for him? I'd like to be sure, one way or another..."

She'd avoided thinking of Wiley too much up to this point. The constant danger had been welcoming in the respect of offering distraction. But now that she was relatively safe, she was going to have far too much time on her hands to worry and wonder.

"If he is not dead, he will likely wish he was." Easton's gaze shot upward, her surprise turning to frustration. Hook held up a hand.

"That was not a threatening statement, Vermillion. It was simply a statement of fact."

"He's a good person. One of the best men I know. He's not a threat to you or your people. You could put him to the test with your binding thing to prove it. But you'll have to leave his hands free."

"Oh?" Curiosity flared in Hook's eye.

"His voice doesn't work. He speaks only through his hands."

"I see. That fact might make his situation even more dire, should he still be alive."

"What do you mean?" Dread pooled in her gut.

"There was once a man from a village not far from here. He was afflicted with a similar difficulty as your friend, though it was of the ears, not the voice. The villagers feared him and segregated him. It left him easy prey. Pan took him for sport. He set him free to run about in a maze while his lost boys hunted him.. They enjoyed the noises of fear he made. Needless to say it didn't end well." Hook held her gaze.

"So you see, it is not I that threatens your friend, Vermillion, but our enemy. Pan has a way of...changing a person. If Pan has your friend, if somehow he looks past his inability to speak and accepts him rather than killing him, there will be nothing left of the man you once knew. There will be no saving him. It is better that you wish him dead on the watery rocks, than the fate of being captured by Pan." E swallowed, staring at her hands once more. Hook sighed, rubbing at his face.

"I apologize. Let us continue beyond this sensitive subject. You asked why I was helping you..." She nodded, sliding into the chair at the table, "I own that I don't trust you yet. I don't trust easily, or often." She blinked.

"Understandable. I figured as much when I found the guards outside my door, and was followed over by the faithful lapdog. I get it."

"Lapdog?" His face cleared, a slight grin tugging at his lips. "Oh, I see. Smee. He would appreciate that title, I think." He chuckled mischievously. It made her heart feel warm.

"Those restrictions were actually put into effect for your own protection. The guards at the doors were to watch over you while you slept so heavily you could not defend yourself if needed. Smee walked you over to be an extra set of eyes for you. The people here are not as hardened and suspicious as those outside of the Sanctuary, but some of them are…uncomfortable with new comers."

"Especially those with red hair," she surmised.

"Yes." Hook's smile gained a wry edge. "I made you a promise of safety, and I mean to keep that promise. And though I do not trust you yet, I do respect you. You have acted with reserve and caution, yet wisdom and swift action from the moment we met. I can see your mind constantly working through the matters at hand, sifting through every factor that might have an impact on you. You know how to protect yourself. Yet you understand the importance of protecting your assets as well, including people. You immediately went on guard when we were attacked, you fought along with us, protected our backs. Slaying that giant has earned you many…what was it you called it… brownie points?" She nodded, offering a wry smile. "You have earned many brownie points not only with my men, but with me. Had you not acted, I would have lost many more men than I did in that moment."

"I've seen your concern for your men. Which is admirable for any leader," she paused, "but what about your own life? You seemed a little too excited about impending doom."

"When you've lived such as I have, death would be a mercy, Vermillion."

"You know my name now." She reminded him, avoiding delving into his rather depressing reply.

"I do. But names have power. You have my respect, but not my trust. When you've earned both, I'll share mine along with using yours."

"I already know your name." She leaned back with a haughty grin, feeling playfully smug.

"Oh?" His gaze sharpened.

"James T. Hook." Hook's expression shifted from wary, to outright humor. With a deep, rough laugh he stood and strode away.

"Smee will see you back to your quarters. We'll discuss other matters tomorrow."

He called over his shoulder, the swinging doors flapping in his wake, the sound of his laugh once more filtering back to her. E frowned in confusion. That hadn't been the reaction she'd expected at all. Jumping to her feet, she raced out the doors. Smee grumbled a surprised curse as she nearly plowed into him. He made a grab for her, but she deftly dipped under his arms, eyes searching the night for Hook. Smee followed, but with her head start, she managed to catch up to Hook before Smee caught up to her.

"Wait!" She purposely called out, alerting him to her approach. She'd immediately recognized Hook's taut body language for what it was, and hadn't been too eager to get a butt beating before he realized it was her. He turned toward her, lips fighting a grin. He waved the red-faced Smee away and the giant man lumbered a short distance off, scowl heavily mapping his face.

"Yes?" Hook's lips still quirked with that barely concealed humor.

"You want me to believe you aren't James T. Hook. Why? I already know the truth, I read about you in the book. So why try to evade the facts now?"

"Let me first ask this. Hook is portrayed as the enemy, in this book of yours. And Pan as the hero. Yet you say you never saw Hook as the villain. Am I correct thus far?"

"Sure."

"I would like to know exactly what it was about the man that drew you in."

"Well…" she cleared her throat, trying to formulate a thorough explanation. "I couldn't stand bullies. I've had to deal with them my whole life. I always saw Pan as a spoiled punk kid that was devious and liked hurting people for his own enjoyment. He cheated at everything he did. The guy could fly, and had the whole island of Indians, fairies and Lost Boys on his side. He could leave Neverland whenever he wanted, and he stole kids out of their beds for crap's sake!" She threw her hands in the air, pacing slightly side to side as she ranted.

"Meanwhile, Hook had to fight him off with no special powers and was stuck in Neverland. He didn't have the ability to fly. He was chased constantly by a giant reptile that took his hand and wanted to finish the rest of him. And to top it off, he didn't have everlasting youth on his side. But through it all, he never once gave up. Growing up...I needed that kind of example to look up to. Maybe I'd have to make hard choices to survive, choices that weren't always right or legal. But as long as I stayed true to who I was, I wouldn't ever be completely lost. And despite the bullies in life, I couldn't let anyone tear me down or lose track of what I wanted."

She cut off her impassioned speech, cheeks heating under Hooks intense stare. His eye held a mixture of emotions flickering in its depths for only a split second before disappearing. She had seen what looked oddly like respect, and even stranger still, regret.

"You saw all that, in this man of your book?"

"Yes."

"That is very insightful for one so young." Hook cleared his throat and stood straighter. "But I feel I must inform you of one very important detail. I am not that man. James the Hook began our quest to defeat the Fiend, but the man you came to know and admire in your book has not been amongst the living for many, many years; hundreds of them, if I were to venture a guess."

"Wait, wait just a minute. James *the* Hook. You're telling me that the 'T' stands for 'the'?" Hook shrugged, unrepentant. "Seriously? How lame is that? I was expecting Tristan, or Theodore or something!"

"Theodore?" Hooks eyes scrunched, unconvinced. She threw her hands in the air in exasperation.

"Anything would be better than 'the'. 'The' is just so... boring!" Hook offered a small chuckle, which earned him a grumpy expression in return.

"But I don't understand. Everything is the same. Neverland, Peter Pan, Hook, there's even a Smee in the stories." She waved her hand vaguely in the direction of the grumpy man. "Granted, he was usually represented as a happy, fat, short, scatterbrained old man.

And you looked a bit different too..." she waved her hand in the air, frustrated, "but still!"

"There are small differences from what I read, but way too many similarities for you to not be James T. Hook. Everyone calls you Hook. Or was that some elaborate ruse to trick me? Plus, what about the actual hook? It's not like wearing a hook is a fashion statement here, is it? Call me crazy, but chopping off your hand for a fashion statement seems a bit extreme."

"I am sorry to disappoint you, but don't turn your dragon fire on *me*, Vermillion. I didn't write your little book. I know everything about its origin, though I must admit the contents of it have become increasingly ridiculous as the years have passed. It was originally meant to serve as a guide, a call for help to those who would read it. Pan's power in Neverland has been corrupting it as time passed, twisting it more to fit his purposes. It is no wonder that the Arrivals are so easily turned to his will upon coming to Neverland. The book has honed them to liking him immediately, and seeing Hook as the enemy."

"As for Smee. Technically he is old, we all are, we just don't look it. He is not the least bit happy, or small, nor would I consider him a friend at present. But he is loyal to the cause, and a good deal of help in battle."

Holding the hook in the air between them so that she may better see it, his eye the color of sea foam locked with her own.

"As for this? 'Hook' is a title given to those assigned to the very serious cause of bringing death to the Pan. Hooks are the only ones with the power to do so. This was not the consequence of a stolen hand. It was an *earned* privilege, an exchange that I made freely. I honor the hook, respect it, and am humbled by it. Never let me hear you speak of it as though it were a dishonorable thing again. To do so will avail you nothing but my distrust and temper."

Easton frowned in confusion. The Hook of her childhood book had always seemed to hold a twisted sort of relationship with his weapon. He appreciated its cruel usefulness, but he despised what it stood for; a forever reminder of defeat through both its presence and the constant hunger of the crocodile. This Hook, however, seemed to revere it, cherish it even. What kind of man freely agreed to have his hand chopped off, and a hook put in its place? Her eyes shifted to stare at the weapon. Rather than hiding it away, Hook left it in plain sight, readily available to appease her unabashed curiosity.

"Do you understand your Captain, little butterfly?" His strange tone broke E from her observations. He wasn't threatening her, simply stating facts and asking her to respect them. Much like a teacher schooling a child.

"Yes, I understand. I'm sorry. There are so many differences and similarities, it's confusing. But I'll learn," she promised. Seemingly understanding of her reply, he nodded and stepped back. Without so much as a goodbye, Hook turned and sauntered away. Easton watched him with awe.

There had been no artifice in his actions, not like there had always been with Jag. Hook's grace was the reflection of a man so knowledgeable of his own danger to others that it permeated to his very core and oozed through his every move. He didn't have to *try* to be intimidating, he simply *was*. Hook was definitely a man that Easton should be afraid of. Yet the ever growing respect within her stopped any fear she should feel. He may be scary, but he was entirely honest. And honesty, complete honesty inside and out, was a rarity. *Hook* was a rarity; one that E found herself thirsting to be near. A cleared throat caused her to jump. She'd forgotten about Smee.

"Did you miss me, darling?" she asked cheekily.

"Deviant." He groused in return.

"Didn't miss you either."

Smee stepped closer, ignoring her glib attitude.

"Obviously you passed the binding test, or you'd not be here. But hear me now; if you've plans to turn coat on the Cap'n, I'll run you through." Whether it was from her expanding good mood, or the fact that she was still too tired to have a serious fight with the man, she ignored the impulse to keep poking at him.

"Settle down, Smee. I'm not going to turn on the Captain. Look, you weren't in the binding thingy to hear what I had to say then. So I'll say it now. There is no way I could try to kill off Hook. I grew up hearing stories about him. I idolized him. The book that sucked me into it was a book about the adventures of Peter Pan and his enemy James T. Hook. My mother used to read it to me, before everything changed and I ended up on the streets."

"You are an orphan of the streets?"

Easton glanced away from the surprising shadow of sympathy in Smee's eyes. Apparently even rude pirates pitied orphans.

"Something like that. Anyways, point is, I begged her to read it every night. But I called it 'The Book of Hook', because I refused to think of Peter Pan as the hero. Now, Captain Hook might not be the same man as James T., but he has already shown a lot of the same characteristics of the man that I grew up admiring. I've waited my whole life to meet someone like that man. Everyone else fell flat. I'm not about to turn on the one guy that matches up. Hook has done nothing but treat me with respect since I showed up, even gone out of his way to help me. So I'm going to do my best to carry my own weight."

"That is...unsettling." The absurdly disquieted expression on Smee's face sent Easton into a round of giggles.

"Yes, yes it really is! But now you see the truth of my innocence." Smee's brow rose, challenging that statement. "You'll figure it out. Now. Let's get some more food. I'm starved."

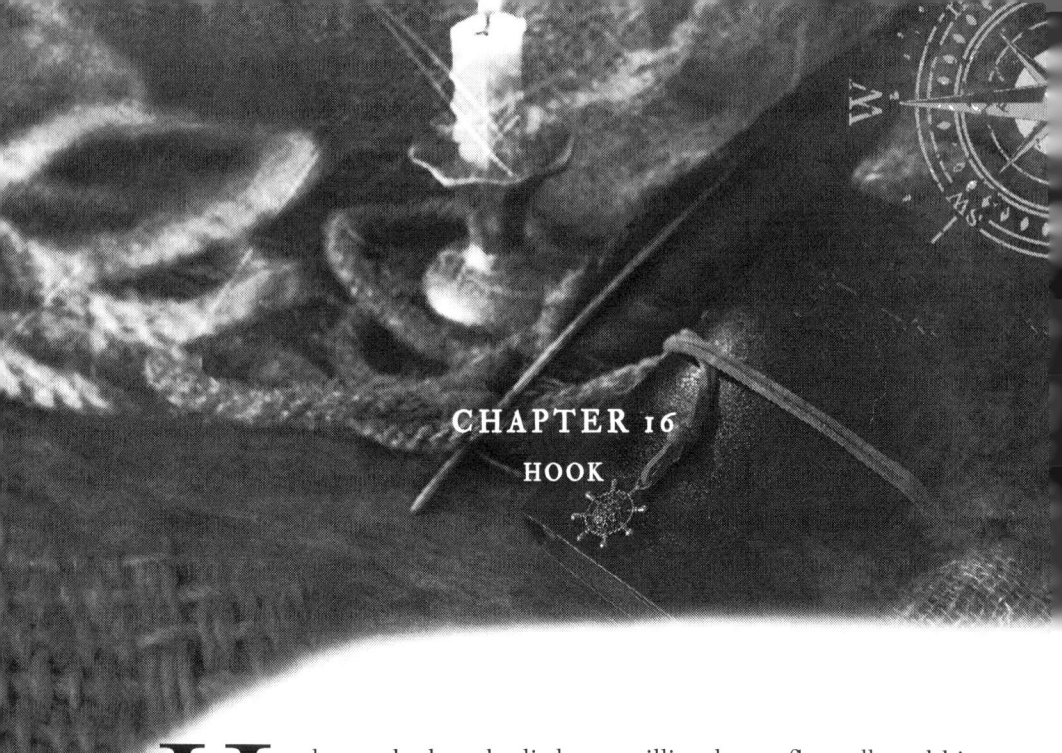

CHAPTER 16
HOOK

Hook watched as the little vermillion butterfly walloped his Bo 'sun over the head. She was getting good. Roughly five months had passed since she'd joined his ranks, to his best estimation. It had been a rough start, and he had questioned his sanity in bringing the girl on. It was clear that, while his men had appreciated her prowess in slaying the satyr, they didn't trust her nor appreciate her presence in his crew. As a lovely thing to enjoy the view of, yes. But part of the crew? No. Seamen had long looked at having a woman in the crew as bad luck, and despite years of being isolated on land that hadn't seemed to change.

Hook had never gone back on a promise in his long lifetime, but in that first month he found himself considering whether he should rescind his promise of her place amongst his crew. Not because of the displeasure of his men, or superstitious stupidity. But rather because of his concern for her safety. The first day he watched her best one of his men, however, he decided to let matters lie; to give the butterfly her wings and watch them unfold. He hadn't regretted it.

Each day the men would find a way around his orders or under his visual observation to taunt the girl, bullying her in an effort to make her leave. If the men went too far in their badgering, bordering on physical abuse, Hook was swift to discipline them.

However, the rest of the time, he let the men push her. If he were to coddle her, the men would torment her with renewed vigor, and he doubted the girl herself would appreciate the gesture, well-meaning as it might be. Truth be told, he had been curious to see how she would react, what her temperament was made of, and how she would handle the situations.

What he found was that the girl was remarkably resilient. She was a swift learner and the intelligence in her eyes was easy to mark as she quietly gained the upper hand on each man through observation and manipulation of their weaknesses. Slowly she worked her way up the ranks, earning her place in line and in their respect. And somehow she managed to do it all without hard feelings residing amongst the crew.

Being as true women were in short supply in Neverland these days, Easton was a rarity. The women that did survive the Fiend's attacks were afraid to leave Sanctuary, knowing it would mean the end for them if they did.

Hook had explained to the girl about the shortage of women. How Neverland had sickened under the growing power of the Fiend and in reaction to his hatred toward them, began corrupting the women turning them into sirens of the sea to do his bidding. She had shivered in revulsion when he explained that those women not corrupted, the Fiend used as resources for harvesting children that would grow up under his control, readily available for his soulless armies of Lost Boys. For the Fiend fed off the souls of children to sustain his own life.

His efforts failed, time and again. No heirs of Pan would manifest, yet another curse of the Pan. The women had all become entirely barren. In his fury, he hunted them down and destroyed those still free of his corruption.

Hook had expected the news to send the girl running to the Sanctuary for protection, withdrawing from the ranks. It had the opposite effect. She had doubled her efforts, served each day with vigor and determination. She'd practically been frothing at the bit to get outside and get her hands dirty.

Hook had found himself being the reluctant one. A woman of Vermillion's caliber was truly difficult to find. If the Fiend did not have his nose to the ground in search of her already, he would soon catch wind of her spectacular spirit. Hook knew she held prowess in fighting, some of the greatest he'd seen and a marvelous fiery soul. But the Fiend would be relentless in his efforts to own her for those reasons, if not simply for her gender. And Hook would see himself dead in the ground before Pan got his hands on her.

Yet he could hardly deny her the rights to patrol with the rest of the crew. To do so would mean degrading all the work she'd put in, climbing the ranks. She would immediately become the girl that was humored within Sanctuary, but set aside when the dangerous work began. The men would lose all respect for her. Besides, he'd been the one to ask her to join his crew. He wouldn't go back on his word.

So he'd dressed her in men's clothes, sat her down in a chair, cut her beautiful hair to average shoulder length, covered it in dark brown chalk, and took her on patrol with them. It was another decision he hadn't regretted. The girl was a veritable lucky charm. She had a way of sniffing out the trouble spots, finding the dangers and suggesting good lines of attack. They hadn't lost a single man since she came to them, and their patrols were never uneventful.

The men had taken to kissing her vermillion hair before each mission, not letting him chalk it until they'd done their ritual. Thus the coloring that had made her a pariah was now held to be the revered luck of his men.

They all trained and patrolled together in the day, and at night they joined together in the restaurant, laughing and sharing stories well into the dawn hours. Vermillion had brought color to their world and healing that can only be found in a good, long, hearty chuckle. While Hook knew the happiness that had fallen over Sanctuary couldn't last forever, he was determined to drink it in while it lasted. It had been so long since he felt anything but hatred and guilt, mixed with a soul-weary determination to end the tyranny of the Pan. For the time being, the Fates had smiled upon them, dropping this bundle of irreverent healing in their laps. And if the Fates continued to favor them, that irreverent healing just might lead them to respite.

The woman in question suddenly went sliding across the ground at his feet, and for a split second he feared Smee had taken their tussle too far, his temper getting the best of him under her persistent badgering. The thought was swiftly banished as she bounded to her feet with a curse and a smile. Her hair was filled with grass, patches of the green blades hanging out of her shirt with tufts of dirt still stuck to them.

"Smee, I'm going to skin you for that one, you limp-haired ape! You've gone and made me get dirt all over the Captain's shiny boots!" She turned to grin up at Hook then, eyes dancing with pure excitement and humor.

He'd seen to it a tailor fitted her for proper apparel the day after their meeting in the restaurant, and the garments flattered every ounce of her. The green shirt she wore today brought out the brilliance of her hair, the corseted belt at her waist accenting her hourglass figure, and the pants fitting a bit too perfectly for the mental health of his men. A short sword and dagger sheath normally hung about her curvy hips, but had been discarded for the purpose of her current tussling. Hook was proud to note that in the months she'd spent with his crew, she had been eating well, her curves filling out to lovely proportions. She had been too scrawny and malnourished upon Arrival. She was every bit a pirate wench now, as she proudly boasted daily.

"Try keeping the grass on the ground, not in your teeth." Hook said sternly, though he knew she wouldn't listen to a moment of it. As expected, she offered a mock salute with the flip of two lazy fingers at her brow, mischief in her gaze.

"Of course, Captain." Plucking it from her shirt, she shoved it down the front of his own and sprinted away. "You wear it much better, anyways!"

She threw a jaunty grin over her shoulder as she moved in for another attack on Smee. Hook dug the grass out from inside his shirt as he watched their display of playful violence. Now that was an odd relationship, if Hook had ever seen one. Those two picked at one another like savages. He was surprised they had any metaphorical skin left on their bones. For all appearances sake, Smee and Vermillion hated one another.

Yet there was a bridge of respect that seemed to have grown out of that hatred. Smee looked after her as Hook had ordered still the same, stepping in to clout someone over the head when he felt it was needed. Of course if you'd asked him why he did it, he'd grumble about her stirring up trouble amongst the men and how he wasn't allowed to hit *her*.

And if any of the men ribbed Smee too hard about some matter, leaving the man a silent grumpy brooding figure, the girl would step in and rib the men harder than they'd given. But she'd only admit to wanting to knock their arrogance down a notch or two, if asked why she'd done it. They seemed to hold an uneasy, unspoken truce between them, and Hook found the entire matter rather entertaining.

"If you two love birds are done romancing, I need Smee to gather up the men for rounds," Hook commanded, shaking another clump of grass out the bottom of his shirt.

Smee stopped abruptly, a look of appalled disgust on his face. The girl pinched his cheek and cooed, earning her a scowl and swat to the shoulder that sent her stumbling away, giggling. Smee swiped his weapons up off the grass as he went, grumbling under his breath, eager to do his Captain's bidding and be gone from the now awkward situation. Hook grinned.

"Have a good day, darling!" the girl called out, just to spite the man. She always had to get the last word.

"Vermillion, with me," Hook ordered, heading toward the Inn. She immediately joined him, buckling her weapons belt in place as they walked.

"Time for some good ol' chalk dusting, huh?"

"Aye. Though it might be more trouble than it is worth, picking all this grass out. I've never met a woman more at home in the dirt in all my life." He plucked a silky, grass-sprinkled strand off her shoulder, holding the burnished red color in the rays of the sun.

"Yes, much too much work. It will be the day after tomorrow

before I am finished. Maybe I'll leave you home today." He barely contained the chuckles of mirth as Vermillion's brow lifted, immediately turning defiant.

"Maybe you need some sense kicked into you, next? I'd be more than happy to teach you a lesson in humility, Captain."

"Indeed, humility isn't my strongest asset," he acquiesced. "You know, vermillion truly is a handsome color on you. Its fire matches your disposition. I'm half tempted to leave it as is. Perhaps when the villagers are busy attempting to roast you for it, and you are attempting to teach them humility, I could get a moment's peace. I might even take a nap."

He smirked, enjoying their ongoing game of banter. She always seemed to manage to bring out hints of an old part of him that he had thought long lost. The part that was able to make jokes, tease and be playful. It was a part he'd been painfully empty without. When she brought it to the surface during their daily chats, he felt a glimmer of life within his barren soul again. It was both disconcerting and liberating at once.

"Cute. But you'd be lost without your lucky charm, Captain, admit it." She taunted, leaning over to pluck a stray blade of grass from his chest hair, not the least bit perturbed by his empty threats.

"Perhaps you are right, little butterfly. Lucky charms are difficult to come by these days." He sighed dramatically. "Come along then, Vermillion. I am certain your adoring public already awaits their obligatory hair kissing."

"You first." Her eyes gleamed with a silent challenge already won long ago. Hook stepped closer, fingers dipping into the soft strands. Holding her gaze as he leaned forward, he pressed a slow kiss to her fiery hair. He didn't miss the way her eyes widened the slightest bit.

"I wouldn't miss it. A Captain isn't worth his salt without his lucky charm."

Winking, he straightened and led the way into the inn. Within the hour Vermillion was changed over to her usual men's attire, hair dusted to a much tamer coloring of mud brown, and they were walking through the countryside with ears to the ground searching for danger. They already had two fights won and under their belts.

With Vermillion on their side, Hook was confident that they were picking holes in Pan's army, and it brought him a deep-seated satisfaction previously unknown.

Vermillion sent him a sassy wink, as though she could read his thoughts. Popping a spice leaf in his mouth to chew, he offered one to Vermillion. She was just reaching for it when she froze. The men immediately followed suit, holding their breath. Shaking her head, she started walking again, only to freeze moments later. Hook doubted she noticed the way they all followed her movements, so well accustomed to her 'hunches' they'd become. Confusion clouded her face as she glanced around.

"What is it, Vermillion?" Hook asked, voice low as he stepped closer.

"Do you hear that?"

Silence fell heavily as they listened. A vague, barely there ticking sound emanated from the dark forest to their right. Hook blinked, glancing sharply at Smee.

"Croc," Smee agreed grimly.

"Croc?" The girl asked. Her eyes widened. "You mean the crocodile is real?"

"He is a man, though he's become more animal with the passage of time." Hook's gaze held hers. "I assume Croc was in your book, as well?"

"Yeah. At the end of the book the Fiend wins and Hook is eaten by a crocodile."

"Ah." Her brows went up at the significant glance shared between the Captain and his Bo 'sun. "Croc and his followers are cannibals." Hook finally explained. Her face screwed up in disgust.

"Oh that's nasty! I always hated the end of the book but this information just gave a whole new depth to the why."

"I must own that I am not too fond of the idea myself." Hook's gaze held hers, lips quirking in a sideways grin of triumph. "We've been looking for him for a very, very, long time. And you, my lucky charm, have just led us to him."

He pulled her close kissing the top of her hair. Another time he might have enjoyed the way her cheeks flushed, but he was already sliding further into the trees on the hunt. A few moments later, they stopped. Sprawling in front of them was a large camp. In the center a bonfire lit the darkened forest, and figures danced silently around it. Tents formed an enclosure of sorts around the fire, speaking to their nomadic ways. If they so much as heard a twig break in the forest they would pack up and run for their next place of hiding.

"Ew. Creep town. Why is it so quiet?" Vermillion whispered.

"Croc demands absolute silence so that he can always hear the ticking of the clock." The weight of questions in her eyes felt like a physical caress as her gaze shifted over his tense features.

"You want the clock."

"Yes. I do." Hook looked to her with a smile. He loved her instinctual intellect.

"So let's go get it." His grin grew. Always so eager.

"Calm, butterfly. We have to be careful about this one. If they so much as suspect attack, they will scatter, and they are far too good at disappearing in this forest. It's what has made them so difficult to hunt down. We've only found them two other times. They fled before we got close enough to act. Croc is slippery."

"Which one is he?"

Hook leaned close until his cheek pressed to her own, finger lifting to guide her eye.

"There, toward the edge of the light. He ensures his followers all dress alike and have similar indistinct features to help him blend in and be harder to find. He's slightly shorter than the rest however; and his face is more mottled, belly rounder. The watch is held on a thong around his neck under the shirt." He watched as her keen eyes sifted through the throng of people, noted her grimace of disgust when she found him. "Don't let his physique fool you, he can move faster than any of them. We'd have to be silent and swift as the shadows to catch him off guard."

"Guess I know how he got his name. He looks all scaly." Vermillion shuddered.

"A skin malformation from the time of his birth. It continued to spread with time, but halted once he gained the watch."

"And control of time. Got it. So it's safe to say he won't love us taking it. Will he chase us immediately, or call the Fiend for aid?" She asked, a new intensity about her face.

"I'm afraid we don't have any knowledge to answer that question. He's only ever run in the past, but then he had the watch with him. If the watch is taken, who knows how he will react."

"Could we handle them, if he charges?"

"It would be best to escape him rather than fight. They all wear claws that are dipped in poison. I don't think they are much of fighters, but they would be deadly if they find the will. Especially when quite a few of them look underfed. Hunger and anger are tremendous motivators."

"So we'll have to run fast if we don't want to be dinner, got it."

He reached out to grab her wrist when she moved to leave.

"Vermillion…"

"You've tried twice before. It's my turn." She gave him a saucy wink. "I got this. I'm pretty good at the shadows thing. Make some noise when you see my signal, then be ready to disappear."

Prying his fingers from her wrist was akin to prying away his own skin. But her eyes sparkled, asking for his trust. So he gave it. Whispered orders were sent to his men to prepare to disperse, the ones closest to the back already stealthily slipping away. Grabbing a thick branch, Hook turned back to Vermillion. She was gone. He startled, eye searching the shadows for her form. He found nothing. How could he act, when he couldn't see her signal? Smee sent him a loaded glance, clearly wondering the same thing. Hook handed him the branch and focused on Croc. He had to trust that that's where she would show. He couldn't trace her in the shadows, so he would focus on her target and be ready.

Croc pulled the watch out of his shirt, idly caressing it, before letting it fall back atop his chest. Staring hard at Croc, Hook saw only the tiniest flicker of movement behind the man's chair, gone the instant it was realized. He knew it had to be her. Croc scratched at his neck, drowsily watching the dancing. Slowly, two fingers rose behind the chair above Croc's head, giving a little wiggle like bunny ears. Hook immediately nudged Smee, who snapped the branch in half. As silent as the woods were, the snap echoed through the trees.

Croc jumped to his feet, intent on their hidden position. As he stood, the watch slipped down his chest, falling from the severed cord. Croc's eyes rounded as he dove for the watch, but a deft hand reached out from beneath his chair to grasp it seconds before he could. Croc spun, but Vermillion was already melting into the shadows. Croc threw his head back and bellowed in rage, the sounds grating painfully against the ears. Immediately his followers followed suit, their enforced silence broken.

"Time to go." Vermillion hissed, darting past them into the trees. Hook and Smee followed.

Joining his men, they ran silently through the trees, putting as much distance as possible between them and the furious disfigured man. His screams fell further and further away. But still they ran, not willing to risk it. When too winded to keep their pace, they slowed to a fast walk. Hook lifted the watch to inspect it. Twisting the dial at the top clockwise one time, he pressed it downward until it clicked. Immediately a stiff breeze pulled at their clothing, an audible sigh issuing from Neverland itself.

"Did it work?" Smee asked as the wind died down.

"Only one way to find out. Time itself." Hook grinned broadly, feeling a weight lifted from his shoulders. Throwing an arm over Vermillion's shoulders, he drew her close and placed a noisy kiss atop her head. "You magnificent lucky creature, you." She laughed, shoving him away, cheeks flushing again.

"I told you, I'm good at doing the sneaky shadow thing. I'm a bit rusty though. Took longer than I wanted." She waved away the men's denials that sprang up all around her, staggering around under their playfully strong pats on the back. "So why is the watch so important, anyway?"

"This, little butterfly, is what was keeping Neverland from moving at the normal pace of time. And hopefully what added to the Fiend's power. Without its interference, we can hope we've put a chink in his armor."

"Wow. Pretty big deal then."

"Yes, Vermillion, a very big deal. The Fiend stole it from James as he lay dying. He taxed me with ending the Fiend, and returning the watch to its rightful owner."

She opened her mouth, countless new questions at her lips, when his muscles went rigid with the dangerous shift in the air. Vermillion felt it a moment later. Licking her finger she made a mark in the air.

"Point to you, Captain. Don't get used to it; I plan to outdistance you again by the end of the day." The girl promised as she put her back to his, Smee silently bringing up the other side of their defensive triangle. It was a habit formed from that first fight so many months ago. They were a good team, the three of them, and together Hook and Smee could safeguard their treasure between them.

"You can certainly try, Vermillion. You'll fail, but you are most welcome to try all the same," he replied, eyes searching for the danger he could feel closing in on them. The ground began to rumble, coming from the direction of the forest to his left. This was bigger than just Croc and his minions.

"Mr. Smee…"

"At arms, men!" Smee shouted, issuing commands immediately, allowing Hook to focus solely on the imminent threat.

"Any ideas, yet?" Vermillion asked.

"Something big. Perhaps…perhaps many somethings." Hook's gaze found the girl's, the worry he saw there confirming his own. "Smee, take the watch and head for Sanctuary. We can't let it fall back into his hands. Don't stop, don't turn back."

"Capt'n…"

"Go Bo 'sun!" He shoved the watch into his hands. Smee growled in anger, but moved to do as commanded. Easton watched as he found some energy he must have held in reserve somewhere and sprinted away. Hook turned to the rest of the men.

"Spread out and head for the cover of the trees!" Hook shouted. The warning was drowned out by the sound of crashing trees, bursting to make way for the thundering stampede headed their way. Cursing, Hook spun and grabbed Vermillion around the waist, turning her about as he ran, urging her along. His men scrambled, spreading out as instructed, all trying to get out of the way of the herd of Wilders. Large and shaggy with great horns on their heads,

Vermillion often referred to them as something called "buffalos on steroids".

"What are those doing here? I thought you said they were migrating the other way!" Vermillion shouted above the terrified shrieks of the animals as they pounded increasingly closer. The beasts had been well on their way to the other side of Neverland, last Hook knew, taking their biannual migratory trek to more abundant areas.

"They're afraid! Something must have turned them around!" Risking a glance over his shoulder, Hook found the source of the animal's terror. Small black creatures ran at their feet, stabbing at them with sharp spears. "Pigmites!" Hook growled. Croc must have sent them his way. They hadn't outrun him, he'd gone for reinforcements.

"What?" she cried over the sound.

"Never mind! Just run!" She complied all too eagerly, lithe legs picking up speed. They leapt through the tree line, dodging trees in their path. And nearly running head first off the edge of a steep cliff. Before they could correct their course, a Wilder burst through the trees behind them. It crashed into them, sending them flying off the cliff with trees, rocks, and the Wilder tumbling after in freefall.

Hook blinked, fighting against the threat of unconsciousness, adrenaline his only ally in the cause. Glancing to his left, he found Vermillion laying on the ground about four feet away, the rock beneath her head dripping a red that rivaled her natural hair color. He prayed it was only sleep that found her in the fall, and not death. His hand extended, lower body and hook trapped beneath piles of jagged tree trunks and rocks keeping him from moving to her side. Fingers grasping, he sought the edges of hair fanned out about her.

"Vermillion!" Wrapping one thick curl around his finger, he called out for her, voice raw from the dust he inhaled. "Easton! Wake up!" she remained unresponsive and he let his head fall back against the ground, trying to think against the fog in his mind.

Skittering and clicking sounds suddenly issued from the cloud of dust in the air. Swallowing hard, Hook prepared himself. Slipping a knife from the cuff at his wrist, he waited. Slowly the figures emerged, slinking closer, curious sounds emanating from their lipless mouths. He sneered in revulsion. The little savages enjoyed acts of self-destruction, cutting away pieces of their body in what they considered signs of beauty.

The blackened bodies moved closer. When one grew too near the girl for his comfort, he let his dagger fly, impaling the creature in the neck. The others pulled back with hisses. It only deterred them for a moment, however, and soon they were close enough Hook could smell their putrid stink.

"Hooksss," A pigmite with a crude feathered hat atop his head hissed; the Chieftain of the pigmites. The others did a strange hopping dance, clicking in excitement over their catch. Another pigmite approached Vermillion. Hook shouted a curse, chucking a rock at its head before it could touch her. The pigmites hissed again, the strange skinless bones in their necks rattling together in unison to make the threatening sound all the more menacing. Yet when the same pigmite moved forward again, the Chieftain growled a smat- tering of garbled words and clicks together in warning.

"Leavesss it! Pan wantsss." The others seemed dejected, but bowed to the will of their leader. The Chieftain pigmite crawled closer, poking Hook's chest with its spear, drawing blood. Hook barred his teeth and yanked the spear from the creature's grasp. The pigmites clicked and hissed in angry horror when Hook slammed it over the Chieftain's head, snapping the stick in two. The leader stood with a vacant gaze on its grotesque face for several long moments. Finally it blinked in rapid succession and snapped out of it.

"Cavernsss!" The Chief roared, much to the pleasure of his followers. With what might have passed for a grin, had he still both lips, the Chief leaned closer. Opening his gnarled fist, he blew a grey dust in Hook's face. He coughed and groaned as the world tilted above him.

"Pans wantsss. Can hasss you when drowned." Hook's vision faded out to the sound of whooping cheers.

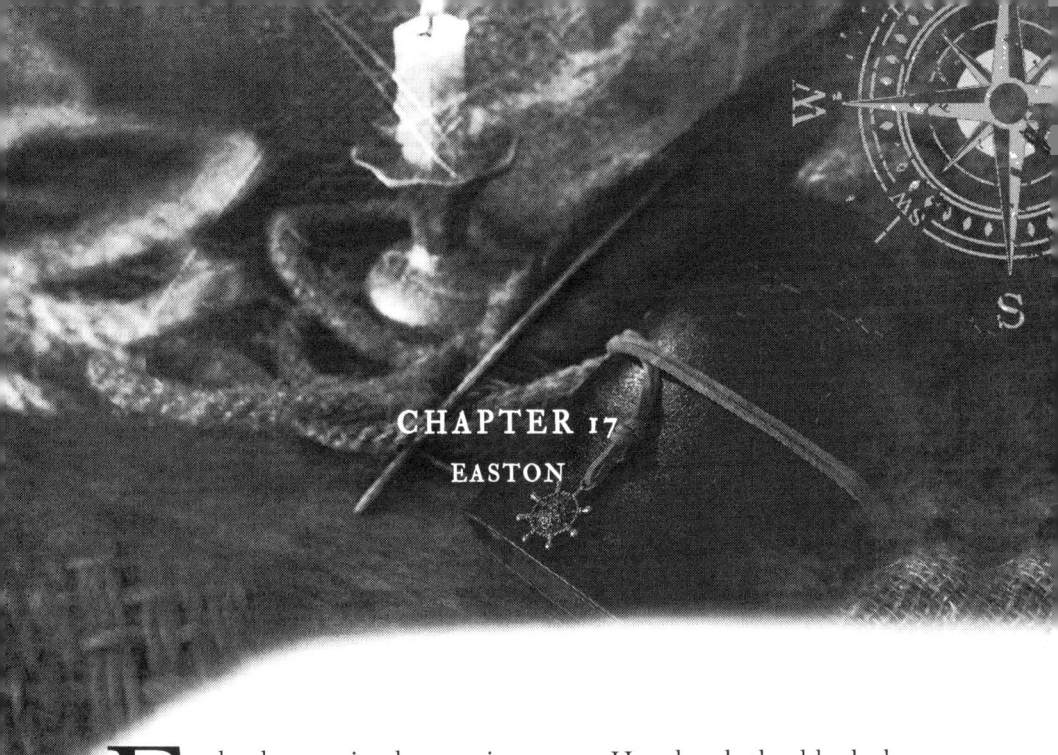

CHAPTER 17
EASTON

E slowly regained consciousness. Her head throbbed, her body ached, and her hands were tingling like they were stung by a nest of bees. Heavy head lifting with a groan, she blinked blurry eyes in an effort to gain her bearings. Bit by bit the blurry images sharpened into slimy stone walls, and flickering torches.

She was in some sort of cavern, standing on a stone pillar surrounded by black nothingness below. Swallowing, she forced her attention away. Glancing up revealed her hands had been tied to a long bamboo style pole above her head. While unconscious her whole body weight had been on her tied hands, which was effectively cutting off the circulation. E groaned again, forcing her gelatin legs to stand firm beneath her. It took several tries, but finally the weight was taken from her hands. The resulting increase of pain from renewal of blood flow was mind-numbing.

"Are you alive, little butterfly?" Hook's voice called to her from a distance. E swiveled her head to the side in search, only to find him restrained across a chasm of sorts.

"Maybe." She called back, trying to make her voice carry over the noise in the cavern. "I'm not sure yet."

"Let me know when you figure it out." His voice was filled with a dark sort of humor that couldn't help but stir an ounce of it in her as well.

"What happened?"

"A buffalo on steroids fell upon us, and then we were assaulted by little lipless creatures."

"Um…I don't think I want to know the rest." She amended, much to Hook's enjoyment. "Can you get free?" E called over the rushing noise in the air.

"No. They've trapped my hook in some sort of metal cage with a lock."

"If your hook was free, could you get us out of here?"

"In a heartbeat." Hook promised. "But I have no way of freeing it. I've been trying the whole time you've been napping." E rolled her eyes.

"Well, everyone needs their beauty sleep. You should try it sometime."

"Some of us come by it naturally, my dear. Should I gain any more beauty, your mortal eyes couldn't handle it." E laughed, enjoying the tilt of his lips from across the dimly lit space.

"In that case, stay ugly."

"As you wish." Hook's smile grew with good-natured mischief.

"And it was so nice of whoever put us in here to leave behind torches for me to see those grotesque features of yours," she added sarcastically.

"Indeed. Though they were left as more of a twisted torture than a courtesy. The pigmites enjoy leaving prey to watch their demise slowly approach them; that and being made to watch their friends die alongside them. When the end is near, the pigmites return and watch the whole thing from those small holes above." E squinted upward with a frown.

"Oh, lovely. So we just watch each other starve, is that the goal?"

"No, no, we'll drown long before we starve."

Hook laughed his dark sort of laugh he typically reserved for danger and battle. It was in those times that E wondered if he truly did relish the idea of impending death, welcomed it closer with open arms. Easton's eyes rounded as she bent to follow Hook's glittering gaze. Sure enough, there it was: impending death. Her breath caught as her eyes landed on the tumultuous waves just visible below. That would explain the annoyingly loud sound echoing off the walls.

"We need to work on your screwed up love affair with death," E grumbled. Hook's smile merely grew. "Do you know how to pick locks?"

"I've had my hand at it a time or two. But I'm afraid I left my lock picks in my other eyepatch." Hook replied wryly.

"What a terrible day to wear the wrong patch, Hooky."

Experimentally, E tested the ropes at her wrists once more, wriggling them back and forth. She pulled herself upward, slowly testing her range of movement. Over and over she lifted herself upward, trying to reach her hidden weapon, only to tire out too quickly and have to lower once more. With her wrists tied together over the top of the pole, she could gain no grasp to help lift her body. Her efforts failed time and again. The angles were all wrong, and the weight on her awkwardly tied wrists was excruciating. In addition, each trip upward not only cost her upper arm strength, but also made sticky blood flow in wider rivulets down her neck. Apparently she'd obtained a pretty nasty head wound earlier.

"While I find it rather enjoyable to watch you exercise, it's a bit late in life to build up your muscles, don't you think, Vermillion?" E ignored Hook's comment, eyes taking in her surroundings once more. He might be glibly anticipating death, but she wasn't ready for either of them to die.

Finally her gaze snagged on hope. Doing a few jumps, E let her full weight pull at the pole on her way down. The pole bent, but stayed fairly stable. The second part of the plan forming in her mind, she twisted about in an effort to see the wall behind her. That proved difficult, given her position.

"And what kind of exercise is this one?" he asked coyly.

"The 'possibly escape-worthy' kind. Now, look at that wall behind me and tell me what you see, will you?"

"I see...rock. Lots of rock."

"Very insightful, thank you. Is there a sort of shelf, ridge-type of thing that my pole is resting on?"

"Yes."

"Can you tell if it goes all the way along the wall to your position?"

"It would appear that it does, though I can see a few dark areas that likely have broken free at some point." He paused, looking over his shoulder at the wall behind him, having more mobility in his movements. His tone took on a cautionary air. "You wouldn't be considering sidling your way over here, would you, little butterfly?"

"Do you have any better ideas?" Hook's silence was answer enough. With a deep breath, E picked up her feet and began swaying back and forth. She bit her lip to cover her cries of pain as the rope bit into her swollen skin.

"Vermillion…" Hook attempted a warning once more, cutting off abruptly as she made her first leap to the side. At that point, she figured they were both holding their breath, watching the pole shudder under the momentum and her weight.

The ends of the pole skittered along the rock ledge, the pole sagging a bit more than her first experiment had suggested it would. But it was too late to go back now, she was a good yard and a half away from her pillar and the outreached toe of her boot couldn't even touch it.

"Onward you go, then." Hook stated solemnly.

"Right."

E tried to not succumb to the panic-filled knowledge that she was now hanging helplessly over swirling black water, with only a rope, pole, and crumbly ledge to rely on. Swinging her legs back and forth to gain more momentum, she managed to scoot the pole further along the stone ridges without having to put much effort into it. Her heart momentarily lifted in hopes that she just might be able to pull this off, when Hook's warning stomped on it.

"There's a shadowed area coming up, Vermillion. It's about a foot wide. You're going to have to jump the pole over it."

"Right…" she breathed out with a shaky laugh, "any suggestions on how I do that?"

"You're going to have to build up a lot of swing. When you get as high as you can without slipping the pole along the wall, pull your legs up, kick out toward the direction you want to go, and push up with your arms at the same time. Hopefully it will be enough momentum to get you across."

"Great. Okay. I got this." She assured herself, repeating it over and over with each swing of her legs.

"Yes, you do. You're a butterfly, after all, and flying is what they do best."

Hook added his assurance. It was firm, steady, acting as an immediate calming balm that seeped into her muscles. Hook said she could do it, so she can do it. *Time to grow some wings. No letting the captain down now*, she demanded. Her swings took on a more determined mode of motion, the pole bending and swaying with her.

"Good. On the count of three, you are going to jump. No hesitation. Understood?" Hook commanded. E nodded.

"Yes, Captain!"

"One." Swing "Two!" Swing. "Three!" E tucked her legs upward and kicked out, shoving upward with her arms best she could. For one heart stopping second that stretched into an eternity, E floated through the air. Then time choked within E's throat as the pole came down, jarring onto the rock ledge and sliding onward with the momentum.

"Whoa, whoa, that's enough!" Hook cried out, though she wasn't entirely sure who he was yelling it at. It wasn't as though she could stop the forward movement now.

"Jump again, Easton, now!"

His jarring shout, along with the surprising use of her name had E reacting without conscious thought. The pole flew upward again on the burst of her adrenaline. A squeak of fear leapt from her throat as the pole bowed frighteningly far beneath her weight upon landing. A horrible grinding noise followed, and the air was heavy with trepidation.

"Was that what I think it was?" The words came out strangled and fearful.

"I need you to hold very still, Easton." Hook spoke slowly,

cautiously, as though approaching a spooked horse. E swallowed and fought to calm the urge to flail her legs about in panic. "That's right, good. Now, when I say, I need you to give a good, strong push upward with your arms. Can you do that?"

"I think so." She breathed out, "I can't feel my hands anymore."

"Never mind that. Just focus on my voice, and do what I tell you. I'll see to it that you make it through just fine."

"Okay."

"Alright, on three, push up. One, two, three." E gave a little kick with her feet, pushing upward with the lagging strength of her arms. The pole gave another sickening grinding sensation, then sprung upward coming to land on the ridge once more. With a sickening sinking feeling, E realized her fears had been correct. The pole had come off the ledge and could have dropped her into the abyss below at any moment. Panic rose with the force of a gale, dropping away any lingering fears of action.

"Are there any more holes?"

"I don't see…"

"Good." Without a second's pause E swung, skidding recklessly across the remaining distance.

"Slow and easy, Vermillion!" Hook warned.

"Slow and easy will see my arms and hands falling off, and me going for a dip!" E groused, more than eager to end her impromptu leap into adventure. Her final scoot sent her careening into Hook's side. Better braced with his arms around his rock pillar, Hook quickly scooted to the side as much as his bindings would allow, giving her room she would need to stand on his pillar. Using his body as a breaking force for her momentum, he reached out with a strong leg, sweeping it out to pin her against the rock before the impact rebounded her in the wrong direction. She squeezed her eyes shut, trying to calm her churning insides.

"Are you alright?" he asked.

"Yeah, just remind me not to do this again anytime soon, okay?"

"Indeed. Though I think you did rather well, Vermillion. Honestly, I didn't hold much faith that that last little trick was going to work. So, well done on your execution." Her eyes opened in surprise.

"You didn't know it would work? You sounded so certain…"

"Well. One of us had to be."

E stared at him for one more long moment before a mad little laugh of her own bubbled to the surface. Closing her eyes once more, she rested her head back against Hook's pillar and simply laughed, releasing the last of her pent-up freak-out from the journey across. Somehow it all seemed ridiculously hilarious, now that she was safely on his side. Opening her eyes, she caught Hook watching her with a soft smile, enjoying her display of crazy. Caught, his smile turned serious, and he nodded toward his leg that still pinned her to the rock.

"Are you steady now?"

"Yes, I think I'm good. Thanks." With a nod he slowly released her, cautiously ensuring she had her balance firmly rooted in her feet.

"Okay, time for the next step of the plan," she breathed.

"There's more?" Hook grinned.

"Of course. Now hold still." E took a deep breath, pulled on her aching hands and arms once more to lift herself upward. Hook opened his mouth to say something but was quickly shut up when her legs came down on either side of his head to sit on his shoulders, her crotch basically shoved in his face. He froze, silent as the dead. She grinned. For once the man was speechless without a single sarcastic word to say. It didn't last long.

"So…this is what you had planned when scooting clear over that chasm? What will the tea committee say?"

The tea committee was a group of old women that liked to sit on chairs lining the streets of Sanctuary. Some of the few women to escape into Sanctuary before being corrupted, they apparently had nothing better to do than sip tea and gossip about every person that walked by. Most of it was pulled out of thin air, not an ounce centered in truth. Easton found it entertaining to give them plenty of gossip to spread amongst themselves about herself each time she passed by.

"You're my ladder. And ladders don't talk. So shush."

He sat quietly then, both of them pretending it wasn't entirely awkward that she was sitting on his face. E focused on getting her hands, which had turned an ugly shade of mottled purple on her trip over, to cooperate. With her new vantage point, E was finally able to get close enough to her hands to work toward her earlier goal: getting a hold of the lock picks hidden in her bra. Finally she grasped one. Her exhale of relief quickly turned to a curse as the pin fell from her numb fingers.

"Okay, plan B." Easton held herself upward as much as possible on the pole, shifting first one leg, then the other down through the circle of his arms.

"That's going to leave a bruise ." Hook groaned under her jostling.

"Never mind that," she said, using one of his favorite phrases in return.

Her legs finally managed to slide down between Hook and the rock he was bound to. It was a tight fit, but at least she didn't have to support her whole weight on the pole anymore. Her hands screamed in agony and relief alike as his body and the rock supported her. Hook watched her carefully, eye bright with intensity as he stared up at her, the top of his head just at a height with her collarbone.

"What now, fearless butterfly? I'm all ears."

"Okay, don't get weird," she warned cautiously.

"I make no promises."

"In my bra I have two more lock picks. I can't get to them; my hands are useless right now."

"Magnificent! Where is this bra?" Hook's eyes scanned all over her, trying to discern what accessory she was talking about.

"Oh for the love of…it's the thing that covers my…chest!"

She spit out in embarrassing frustration. Something about saying the word 'boobs' to Hook the pirate seemed all kinds of awkward. Hook's brow rose before understanding flashed in his eye. Excitement followed the understanding.

"Brilliant! Hiding picks in your breast binding…" He shook his head, "women have all the best hiding places."

"Yeah, okay, I'll give you that. But we're kind of running out of time here, so…"

"Right." Hook's eyes narrowed in concentration as he zeroed in on the laces of her shirt. She bit her tongue as he dived in, ripping the laces free with an expert ease.

"Do this often?" she muttered, oddly nervous.

"This would be a first for me, actually." Hook grinned up at her roguishly, one lace hanging from clenched teeth. E rolled her eyes and looked away, concentrating on anything but the debacle taking place. Finally the laces were gone, and Hook was all concentration again, though this time it was focused on her dark green bra, the one thing from her past life that she continued to hold onto.

"What a strange binding," he remarked.

"Okay, never mind that!" She was starting to see why he liked that saying so much. "The pins are the jeweled things in the middle."

"I see. Their lengths must run sideways into the material, leaving the ends to… look as though part of the design?"

"They're less likely to get taken from you, if people think it's just part of your clothes. Even the police pat downs never caught them." Hook grinned that rogue's smile once more.

"Brilliant."

"Uh, thanks. So, if you can just…grab one with your teeth, I guess, then you can reach around me and maybe make it to your hand…"

"Got it."

Without further ado, Hook dove in for the kill. If their situation hadn't been ridiculously desperate and she weren't covered in dirt, blood and sweat, the actions might have been more erotic than awkward. Easton cleared her throat and stared at the top of his wavy hair.

"So. You used my name."

"Yes?" Came Hook's muffled reply. She cleared her throat against the squeak that nearly escaped it.

"Yes. And since we very well may still die, I think it's only fair that you tell me your real name now."

"Oh?" Another muffled reply.

"Yes!" She huffed, short of breath. "You did promise that once you used my name, you'd give me yours. And... for crap's sake, what's taking so long down there?"

Hook's head popped up before she hyperventilated, one jeweled pick between his lips. Ducking around her he pressed forward to reach the pick to his hand, outright squishing her in his efforts.

"Maybe I should have moved first." She grunted.

"No need, I've got it. If we move now, I may drop it." Hook returned, breath fanning across her chest as he strained to work his hand behind the rock pillar at her back.

"So..." she cleared her throat. Okay, maybe even despite the perilous situation and her dirty grossness, their current position was getting to her. A lot.

"So." He looked up at her, a deliciously spicy, sweet scent from the leaves he'd chewed earlier washing over her face.

"Name?" she cleared her throat and tried again to gain an answer. Her throat would be raw by the time they made it free if this lasted much longer.

"Damn it all to the sea's depths!" Hook hissed, startling her. "It broke. I nearly had it and it broke!"

"I have one more." She reminded him. His frustration shifted immediately to mischief that danced at the corners of his lips

"Do you think you could bear it?"

"Just get the stupid pick, Hook!"

With another playful grin, Hook dove down again. This time, E bit her lip, closed her eyes, and waited it out. It was better than saying something stupid, which is exactly what would have happen if she opened her mouth again.

"Octavian." His lips brushed across the overheated skin of her chest.

"What?" E blinked, lost in an overheated haze as he continued to root around in her personal space. Hook pulled away and moved around her once more to shift the pick to his bound hand. When his head came back around, face once again tilted close to hers, it bore a serious expression. She found herself drowning already, in the intense sea-colored depths of his eye.

"My name."

She blinked at him in surprise. He'd just given her his name, something he felt had the utmost power. She'd asked him for it, but she hadn't actually expected him to give it.

"Octavian?" She tried the name out on her tongue, trying to match it to the face she'd grown to know. He stared at her solemnly for one more long unfathomable moment. A loud clanking sound broke the heavy atmosphere between them, and just like that his killer grin was back in place.

"Got it!"

A rough slicing sound signaled that his hook had cut loose the ropes tying him to the pillar. E drew a deep breath as Hook pulled away. She shook her head. *Octavian.* She was going to have to get used to thinking of him with that name, rather than simply 'Hook'. His gaze found hers, holding her in that impenetrable way of his.

"The pigmites took my daggers. I need you to hold *very* still, Easton," he spoke slowly, carefully tasting her name on his tongue in much the same way she just had. "Don't move an inch."

She nodded, understanding dawning. He was going to cut her free with his hook, and was worried about cutting her. She wasn't fully informed on what made the thing so dangerous. Typically when they battled, he used his sword. On the occasions he used his hook, she was too busy surviving to notice anything out of the usual. But she gathered it came with some seriously bad juju, and the last thing she needed was more bad juju.

Moving with exaggerated care, Hook sliced through the ropes binding her wrists, like they were butter. No sooner had the ropes been cut did Hook slide the crystalline casing back onto the weapon. He took a small step back, allowing her as much room as the area around the pillar could afford. Quickly lowering her hands, E shook out her swollen, raw limbs, wincing. Hook leaned forward, grasping one hand with his. His fingers worked rhythmically in a twisting motion back and forth, inch by inch down her hand to the tips of her fingers.

"Rub them like that; it'll help the feeling return faster. It'll hurt terribly, but it's better than losing your hands." Leaving her to it, Hook turned in a full circle, scanning their surroundings.

"Thanks," she whispered, enjoying his ease of care. She really loved the way Hook treated his crew like family. The thought warmed her beyond the pain in her hands.

Strange skittering noises reached her ears, clicks and odd jumbles of words mixing to form the sound. Glancing upward, E realized the pigmites must have returned. Their time was up.

"So what's the plan?" She tried to ignore the rising black water, and how during their efforts to escape it had risen to lap just below their feet now.

"You're the one with the plans. I was just waiting for you to announce the next move." His face was so nonchalant that E actually panicked for a minute. But eventually that maddening grin broke out on his lips once more. With a relieved huff, she shook her head.

"Very funny. You've got a plan already; you're just messing with me."

"I absolutely have a plan." He acknowledged. "How are you at holding your breath?" E stared at him, mouth dropped wide.

"You're kidding again…right?"

"I'm afraid not." His face smiled, but his eyes were deadly serious. Realization smacked into her gut so hard it stole her breath.

"We're going to die."

This whole time she never doubted they would escape. She knew if she could just get to him he'd save them. Now, that certainty was gone. He'd simply been trying to keep her calm, to help her keep sanity about her just a little longer.

"Come now." Hook kicked lazily at the water pooling about their boots. "Where's your sense of adventure, little butterfly? You've got wings!"

"Butterflies crash and burn when their wings get wet, just so you know." She hugged herself as the water climbed to her calves. Hook's wild grin positively beamed as he wrapped an arm around her waist, pulling her close.

"Not this butterfly. This one's my lucky charm. Perhaps the

butterfly will grow fins instead." He pressed a kiss to her hair. She offered a shaky smile, leaning into him as the water hit her thighs.

"The water's rising faster!" She gasped.

"The tide is nearing its peak," he agreed. When she began shaking, Hook tilted her chin upward to meet his gaze. "Easton James, surely you're not scared of a little adventure with the infamous Hook, are you?"

"Just a little worried about the drowning part of it, is all. Is there no other way?"

"The tide is too strong, the corridors too long to swim down and out while it fills. Likely they have the entrance barred, and we'll need to pick it to escape. That will take some time. There is no other way."

The cold water stole her breath as it rose to her waist. Her fingers clutched at his shirt, eyes wide with desperation as the torches along the wall began to sizzle and splutter. Hook once again captured her chin, gazes locking.

"Have a little faith in your Captain?"

Their feet lifted from the rock, bodies rising with the salty water. Panic once again had her limbs wanting to flail about for purchase. The inky darkness, the water closing in, it called her claustrophobia to the surface. Yet locked within his gaze as she was, she found herself drawing on the strength that was Hook. He was fearless in the face of death, calm and resilient. He was being strong for her, trying to make their coming demise easier for her.

"Okay."

Hook smiled, moving arm's length away so that she could use her limbs' full range of motion to keep afloat.

"That's my lucky charm. Now, just relax, let the water carry your weight. Lie on your back and float for a time if you must. Breath slow and easy, you'll need your lungs working for the top."

"Okay," she repeated, trying her best to do as he said, staying calm. And it was working, until the lights hissed with a final farewell, plunging them into bleak blackness.

"Calm, Vermillion. Breathe. I'm right beside you." His fingers shifted up her arm, offering a soothing squeeze.

"Okay, sorry, I'm sorry." She pushed the words through hyper-ventilating breaths.

"Apologies are not needed here. This is a difficult test for you, but you are weathering it well. Shall I tell you about the time that I was sailing the Atashio seas?"

"Please." Tears leaked from her eyes, joining the water at her chin.

"It was my first journey to the seas on my own command. I had a brand new ship that I was devastatingly proud of. It was gifted to me by the King, my father."

"Your father was a king?" she asked, teeth chattering. Hook moved closer, one arm wrapping around her back, keeping her legs free to swim yet offering some of his warmth.

"He was. King of a vast array of seas and islands, lands as far as you could see."

"Then, that would make you a prince?"

"At one point, yes," he acknowledged. "But that was long ago. Shall I continue?"

"Yes, please." She squeezed her eyes shut as the holes at the top of the cave loomed closer, the light of the sky dimming to night with unnatural speed, as though eager for their deaths. She held tightly to Hook, trying to soak up his courage through her contact with him.

"At age fifteen, I was thrilled to be sailing the vast seas, embarking on a journey across the expanses of my future kingdom. My father had received the call that asked for help, asked for volunteers to join the ranks of Hooks. I eagerly jumped at the opportunity, begging that he give me the honor of accepting the call." She could hear the roguish grin that split his face. "I thought I was quite something then; I'm afraid I was a bit arrogant and wild."

"Never." E returned the contagious grin. Hook chuckled.

"Indeed, I was! Eager to be among the first to arrive, I pushed my ship as fast as I could. When the storms came, the sailors urged me to hold back. In my arrogance I thought my grand ship could fight through any tempest. So we sailed onward. I should have listened." He toyed with the numb fingers of her left hand as he spoke, his touch barely discernible. "The tempest capsized my father's present, and all of my crew was tossed into the seas. The waves pulled us under with a vengeance. Clearly Devus was angry with my arrogance to sail his seas so brutally."

"What happened?"

"I grew gills."

E's disbelieving grin disappeared as the sound of metal ringing against stone met their ears. Their upward momentum had ceased, his hook pressing to the ceiling in an effort to protect their heads from bumping into the stone. Their time was up. The excited chatters above rose in chorus, the pigmites excited to see the end of their prey. Her body shook with uncontrollable tremors and sobs, tears spilling freely. Hook grabbed her about the waist once more, pulling her close. He pressed her cheek against his chest, holding her tightly.

"Easton, when your air runs out...it's okay to breathe."

E choked back a sob, nodding against his chest, holding tight to his waist. It all had to end one day, it ended for everyone. And while she would have chosen a different way to go, she couldn't think of a better man to die beside. Even to the end he was comforting her, helping her face acceptance of death with dignity. One last breath filled her lungs as the water plunged over top of her head. Hook held her close, keeping her tightly pressed to his chest.

As the need for air crowded in on her, she jerked in his hold, body reacting without her consent, fighting for air that wouldn't come. Still he held her tightly to him, securing her in place. His lungs suddenly expanded against her ear, and she knew he had drawn his first and last breath of the sea. Still her body fought with itself, one part of her refusing to let it end like this, the other begging for a breath. Hook's chest rose and fell against her once more. Then there was no more time for thought as the frigid water gushed into her mouth, filling her lungs.

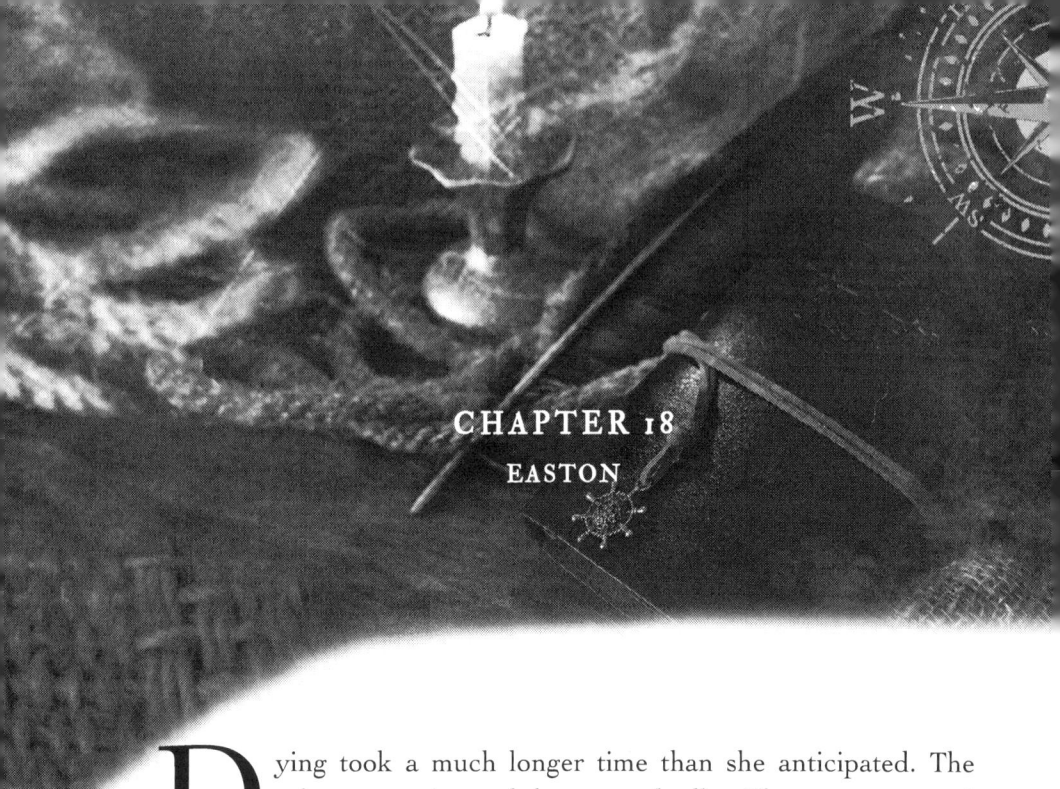

CHAPTER 18
EASTON

D ying took a much longer time than she anticipated. The salty water burned her eyes badly. The water poured through her mouth and nose, yet somehow she wasn't drowning yet. She could practically hear Hook coaxing her, reminding her it was okay to breathe. It wasn't until he grasped her hand and pressed it to her neck, that understanding flooded in with the water. Hook may not have given her fins, but he had somehow managed to give her gills. The final words to his story rang in her ears, *"I grew gills."*

Though it went against every ounce of her instincts, Easton found herself breathing water. Her efforts to fight stopped abruptly, and she clutched him closer. Blindly navigating her hands across his body, she found her fingers skating over gills on his neck as well. Suddenly, anger filled her. She threw out a punch, hitting him in the chest in what felt like slow motion due to the dense salty water.

He knew! He knew what he could do for them, and he didn't tell her! He let her think they were going to die in a watery grave, let her blubber like a baby, when he could have just told her 'hey Easton, I'm going to turn you into a fish'. Simple enough!

"They were listening. I couldn't let them know we had a way of surviving, Vermillion. It would have ruined any plans of escape."

E balked, fists freezing in mid-punch as Hook's voice sounded within her head. His hand landed on her hip, keeping her close.

"I know it's a lot to take in right now, but do try to not drift away. Your eyes will adjust soon, the burning will ease, and you'll be able to see. But we don't know what else the tide brought within this cavern. For the moment I think it wise we stay close to one another."

"Are you...are you actually talking to me, in my head? Or am I dead right now? I'm really dead, aren't I?"

"No, you aren't dead, Vermillion. Calm down." She could hear the laughter in his voice, teasing her.

"How is this happening? How did you turn me into a fish?" Her eyes swept back and forth, desperately searching the inky surroundings for ninja water creatures.

"Let me know when you are done assaulting me with fists and questions, and I'll gladly answer the best I can. Perhaps try counting backwards to calm yourself."

She knew that tone all too well. Normally his level-headed approach would calm her, but in this whole realm of crazy, it wasn't helping. If anything, it made her want to kick him where it counted, or any number of other places running through her head.

"In this state, all thought carries over to words. All thought. That means I can hear everything going on in that little imaginative head of yours, Vermillion. And it would be incredibly difficult for me to get you out of here if you crushed the family jewels, so you might want to rethink that last bit."

She blinked at the darkness where he floated, shock momentarily overriding her anger.

"Oh."

"Yes. Now, calm down. You are more shaken than angry. You promised to have a little faith in your Captain," he tsked.

He was right. Her anger stemmed from the fact that she was a raging mess of screwed-in-the-head right now. She'd just faced her death, and it hadn't been pretty. She had outright panicked, something she was becoming frustratingly familiar with in Neverland.

"Are you calm now?"

"*Yes.*"

"*Good. Your eyes should begin to adjust soon. Can you see me?*"

Just then something moved not a foot in front of her, but before she could karate chop it, she realized it was a dim outline of Hook's arm. Slowly but surely, bits and pieces of him became more clear, and soon she could see the distinct outlines of his features, though the details were still too dark to be seen.

"*I can see you. Vaguely.*"

"*Good. We need to swim down to the bottom of the cavern and find our way to the entrance. There, with any luck, we can escape unnoticed. By the time the tide recedes and they come back to claim their prizes, we will be long gone.*"

"*What will happen if they catch us? If we can't escape in time?*"

"*Pigmites are… unpleasant. You'd rather not know what else they are capable of, and I'd rather not discuss it. Bad luck to speak of them too much.*" He pushed the sides of her shirt open and slid the lock pick back into its hiding place before she could register the intent of his actions.

"*You'd best keep this in there. Don't want to lose our last key to survival.*"

"*Right.*" She cleared her throat, or tried to. It was an unsettling sensation, and made no sound at all. Hook grinned as he grabbed her hand, urging her to swim down with him.

"*Vocal cords don't work so well when engulfed in water. It is why the Mer people communicate through thought.*"

"*Mer people? Are you a mermaid then? Mer..man? Am I? No. That makes no sense.*" Hook was quiet for a long time. It wasn't until they reached the bottom of the cavern that he finally spoke, his tone reflective and cautious.

"*Take this stone. Cup it between your hands and think of light.*" E held the palm-sized rock in her hands that he pulled from his belt, and did as instructed. Slowly a light formed within the rock, filling the cavern around them in a warm glow. "*Keep the stone in your hands. I'll keep my eyes open for dangers and protect us if I must.*" E followed his gaze to a large black hole in the wall.

"*Exit's down the dark scary tunnel, huh?*" Hook nodded, silent, face determined.

She'd be a fool to question him now, he'd proven himself time and again, and always kept his word to protect her. She swam forward, making the first move. He kept one hand at the small of her back as they slipped through the gentle currents, keeping them in sync as they progressed, their eyes searching every nook and cranny of the huge dark tunnel.

"You remember my story? The ending?"

E had been so engrossed in the creepy journey that she jumped at his soft-spoken thoughts. His hand at her back gave a gentle rub, assuring her and apologizing at once.

"You grew gills," she recited.

"When I was thrown into the water, I was pulled deep by the currents. I knew I was about to die, and that it had been my own fault. I knew others were losing their lives because of my impetuous fool-hearty choices. In my dark sorrow, I welcomed death. But, I didn't die. I was rescued by a blue-haired mermaid with a gentle smile and dancing eyes."

The fondness in his voice riveted Easton to the story. Hook had loved this mermaid, that much was evident. And E found herself inexplicably drawn to knowledge of anyone loved so deeply by the pirate Captain Hook.

"The Mer People had been divided for the first time in their existence, as they have stayed to this day. Half of them were convinced to join the Fiend. The other half fought against his efforts of control. They had banded together with the Fairies and other free creatures of Neverland to issue the call for help. It was the rebellious Mers who brought word to my kingdom, asking for help. When the Fiend learned of the approaching allies, he sent his faithful Mers to attack us. They are the ones who eventually were corrupted and turned into sirens."

"So the crew thought I was one of the Fiend's pet sirens come to steal away the new Arrival?"

"Aye. Mers of every variation have connections to the elements. The Fiend often sends his Sirens to persuade the Arrivals to his side, as their voices are incredibly hypnotic. Coming in contact with water always reveals their true natures."

"That makes a lot of sense. I was so confused." She laughed. *"Continue, please."*

"Bound to the elements as they are, their whims can stir up the sea to anger. So it was that they set the trap. My ship was but one in a full fleet of

allies. In my haste, I had become separated from the fleets, thus triggering the trap set by the Mers, trapping us alone. Some say my impetuous actions saved the others in the fleet from death. With the storm triggered, they couldn't get close enough to be brought to harm. And once the trap was set, the dark Mers could not orchestrate another devastating enough to destroy them." He glanced her way.

"It takes a great deal of their strength to create a storm of such intensity. Some have called me a hero for it. I despised that word. I did not deserve it. Whether I saved others or not, it doesn't change the fact that I sacrificed the lives of my crew. It wasn't done as a selfless act to trigger a trap I saw ahead of time. It was simply the act of a foolish, overly eager boy." He shook his head, sorrow and guilt lining his face.

"When the good Mers discovered the dark Mers' actions, they moved to counteract. So it was that the blue-haired mermaid found me. The others tried to save my men, but they were intercepted by the Fiend's numbers, and in battling for their own lives they could not save the others in time. I still don't know why I was saved. Why it was me that Avida found, and not one of the other more worthy men."

"Avida." Easton searched her memories, trying to recall where she'd heard that name before. *"The ring, the one that you had during the judgment. It was inscribed to Avida. O.R.B?"* He nodded, acknowledging her unspoken assessment.

"Octavian Ryes Bendal."

"Those initials were yours. So that means…" she thought back to the engraving on the ring. He waited patiently, allowing her to piece together the puzzle. *"Her ring was engraved with your initials. The woman you loved."*

"Yes, it was her. Mermaids are clingy creatures, and once they find something that calls to them, they won't be happy until they own it. But she couldn't very well own me if I drowned. So, she gave me gills."

"How? How did you give me gills, for that matter?"

Hook stopped swimming, carefully lifting her left hand. E stared at it in surprise. On her middle finger was a delicate rose gold ring, with a large pink ruby at the center.

"Where…this is the ring…how?"

Her thoughts stalled out, mind racing to understand how she had ended up wearing Hook's love's ring.

"Yes, this was her ring. It is all I have left of her. The ring's magic is what allows you to live now. It is how she saved me that fateful day."

Her mind halted on the memory of him playing with her fingers as he told her the story, before the water covered their heads. That must have been when he slipped the ring on her.

"How does the ring give you gills?"

Hook urged her to begin swimming once more.

"Each Mer carries two rings on their hands during their lifetime. Mers are birthed on land, and given these rings upon their birth. In such a manner, they have found ways to live on both land and water. Being birthed on land, and the rings bonded to them in that moment of their first breath, the magic contained in the ring gives them the power to live in both realms. The rings grow with the Mers as they age. The first ring on their right hand stays with them. The ring on their left goes to the person of their choosing, the one whom they choose to wed. If it be another Mer, they simply trade rings, and are bound. But, if it be to someone outside of their race, such as a stupid human boy? It bestows the same power to that mate as the power of the Mer who gave it."

"That's how she gave you gills. By giving you her ring, you could breathe in the water."

"She put the ring on me, binding me to the magic, but to her as well. As her husband." E's eyes widened in surprise.

"But you were only fifteen. I mean, I understand that it was the only way to save you, but...marriage, at fifteen, and to a stranger? That had to be awkward."

"Is this not an acceptable age of marriage in your world?"

"No!" She choked. *"We tend to get married in our twenties, or even later. Anything earlier than that is usually frowned on."*

"Interesting that you waste your best years before devoting yourself to someone," Hook murmured.

E blinked, that line of thinking never occurring to her before. Was that true? That you wasted your best years before deciding to marry? She shook her head, not having time to delve into the matter.

"So, she rescued you. Then what?"

"I continued on my way to the gathering place. I became a Hook. Marriage was barred to those in the Order of the Hooks. But given my circumstances, they were forgiving. They couldn't very well deny a time old Mer custom, and chance losing an alliance they needed so badly in the battles to come. I was allowed to visit her, and she me. But we were forbidden to start a family, or do anything that would compromise my position as a Hook. I continued my training as a Hook, seeing Avida only a few times a year, until I was twenty-three. And then, she died." E gasped, silently sucking in a lung full of water.

"What happened?"

"Pan."

"He killed her?"

"She couldn't bear our time apart. She begged me to demand more time from the brethren, but I refused. I couldn't ask for more exceptions than they had already allowed. It wasn't fair to the others. So one day, she took matters into her own hands. When I left after our time together, she followed me. She saw how I entered into the secret passage of the Hook Brothren's holdings. It was the only weak portion of the magic shield that protected our fortress from Pan."

"Afraid of what would happen should truth of her forbidden knowledge come to light, she begged me to keep it a secret. Wanting to protect her, wanting to be a good husband, I agreed. Foolish, foolish naive mistake. Soon, secrecy wasn't enough for her. I think she knew that the long passage of time between our meetings was affecting us differently."

"Still very much a boy upon our marriage, I had done much growing and maturing in the years that followed. With that growth brought the yearning for independence, and a slow falling out of youthful fancies of what I thought had been love. I came to think of her more as a cherished friend, but little more." He shook his head, jaw clenching.

"While the passage of time pushed me away from her, it only made her cling to me all the more. She vowed to enter the fortress itself if I didn't show up every night to see her. She wouldn't listen to reason, and knowing Avida's strong will as I did, I had no doubt that she would carry through on her threat. For weeks she and I would meet in the secret passages, disregarding the rules that had been placed upon me as a Hook."

"Toward the end, Avida and I fought. I still loved her in my way, but it never felt right that I should go against my brethren, betraying their trust and *safety for my own selfish reasons. I could no longer in good conscience disregard the rules. I had matured in my years, come to understand that my wishes could not be put over others, simply for my own pleasure, or that of Avida's. The loss of my crew had taught me that. I simply hadn't had the courage to deny her before that moment. I hadn't wanted to hurt her. But no longer could I ignore the dictations of my duty to my fellow Hooks. And to be honest, I didn't feel it fair to Avida that she was forced to stay with me. The growing distance was painful to her heart, I could see it. Yet short of continuing to lie, there was nothing I could do to change that."*

They stopped suddenly, heavy metal gates looming ahead of them. They had come to the end of the tunnel. E quickly moved to grab the lock pick from her bra, handing it over to Hook.

"Can you not pick locks? I find that hard to believe, as you carry them with you." he pulled back, giving her room. *"I would like to see you in your element."* E felt her nerves jangle. She was pretty good at locks, but she was also nervous. If she screwed this up, it would be her fault they didn't escape.

"Are you sure?"

"Of course. I have every faith in your capable hands. Two hands are better than one, after all." He winked, motioning her forward. E shook her head.

"I don't agree with that statement," she argued quietly, moving to pick the lock. She definitely wasn't as adept as Sad. But she had picked a lot of locks in her lifetime, and much to her relief the lock popped open, gate swinging easily despite the time it often spent underwater. The pigmites must maintain it on a regular basis. Hook grinned widely.

"Lucky charm."

E blushed as he closed the gate behind them, careful to ensure it locked once more to avoid early detection of their escape. Glancing about to check that the coast was clear, they swam alongside the cliffs that harbored the caverns, hoping to soon come across a shore. E waited on edge, eager for Hook to finish his story. Yet she was too intimidated to ask him to continue. It was an intimate matter close to his heart that had clearly been damaged at many points throughout the story. Asking him to continue seemed crass. Or was it crass to act as though she didn't care to ask him for the rest? Luckily, he saved her the uncertainty, and continued on his own.

"I told her I would no longer meet her in secret. That she would have to be okay with the time that we were allowed to be together, or not at all. She declared she would still return the next night and wouldn't leave until I came. I told her she would be waiting alone. We left one another under disagreeable terms. She sobbed on the shore all the next day. I could see her from my window, and I knew she knew that. She wanted me to see her sorrow and be forced to break my new vow."

"I hid myself away in rooms with no windows, and refused to fall. I thought I was doing my duty, that I was doing the right thing. Doing the right thing would have actually entailed admitting my misdeeds to the others, coming clean about everything. At least then, they would have had a chance." Hook shook his head, his next words bitter.

"But I was still just as foolish as the day I rushed into that storm. It was then, while she languished on the beach, that the Fiend happened upon her, intending to use her as bait. As our meetings had always been in secret, she was alone, unaccompanied by her usual protective guards. She made an easy target. There was no one to come to her aid. I did not know he took her away, no one did. When she did not show up on the beach the next day, I thought she had returned to the sea to wait me out."

"During the time Pan held her captive, he turned her toward sympathy for him. Avida was demanding as are many Mers, but she was also a delicate soul. She was more suited towards loving than the sneaky ways of war. In her pain that I had caused, Pan wriggled his way into her sympathies, playing on her insecurities." Hook's jaw clenched.

"She told him of the secret passageways. Whether she did it out of hurt anger towards me, or out of a shift in loyalty for the Fiend due to corruption, the results were the same. One night, everything changed. Smee was a guard at the time, young and loyal. He was also a friend."

"Friend?"

"Our relationship might seem to only be one of Captain and begrudging Bo 'son. But once, we were friends. We shared a similar air of… arrogant confidence and eagerness for mischief."

"Arrogance, I could see. Mischief? Smee doesn't strike me as the mischievous type."

"Time changes all." The muscles in his jaw twitched. *"It was Smee's birthday. I talked him into a night out at the local village with me and a few other men, who you now know to be a large portion of my crew. They were a mixture of the crews of others who came on the ships after me. We had bonded over the years. We often would go on outings together when deemed appropriate by the other Hooks. So this night was no different, in the beginning."*

"Yet when we returned, it was to carnage. The Fiend and his minions had attacked while the Hook's slumbered. They were completely unprepared for attack, not knowing their secrets had long ago been breached. The Fiend's minions had slaughtered most of them, cutting off their Hooks before they were even aware of the dangers lurking around them in the dark."

"By the time I got there, only a few of my brethren remained. They had taken down many of the invaders, but it was clear they were already mortally wounded themselves. In my fury and anguish, I attacked the Fiend. My sense of vengeance gave me strength. I nearly killed him. He knew it as well as I did. I could see the fear in his eyes."

"But at the last moment, as my hook was descending upon him, Avida jumped in the way. Blinded to everything but my foe, I hadn't noticed her lurking in the shadows. My hook found her flesh instead of his. The Fiend flew, taking his few remaining minions with him, leaving me alone in the anguish he created. Avida was lost due to my blind fury and blatant idiocy. And Smee? Though he remains loyal to my cause, he has never forgiven me my foolish heart that had yet again cost so many lives." E stopped short, hand resting on his tense back.

"I am so sorry." She whispered in his mind. Hook nodded, looking away into the distance. His eyes suddenly sharpened.

"There is land ahead. Pigmites have excellent hearing. Once on shore we must move quickly, and as quietly as possible."

Putting a finger to his lips, he motioned her to silently follow him. They reached land, swiftly scuttling up onto the shore and into the cover of trees. Exhausted, they stumbled through the forest as quickly and quietly as possible. But luck was not with them now. A curious chirrup in the trees above their heads froze them to their spot.

"Stay clear of my hook." He warned in his gruff voice, giving her hand a final squeeze. Then he shoved her into a nearby bush.

E rolled under the bush as far as she could and stared wide-eyed through the leaves. Without a weapon she would just be in the way, and the last thing he needed was a distraction.

Small black bodies leapt into view, trying their best to land on his back. Hook moved with such a fluid grace that it was awe-inspiring. She'd seen him fight this enemy once before, but then she had been fighting for her own life against a giant goat man. She hadn't been able to soak in the entirety of his prowess. She also hadn't seen what his hook was capable of.

Each slash that found the body of a pigmite left behind a vivid bright blue streak. The streak opened wider, glittering with stars of a vast universe. Then, a horrible sucking sound issued from the hole, and the bodies of the pigmites slowly caved in on themselves until nothing remained but their distant screams. When the last pigmite was cast into nothingness, Hook sagged against a tree, breathing heavily. E tumbled out of the bush, rushing to his side.

"We must continue on. If others heard the noise they will soon be upon us and my strength is flagging," Hook commanded, though he accepted her efforts to help support his weight, an arm thrown over her shoulders. Soon they were on the move once more, rushing into the dark foliage. When they finally felt safe enough to slow to a walk, they were both exhausted, and a long ways distant from the beach.

"I think we can afford to stop for a bit. Those were mere scout pigmites. Had the whole group of them been near, we wouldn't have made it this far," Hook assured her, slumping against a tree.

"What was that? What did your hook do to them?"

"When a cut is made in the flesh with my hook, a portal not unlike that of your book is made within them. They are sucked inward through the portal, and sent to a hellish plane where they suffer anguish for all eternity." E digested his gruff statement, the black cloud of emotion over his features.

"So… your wife?"

"Is there languishing amidst the sea of demons put there by my own hand. And I have to live with the fact that when I vanquish the Fiend, I will be sending him to an eternity with her as well. But for the sake of all Neverland, for the sake of every life that rests on my shoulders, I must do it, and continue to do it every day until it is done." He paused, face twisted in guilt.

"Do you know what her last words were?" E shook her head, fighting the sting of tears in her eyes.

"It was as though in the moment of her impending death, Pan's influence over her lifted away. And she begged with her last words, that I forgive her." He scoffed, rubbing the crystalline sheath over his hook. "Was it I who should have begged for forgiveness? Did either of us deserve forgiveness? We both played a role in the death of the Order of the Hook." He glanced her way. "Including your dear James T. My mentor."

E blinked in shock.

"But...you said he's been dead for hundreds of years."

"He likely has been, by now." Hook tiredly pushed away from the tree, walking onward into the forest. E followed in confusion.

"I don't understand."

"Until we retrieved that clock time did not pass in Neverland, Vermillion. Not as it does in the rest of the world. When the Fiend killed all but one of the Hooks, he gained a power unlike any he'd ever had. He stole the watch from James, and with it he stopped time, stopped the progression of life itself. He froze Neverland, so that he could rule it forever. James was my mentor. In the time that I had been amongst the Hooks, he had become like a second father to me." His jaw clenched.

"And as such, my betrayal was that much more heart-rending. I found him amongst the dying, torn to shreds. He barely clung to life. I pulled him into my arms, begging his forgiveness. 'What have you done, Octavian?' he said, staring up at me as though he no longer knew me. I confessed everything in that moment, mourning my actions. When I finished, he drew the tip of his hook across my eye." E gasped.

"Being the first of us, the strongest of us, he'd learned the strength to stop the progression of a rift. He could open a rift, then close it, seal it away if he wished. It was difficult, but he had the power. The rest of us could never dream to achieve it. He promised we were capable, but we never believed. With the last of his strength, he opened the rift over my eye, but stopped its progression beyond that. 'So that you may understand the depth of your transgression', he said. 'Return the watch to its rightful owner. Find redemption and you will close the rift. Or forever suffer in consequence'. And then he was gone."

"...You have an open rift over your eye?" She gaped. "I thought you'd lost it in battle."

"Whether my eye still functions properly or not, I cannot tell. I wear the patch for the safety of others. It only took one glance for a crew member to lose their mind by staring into the rift. It was then I realized the danger it posed even to those in the living world. So I covered it."

"Does it pain you?"

"Does it pain me?" His grin was brimming with irony. "I can see into the rift in my every waking moment. Even in my dreams, I often find myself plagued with visions of it. I can hear the constant mournful cries of those I have sent there. Avida amongst them. I believed I would go mad from it, at one point. Yet somehow, here I stand in all of my horrible sanity." He sighed, rubbing the patch. "Yes, it pains me, Vermillion. In so many different ways." They sat in silence for a long, painful moment.

"You can see into the Rift, so does that mean you can talk to the people there? To Avida?"

"No. I hear them, I feel their pain, I see anguished blurs of perhaps those I once knew. But I cannot interact with them. I cannot speak to her of regrets, or..." Without another word, Hook pushed away from the tree and walked on.

E followed in his wake, heart trembling for her Captain. A stray ray of sun glinted off the ring on her finger and she quickly moved to take it off. She knew how important it was to Hook, and now that she knew the tragic story, it didn't feel right for her to wear it any longer. She tugged harder on the ring, but it wouldn't budge. Her new friend Panic came back for a visit.

"It...it won't come off." Hook stopped walking, though he didn't look her way, his tense back kept to her. "I'm so sorry! My fingers must be too swollen still. Just give me a minute..."

"Don't bother trying to take it off, Vermillion." His voice was calm, devoid of any emotion. He was probably regretting putting it on her, but too gentlemanly to say it. If she couldn't get it off, it would mean he'd lost the one item left of his wife.

"No, wait, I can get it off. I just need to pull harder... and twist, maybe."

"Easton." Her horrified eyes slowly slid up to meet his face as he turned toward her, dreading his look of loss. Yet instead of loss, she saw only an expression of guilt.

"I don't understand." The words escaped her lips as a lost whisper.

"Once the ring has been placed upon your finger, once the magic has been used on you, it is yours. You are forever bound to the ring until your death."

"Bound forever. Like you were after she put it on you..." Her breath caught.

"Yes. Which means you are forever bound to me as well, little butterfly. Though we are human, I am still bound by Mer law." He held up a hand, showing her the matching ring still on his finger where Avida had placed it. "And as such, so are you. As far as Mer custom is concerned, you are now considered to be my wife."

Turning, he walked away, leaving her stunned. Eventually her feet found their way out of the shock, following in Hook's path. They walked in silence for hours. As the sun once again threatened to give way to night, Hook made camp. At least it seemed the watch had fixed the progression of day and night, time flowing smoothly once more.

Easton helped with preparations, working alongside him in that same heavy laden silence. It wasn't until he moved to hand her a piece of their roasting forest creature dinner that E could find her voice. Taking the meat from his fingers, she met his eye.

"You knew." He hesitated, then pulled away. Staring into the fire he remained silent, not acknowledging her statement. She pushed onward. "You knew that you would never get her ring back, once it was on my finger. And you still did it." Still he remained silent. "Why? I know how precious this ring is to you, to her memory. I saw the relief in your eyes when you recovered it in the judgement room."

"*Life* is precious, Vermillion. Memories are always with us, but life can be stolen away. I couldn't let you lose your life, not while I had a way of saving it."

"But..."

"You are part of my crew, Easton, my family. I told you I would protect you. And I always keep my word." E bit her lip, looking down at her hands. The food was gone, and the fire banked before she had the courage to speak again.

"So...Octavian Ryes Bendal?"

"Yes. That was my given name, once upon a time." A small smirk graced his lips, mind clearly reliving happier times.

"It's very...royal sounding. Kind of a mouthful, though. Mind if I just call you Ian?" Hook stood, fanning his cape out on the ground near the embers, the curve of his lips shifting to a solemn expression once more.

"As you will it. You may call me whatever it pleases you to, Easton. We are bonded now. As such nothing is forbidden you. Now, my cape has dried and will provide a small comfort against the ground. You can take your rest. I'll be on first watch."

Hook melted into the shadows to stand against a tree, becoming one with the night. She'd had the whole trek here, and all through dinner to contemplate their new and unexpected relationship status, yet she still couldn't quite grasp the gravity of the situation. Technically, E was now a married woman. She was married to a man who used to be fiction. A man who was once married to another once-fictional mermaid, who he accidentally killed in his efforts to end the life of yet another once-fictional character.

Life prepared you for all sorts of things, but she was pretty sure it never prepared you for this. It certainly hadn't prepared her, anyway. So, what did it mean, to be married to a Hook? Easton stood, hesitating as she eyed the cape on the ground. Decision made, she tromped towards Hook, throwing her arms about his waist for a quick hug.

"Thank you, Ian." She put as much of her sincerity into those words as she could, hoping they conveyed what her heart couldn't put into words. She spun and headed for the cape, careful not to meet his eyes again. E wasn't normally a touchy feely kind of girl. Her life had brought her up in a very hands off sort of way. Letting someone into your personal space was dangerous, in so many more ways than one. But somehow, this situation felt like it called for a hug, a physical display of her gratitude.

"You're welcome, little butterfly." Had the night not been so still, she would have missed his reply entirely.

The fact that he had given up something so precious, the only memento of his wife, to save her life, not to mention the weight of commitment such an act brought with it? It boggled her mind. It was such a huge gesture that E didn't know how to repay it. So a hug was the best she could come up with in that moment.

And if his soft reply was any indication, he'd needed it as much as she did, and likely been just as confused by it. She lay with her back to him, wrapped in his warm cape, staring at the slowly dying embers. She admired the sparkle of the pink gem as she spun the ring around the base of her finger, thinking. For such a delicate token, it carried a huge impact.

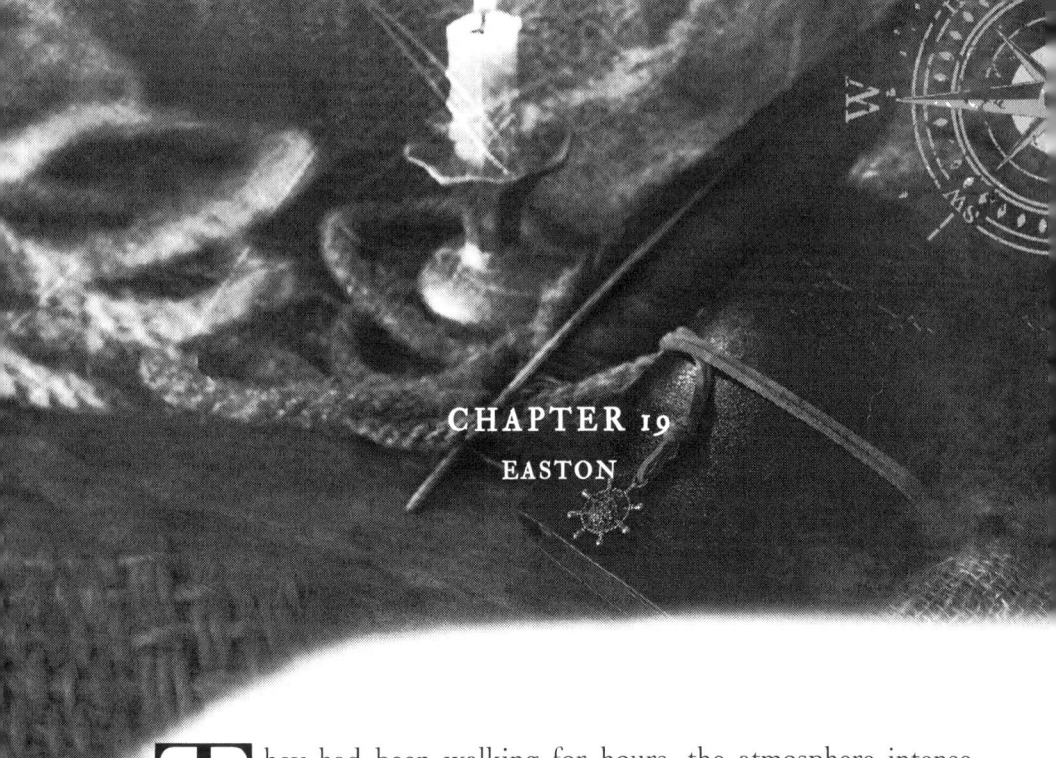

CHAPTER 19
EASTON

They had been walking for hours, the atmosphere intense with both the threat of enemies, and the change in their relationship status. He had changed watches with her after letting her sleep for a few hours. Though, from his tense frame, she doubted he had slept at all. But Hook, Ian, was anything but unfair. He understood the importance that came along with leadership, including allowing others to take the mantle of responsibility on themselves now and then. Still, he'd eagerly jumped up at the first break of dawn, and they'd silently doused the fire and were quickly on their way.

At a few points in the journey they had encountered dangers, during which time she got to once again see him and his hook in action. It was fascinating. He didn't always take the hook out. She asked why that was, to which he replied with a somber 'not all creatures are dangerous or evil enough to face the wrath of the rifting.' She'd silently admired his character, her appreciation of him growing in that same steady fashion that it had since her Arrival. The weight of responsibility he carried was enormous.

That was the most conversation they had carried all day. It was obvious they were both desperate to move past the awkward weight over their heads, but unsure how to progress. Awkwardness between the two of them was a foreign matter. When they were together, it was as though a strange well of mischief and playfulness built up within. If it wasn't released, there seemed to be an electric discomfort in the air. It was almost like a wild thing that needed to be released, needed room to run freely. *Her* well had reached 'bursting capacity' hours ago. If his twitchy behavior was any indication, his had, too, so Easton jumped in head first.

"So, what exactly does it mean to be the wife of a Hook? Please do explain what I've gotten myself into, kind sir."

She fought the tug at the corners of her lips, trying to restrain the telltale signs of mischief. It must have danced in her eyes, however, because Hook immediately played along. The relief in the air was palpable.

"Well, let me think on that." His lips pursed, feigning deep thought. "There will be endless hours of adventure, and a good dose of danger."

"No!" Her mouth dropped wide, eyes rounding dramatically.

"I'm afraid so," he sympathized. "And there will also be hours upon hours of being surrounded by dirty, sweaty men who bear not an ounce of my charm."

"Oh, I don't know if I can handle that one."

"It is a difficult burden to bear," he sighed heavily. "And of course, there is the fact that by aligning with me you have made a powerful enemy. Similarly, by becoming my wife, you'll be an even bigger target to the Fiend. You know well by now that my world is not an easy one, nor my daily breath guaranteed."

He stooped to scoop up a handful of rocks, sending them individually skipping into the forest ahead of them as they walked. Animals skittered out of the pathway of flying rocks, serving to stir up any concealed dangers ahead of time, whilst also entertaining the Pirate Captain. Clearly the discussion at hand was bringing to light real concerns he faced, but being Ian, he tried to put a silly twist to them to lighten the burden for others. She loved that about him. He cared far more for others than he gave himself credit for. Besides, life sucked too much to be serious about it all the time.

"Hmm, okay. What else was in the fine print of this marriage contract?"

"I'm glad you ask, as the list is quite lengthy. Chances are quite likely that the time will come in which I will not return home, and to be honest, there are days I am rather amenable on that matter. However, should I perish, as the only remaining Hook with the power to destroy him, the Neverland we know and love will be utterly destroyed, and the Fiend will reign without limitation. You and the rest of the crew will likely suffer gruesome fates at such a time. Of course, I will try to avoid such an instance, especially as I now have a wife who will likely be barefoot and with child in our kitchen one day in the future." He smirked over at her as she punched him in the arm.

"As if. Perhaps you'll be the one in the kitchen."

"That would truly be a feat. Hooks are capable of much, but I think that bearing offspring isn't on that list."

"Okay, okay. Keep going. This list is becoming quite interesting."

"You'll have to face the increased danger of being near my hook, as it is a weapon I can never be free of until the curse on this land is freed with the Fiend's death. *And* you will face the indignity of suffering under occasional leering looks from yours truly."

He offered a perfect example of said leering, drawing an irreverent laugh from her lips, though she tried valiantly to hold it back for the sake of their little game.

"Is that part of the danger you mentioned?"

"Absolutely."

"So, basically it will be just like everyday life. Is that what you're saying?"

"Hmm. You may have a point."

"Pity, I was expecting something breathtaking and shocking."

"Well, if it is breathtaking and shocking that you want, I'll let you in on a little rumor I've been made privy to." He glanced around conspiratorially. "There are some who suggest that Hooks are well known for their devilishly stolen kisses and breathtaking prowess in the bedroom."

"Oh no, now you've gone too far, sir! Say it isn't so!" She gasped, pretending shocked impertinence.

"I can only tell you what the rumors have garnished, my dear, no matter how shocking they may be." His grin was infectious, and she felt a self-congratulatory pride rising within. It had become a sort of pet project of hers, making that smile appear. Each grin added up on the mental tally system of triumph she had going on.

"Well. I suppose I can handle most of those things. If the rumors turn out to be true, I might have to change my thinking on the matter; for the tea committee's sake, of course." She offered an impish grin.

"Of course. The poor dears would suffer terribly from having to share such gossip. It won't be all fun and games for us either, though. I feel I should warn you of one last danger."

"Oh, no. There's more?" she feigned exhaustion, fanning herself. He remained quiet for a long moment as they walked. When he paused, stopping her with a hand at her elbow, his face bore that intense sober nature she had come to recognize through their months together. She was suddenly unsure if she wanted to hear this last one.

"A terrible, life threatening danger." He agreed. "I fear that my feet stink something terrible at the end of the day." The gut laugh that escaped E's throat was raucous enough to send birds in the trees flying away with startled squawks.

"Heaven help me! I could have borne anything but that! Please tell me it isn't so." Grinning softly, Ian turned and looked off into the distance.

"Sanctuary is just around the bend, and there is a matter we must agree upon now. Given the later age range in which your people typically marry, I can see that this is possibly something you wouldn't have wished for."

"It's true I've married far too young. What would the people of Chicago think?" she teased.

"And, given my confessions earlier, my past relationship woes, and my status as a man that lives his life by the obsession of killing another man...well, I can see that possibly adding to the foreboding you might feel on the matter. I can't change the fact that we are wed, nor would I try. Your life was saved by the action, and I can find no guilt in the matter. That being said, I will not force you into the role of wife. If you wish it, we can be wed in title only."

She hadn't expected that. E took a deep breath and watched his expressions closely, preparing to read the full truth of his answer to her return question.

"Do *you* want this? It can't be easy for you, forced into marrying again, after Avida's death. I know the situation was crazy, but she was important to you. I don't want you to feel a sense of obligation to me, especially if it shadows your heart." Blinking, he carefully chose his words.

"Avida was…" he swallowed, and looked into the forest. "Avida was important to me. For a time, she was everything. But with time, much passes into memory, even feelings of the heart. To be honest, I have not been a man of heartfelt feelings for a very long time, Easton. My life, my very essence, has been devoted to the single-minded purpose of that of my brethren; destroying the Fiend. I did not think I would live beyond that purpose, much less see myself wed again far before that purpose was fulfilled. I worry if I have the capacity within me to divide my being in such a manner."

He looked up, meeting her gaze, hand finding hers. E felt her heart do a strange little hop inside as the intensity behind his gaze seemed to soak into her bones.

"I find you to be an intriguing woman, Easton: brilliant, brave, noble, valiant and capable. You are wise enough to carefully choose your path, yet you bear wildness within you that can be quite strik- ing, not unlike your external beauty. It is a rarity to find such quali- ties as I see in you. I can think of no other with whom I would trust, with whom I would share my burdened world. I will endeavor to be a far better husband to you than I was to Avida; whether in title alone, or of true all-encompassing union." Mischief bloomed, covering the intensity that had stolen her breath.

"You also have a perfectly lovely pair of breasts, and I am not at all opposed to being their companion for the rest of my years." Easton's eyes widened, then yet another full gut laugh escaped her lips, tears welling in her jovial eyes.

"There you are! For a while I was worried I might have escaped with the wrong Hook."

"I'm afraid not. I am the one and only." Behind the shielding humor, she saw the guilt and the heaviness of that burden. He truly was the last of his kind. Pulling away, he fussed with the belt hanging low on his hips, readjusting it.

"Whatever you choose, I shall follow your wishes. But, a decision must be made before we enter Sanctuary. The men will undoubtedly notice the change in our relationship, and they will not be appeased until they receive an answer."

"How will they know?" she asked, curious.

Really she was grateful for any distraction to give her a few more moments to think. Once again he picked up her hand, fingers spinning the ring on her finger with a significant look that shouted, 'how else?' Dropping her hand he turned back to the task of adjusting and readjusting his weapons.

"One doesn't live for hundreds of years amongst the same people, without them learning most everything about you, little Vermillion. Endless time has a way of destroying any hopes of anonymity and privacy."

"Oh, come on Ian. You really think a bunch of guys are going to notice me wearing a ring? Hyrel didn't even notice when his butt was on fire two weeks ago."

"To be fair, he has far too much padding back there. The fire probably could have burned a full week on that much lard without him noticing."

Hook laughed, clearly reliving the memory of their village visit, during which one his crew members, a scrawny but oddly big-butted, scraggly-toothed weirdo, had pressed his oversized derriere too close to the baker's oven while making repairs to the old man's floor.

"Exactly my point. A woman's jewelry would be no different."

"Do I smell a wager coming, little butterfly?" His gaze lifted to find hers, seafoam green glinting with excitement.

"I think you are confusing it with the smell of defeat. It smells an awful lot like your stinky feet, I bet."

"Feisty wench." Hook leered playfully. "What shall we wager then?"

"If I win, you give me a foot massage at the end of every day for a month. It's only fair, with all the walking you make me do."

Her poking at his commanding orders had Hook's eye narrowing slightly, though the corners of his lips twitched in a fight to move upward. He knew she didn't mean it rudely, and he also knew he didn't much care for all the walking himself. She'd seen him covertly rubbing his own feet with a grimace at the end of the day. Standing straighter, Ian leaned closer.

"Fine. And if I win, I get a kiss."

"A...a kiss?" she stuttered, defiant playfulness stalling out in surprise. Her cheeks flushed. "What happened with your 'I won't hold you to the role of wife' idea?"

"For one, you still haven't answered me on that decision. And for another, you don't have to be wed to kiss. Or at least you don't in Neverland. This won't be a kiss from a husband to his wife. Only a man to a woman. That is all."

"So...you just give me a kiss. That's it?" she asked, suspicious.

"No. *You* give *me* a kiss. And it has to be spontaneous. None of this 'let's plan it out and mark a date on it' business you seem to like so much. A kiss is not meant to be put on a list of things to get done in a day."

"Okay, fine. It won't matter either way, because I'm going to win." They shook hands, sealing the deal. She tried to ignore the burning certainty in Ian's gaze that told her she'd just sealed her fate. Her fingers rose to play with the laces on her shirt. Hook had stripped them from his own shirt that morning and handed them over, since he'd yanked hers out in the cavern. At least now she wouldn't be flashing her goodies to everyone, ever the chivalrous pirate Captain.

"So, what is your decision? We should get to the cave before night falls again," he teased.

"Got any more of that liquid courage to share?" She grinned, only half joking.

It wasn't that she didn't relish the idea of being tied to Hook. She did, a little more than was likely healthy. However, being in love with a legend on paper for most of her life was less intimidating than finding herself caught up in the arms of the spicy hurricane that was the real man. She wasn't a blushing bride by any means, but the idea of being with the guy she idolized had her twisted in a sudden bundle of nerves.

"Uh…no. No, I don't." Hook actually stumbled over his words, something shocking enough it snapped her attention to him. "You drank it all." He finished, staring out over the landscape, steadfastly avoiding her gaze.

"Oh. Sorry. I'll have to buy some more when we get to town."

"You can't."

"Why?"

"There is no more."

"In Sanctuary?" she probed, wondering why he was being so evasive.

"In Neverland." Her brows rose, uncertain if he was messing with her or not. Finally, he caved. "The draught was a specialty from my homeland. We had brought several cases of it with me on my journey here. Most of it was destroyed in the wreck, but I was able to retrieve some of what was left from the bottom of the ocean." He paused. "What little I could save, I have been nursing since James T. created the rift over my eye. It helped to numb the… discomfort."

"And it's all gone now?"

"You drank the last of it before the judgment. And being cut off from the rest of our world as we are, I am unable to attain more." Her stomach bottomed out.

"You gave me the last of your supply?" He didn't answer, still gazing at the trees. "Ian?"

"In all fairness I didn't know you were such a lush." He smiled.

"I'm serious. You gave me the last of it. It was the only thing that brought you relief, and you shared it with me. Why would you do that?"

"Perhaps I'm a soft-bellied cod fish," he offered, with a shrug. "Or perhaps I felt that you would be important to me, and I am too selfish to risk losing you." His words came softer. "Perhaps because I was inexplicably drawn to you, and I couldn't stomach the idea that an innocent little butterfly might fail a test simply because I was too greedy to share what comfort I could." He shrugged, straightening. "Take your pick, any will suffice."

Her large brown eyes stared up at him in wonder. Twice he had sacrificed things that were precious to him, for her. Things that were irreplaceable to him. Her Captain had taken care of her, protected her, had been on the end of sacrifice while asking for nothing in return. Slowly her hand rose to his face, palm reverently cradling his jaw. He turned to her, surprise evident in his eye.

"You asked for an answer, so here it is. I understand the dangers I face at your side. But I'm not worried. Because I'll be fighting at your side, and you aren't going anywhere without me. Just like I know I'm not going anywhere without you. And, you may not know this yet Octavian Ryes Bendal, but your wife can be incredibly stubborn when she puts her mind to something. Now, let's go. I have a bet to win, a marriage announcement to make, an empty stomach to fill, and you have feet to rub." She walked away with a smug grin. After a long second's pause, her grin grew at his swiftly approaching footsteps.

"That was quite the speech. Though, all you had to do was say thank you."

His devilish grin, covered in a sunny patchwork of leafy designs from the thick canopy of tree fronds above them, was contagious. In keeping with her end of their little game, she gave him a hard elbow to his ribs.

"Thank you."

Ian laughed, threaded his fingers through hers and brought the back of her hand to his lips. Her stomach did a nose dive, then rose on a horde of butterfly wings.

"Come along then, my dear, we've a wager to decide."

"Why's she got your ring on, Capt'n?" Easton's determined stride, along with her smug grin, disappeared the moment Hyrel's mouth opened. All the men around the tavern turned in unison, eyes riveting to her hand.

"Why didn't you tell us you two was getting married, Captain?" Another asked, while still another added his two bits.

"And why's she wearin' your shirt laces?"

E's eyes rolled heavenward as the questions continued to pour in. Of course they would notice the laces, too.

"Here we were worried you'd gone and got tossed in an early grave. Guess we were right." Several jeers, chuckles, and elbow nudges followed. Hook walked by her with a bawdy wink, though he wisely kept his mouth shut. He didn't have to say a word to let her know he was going to enjoy waiting for that surprise kiss. E's eyes narrowed. Stomping forward, she stood on tiptoes and slapped Hyrel upside the back of his head.

"Oiy! What was that for, Vermillion?"

"You don't notice when you're butt's on fire, but you can zone in on a ring from twelve feet away?"

"Pa always said Rel had the eyes of a hawk and the brains of a

Wilder!" Tove, Hyrel's brother, shouted over the laughs at Hyrel's expense. Hyrel shrugged in confusion, still rubbing his head. E sighed dramatically. Raising her voice just loud enough, she let loose.

"Fine, then. If you must know, I've decided that Smee isn't going to do it for me in the husband department. Sorry, darling, but it just never would have worked."

Smee's face turned a mottled red color, eyes narrow, big shoulders hunching as the other men poked fun at him. She'd be in for a good brawl later for that comment. TheTea Committee gasped, immediately whispering at her back. E grinned. Two birds with one stone. Hook caught her eye then, casually leaning against the frame of the door, Cheshire grin of his own in place as he watched her poke fun at his men. He thumped a hand down on Smee's shoulder.

"Be glad you escaped, Smee. The woman nearly drowned me just to win me over as her husband."

Easton fought a snort at Hook's hardly true statement. The effort to conceal the snort grew more difficult when the crew sent one another unsettled expressions. Steeling her resolve, E strode toward Hook, slid one hand around the back of his neck and pulled him down, planting a quick hard peck on his cheek. His brow rose, then his eye narrowed, depth burning with unspoken promise of trouble.

"You call that a kiss?" he murmured.

"I call it payment of a bet. You're the one who didn't make the details of your wager clear." Face schooled to one of indifference, she eyed the crewmen. "Let that be a lesson to you. Vermillion always gets what she wants."

The Tea Committee exhaled another group gasp of shock. This time she did grin. It only seemed to unsettle the men more. The men quickly parted, perhaps afraid she'd try to drown them, too, on her way into the tavern. This whole marriage thing was going to be even more fun than she thought.

Sitting together, she and Ian stuffed their faces, famished. In between bites they took turns regaling those in the restaurant with their tale. When the truth was revealed as to how she came to be in possession of the ring, the men groaned and threw bits of roll and meat at her. She smiled, entirely unapologetic.

The only time her grin lost its edge was when Smee found a smile of his own. A smile on Smee's face never meant good news. She kept a careful eye on him, but other than speaking to Lenay - wife to the owner of both inn and restaurant - Smee never moved from his slouched spot at the bar. The matter was made even worse when he lifted his mug to her in a toast. What was that ruffian up to? Her eyes narrowed; his burned with some hidden joke, no doubt at her expense. She jumped slightly when Hook stood at her elbow.

"I'm to bed. The lot of you be prepared for life to get back to normal on the morrow. You've been lazy long enough in our absence. We've still a Fiend to destroy."

The men raised a disjointed chorus of farewell, immediately diving back into their mugs and plates. E watched him go, eyes lingering perhaps too long, since he turned at the door and caught her gawking. He offered a cocky grin and she stuck her tongue out. Unfortunately he'd already turned and walked out the door, nullifying her efforts at being bratty.

"You're a fine bunch of men." She retorted, suddenly eager to pick bones with someone. Her stomach had been in knots since she kissed Ian's cheek outside the restaurant. It hadn't helped that the men had been sending her a constant stream of looks, kissy faces, and mumbled innuendo about her new relationship status. "We come home to find you're all sitting in the comfort of Sanctuary, and you don't even offer a single 'are you okay'? What happened to a good old-fashioned search party?" The men ducked their heads, not meeting her eyes. Shamed silence hung heavily over the lot. E felt the first stirrings of guilt.

"Capt'n Hook forbade us long ago to never come in search of 'im. He says if he was ever to disappear, we was to stay here and wait for 'is return. And if he don't, we batten down the hatches to protect everyone here and pray the Fiend don't find us." Muck, the nervous cold-handed man she met in the Sanctuary tunnel's darkness was the first man to raise his voice.

E's eyes shifted over the rest of the crew, the men she had grown to respect if not care for over the last five months. She hadn't known about that rule. Guilt pounded her over the head. She felt a closer kinship to most of these men than she did with her other friends back home, save for Wi. She felt like a total jerk for taking her emotions out on them over something that was obviously a sore subject. She'd meant it to be playful, but being distracted and frustrated as she was, she hadn't thought through the full impact of her words or their delivery. The men, usually a thick-hided bunch, looked like abused dogs.

"I only meant to tease you, but my words were in poor judgment. You all did exactly what you should have. You're a brave bunch of men. It takes bravery to follow orders, despite having someone you care about being in danger. And I do know how much you care about the Captain. You showed your loyalty and depth of character by waiting for him. He needs men he can trust and rely on like that. You've made your Captain proud. Please forgive my tired tongue."

After a moment's pause the men smiled, sent half-hearted crude jokes her way, and soon the room was once again filled with ridiculous amounts of noise and cheer, like it should be. E stood, determined that she should get some sleep too, before she said or did something else stupid. Lack of sleep was never a person's ally.

Smothering a yawn as she climbed the stairs in the inn to her bedroom, E ran face first into Smee. Instead of cursing her, he merely smirked. Her eyes narrowed.

"What have you been smirking about all night?"

"Don't know what you're talking about, Deviant."

"I know you're up to something, you big ape."

He simply offered a shrug before slinking off to his room. E glanced down the hallway where he'd just come, eyes fastening on her door at the end. She walked carefully toward it, nerves making her slip back into her thieving days, crouched stride smooth and quiet. In front of her door, her hand hesitated over the latch. Glancing back toward Smee's door, she saw the jerk hanging out of his room, watching. He'd obviously done something to her room. Nerves on higher alert, she swung the door open, and gasped. There in the middle of her bed was a large hairy man very much naked and in a state of behavior that she'd never be able to scrub from her memory. Instead of being embarrassed, she was furious.

"What are you doing in my room? On my bed no less? Get out of here!"

"Oiy, unless you're going to join us, get out of me room." The burly man replied, ignoring her claim on the room completely.

"This is my room!" Still he ignored her. Glancing around, she realized the room was oddly sparse. Her things were gone. "What did you do with my stuff?"

She took a step further into the room, fully intending to start kicking some butt. After the man threw his underwear at her head, however, she quickly vacated. Some battles were better fought at a distance. Stomping past Smee's empty doorway, E searched out the owners. Lenay greeted her with a bright grin in the foyer. One of the few younger women to escape the machinations of Pan, the beautiful blond woman was tall, stick straight, and bearing the demeanor of a saint. E was rather fond of her. Smee sat in one of the chairs, feet propped up, pipe in his grinning mouth. She wasn't so fond of *him*, however.

"Can I help you, Miss Vermillion?" Lenay skipped forward, bright smile in place.

"Lenay, I think there's been a mistake. There is a rather…obnoxious person in my room, and my stuff is missing."

'Oh, no mistake, Miss. Mr. Smee informed me of your nuptials." E stared stupidly at the woman's overjoyed grin.

"Huh?"

"You, being wed to Captain Hook on an adventure that nearly cost your lives." She sighed dreamily. "I think that's the most romantic thing I've heard in years. That man needs some love, if you catch my meaning. If I weren't married…" she sighed again, fanning herself. "But of course, I'm happy with my Eber, and I'll wager Captain Hook will be plenty happy with you."

E's eyes shifted to land on the Bo 'sun as a few snorts made their way out of his crooked nose. Fighting for patience, she turned back to Lenay with a smile.

"Um…I'm sure you're right. But where's my stuff?"

"I took the liberty of having it moved to the Captain's room while you ate. I remember how those first weeks of wedded bliss are. You can't get out of bed long enough to eat, much less move your things from one room to another. And just in time too, what with all the travelers from the southern side of Sanctuary trekking into town for the festival at week's end. The rooms are all stuffed to the brims. That vacancy couldn't have come at a better time."

E looked to the ceiling, breathing deep as Smee's snorts became full-out guffaws. She was really going to make her best efforts to straighten that nose out for him with a few well-placed punches. Lenay's face became concerned.

"Is something wrong, Miss? Have I offended in some way?"

"No, no, not at all! I'm just really tired, and realized I forgot to ask my… husband which room was his…ours."

"Oh, I can easily show you…"

"Don't you go worrying about that, Lenay. I'll show her on my way out." Smee happily bounced to his feet, knocking what was left of the contents out of his pipe on the outside of the window frame.

"Well, that's mighty kind of you, Mr. Smee! Busy, busy, busy!" Lenay grinned, quickly scurrying out of the room to attend to her schedule.

"This way, *Mrs*. Hook." The Bo 'sun bowed dramatically, motioning to a hallway that led toward the back of the inn. E moved ahead, fists stiffly held at her sides.

"I suppose you think you're funny."

"On the contrary, Mrs. Hook. I *know* that I am funny."

"Shut it, Smee." She grumbled. Finally reaching the end of the hallway, Smee happily knocked his heavy fist on the door. E turned toward him with an angry hiss.

"I'm perfectly capable of knocking on a door, thank you!"

"Of course you can. But it's the least I could do for the new bride. I'm sure you'll need *all* your energy very soon."

E raised her fist, fully ready to make good on her promise to straighten his nose. The door opened, and her attention shifted to the sleepy, messy haired, well-muscled, shirtless Captain Hook. Glancing at him from the corner of her eye, she offered a chagrined smile. Groggy expression screwed up in confusion, he stared from her, hand still raised to punch his Bo 'sun, to Smee himself, who was beaming happily.

"Vermillion, Smee?

"I was just showing your blushing bride where your quarters were, Captain. She was most eager to find you."

Hook's brow rose as he nodded to Smee, dismissing him, eye immediately seeking her out, checking for an obvious sign of what brought her to his door. Smee turned smartly on his heel and headed down the hall. E poked her head in the door, grabbed the nearest thing she could find, and chucked it at the retreating man.

The cup of shaving cream, brush still inside of it, hit the Bo 'sun square in the butt. White cream splattered all up and down his back. Smee spun about, eyes burning with retribution. E and Ian both stared at the man. E with grim retribution of her own, and Hook with wide-eyed, newly awoken surprise. Slowly Hook's hand rose, one graceful finger pointing at her in blame. Smee grunted in annoyance, then stormed off.

"Are the ex-lovers having a spat?" Hook asked innocently.

Smee tripped on the first step of the stairs, grumbling and cursing as he went. E trotted toward the discarded shaving cup, wiped off the few random splatters on the wall with the tail of her shirt, and returned to Hook with a grin. Instead of taking the cup, Hook stepped back a few feet so that she could enter the room. Swallowing, E followed the silent command.

"As much as I enjoy your squabbles, I can't help but wonder if you and Mr. Smee truly needed to continue them quite so soon after returning. I had hoped to gain at least a few hours of sleep before the wars began anew."

"Uh... sorry. About the cup, and waking you, I mean."

"Is everything well?" His concern warmed her in a way it probably shouldn't have.

"Oh, yes. I'm fine, thanks." He watched her a moment longer, then nodded, satisfied in the knowledge that she would tell him if she wasn't.

"Care to explain further?"

"I..." She felt her cheeks annoyingly heat under his sleepy gaze.

His gaze suddenly sharpened, and he shifted from one foot to the other.

"Did you intend to stay with me, now that we are wed?" He ran a hand through the mess of wavy curls in his hair. "I apologize, I didn't think to ask. I assumed from your chaste kiss earlier that you wanted to maintain some amount of space."

"No, I mean, yes, I…" She sighed in exasperation, calming the butterflies in her stomach. Why must the man always have that effect on her insides? "When she heard that we got married, Lenay sent my items here and gave my room out to someone else. She was trying to be helpful."

"Ah. That would explain the surprise in my drawers." Ian nodded, heading toward the bureau against the wall and sliding open a drawer. His hand exited the shallow drawer with a pair of very feminine undies on one finger.

"I was concerned Lenay was making an overture after all these years. She's a lovely woman, but I respect the vows of marriage as well as my friendship with her husband. I'm glad to hear they are yours." He examined the lacy fabric a little closer. "Although on closer inspection, the cut does seem better suited to a well-formed figure such as yours."

He grinned roguishly as she yanked the fabric from his hand and stuffed it in her shirt. He shook his head, leaning against the bureau with a lazy smile.

"All the best hiding places."

"Okay, Casanova." E blew out a shaky breath.

"Who is Casanova?"

"Never mind, it's not important." Still holding the cup in her hands, she examined his face with a frown. "Why did you have a cup full of shaving cream, and a scruffy face?"

"I was going to shave, but decided I was too tired, so I went to bed instead."

He itched at the black hairs on his jaw, the contact making a rough scratching sound. Her fingers twitched, wanting to give it a try herself. Taking a safe step back, E looked everywhere but at him. What was wrong with her? She wasn't afraid of him, and she definitely was attracted to him. But, for possibly the first time in her life, Easton had a hard case of shyness going on. She really needed sleep. Hook watched her step back, and took a step forward. When she took another involuntary step back, a smile grew in his gaze. Stepping away, he moved to sit on the bed, giving her plenty of space.

"Vermillion, you know you are welcome here. I told you, you are my wife, and nothing will be denied to you. My room is your room, my bed your bed. Come. You are obviously exhausted; I can see the shadows under your eyes from here." He stretched out on the side of the bed closest to the door.

"You'll have to take the side by the wall. I always have to be closest to the door, or I can't sleep." He left it at that, throwing an arm over his eyes. When she still hadn't moved for a few minutes, he peeked up at her from under his arm.

"I promise to leave your virtue intact. I might speak like a rogue, but I never overstep a lady's bounds. You *are* safe with me, Easton." His eye disappeared back under the arm, leaving her to choose as she would.

"I know," she said.

And because she really believed it, she set the cup aside, toed off her boots and moved around the bed to climb onto the side he'd offered. Hook didn't look at her as she snuggled under the sheet, though his lips curled into a lopsided smirk.

"And next time we make a wager, I will be sure to be more exact in my details."

"You'd have to win again for it to matter." She replied with a grin, watching his chest rise and fall with deep even breaths.

"Someone is in denial again," he whispered, sleepily.

"Ian?"

"Hmm?"

"Your feet really do stink at the end of the day."

"Minx." Hook released a mumbled chuckle, falling asleep almost immediately afterward. For the first time since her parents were taken from her, Easton fell asleep with a smile on her face.

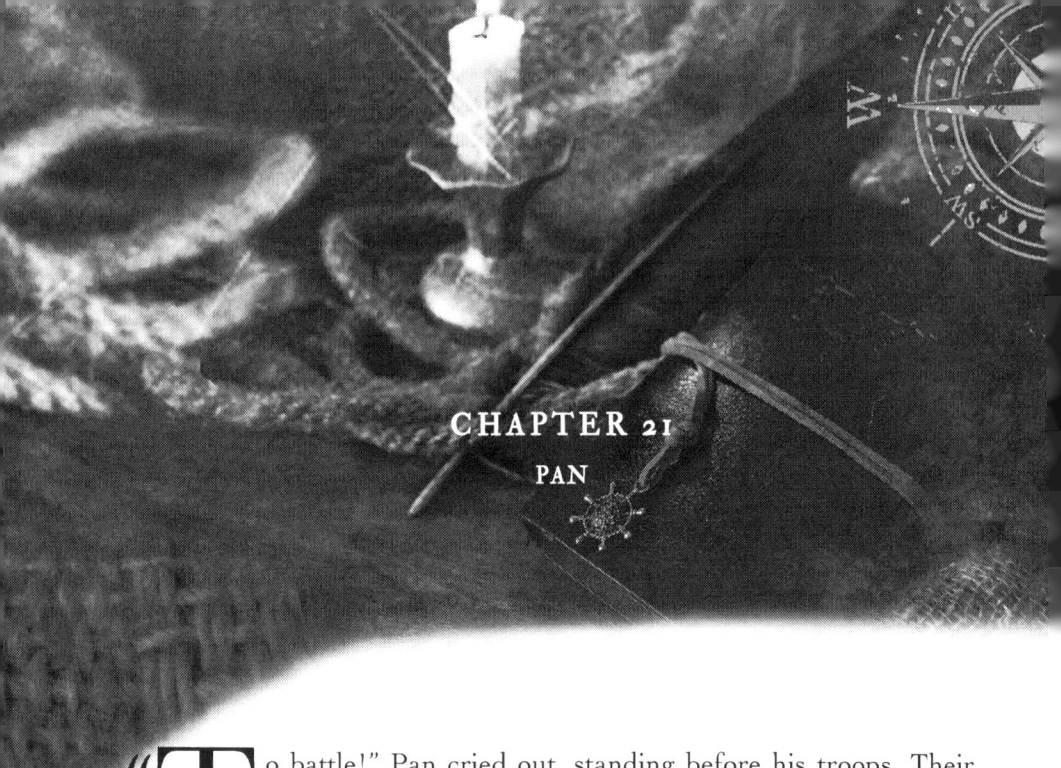

CHAPTER 21
PAN

"To battle!" Pan cried out, standing before his troops. Their answering shouts gave him power, lifting him off his feet to hover above their heads. "These worms think they can run through our forests without permission! They think they can spy on us and tell our enemy where our home is!"

The Lost Boys booed, his words fueling their anger and aggression. They made a beautiful team, he and his Boys. He gave them adventure, and they gave him power. They would be so lonely and bored without him, living dull lives that were empty of anything but dumb grown-up notions of work, lies, and betrayals. They needed him to save them! And he needed them for...

Pan shook his head, glancing down into the pits, eyes fastening on the ten spies they found lurking in their forests. The pathetic worms sent by Hook in yet another of his latest attempts to search the Pan out. Well, just like all the others, these had failed. Perhaps they had found him, but they would die for their efforts, and Hook would be none the wiser.

The Hook had become troublesome of late. Since that day the Hook nearly bested him, Pan found the Hook became lost, no longer much of a threat. He'd become nothing more than a play thing to

Pan, fun to bat around and watch him spit and hiss. But lately Pan had noticed another distinct change. There was an unerringly pointed poison to his efforts suddenly. He uncovered the spies and allies Pan spread throughout Neverland. Pan had always found them to be resourceful in their deceptions, Hook never suspecting as they spread Pan's influence.

Somehow, Hook was now sniffing them out as easily as if they had a large red x painted on their foreheads. Ever so slowly, Pan's resources were dwindling. And with the loss of those resources, Pan began to feel his power lessening. Hook was becoming an annoyance once more, and Pan was losing his temper on the matter.

"Should we teach them a lesson, Commander? String them up by their insides on the outsides?" a tall, scrawny shadow asked; a boy that was once named... well, something. Pan couldn't remember and it didn't matter anyway. Pan had changed his name to Smartybum, because the Boy always came up with the best ideas. And now the name was a badge of honor for the boy, because his Commander had given it to him, and they all loved their Commander. As they should. Pan's grin grew.

"Smartybum brings up a good plan of action. What say you, Boys?"

His shout was drowned out by their exuberant war cries. Pan leered over the railing, eager to see the fear in the eyes of the enemy as they watched his power at work. The spies below nervously shifted from one foot to another. One was babbling and two had even peed themselves. Pan's eyes froze on one form out of the ten who did not cower in fear. In fact, the spy stared up at him in defiance, dark eyes burning with fire of hatred.

A stirring of interest flared to life in Pan's chest, a feeling he knew all too well. This one had potential. This one could need him, just as the others had. Pan blinked as the spy was the first to break eye contact, turning his back on him to calmly stride into the maze. Pan's eyes narrowed in fury. Maybe the spy was broken, but that was no way to treat your possible future leader!

"To battle, Lost Boys! Make your Commander proud!"

With whoops and hollers, the Boys leapt over the railings,

chasing their fleeing prey. The spies bleated like frightened sheep, splitting off into different directions. It would do them no good. His Boys were unbeatable. It was still entertaining to watch them try, though.

And yet Pan couldn't concentrate on the battles below. His fire-brand eyes desperately sought out the one who had defied him. Where had he gone? With the screams of the dying, the fear, the slow drain of their souls, Pan floated easily to the air. Hovering over the maze, searching each twist and turn, he led the Boys on the hunt for the last remaining victim.

Fanning out, they quickly covered the distance, but still the defiant one was elusive. Moving back to the beginning of the maze, Pan landed on his feet, the Boys at his back. His eyes surveyed the carnage left of their prisoners. Where had he gone? Ears turning to the plants around him, he listened, beckoned for their answers. The vines shivered, groaning in protest. Eyes narrowing he pressed harder, and their cries of pain mixed with repentant answers. A whoosh of air ruffled Pan's ear only seconds after the plants had given up the spy's location, the thick branch just missing his head as he twisted out of the way.

"You tried to hurt me!" Pan shouted angrily, spinning into the air.

The last remaining spy jumped down from the vines and crouched low, the thick branch clutched loosely in his large hands, wild eyes watching the Boys that surrounded him with shadowed foul intent. Mud smeared him from top to bottom, branches covering his body. Pan felt his anger melting slightly as he stared, that pang in his chest once more calling out to the enemy at his feet. He was meant to help this one, to be his Commander, his father.

The Lost Boy, Feisty, leapt forward, shadowed hand gripping for the defiant's throat. The spy dove out of the way, bounding to his feet with a hard backswing of the branch. Had the Lost Boy been a weak Neverlander, the branch would have likely knocked his head clean off. Instead, the branch passed immediately through the shadowy figure, momentarily knocking the defiant one off balance. Immediately the rest of the Boys moved in for the kill.

"Wait!" Pan's shout rang through the maze, the vines shrinking away from him, just as his Boys did. The defiant one looked up at him, those brown eyes still filled with hate and a proud refusal to go down easily.

"This is the last of them. Let's play with him a bit." Pan offered, his smile finally returning. The Boys, all too eager to please, jumped into the fray. The spy gave it his best efforts, continually searching for ways to bring down his impenetrable enemy. Of course he failed, but it was the fighting spirit Pan was looking for. Instead of fear taking over his heart, his failures seemed to only fuel the spy in his efforts, his mouth open wide in a silent growl of anger.

Intrigued, Pan sent a thought of action to his Lost Boys, and as one they acted. Using their power, they tossed objects at the enemy, dirt in the eyes to disorient, sticks poking and hitting from all angles, rocks pelting his weak points of muscle. And throughout their game, not once did the spy cry out in anger, pain or fear. Even as he sagged to his knees in disorientation and pain, the fire burned in his soul.

"Enough, Boys!" Pan called out. Sinking to his feet before the spy the Boys moved back to give him more space, though he could still feel their protective nature surrounding him. Head cocking to one side, Pan observed the man before him. No. Not a man. He was a boy, a true Lost Boy at heart.

"We shall name him...Fink, because he's a dirty little elusive Ratfink!" Pan grinned and the boys cheered. Yet the boy at his feet didn't cheer, he didn't even smile. Pan chuckled.

"You aren't very smart, I can see. But I will explain. Giving you a name means you have been accepted in our ranks."

The boy's face grew stormier, eyes narrowing. Pan shook his head, finding it oddly endearing how dense the boy was. He was offering a beautiful gift, yet the simple boy couldn't see it. Pushing gently out with his power, Pan touched the fringes of the boy's mind, sending feelings of wellbeing and eagerness. The boy shook his head, shuffling back a step as he shrugged off Pan's efforts. Pan's smile faded at the edges.

"You fight me. Why?" The boy said nothing, hands gripping the wood tighter. Pan tried a new tactic. "You are very quiet." Pan's voice became hushed in an unconscious effort to replicate his silence. "But sometimes quiet can be a good thing." He poked at the mud on the boy's face. "You used nature to hide from me. It made you silent, invisible. You were so quiet, even the plants did not notice you."

The Boy's ooo'ed in appreciation, and Pan nodded his own agreement. Pan could acknowledge when someone else was good. As long as they didn't try to be better than him, to take his place as father, he even encouraged their inventiveness. Mischief was the way of a Boy's heart, after all. Again he tried to push his power on the boy, and again the boy shrugged it off, retreating further. Pan felt his irritation growing. Stepping forward quickly he pressed his palm against the boy's forehead. Instantly the spark in the boy's eyes dimmed, gaze taking on a dazed appearance. Pan sifted through the well-barricaded mind.

"Your old name was Wiley. You came here from," he frowned, brow pinching in concentration, pushing harder, "you came from...a book." The spy was an Arrival. Pan blinked, taking in the overall appearance of the boy.

How had he not noticed before, how had he not sensed the Arrival this time? Pan's jaw clenched. He was not getting weak! The boy's attire had been so dirtied and torn that Pan hadn't immediately noticed it until now, that is all. In his frustration, Pan pushed a little harder on the connection in the boy's mind. Fink shuddered beneath his power. The Lost Boys were excitedly whispering amongst themselves, many of them likely feeling an instant kinship with the boy. Pushing his feelings to the side, Pan continued reading the boy's mind.

"Your past is pained." He winced as the boy pushed back, not wanting him to delve into his past. He shifted to a different venue. "You are worried about someone, someone special to you..."

A wall slammed down, tossing Pan from Fink's mind. The boy scuttled away, holding the stick out in front of him, lips pulled back in a grimace that promised pain to anyone who neared. For a moment Pan was tempted to take back his promise, to not let the boy into their group. But, that would mean losing out on everything the boy held inside, which was so promising it made Pan's mouth water.

He hadn't had a real challenge in a long time. The power he could get from this one! Taming his opposing sides into one determination, the smile formed in full glory once more.

"I understand, you have secrets. But that is alright. We all have secrets. No one will take them from you."

Pan wouldn't *have* to take them. Once the boy was fully dedicated to him, there would be no urge to keep them secret. Fink would want him in his mind, would want him to know every secret, he would lay them out before his Commander like gifts in a row. Pan would have full access to everything in his mind, and the power his soul offered. Pan's mouth watered once more, but he held it in check as Fink's eyes shifted toward him, unsure.

"You are nervous. You are in a new place that you know nothing about. But look around you. Most of these Boys have also come from the land you are of." He pushed out with his power, ensuring Fink saw what he wanted him to see. Normal, healthy boys, around the same ages as himself. Fink blinked, shaking his head slightly as he looked at those around him. Pan pushed harder with his power, and Fink's eyes dulled slightly. Pan felt victory on the horizon.

"My job in this land is to protect, to keep those like you safe under my wing. These Boys are your friends. I am your friend. I will take care of you, protect you. I will give you so much more happiness than you ever could have had in your past. There are no limitations here. With my help, the universe will be yours." He was gaining ground, but not quite fast enough for his limits of patience. He tried a new front.

"Power will be yours. You'll have power to protect those you care about." Fink's eyes lifted to his. Yes! That was his key! "The one you worry for. I can give you the power to protect them in this unforgiving place, until they too can find safety. You saw what the Boys were able to do while you fought them. They were indestructible. With that power you can protect endlessly."

Before the boy had time to think, Pan once more placed his palm to his forehead. As Fink's eyes dimmed, Pan's brightened. He stretched within Fink's mind, searching for the connection that would give him full access. A euphoric sigh hissed through Pan's lips as just a taste of Fink's soul slipped inside his own mind. Pulling back was far more difficult than he would like to admit, but it was necessary. If he pressed this one too quickly, he would lose the gift proffered him.

Fink's disoriented gaze found his, and Pan knew he had him; at least, for now. The boy was now a Lost Boy. Defiance still lurked in the background of that dark gaze, but the lock to the window was open. All he had to do was entice and entertain until the Boy inside opened the window to him. Then there would be no stopping him from stealing away the Boy's soul to join his own.

"Come, Boys! We must throw a feast in honor of our new friend! Let's show him how full the life of a Lost Boy can be!"

The Lost Boys whooped and urged Fink forward, whispering promises and adventures in his ears. Fink stumbled awkwardly in their midst, eyes conflicted. But still, he followed. Pan's grin darkened. Soon he would be given access to that window, and all the treasures held within.

Easton's mind was filled with horrors.

She fought her way through a green jungle of fear and menace. She was cold, wet, and afraid. Her muscles trembled under the strain of placing each foot in front of the other, ears hanging on every sound. The branches reached for her then, the vines twining around her arms and legs, slowing her progress. Mouth opening in a silent scream of fury and panic, she lashed out, ripping at the plants and tearing them from her body. But the plants fought back, their tendrils puncturing her flesh, entering her body. Suddenly it was no longer her face screaming in silent agony, but Wiley's. His wide, expressive brown eyes stared at her, begging her to save him. And then, the vines filled his silent mouth.

E gasped, body jerking, thrusting her back into the world of wakefulness. Hook rolled over her in a flash, hook held near her throat, eyes glowing a malevolent crimson. She stared up at him with a mixture of terror and awe. She had seen him in that mode other times, sure. And it was awesome then, but being the object of that intense ferocity? That was scary as hell, and flat out amazing!

"Wow." She whispered, unable to contain her inner fan girl awe. Hook blinked in uncertainty.

"Butterfly?"

"Hi, Ian."

Horror replaced uncertainty as Hook threw himself off the bed. Stumbling backward over his boots on the floor in his haste to reach the other side of the room, he plastered himself against the door. E's body shook as she slowly pushed upward to sit in a huddle of sheets.

"Easton, are you well? Have I hurt you? Are you cut?"

E stared wide-eyed. She'd never seen Ian so worked up. Ever. In the face of danger, even death, Hook was cool, calm and collected. Now, he shook like a leaf, and for the first time, that deep fierce gaze wouldn't fully meet hers.

"Ian, I'm fine," she assured, sliding off the bed. He flinched back against the door as she approached, wood creaking under the pressure of his retreat.

"Stay back!" he commanded. E didn't so much as pause, a decision long ago solidified as to where she stood; her place was at the side of Hook, no matter the dangers. Slow steps continued to carry her forward, movements cautious for his sake, not her own; he looked ready to bolt.

"For all that is good and true of Devus, I just attacked you! Steer clear of me, woman!" He tried again, desperately pushing himself further against the door. When his hand twitched toward the handle, E paused, giving him a moment to catch his breath. She wouldn't make him run; not from her, not ever.

"Ian, look at me." She waited until his eye finally met hers. Her heart skipped a beat as she met the strange mixture of sea foam and crimson in his eye. If she didn't think it was so cool, she'd be a little creeped out by the surreal appearance.

"I apologize, Easton. This was a mistake." Hook's hand shook as it shifted away from the door to press to his eye. "Cursed eye, why does it persist! There is no danger here!" He growled to himself. "I should have been more careful. It's been so long since I shared a bed with anyone... I should have recognized the possible...difficulties." She watched as Hook scrubbed at his eye again.

"Ian, I'm not going to be another Avida." He paused at her words, a shudder running through his tense muscles. "I am not going to meet the same fate at your hook. You won't allow it. Good men do not harm the innocent." Hook released a halting breath, sliding down the door. Head falling back against the door with a thud of exhausted defeat, Ian stared into the distance.

"Your intentions are good, but your statement is faulty. I took Avida's life. And my actions led to the deaths of all my brethren," he reminded her softly. E sunk to the floor and crawled the last two feet to sit at Hook's side, their arms barely touching.

"I know you cared for her. But Avida was hardly innocent. From what I know of Pan, he can only twist and entice the selfish feelings that are already in your heart. And even before Pan tainted her decisions, she made choices that placed you in difficult, even dangerous situations. She asked you to lie to your brethren, keep secrets, just so that she could have you to herself. And don't give me that look." E held up a hand, stopping him short.

"I don't judge her for wanting more time with her husband. It was a difficult position to be put in, for anyone. And unless I was put in a similar position, I couldn't say what I would or wouldn't do. However, I can say this. No matter how naïve a person may be, a woman knows when she is making a move that could be detrimental. When Avida followed you to that secret entrance, she knew what she was risking, what she would be forcing you to risk. She did it anyway. She knew asking you to meet her so often was a danger not just to you but your brethren. Maybe it was out of desperation to be near you, but she certainly wasn't innocent of her decisions, or ignorant of the consequences that would follow. And it was those decisions that set her on the path to her end, and your eternal guilt and sorrow."

She watched him carefully, gauging his reactions, praying she wasn't overstepping. Other than his prolonged silence, she noticed no difference in his demeanor. He knew Avida was as much to blame for her fate, and the brethren's, as he was. He'd admitted as much to her. But that didn't change the fact that he had loved her, and that in the end he had been the tool of all their deaths. Easton's hand settled on his forearm.

"I'm hardly an innocent soul myself, I know this. But you said once that I had passion, yet acted with a clear head. I never once have tried to hurt you and those you protect. And I never will. I will never betray you." His eye slid shut on a tired sigh, muscles relaxing slightly under the cadence of her assurances. "The only thing you are guilty of in this moment is reacting in a completely natural way. You've lived hundreds of years with the constant need to protect yourself, to always be ready for a fight, especially when sleeping, I am sure. Living on the streets, and the life I had before, taught me the same. I gave quite a few people bloodied faces, and worse, when they woke me."

He watched her carefully, gauging her statement, digging through the words for a deeper understanding of the life she once lived, the things she might have done. She looked away.

"I know how it feels, and I know how easily it can be triggered."

He shifted, expression awash with awe. Slowly, he reached out to caress her jaw. When she didn't flinch, but rather leaned into his touch, his gaze lit with warmth.

"You are truly a wonder, Easton." His voice was almost reverent in tone. "Do you not fear me?"

"Of course not." She laughed, a little breathless as his trailing fingers continued from her jaw to sink into her hair. "It surprised me a little, but I was never afraid of you."

"Such bravery."

"I trust my Captain." His gaze gathered more heat at her firm statement, and she blushed. "Besides, it was my fault, anyway. I had a bad dream and it jerked me awake, which startled you awake. It's no wonder you reacted as you did, and I don't blame you at all."

"Dream?" Hook froze, commanding intensity momentarily over-shadowing his curious touch. "Tell me every detail."

E hesitated, not eager to relive the fear of the dream. She shoved the hesitation to the side. She had refused to be a prisoner to her dreams long ago, and that remained true now. Especially for Hook. She wouldn't keep anything a secret from him.

Carefully mapping out the details, she retold her dream to the best of her memory, the details swiftly disappearing already. Ian listened carefully, intelligent gaze proof that he was soaking in the details. When she finished they sat in silence for some time.

"The Fiend has your friend, then." The gravity of Hook's words settled like ice in her stomach.

"What? No, it was just a dream."

"Dreams in Neverland are never simply dreams, Easton."

Holding up his right wrist, Hook unsnapped the leather bracer that encased it. E stared in rapt attention at the skin revealed just below the hook. The skin wasn't burned, jagged, puckered or scarred in any way as one might expect their appendage to appear after having a hand lopped off and a hook placed in its spot. The skin flowed seamlessly from forearm to the cuff of the hook. Where the bracer had been on his wrist, the skin was smooth though slightly less tanned than the skin that was regularly exposed to the sun. And directly in the center was a branded compass, lain over top the relief of a hook.

"Hey, I've got a compass, too!" She showed him her wrist where she and her friends had tattooed their team name in the form of a compass. Her E tattoo held only one letter, a large capital E.

"Indeed." His thumb ran lightly over the tattoo, voice soft. But before she could examine his further, Hook presented the bracer to her.

"In the center you will find a small key, in a hidden fold." Following the unspoken command, E pulled the plain silver key from its hiding place. "Good. Now, in the bureau, you will find the backing to be a false wall. Press it to release the mechanism. Use the key to open the revealed drawer, and bring back what you find." Soon E was returning with a thick brown leather bound book, the words 'Brethren of the Hook' stamped on the front.

"Read." He took the key and returned it to the hiding place, snapping the bracer back in place.

"What is it?"

"A journal of sorts."

"Going to share all of your dark fantasies with me now?" she teased.

"A dark secret, perhaps." He acknowledged. Sword-calloused

fingers fell to cover hers where they rested atop the book. "It is time you realize your purpose in Neverland, Easton James Bendal." She blinked up at him, heart speeding at the use of her new married name.

"My... purpose?" Hook nodded, then leaned his head back against the door, eyes closed.

"Inside the book, there is a marker. Read the passage you find there." Once again E followed the enigmatic directions. Clearing her throat she read out loud.

> *"When the Blood of Pan returns, foretold is his undoing*
>> *With the Vermillion weapon, Hook shall halt the Fiend's last breath*
>> *Then the land of eternal viewing*
>> *Once more shall understand death*
>
> *But wary must be He of the Everlasting Unrest.*
>> *Temptation leads astray, heart's purity the only assuring*
>> *The Hook and the Descendant, together must quest*
>> *A taste of freely offered eternal destruction, to shift fortunes discerning*
>> *Then, controlled gifts shall lead to full life blessed."*

"Wow." E breathed out a shaky laugh. "You're a poet and I didn't know it."

Her lips couldn't quite play the game this time, the tips wobbling in her efforts to keep them upturned. Something about that poem had stolen the breath from her lungs, left her weak to the marrow.

"It is true that I am... careful of my surroundings, especially when at my most vulnerable in sleep," he admitted, voice holding a determination that can be found only in what one felt to be the truth. "But after hearing your dream, I feel it only a verification of something I have long since suspected." His eye held her paralyzed.

"You say I reacted; that much is true. My Hook and eye react to threats. I was pulled from sleep not by surprise, but in reaction to the presence of Pan." That was enough to pull E from her stupor, and leave her looking around the room with unease.

"But you said he couldn't get inside Sanctuary."

"I felt the Pan's presence, Easton, but I felt him through your dream. I felt the Pan, through you." E choked on the sarcastic reply as it dried to a husk in her throat. Now wasn't the time for jokes.

"I...he can do that?" she asked shakily. "How does everyone else keep him out?"

"They don't have to. Not within Sanctuary, and not within dreams. Only those touched of the Pan can dream in this cursed land. Pan used his power to ensure that he stole even our most personal of treasures."

"But that doesn't make sense. I've clearly never been anywhere near the guy. So, why me? Can I dream because I'm an Arrival? Are the rules different for me?" Hook watched her for a long moment, waiting. Finally, his unspoken thoughts seemed to rebound in her mind, along with the poem she'd just read. Her eyes flew back to the paper.

"Returning Blood of Pan... the Vermillion weapon." Throat dry, the words whistled out like a dying man's breath.

"He is of your blood, Easton. You *are* a Pan." Ian's rough voice filled the deadly quiet of the room, wrapped itself around her more securely than any binding. "Your dealings with Croc should not have been so simple, Easton. The way the shadows clung to you, melded around you at your bidding for protection. I have only ever witnessed such skills from the Pan himself."

How many times had she sunk into the shadows, relied on them for protection and never once been caught? E swallowed hard.

"I'm good at what I do. One of the best, even. That doesn't mean I'm a Pan, I'm just... good at being bad."

"I see. And have you had one of my men teach you the Neverland language?"

"No? What does that have to do with anything?" She frowned, confused.

"Everything you read on that page was written in Neverland's language, Easton, a language that takes years to master. Such is the reason why I offered to teach you if you planned to stay. It is not something one can master in such a short amount of time." She blinked down at the pages, wondering if he was screwing with her. It

245

looked like English to her. Ian nodded resolutely. "Only those with the magical blood of the Pan flowing in their veins would be able to decipher the words with no knowledge of the language."

"But… I don't understand. How is any of that possible? Ian, I'm not even from this world."

"When the prophecy you just read came to light, and the Hooks were formed, we took action. A powerful sorceress cast a magic spell. The only heir of Pan was sent through a portal, into your world. And with the creation of that portal, we were able to strike two blows at once. First, the Pan could no longer travel from one world to the next. And second, he had no access to his offspring, the one link to his future doom." E threw her hands in the air.

"Just because I have red hair, it doesn't mean I'm anything like him, much less his descendant. There's tons of people where I come from who have red hair." She wanted to scream, to rage, to fight against the truth that her heart quietly mirrored, traitor to her denial. "Where did you get this dumb poem, anyway?"

"Prophecy, Easton, not poem," Hook reprimanded her gently. "It holds far greater import than any poem. I have lived, breathed and fought according to this prophecy. Just as my hook, it deserves respect."

"Sorry." She sighed sullenly, her insides feeling like they'd been thrown into a blender with a whole heaping of hell mixed in. "I'm just…"

"Confused and upset. I understand." He nodded, letting the matter go. "The prophecy was formed at the beginning of this war, declared by my father's renowned soothsayer the night word of the Hook gathering reached us. It is part of the reason I came to be of the Brethren. My father tasked me with the deed of bringing this prophecy to James. Very few people have ever heard or read it. Very few."

"Let me guess. Pan isn't one of those few."

"Good guess. None outside the order of the Hooks, and those of the council, know."

"So, Pan doesn't know the danger of his descendants?"

"No. And we hope to keep it that way. It is our one advantage in this war."

"Isn't that a bit of a risk, then? Telling me all of this, when he can obviously get inside my head?"

"I hold no doubts in you, or I wouldn't have shared the information, little butterfly." Shifting his weight on the floor, Hook scratched at the scruff on his jaw, gaze distant.

"I will own to you, there is danger in this knowledge. I risk much by sharing it with you. Yet I feel you have long ago proven your loyalty. It is time I return the favor." He shoulder-bumped her with a soft, irony-filled smile. "Besides, it is only fair that one is told their paths of destiny, so that they might better prepare to walk them. Don't you agree?"

She could see in that moment just how much the prophecy must have weighed on him, all this time. He'd known from the beginning that a Hook must be the one to destroy the Pan. And now, he was the only one left living, leaving the prophecy resting squarely on his shoulders. Instantly, all of her fight deflated, seeping from her muscles.

Hook had faced this great burden alone for what was likely hundreds of years, living each day knowing he was Neverland's last hope. Impossible and terrifying though it may seem, destiny was now offering her the opportunity to help him shoulder some of that weight. How could she say no?

"So… you think that I'm this descendant of Pan? The Vermillion weapon?" Hook retrieved the book, carefully replacing it in the hidden drawer, taking the time to think before replying.

"Are Jaguar or Wiley related to you in any way?"

"I… I don't think so? I mean, I'm an orphan, so…" She hesitated, thrown off by the shift in conversation.

"All Arrivals to this point have been descendants of Pan, to very limited degrees. The blood was most often diluted to the point that no physical vestiges of the bloodline could be seen. No one has ever had truly vermillion hair. Only those of Neverland that have been touched in the mind by the Pan bear hints of the coloring of vermillion; nothing more than a glimpse when seen in the sun, really. It is a color that comes *only* from the Fiend." He tiredly rubbed the back of his neck.

"The fact of Wiley and Jaguar's presences in Neverland is quite a shock. The portal's only purpose is to bring those of Pan's blood, those that the prophecy could work through to fulfill destiny. Either the portal's power is weakening, or your strength is more than that of the books. Perhaps even still, they were meant to come through, to play some purpose in your destiny here." She held his gaze, dreading the answer to her coming question.

"So Wiley really is here. I'd hoped… I'd hoped he'd just never been pulled through the portal."

"I feel your dream is a clear reflection of this truth, yes. Your friend is very much in Neverland, and very much in danger. I am sorry we did not find him before the Pan," he offered quietly.

"I know." She rubbed at the growing headache between her brows. They'd looked for him as quests allowed, but time spent outside of Sanctuary was more often than not about survival and fighting, than hunting. Though she'd tried, in the end she'd still failed him. "And, the threat you felt from my dream? Was it actually from Pan, or from me? Since I'm a Pan too…," even saying the words made her feel disjointed and lost.

"The threat was not from you, little butterfly. I've been near you all these months and felt no threat." She glanced up at him.

"What's to keep that from happening? What's to keep me from being turned by Pan, and becoming a threat?"

"I'll not lie to you, Vermillion. There is risk to be found in this matter. You and Wiley clearly hold a strong bond. With the Pan now owning your friend, he has access to this bond. That much is clear from your dream. If your friend is strong, perhaps he can hold out the truth of your appearance for some time. It could be that this dream was merely Pan searching for a taste of the other end of such a strong connection. If nothing else, Pan is very curious about rela-tionships. Mostly about destroying them." Hook sneered, wry voice packed to the brim with having lived those facts. His fist clenched in his lap.

"But eventually, Pan will find an interest in you, and he can use that connection as a pathway to your mind. With that power, he *could* try to corrupt you."

"So, Pan has my best friend, is doing who knows what to him, and now thinks he can waltz around in my head whenever he wants?" Indignation rose within, swift and fierce. "I'd like to see the little fat head try it again. I'll show him real fear." Hook chuckled, giving her knee a reassuring squeeze.

"The Fiend has another thing coming to him. He's bitten off a bit more than he can chew with you, I think. You lived the rough life of a street orphan, and came out triumphant. You rode the book's portal and somehow managed to take along two, non-related, guests. Your strength kept them from being lost in the portal voids, with no knowledge of even owning that power. You won my hardened and uncouth men over to your side with nothing but smiles, a sharp tongue, and wickedly dirty fighting styles. You've killed a satyr from the inside, outrun Wilders, and escaped the death caverns of pigmites."

"You forgot survived the smell of your feet."

"True enough. That is a feat of its own." He tossed the cheesy play on words right back at her without missing a step. "Aside from all that, you're loyal, not to mention as stubborn as they come. Once you've chosen a side, you won't give it up easily. Lucky for us, you've chosen our side. You'll never betray us."

She felt her temper melting away to a low burn, a smile twisted her lips. He'd just repeated her earlier promises, his tone reflecting the fact that he believed it. Glancing up, she met Ian's gaze. He looked back, a roguish grin reflected in an eye that still retained just an ounce of red, though most of his sea green was back now.

"Are you sure I am what you think I am? Maybe the real descendant was Wiley or… Jag." She swallowed, forcing herself to speak his name. She refused to be a slave to him in any way any longer. She smiled, immediately feeling strength within. Ian was right. Names truly did hold power. Even the power of freedom.

"For all you know this isn't even my real hair color. Maybe I liked to dye it, maybe I'm really blond." Obviously that argument wasn't a worry for him as her roots would have shown him otherwise long ago, but she was pulling at any straw she could to weed out even the tiniest bit of doubt he might have.

"I can't be sure of anything in my world, Easton. But I am certain of one thing. I felt the beginnings of hope when I first saw you walking down that long dusty road, giving Smee and his men your best sassy attitude, not backing down to their bullying. I didn't trust you then, but I felt hope despite. I didn't believe it was possible for the blood of Pan to be on our side."

"Being witness to your stubborn fire, however, I began to wonder if maybe you were too willful to fall to his whims, to be told what to do by anyone. That you might actually be able to make up your own mind as to whose side you wanted to fight for. The Light Binding reinforced that hope, when the coloring of your hair intensified. That is most certainly your true hair coloring." He smirked knowingly, picking up a stray strand to rub between his fingers. She sighed, glaring accusingly at that strand in his fingers.

"So, my hair really did get crazier? That's a relief, knowing it wasn't in my imagination. But why did it happen?"

"The Light Binding brings to the surface, and enhances, one's true self."

"So, the brighter the red, the deeper my connection with Pan."

"Yes. Therefore I knew you were a strong blood descendant. The dream is merely a confirmation of your strong blood connection to Pan. I didn't know, in the beginning, the truth of your heart; I didn't know if I could trust you to be loyal. Working at your side all this time has solidified that truth for me. You are the miracle we have waited for, Vermillion. You've already started saving Neverland, helping us restart time's flow." Leaning back against the door, she scoffed.

"I knew you had to have been watching me long before the Pub." She shook her head, remembering that sinking feeling she'd felt then, knowing the mysterious hooded man had been stalking her, watching her interactions with Jag.

"You were even more astute than I gave you credit for. Even Smee didn't know I was following along on the journey. We were to meet at the tavern." He grinned, lips stretching to form a proud gleam of white teeth. "I like to observe possible enemies from afar, before they are aware of my presence. This time, however, I felt restless and compelled to watch longer."

"And what did you find?"

"That you were a firebrand of a woman who would cause my men and I a lot of grief. But I hoped you'd cause the Fiend more. I'm not entirely sure I came out on top of that bargain." E elbowed him in the ribs, earning an unaffected grin in return.

"Okay. But what about now? I know how you used to feel. Now that you know of the connection in my head, don't you feel threatened by what I am? What I could become?"

"Easton, when you've lived as long as I, encountered the betrayals and losses that twist life's light, trust is not an easy commodity to acquire. Yet when it is finally obtained, it is not an easy thing to shake free of, either." He gave her hair a gentle tug, before reaching out to grasp her hand in his.

"I would like to think my dedication to the understanding of the worth of your soul is obvious now, but not simply tied to the well-being of Neverland. I do not make promises lightly."

His fingers grazed over the ring on her hand. She smiled softly, a slight blush warming her cheeks. She wouldn't be wearing that ring if he hadn't thought her worthy of binding himself to her. He leaned close, holding her gaze.

"You've won my trust, little vermillion butterfly. It is a young and fragile thing, delicate and hesitant in its lack of use and bruising through the long years. But it is there, growing steadily with each passing breath. While I know the dangers the Pan poses to you, especially now, I also know the depth of your character. I've seen what I feel confident are reflections of a pure heart. And I hold utmost confidence that you won't be led astray. I wouldn't be so proud to claim you as my crew member, and wife, if I didn't."

"Thanks." She grinned, jabbing his arm with her finger. "I kind of like you, too."

"Kind of?" He wrapped an arm around her shoulders, pulling her tight against his ribs. "I'll accept that. Saucy wench."

Grinning, she snuggled into his freely offered embrace, soaking up its comfort. Still, her mind wouldn't stop shouting at her, her stomach rolling with waves of worry. Even Hook's warm embrace couldn't keep the smile in place in the end, and she finally voiced the war within.

"You know, I had almost convinced myself." Ian looked down at her.

"Of what?"

"I'd almost convinced myself that Wiley was fine, home and safe. I know... " she took a deep breath, "I know you said that once Pan gets someone, they're no longer the same person. But I know Wi. He's strong, and he's independent. He won't let Pan change him. If we could just find him..." Hook's face had taken on the expression of compassion as he listened.

"I know that you want to save your friend, Easton. And I am pained for you, that he has been taken. I wish that we could have been the ones to find him. At least we can assume that the Pan hasn't had him for long, or your dreams would have been invaded sooner. He must be very good at evasion to have stayed free of Pan all this time."

"If Wi doesn't want to be found, he won't be. He's really good at blending in, despite his size," she agreed.

"That alone speaks to your friend's strengths. However Pan is renowned for his strengths as well; he is inscrutable, and merciless. No one has ever escaped the machinations of the Fiend once he has them in his grasp."

She shook her head, tears prickling her eyes. She fought to contain them, to keep them from her voice. In their place, anger and helpless frustrations shouted her pain.

"It's my fault he's here, Ian. It's my blood that caused this. I didn't know anything about my being a descendent of Pan, I never would have expected this fate to fall on my shoulders. But it has now, and I willingly accept fighting at your side until the end. But I can't accept the loss of Wi. He has been there for me through it all, and like you said, I don't toss true loyalties to the side so easily. I won't betray you, and I won't betray Wi by giving up on him. I can't do that. I can't abandon him. Now that I know he's here, I have to save him." Hook held her closer, his chin resting atop her head.

"I wish that I could give you your heart's desire, dear wife. I wish that we could save your friend. Wiley will be hidden away in Pan's lair until his loyalty is unquestionable, until he has lost his soul and become a Lost Boy. You are a force to reckon with Easton, but when Wiley loses his soul to Pan there won't be a force in all the lands that can save him. We don't even know where to begin the search. We don't know where Pan's lair is. If we did, we would have taken the fight to him long ago. He's found a way to mask his presence to us, just as we have from him. The Fiend can be damned elusive when he chooses to be. You've never once seen him, the whole of the time you've been here. Devus' blessing upon us."

"Does the obsidian work for him, too, you think?" E asked, thinking of the rock enclosure that kept them safe. Hook had long ago explained that the rock somehow enhanced the magic of their sorcerers, protecting them from Pan's abilities to find them, or hear their thoughts. It was also the reason that Sanctuary lacked echoes. She'd never questioned the science of the matter. Neverland, after all, was the land that defied the laws of nature.

"No. This is the only structure of such making in Neverland. Trust me Easton, we've looked long and hard. Of course we will continue to look, but I won't give your heart false hopes. We can't find Pan any more than he can find us. We've been locked in a stalemate for endless years." He lifted her chin with one finger, directing her gaze to him. "If I could find your friend, I would."

"I understand."

"That's it? You understand?" He watched her like he would a rattlesnake, waiting for it to strike. "I expected more of a fight."

"No fighting. We'll just have to find a way and make it happen. Either we will catch Pan, or we will catch someone who can lead us to Pan."

"They'll never betray him. He's the owner of their souls. The idea wouldn't even so much as take root in their minds," Hook warned.

"Maybe they've just never been scared of anyone more than Pan." She replied, sinister depths within the words. "I'm getting Wi back. And when I find Pan I'm beating him to a pulp, along with anyone who tries to stand in my way." Ian's answering grin danced in his eyes and words.

"If anyone is capable of it, it is you, little Vermillion butterfly." He squeezed her tighter before climbing to his feet and offering a hand. Once she stood at his side, Ian threw on a shirt, pulled on his boots, and encouraged her to gather her own. Shoes on, they headed outside.

"Where are we going? Aren't you still tired?"

"Weary to the bone. But there'll be no rest till you've had calm in your heart. So we're off to find some. Otherwise you just might bite my head off whilst I sleep."

"Who needs to wait for sleep?" she teased, snapping her teeth at him playfully.

"Perhaps we will further explore that threat upon our return." His roguish grin glimmered with dark promise that quickly had her blushing to the roots of her hair. One big red tomato out for a stroll in search of calm, that was her. Laughing, Easton leapt onto Ian's back. He easily held her with one arm, carefully avoiding touching her with his hook. Keeping her firmly planted on his back, Hook gave a whoop and ran the rest of the way, his contagious laughter easily overshadowing any reservations she still held. Villagers and crew members alike stopped to stare at the odd couple as he ran through the streets, just a wild man with a hook for a hand, and the red snorting tomato on his back.

With a grin, E held Ian tighter, and thanked whatever fates had brought her here to this man. If those fates demanded she take down Pan in return, she was ready and willing.

CHAPTER 23
EASTON

"What is this place?" E whispered as she slid to the ground, walking around Hook's form to take in the surroundings. The air held a sense of something almost sacred.

E had never gone to church. She'd never had the opportunity, or the peace of soul to dare trying. But standing in this small grassy area, deep within the heart of Sanctuary, E felt what she could only imagine such a special place to feel like. Guards had stood at the entrance of the heavily gated area, dangerous eyes watching her every move. That alone had been enough to warn her of the special nature of the area they were entering. The feeling in the air was reinforcement of the matter.

Ian walked up behind her, mouth near her ear, chest pressing to her back, hand gently cupping her waist. When he spoke, his gruff voice was just as quiet as hers.

"This is Neverland's greatest secret, little butterfly. A secret I am sharing with you. If ever there was a doubt in your heart about my dedication, and my faith in you, I pray this puts it to rest." Straightening, but not relinquishing his gentle touch, Ian released a long sequence of whistles into the air. Arms wrapping about her midsection, he held her tightly and waited.

"Try not to make any sudden movements. They startle easily, and will release painfully high-pitched screams at a moment's notice." E froze in place at Hook's cautionary tone, eyes scanning the horizon for the coming threat. The sounds of happy cheers met their ears moments before the little bodies appeared in the distance. Tiny arms waved in greeting as the bodies jumped up and down with excitement.

"Are those… children?" E gasped.

Hook released a long pent-up chuckle, clearly enjoying the false suspense he'd just instilled in her. Easton elbowed him, hard. Which of course only made Hook laugh harder. She increased her efforts to poke holes in him with her elbow, the only appendage she could move in her currently bear-hugged position.

"You big jerk, you had me ready for a fight!"

"Hey! My warnings were perfectly honest! Those little devils have nearly burst an eardrum or two over the years!" Finally, offering surrender, Ian grabbed her hand and pulled her forward. E watched the children in wonder as they drew closer.

"I haven't seen a single child since I arrived. What are they all doing here?"

"Remember, the Pan steals children away to become his sustenance, dear one." E blushed, enjoying the progression of Ian's endearments since their impromptu marriage. He had always called her little butterfly, etc. But as their friendship grew, so did the inflection behind those little harmless phrases.

"These are the last of the children in all of Neverland. They are the ones we fight to make a new world for, they are the greatest treasures we have to offer that world one day." He pressed a light kiss to the tip of her nose. E swallowed hard at the tenderness in his gaze when he pulled away. "And thanks to you, Easton, they will now have the chance to finally grow up."

These were the last children in all of Neverland. They were secretly kept here to protect them, to keep them safe from Pan. They had been trapped as children for an eternity. But now that they'd taken the watch from Croc, time was moving in Neverland again.

And Ian had shared that secret with her. Either he had a million times stronger faith in her than she did, or he was crazy. Reaching the top of the hill, only feet away from the children, Easton could see a whole little village huts in the dished out valley below the ridge. From down below you'd never know it was there. Releasing her hand Hook stood purposefully in front of her, like a shield.

"Ho, there you savages! This here is my new, shiny toy, and I'll not have you tearing her to bits, is that understood? If you're very nice, I'll share her with you. She is very good at playing dirty and kicking shins. She is even sometimes good at real games, too. But we must take turns." The children all giggled.

"She's not a toy, Hook! She's a lady." A pudgy, staunchly opinionated boy stated, fists on hips.

"She's not?" Hook turned to her in confusion, lifting her arms and bending them at the elbows as though checking for defects. "No, I suppose you are right." He sighed heavily. "I supposed I shall simply have to keep her as a wife then."

"But you already married her, Hook!" A girl who looked like she was four, chastised. "Did you forget?"

"Well, you're all a serious bunch." Hook chastised back playfully. "What will I do now? I came here for a game of Kick Nick, but now I can't find any kids to play with. I suppose I'll simply have to leave and come back later." The children all rang out in a discord of arguments.

"Well now that's more like it. The savages have reappeared. Go and fetch Nick then!" Half the children ran down toward the buildings below, laughing and screaming, while the other half crowded around, dragging them along behind.

"Kick Nick?" Easton asked, leaning closer.

"Well, it started one day when I told the children we were going on a picnic. I stepped on a rogue ball hidden in the grass mid-sentence, nearly fell and broke my neck. The children misunderstood me, thought I meant to play a game of kickball called 'Kick Nick.' I went along with it. Children are impossible to argue with, in case you didn't know."

"Sounds like someone else I know," E teased. Hook winked, pulling her along faster. The children reappeared with one large ball, and a strange oven-mitt-looking thing.

"There's a good lad." Hook thanked the boy who handed him the mitt. Securing the heavy leather glove over his weapon, Hook sent another wink her way. "Must play fair now. No gutting the little flopping fishes whilst I play."

The children laughed and yelled their displeasure at being called fishes and being gutted, enjoying the teasing in his tone. It was clearly an old joke Ian said to them often. But Easton easily heard the concerns below his humor. Though he had the crystalline case on his hook at all times, he clearly still feared its danger. Hurting these precious treasures was the last thing Hook could ever allow himself to do.

With a triumphant shout, Hook led them onward in a rowdy, disjointed game that seemed to have ever-changing rules, dictated by the whims of the miniature savages that surrounded them. After multiple bruised shins and a stomach that hurt from laughter, E found herself 'out', standing on the side lines.

"Peter so loved children." The old lady came out of nowhere, standing beside her in a hooded cloak.

E jumped away from the woman in surprise, thumping into a googly-eyed goat that had come out to watch the game half an hour earlier. That creature accounted for a good number of bruises to her backside. It had an odd love for head-butting into people anytime they bent to grab the ball off the ground. Which of course led to obnoxiously loud rounds of laughter from the kids. Apparently it was their favorite part of the game. It seemed to enjoy attacking Easton most. She suspected it knew how much she disliked goats now, given her past encounter with the satyr. Maybe the satyr had even been a relative.

Giving her one of those hard rams to the hip now, the disagreeable creature ambled off to the other side of the games, searching for its next target. Honestly, E had hardly noticed the attack, her eyes glued to the figure beside her. The fact that she was one of the people who had been responsible for whether she lived or died months earlier, her presence was more than distracting.

"Um…" E stuttered, not at all sure what to say. Turning, she caught Ian's eye, silently asking if she should run. Hook nodded toward the woman, his expression serious. Then, without so much as an apologetic grin, he turned and continued the children's game, leaving E alone with the creepster. Nice.

"So." E rocked back on her heels. "I'm not supposed to be here witnessing this, I suppose. Am I going to have to go through the white dome of hell again?" A rich laugh issued from the hood.

"No, no, you've done nothing wrong. Actually, you seem to be doing everything rather well. So far." E's brow rose over the 'so far'. Clearly they were still carefully watching her.

"Duly noted."

"Trust does not come easily to the inhabitants of Neverland." The woman openly acknowledged the threat in her earlier statement. While it was intimidating to know their eyes and ears were still on her, it also was refreshing. Blunt honesty was always more welcome in E's world than threats hidden behind smiles and pleasantries. And, as always, people doubting Easton only pushed her to fight harder. She'd just keep proving herself until they didn't have anything left to doubt.

"The Hook bringing you here is, however, a surprise."

"Yeah. He keeps springing surprises on everyone today, it seems." Her mouth fell open as the woman pushed back her hood. "And apparently you enjoy surprises too."

E had seen the judges wandering through town now and then, their features always carefully disguised. Hook told her that protecting their identities was the Neverlanders' way of ensuring anonymity and justice. The fact that she was seeing this woman's face now didn't bode well for her survival. The Monk Mafia was going to take her down.

The old woman before her was average height, though had her back not been humped at the shoulders as old people sometimes were, she probably would have been a good six inches taller than E.

Her white-yellow hair gleamed with a dull sheen in the dim sunlight. Sharp blue eyes sparkled with a keen humor and intellect that made E instantly wary. This was a woman not easily fooled, and one to whom she should give a healthy dose of cautionary respect.

"Yes, I must admit a partiality to mischief, myself." She winked. "It's probably what first attracted Peter to me."

"Attracted to you? We can't be talking about... the Peter, can we? Pan?"

"The very same." A frail, age-spotted hand extended. "It is time we were properly introduced, Easton of the Arrivals. I am Bell of the Tinkers."

"Bell of the Tinkers?" E's eyes widened. "You're Tinkerbell!"

"Tinkerbell." Her eyes grew distant, a sad smile gracing her lips. "I haven't heard that name in quite some time. Peter used to tease me with it every day. 'Tinkerbell, winkerbell, laid a stinkerbell'. He wasn't very good at rhyming." She confided with a good-natured wink.

"You're here, which means you must be on our side. But in the book, you were Pan's closest confidant. And it definitely sounds like you had a friendship going on..."

"So, where does that leave us, Arrival?" Bell grinned, that mischief back in her gaze. E felt as though she were in that stupid white room again, being tested.

"Everything in Neverland has similarities to the book, yet some things are so different. Hook is good, Pan is bad, Smee isn't anything like he is in the book. And you were a forever young, pint-sized fairy in a skimpy dress. Honestly, I never know what to believe."

"Mercy me! A pint-sized fairy in a skimpy dress. Hook wasn't exaggerating when he told the Elders that the book was changing from its original version. What a joke Peter has played with that description," she chuckled.

"I'm hardly pint-sized. In my youth I was much taller than I am now. Also, my family were renowned magic smithies called Tinkers. As such, long clothing was a must in our profession. Until I met Peter, I never wore a dress without sleeves, a neck lower than the collar bone, or higher than my ankles." Her smile became tainted with a wry sadness that tugged at Easton's insides. "Though the youth part of the story doesn't surprise me at all."

"You sound as though you were very attached to him."

"And you want to know what happened to change that." She patted E's arm. "Of course you do. This is as much your story as it is mine. And from what I've seen, you've got a healthy dose of both mine and Peter's yearning for knowledge." E blinked under the scrutiny of the old woman, who was clearly waiting for a reaction to the answer Easton hadn't even known to ask.

"The baby sent through the portal was yours, wasn't it? Yours and Peter's."

"Yes, child. And that would make me your great, great, great however many times over grandmother."

Easton reeled. She'd been without a bloodline family for a long, long, time. Even the only true parents she'd known hadn't been her blood family. The idea that she was currently speaking to a very distantly related grandmother was staggering. The fact that Pan was her very distantly related grandfather? That was worse.

"You look as I feel most days: dizzy, confused, and exhausted. Come and have a seat with me on the porch." E did as requested, offering her arm to aid the woman in her trek toward a nearby house that sported a good view of the rowdy game still playing out on the field. Once seated, Bell turned to E once more.

"I didn't have the chance to know my daughter, before sending her to your world. And, as you're the closest I have ever been allowed to an Arrival, I'd love to know my granddaughter. If you'd care to share, of course. I'll not force you."

Easton hesitated, eyes shifting to watch Ian as he ran about the field, kicking the white goat-skinned ball about, lithely dodging the cantankerous living goat. As though sensing her gaze, he glanced up. With a cavalier salute her way, he was back in the action. It was uncanny, the way the slightest glance, smile, wave, or mere thought of him, was enough to bolster her. With a deep breath, Easton dove in.

"What do you want to know?"

"I already know the life you lead immediately before coming

here. I want to know the rest. Start from the beginning, the very beginning."

"Alright. Well. I never knew my birth parents. I was left at St. Alice's hospital doors, when I was what doctors estimated to be only a few hours old. No one saw the woman or man that left me behind."

"That is as to be expected. Born with a wanderer's soul, no descendent will ever stay with a blood relative so long as Peter's curse remains. They also have a difficult time staying in one place for long. It was a safety built into the magic protection spell put on my baby, a way to prevent Peter from finding his true descendants, if he were ever able to make his way through the portal."

"Oh. That explains a lot then, I suppose. Anyways, I was adopted by a couple in their early forties. Their names were Sebastian and Lacey Howe, and they were wonderful. They became my parents in every way. My mother would read to me every night. She was a librarian by choice, she loved being surrounded by books. My father was an undercover policeman." Bell's brows rose.

"A policeman? And yet your actions all these years have been those of a thief."

"Yeah. Pretty screwed up, huh?"

E swallowed hard against the surprising appearance of guilt that threatened in the back of her mind. She'd always felt the guilt of her life, but she'd never fully acknowledged it, shoving it to the back of her mind and saying it didn't matter anymore. Now, years of pent-up emotion seemed to be begging for attention. Bell's hand found hers, and while Easton's typical reaction would have been to politely pull away, E found herself savoring the physical contact. With the contact, her memories flooded back to her, crystal clear. Memories she had suppressed so often it became a habit. Pain wasn't something Easton treasured, painful memories included.

"One night, my mother hid me away in a safe room under the stairs. She said we were playing hide and seek, and to not come out until dad found me. I was too small to understand the depth of what would happen. I was only five." Bell's hand tightened on hers, reassuring her.

"But it was no game. Men had broken into our house to kill my parents. You were there in the dome when I found out the truth. That it had been men angry at my father for having put a large portion of their gang in jail. He'd been undercover then, a spy I guess you'd call it. Now I think of it, I am sure many of the men who killed them that night were the men he'd pretended to be friends with for three years. That night, the consequences of my dad's crime-fighting past finally caught up to us."

"I remember hearing shouts, and my mom crying. Then sirens in the distance. They say my dad had managed to get out a signal to the local police department when the men first broke in. The threat of capture didn't stop the criminals from lighting our house, and my parents, on fire. The stairway door was locked and I couldn't get out. I lay down on the floor and waited, crying in the black confined space. The fire destroyed most of the house."

"They called me a miracle because the stairs hadn't been touched. It was about the only place in the house not engulfed in flames when the firefighters finally heard me crying. Aside from the trauma of my parents being killed, a fear of confined spaces and not being able to breathe, I wasn't hurt. Given the delicate state of my father's officer status, along with my age, the case was treated very discreetly. They didn't bother trying to contact Vye and Charles' family. There was none."

"Your survival; that would be the magic, too," Bell nodded. "All descendants are surrounded with an amount of protection. Given the fact that you are so far down the line, I am surprised the magic held that strongly for you. But then, you carry so much of our blood within you." Bell carefully touched E's red strands. "There is much strength in you, Easton. Even from your youngest years."

"That's what they said, too. That I was strong and so very brave. But it wasn't strength or bravery that kept me together after my parents' deaths. Or even through all the abusive foster homes that followed, or the years lived on the streets dodging rival gangs and the police that had once helped me. It wasn't strength or bravery that kept me going when I was trapped into the street guild of a man who was the son of the gang members that killed my family." E kept her gaze fixed on Ian, though her attention was far distant.

"It was the fact that I was broken inside. Something snapped in me the day that my parents died. I was empty and hollow, literally incapable of caring one way or another about most things. All that was left to me was the memory of a fearless Captain Hook, and the need to survive. Even now when I found out the man I played servant to for so many years played a monumental part in my parents' deaths…the tears just won't come." Her shoulders lifted in a half-hearted shrug.

"People where I come from have a saying: 'Time heals all wounds'. I'm still waiting for that to happen. Maybe I'm just too broken to fix," E admitted. Bell sighed, staring off at the children as they played.

"Not all wounds heal. Even if they close up, there is always an ugly mass of scar tissue left behind, something that can be more painful than the actual wound at times." Suddenly Hook let out a wounded cry of defeat, falling to his knees.

"Beaten by little midgets at my own game? Impossible!"

The goat chose that moment to head-butt his back, sending him face first to the ground. The children cheered, piling on top until he was at the bottom of a squirming lump of tiny bodies. E smiled, warmth stirring within. Bell's soft, wrinkled knuckle slid down the side of E's cheek.

"And sometimes, new things come along to warm our souls. Maybe the old wounds aren't healed, but the new things can bring happiness so bright it fights the shadows to the farthest reaches of our lives. Maybe that is the best people like us can hope for. Sometimes, being broken can make the best of heroes. Because those who were broken, yet still survived, can carry on with strength unlike any other. They are often the ones who can beat insurmountable odds, and save others from being broken, too. They are the hearts of our strongest warriors."

E looked out at her husband, watched the way he rolled around in the grass with the children. Despite all of his past sorrows, despite his broken story, he found purpose and joy in his duties toward others. Despite the soul-deep weariness he carried, Ian carried the others in this hopeless little world, too. He carried their hopes and their existence, carried their beings within his broken one. And his purposes brought him joy in a world of bleakness. His warrior's heart was a beautiful thing.

"We're all a little broken, just in different ways," she whispered, Wi's words coming back to mind once more. "Thank you. You're right, Bell. I needed to hear all of that."

"Sometimes our strength runs a little dry. It's not gone, just thirsty. All we need is for someone else to give us a drink."

Bell looked at her, sage knowledge only found in a long life of trial reflected in her keen gaze. Bell's words were exactly what Easton had needed to hear. She hadn't realized it, so wrapped up in her shell of survival. But Easton had been dying of metaphorical thirst all her life. After finding out the truth of her bloodline, about Wi being captured, her internal numbness had spread. Confirmation of being a monster down to her DNA, being part of what was destroying this world and making it impossible for her to fit in her own, it had been too much. She'd been teetering on the edge, halfway happy to give up and fall into oblivion, though she wouldn't have admitted it out loud, or even to herself, until this moment.

That fact stirred Easton's ire. Easton James never let life destroy her. Well, Easton Bendal would be no less strong and determined. Now that she had Hook at her side, she had worlds to conquer. She'd been looking at it all wrong. If anything, her blood was an advantage, her past was an advantage. With her help, maybe Hook really could destroy Pan, and then maybe they'd both be free to find a life without the broken edges.

"Bell, I'm going to help Hook find Pan, and we're going to kill him." Easton said to her companion, cautiously honest.

"You are prepared to accept your role in the prophecy, then?" Bell's voice was distant, disconnected.

"Yes. I still doubt my place in the role destiny has given me, whether I have the strength and ability to be what it expects of me. But Pan needs to be stopped."

"And you are now the wife of a Hook." Bell nodded significantly at the ring on her finger.

"Yes." Easton whispered quietly, spinning the little circle. The

265

words husband and wife were still so foreign to her. She'd never thought of herself as being a wife one day. She'd been too busy trying to survive. But the reality had slowly been seeping inward, leaving a pleasant acceptance in its wake. Things were still new, and delicate. But she rather liked the fact that she was so tangibly connected to Ian now. And, she was excited to watch that connection grow.

"Wife of a Hook, with the blood of a Fiend." Bell mused humorously. "Such complicated offspring we've created, Peter."

"You still speak of him as though he's special to you. Is he?" E stated bluntly.

"He is, in a way. He's my husband, the father of a child we created. He will always hold a special bond within my heart," she replied quietly. "But have no fear of my betrayal, child. Just because you love someone, doesn't mean you must protect them and support them from their consequences. The Pan and the man, they are separate in my heart, yet in reality they are one in the same. And that is something I'll never overlook again." The old woman released a burdened sigh. "Perhaps you'd care to hear my story now? Perhaps it would help you to understand."

"Yes, please."

"My mother had sent me to gather water one day. My father had died a year before, and with three younger siblings, I had to pick up much of the Tinker work. Water was vital to our work's formations. I won't bore you with those details. Only know that I was normally a good girl and went to and from the stream without a moment's hesitation." She smiled softly.

"That day was different. I was only ten then. I filled my buckets, made my trips. But on the last one, I faltered in my diligence. I imagined the other village children, what they were doing at that time. For the first time, I found myself wishing I could be doing the same; wishing I didn't have to do so many grown up duties, that I could have fun. And then I saw *him*." The wizened face took on a soft glow of childhood remembrances.

"Sprawled across a boulder in the river with a rakish grin on his face, he appeared to be only a few years older than me. I watched him carefully at first, ever mindful of the danger of strangers. He winked, lifted a flute to his lips, and played the most beautiful melody. Yet it wasn't the music that held me enthralled, but what it did to the water." E leaned closer, drawn into the woman's captivating presence and story.

"Ever so slowly, the water around the rock began to flow in a different direction than the current. It spun around the rock like a whirlpool. Beautiful colors reflected in its depths, glimmering in the sun. With a jiggle of his flute, the liquid lifted, rising high enough to rain a beautiful rainbow of colors down on him. And then it moved to hover over me. He watched with a gleam in his eye as I was encircled with the glimmering water, perhaps eager for my cry of outrage. But instead, I was enchanted. I stepped into the ring of falling water, laughing as I spun about. The water droplets sounded like fine glass as it rained down, the colors beautiful and brilliant." Her eyes lit with an inner light. "After that moment, he was as enchanted with me as I was him."

"He came to the shore, and we spoke for many long hours. It wasn't until my mother came storming into the clearing, chiding me for leaving her alone to work, that I realized how long I'd been there speaking to him. He'd disappeared as though he never existed, slipping into the shadows until her back was turned. Peter was always at home in the shadows. They wrapped around him like the best of friends. He was very good at sneaking." She sent E a knowing look.

"I'm pretty good with shadows myself," she offered with a blush. Bell nodded as though she suspected no less.

"He left me with the memory of a roguish smile, drenched in mischief and promises of fun. He was unlike any other boy in the village. And each day, he returned. Always when my mother was elsewhere, when I was alone and free to talk. Peter told such wonderful stories. As one could expect from a mysterious young man, brought over from a different world."

"A different world? My world?"

"Are you familiar with the story of the Pan? Not in the book you read of Peter and Hook, but of the Pan himself. Our worlds are vastly different, but I believe you know much of our histories to be only myths in your land."

"I took a mythology class in school once. But, my record of school attendance wasn't great, and eventually I completely dropped out." Bell nodded.

"I see. Well, perhaps I shall refresh you. The Pan has existed throughout time. Though, he was not just one man. The Pan has never been immortal, only living the typical lifespan of each individual race. Eventually one Pan grows weary of life and they can feel their magic dispersing, so they choose a successor. The Pan before Peter was a satyr. Half man, half goat, and they are long-lived creatures. It is not uncommon for them to live two hundred years." E shivered, which caused Bell to giggle.

"Yes, I hear you have quite a history with satyrs. Though this satyr was the size of a normal man, not mutated by Neverland's curse as the one you fought. He had quite a history with our people, too. No one cared for him overly much. He was always stealing away the virtue, if not the hearts, of the village girls." The disapproving expression on Bell's face let Easton know just what the common mindset on that behavior was.

"His predecessors had often been looked to for help with cultivating our fields and livestock. The Pan's skills were renowned for their abilities to help crops and animals thrive and become bountiful. The satyr Pan, however, brought a scourge upon the once honorable title. The Pan was rarely sought out after that, people going to such lengths as to ban him from their lands."

"He couldn't have liked that too much."

"No indeed. He withered their crops, and cursed them with all manner of foul tricks, determined it would force them to come back to him, beg his forgiveness. However, it only made them bitter. And with the lack of their approval, his magic also dwindled. Likewise, he gained power from the growth of plants and animals. He wasn't the wisest of men," she scoffed. "As those were withering and dying, it only further drained his power. The less he worked, the less power he had, and the closer to death he grew. So, in his desperation, the Pan sought out an apprentice, an act that would give him a magical boost in power. Yet, hated as he was, no one was eager to apprentice with him. Using forbidden magic, the Pan moved to a different world, and sought out his next apprentice."

"Peter," E said with certainty, sorry for the child that would be taken. No matter the sins of the adult, the child version hadn't deserved to be stolen away into a fate such as the one he now lived.

"Yes." Bell nodded sadly. "Peter was but a babe when the satyr stole him from his bed, two years old. The Pan wanted an apprentice that would grow to love him, to think of him as a father and deny him nothing. The Pan went to an orphanage, where a child would have no connections to family, nothing holding their hearts. Peter told me once that the Pan had chosen him after seeing the toddler bite an older child for stealing his toy. The Pan thought it was such good fun, the way Peter made the bigger child cry. And the coloring of his hair set him apart from all the others, making him a unique commodity to the satyr, who loved to collect special things. And so, Peter came to Neverland."

"The satyr raised Peter and taught him every cruel joke and mischief he could. Despite it all, Peter had a good heart. He retained the mischief with none of the cruelty. That changed, when others discovered our friendship. Peter and I were eighteen when we were discovered. We had been secretly wed earlier in the year. When my belly began to grow, it was no longer possible to hide our relationship. Adults who had been made destitute by the pranks and cruelty of the satyr demanded that I shirk Peter. He admitted to being part of their sorrows, causing their problems. Though he was not cruel like the satyr in his actions, Peter still played the games. He had little choice. To do otherwise would mean denying the only man he'd known as a father."

"Peter encouraged me to do as they said, to leave him so that our child might have a normal life. In my young love, I refused to turn my back on him, to raise our child without a father. So, he tried to make amends with the villagers. They refused to accept it. Persecution grew, and the villager's hatred spread to other nearby villages. With the growth of their hatred, also grew Peter's frustration. He began to play pranks on them in earnest, even blatantly telling them that their childish behavior deserved retribution. The aggression spread like a disease. Soon, those who used to come from all over Neverland for our Tinkering, refused to do business with us, only further angering Peter."

"I begged Peter to take me away from all the chaos. I loved him and wanted to be with him, but I couldn't stand to see my family persecuted any further. I also couldn't stand to see the changes all of the strife was bringing about in Peter. He was becoming more like his father with each confrontation. So, I ran away with Peter to a secluded area amongst the sirens. Sirens have long been loyal to the Pans, and they welcomed us with open arms, eager to help. Their much larger group of cousins, the Mers, were not so easy to convince. But they left us alone, so long as we agreed to stay clear of the village people. We lived happily for a short time."

"The unrest didn't dissipate with our departure, however. The satyr continued to try to ply Peter away from our happiness. He demanded Peter return, that as his last heir it was his duty. Peter was torn between us, but in the end, he chose me and our unborn child. The satyr acquiesced, but I could feel him quietly biding his time. The creature had never liked me. He loved the unrest our relationship caused amongst the people, but when Peter chose me over him with increasing occurrence, his dislike of me grew. He was a jealous creature, and did not care for the love I stole from his power source."

"As the final weeks approached before I would give birth, the satyr returned; not with gifts of adoration, but rumors of hatred. The villagers had begun to claim my child would be a devil, that I carried the destruction of our world in my womb. The satyr promised Peter that when I gave birth, they would be determined to hunt us down, and kill us all. When the sirens confirmed the satyr's claims, Peter was furious. He stormed into the night, such darkness in his eyes, even I was afraid of him. He returned the next day, a man completely changed and wild."

"He was murderous in his intent to make the adults pay for their hatred. He began hunting villagers in the night, making it a game. He told me it was the only way to instill the fear in them, the same fear that they would wish to instill upon our child. The fear of being hunted, always. I tried to remind him that we were adults now, too. He angrily rebuked me, claiming he would never grow old to become such a single-minded creature. He became obsessed with it, not sleeping for days at a time."

"Then one day, he disappeared. This time when he returned days later, he swept me up in his arms and kissed me as though his life depended on it. The madness in his eyes as he told me of the deal he'd struck with an old sorcerer deep in the swamps curdled my soul. He would never age beyond his current years. He would never become old. And the sorcerer had promised he could do the same for me. That he could forever keep me in my present state. Including our babe, locked away in my womb, the only way Peter determined we could keep her safe. He told me our kiss had sealed the deal, that I was now forever the same as he."

"I was horrified. I begged him to reverse the spell. He didn't listen, promised in time I would see the brilliance of his ways. But with time only came pain. I was in discomfort, always in discomfort. And the babe within me? I could feel her pain and confusion, her yearning to be free. I wanted her free of me, just as much as she wanted it. Nature is not meant to be subverted; it turns cruel. Peter saw my growing sadness, and was lost as to how to fix me. That was when he began stealing children."

"He followed his mentor's path, moved into your world, and stole children from their beds. First it was one child, a child he hoped I would find suitable to replace the one trapped within my womb. Then, the children began to show up in droves. He told me they were orphans, just like he once was. That he was giving them life in a way none other could. That through us, they would find happiness, and so would we. None of them brought me solace; they only compounded it. Peter turned to the children to cover his own fears and confusion. He spent all of his hours in their presence, playing and conversing as children do."

"It was then that I saw what was happening to them. The life of a Pan is sustained by love and growth. Peter found none of that in the land he was destroying. But within the children he stole? They looked to him as a father, just as he once had with the satyr. They

271

adored him, hung on his every word. Soon, it was as though they could read his thoughts, and he theirs. Then, their bodies began to fade into shadowy creatures of their past vestiges. Peter was slowly sucking their very souls from them in an unconscious effort to sustain his own life. Every use of magic exacts a price. Peter thought he'd cleverly escaped any consequences. But the consequences presented in the children he loved so much. They became specters forever locked into subservience to him, all in exchange for Peter's deal, to cement our eternal youth."

"When I confronted him about it, he flew into a rage. He refused to believe that his 'gift' would exact such a price. Instead, he claimed that their transformations were simply paths to new and everlasting life, a gift of power from himself to them. Still, as their forms faded into shadows of specters that followed in his wake, Peter grew agitated. His features drew wane, his restlessness a neverending torture. Compelled onward in an uncontrollable path, Peter returned to your world, intent of bringing more children to fill his void. And that night, while Peter was in your world, I did what I should have done years earlier. I fled."

"Wow." E stated, feeling completely adrift. "So, what happened? Obviously you had your baby, since I exist. And clearly you aged."

"Yes. I had a good friend, a sorceress named Celeste. She didn't approve of my relationship with Peter, but still she remained my friend. She had the power of premonition. She'd known about his potential for darkness from the beginning, when I confided in her about my forbidden love. She warned me that our relationship would end in pain and sorrow, but she wouldn't stand in the way of my choices. When I fled, I went immediately to her home." Bell looked up at the warm brown sunlight sifting through the stone.

"Gathering her few belongings, Celeste brought me to these obsidian caves, using their attributes, mixed with her magic, to shield us. We worked for months on a plan to reverse the spell of the dark sorcerer, to find a way to stop Peter's destructive force."

"Meanwhile, Peter ravaged the land, growing more dangerous and more juvenile with time. It was as though the spell continued to work, rewinding his mentality as he threw a temper tantrum over all of Neverland, furious at my disappearance. I nearly gave in to his behavior if it meant stopping him. But I knew it wouldn't end. I knew that by going back to him, I'd only doom myself and our child, and it wouldn't change Peter's plans. And if I'm honest, I was afraid. Afraid of what he would do in his unstable nature. Eventually, Celeste made a discovery. It was a discovery that would see us both making the greatest sacrifices possible."

"The spell would drain my life essence, ensuring that I lived forever but without my youth. An eternity of old age. With the force of my life, I could birth our child into the world with a spell that would preserve her, protect her. But to do this, I would have to immediately send her through a portal to a place I knew nothing of, a place I could never visit. I could never see my daughter again, and would have to trust in the kindness of strangers to protect her. She couldn't stay here; the force of the spell was powerful enough it would destroy Neverland."

"She had to go somewhere without magic, to nullify the sheer power that would roll off her in waves otherwise. With the essence of Peter and a Tinker, then encompassed in a magic-infused womb for countless years, and further infused through the spell of Celeste's magic, the child was an explosive danger. In the hands of Peter, our child would be an indestructible force that would bring all worlds to their knees."

"Using the power of her mind, Celeste called a gathering of her people to the caverns. Powerful magic casters, they all conversed in efforts to come to an understanding of what it would take to free the land of the scourge of my husband, and to free the land of the power growing within my womb. The Brotherhood of the Hook was formed. Decisions were made, and envoys were sent in every direction by land and sea. When Prince Octavian Bendal came to the Brethren with a prophecy, we finally had the final pieces of the solution for my child."

"To send the babe to such a magicless land, my only friend would usurp Peter's portal, and use it to send my daughter to the next world. Tying the portal to her life essence would ensure Pan couldn't control it any longer; he couldn't follow and continue to gather his army of soulless children, or find our daughter. And in the process, they would seal Neverland away, its borders becoming an inescapable thing. The world would be safe from us and eventually forget our existence. It would ensure Peter could never leave Neverland again."

"The price of such an expenditure of power would not only cost my youth and my daughter's absence. It would cost the inhabitants of Neverland's freedom. They would forever be entombed with a mad man and his quest for a soul's depth. It would cost many brave men their destinies and families; a loss of a hand for the pathway of eternal battles, loneliness, and death. And it would cost my friend her life as well. She would become the portal, the only pathway for my descendants to return, the keys destined to be instrumental in the downfall of Peter. Our child would be the catalyst of death to her father, my friend, and quite possibly Neverland."

"That would be a difficult burden to bear."

"It was. It is still. Especially when I look at these poor children, trapped forever in their youth, unable to grow up and gain the responsibilities of adults that are in mankind's nature to crave." Bell grasped her hands in her own. "For that, I thank you. They can now experience life as it is meant to be experienced, even if only in the confines of Sanctuary. You've freed me of one burden already. I'm sorry I must ask so much more of you."

"I'm glad I could help. I hope I can do what everyone else expects of me." E pursed her lips, carefully watching the old woman. "How exactly did Celeste draw your descendants to the portal?"

"Through the book of course. I never pretended to understand her magic, but from what I gathered in our time together, she needed a physical object already in existence to tie her magic to. As the book did not exist before Celeste's arrival, I would assume she found a way to enter someone's mind, feed them the story, and then waited until the book was brought into existence so that she could tie herself to it. It would have been exhausting for her, holding herself and the portal in such a state of limbo. I imagine this is part of why she knew it would cost her life."

"You say Celeste became the portal. Does that mean she's not entirely dead?" Bell's face drew downcast, and E quickly spoke her thoughts. "What I mean is… I think I saw her. I kept hearing a woman speak to me, and then eventually I swear I saw just a glimpse of her. She was really ghostly-looking, but she did exist. Scared the crap out of me, if I'm honest," E grudgingly admitted. Bell chuckled.

"That certainly sounds like something Celeste would enjoy. She had quite the dark sense of humor when it came to her magic. It probably played a part in why she never trusted Peter; they were too similar in their liking of mischief."

"Well, I just wanted to let you know that she isn't completely gone."

Now that she said it, E wondered why she'd ever thought it would have been comforting. She basically just told an old woman that her dead friend was a ghost. Bell patted her hand once more before pulling away and looking into the distance.

"I understand you mean well, Easton. And it is a comfort to know that she is not gone entirely. It means there is still hope. But the end is near; I can feel it as surely as I feel you."

"Now that the time is here, are you ready to allow the next step to happen?"

"The death of my husband, by one of my long-descended grand-children, you mean?"

"Yes."

"Peter was my husband; he always will be, in my heart. But the Pan has become a far different creature than my husband. He has taken countless lives, and I dare say lived in a mess of confusion and guilt. It is time that we both find our rest."

"Both?"

"When Peter is at rest, I'll finally be able to find mine as well." Her eyes drifted shut for a time, a peaceful expression washing over her face as though she could imagine the rest to come.

"I am old, Easton, and I am so very tired. My mistakes, my passions, and my heartaches all bind into one, and it is exhausting to the heart, child. But seeing you here now, it stills the trembles of a ravaged soul. I find comfort in the knowledge that Celeste was wrong on one thing. Good has come from mine and Peter's union.

Good found in you, and found within the Hook." She grasped E's hand, holding it with her frail ones.

"Child, this is a heavy burden that I pass on to the two of you. Yet, should you and the Hook succeed, this land and everyone within it will be freed." Responsibility grew heavier on her shoulders, suffocating her. As though she could see it, Bell shook her head.

"No doubts. You can do it. Never underestimate the power of love between a man and woman." E looked to her in surprise, denial on her lips. "Don't bother arguing, child. Perhaps it is too soon to love so deeply. But love begins in all forms, and can grow with the swiftness of the winds. If the love of one man and woman can destroy the world, the love of another can mend it."

"Thank you for telling me all of this." E stood.

"I… I wonder if I might ask one more thing, before you go," Bell asked, wearily pushing to her feet as well.

"Yes?"

"I was never able to hold my child before she was sent through the portal. She was taken directly from my womb, sent into the great unknown without me so much as being able to see her, much less hold her. I wonder if I might hold you, the last I have of my child; if but for a moment."

E answered silently, moving to enfold the woman in a hug. What began as an awkward movement quickly became one of warmth and security, Easton enjoying it just as much as her great however-many-times grandma.

"What was your daughter's name?" Easton asked quietly, still enfolded in the embrace. A soft, wrinkled cheek lifted upward against hers.

"Emery."

"That's a good name."

"Yes. It is." Bell nodded, pulling away. Her face glowed with a serenity that it hadn't held earlier. "You are beautiful, child. And special. I can feel it. Together, the two of you will bring us peace."

"I hope you're right."

"And Easton?" When E turned back, Bell smiled reassuringly. "If you can get to your friend before his body is shadowed, there is a chance he can be saved with the death of the Pan. But once his body has become spectral, the most merciful thing you can offer him is a swift death."

"I understand," Easton whispered. It was a hard truth to hear, yet she was grateful the woman respected her enough to say it. Turning, E set out to extract her husband from the layers of giggling children still piled atop him.

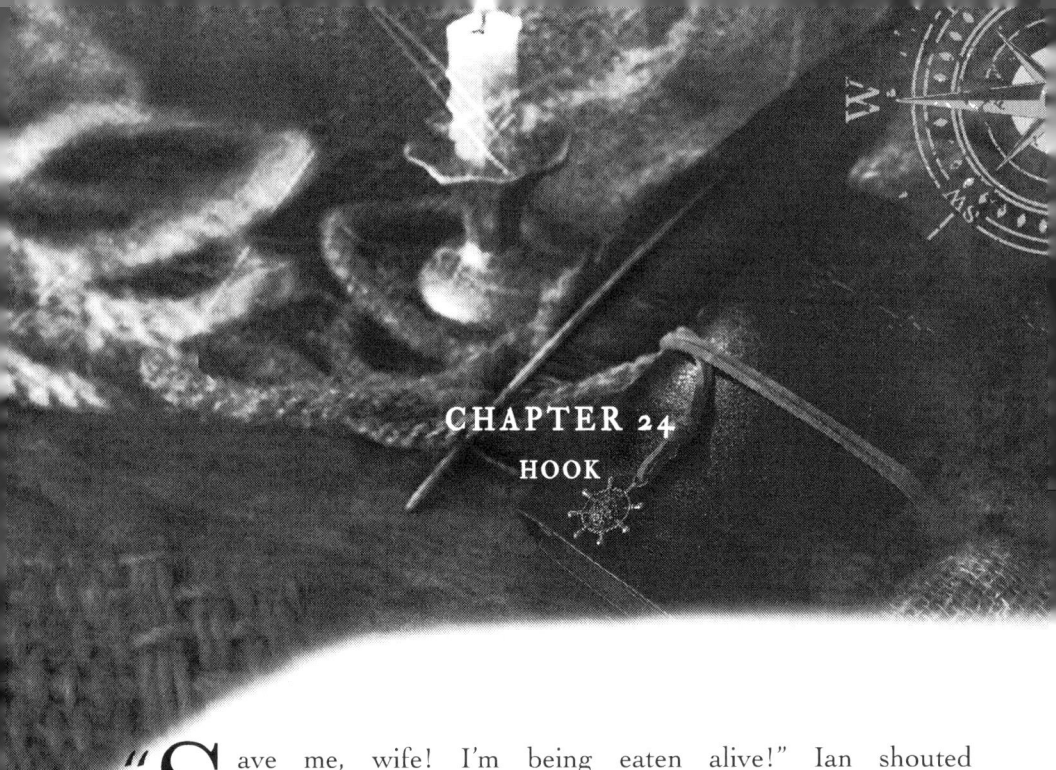

CHAPTER 24
HOOK

"Save me, wife! I'm being eaten alive!" Ian shouted dramatically.

He loved seeing her bright grin as she lifted one bundle of mischief off him after another. He could have easily gotten up, but where would the fun in that be? And once in a while, Ian needed some fun. So did his little butterfly.

She had been floundering, he could feel it. Her tormented soul stretched to a breaking limit. So much had been thrown her way in the last few days, and he was endlessly proud of how beautifully she handled it. Ian had always seen that in her. She was a survivor, a delicate girl with a warrior's heart. But even the most hearty of warriors needed a shoulder to lean on, a respite from the battles.

And when those moments arrived for Ian, he found peace here with the children, the last hope of Neverland's dreams. And Bell had a way of replenishing a heart with her wisdom. When she wasn't teasing you with information she wouldn't share until you figured it out yourself. Based on Easton's warm, casual smile, it seemed she'd found some of that peace.

"I think maybe you'll have to stay there forever, Hook," she teased, melting his heart.

He so loved their little ploys, the way they played together so well. She made life bearable, she made it fun again. Easton brought beauty to the world of sullen grays they all lived within now. The children cheered, clambering atop him again.

"Abandoning your Captain in his time of need? You minx!" Ian grunted as several well-placed knees found his stomach and thighs. When two very nearly unmanned him, he rolled to the side, sending them rolling and giggling across the grass. Climbing to his feet, three little monsters still hanging onto his arms and back, he met her eyes. A soft, sympathetic smile was held in their depths as she carefully dislodged the wee ones.

"Never, my Captain." Her gently spoken promise clenched at his heart. The warm depths of those sparkling eyes held him as surely as an anchor.

"All right you ruffians, off to dinner with you!" Ian shouted, never glancing away from the woman that was now his to treasure for the rest of his living days. The children immediately ran toward their houses, eager for their meals. The piranhas were always hungry. E stepped closer, pulling pieces of grass from his hair, still locked in his gaze. When she adjusted his eyepatch so very gently, he couldn't resist touching her. Grasping her wrist, keeping her hand pressed to his face, he spoke.

"Have you found rest?" His rough voice, a testament to an old neck wound from the Fiend long ago, seemed to always capture her attention, gaze dropping to his lips in a way that was far too adept at stirring warmth within him.

"Yes. I think I have." She replied, eyes moving back to his. "Thank you, Ian. I needed this."

"I know. We both did."

"You knew what Bell would tell me? About her and Peter, and who she is to me? About their story?"

"Yes." He watched her intently. "I hoped she would share the knowledge; I hoped the news would offer some solace and grounding for you both."

"I think it has. Thank you." She thanked him again, the depth of internal healing reflected in her gaze. It was breathtaking.

"Nothing denied to my little vermillion butterfly." He murmured. Her eyes widened slightly, body unconsciously shifting towards him.

"The children are running low on supplies, Hook."

Bell's wry voice had both he and Easton jumping. They'd been so wrapped up in their own world, they hadn't noticed her approach. Which said much for Ian. It was good they were within the safety of Sanctuary. He'd have to be careful when being trapped within Easton's gaze from now on. The growing power she seemed to hold over him could get dangerous otherwise. A moment of unease rippled through him. Was it wise for him to be allowing such an immersion of himself within the girl?

Avida's face flickered through his mind, trailing along another wave of unease. As though summoned by his thoughts, her voice seemed to wail louder at him through the rift in his eye. Shuddering, Ian took a step away from Easton, turning to the frail old woman instead. He tried to ignore the blink of surprise, and confusion, in his wife's gaze.

"I will send Smee with more supplies, Bell. If you've a list of particular items, I'll be glad to send them along with him as well." Untying the mitt from his glove as he spoke, he handed it back to Bell. Her withered hand patted his cheek, a smile of affection on her lips.

"Such a good lad. Always looking out for us." Her wizened eyes turned to Easton. "After the portal was made, we formed a safe haven here. With the other worlds closed off to Peter, Neverland sealed away to keep him from attacking the rest of the lands, the Pan was forced to turn to stealing the children of Neverland." Bell sighed heavily with regret, and Ian gave her frail hand a pat. He understood regret over matters that were outside of your control. With a grateful nod, Bell continued.

"We secretly moved as many of them as we could here. Having to move cautiously so the Pan wouldn't know where our safe haven was slowed us down. We weren't able to save them all. But we saved as many as we could. Celeste's people stayed here, forming the Council of Judgement, waiting for the inevitable return of my descendant. I joined them, but I prefer to stay here with the children. I feel it my penance, my truest calling in life, protecting these small treasures. It fills the hole in my heart."

With a sad smile, she stuffed the mitt under one arm and grasped both Ian and Easton's hands. Without saying a word, she conveyed every hope she had in them, in their ability to mend all of Neverland, hearts included.

"I'll fetch my list and send it to you by way of the guards. You two look after one another. The world is a sad enough place, it needs more love. It does my heart well to see the two of you frolicking around like a bunch of fools." With a wink, she turned and followed the path the children had taken.

"If you're done playing around, wife, I'm tired and would like to take a nap." Ian smirked at the imperiously lifted brow she sent back his way.

"Careful, husband; you sleep in the same room as me now. I could do all sorts of mischief to you as you sleep."

"Good point," he conceded, offering his arm. "Shall you walk this time, or shall I carry you along like a lumpy flour bag on my back once more?"

"Maybe I'll carry you, old man." Her eyes burned with that feisty fire he found irresistible.

"You couldn't carry me if your life depended on it, you saucy wench." Spurred by his challenge, she moved toward him. Grabbing one arm, she bent low and pulled him to lie across her back. One arm wrapping around the backs of his thighs, she gave a grunt, and lifted. To his surprise, she actually managed to lift him off the ground without falling flat on her face.

"Told you!" She gasped under his weight, but was too stubborn to put him down.

"So you did. I see I have miscalculated your strength," he stated calmly, not fighting her. If he fought her on the matter, she'd do something foolish like stubbornly trying to carry him down the hill. With a satisfied grunt, the little firebrand planted him back on the ground. He steadied her as she stumbled to the side slightly, face red but triumphantly beaming back at him.

"Stick that in your pipe and smoke it!"

"Had I a pipe to smoke, I surely would. You proved you could lift me like a real Neverlander brute of a woman. Well done." She stuck her tongue out at him, but continued to beam. Mischief swelled within him. Yanking her close, he tossed her over his shoulder.

"But this is the way it's done."

"Ah! Hook, you devil dog! Put me down! I won that fair and square."

"Aye you did. And nearly burst an organ in the process, I'd wager. Well done. Now hush your sassy lips or I'll carry you this way everywhere we go and let the men use your backside as target practice." He gave that healthy backside a hearty swat, grinning when she gasped in surprise. She slapped his backside in retribution along with several more bantering remarks, but happily allowed him to carry her. Before reaching town, he let her slide to the ground, giving her the dignity of the men not seeing her tossed over his shoulder like potatoes.

She offered a shy, sweet smile, her cheeks rosy and face glowing with a zeal for life. He'd hoped she'd find that fight for life once more, after speaking to Bell and playing with the children. He always yearned to see that peaceful smile in her eyes. Falling into an easy silence, they strolled through town. Yet as they neared their shared room, a heavy air of suspense fell over them. He didn't have to ask to know she was just as nervous about entering the small room as he was.

Waking to find himself poised over her, hook to her throat... it had ripped his insides to shreds, gutted him more surely than any weapon ever could. Ian had been in so many terrifying positions in his lifetime. He'd lost good men and friends, suffered grievously painful wounds. But in that moment, he'd found himself more terrified than he ever had in his entire existence. He relived the death of his first wife all over again, but the terror was magnified a hundred fold. He'd hugged the walls, torn between wanting to gather her in his arms to never release her, and fleeing down the hallway, never to see her again.

The loss of Avida had been heart-rending, the guilt insurmountable. Yet, looking at the differences between his wives now, Hook felt a disconcerting imbalance. He'd loved Avida. She'd saved his life, been his first love and lover. She'd taught him to not look at the world with such a stern vision.

But it was Easton who set his blood afire. It was Easton who pulled him into her heart with the force of the rift itself. It was she who kept him guessing and yearning for more of it. And it was she, he knew, that would destroy him beyond redemption if he ever lost her. He had long held himself aloof on the surface, tried to keep her distant to protect himself, and her as well. But the girl had found every crevice of his soul, wormed her way in, and filled up the cracks behind her. She was forever a part of him till the end and beyond if there was such a thing. He couldn't pry her free of him even if he wished.

Avida's mournful wail rose once more within, and guilt spun wildly in Ian's heart. He wished he had been able to love her as fiercely as she claimed to have loved him. He had wanted to believe she loved him. But a part of him always wondered if it wasn't just the ring, the bond, and the possessive heart of a Mer that drew her to him.

He had felt the love of gratitude towards her for saving his life, for helping him climb free of his mire of guilt over the death of his men. He felt the budding love of a young man embarking into his first true foray into romantic relations. The protective nature of wanting to keep safe the woman he was responsible for, and of course, the inevitable feelings of love that came along with the connection a man felt with a woman when intimately involved. He felt the guilt for loving another woman more deeply than the woman who had given him the gift of life; the same gift that also allowed him to save his new wife.

He felt the guilt of danger he posed to Easton. How could he promise her safety as he had when he was the most intimate danger to her? Falling asleep with her in his bed had been so easy. Far easier than he'd expected. And he couldn't deny the feelings of pleasure that coursed through him upon learning that she would be staying in his room. Yet now, Ian found himself very much afraid of what he might do next. It had been the threat of Pan, the Fiend lurking in her dreams that set off his hook's instincts. But what if it happened again? He'd kept the sheath on the weapon this time. But what if he didn't next time? What if he was too slow to wake?

The fact that the Pan was sending her devious messages in her most vulnerable moments, threatening her where a Hook couldn't protect her, it made his blood boil. Bell still held a soft spot for the Fiend, her heart tied to the old memories of her love. She was wise enough to understand that man was no longer alive, thankfully. Yet she stayed carefully away from any chances of being near the Fiend again, because of those protected feelings and memories. Ian held no such restrictions. His only feelings and memories involving Pan were murderous ones. The Pan had to be stopped; the suffering and fear he caused had to be ended. Now that Ian had yet another soul depending on him, one far more intimately dear to him than any other, that need rose anew within him.

But that would have to wait. There was a far more immediate danger facing him now: the door to his bedroom. How had they arrived at it so quickly? In this moment he wished he had the free use of both his eyes. He'd love to glance at her from the corner of his eye, to discretely see her reaction. Was it similar to his own? Hesitation as they stood at the brink of territory little explored? As it was, he'd have to turn his head fully to see her, being as she was standing on the side of his patched eye. So he stayed frozen, contemplating.

Her hand suddenly appeared in his line of sight, fingers wrapping about the handle of the door and pushed it open, and then pushed him forward. The saucy little minx had just surpassed all of his concerns, and then shoved him in to face them first. Reaching behind him, he yanked her in with him. Laughing, she lightly pinched his back, and moved to sit on the small chest at the end of the bed, unlacing her boots.

"Can I ask you something?" Her soft question shook him from the act of leering at her like a fool. Turning toward the closet, he set about searching out additional blankets and pillows.

"Anything."

"Is that why you started calling me Vermillion? Because you

think of me as the prophecy? The weapon to be used against Pan?" Hook hesitated, back turned to her.

"I've never lied to you, and I'll not start now." He repeated his familiar promise to her. "I began calling you Vermillion because I needed a way to keep myself distanced. From the moment I saw you, I felt a connection form, a bonding in its own way, long before any ring was involved. It unsettled me. In that moment, you were a Pan, an enemy until proven otherwise. I felt I should treat you with respect, yes, but not feel such a strong connection. So, I called you the one word that should have kept my feet firmly planted on the ground, eye on the goal." He offered a lopsided grin over his shoulder.

"Instead, I found only beauty of heart and soul reflected toward me each time I glanced your way. And you were too often on my mind, like the delicate fluttering of graceful butterfly wings in my head. A delicate and graceful dance so clearly at odds with the warrior's heart you displayed on our journey. My brave little vermillion butterfly. As you can see, it quickly transformed from a stern cautionary expression, to a term of endearment." He shrugged unapologetically. "Life is rarely what we would plan it to be. Yet it often works out well enough in the end, if you survive it." Easton grinned up at him, stood and sunk one hand into his messy hair, ruffling it into further disaster.

"Aww, Hooky, you do care."

"Aye, and I'll not deny it." Pulling her closer, he planted a sloppy, wet, comedic kiss on her forehead, smearing it left and right until she gasped for breath between giggles, pleading him to stop.

"All right then. Enough games. Off to bed with you, you minx." He tossed the blankets and pillow on the floor, yanking off the shirt over his head. He almost wished he could stay cocooned in the fabric, feeling the weight of her imperial temper on him. But Hook was no coward, even in the face of a woman's wrath. Emerging, he faced her expression.

"Your face is going to wrinkle, staring at me like that."

"You're not sleeping on the floor, Octavian Ryes Bendal." His brow rose at the full use of his name, surprised. The serious shield over her face cracked, a giggle escaping her lips.

"Okay, sorry, that was all crazy wench tone right there. But seriously. You're not sleeping on the floor. That's just dumb. I thought we already went over this."

"My wanting to protect you is not 'dumb', Easton."

"I didn't mean it like that." She growled in frustration, throwing her hands in the air. Moving into a tornado of motion, she returned with a small leather messenger pouch. He tensed as she grasped his wrist, just above his hook, torn between wanting to jerk it safely away from her and afraid to hurt her in the process. Deep brown eyes met his seafoam gaze, holding it.

"We went over this. I am not Avida. I won't betray you; I won't hurt you and you won't hurt me." When he still hesitated, she stepped a little closer. "Have a little faith in your wife." Swallowing, he relaxed his hand, allowing her to lift it. As the hook neared her body, his pulse began to pound, his skin to flush with a sweat of panic. It was an uncomfortable feeling and one he didn't relish. He shivered with a mixture of feelings as her fingers deftly slid along the length of the crystal-encased hook, up to his wrist. The leather bag followed, slipping over the weapon.

"You are my husband now. And a husband's place is with his wife, and vice versa. If you choose to sleep on the floor, I will sleep on the floor. If you sleep in bed, you blessed saint of a man, I will sleep in bed." Hook couldn't deny his grin entrance to the world, smirking at her obvious pleading for him to choose the bed. The ties of the leather pouch wrapped about his wrist, securing it in place.

"The same idea worked well enough to roughhouse with rowdy children. If you trusted it then, you can trust it now. If you have another reaction to me, you'll have to untie the bag, and pull off the crystal sheath to get to me. And if you want it that bad, well, maybe I did something to deserve it." Awed and humbled, Hook's hand found its way into her hair, gently cupping her neck.

"You are a magnificent woman, Easton Bendal."

"And most of the time, I don't even have to try," she smirked back at him.

"Well, then, time for bed I suppose. I'll not fight you on it a moment longer." Flopping onto his back on the floor, eyes closed, Ian fought the grin that wanted so badly to unleash itself upon his face. He waited a full thirty seconds before he felt her settle onto the floor next to him.

"At least give me your shoulder for a pillow then," she groused, only half ill-tempered at being made to sleep on the floor. Curling up against his side, using his shoulder for a pillow, she closed her eyes and settled in. She really was going to sleep on the floor. Hook chuckled, earning a grumpy frown.

"Stop it. I'm trying to sleep. Pillows aren't supposed to move," she grumbled. He laughed harder.

"As much as I love your chivalrous effort of sleeping arrangement loyalty, I'd much prefer to sleep on the bed after all."

"Hallelujah!" she sang. He winced dramatically as she slapped his bare chest in retribution for his tricks, leaving behind a red hand print. She didn't give him the satisfaction of sympathy, grabbing his hand and pulling him up behind her as she eagerly rushed toward the bed. Kicking off her boots the rest of the way, she bounced onto the bed and patted it.

"Hurry, I need a pillow."

"Fine and well enough," he agreed amiably. "But next time, I get to use your gloriously fluffy pillows for my head." Easton's eyes rolled, though a pretty blush kissed her cheeks as he sank into bed next to her. Pushing her way under his arm and wrapping herself around his torso, she sighed with pleasure.

"So much better than the floor."

"Mm." He agreed, exhaustion descending upon him once more. She squirmed impossibly closer, one leg thrown over his waist. Ian smirked, lazily running the tips of his fingers up and down her side.

"By all means, make yourself comfortable, woman."

"Nothing denied to me, pillow," she murmured around a yawn. He pressed a soft kiss to her head.

"Indeed." He closed his eyes, enjoying the feel of her wrapped about him, happily snuggled in. A corner of his mouth lifted in one last jest.

"You've kept a secret from me wife."

"Nuh huh." She mumbled.

"Indeed you did. Your feet are just as stinky as mine at the end of the day." Her lithe body jiggled against him as she chuckled, not bothering to deny his accusation.

CHAPTER 25
HOOK

He'd woken two hours earlier, having slept only a total of four hours. His mind had been restless, unable to calm itself, urging him out of the warm embrace of the beautiful woman in his bed. He glanced up toward her now, allowing a crooked grin as he took in her current position.

Splayed across the bed, she'd quite taken over the moment he rolled out of the covers. Arms and legs thrown wide, vermillion hair cascading in waves around her head, a few strewn artfully across her face, she made a beautiful portrait. So beautiful that he'd found himself distracted often since waking, catching himself staring at her prone figure, drinking in the nuances that made her quite simply irresistible. Perhaps one day, he'd have to try picking up his old habits of painting in an effort to capture that passionately wild beauty. Frowning, he pried his tired eyes back to the maps before him. He'd paint when the Fiend was dead.

Ian's restlessness had led him to pouring over his extensive collection of maps, searching for any blank spaces they hadn't searched, anything that might have slipped through his notice. Nothing had presented itself thus far. Where the devil was the devil? Dropping his ink quill on the table, he pressed a palm to his eye.

How long had he been searching for the Fiend? He'd told Easton it was hundreds of years, but it could have been thousands, as weary of the hunt as Ian felt. Oh, how those years, and the torment they offered, had never ended. Hook and his men stretched thin, as Pan and all of Neverland grew wilder and more vigorous. How often had the Pan managed to dupe him throughout those years, as easily as child's play? The past mattered not, however. They'd struck a heavy cord against the Fiend with the theft of his time keeper's watch. Pan's ire would be immense. The present called for nothing short of swift success if the future were to be bright. Failure in this moment was no longer acceptable, time an essence now in short supply.

"You're up early." Easton's soft voice startled him.

She was climbing out of bed, the lightly curled mass of brilliantly colored hair tumbling at her shoulders, surrounding a face that took his breath away, even fresh from sleep.

"I couldn't sleep." Clearing his throat, Ian looked down to the maps, trying to turn his thoughts back to the business at hand. Just as he tried to ignore the sway of her hips as she headed toward the basin near the window, tiredly stripping the red leaves from potted plants there that served as mouth cleansers. She had confided in him on several occasions that the leaves 'beat the crap out of toothpaste', whatever that meant.

"Did I push you out of bed? Sorry, I guess I'm a bed hog." Happily munching on a bunch of the leaves, she leaned against the window, waiting for an answer.

"Not at all. You are quite a dulcet bed companion," he disagreed, though the contradictory smile couldn't be entirely hidden away. "The snoring could be a problem, however." She didn't snore at all.

"I'll work on that." She assured him, playing along so well with his games. The promise of future nights in bed made his stomach bottom out in an entirely pleasant way. Spitting the leaves in the refuse bucket, she moved to his side.

"So, what are you doing?"

"I'm going over my maps."

"Yes, I see that, and they are very impressive maps." She grinned, spicy fresh breath washing pleasantly across his face as she leaned over his shoulder. "But what are you looking for?"

"I've been pouring over these maps for hours." Ian groused, poking accusingly at the maps, shifting them about so that she could see them all. "But I haven't found a single space we've missed. It's maddening, and time is running short. But I haven't a clue as to where to begin." He drew her attention to a particular spot on the man.

"You were found here, on the far side of our mountains, the Destridges. If it was as you feared, and he fell through the Twin Sister's Waterfall depths, that would bring him out down around here. With seasonably high water flow, the current would have pushed him farther south on this path than it would in dryer seasons. It would have carried him down the second set of falls, and then left him near the Forest of Idin," he stated, drawing his finger over the lines as he spoke.

"However, your friend has been on the run for quite some time. I've never known someone to survive alone in Neverland for so long, escaping the Pan all this time, no less. He had to have kept his nose to the ground, not gone into any of the villages. As you've learned, strangers are not easily dismissed in Neverland." He offered her a wry smirk.

"You're looking for Wiley?" Her voice was quiet, eyes locked on the maps. Ian nodded, rubbing at the scruff on his face. He'd have to find the time to shave it soon; it was itching madly. He had intended to upon waking, but the maps would not relinquish their hold on his current obsession.

"So we find ourselves faced with the question: has he been on the move this entire time, or did he hunker down near the falls? I sent men to scout about the area after you told me of the possibility of him having Arrived. They found no trace of him. I would venture to guess he did not stray far from the falls, perhaps until recently. But I have no way of knowing. All this time, we've uncovered no trace of his having been in Neverland. Either he is very good at hiding, or the land is helping him for some reason. Or perhaps, just foiling us. That seems more likely." Frowning, he readjusted his eyepatch. The cursed thing seemed to bother him of late.

"I've been staring at these maps, hoping to follow this line of thought in an effort to triangulate an area of search for where Pan's lair might be, but I'm afraid we are just as lost as before; there is simply not enough information. The Fiend's lair remains as elusive as ever," he growled, roughly shuffling through the maps once more.

"We've searched to the south in Dead Man's Noose a hundred times," he pointed to the rocky barrens of land that covered half of Neverland, "across the expanses both south and north to Fearsome's Peak and Traverse's Peril. Cannibal's Cove is difficult to search as the Sirens prefer that area, and I've lost far too many good men to them to attempt it again. However, the Mers loyal to our cause assure us there is no sign of Pan being under the water, or in the Cove. "

"To the East we have Mermaid Lagoon and Saint's Mire." He poked the bog in disgust. It was definitely one of his least favorite places. "The Natives of Indian Camp to the northwest won't allow us on their sacred ground, much less the Pan. They protect it fiercely. Aside from Sanctuary, it is the only place free of Pan's taint. I have no doubts of it staying that way." His gaze moved to the mountains in the center of the island.

"This is where we are, deep within these mountains. Pan's not here. That much I know. I suppose there are patches toward the east we have yet to cover, though I find it doubtful either of them could slip beneath our notice so close to home…" He paused, glancing out the window. "We'll search them either way. Now that the passage of time has returned to normal, it will be safer questing for longer jaunts during the daylight hours." It was then he realized Easton was no longer looking at the maps. Her attention was focused solely on him.

"You're looking for Wi? You've been looking for him this whole time, not just the times we managed to search together?" She sounded bemused and surprised. Ian blinked. Hadn't he already mentioned he had? She must still be half asleep, if she missed the entire point of their current discussion.

"I promised I would continue to search for your Wiley, little butterfly," he reminded her.

"You did," she agreed, though her voice held none of its power, escaping as only a ghost of its usual tone. Understanding dawned.

"You did not believe me." He ignored the underlying inclination of hurt, kept it from his voice. Neither of them were strangers to the delicate nature of trust. He had no right to be offended over her lack of it, when it came to such a large matter of the heart. Trust would continue to grow with time.

"I... you never mentioned your searches in the past. And when I asked you earlier, you just sounded so final. Like there was no hope at all for Wiley, so why bother continuing to search," she whispered again, moving opposite of him to sit on the desk.

"I told you from the beginning that we would search for him. And I reassured you of our searching for him after your dream." When she did not reply, Ian stood and slowly approached. Hand and hook placed on either side of the desk at her thighs, he studied her carefully for a moment. "You thought I only spoke calming words to placate you. That I had already long ago abandoned your friend, as well as your heart's desires?"

She stared at her hands in her lap, refusing to look at him. He didn't care for that at all. She had always met his gaze. Stubborn to the bone, even from their first encounters, she'd defiantly stared him down on more than one occasion that would have sent a lesser woman running.

"Easton. Why won't you look at me?"

"I'm embarrassed and ashamed. You've done nothing but help me this whole time, and sacrificed so much for me. I do trust you. Yet, somehow, I still doubted you. It's ridiculous and stupid."

"Easton. Please look at me." His gruff voice was gentle, encouraging. When she finally looked at him, he held her gaze solidly. "You and I are still new to this realm of trust. Our instincts remind us to be cautious, to never get too comfortable. Those instincts have kept us alive, have they not?" She nodded, remaining silent. "Then we can surely give them time to come to terms with allowing others into our circles of trust."

She swallowed, eyes bearing the sheen a woman wore before tears leapt to the surface. Yet she didn't relinquish his gaze again, staring him down. There was his brave little butterfly. He ran a finger down the length of her nose, gently tapping the end of it.

"I respect and adore your passionate fire, Easton. Never feel that you are unable to meet my gaze, nor speak your mind and heart to me. Perhaps you are part of my crew, but you are also my partner in every way now. Your concerns are mine; your pains, mine. And your friends are mine. If there is time left to him, and it is within our ability to find him, we will save Wiley." He leaned closer, thighs touching her knees where they bent over the edge of the desk. "And when I promise you something, beloved one, know that I will keep it until my last breath." Her lips parted as she gazed up at him, nut brown eyes misting further.

"Ian...?"

"Yes?"

"It occurs to me that I never fully paid the debt of my wager to you."

"Your wager?" His tired mind perked up at her breathy tone. "The wager of being able to lift me? We never made any terms on that."

"The wager of the kiss." He froze, gaze dropping to take in the delectable view of her pink lips.

"I seem to recall a chaste pressing of lips to my cheek fulfilling that payment."

"It wasn't enough."

His gaze shifted back to hers, locking down tight, ensuring he understood the meaning behind her words. Her knees pressed outward to the sides, silently beckoning him closer. He eagerly accepted, moving into the new space afforded. He felt it safe to say he understood the line of her thoughts. His heart rate quickened, eager to turn those thoughts to actions. He was rusty, long out of practice, and he was strong enough to admit that he was nervous. But he was also ready, and so very willing, to take their next steps into this impromptu marriage they found themselves in. Because it was Easton who called to his heart, Easton who enraptured his soul, and only Easton who could complete him.

"No," he agreed. "Though with you, wife, I have a feeling it would never be enough. I would always hunger for more."

She closed the few inches of distance left to them, soft lips pressing to his. Warmth rushed past his mouth, spreading to each limb and ounce of his being; she'd unleashed an entirely unexpected inferno raging within his soul.

"Was that enough surprise for you?" she asked, referencing the terms of their wager, her breath coming in small panting puffs against his lips. He shook his head, arm wrapping about her back, though always mindful to keep his hook distant.

"Not enough. Surprise me again." His hand sank into her hair as their lips connected once more, bodies pressing together, every inch of his skin ablaze. Devus, but he'd never felt so alive than in those moments!

A pounding sound shattered the moment. Easton broke away, looking at the door. Hook turned her face back toward him with one finger, reclaiming her lips around her giggle. The pounding came again, louder. Hook sighed, forehead falling against her shoulder as he fought for steady breath and patience alike. He won neither.

"Capt'n?" Smee's questing voice issued through the thick wood.

"Be gone, you black-livered harbinger of ill timing!" Ian growled in reply. Blessed silence followed. Easton's giggling began anew, shoulder bouncing beneath his head. Pulling her closer, Ian nuzzled his nose into the crook of her neck, drawing deeply of her scent.

"That tickles!" She squeaked and squirmed beneath his ministrations. With a roguish grin, Ian added his lips to the torture. Her squeak of protest came louder this time, intermingled with breathless laughter that only encouraged him.

"Capt'n." Smee's voice came again, more insistent than before. The mongrel wasn't going to leave.

"Blast it all to the ocean's depths!" Ian growled, pushing away from his tasty morsel. Wrapping an arm about her waist he pulled her off the desk. "Come wench, we've urgent business to attend, it would seem." She rolled her eyes, that enigmatic smile that never failed to draw him in growing impish.

"Perhaps we shall continue negotiating the wager later, my Captain."

"Perhaps we shall negotiate new ones as well, my minx." He gave her backside a friendly pat as he pulled open the door, once again earning that impish grin. All of his levity deflated in an instant as he saw who stood at the door. Sensing his mood, Easton's grin dimmed as she glanced back and forth between him and their visitor.

"The Mer Prince, Capt'n Hook," Smee intoned uncomfortably. At Smee's side floated the oval-shaped bubble of a Seeing Orb, its form shifting colors of iridescent black. And within its depths reflected the image of a very unimpressed Mer Royal.

"So, it would seem the rumors are true." The Prince ascertained, eyes falling blatantly on Hook's new wife's ring. Easton's eyes narrowed in defiance. She didn't have to know the lay of current relations between him and the Mers to understand the heavy threat that lay in the air. She had always been vastly adept at sensing danger, he had found.

But instead of hiding the ring away, his brave little butterfly narrowed her eyes defiantly, and took hold of Ian's hand. Posture straightening, she just as blatantly staked her claim against the Prince, challenging him to deny her right to be at Ian's side. Thankfully she kept the violent thoughts accumulating in her dark gaze to herself, for now. He prayed that would last, at least until he'd had a moment to temper the situation. As much as he loved her fire, the last thing they needed was a brawl with the Mer Prince.

"Hello, Acquis." Ian sighed, lightly squeezing Easton's hand in reassurance. "Time for a little family reunion, is it?"

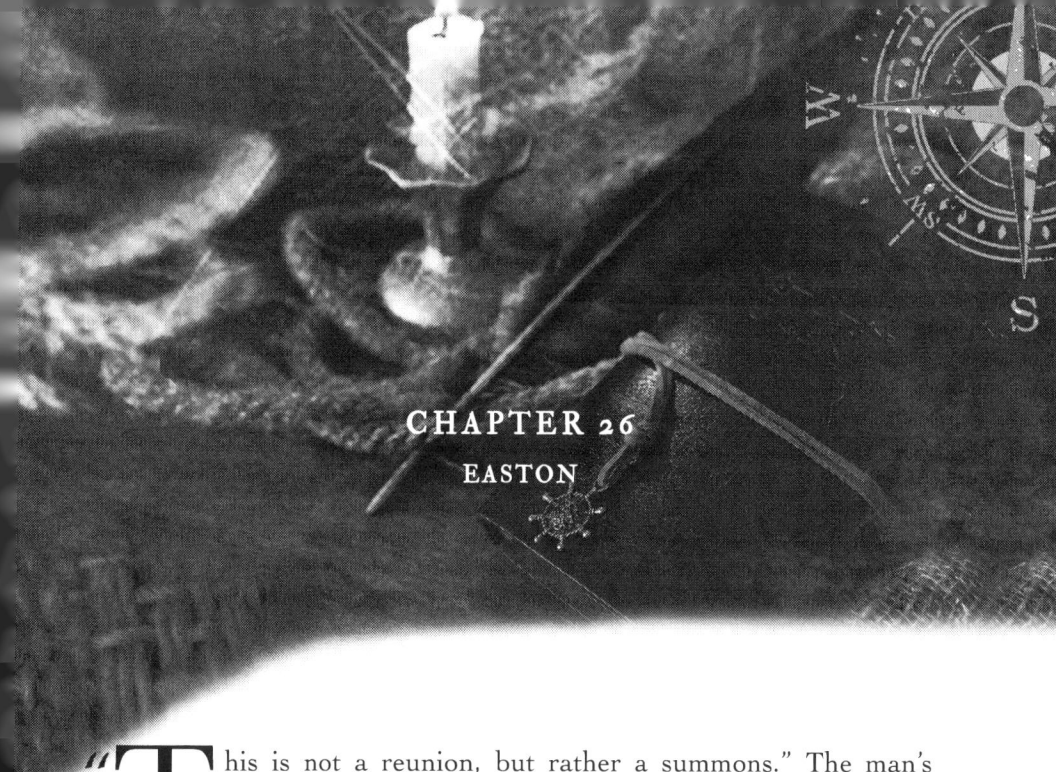

"This is not a reunion, but rather a summons." The man's voice replied in its odd hollow echo from the bubble. Ian's jaw clenched.

"Very well. I will find my way to the Mer realm within the week."

"The summons is immediate and all-encompassing."

Ian went still at her side, and Easton felt her stomach clench. She'd grown accustomed to his body language in their time together; a still Hook was not promising of anything but battle.

"I will go with you, Acquis. But the girl shall stay here. You have no quarrel with her; she has broken no laws," Ian stated firmly, though he managed to maintain that ever diplomatic tone she thought would have served him well in his life before becoming a Hook. Something the man before them could certainly use more of. The contrast between a once-prince and a current prince was rather striking in that moment. The Mer Prince's lip curled as he assessed her from the top of her red head, to the tips of her bare toes. Clearly he wasn't impressed so much as he was disgusted.

Since she had no idea how these bubble things worked E couldn't say if the image reflected was a true-to-life size or not. But from the reflection, the Mer was at a similar height to Smee, though more on the thin side. Perhaps that leanness carried some amount of muscle, but it was hard to tell beneath the flowing bulky robes he wore. Long blond hair fell to his waist, and she noticed with some surprise, his nails were long and curved like blue talons. His yellow eyes were the most captivating thing about him. Otherworldly as they were, they were a striking shade and complimented his angular face well. Too bad he had to open his mouth and prove himself to be a jerk.

"You have one touched of the Fiend living freely in your midst, and taken her as your wife no less. Her very existence breaks the rules of nature, and our laws," he stated bluntly. "She is to be judged by trial just as surely as you." Ian's jaw clenched at the Prince's harsh words, but surprisingly, he didn't say a word. So E did it for him.

"Judged?" she scowled. "What business is it of yours who I am or who he marries?" Ian squeezed her hand, this time in silent warning. She ignored it.

"Obviously I'm new around here and don't know all the in's and out's of the politics. I'm an outsider, fine, whatever, I get it. But to my knowledge, the Mers don't control Sanctuary, much less have a place in judgement of the inhabitants within it. The people have accepted me in Sanctuary, I don't see any reason why your opinion should matter."

Ian released an almost inaudible sigh. She sent him a sidelong look, only to be met with a long-suffering expression. Maybe she should have kept her mouth shut, as Ian's expression clearly concurred. But her temper was stoked and for some reason she was having a difficult time reeling it in.

"Have you nothing to say to such willfully obnoxious behavior, Octavian of the Bendal Isles, last of the Hook? Should the wife of a Hook and Mer Royal not show more common sense? Should she not hold respectful silence?"

"Should a wife not betray her husband and all of his brethren to her sworn enemy, leading to their deaths, simply because she did not get her way?" Easton shot back smoothly. This time, Ian's groan was anything but silent. The groan swiftly shifted into that mad sort of laugh, one not unlike his laughter in the face of death. That didn't bode well.

"Acquis, my old friend, perhaps you should rethink bringing her down to the Pearl Cities. You'll find she is not easily intimidated," Ian grinned.

"Intimidating her has nothing to do with justice and judgement. She will attend, and she will be judged. We will know of her guilt, and we will punish it accordingly. Old *friend*."

E didn't care for the twist Acquis had put on that last word. Obviously the Prince was holding a fierce grudge against her husband. She also didn't care for his 'guilty until proven guiltier' mindset. She was tempted to throat chop him. It might be entertaining to see how the pampered prince dealt with a scrunched-up trachea. Even sprouting gills wouldn't do him much good then.

As though sensing her train of thought, Ian gave her hand a slight tug, carefully pulling it behind his back, their linked hands serving as a leash of sorts. It would seem he knew her thoughts all too well. Okay, so she wouldn't actually throat chop the Mer. She had that much control of herself. Not to mention the fact that he was just a reflection of himself, and not physically there. So no, she wouldn't throat chop him…yet. But she didn't have to shut up either. How was that for diplomacy?

"I have nothing to hide. I've passed Sanctuary's tests already."

"Oh I'm quite certain that you did. However, we Mers have our own form of truth telling. One that cannot be wrongfully passed." He grinned maliciously at Ian, producing a mouthful of sharp pointed teeth. That was just wrong and creepy-looking on someone who, for all intents and purposes, looked like a regular human.

"That won't be necessary, Acquis." Finally Ian broke his complacent silence, tone gone deathly calm, a sure indicator that he was on the verge of gutting someone himself.

"Either she faces judgement amongst our people, or I carry out judgement here and now.

"You could certainly try." The grin on Hook's face wasn't fooling anyone, especially E. Maybe throat chopping was frowned on, but E was pretty sure that gutting the Mer prince would likely be considered a lot worse. E was the one who squeezed Ian's hand in warning this time, speaking before the Mer could.

"I have nothing to hide. If the Mers have to rely on their own form of tests rather than trusting the good people of Sanctuary, then so be it." She turned her gaze back to the prince, "I have no reason to be afraid."

"You have yet to meet my people."

A sinister curve curled the Mer's lips, leaving him to look like that hungry shark again. Still the same, no matter how creepy he was, E didn't back down to anyone. She'd dealt with his type her whole life, and he stirred the same reaction within her as they always had in the past: defiance. Taking a step forward, she held his gaze, eyes glowering up at him in challenge.

"It doesn't matter. I'll do whatever it takes. I've proven myself time and again in life, and I will continue to prove myself until my dying breath. My place is at Hook's side. No one will stand in the way of that. No one. Got that, Legolas?"

Ian choked in his efforts to stifle the mad laugh once more. E's mind scrambled. Obviously no one in Neverland knew the Lord of the Rings reference to the elven archer; she had said it more for her own rebellious entertainment than anything. So what the crap was Ian laughing all crazy about now? The prince huffed, face shifting from what seemed to be a natural, very faint pale green, to a deep mottled moss. She took that to mean he was pretty miffed. She held her ground, though inside she was wondering if she'd taken things a bit far.

"We leave within the half-hour! Meet at the water gate." Acquis growled, before spinning on his heel and stalking away into the depths of reflection until it disappeared.

"Ensure the crew is prepped, if you please, Mr. Smee."

Smee, who had been stunned to silence throughout the conversation, nodded and quickly moved to carry out the command. Ian slowly shut the door, leaning his forehead on it.

"So… how much trouble did my big mouth just land us in?" she ventured carefully, not sure what to expect from him. She'd never seen him so silent for such a long time. And now that the infuriating Mer-tuna was gone, she felt her frustrations wither away, seeping from her, leaving her muscles oddly weak.

And then, Hook's mad little laugh was back. Turning, he leaned against the door and laughed and laughed.

"That bad, huh?" she winced.

Still grinning, Ian pushed away from the door and slunk closer. Sifting his fingers through the hair at the side of her face, he pulled her in for a slow deep kiss. The kind that made your toes tingle, and stole the breath from your lungs, yet left you begging for more of the sweet torture. Pulling away, Ian leaned his forehead against hers.

"You beautiful, fiery, daft little thing," he chuckled. "What were you thinking?"

"I couldn't help it. He made me mad. I hated the way he was treating us. He was a complete jerk to you, and he's got no place judging me." She sighed heavily, frowning. "I usually keep better control of my temper. He got under my skin somehow. The big jerk." His grin softened, thumb running across the lower lip she hadn't even realized popped out in a pouty angle.

"You are still unaware of so much of Neverland's workings; you seem so natural here that I forget that at times. Allow me to fill you in." Ian gazed down at her, all seriousness now. "You always have the right to defend yourself, and I will stand by your side. Yet, given the situation, it might have been wiser to keep your mouth still, my dear. Speaking back to a Mer Royal is dangerous on a good day. But calling him a Legolas? Where did you even learn such a word? It can't have been from one of my men, they don't have such a death wish."

"Where I come from, Legolas is an elven archer in a story."

"Is he quite hideous?" The corners of his mouth kicked up a notch.

"No, actually, a lot of women think he's pretty hot stuff. Personally I think he's a bit on the feminine and prissy side. Not my cup of tea."

"He's no James T, then?" her cheeks flushed, remembering her light-bound admission to Hook being her cup of tea.

"No. He's no Octavian R, either." He pressed a kiss to her forehead.

"The one and only." He murmured before pulling away with a

wry grin. "Well, you'll be pleased to know that you just called the Mer Prince, in his own language no less, a pregnant sea cow."

"Oh. Yikes."

"Yes." He grinned crookedly.

"Well, he's hardly the first person I've ever called a sea cow."

"I see. This is a typical slanderous phrase of yours, is it?"

"I've been known to use it now and then. Usually it's a 'fat sea cow'. I had no idea I'd figured out how to bridge language barriers and upgrade people from fat to pregnant. Especially men."

"Hmm, must be a latent talent of yours, I suppose." Hook smirked down at her, managing to capture the humor of the moment, while still giving her a silent caution.

"Okay, I can see how that would be bad." She nibbled her lip. "But come on, really. Who did he think he was, anyways? He doesn't have any right to come stomping in here demanding we follow him around. Or was I wrong about that, too?"

"No. The Mers have no command within the Sanctuary laws, they aren't even allowed knowledge of where Sanctuary is. Thus his use of the seeing glass. We can't trust them enough to share such knowledge." Her shoulders relaxed, a smile lifting her lips. "However, when I wed Avida, I became a member of the Mer society. With her death, nothing changed. I may have been free to choose to live apart from them, but I still must abide within their laws. And when you wed me…"

"I got tossed onto the Mer welcome wagon too."

"Perhaps you should try to enjoy the ride, and stop sticking our legs in the wagon wheels as we go." He winked, moving toward where their weapons belts hung on the end of the bed.

"Got it." She bit her lip as she watched him belt on his swords and other items. "Are you sure you're not mad at me? I wouldn't blame you. I just couldn't keep my mouth shut. Usually I'm better at that." He lifted a brow at her. "Okay. Sometimes I'm better at it. This wasn't one of those moments, obviously." Shaking his head, Ian began buckling her weapons in place about her hips.

"I'm not angry with you, little butterfly. As I said, you always have the right to defend yourself, and I will always support you.

Besides, it wasn't entirely your fault. Mers have a way about them. They elicit the deepest passions of those around them; if you are not prepared for it, they can have you murderously angry, or crying under the bed. Considering the situation, I think you did rather well."

"Really? Even through a mirror?"

"Aye."

"Do they do that on purpose?"

"Mer Folk are creatures of a twisted nature. Within them lies a darkness, one that demands mischief. Yet, they also have a side within that yearns to do good; to do what is right and helpful. Through time, they have sought to overcome that darkness, to align with the lighter side that yearns to do good. Some are better at it than others. Some must fight themselves, to keep the dark pull from surfacing and taking whatever they want from others. The Sirens never wanted to align with their goodness; they loved mischief too much. You can see how Pan pulled them to his side."

Ian knelt to tie the stay strings that would hold her dagger sheaths in place against her thighs.

"Not all have the strength to use this gift as they will. Acquis holds a small amount of that strength, and I think it fairly likely he was using it against you. I certainly felt him trying it on me. I've had years to build an immunity to it, however. Given your sharp, keen-witted responses that cut to the bone, I feel it likely that he will exercise that gift much more often on you now."

"Oh. Great."

"And, there are others who are more adept at it. I'm certain we will meet them within the City as well. You have a fiery glow about you that shouts willingness to battle."

"All part of my charming personality, I suppose."

"Indeed. Just try to focus on the matters at hand, detach yourself from emotion the best you can. I'll be at your side the whole way."

"Care to share what kinds of tests we will be up against."

"Not particularly. There will be time for that later. I don't quite have the stomach for it at the moment."

"Understood. One more question?"

"Of course." The grin in his voice said he expected no less.

"Was Avida a princess?" Ian froze, hands stilling on her thighs. "I just realized Acquis said 'the wife of a Mer Royal should know better'. So, I'm guessing that means Avida was a princess, and therefore likely also his sister. Am I right?"

"Yes." Ian murmured.

"Which means my remark about her less than stellar final actions in life probably made things a hundred times worse for us." Ian looked up at her with mischief in his seafoam gaze.

"You certainly know how to make a first impression, dear one." E sunk her hands into his hair, cradling his head against her chest. He wrapped his arms about her, hugging her close, sharing a silent moment packed full of the knowledge of dangers to come.

"Well, we like a challenge, you and I. We'd get bored otherwise." She whispered. He nodded against her.

"Mm, very true." His voice held a sleepy purring quality to it, and she grinned, knowing he was thoroughly enjoying his current position.

"Shouldn't we be getting ready?" She asked, though truthfully she'd rather keep him exactly as he was. Would rather ignore the upcoming challenges that just might see them dead, again. They seemed to run into a lot of those lately.

"We don't take anything with us, only our weapons. We only take those to safeguard us until we reach our destination. Once within the gates of the Pearl City, we must relinquish them to the Royal Guard."

"Of course. They wouldn't want us making tuna dinner, after all." Ian pulled away to grin up at her.

"You are trouble, wife. But I wouldn't have you any other way. I'm sure that makes me quite mad, but it is what it is."

"Any other last-minute advice, other than keep my mouth shut and temper in check?" Standing, Ian tucked her hair behind her ear.

"Remember that in the Mer form, your thoughts are projected to all. If you wish to speak privately to me, we must be touching, and you must concentrate on only me. With time, our connection through the ring will grow to the point that we can speak to one another without touching. Otherwise, don't be surprised if everyone in the city knows what you are thinking."

"That would suck. So I probably shouldn't be thinking about how I wanted to turn them into my dinner?"

"Probably not" he grinned. She took a step closer. "Or how I insulted their prince?"

"Definitely not." She leaned into him, playing with the strings that secured his shirt.

"And, considering your history with their princess, I should probably not think about the way I feel when you touch me?"

"Debatable." He swept the hair over her shoulder, then ran his fingers gently down her spine, leaving a trail of searing goosebumps in their wake. "You're my wife. I think it is only expected that you know pleasure in my touch." A glimmer took residence in his eye. "Besides, I'm a Hook. I think it fair to assume they already know of the power of my skills."

"Right, how could I forget? Rumors of the Hook's seductive prowess and all," she grinned.

"However, they won't know the prowess of the vermillion butterfly. I shall have to guard my thoughts carefully as well, or I'll not be able to guard your virtues from the others."

"Then I suppose it's a good thing you don't know any of my more intimate virtues yet," she teased.

"No. But I can imagine, until I do." His gruff voice growled softly in an entirely enticing way, fingers flexing against her back.

"Oh?" she suddenly felt breathless, staring up into his eye. "You're very confident."

"I have a remarkable imagination." His gaze roved over her. "I've drunken in your form often enough that I feel I could correctly envision much. Though in none of its full beauty. I pray I one day get to uncover the perfection beneath what only my imagination has touched." E swallowed, hands slipping upward from the strings, wrapping about his neck to hold him closer.

"Maybe we should give you some more detailed information for them to hear, then." Ian groaned, forehead falling to hers.

"You'll be the end of me, woman."

"Only if I can promise a new beginning afterward," she promised. He pulled away, staring down into her eyes as though she'd just said something profound.

"You're a vision, do you know this?" His fingers slid through her hair. "I never thought to love this coloring. Never in my existence did I imagine I would think so fondly of it." He wrapped a thick length of strands about his fist, lifting it to caress his still scruffy cheek with it. "Now, I find my world would be so dark and void without your fire." He held her gaze, locking it down.

"We must come out of this alive, little butterfly. Neverland relies on my hook as its one chance of survival. It depends on you as well. We may not know your role in the matter as of yet, but all shall be lost without you, I am certain of this. *I* shall be lost without you. No matter what comes to meet us below the waters, you must survive for me, wife. I feel I would be quite irrevocably destroyed if you were to be taken now. You've managed to slip your way into my soul, Easton Bendal. See to it you stay."

"We're a team, you and I. The fates declared it. This is just an… underwater vacation of sorts. We're not going to be separated. We have too much to do. Together."

"You've made a promise now. As have I."

"And you always keep your promise. As your wife, so do I."

"Good." He pressed another kiss to her forehead, then stepped back. "Now, sentimentalities aside. Our time is nearly at an end and we must do something about your hair. We'll be passing through the villages in order to gain entrance to the Mer path."

E nodded, not eager to pass through the villages without her hair's disguise in place. E had once asked Hook why they didn't simply move all the people of Neverland within Sanctuary. Aside from the fact that there wouldn't be enough room, nor food and water, Ian pointed out their very different mindsets.

The people had first chosen to stay, declining to leave the homes they had fought so hard to build. But after living in the lands tainted by Pan for so long, by the hardships of their lives, the people had changed. They'd become a harder, single-minded and cruel lot, violent and suspicious. It was often that people ended up bludgeoned, or some other barbaric form of death, simply because the villagers found them guilty of the taint of Pan, or some other horrible sin in their eyes. Hook was understandably hesitant to bring such mentality within the comfortable and calm environment of the Sanctuary. E was particularly grateful for such a decision. The villagers didn't so much as bat an eye at her when she and the crew walked by. However, if they saw the true nature of her hair, if they saw her without her men's clothes on? She'd be strung up immediately. Or worse. They'd certainly try, anyway.

Instructions were left with the crew, and they were ready to be on their way within twenty minutes. Still, they waited for another forty minutes, loitering about for seemingly no reason. E didn't say a word, trusting Ian's lead. If he wanted to be late, they'd be late. She soon understood why they waited so long, however. Tromping through the forest for only five minutes, it wasn't long before they heard the sound of whirling water.

"What's that?" she asked in a hushed voice.

"The Mer gate," he replied just as quietly, both of their senses on alert.

"The gate to the Mers is so close to Sanctuary?" She glanced at him sharply, alarm growing.

"It is. Keep your friends close…" He shrugged.

"The rest of that saying back home finishes with 'and your enemies closer'."

"It is the same here as well," he acquiesced.

"Then since they don't know where Sanctuary is, I'm assuming you aren't entirely sure of the Mers loyalty."

"It is why we waited until nearly the full hour elapsed before setting out."

"Because you don't want it to be obvious how closer we are."

"Sadly, I've learned to never fully trust anyone , Vermillion. Even those closest to me."

He kept his gaze straight forward, but she felt the weight of those words. She took a moment to ponder them, to see if they stung. They didn't. She understood all too well. And felt he was wise to feel that way, considering she didn't fully trust herself either. He allowed her far more trust than she deserved given the circumstances of her birth, and she would gladly take it. Once the Pan was gone, his heart could be free of doubt. She would eagerly continue to earn it.

Entering a small clearing, they found the Mer Prince impatiently waiting. Acquis took one look at her hair and sneered.

"I see your hair changed color."

"Actually, I'm perfectly happy with who I am and how I look. This is more for the benefit of those who can't handle it." She added a bit of pity to her voice, lip pouting slightly in 'concern' for him.

"Such levity. We shall see how much of that remains when you are leagues below the surface. No amount of dusting will conceal your true coloring there."

Ian tensed at her side and she could feel his gaze on her, his jaw clenching in efforts of silence. E's mouth opened to reply with another snarky remark when she realized she was being baited by whatever sway the Mer held on her emotions.

Armed with knowledge, she fought the urge, pushing down the emotions that swelled within, the ones that demanded verbal and, quite possibly physical, retribution. With much effort, E clamped her mouth shut, leaving only a polite grin. Acquis scowled, then spun on his heel and headed for the pool of water. Ian grinned proudly, giving her backside one of his friendly pats.

"Well done, little butterfly," he whispered with a wink. "Our legs are *mostly* free of the wheels after that one." E allowed herself a proud grin, too, trying to ignore the butterflies Hook's proud grin and newly favored butt pats set scuttling about in her stomach.

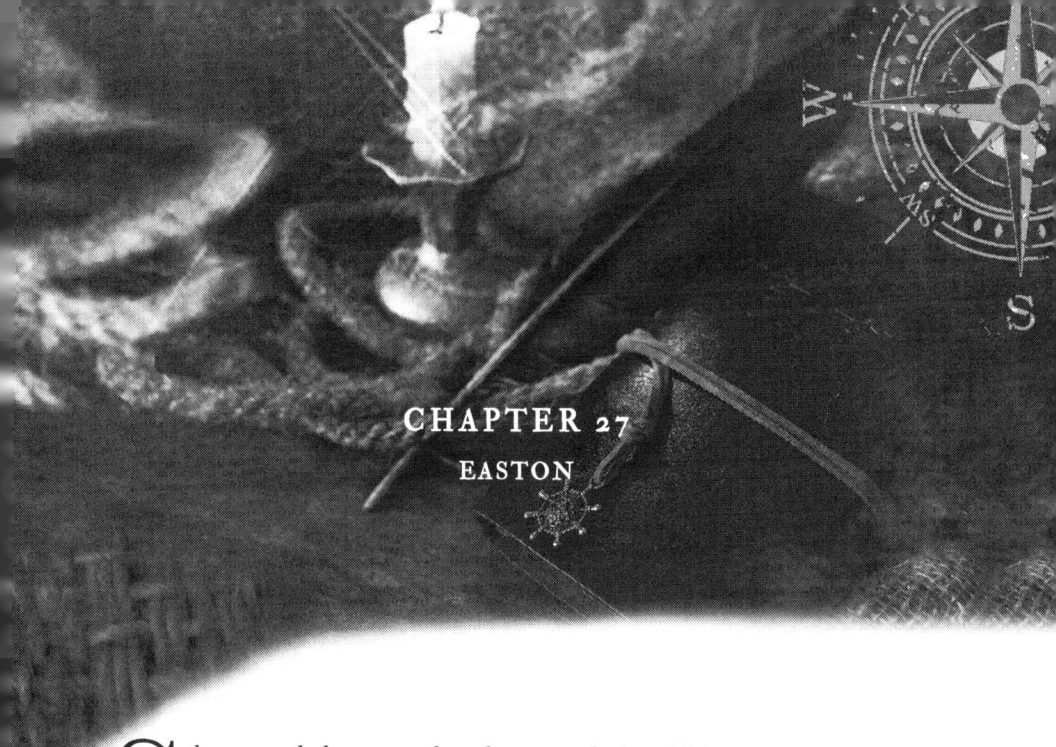

She stared down at the churning hole of black water ten feet away from her toes. Apparently this was the gateway to the Mer Path. It looked more like the gateway to Hell. Which, in their case, just might be true.

"Is that fear I see in your eyes, Fiendling?"

E's eyes rolled heavenward as Acquis approached. It was hard resisting the urge to poke the Mer with her dagger, but she promised herself she'd keep getting better as the moments passed. She could tell that Ian was pleased with her when she merely smiled sweetly back.

"Not at all. It looks quite charming."

"Then by all means, be the first to enter." He grinned, flashing those unsettling chompers.

"Is that not the calling of a prince? To lead his people?" Hook stepped closer, carefully wedging his shoulder between the two of them. He might have trusted her to not stab the Mer, but he clearly didn't trust Acquis.

"*You* are not my people," the Mer prince hissed. "And I plan to see to it your blight on our people will be dissolved by the trial's end." His gaze shifted to E. "And you'll be the first to taste of my judgement."

"Gross. No thanks." The words escaped her on a scoff of disgust. She only felt a little bad about that one.

"Such disdain for your betters. Clearly Hook does nothing to temper your unsightly spirit."

"I do not, and never will, have the desire to temper her in the least. She is my wife, not my slave," Ian stated firmly, hand resting atop his sword. Acquis' eyes followed the movement, a chilling laugh issuing from his lips.

"Still playing the valiant protector. But when judgement comes, you'll not save her again. No amount of your potion will protect her this time."

"You've been watching me." Ian's voice garnered its deathly still quality and Easton tensed, readying herself for a fight.

"I promised I would, all those years ago. Or have you forgotten?" Acquis hissed, skin shifting back to that dark green.

"I haven't. Yet you seem to have forgotten my warning to do so at your own peril."

"So, let us finish now what we started then, Hook." Acquis held his hands to the sides, sharp nails glinting in the light, shoulders hunching. Ian held perfectly still, but she knew he was poised to act on a split second's notice, he always was. E placed a hand on his shoulder.

"Let's just go in there and get this over with," she whispered, pressing closer to his arm.

"Do not wish to see your protector destroyed, Fiendling?"

"I have no concerns about him dying. Hook is formidable and the best fighter I've seen. I simply have no wish to watch a fish flopping on dry land, dying. I've got more important stuff to do."

Acquis lips pulled back into a snarl. A whoosh of water splattered down on them from the whirlpool. E glanced distractedly down at the water, and flinched in surprise.

"Caol!" Hook grinned down at the head that bobbed merrily in the water.

"Hello, old seadog," the Mer chuckled. There could be no doubt as to the good favor that hung between Ian and this Mer. The Merman pushed himself up out of the water, sitting on the edge of the pool. Swiftly the gills on his neck disappeared…as did his tail, the effect leaving behind a very happy, but very naked Merman. E turned away, shaking her head. Well, that answered a question she hadn't even thought to ask about the men of the Mer Folk.

"You can turn now, Treasured One."

Realizing he must be speaking to her, E turned back. He'd donned some sort of bulky robe much like Acquis', producing it from a waterproof bag he carried along. The smile that beamed down at her shone through a pair of dimples deep enough to get lost in. Aqua blue eyes glimmered with humor, a good match for the deep blue hair that hung in a long braid to his waist. He stepped close, carefully taking her hand in a golden-nailed grasp. Placing a kiss on her skin, he leaned back with a wink. Either this dude had no idea she was a 'Fiendling', as Acquis liked to call her, or he simply didn't hold the same prejudices.

"Who is this sweet morsel, Prince of the Isles? A gift for me?"

"Afraid not. You're slobbering on my wife," Ian chuckled. Caol's brow lifted in surprise and a whole lot of curiosity. Walking a circle about her, he lifted a few strands of her hair, nodding.

"Ah, I see, you've disguised the color. Good thinking, Hook." He winked over her shoulder. "You've always been a thinker."

"It was actually her idea," Ian grinned roguishly.

"Forgive me, my lady." Caol bowed deeply to her, donning his own roguish grin. She could see how Ian and Caol were such good friends. They were both mischievous knuckleheads. She had a feeling she was going to like Caol. All three of them turned toward the disgruntled throat clearing of the Mer prince.

"You are aware then, that you are happily cavorting with a Fiendling, Caol?"

"Don't get mud in your gills, Acquis. She is our brother's woman." Caol frowned, seemingly not intimidated by the surly prince.

"He is no brother of mine. And she is a Fiendling, touched of the Pan so much that her whole head bears a striking resemblance to the Pan himself."

"Keep saying his name and he'll show up to hold this conversation with us, Acquis," Ian warned darkly. Acquis ignored Ian, turning his ire on the newcomer.

"What are you doing here, Caol?"

"It seems the council didn't trust you, dear Prince. Upon returning from my guard duties at the ridge of the sea, I found quite a surprise. I was told that *I* was meant to accompany these two back to the cities with diplomatic intent. Not you."

"She is to be judged!" Acquis seethed.

"She is to be brought before the council to ascertain if a threat resides within her. If not, we are to congratulate them on their wedding, and properly give welcome to a new sister."

"Congratulations? Have we sunk so low that we align with the tainted? I think not."

"They thought you would have such an outlook. I left with haste the moment I heard you'd run off to bring them in yourself. It would seem such action was wise, considering I happened upon you in the act of challenging the Hook and his bride, daring to declare judgement upon them yourself. Such behavior smacks of disloyalty to the Mer, *my Prince*." The last came out as a sneer.

"As Prince, it is my duty to secure the safety of my people."

"That includes all of its people, Acquis. Including the Hook and his bride."

"We shall see. And I shall speak to the council of your disrespect upon returning, mark my words, Caol," Acquis threatened. With that, he discarded his clothing and dove into the pool, leaving the men fuming and E's stomach churning. These Mers had no grasp on body image issues.

"Selfish tadpole," Caol scoffed, turning his back on the water hole. "Please forgive my brother his stupidity, sister." E blinked up at him.

"Are you and the prince really brothers?"

"We are. Though you'd not think we were spawned together. Avida and Acquis were always closer than they and I," he admitted.

"The three of them were born together," Ian offered, clearing matters.

"Triplets? Wow."

"I'm the fun one," Caol winked. Ian patted him gruffly on the back.

"You have impeccable timing, my friend."

"And you have impeccable taste," Caol grinned, leering at E. "So, brother, where did you find this wonder before us? Did you steal her away from someone else? Please tell me you found a hidden village full of beautiful women?"

"Caol enjoyed visiting the local villages before the Fiend's taint destroyed everything." Ian quirked a brow at her.

"Ah, a ladies man?"

"The dirt dwellers were far more entertaining than the girls below," Caol winked. "Come then, we must away before discovery."

Ian grasped Caol's arm.

"Is it truly necessary for her to accompany us?"

Caol sobered, dropping a hand on Ian's shoulder.

"I am afraid so, brother. You know the laws." Ian sighed, but nodded. Caol turned to E, dimples appearing. "Are you ready to see your second home, sister? There is quite a lot to impress you. Octavian and I can show you much of its wonders during your visitation." E shook her head.

"I wish I had time to see more of it. But I have to hurry back to the surface. A friend of mine is in danger." Caol paused, glancing uncomfortably at Ian.

"I am afraid it will be three days' time before you resurface, sister."

"Three days?" E gasped. "Why so long?"

"It is the timing of the Mer. The council must be gathered, and we must be allowed time to be near you. It is part of the preparation of the trials."

"I'd forgotten the time allowance." Ian sighed, rubbing his eye.

Reaching out to grasp her hand, he looked deeply into her gaze. "The choice is yours, little vermillion butterfly."

E glanced behind her, eyes searching the land in vain. It wasn't as though Wi was going to pop up and say, 'Here I am! We can go see the tuna now.' Even if he did, there would be no way to take him with them. She knew what she must do. Though Ian was giving her a choice, it was one that would only bring both he and Neverland pain.

"If I don't go, if Ian supports me… what would happen?"

"You would be allowed to return to your Sanctuary." Caol hesitated.

"But it will put a rift between the alliance of the Mer and Hook's people," she finished, already knowing the truth, but needing to hear it confirmed.

"Yes. We can be a joyful people, but our laws are a matter upon which we are very stern. Laws are what our people are founded upon, what we live by. I am pained to make you choose responsibilities over your friend's life, but the choice must be made." E's eyes swept the land one more time before she closed them against the burn of threatened tears.

"I'm sorry, Wi," she whispered. Then, turning her back on the land, and for the time being, her dearest friend, E nodded. "Let's go."

"You have a wise mind, little sister." Caol bowed over her hand once more. "Avida would not have chosen so well."

"She didn't." E agreed. Caol winced in regret.

"She didn't. But I feel you will do better for Octavian and the land." He turned toward the water, then paused, casting her a grin. "You'd best cover your eyes, sister. I understand nudity is awkward for the dirt dwellers, unless it is between the sheets. Which would be awkward also, considering you've wed my brother."

"Okay, I get it." E laughed quietly, covering her eyes. When she heard the splash, she peeked from behind her fingers. Caol bobbed in the water, happily pushing the blue hair from his face. Ian rubbed a thumb down the edge of her jaw, drawing her attention.

"If there was another way…"

"It's okay. I understand, Ian." And she did. Life was full of difficult choices, burdened by responsibilities. She couldn't choose herself, or even Wiley, over Neverland and all of its life. She couldn't turn her back on Ian. She squeezed his hand, offering a soft smile.

"Brave butterfly." He murmured, eye reflecting silent respect. His hand dropped to slide the length of her throat. "Remember: when you run out of air, it's okay to breath." She nodded, then turned to the gate. Legs dipping into the water, E resisted the urge to look back once more, and slipped beneath the surface.

CHAPTER 28
EASTON

Breathing water was just as disconcerting as it was last time, Easton decided. Perhaps more so. The first time her lungs were desperate for air, the reaction to suck in was entirely out of her hands. This time, she had known what to expect, and she had made the conscious decision to draw the chill water in. Going against what has been natural your whole life has a way of twisting your mind around on itself. She'd been breathing the water for a good half hour now, and she was still fighting the urge to panic; something that didn't go unnoticed by the two men at her sides. She had planned to use the trip to the Pearl Cities to calm her mind and practice not projecting every single thought, but that wasn't working out so well.

Caol thought it was endlessly entertaining. Her eyes riveted to the Mer as he swam slightly ahead of them. His tail reflected a beautiful sheen of blues, greens and gold as the dim rippling rays of sunlight splayed across his scales with each powerful flick of the fins. The colors and strength of his fishy form were actually pretty cool and more than a little breathtaking. Caol looked back at her with a grin.

"Thank you. I'll let you touch if you're really nice." He tossed a glance Ian's way, who shook his head and grinned.

"Not sharing, Caol. Find your own." E threw her hands to the sides in the water. What would have come out as a groan of frustration, issued from her mouth in a silent gush of water. Even if she ever became accustomed to breathing water, she doubted she would ever become used to the lack of sound from her vocal cords.

"That's so not fair! You guys can privately chit chat all you like, and I'm stuck shouting it to the world."

"You could do the same, if you concentrated, little butterfly."

"Little butterfly. Why do you call her this?" Caol asked, curious.

"Because she flits about with the grace of one, and is brightly colored." Ian teased.

"She certainly is," Caol snagged a handful of her hair where it drifted in the gentle current, *"I heard the stories, but I didn't believe them fully until I saw it myself. Such a striking color. Like the fires of the sun in the palm of your hand."*

"Aren't you worried about what my red hair means, like everyone else?" She watched him curiously, still surprised by his easy-going nature, now that her hair had returned to its red glory.

"I know what it could mean, yes. But I trust my brother Hook more than superstitions." He gave the hair a tug and smiled.

Caol had been fascinated with her hair from the moment she slipped into the water and the coating washed away. He'd scared her half out of her wits when he grabbed hold of it, examining it in the darkness of the cavern they'd dropped into. Being a natural-born Mer, his eyes adjusted instantly. E's took longer. So him grabbing her in the dark like that, she'd all but had a heart attack, kicking out like a mad woman. Lucky for him, the water slowed her movements, so her attack was easily dodged.

They had swum for ten minutes through those black caverns, E holding onto Ian's belt as he led the way. Apparently being part Mer for hundreds of years made your eyes adjust quicker too. It wasn't until they had exited the tunnels that E's eyes were fully adjusted to the darkness.

"How much longer do we need to swim? My arms and legs are about to fall off."

Easton wasn't one for complaining like a wimp, but she was honestly wiped out. Caol looked to Ian, that silent communication shifting between them once more.

"Only if you drag me along for the ride, too. I go where she goes." Ian shook his head. Caol caught her eye and smiled sweetly at her silent frustration.

"Ah, I apologize, little sister. It is our nature to commune so easily between one another. I forget you have yet to attain the talent. I asked Octavian if I was allowed to give you a ride, so that we may swim faster. We are still quite far away from the Pearl Cities. At our rate of progress, it will be many more hours before we reach them."

"Could you drag Ian along too?"

"Of course," he replied modestly.

"Then by all means, grab ahold!"

She held her arms to the side, eagerly waiting for him to grab her anywhere, as long as it meant she didn't have to fight her way through even the gentlest of currents for a while.

"I think perhaps I've found the one thing that puts you in a complacent mood. Next time you get fired up, I'll suggest a swim." Ian chuckled.

"Ha ha" E stuck her tongue out, then wiggled her arms at Caol once more. *"Come on then, fishy brother, help a girl out."*

"Demanding isn't she?" Caol turned to Ian.

"Tell me about it."

E couldn't help enjoying the teasing between the two men, loving the way the 'brothers' bantered with one another. It was fun seeing Ian so relaxed and with his family of sorts. Caol moved forward, wrapping an arm about her waist with a wiggle of his brows. She grinned and shook her head. He was just as friendly with Ian though, also wrapping his arm about his waist and wiggling his brows at him, too. Ian squished his cheeks the way he would a child, then offered him a slow-motion slap. The three of them set off in higher spirits than they had begun.

Caol sprinkled her with stories about the times he and Ian got into trouble together. While Acquis had never taken to Ian, likely because of jealousy for Avida wanting to be around him more than her old best friend, Caol had immediately hit it off with the pirate captain. Considering how similar their personalities were, that fact didn't surprise E at all. She was enjoying the stories so much, her heart lifted so high, that by the time the Pearl Cities came into view, the sight didn't intimidate her as much as she had expected it to.

The cities rose in beautiful golden and pearl spires, glimmering in the oceans depths. The entirety of the huge city was encased in massive ornate gilded cages that clearly served defensive as well as decorative uses. Three other identical cities sat in a squared pattern, all interconnected with more of those ornate caged domes, protecting the throughway connections. *The Little Mermaid* movie had nothing on this city. Caol caught her awed expression and grinned.

"She likes it. You two just might have found a new home."

"It's beautiful. It's so much... more than I expected," she admitted.

"Have you seen many Mer cities, then?"

"Just in the movies," E replied distractedly.

"Movies?" His brow scrunched in confusion.

"Um... stories that are told through little drawn pictures put together in a sequence of events that makes them appear to move and talk. Some movies are made with real people, acting out stories."

'Tell me more of these movies," Caol demanded eagerly, like a child listening to their favorite bedtime story.

"There is one, a drawn picture version, and it's called The Little Mermaid. It's about a girl, a mermaid, with long, flowing red hair, who tries to convince her prince to fall in love with her in three days."

"...is this story about you, little vermillion butterfly?" Ian stared at her in confusion.

"No." She smirked, then paused. Come to think of it, the story did have quite a few similarities when you looked at it in a certain light: red hair, falling for a prince, and three days in an underground city of Merpeople. The thought made her laugh... or at least throw her head back and look like a possessed fish choking on something, more than likely, since no sound issued forth.

"Maybe I'm playing the part of a mermaid right now, but I'm missing the tail and sea shells."

"Sea shells?"

"Yeah, she wears them like… well, like a breast binding." Ian and Caol quickly glanced at one another.

"Similar to yours?" Ian's voice sounded stunned in her mind. She chuckled to herself. Men.

"Well, yeah, pretty close. But with sea shells." The two of them shared a look, at which point Caol's eyes rounded out like saucers.

"I think I should like to see these movies of yours, little sister."

Somehow she doubted the Mer council would appreciate her little story about movies, if Caol was going to go around in a daze like this. Obviously they didn't have anything like that in the Pearl Cities. She glanced at Ian, who still seemed a bit dreamy himself.

His eye shifted to meet hers. A mental image of her bra peeking out of her shirt in the pigmite caverns suddenly popped into her head, sending her blushing again. She now had an idea of what caused Caol's eyes to widen like that earlier. Ian hadn't been joking when he said he needed to be careful to lock down on his mental imaginings of her. She sent him a wry frown in a playful rebuke. He had the decency to blush. It was such a rarity for the man that she couldn't be annoyed with him for the mental projections of her underwear.

Caol released them both, nodding toward the large golden gates at the front of the city.

"It is best you swim under your own power from here. Weakness is not the best of appearances for you during your visit."

E agreed, not wanting to get off to a bad start with these people. Her arms and legs would be sore tomorrow, but for now they had enough power left in them to get her to the gates. They swam forward, halting before the guards at the gates. They bowed to Caol, and greeted Hook well enough. Their eyes froze on her hair, however. She smiled charmingly, and hopefully disarmingly.

"I know. I get that reaction a lot."

The men stared at her a moment longer, before looking back to Caol. Upon his nod of encouragement, the gates slowly opened, bidding them enter. Three Merwomen drifted near the gates, watching their approach. Their chests were covered in a gleam of fish scales that were as natural as the ones on their tails. The scales modestly covered their assets much like a tube top. That explained why the shells idea was so shocking to Caol; unless on land, the mermaids wouldn't even have visible cleavage, much less a need for a bra. She glanced at her somewhat brother-in-law, only to find him eyeing the females with a calculating gaze, as though trying to mentally picture seashells.

The three mermaids moved to stand in line before her. Greeting E first was a beautiful blonde. She leaned forward, wrapping her arms about her in a stiff-armed sort of hug that consisted more of pressing biceps against shoulders, and not encircling her with her arms. The Mermaid quickly moved on to Ian and then Caol, repeating the odd hug. Next came a brown-haired Mer, who pressed a kiss to both cheeks, then her chin and forehead before moving on. E's eyebrow lifted at the odd greetings, but she mentally congratulated herself on receiving such a welcoming reception.

The last girl, one with glistening black hair, approached and E waited to see what kind of greeting this one would hand out. Hand it out she did, both hands coming up toward her quickly, slapping her cheeks in unison. E's eyes flew wide. The girl moved on to do the same to both men, before all three of the girls swam away, whispering excitedly to one another. E stared after them in shock, hands covering her cheeks. Mers moved much quicker in water than she did, because those slaps actually had some force to them. She'd just officially been fish slapped. Caol looked to her with a bright grin, and matching red cheeks.

"Well, now that you've met the welcoming committee, shall I show you to your lodgings?"

Ian smiled at her, grabbing her hand as they swam after Caol.

"That is the Mer way of saying hello. The hug is to wish you strength in your swimming, which is life itself to the Merpeople. Kisses are not a strictly sexual thing here. They are seen as a bonding of family. The father of the forehead, the sisters and brothers of the cheeks, and the mother at the chin. And the

slaps? Those are to bring a rosy color of health and vigor to your countenance. It may or may not also be a sign of sexual attraction amongst the Mers."

"*Slapping means 'I like you'?*" she repeated in stilted confusion. Ian merely winked and led her along. If that was their usual form of a cheerful greeting, E hated to see what an unwelcoming hello from the Mers would have been like.

CHAPTER 29
PAN

The Lost Boys' joyful sounds melted into the distance as his mind turned inward. Closing his eyes, he allowed himself to drift.

Immediately her face was there; her smile a beam of sunlight that pierced his chilled heart with warmth. The blond wisps of hair that he so loved to wrap around his fingers, floating in the breeze as she ran and giggled, daring him to chase her. He could almost feel the silken strands slipping through his fingers now, smell the scent of berries and smoke that always seemed to linger there no matter how long she'd been away from the forge. Tones that played across his ears like the sweetest music, that had been her laughter; enchanting, enticing.

He chased after her in his mind, allowing the faintest smile to grace his lips as she giggled and dodged away from him, lithe on her feet despite the growing babe within her womb. His heart gave a hard twist, eyes burned with traitorous tears. How he missed his Tinkerbell. He wished he could go back, to have held her that night, to keep her safe in his arms so she couldn't have been led to run away from him. To learn to fear and hate him. He ran after her in his mind, desperately trying to do just that. Maybe, if he could just touch her, maybe…

Time slowed as she turned back to him with a smile, golden hair haloing her face as she laughed and reached a hand toward him, beckoning him into the sun with her. He felt a moment of pure joy as his fingertips brushed hers. Her beautiful clear eyes widened in horror, wrinkles flooded her skin as it weathered and sagged, the sun-kissed color washing away to the sallowness of old age.

"No!" He screamed, pulling her close. "Don't!"

She continued to wilt inward, body shrinking, aging in his arms. Her belly flattened into nothing, their babe gone before he could try to protect it. Peter screamed in helpless frustration, clutching her closer, desperate to save her. As she withered away, he grew stronger, pulled her essence within, stealing her joy and happiness for his own. Yet, even knowing it was his touch that caused her suffering, he still couldn't release her. He sobbed, rocking her frail body in his arms.

"Tink. Come back. Please don't go." Her dry cracked lips parted, sunken eyes full of pained accusation.

"Monster!" The whispered words carried the force of a typhoon, crushing his soul.

"No, I'm not a monster, Bell…"

"Monster." Her body burst into a poof of ash, immediately carried away on a gust of wind. He scuttled backward away from the swirling remains of his wife.

"I'm not a monster!" Her words seemed to linger long after the evidence of her demise was scattered. He pressed his hands to his ears and screamed. "I'm not a monster!"

Sudden silence fell, the heavy presence of eyes on him drawing him back to reality. Slowly his eyes opened, and he looked out over the table. His children all watched him carefully, confusion maring their usually joyful faces.

"Father?" Smartybum drifted closer, one wispy hand held outward in concern. He stared at the blackened hand with apprehension. The shadowed bodies of his Lost Boys seemed especially dark and empty tonight. In that moment, he saw them as he had Tinkerbell. Wasted away, sucked into his own soul. He could feel them whirling there now, deep inside. The word monster hovered in the air. Peter took a step back, flinching.

"Father? What's wrong?" More voices joined in, more bodies pressing forward. The word monster echoed always at the edges of their voices. His gaze snagged on the new boy, the suspicious tint in Fink's still solid gaze. Suspicion and still more accusation, distrust. Hatred.

"Enough!" Peter shouted, hands covering his ears once more. He breathed heavily as the silence slowly descended once more, shrouding him. Slowly the shivers racing his skin shifted from fear and self-hatred to anger, malice, revenge; emotions that always protected him from the things that tried to harm him.

"Attention, Boys!" Pan shouted. The boys immediately shifted their misty bodies into upright forms any soldier would be proud of. "I'm going for a fly. When I come back, I want a feast prepared to fit a king!"

The boys hooted in excitement, scrambling past one another to begin preparing. Turning on his heel he ignored the lingering stare of Fink. Shoving past the writhing bodies of pigmites, he ignored them and filled his thoughts with dreams of conquest and gutted cod fish. He closed his eyes as the air lifted him into the dark sky. He'd listen to what the pigmites wanted to tell him later. For now, he needed to fly, to let the wind whip away the nightmares that plagued his waking hours.

"Oh, Peter." Her sorrowful voice drifted across his heart, soft tear-filled eyes flashing in his mind. He quickly shoved it away.

"No, Tink. I'm no monster," he vowed. "You left me, you made me what I am, it's your fault. Your fault! I'll make sure you rue the day you took everything from me. I'll make you sorry. And when you beg to come back to me, I won't let you. I won't!"

With another burst of speed, he flew through the darkness that still felt lighter than his soul.

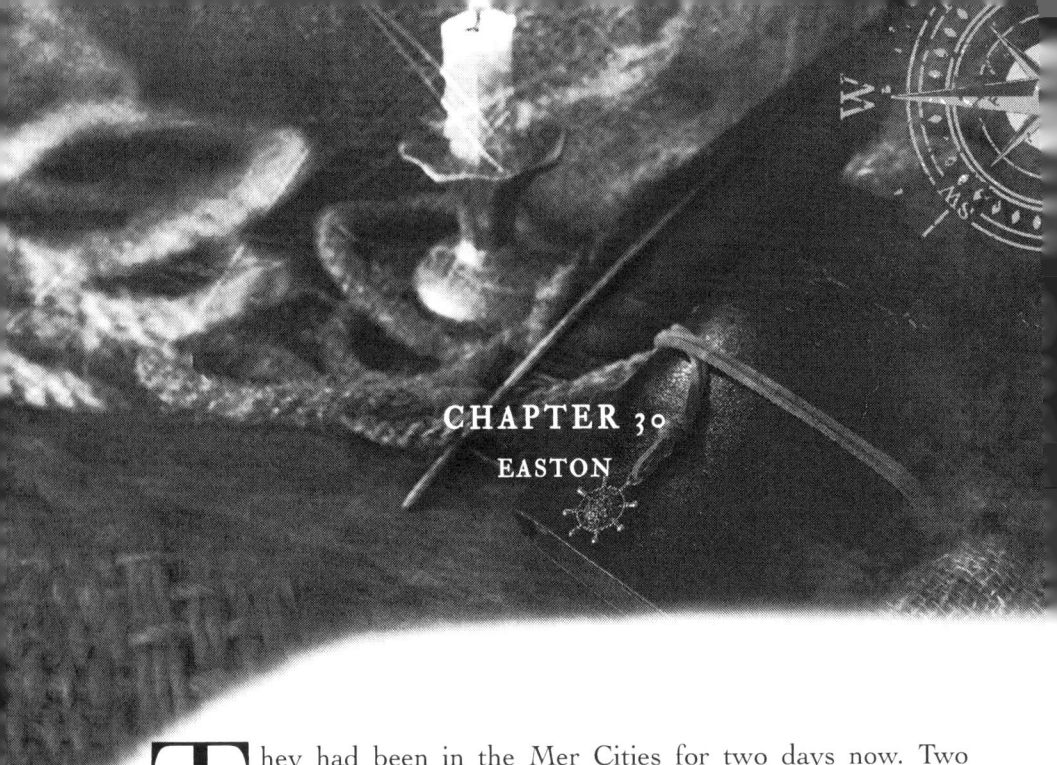

CHAPTER 30
EASTON

They had been in the Mer Cities for two days now. Two days, and she was exhausted. She lay sprawled out on the bed, too tired to move, thinking back. Ian and Caol had shown her up and down pretty much every inch of all four cities. Caol insisted it was part of the trials to come, that the Merpeople had to become acquainted with her, see her on a regular basis, get a feel for her 'aura' of sorts. For the most part, E had felt welcomed. The Mers had watched her with a mixture of curiosity and caution in the beginning. But after being touted about the cities, and then tossed into multiple Mer games, one after another, they began to welcome her with laughter and smiles.

Ian stayed close, fending off some of the more…virile of the race. Apparently 'dirt stompers' were a sought-after commodity amongst the Mermen, now that they had basically gone extinct. Having one come to them was even better than having to go to the surface to find one. The fact that she had the 'Fiendling touch' tainting her didn't seem to faze them overly much. If anything, it seemed to make her a higher commodity, the men vying for the rights of who would be strong enough to tame her. Ian diplomatically reminded them he had already tamed her and claimed her, which made them both laugh; they knew the taming bit wasn't true.

Back home, Merpeople were considered beautiful and fantastical, something of your dreams, movies, or things you read about in romantic books. Seeing them in person was an eye-opener for Easton. They were beautiful alright, but they had a deadly, downright scary side to them. Those teeth could rip out giant chunks of flesh in a heartbeat, and those strong tails could easily break a neck with a single slap. Not to mention their sway over emotion. Caol told her they had to be careful not to indulge in the use of compulsion too much, however, lest they become like their Siren relations.

E found she could appreciate their beauty, yet simultaneously respect their dangerous sides enough to happily keep her distance.

Easton sighed, staring at the sparkling pearl ceiling over her head. Not all of the Mers were appreciative of their presence in the city, however. A portion of them seemed to be of Acquis' mindset. Thankfully they hadn't seen Caol's snotty brother again during their stay, but E could almost feel his angst surrounding them every time they were near other Mer who clearly shared his feelings. Caol confided in them that he feared there would be another 'culling' soon. A battle where those who were partial to Pan's way of thinking were either killed or banned from returning to the Cities. Ian didn't say it aloud, but E knew he was worried about such a prospect. E certainly was. Pan was slowly eating away at their allies, dragging them to his side, building his army while destroying theirs. Things needed to change.

"You look like a creature in the road, flattened by a wagon wheel."

Ian's snarky comment floated to her ears. Turning her head with great effort, she found him leaning in the doorway, arms folded across his chest, the picture of ease and arrogance. She grinned.

"I feel like one, too. I swear, if I have to play one more game of Wave Tumbler or Eel Ball, I'm going to feed myself to a shark." Ian shook his head, moving to the bed. Flopping onto his back at her side, he stared at the ceiling with her.

"Don't do that," he cautioned playfully, moving to wrap his arm around her shoulders. She happily rolled into his embrace, head pillowed on his chest. He placed a kiss atop her head and gave her a comforting squeeze. "No more games. We'll stay in the rest of the evening if you wish, little butterfly."

"Mm, that sounds great." She paused, "That won't offend them though, will it?"

"I think we're safe staying in just this once." She squirmed closer, enjoying the warm humor in his tone. "You've done remarkably well, Easton," he murmured; the hand splayed across her hip gave it a proud squeeze. She smiled sleepily.

"Thank you, Captain." The quietly returned chuckle rocked her gently into slumber.

The fall into dreams was so swift she didn't even register the transition. Suddenly she was sitting at a massive wooden table loaded with food. Rowdy, masculine laughter filled the air. Blinking blearily, trying to orient herself, E looked around. Shadowy figures of boys of all different ages pushed, shoved and pointed, bouncing out of their seats, falling over one another as they roared in laughter. E followed their line of sight, wondering what could possibly be so funny.

In the center of the table, a man knelt chained to the table. Bald head bowed, sobs shaking his naked shoulders, his thin white linen pants soaked up the drinks and food that were thrown at him. Hands chained behind his back held him secured to the table, while a matching chain about his neck leashed him from the front. In such captivity, he was entirely unable to defend himself. The boys continued to laugh and taunt the man as they hurled their food and drinks at him. Then, the chant began.

"Cut it, slay it, eat it! Cut it, slay it, eat it! Slay the dragon!"

Their shadowy fists pounded the table in a drum beat of war. E shuddered, slowly pushing out of her chair, trying not to draw attention to herself. And then, she froze, heart lurching in a sickening jolt. Wiley stood on the other side of the table, and though he was still mostly solid, his outline was a shadowy, blurred hue that hurt her eyes to look at. But most painful, was the wicked contortion of his face, and the huge knife held over his head, aimed directly at the poor soul chained to the table.

"Wiley, no!" E screamed, no longer caring if anyone noticed her presence. She threw herself onto the table, stomping through all of the plates as she rushed to intercede. "Wi, stop!" she continued to scream. Wiley suddenly faltered, blinking as though waking from a dream. He turned toward her, and hope lit in his eyes, a grin blossoming on his previously snarling lips.

"E?" he signed, moving his hands as though he wished to say more.

His grin melted into an expression of sheer horror as he realized his other hand was full. His gaze shifted from the knife to the man on the table. The knife clattered to the table, Wi stumbled away, mouth moving in mute mumblings of denial. The shouts and cheers immediately cut off, silence falling over all present. Wiley's gaze locked to hers, and her heart ached for the pain and fear reflected there.

"Run, Wi, please run!" E begged.

Wi stared at her for a moment longer, then spun on his heel and stumbled away. He disappeared from view as the shadowed figures stepped forward, turning her way with malevolence.

"Someone has entered our sacred hallow, Lost Boys." A taller shadow hissed, black eye sockets searching blindly. For whatever reason, they didn't seem able to see her, but they could definitely sense her.

"Tis a she, Smartybum!" A shorter, plumper shadow leered, sniffing the air. The fact that it could tell she was a girl simply by smelling the air made E queasy. "He doesn't like she's. Might we catch her, to feed her to the Pan?" Other shouts of agreement rose in reply, eager for the hunt.

Content that Wi was for the moment safe, E turned her attention to her own survival. Leaping over the shadowed boys, she sprinted into the dark forest that seemed to entirely surround them. Crashing into the trees, E cut through the night. She had no idea where she was running, instinct for survival alone propelling her. Unearthly howls of excitement filled the night at her back, and E pushed her legs harder, leaping from shadow to shadow.

Then, as dreams were wont to do, reality shifted. E's feet lifted from the ground, propelling her forward with the ease of flight. Her stomach bottomed out, a rush of her own excitement filling the void. The Lost Boys faded into the distance as she flew. She was free. Eventually, despite how exhilarating the sensation of flying was, exhaustion pulled her back to the forest floor. E leaned her back against a large tree, trying desperately to catch her breath, and willing herself to wake.

"Come on E, snap out of it. Dreams are dangerous, remember?" She hissed to herself, shaking out her hands.

Her breath caught as new voices floated her way. As though a marionette on strings, E's feet carried her forward to the edge of the forest, drawn to the voices. Just before the trees gave way, her feet stopped, and E stared in wonder. Two men stood in the clearing beyond. One was Acquis. And the other could be none other than her great-great-however-many-times removed grandfather, Pan.

His red hair was fiery, bright and undeniable. It fell in messy lengths, making it obvious that he was responsible for cutting his own hair, with a dagger most likely. The edgy locks glimmered in the unnatural light that seemed to fill the clearing ahead. Russet-colored eyes sparkled with mischief and a little bit of madness; a captivating mixture. A strong nose, brow, and cheekbones, rounded off with a crooked grin that could snag any heart's attention. The combination of attributes made Peter a striking figure. E understood how Bell had lost her heart to the mischievous man before her.

"I need to see her!" Acquis was demanding. Pan cocked his head to the side and grinned, feet lifting into the air so that he could float with legs crossed beneath him. E felt a tug at her heart, as though something were trying to pull her closer. She ignored it, forced herself to focus. What was Acquis doing here?

"Why?" Pan asked, wearing that same charming, yet oddly childish grin.

"Why must you ask me this accursed question each time I come?" Acquis growled. "You promised me!"

"What promise was that, again?" Pan was toying with the Mer and loving every minute of it.

"You promised she would always be safe with you, that she and I would always be together. Then you let him take her from me!"

"I don't remember actually saying the word 'promise'. If I didn't say the word, it doesn't really count." Pan grinned.

"We made a pact of blood and magic, one that can't be undone! I have kept my end of the bargain. I gave you the key to destroying the Hooks. Avida led you right to them! Now you have to keep your promise!"

"I don't like it when people yell at me. Did you know that?" Pan asked, still cheerful in countenance, though the goosebumps on her arms left her with little doubt of the threat beneath the surface. "It makes me cranky." Acquis immediately mellowed, clearly hearing the threat as well, though his hands clenched at his sides in repressed anger.

"I apologize." It was an apology of grating gravel and broken glass, but it was an apology. E stared in shock. Acquis had been a part of what led to the fall of the Hooks? She blinked, shaking her head. What kind of screwed up dream was this?

"But a pact is a promise, and you must keep it or you lose power," Acquis reminded. Pan's grin faded, feet sinking back to the ground.

"Fine! But my patience on this promise is running out. If you aren't careful, I'll find a way to make sure you and she are always together, within the Rift!"

Acquis paled, wisely keeping his mouth shut. Pan's hands lifted into the air, covering his face. A quiet murmuring began, muffled behind those golden hands. Then, slowly his voice rose and his hands pressed to the side. When the chant was complete, Peter's face glistened with a sheen of sweat, and his shoulders slumped.

"You have until the night falls. Then you don't come back for a long time, understand?"

"Yes, yes." Acquis waved away Pan's demands, distractedly searching the trees. Pan glared, but motioned to the trees behind him.

"Come out, sweet one. Your fish-mouthed brother has come for a visit." Peter's grin was back, clearly enjoying his joke.

A pale figure stepped from the trees, a striking beauty even from this distance. Her waist-length blond hair had streaks of blue running through it, a clear mixture between Acquis and Caol's coloring. The dress she wore sparkled a pale green in the bright lighting. Her face stayed entirely impassive as she approached Acquis, who held his arms out imploringly, a loving expression on his features.

"Avida! How I have missed you!"

Pan scoffed.

"I'll leave you to your sickening displays of affection. One month Acquis, not a moment sooner." Without so much as a backward glance, the Pan disappeared into the black forest. Acquis wrapped his arms about Avida, who flickered under his touch.

"How I wish I could truly hold you," Acquis despaired. The reflection of Ian's once-wife frowned.

"Why do you continue to call me here?" Displeasure practically radiated from her.

"Why should you ask such a question? I miss you. Do you not miss me?" The Mer Prince pressed a hand to his heart as though her words had speared him.

"I tire of this, Acquis. You must stop pulling me to you. You can't have me back. And the fates do not pity those who defy consequence."

"Don't talk so, sister," Acquis pleaded. "You would not be forced to face such a consequence had it not been for that foul Hook..."

Avida's hand shot outward, slashing through Acquis's head in what would have been a searing slap had she been a true physical manifestation of herself. Acquis blinked, stunned as surely as if her true palm had met his skin.

"Never speak thus of Octavian! Never! He is far better a man than you could hope to be, nor I could hope to deserve. You and I are where we are because of our choices. I've accepted mine. You continue to deal with the devil, trying to free yourself in ways that can never be yours now. The Pan can find no happiness of his own, what makes you think he could grace others with it?"

"Avida..."

"No, Acquis. I am done with this world. I am worn through. The

Rift drains me of any peace I may have once hoped for. Bringing me here leaves me in far more agony than if I were left to the Rift alone."

"That can't be true. This is a place of peace…"

"Perhaps, as momentary as it might be. Yet when I return, the agony has increased two-fold what it once was. Countless times you have called me to you, and each time the pain is doubled upon return. Can you not understand the burden you continue to press upon my ravaged soul?"

"I can't believe that," Acquis argued stubbornly.

"As I told you, the Fates do not pity those who defy consequence. Your selfish efforts to see me, to alleviate your own feelings of guilt, they leave me suffering far more than you could ever imagine." She held up a hand to stave off any further argument.

"I have but a short time left to me on this plane. Leave me now, so that I might enjoy this last moment of peace." Acquis opened his mouth to speak, but dejectedly turned away. "And, Acquis," she called after him. "I shall never forgive you if you call me to you again."

"I'll be back soon," he whispered in a hoarse voice before disappearing.

Avida hung her head in despair. And for the first time after hearing of Avida's betrayals, E felt a stirring of sympathy toward the woman, dream or not.

"Step from the trees and join me, wife of that which was once mine." E jerked in surprise, heart lodging in her throat. A sad smile twisted Avida's lips as her eyes immediately locked on E's hiding place. "You have nothing to fear from me. Quickly now, my time is short, and I wish to look upon you." E hesitated a moment longer, then stepped resolutely from the forest, chin held high. Avida's lips twisted into a wry grin.

"Ah, yes, I can see why Octavian is drawn to you. There is fire in your gaze." E slowly walked closer, glancing around uncomfortably as she stood in the middle of such an open and bright area where two of her enemies had stood moments before.

"My ring looks well on you." Avida stared pointedly at Easton's hand. E fought the urge to hide it away.

"How did you know I was here?"

"My ring, of course," she acknowledged. "I'm still bound to it in a way. To Octavian, and now you as well. It is how I pulled you here to this clearing."

"*You* drew me here?" She fought down the moment of panic. "Why? To deliver me to Pan?"

"No. I wished to see my replacement." Avida grinned, flashing her sharp teeth. "And I have much to share with you."

"What could you possibly share with me? You aren't even here. I'm not here. This is all a dream."

"Not true. You and I both are here, in this moment. To the extent in which our souls are capable, that is." Avida frowned. "Pan uses his power to draw a reflection of my soul to this place. I can only exist on this plane for a short time, and it drains the Pan of much of his power. It is why he so dislikes his agreement with Acquis. And you came to this place because your soul is desperately seeking someone."

"Acquis helped you and Pan destroy the Hooks," E accused, ignoring Avida's own accusation. The Princess nodded, eyes distant as she stared over E's head.

"My brother came to me one night. I was sobbing into my pillow as I was wont to do after my visits with Octavian. When Acquis found out that Octavian had cast me aside, he went into a fury. He went to our sworn enemy, the only man who hated Octavian more than he did."

"Pan."

"Yes, Pan. He and Pan formulated a plan. I was told that Pan would imprison the Hooks, send them out of Neverland where they could never return, leaving Octavian free from his pact to be with me. I couldn't see past my youthful emotions. I often struggled with my darker side. Acquis was regularly mired in his own. Caol was the best of us. I often wished I could own his strength." She smiled sadly.

"Alas, I didn't. I was weak. I couldn't see past my own pains and demands. I agreed to the plan. I took Pan to the secret passageway, and allowed him and his shadows within. When the destruction began, I knew I had been led astray; by my brother, by the Pan, and mostly by my own foolish greed. I hid in the shadows, terrified of what I had brought about. When Octavian returned, I threw myself in the path of his hook. I couldn't bear the guilt and sorrows caused by my actions. I couldn't bear the look of disgust I knew would be in his gaze each time he looked at me. So I let him send me where I knew he could never follow."

"And doomed him to live an eternity of guilt and heartache for being the one to send you there. He thinks Pan kidnapped you, he thinks you were lost under his compulsion and threw yourself in his way to protect him," E growled.

"Yes. It was selfish. Though in the end, I have gotten what I deserved." Avida sighed, pushing the hair from her damp eyes. "However just and deserving my pain may be, it is still his pain as well. A pain that he doesn't deserve. This is why I called you to me in your dreams. I wanted, needed, to help."

"Help. Right," E replied stiffly.

"I can see the distrust in your eyes, and I don't think badly of you for it. I earned such distrust." She turned away, ringing her hands. "Existence in the Rift tends to leave a woman with plenty of time to reflect. I have looked upon my errors in life, and I wish to atone for them."

"I don't know that there's any way to atone for causing the deaths of so many, along with the eternal guilt and torment to the soul of another that you supposedly loved," E stated bluntly.

"Yes, I suppose this is true. The Fates are not forgiving, this I know intimately. However, I will do what I can." She turned. "Just as I am still bound to you and Octavian through the rings, I am like-wise connected to Pan." She held up a calming hand, asking for patience.

"There is no need to fear. My connection to the rings simply allows me to feel your emotions, pain, happiness... and love." She studied E closely. Easton didn't flinch away from the word, as she might have once.

"I can feel them, but not interfere. Not until tonight. I poured every ounce of what is left of my power into pulling you here. I'm afraid I don't have much to offer. But as I am connected to the Pan, I can tell you this. Your friend has awoken from the compulsion of Pan. I had nothing to do with that. Your searching soul found him. You reached him under your own power, the power of what I can only assume is inherent in your blood. The blood that gave you the power to walk this dreamscape twice now. You freed him of his unwelcome slumber, and your friend is fighting to escape Pan's lair as we speak. I simply enticed you to this place from there."

"Wi is free?"

"He will be soon. She seems to be helping him."

"She? She who?" Avida ignored E.

"Once he is free, you must find him before others do. You will be his only hope in that moment, as her physical power does not extend beyond Pan's lair."

"*Who* is she?" E pressed. Again she was ignored.

"Save your friend, wife of the Hook. Do not let him become as I did, a slave to the Pan." Giving up on answers to the identity of the mysterious 'she', E pressed on with different questions.

"How much time do I have?"

"Not much, I should think. Pan will be drained from bringing me here, but he will recover quickly, and when he discovers one of his Boys has deserted him, nothing will stand in the way of him seeking retribution."

"I'm stuck underwater right now, with your people. Acquis forced Ian and I here to be judged."

"Acquis, such a fool!" Avida hissed, ringing her hands. "That would explain Octavian's feelings of concern." She paused in thought. "How long have you been amongst my people?"

"Two days."

"Then tomorrow night you will be judged. As Prince, Acquis will hold power in judgement. You must find a way to bring him down. If you can prove his guilt of involvement with the Pan, he will be cast from the Mer, and you will be free. But you must act quickly. There is deception amongst the Mer, not only within the heart of my brother, but also many others who secretly follow his lead. They will cause death and disharmony in my people, in the war. You must move quickly to defeat Acquis, warn my people, and save your friend from the Pan. Otherwise, Acquis will surely cause your deaths, and Neverland will be lost." E bit her lip in uncertainty.

"If you are connected to Pan, what's to say he isn't aware of everything we're talking about?"

"Nothing. I can't feel words through the ring, but I can see hazy images, as well as feel intent and emotion. It is quite likely that he can feel the same. So in this moment, he won't know of what we speak, but he will see your face, your hair, and he will know the intent behind your emotions, through me. I suggest you leave quickly when my time has come to depart."

"Can you tell me how to defeat him?" Avida shook her head, taking a step back, fear evident in her aquamarine eyes.

"I can say nothing more on such matters. Seek her. She alone holds the keys to the destiny of the Vermillion Hook."

"What?"

"She told me you would come; the Vermillion Hook who would own the heart of my husband. I was jealous and angry at the time. Now, I am grateful to you." She paused, wincing, her image flickering. "Oh, my time is near! I can feel the Rift reclaiming me."

"Wait!" E paused, swallowing her prejudices and anger. "I'm not saying I trust you, but… thank you for your help. And, Ian would want to know: is there anything that can be done to ease your suffering?"

The words were bitter in her mouth, so many conflicting emotions battling within her. But she forced them out, because if it meant easing Ian's suffering, E would help to ease Avida's.

"Bring an end to Pan's disease on the land. It is the only way Octavian can be free. Help Octavian, bring him happiness; fill the hole I left in his soul. That is all the comfort I require." Avida grasped her stomach, groaning in pain, falling to her knees. "My time is at an end!"

Tear-soaked eyes lifted to E's, her sad smile back in play. And then she was gone, no final words, no last-minute pleas for forgiveness, or messages to give to Ian. She was just gone. E shivered. It was disturbing how quickly your place in this world could be ripped away from you. E froze as a lock of her hair lifted from behind.

"Hair of such vibrant color…"

E spun, pulling the hair free of her unwelcome visitor's grasp. Peter stood before her, eyes wide. Then a grin twisted his lips, dark mischief twinkling in his gaze.

"Hello, daughter." E screamed and stumbled away. Tripping, she fell backward, the ground swallowing her into blackness.

CHAPTER 31
EASTON

She sat up in the bed, gasping for air, the taste of dirt still in her mouth.

"Easton." Ian's tortured voice came to her from across the room. "You've returned. Are you well?" E turned her head to see Hook pressed into the corner of the wall, eyes glowing red, body curled around his hook in an effort to protect her from himself. Pan's presence must have been excruciating for him this time. Avida was right; the dream hadn't been a dream at all. She moved to leave the bed, but Ian held up a hand.

"Please, I beg of you, keep your distance but a moment longer."

She nodded, sitting back on the bed, allowing him the space he pleaded for. They sat in silence for some time, Ian's mouth pulled into a grimace of pain. E shivered, rubbing at her arms. The Mers had placed them in these rooms because they were built to be free of water in their underwater city. As Ian and Easton weren't true Mers, their skin did not hold up well to the constant contact with the sea water. The magic of the rings only went so far. It could help them breath under water, but it could do nothing to make their skin salt-water friendly for long periods of time.

Apparently the other Mers who took above-water-dwellers to

spouse all lived in housing situations such as this. However, while it was nice to not be submerged in water so often, the rooms tended to be on the cold side. Mers' body temperatures were regulated to the cold temperatures of the sea; they didn't often have to deal with these matters. And being under water, fireplaces were obviously out of the question. As such, they had to rely on other forms of heat.

"I'm going to turn the heat up a bit," E warned Ian, waiting for his affirmative nod before moving to the other side of the room. Grabbing the glass wand off the table, E dipped it into the large tank of water at the center of the rooms. Stirring vigorously, she woke the little red creatures that floated in the tank. They angrily snapped at the glass stick, their bodies bursting into flaming orbs. Instantly the water sizzled, steam rising from the surface, moist heat slowly infusing the room. By the time she sat back on the bed, the room was warmer, and Ian was breathing easier.

"It was bad this time," she stated, already knowing his answer. He nodded, slumping to the floor in exhaustion.

"Yes. It felt as though he were right there in bed with us." His gaze fastened to hers. The sea foam depths sought answers, yet didn't accuse her of anything. "What happened?"

"A lot." She fidgeted on the bed. "I saw Wiley. I saw the Fiend and Acquis." She hesitated. "And I saw Avida." Ian went perfectly still.

"Explain."

Taking a deep breath, E repeated every detail of her dream. She watched him carefully throughout her explanation, especially when she delved into her conversation with his ex-wife. No expressions shifted across his face, his intense gaze never left hers. When she finished, they sat in utter silence for so long, E began to wonder if she should go poke him to see if he had fallen asleep with his eye open.

"Don't get that look in your eye, wench. I'm just thinking," he grumbled, though a small smile quirked his lips.

She sighed internally, grateful to see that smile, as small as it might be. The news hadn't broken him. He pushed to his feet and walked to the washing basin at the glass wall that was currently curtained off from outsiders' eyes. Shrugging out of his shirt, he tossed the material on the floor, then splashed what was undoubtedly frigid water all over himself.

"Ian?" she asked timidly. "What are you thinking?"

"I'm trying to decide where to search for your friend, and what the best way to remove Acquis' head from his shoulders would be."

"I'm working on a plan for the last one," she admitted, pushing up from the bed. "But, I think maybe I should do it alone." Ian turned to her quickly, water dripping from his wet hair, running down his stormy face.

"No."

"Ian, think about it," she pleaded. "We both know that I'm the reason we're here. Aquis wants nothing more than to bring you down. He holds such a soul-deep hatred for you it's poisoned his every thought. He will do whatever he can to destroy you. And I'm the perfect key to your destruction." Ian didn't deny that fact, simply clenched his jaw, staring her down with that ocean-deep eye.

"They've been very welcoming to me so far, but that could easily change. If my blood wasn't enough to condemn me, the fact that I'm about to accuse their prince of treason might be. Neverland needs you. If you go, if you leave me behind, you can still hunt down the Fiend and destroy him. The Mers might separate from your cause because of your leaving before the trial's ending. I know it's a risk. But I think they are more loyal to you than you realize. It's me that they don't trust. If my plan works and the trial doesn't condemn me to death, I'll come back to you. Otherwise..." She took a shaky breath. "If you stay, if my plan fails, we're both dead. End of story, end of Neverland. You should go."

"You would have me leave you alone to face possible death?" She tried to avoid his steely gaze, staring at the door as she hurried on.

"Besides, if you go now, you might be able to save Wiley, too. If you can save him, he might be able to help you find and kill the Fiend..." She trailed off under the heat of his defiant stare, no longer able to avoid it. His jaw clenched, something dark burning in his gaze.

"I'm not going anywhere. I'd sooner tie myself to the bed." He folded his arms across his chest, feet apart in a stubborn stance. "I stay."

"Then you better get to tying, because I'm making the call. Neverland is more important than just one person, remember?" she replied just as stubbornly.

Ian stared at her long and hard, fire burning in his gaze. Without a word, he stalked out of the room. E stood staring at the door, her heart skipping, immediately feeling the weight of his loss. She moved toward the door, hand rising to the handle. She froze like that, knowing she couldn't open that door. She couldn't call him back, beg him to forget the stupid words that just came out of her mouth. She'd said what she did to keep him safe, to keep Neverland safe; and he'd actually listened. She could face the next day without worrying about him. Shaking, E took a step back, then two. Leaning against the wall, hot tears leaked from the corners of her eyes. Whether she was glad he would be safe or not, her heart hurt.

She jumped as the door opened, revealing a very intense, very silent Hook. A thick length of rope coiled about his shoulder. She backed away as he entered and barred the door behind him. He set about uncoiling, then knotting the rope. The tumultuous storm in his sea-colored eye never once left her, hand deftly tying knots by feel alone in the way only a seasoned sailor could.

E wanted to come up with some sassy remark, something, anything to say that would break the thunderous atmosphere that wrapped about her and stoked her insides to a vibrating mess of excitement and intimidation at once. Yet her mouth was frozen shut, unable to utter a single word. Splicing two knotted lengths of the rope, Ian finally broke their battle of gazes long enough to tie the two lengths to the headboard of the bed. Without a word, he plopped down on the bed. Tying first his hook to one side, then placing the extra length of rope in his mouth on the left side, he pulled tight on it, securing that hand too. Her heart stopped as his gaze once more returned to her, stubborn set to his jaw, black storms of defiance rolling off him in waves. He'd tied himself to the bed, just as he'd threatened.

"If I leave, perhaps my body would live. But my soul would die.

Far too long have I gone about daily existence with nothing but a dead soul in a weary body. You brought me back to life, Easton. If you were to leave this existence, my soul would perish an everlasting death and Neverland would follow just as surely. I stay."

Her feet carried her to the bed, and they stood staring at each other for a long moment, wills pulling and pushing at one another in a heated battle. Finally, E moved her attention to his feet. One boot, then the other, thumped to the floor. His socks followed, leaving his feet and calves bare. Ian watched her, stalwart in his refusal to back down, though she could sense both an air of caution and intrigue in the mix. Her fingers lightly trailed down the soft expanse beneath his foot, around the heel, across his ankle.

"If you're going to stay, you might as well be comfortable," she whispered.

A shiver trembled through his muscles as her gaze met his, fingertips skating up his bare calf. Her gaze dipped back down as her fingers met fabric. Taking a deep breath, she continued their progress, trailing them upward, over his knee, up the length of his thigh. Her eyes flickered back to his, at his sharp intake of breath, her fingers shifting over his hip. Swallowing, she took the next leap. His gaze hooded as her fingers came to rest atop the laces of his pants, waiting, asking permission from their Captain.

"Nothing denied."

His voice was quiet, rough like velvet skating the wrong direction over her skin. Her heartbeat rose, pounding in her ears like the pretense to a gale. Licking her lips nervously, she leaned forward and methodically stripped away the laces with her teeth. A low chuckle rumbled in his chest at her teasing so reminiscent of their times in the pigmite cavern.

Digging his heels into the bed, Hook pushed his hips upward. E hooked her fingers in the waistband and slowly tugged them down the lengths of his legs. She fought for control of her heart as the fabric fell to the floor next to his boots. Releasing a shuddering, forti-fying breath, E shed her boots and pants too.

"Fair's fair." She murmured as he drank her in like a man dying of thirst.

E climbed atop the bed, settling between his feet before her courage could flag. Leaning forward, she pressed a reverent kiss at his ankle. The kisses slowly spread, meandering up his calf and thigh. Pausing at the thin scrap of modesty that covered his hips in the form of piratey boxer briefs, she lingered just a little longer with her kisses. Jumping across the fabric hurtle, her lips pressed to the V of muscles on a man's lower stomach that never failed to send girls into a squealing faint of desire. Ian's head fell back against the headboard, eye closed, face screwed up as though in pain.

"Who knew butterfly kisses could be so torturous to a man's heart."

"Should I stop?" she asked quietly, lips hovering above his skin, looking up at him from beneath heavy lashes.

"Only if you wish to kill me, wife," he avowed.

E grinned, pressing another kiss to the heated skin. A mischievous grin of his own quirked his lips. Oh how she loved that roguish gleam in his gaze. The kisses continued across from one side of the V to the other, then back to the center and up toward his bellybutton. Her nose slid around it in a small circle, teasing a shiver out of him that verged on the edge of ticklishness. She grinned, determined to explore that factor later. She graced each of his eight delicious abs with their own kisses as her fingers trailed up his sides. Lips smoothing across his chest, her hands moved up his arms to the ropes, then back down.

Ian lifted his chin, elongating his neck so that she'd have more ground to cover. She could feel how quickly his pulse came against her lips, how quickly his breath came as it rose and fell beneath her chest, until it became a dance, both of them fighting for air. His scruff left her lips tingling as she kissed her way across the dark hairs spread along his jaw. Finally, her lips' journey halted at the corner of his mouth.

"Thank you for staying with me, my Captain." She placed a single, long-lasting kiss there. She could feel the muscles of his body tense as he fought the urge to turn into that kiss, to take away the current power he afforded her in their ever-continuing games.

"Till the end of time and beyond if it be within my power to choose, little butterfly." He promised.

Leaning back on the trembling legs that straddled his waist, she locked into his sea-colored gaze. Arms crossing at her waist, she latched onto the hem of her shirt, and ever so slowly pulled the fabric over her head. His eye grew feverish, and his throat bobbed on a heavy swallow. Leaning forward, E began untying his hook. He tensed, and she glanced down at him, eyes asking for his trust. Like ice thawing before an inferno, his muscles loosened, silently giving her that trust.

E carefully wrapped her shirt about his hook, covering the length with a layer of padding. Shifting to the other side, she untied that hand too. He slowly lowered the limbs. The hook still safely held to the side, his hand settled on her knee, asking his own permission. In answer, she placed her hand over his and encouraged it to slowly slide upward.

"Smooth as the finest cream," he murmured, watching the progression of their hands. He paused at her panties, the tip of one finger sliding just under the edge so that he could rub the fabric between his fingers.

"What is this material called again?"

"Lace."

"Lace undergarments." He shook his head. "I think I should enjoy some aspects of your world, little butterfly."

"Well, enjoy them while you can. They are my only pair, the ones I wore when I came here. The others I own are just like yours." She smirked. "I had the seamstress in town try to replicate these, and she did the best she could, but our fabrics are different than yours. They ended up looking like flour sacks. These can only be washed so many times before they wear out."

"They are very soft," he acknowledged, rubbing the fabric between his fingers again. "We don't have anything like this in Neverland." E bit her lip as silence fell on them once more. Then, a thought struck her. He was stalling. Leaning forward, Easton slid her hands into his hair, chest pressing to his.

"Do you want this, Ian?" The last thing she wanted to do was toss him into another relationship he didn't choose. "After what I just told you about Avida, I'd understand…"

"I want this. I want *you*, only you. Far more than I'd ever believed possible. I promise you this."

The tone of his voice, the expression in his gaze, obliterated any doubts she might have had. He never made a promise he didn't mean, nor intend to keep. He lifted his head, closing the distance between their lips, drawing her into a deep, soul-searing kiss. His hand slipped upward the rest of the way, firmly cupping her butt. She grinned against his mouth, earning one in return.

"Grinning in bed, wench? I don't know whether to be insulted or proud."

"I'll let you know. But for now, I'd say you're on the way to 'proud'." His grin kicked up a notch to roguish levels. "I only have one suggestion." She reached out, grabbed his hook, and placed his arm at her back. His grin stiffened, his mind ever wrapped in the dangers of his weapon. "I'm not made of glass, Ian." She pressed down into him, lips hovering over his. "Hold me, and never let go."

His eye moved over her face, soaking in her determination to get what she wanted, and what she wanted to give him in return. Confidence to be free. She gasped as he pulled her closer, both arms holding her tight as his lips molded to hers. The kiss deepened with every breath, hands explored freely, the air in the room heated to scorching intensity without any help from the creatures in the tank. Rolling her to her back, Ian leaned on his hooked arm, mouth claiming her gasp as his hand roamed over her chest. She arched upward, encouraging. Breaking away, breathing hard, he stared down at her.

"Such a beautiful invention." He marveled once more at the bra, hand splayed across it. Her giggle was cut short when his blisteringly seductive gaze found hers. "Teach me how to remove it?"

Swallowing, E grasped his hand and slowly slid it around to the back of her bra. He leaned to the side to better see what he was doing. When the material popped free, he stared at her in awed wonder.

"Hooks?" She blinked, dazzled by his grin.

"Hooks - always." She replied, suddenly loving her bra. She'd never thought of the closures to a bra that way before, but now she always would. Ian slipped the material free.

"You are a wonder to behold, wife. I'll gladly spend the rest of my days adulating every inch of you. My captivating little butterfly."

"Better get started on that then. I want to see some of that Hook prowess I keep hearing about." She winked, both hands reaching down to grab handfuls of his backside. He jumped in surprise, then chuckled, arm wrapping about her to hold her impossibly closer.

"Naughty little minx." His kisses stole away any replies she might have made, as well as claiming the last of her heart and soul.

CHAPTER 32
HOOK

She stirred in his arms; a sleepy, well-pleased smile curled the lips he'd had the satisfaction of dining on for hours earlier. Ian gently shifted a thick wave of vermillion hair away from her face. Devus, but she wrenched at his heart with her astounding beauty! The shiny hair was smooth against his lips as he pressed a kiss to it. She wiggled just a little closer to him, milky, soft skin touching his from head to toe. Ian grinned, loving how she clung to him in her sleep.

Wakeful Easton was not a clingy creature; she was not cold by any means, but she carefully maintained a safe, respectful distance. The life she'd lived before Arriving had clearly taught her how to protect herself, to stand on her own two feet, to not rely on others. Sleeping Easton, however, was a different story. She snuggled up to him, never seeming able to get close enough. On a few occasions, her snuggling had practically pushed him off the edge of the bed. The memory brought a grin to his lips.

He found that he loved both sides of his little butterfly. He loved that her guard was down in sleep, that she unconsciously clung to him for comfort in those hours. Yet he respected her ability to be strong and not solely rely on him for her every need in life. That was something Avida had never understood, nor mastered.

Careful not to disturb his wife, he shifted his arm to cushion the back of his head as he stared up at the elaborately decorated abalone ceiling. Avida. That had been an unexpected development. Hook still wasn't entirely sure how to feel about the matter. Though he had carefully schooled his emotions and expressions upon hearing the news, an internal battle waged. His late wife, whom he'd accidentally sent to eternal doom, visited his current wife and offered approval and repentance at once.

Ian felt that ever-present guilt loom within him, weighing heavily on his soul. Hearing that her eternal torment was far greater than he expected did little but add to it.

Ian frowned, eyes tracing along the engraved patterns of sea life above. The specter Easton spoke of sounded very little like the woman he'd been wed to so very long ago. Avida had been beautiful, delicate, quiet yet demanding. She was a spoiled princess, long accustomed to getting her way at a heartbeat's notice. Life with Ian had not fulfilled those demands. She'd had to wait for time with him; an entirely foreign idea for Avida. She'd been selfish to a deadly fault. But then, so had he. He'd cost lives in his youth as well. He couldn't condemn her for the thing he himself had also been guilty of.

There had been a softer side to Avida as well, a side that always spoke to him. But what he had held with Avida had been shallow. He knew that more so now than ever. Ian's fingers slid down Easton's side, skimming over her delicate skin. Now he understood the true depth of what love could offer. The woman was his completion in every way possible now. The depth of it was both awe-inspiring and intimidating. What he felt for Easton was far different from what he'd felt for Avida. That knowledge forced him to acknowledge a few facts of his past.

Those endearing feelings he had held for Avida were centered on the feeling of a life debt, the feelings of a youth in awe of a new lease on life. He'd wanted to love her as deeply as she professed to love him. And perhaps he had. But his expression of love was born from gratitude and duty, rather than that of the heart. And, Avida?

Perhaps she'd cared for him as she professed, but Ian felt in his soul that the majority of her love had been that of infatuation born from the new and different, born from the feelings of a guardian of life given. Born from the feelings of fantasy and the internal makeup of her race alone. Perhaps even born of the secret yearning for rebellion.

Whatever the case, their love had been nothing short of youthful shortcomings and games, make-believe that turned deadly wrong. Much time and sorrow had passed since those long ago memories were formed. Ian had changed in the ways necessary to survive this world and his lonely duties. Until Easton's arrival, Ian had strove to keep his heart far removed from any of his dealings and relationships with others. The girl in his arms had changed that.

She'd waltzed her way right into his frozen heart, into his very soul, and possessed it as assuredly as he drew breath. She'd thawed him from the inside, warming him with her fiery persona and laughing eyes. She'd given him hope that he hadn't even realized his soul yearned for. Had Avida's specter shown at any other time, to any other person, Ian wasn't sure how he would have handled it.

Now, hearing the conversation held between Easton and Avida, Ian found himself oddly proud of his once-wife. As harrowing and horrendous a place she found herself in now, as much as he'd eagerly take her away from it, Ian found himself grateful for the changes it had made in her personally. Perhaps such gratitude would be seen as cold and cruel to most. It was, truthfully. Yet Ian knew much of the cold cruelties of the world, and their necessities in changing a man's, or woman's, path.

As much as one would wish to avoid them, their presence set into motion one's ability to choose the person they would become. It tempered them, molded them into a stronger, or more brittle version of themselves. Ian was grateful to find Avida had chosen to make the tempering process one of strength and reflection, rather than that of cruelty and woe. It was a terrible shame that it took an everlasting hell to change them both.

Easton shifted, pulling Ian from his morbid thoughts. She stretched luxuriously, melting into the bed with a sigh of pleasure at the end. Ian felt his heart warm once more, his previous troubling thoughts darting into the shadows to be forgotten for another time. Warmth colored her cheeks to a rosy hue that complimented her skin tone and hair beautifully. That satisfied smile she wore in her sleep had only grown, setting her face aglow like an angel.

"Like a cat fat on her fill of cream," Ian teased. Peeking out one eye, she met his gaze, and the grin grew impossibly deeper.

"If I wasn't so sleepy, I might take offense to you calling me fat."

"Sleepy? I think perhaps, my dearest, you mean spent. You've had a long night of heart stopping satisfaction. It's a wonder you didn't sleep the whole day away."

"So smug." She smirked, eyes closed as she still basked in her afterglow. Sighing, she rolled to the side, fiery tendrils cascading over each shoulder like a waterfall. "I slept like a rock!"

"You seem to prefer me to the mattress."

"Mm. *That* must be the prowess everyone has been raving about. Hooks make great mattresses."

"What's that wench?" He snarled playfully, rolling her to her back and straddling her hips. "Do you mean to insinuate you were not well pleased?"

"Oh no, I was." Her lips twitched with the effort to control the playful twist of her mouth. "You aren't lumpy at all. Perhaps a little stinky, but delightfully warm. Yes, I'm very pleased with my mattress." She broke off into a fit of giggles as he slid masterful fingers all over her exposed skin, tickling her without remorse.

"Stop!" she squealed, wriggling beneath him, "you're going to make me pee!"

"Do you admit defeat to my prowess?" he challenged.

"Never!" she gasped, trying to knee him in the back. With a devilish grin, he stretched out atop her, the connection of their heated skin effectively silencing her giggles.

"Then perhaps you need further demonstrations, wife."

"As you command, oh Captain." Her features took on the look of mischievous seductress, and his heart skipped a beat. He was in deep with this one, and he planned to sink only deeper still. Her hands slipped up his chest, coming to rest in the lengths of his hair. He closed his eye as her fingers sifted through the locks, murmuring a groan of approval stirred to life by her touch.

"Holy crap, Ian! Your hair!"

"Is ridiculously handsome, soft and luxurious, I know. No need to shout about it, my dear." He grinned, eye still closed.

"No, Ian, your hair! Some of it's turned red!" His eye cracked open at her tone, took in her shocked and somewhat mortified appearance. This was a new twist to their games, and her expression was impressively realistic in its expression of horror.

"Vermillion, you say? That's not possible. The hook protects me from the Fiend's touch."

"Well apparently it doesn't protect you from mine!" He moved to the side, releasing her when she pushed at him. Rolling off the bed she bounded, quite plainly nude, across the room to gather up a hand mirror. Ian smirked at her, giving her a roguishly full body leer upon her return. Easton frowned, holding the mirror out in front of him.

"Stop gawking at me and look at your hair."

"I'd much rather look at you." Still grinning despite her censure, he took the mirror and did as she so insistently bade. His brow rose in surprise as a rather blatantly bold streak of vermillion presented itself at the nape of his neck. He toyed with the bit, more curious than appalled.

"What does it mean? Did I break you?" She worried at her bottom lip, the most adorable expression of guilt on her face. He shook his head, landing a soft slap to her backside.

"Come to bed and break me a little more."

"Ian, I'm serious." He pulled with the hand still firmly resting on her backside, toppling her against him.

"So am I." He insisted.

"I shouldn't be anywhere near you," she argued, valiantly fighting to escape his grip. Her efforts were in vain; Ian had no plans of ever letting his little butterfly escape him. For the first time in his knowing her, tears sprang to life in Easton's eyes.

"You should have left when you had the chance. Now you'll go to judgment with my Pan taint so clearly visible on you. We're in enough trouble as it is and my touch made it worse." When her bottom lip trembled, he sighed and gently grasped her chin, hooked arm pressing her closer at the small of her back to keep her in place.

"Stop worrying for me, wife. You've not broken me. The hook would never allow the Fiend's taint to negatively affect me; this is common knowledge to the Mers. After all, they are the ones who gave us the metal to form the hooks. They are well aware of its workings and protections."

"They did?" Beautiful glistening brown eyes widened in surprise as she stared down at him.

"Aye."

"You don't really think they'll understand, do you?"

"Your time here has not been useless. The Mers have grown to accept you already. The Trials will eradicate any lingering doubts they may have. If anything, this vermillion streak is simply further proof to them of your purity and intent. The hook has accepted your touch, just as I have."

"Are you sure?" He smirked.

"Aye. And I'd accept a bit more of it just now, if you'd be so kind." Finally, her muscles began to relax against him, relief forming across her features.

"Is that a command, Captain?" she whispered.

"I can certainly make it one, if your little minx heart so desires it." He held her closer, hand slipping to wrap about the nape of her neck and pull her in for a lusty kiss. She moaned against his mouth and climbed under the covers without so much as breaking the dance of their lips. It was his turn to moan as her warmth settled fully against him, adding a little wiggle for good measure.

"Have a care lest your feminine wiles put me in an early watery grave, minx. We've much to do still in this world, you and I."

"Are you saying my prowess rivals yours, husband?"

"Well, you are a Hook now, so to speak." He smiled softly, rather liking the sound of that, the knowledge that she was his. "And you know the rumors..." She stared down at him, eyes and heart open to him. He'd venture to guess she was just as enamored with the idea of their relationship as he was.

"Maybe you can still teach me a few things. You're very good at making things enjoyable."

She actually sounded surprised by that. He zoned in on the underlying meaning to her words, though he could have easily ignored it and bantered. His mind rushed over what he knew of her past; the tidbits he'd garnered through discussion with her and that of her with the rest of his crew. She'd had a hard life, he knew this. She'd been forced to do many illegal actions that put her in dangerous and unwelcome situations, by those who were meant to care for and protect her. She often made vague mentions of these so-called foster homes; the lifestyle where adults took in children that weren't theirs, in return for payment.

It was an odd concept to Ian, being paid to care for children. The existence alone of children in Neverland was considered a treasure, a blessing. Being paid to care for them would have been seen as a slap to the face of their morality. It was conceivable to Ian that the lowest of man would demand payment to care for such treasures, and therefore not surprising those treasures were mistreated so often. The knowledge of such occurrences happening to his wife did not sit well in his stomach. It wasn't difficult to garner from her body language during past conversation that these foster homes had also introduced her to such matters of man and woman. A harsh introduction.

"I'll spend the rest of time granted to me by the Fates creating memories more powerful for you than those of your past," he promised, gently pressing his hand to her cheek, thumb caressing her lips. Her hands gripped his face turning into his touch. Unshed tears glistened on her lashes as she pressed a kiss to his palm.

"My experiences made me who I am. They sucked, but they served their own purposes. And now, here I am. Because of my past struggles, I have the strength to help you. And I can't see anything bad about that." He stared up at her in wonder.

"No greater treasure could a man ever pray for, than a woman such as you, Easton Bendal." She pressed her lips to his.

"You're not so shabby yourself, my Captain Hook."

CHAPTER 33
HOOK

"**H**ow far do you think we could get if we made a swim for it, right now? Think we have a chance?"

"*You think we should run?*"

Ian grinned down at his little butterfly, her hand squeezing the life from his. They stood before the gates of the Judgement Hall, awaiting their announcement to enter. His wife looked resplendent in the deep green dress traditional of a Mer Judgement. The material clung to her delightful curves, glued to her by the water's gentle caress. Short split sleeves fell to either side of her shoulders, baring the soft skin there as well as the length of her legs from the middle of her thighs down, floating like seaweed in the light current.

Vermillion tendrils floated about her face as though in the midst of a graceful dance with the ocean. The sight was breathtaking, and for a moment, Ian wished they could run, too; run back to bed. Her wide expressive eyes rose to meet his, and thoughts of running evaporated. There would be no running. They'd stand judgement together; he would see his wife gain redemption, or meet the same fate as her.

"*We wouldn't make it past those doors, would we?*"

Easton nodded toward the first set of gates they had entered, answering her own question, her dry tone in his head sounding altogether annoyed. Ian pressed a gentle kiss to her temple.

"Not a step."

"That's what I was afraid of," she sighed.

"What's this? Easton James Bendal, afraid?" he teased.

"I've never had anyone else's lives dependent on me. The guild looked out for one another, sure. But when it came down to you or them, you ran for it," she admitted, not meeting his gaze. *"Even in the pigmite caves, it was our mutual survival on the line. Now? Now your life and all of Neverland's future are on my shoulders. This is my fault. And if I don't fix it there's going to be hell to pay. I can't let them take this out on you."*

"I'm still at your side, Easton," Ian stated gently, his heart softening further under her statement of dedication.

"I know." Her mental whisper caressed his mind. Her face screwed up in annoyance. *"What's taking so long? It feels like we've been out here for an hour. I'm getting all pruney."*

"Patience, oh pruney one," Ian teased, *"Caol is singing your praises to the Mers in attendance. Other Mers that were in close contact with you in the last several days are being called as witnesses to your character."*

"I'm not allowed to be in there to hear it?"

"Caol and I decided it might be best if we remained out here until the witnessing has come to an end. Your presence can't be made to blame for influencing their statements."

"Acquis would blame me for something stupid like that," Easton scoffed. But the way her eyes quickly bounced toward the vermillion in his hair and then away led Ian to believe she was actually wondering if that were a possibility. A grin fought the corners of his lips.

"Yes, he would. Of course that would be preposterous to think you would attempt such a thing, even if it were possible. Such an action would immediately doom you to guilt."

"Of course," she quickly agreed, turning to him with wide, innocent eyes that didn't fool him for a moment. Seeing his grin, E chuckled quietly. It didn't last long enough, dissipating the moment her eyes returned to the gates before them.

"Does it always have to be so freaking cold in the ocean?" Her hand released his to rub at her arms, covering her shiver of nerves. Ian

floated behind her, enfolding her in the warming shelter of his arms. Ducking to rest his chin atop her shoulder, Ian nuzzled her ear.

"Be at ease, little butterfly. I will fight to the ends of the earth and to the deepest depths of the ocean for you. No one will harm you so long as I draw breath. I promise you this."

Her head fell back against him, eyes closing as she reveled in his touch, letting a bit of her anxious shield down to accept the comfort and support he offered. Ian held her all the tighter for it.

"I couldn't bear it if he was ever hurt, but damn I love that about him. A promise I know I can actually trust."

Her silently mental thoughts floated towards him. Ian could tell from the taste of it that it had been meant as a personal thought, not one she'd wanted him to hear. He pretended not to have heard it, though he couldn't pretend his heart didn't swell under her depth of rarely given trust. Turning in his arms, she faced him and projected a clear response that was meant for him.

"Thank you, Ian. Thank you for having my back."

"Such a lovely back it is, too."

He grinned, long ago learning to understand much of her other-worldly lingo. Her realm was one of constant metaphors and what she liked to call 'slang'. He'd found it confusing and difficult to accept in the beginning. Now it was endearing, and utterly unique, just like his butterfly. Her fingers lifted, sliding along the length of vermillion in his hair. He'd tied most of it in a que at the base of his skull, but the vermillion he wore proudly, its length braided and blatantly obvious to the eye.

"I still can't believe you're so calm about this."

"Why should I not be? It's a gift from my beloved one. I wear it proudly."
Her eyes locked on his, hands moving to grip the front of his green and silver embroidered shirt. Her eyes shouted the words his heart longed to hear, and as always, he waited patiently for her to form the words to existence. She hesitated a moment, biting her lower lip.

"Ian, I lo..." Suddenly the gates at their backs swung outward, warm water flowing over them in its wake. Easton tensed as it washed over her back, eyes wide. She was afraid, uncertain of her place in this watery place, afraid of making a wrong step.

"No. Don't worry about censoring yourself. No more treading softly. Just be who you are. Do not apologize for your beautiful soul."

Ian spoke fiercely, words meant to fortify and reinforce his support of her. His thumb stroked her lip, insides jumping as he watched fiery determination stoked to life in her eyes. Devus, but he loved her fire! She grabbed his hand, and stared him down hard.

"I love you, Ian."

And there it was. The purposely spoken words sounded even sweeter to his heart having felt them through their mental connection. His grin surely could have blinded the entirety of Neverland.

"You're not so bad yourself, my Vermillion Butterfly."

He winked, tossing back her usual playful reply to sentimentality. She grinned, mischief joining the fire in her gaze. In that moment, Ian knew they would win. Not just this momentary scuffle with the Mers, but the battle for all of Neverland. With such a woman at his side, how could he not be victorious? Hand in hand, they drifted through the gates together.

Ian was so fond of calling her his butterfly, but E had never felt the name so fitting as now, when her heart fluttered in her chest like the frantic beat of wings. The fact that she could be swimming to her death at this moment should have unsettled her. Yet it was the epic moment she'd just had with Ian that sent her nerves skittering. She'd told him she loved him.

She was married to the guy for crap's sake; it shouldn't be such a shock to say those words. And truthfully she'd begun forming those feelings of love from the moment she'd met him, slowly building on attraction and fantasy, their bond growing from respect and friendship to that depthless pit of emotion inside her now. But it did come as a shock for her. She hadn't said those words to anyone since her parents were alive. Not to any of her friends, past boyfriends, not even to Wiley. She kept herself carefully distanced.

She'd cared for Sad as a friend, and cared for Noah a little deeper than that...like a cousin maybe. But the moment she left her world, E had quickly put them out of her mind. Wiley was as close to a brother to her as she could ever hope, but she had still kept her emotions tamped low. Her fears for him had raged within, a part of her mind always screaming at her to find him. But she'd refused to think about the implications of what his absence might mean, refused to accept the idea of his loss, muted her feelings so that she could breathe each day. E had spent her entire life putting love out of her reach, refusing to embrace it. Love was a weakness she couldn't afford. Pain, fear and anger were her allies; they kept her wits sharp and her body alive.

Yet this, now, with Ian? This was beyond her scope. She kept trying to keep part of her separate, but if she were honest, that had been a failing cause from the moment she realized he was a Hook. Perhaps that was stupid, superficial and childish. But it was what it was. Hook had been her hero from her farthest memories. She had dreamed of going on adventures with James T. Hook. The man in flesh at her side held a far more intimate connection to her. What had begun as a childhood fascination grew into what she trembled to know was love. She'd fought love so hard, and now it had claimed her. And now that she loved him so deeply, now that she had acknowledged it? Losing him would break her more surely than any form of torture or physical attack.

It was that fear of losing him that had her trembling outside the gates. She hadn't feared death in a long while. It was Ian's death that she feared. She'd been terrified to say the words aloud, because it felt like that would make her intentions toward him official to the universe. It would make Ian open game for the universe to snatch away from her.

When he'd looked her in the eyes and fiercely told her he would wear her color proudly, that he would fight to the ends of the earth and depths of the ocean? When he'd told her to be herself, to be proud of who she was to the core and he would stand at her side? That had been her undoing. She'd told him the words he had earned, gave him that final key to her heart. And with those words, she'd declared war: war on the universe, war on anyone who would dare to take him from her. And now, as she swam into the Mer judgement arena, she let those thoughts broadcast as clear as if she spoke them.

"Hurt my Hook, and I'll eat you all for breakfast."

Ian's face remained fiercely determined, his stance strong and ready for a fight, but she could feel his inner smirk of humor to her core. Though somehow she knew his humor had been directed for her alone to feel. Along with the humor came a warm feeling reflecting his pride in her strength. E focused hard on a single thought and feeling, focused on sending it to him alone. Ian promised her that as their Mer bond grew, she'd be able to easily speak to him through the bond without broadcasting it. She felt that day was far away, because even this single thought made her sweat and her head hurt. Still, she managed to get it across to him.

"Mine."

The way his hand squeezed hers let her know he'd heard her; the mischief dancing behind his enigmatic gaze let her know he'd enjoyed it, too. A new voice intruded E's mind; cool and regal, distinctly female, and dominating in its command.

"Well understood. We are here to congratulate you on your bonded bliss, as well as to find answers to a few… concerns. I trust we can remain civil to one another?"

E's attention shifted toward the chairs that sat just below the crowd of Mers who floated in a stadium-seated fashion. Four Mers sat on short, throne-like chairs, two men and two women. Aquis was amongst them, sneering at her like a starved dog.

"Sure I can be civil. I live by the law of give and get. I give back when I get. Aside from a few Mers," her eyes landed on Acquis, who bared his sharp teeth, *"I have had nothing but kind welcoming here. I won't draw blood first. But I will draw the last of it if you try to hurt what's mine."*

"A matter upon which we can come to agreement already."

The voice came again, and this time E could pinpoint which female it came from. A smile quirked the left side of the woman's lips, her pale blue eyes approving. She was a beautiful woman, long hair that gleamed a golden pink in the gentle waves of water about them. The scales across her torso and tail matched her hair, an amazing cast of colors fit for the royalty her regal bearing proclaimed.

E bowed her head slightly in agreement, though she kept a wary eye on the rest of them. They hadn't been allowed weapons, obviously, but E was determined to take them down one way or another if it came to it.

"I am Queen Eventide of the Southern Seas." The woman intoned,

before motioning to the Mers at her sides. *"This is King Bered of the Western Seas. To my left is Queen Allure of the Northern Seas."*

The king bowed his head of black waist-length curls. His tail was an impressive gleam of black oil, the kind that reflected back hints of every color of the rainbow in its dark depths. He was serious, huge and burly, but his eyes were warm. She felt his power of command, yet felt no menace from him. The queen on the other side of Eventide bore pale purple hair that made light green eyes sparkle. Her tail was a calming mixture of purple and light blues, like lavender flowers in a field. She smiled brightly, easily the most outwardly friendly amongst the group.

"And at the other end you will find Prince Acquis of the Eastern Seas in which we preside at this moment. He is acting in the stead of his father, who has been ill for quite some time," Eventide confided. *"We Mers are a hearty lot, and not easily slain, but I fear the Pan's presence in this part of Neverland has weakened King Acquilus to the point that he cannot leave his bed."*

From the glower Acquis sent her way, he didn't appreciate the Queen airing his dirty family laundry. Eventide's sideways grin kicked up a notch as she took in the hot-headed prince's reaction. She reminded E of a mother's wry humor over the temper tantrum of their toddler.

"Pay the Prince's temperament little heed. He is young yet and not well versed in the art of diplomacy."

"Funny you should say that. I had pretty much the same impression of him when we first met." E agreed, ignoring Acquis altogether, joining in on the Queen's approach. She liked this lady.

"Yes, we heard there was a bit of misunderstanding upon your invitation to join us." Eventide's lips lost their humor, royal annoyance portrayed in her features. *"Such an event was not our wish. You are new to our people, and we wished only to extend a warm greeting and congratulatory welcoming. Youth can be such a burdensome time for Mers. Their bodies are not yet in harmony with the Great Tide, you understand. Few can handle its ebb and flow with grace, until they have gained maturity won only with time and experience."* She gestured at Caol, who stood at the opposite side of their arena. When E and Ian turned to meet his gaze, he bowed in warm greeting.

"Caol is one of wonder, a youth beyond maturity in years. We entrust him with much in our kingdoms; he has served in protecting our borders for many years. This is why we wished to send him on the errand of collecting you upon his return from service. However, the Prince took it upon himself to fulfill this matter of duty, feeling it should be carried out more urgently than we were prepared. He did so without the agreement of the combined council, and his youthful temperament saw that he fulfilled the duty poorly, I fear."

"I didn't feel the need to come sniveling for your permission in my own realm, nor wait for my beloved brother's return." Acquis sneered. Caol looked heavenward, clearly not impressed by his brother's aggression. *"I have long been in the seat of my Father, and am well capable of carrying out my duties as seat upon the Council."* His eyes shifted to meet E's, and her spine stiffened.

"As to my behavior, I am true to my people and our efforts. I don't feel the Panling is entitled to such frivolities you are so happy to bestow. Clearly she is touched of the Pan and not to be trusted. However, I feel she is more than tainted, but actual offspring to the Pan himself."

A collective murmur ran through the crowd. Mixed emotions whirled in the air; on the one hand there was shock that he would say such a blatant thing, on the other a fair share of complete agreement. Acquis donned an evil grin, not done.

"I'd have culled her the moment I faced her, had I the chance. Allowing her taint into this place is akin to a pandering cowardice and betrayal I would know nothing of."

"Such vile words are not seemly, Prince Acquis. These are our guests, and they are allowed fair conduct," Queen Allure gasped, eyes wide as she leaned away from Acquis.

Acquis's eyes locked on the gentle Queen's, and though E couldn't hear the words, she was certain he was giving Allure a few of those vile words for her ears only. Allure gasped and paled, though an embarrassed flush swept across her cheeks. Dirty, vile words, apparently. Big jerk.

"Quiet your eel tongue, hatchling!" King Bered rose from his seat, black storms brewing in his silver gaze. His voice thundered deep and heavy like the rolling of thunder across the sea.

"Peace, brother, sister. We mustn't encourage such youthful outbursts."

Eventide placed a calming hand on Bered's massive forearm, and added a gentle pat on Allure's dainty shoulder.

Bered offered one more venomous promise in his brooding gaze, but acquiesced to Eventide and sat in his seat. Allure swallowed and straightened, though E didn't miss the fact that she shifted to sit as far away from Acquis as her chair would allow. Acquis spoke loudly, rising from his seat, hissing to the crowd about his rights in his province, and E's evil, blah, blah, blah.

"Yes, Prince Acquis, we are aware of Mer law on this matter. As we reside within the Eastern province, the majority of the hearing will be directed through you. However, I feel the need to remind you that your word alone is not law, right of province or no. You have seen fit to take the law into your own hands once on this matter already. Something the Council frowns heavily upon, and that we four will speak of together once this meeting concludes." Her attention shifted to Easton and Hook.

"Rest assured, the words of one alone cannot proclaim judgement or decree upon your fates. We are a lawful people, a just people. The majority of agreement amongst the council will decide your fates. Unless your heart proves otherwise, bondmate of Hook, you have nothing to fear from us. Nor does your beloved." Her lips quirked upward in that crooked wry sort of grin as she watched them.

"We thank you." Hook placed a hand to his heart and bowed. E nodded resolutely, following Ian's example and bowing respect to the three royals.

"Yes, we thank you. It's nice to know that we won't be judged entirely without intelligence." Ian stiffened at her side, then relaxed, the humor on his lips a reflection of his earlier words of guidance to be herself.

"We were diverted from our fight against the Pan so that we could come here and be accused of who knows what. I trust that we can count on the three of you to show a more fair judgment on the matter than Acquis."

"Such petulance and disrespect!" Acquis hissed, turning to the crowd.*" Is it not unlike that of the Pan? He daily throws his self-proclaimed betterment in our faces, making himself the king of all Neverland. Is not this girl just as self-centered as the Fiend that bears her coloring?"*

"Aren't you just as self-centered, making this a personal war against a man who's only sin was to honor the bonds of marriage your sister placed on

him? To make it a war on a woman who you are condemning solely on her hair color?" E fired back.

"Only those so deeply rooted in the taint of the Pan bear his coloring!" Acquis seethed, sweeping forward to hiss in her face. *"Everything the Pan touches, his taint stains beyond compare. Only we Mer are safe from his taint, protected as we are by our magic metals."* He held up his ring in defiance, taut expression daring her to argue the fact.

"Indeed, you are protected by the Mer magic. Isn't it that much more deplorable, then, that you readily chose to join Pan's side, even though you are better able to resist than most?"

"Join the Pan? What devilry do you speak now?"

Acquis's face paled slightly, his eyes taking on a wild expression you'd expect on a mad animal. E thought through her words, carefully stepping along the path of her accusations. Ian had agreed to allow her to make the accusations, agreed it would be better for her to take the lead on speaking as Mer law dictated he was there only as her support, until accusations were pressed against him.

"I'm saying you aren't as infallible as you claim. Avida is a prime example."

A hushed murmur of voices rustled through her mind, like leaves caught up in a whirlwind. The mers surrounding them sent significant glances to one another, expressions filled with a vast array of emotion. The majority of it however, was anger and guilty embarrassment.

"You dare to bring my beloved lost sister into this?" Acquis seethed.

"Avida was just like the rest of you. Yet in the end she gave her allegiance to the Pan and brought about the death and suffering of so many." E met Acquis' gaze accusingly. *"Unfortunately, I'd say many more of the Mer than are willing to admit, have been touched by the Fiend in one way or another."* Acquis reared back, momentarily silent. His gaze on her was piercing, searching her for any sign that she owned evidence of his wrong doing. His eyes suddenly shot to Ian, eyes alighting with new fevered hatred.

"Behold the Hook! See his hair! The coloring he so boldly wears in his locks! Vermillion!" The rustling whispers rushed through her mind again, making E cringe with the accusation and overwhelming

emotions from the gathered Mer. *"Is it not obvious that the Pan's taint has found a way to disrupt the power of our precious metals? Is it not clear that the Pan's taint has taken root in the self-proclaimed savior of Neverland? And is it not possible that it is his taint that was responsible for poisoning our dear sister's will?"* He turned on Easton, practically frothing at the mouth.

"Do you deny these accusations? Do you deny your heritage is of Pan?" E stood straighter, chin held high.

"No."

The crowd burst out in a cacophony of conversation. The Royals sat a little higher in their chairs, eyes widening. And for a moment, E felt a flutter of panic at the doubt seeping into their gazes. But it was Caol's blank expression that left Easton feeling the deepest dread. Caol was a very expression-oriented person. To see his face completely blank and unreadable left the feeling of having a sizable hunk of lead in her stomach.

"I request permission to address these accusations, Council." Ian respectfully addressed the Royals. After a moment's hesitation, the Royals sent one another a glance of speech. Eventide waved her hand in acquiescence.

"Speak, then, Hook."

"Yes, let us hear what lies you shall weave for us now, great Hook," Acquis sneered. Ian stepped away from her, walking about the arena for all to see.

"He speaks true, it is vermillion in my hair, and I wear it proudly!" The Mers whispered in shock. *"This is the color of my wife. It is her blood that has turned my locks vermillion, not that of the Pan. She may be a descendant of Pan, yet has remained under my safe protection from the moment of her Arrival. She has made it clear time and again that she is not on Pan's side, but the side of Neverland. She is here to save us, not destroy us!"*

More distrustful and surprised murmurs met this statement. Ian moved back to her side, and E gravitated towards his strength, her own bolstering in closer proximity to his.

"And we are to believe this outlandish statement?" Acquis sneered in disgust.

"The tale of truth is within this lock of hair." Ian grasped the small braid over his shoulder. *"This is proof of her purity! If she were not pure,*

my hook would not have accepted her. If she were not pure, I would have gutted and rifted her long ago, upon my first meeting of her. Yet I didn't. I was wary of her for a time, as you all are at this moment. Yet despite the visual evidence pointing her towards our enemy, I have not for one moment felt a dangerous inclination from her. She went through the Light Binding process in Sanctuary and passed."

"*And while yes, it is true that I gave her a tonic to help relax her,*" Ian cut Acquis off before he could toss more accusations of the worth of his test, "*I did little more than that. Easton has a fear of enclosed spaces, of not being able to move. It is an after-effect of a most painful past. The tonic relaxed her instinctual resistance to the Binding. If my tonic is to be blamed for anything, it is to be blamed for making her less fearful and more truthful. It would not have swayed her ability to speak truth, but rather enforced it.*"

The murmurs were quieter this time, an air of thoughtful consideration growing slowly to replace the fear and anger that had been overwhelming the air moments before. Easton's muscles relaxed slightly under the air of understanding in their thoughts.

"*You have known me for far longer than any other. We have suffered together and triumphed together.*" Ian took them all in, his presence and voice commanding without so much as shouting in his mind as Acquis did. "*I have been faithful to our cause. Neverland may not be the land of my birth, but it has become the home of my heart. I have been faithful to Neverland. I have been faithful to the Mers from the moment you were all joined to me by my marriage. I have lost so many, and been burdened by much. And yet I have remained faithful. Never have I given reason for doubt.*"

"*Avida,*" Acquis hissed. "*You led my sister to her destruction. It is because of you that she resides in purgatory!*"

"*Avida made her decisions,*" Ian stated solemnly. "*She knew what I am, she knew where my loyalties would lie. She chose her own personal selfishness over Neverland.*" Acquis hissed in fury, and several in the crowd joined him, but Ian stood solid.

"*The Hook is correct in this.*" Bered thundered. His voice was quiet, yet Easton doubted a huge man like Bered could ever do anything but thunder. The voices of dissent quieted, and Acquis spun about, hatred in his eyes.

"*You are too close to the situation to gather a realistic truth of it,*" the king stated. *"As one of your hatchling mates, such devotion is understandable and cannot be frowned upon. However, truth is truth. Your sister's choices have haunted us for far too long. We can cover it up and speak no more of it, but the truth remains. She was a traitor to our kind, and to our land."*

"Maybe she once was." E suddenly found herself speaking. Ian looked to her in surprise, yet didn't stop her from going further. *"I have spoken with Avida myself, and I feel she is no longer the girl she once was."*

"Blasphemy!" Acquis hissed. *"No one can speak to her now."*

"We both know that isn't true, Acquis." She replied evenly. He immediately shut up, face paling and eyes once more taking on that fevered speculative sheen. And in that moment, she knew he understood. And he hated her for it.

"We know of only one way to see the entire truth of one's soul." Spit flew from his lips as he raged. *"It is a most unpleasant option, but in our current circumstances I see no alternative. Pans are well known for their ability to deceive even the most stalwart of hearts. Therefore, I demand a Trial of the Between!"*

"No!" Ian stiffened at her side, and the crowd went wild with gasps of shock.

"I agree to the Trial!" E shouted, causing the crowd to quiet in surprise. Acquis' brow rose, his grin one of victory. Ian spun her by the shoulders so that she faced his wild-eyed, brooding glare.

"What are you doing?"

"Facing fair judgment." She replied as calmly as possible.

"Acquis wants death, not fair judgment!" Ian growled.

"This is the best way."

"It is insanity!" he argued. *"We are so close to clearing matters, why would you muddle it with this deplorable agreement?"*

Ian and Caol had discussed the three forms of trial with her the night of their arrival in the Mer city. Trial one was by Witness. This was the trial that Caol and Ian had chosen for them. The mers in attendance would give their accounts of feelings toward the purity of her soul based on the behavior they have witnessed. She would then tell her side of the story, and the Mer royals would declare judgement. Given the fact that the meeting was supposed to be one of only judging her heart as one tainted by the Pan, and Ian's having married one so clearly marked, Caol had assured her this would be all the trial needed. Despite her red hair, the Mer people had been widely accepting of her, aside from a few.

If they hadn't been so accepting, E would have had to face Trial two; the Trial by Blood War. It was a ceremony given to the baser of criminals, one that was already known to be guilty, but given the right to a fair fight. Much of their blood was drained to weaken them, and then they were left to fight against the creatures of the ocean that were drawn to their blood. If the criminal survived, the council would see it as a sign from Devus to give them a second chance. A chance to take it all back into deliberation and likely send them to a literally watered down form of community service and parole.

Trial three was the rarely spoken Trial of the Between. The two men had been reluctant to explain it, covering the details with an eerie sense of foreboding. Caol blatantly told her that the Between was a children's bedtime story told by Mer parents in an effort to scare their hatchlings into good behavior. The Between is a place between Neverland, and the Rift in which the Hooks send their foes. When you enter the Between, all barriers of your soul are torn down. A mediator is able to access all of your memories and project them to those in the arena upon your return. It gives irrefutable proof to your innocence or guilt.

It also puts all of your dirty laundry on display while placing your eternal well-being on the line. Add on top of that, it was a dangerous place from which there is never a guarantee that you will return, in order to tell that revealed innocence or guilt. The Rift at times melds with the Between, only a very thin fabric separating the places. It was known to pull those who entered into its black depths, never to return again. Caol solemnly informed her that it had been attempted at least a dozen times in all of Mer history, and only successfully completed once. If this went wrong, Easton could very well end up in the same oblivion as Avida.

"Ian, you have to trust me on this. If Acquis hadn't demanded it, I would have asked for it myself. Maybe they would pass fair judgement on me and let

us go. But they wouldn't trust me, and they wouldn't trust you. It would hurt our cause." He blinked at her use of 'our cause', warmth sifting through the cold in his eyes.

"It is my cause now just as much as it is yours. We're together on this. That's why I have to do this. Once they saw that red in your hair, they began to doubt. Even Caol doubts." She caught Caol's guilty expression from the corner of her eye. She couldn't blame him. It was a lot to take in. And if she were honest, she doubted herself, too.

"Think of how they will feel when they hear the rest of what I have to tell them? Perhaps they could forgive my blood, but they won't be so forgiving of my accusations. We need all the favor we can get. There's no lying in the Between. There's no deceit, no escape from justice. If there's one thing I've learned on the streets, it's that putting your life on the line only adds proof of your words. No one's going to follow some stranger on a job when that person won't even risk themselves for it."

Ian's jaw clenched, his hand grasping the fabric of her dress in an obvious effort to save her skin from the abuse of his inner turmoil, to hold her close without hurting her with the force of his fear.

"You're determined in this matter, then?" he said, voice tight, though his eyes already held the knowledge of defeat. He knew she wasn't going to back down.

"This may be our only chance to prove your purity, and my heart," she whispered. Reaching out, she slipped her palms to press to his jaw, bringing his gaze back to hers. Her eyes softened. *"You would go to the ends of the earth, or the depths of the ocean for me, Ian. It's only fair that I go to the ends of the Rift for you."*

"Do you understand the implications of this trial?" Bered boomed, serious face examining her closely, even from the distance of his throne. E kept her eyes locked on Ian's as she answered.

"I do." She stated firmly.

"Why would you make such an agreement, knowing the dangers it poses? Were we not clear in our efforts of fair justice?" Allure asked, melodious voice drifting quietly above the rest.

"I need to prove my worth, and the purity of my husband's heart and purpose. I need you to trust us." She steeled herself, turning to face the Council. *"Because I'm going to say something that I need you to know is the*

truth, and not the lies of a Pan." Swallowing, E stiffened her back, staring down the Council. "And I feel that these accusations will assure your place in the coming war."

She didn't dare look Ian's way. She was going a step further with all of this than he had anticipated. He was being supportive in the moment, but she hoped he'd stick with her on this. She'd basically just called the Mers out on their loyalty.

"We know our place in the War of the Pan." Bered's eyes narrowed dangerously.

The Mer had remained mostly neutral in the war. They protected their own. Any battles they fought were in the water, for their own people. The Dark Mers who supported Pan were kicked out of their community, but the Mers did little else when it came to protecting the outside world. Ian had their vague promises of loyalty when the final battle came, mostly out of familial kindness, Easton felt. But those promises didn't extend beyond their watery realm.

The war had once caused major damage to the close-knit race. They had tried hard to mend the damage, and they saw spreading their loyalties beyond the oceans as a danger they dared not risk. But if they were to have any hope of winning, Neverland needed as many on its side as it could gain. They needed the Mers in the coming fight. E needed to know that Ian would have all the help he could get.

"Some of you do, yes. But not all of you. There is disagreement in your people. Sides are being chosen whether you want them to be or not. And those sides will shift to battles, in and out of the water." Bered tensed at her words, storms churning with renewed vigor in his eyes.

"What accusations can you have, that they are worthy of the risk you choose to face now?" Queen Eventide interjected before Easton's words could stir up further argument. E swallowed, hoping her gamble would pay off.

"I am a descendent of Pan." She swallowed as tremors of disquiet echoed in her mind from those in attendance. "And because of that, I have gained certain attributes. I can walk in the realm of dreams. When I sleep, I can go to areas I normally wouldn't be able to. It's how Avida found me. And it's how she warned me of deep-seated deception amongst the Mers." She held up her hand that bore Avida's ring, speaking past the gasps of outrage and denial.

"Avida is connected to me through the ring. It was through this connection that she was able to draw me to her ghostly image. She spoke to me of her sorrow. She told me she wished she'd chosen differently, that she hadn't let her youthful emotions fuel her decisions. She spoke to me of betrayals and dangers yet to come." Acquis had gone stiff. E pretended not to notice, eyes glued to the Council.

"Send me into the Between. Then you'll see Avida's warnings for yourselves and you won't doubt my words or intentions. Until then, I can say no more." Eventide watched her closely for a moment before shifting toward the woman on her left.

"And are you willing to take such a risk, Allure? You are still young for such a tremulous calling in life."

"I knew the risks when I accepted the calling, Queen Eventide. I accept them now, as then, and always. My mother carried the burden before me, and was the only one successful in it. She taught me well. Now it is my turn to walk the lines. I have practiced many times in the past," Allure assured the queen in her quiet, solemn manner.

"Never with others in tow," the queen reminded softly.

"No. But I am strong and I am willing. The accused must always be given their rights to fair trial. If this is what the Hook's bondmate desires for a fair trial, then I shall guide her." Eventide grasped the young woman's hand and gave it a supportive squeeze. Lifting upward into the water, Eventide turned to the crowd.

"The Trial of the Between shall be the judgement of choice."

Acquis eye's met E's, and a twisted sneer lifted the corners of his lips. If he was worried about what she had to say, he wasn't concerned about her surviving the Between long enough to share it. Clearly, he saw this judgement as working in his favor. If only he knew how stubborn a personality Easton had. She was going to crack his little crapfest wide open and share it with everyone. She looked forward to wiping that smirk off his face.

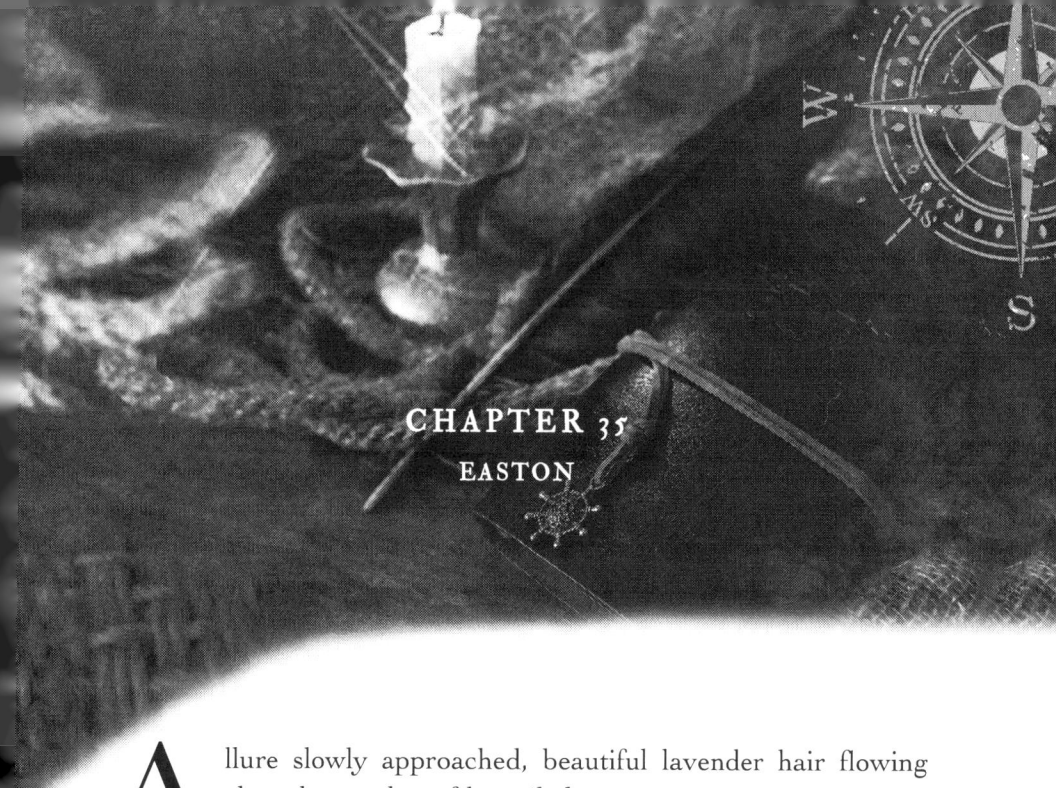

CHAPTER 35
EASTON

A llure slowly approached, beautiful lavender hair flowing about her as she softly smiled.

"Are you prepared to enter, bondmate of Hook?" E nodded, though being face to face with the woman who would be in the midst of risk with her, E suddenly felt that all too familiar guilt clawing at her within.

"I know I'm asking a lot of you, to risk so much."

"I will return with or without you. Did the Hook not tell you that part of my story?" Allure smiled a sad smile.

She held up the wide rectangle of metal that hung on a sturdy chain about her neck. E's eyes glued to it as she nodded. Yes, Ian had told her that part. That hunk of metal was all that was left of what was used to forge the Hook's weapons. It is what allowed them to navigate the Rift's edges. It was passed down through each mediator that dared to walk the lines between worlds. Allure's grandmother had been one of the many to try to guide others through the trial and failed. It would spare Allure, just as it spared her grandmother. But it would not spare either of them the guilt or shame, the haunting knowledge that they led others to their doom in the Rift. E was asking Allure to face what Ian faced each day. Only Allure would know Easton's innocence. Where Ian's victims had always been in the wrong, even Avida, Allure would know that Easton was innocent. And that knowledge would haunt her, just as it always had her grandmother.

"I know you would return physically whole. But emotionally, it's a big thing I'm asking." Allure's eyes took on a sheen of glistening pearly tears, new respect and understanding in their depths.

"Your concern is acknowledged and appreciated." Allure curtsied gracefully in acknowledgement. *"I shall wait near the gate, so that you may say your farewells."* She nodded to Ian before floating in the distance of the large black ornate doors.

"I'm guessing those are the gates to Mordor…" E muttered to herself.

"Mordor? They are the gates to the Between," Ian spoke, wrapping his arms about her from behind, clutching her to him as though she were a delicate thing.

"Close enough." She sighed, happily melting into his embrace.

"You will return to me." His words carried a tremulous force, a firm demand to her soul. *"I'll not lose you."*

Allure wasn't the only one that Easton was asking a lot of. She was asking her husband to risk losing yet another wife to the Rift. She turned in his arms, suddenly shaky. Her nerves had never been a problem in that past. E had used those nerves, pulled them inward and turned them into her driving force during her thefts and adventures. She did so now, only this time when she pulled the nerves to her, she took a moment to cradle them, protecting their delicate being. It was love, and the fear of losing it, that brought her nerves into play today. She stared up into the eye of the source of her nerves now, and made a returned promise.

"I will return to you. You won't lose me."

He grabbed her up, pressing such a feverish kiss on her lips that a hush fell over the arena. E returned the embrace, relishing in it. Kissing under water was an interesting experience. The fact that she didn't have to pull away to catch her breath now and then, her gills taking care of that for her, well, that was something she hoped to further explore in the future. Ian held her tightly, stating his own forceful claim to the universe. Easton was his, and neither hell nor

Rift would keep him from her. She pulled away, shaky for a whole new reason.

"There's that Hook prowess they're always talking about."

A hint of his cocky grin returned. With a wink, she spun and swam across the arena, not looking back. Acquis smirked at her from his seat on the Council. E couldn't help herself. She stopped before the ocean royalty, and bowed deeply...but only to Bered and Eventide.

"King Bered, Queen Eventide. May your justice and goodness continue to protect the Neverland Seas from all that is evil and wrong."

She sent a bold glance toward Acquis, then purposely turned and swam toward the gate. She didn't miss the looks of speculation on Bered and Eventide's faces, nor did she miss the baleful fires on her back from Acquis's gaze as she approached Allure. Easton's lips spread into a devil may care grin Ian would no doubt be proud of. Allure arched a brow as she held out her hands.

"You wear a bold grin into the depths of perdition." She glanced in Acquis' direction. *"Perhaps you enjoy playing with fire?"*

"Smile at the devil and spit in his eye, I say." Allure's eyes widened for a moment of shock, before a soft, delicate giggle issued from her mind.

"You are truly a rarity, bondmate of Hook."

"That's a nice way to put it." E smirked as she placed her hands in Allure's. *"And please call me Easton. If we're risking the Rift together, we should be on a first name basis, don't you think? Make it my possibly final wish."*

"It is not proper amongst our people. But I suppose this once..." Allure hesitated.

"Thanks. Now, what do I do?" The Mer's graceful features swept into the serious expression as she began explaining the ritual.

"I shall speak a chant that will release the doors of their closure. When that happens, you will feel an immense surge through your body, the Rift trying to pull you inward. Do not answer its beckon. Hold your eyes to mine, always. The Between can be a dangerous place that pulls and tugs. Those within will be drawn to your life force and greedily wish to claim it. If you lose your foundation, you'll spin wildly into the beyond and I will not be able to save

you. Once within the Rift, you will never be free. There is no escape outside of the safety I offer. Stay with my gaze, always."

"Staring contest championship. Got it," E muttered, nodding.

"Once we are inside, you will feel me entering your mind. The Between is not a place of words. We will not be able to communicate with one another, even within our minds. My intrusion may... put you at unease. You will feel the need to pull away, to hide. Especially if the memories are delicate in nature. You must force your way past this sensation, Easton. If you block me from the pathway, you can damage both of our minds, and I will not be able to bring us back to this world whole."

"Oh. I didn't know that part."

E bit her lips, new nerves bundling within. She knew they would get to see all her dirty secrets. What she didn't know was that she would have to actually live through them again herself. She'd somehow thought that they would go in and Allure would dig around undetected in her brain while E stared at the scenery in boredom until it was time to go. Allure watched her carefully.

"You have a dark past."

"Yes. A secret dark past that most don't know all the details of; even Ian, though I think he has guessed at some of it."

"A dangerous one?" Allure pressed. *"If it is something that will see you lost, turn back now and confess. It is not too late to regress from this trial to another."* Clearly Allure was assuming that Easton held ties to Pan that she feared to confess. E tightened her resolve.

"No, there's nothing that will keep me from passing the tests of my heritage." E glanced toward Ian, but stopped herself before she could meet his gaze. Allure nodded slowly.

"I see. Matters of the heart, then." E met her gaze, knowing that sympathetic tone all too well. Allure knew the likely sources of her issues. *"We shall face such things when they arise."* The Mer acknowledged, squeezing E's hands in assurance.

"Right, you're right: concentrate on getting back first, worry about the rest later." E nodded, steeling herself once more. *"Let's get this show on the road."* Allure grinned a funny, sharp-toothed grin.

"Yes. Let's... move onto the road." She replied haltingly. E grinned.

"Remember, my eyes only." E nodded and stared into Allure's beautiful light green eyes.

Ever so quietly, Allure's voice lifted into the lilting cadence of Mer language, her words dancing about in the air as the water currents shifted in an ever increasingly smaller orbit about them. Allure's eyes took on a startling appearance, a sheen of mother of pearl washing over their surfaces, her words growing ever louder. The metal hanging about her neck lifted upward in the water, an odd, dull gray light emanating from it. The light spread to join the water currents, until Allure and Easton were both encased in an iridescent gray egg-shaped shield. The shield grew until it encompassed the gates, protecting the bystanders from the effects of the opening portal.

"et aperire portas inferorum. Quaerite verum. anima revelare."

Allure's repeated words sent shivers of goosebumps over every inch of E's skin as an inhuman screaming sounded around them. She didn't understand whatever language the Mer's spoke, but 'inferorum' sounded awfully similar to 'inferno,' which brought to mind Hell. Based on the creeping sensation stealing over her, that probably wasn't too far from the truth.

From the corner of her eye, E could see the vague shapes of the black gates creaking open. Dark light poured out of the opening, spreading along the edges of their protective gray shell. The shield kept the blackness from escaping into the arena, but it also deflected it back towards Easton and Allure.

Allure's hands gently squeezed E's, reminding her to keep their eyes locked on one another. It was harder than E thought, keeping her eyes locked with a shiny-eyed Mer while screams filled the air and blackness assailed you. And then, the sucking sensation on her soul began, and it scared Easton into immediate lock-down on that staring contest. No way in hell, perdition or the in between, whatever you wanted to call it, no way was she letting go of her friendly neighborhood Mer guide's gaze.

The sensation pulled harder, demanding she give in, that she turn and follow its beckoning. E grit her teeth and squinted at the amorphous eyes before her, determined more than ever to not look away.

The sucking sensation suddenly became an oppressive feeling that sent E into panic as her mind connected it to a past occurrence. This is what it was like when E was pulled into the book. This was the exact sensation she felt in that moment. Was Allure sending her back to her world? Had this all been a ploy to get rid of her?

Allure gripped E's hands tighter, not letting go. With the nearly painful grasp, reality slowly shifted back to her. How could this be a ploy to get rid of her? It had been E's idea to even do this form of trial, after all. As her heart rate slowed, E became more sure of that fact. Allure wasn't getting rid of her. But this was without a doubt the same path that E had followed to Neverland.

Allure may not want to send E home, but the Rift definitely wanted to take her. Whether it was to suck her into the Rift or to spit her back out where she'd come from, E fought it. Maybe it was crazy, but E didn't want to even risk going back to her realm. Neverland was her home now. Ian was her home. Losing those homes would destroy her. Gripping Allure's hands just as tightly, E signaled that she was ready. Time to get this over with and be as far away from this place as possible.

The disturbing sensation of Allure entering her mind came as a slow tickling crawl at the back of her mind. It made her want to itch her scalp. Then, it spread forward, like a sheet of silk, covering her mind. That wasn't so bad. It was when the silk clung to her, encasing her, suffocating her, completely cutting her off from everything, that was the disturbing part. E still existed, yet she floated in a strange sort of coma, mentally paralyzed. She could distantly feel Allure sifting through her mind, copying those memories into her own mind, yet E couldn't fully grasp the situation. A dull part of her mind wanted to scream in terror, yet she didn't have enough mental capacity to even grant that.

And then after what felt like an eternity of floating, the sensation retreated as though it never existed. E's thoughts and actions were her own once more. She panted heavily, tightly holding to Allure's hands, eyes locked to the shifting colors of her eyes. But she couldn't help the laugh that bubbled from her lips. It sucked, but she'd done it. Half the battle was over. Allure offered a vague smile, then began the chant that would bring them back home.

As though in answer to her relief, metallic ringing sounds suddenly came from all around. The blackness outside their bubble began to shift and writhe and from the edges of her vision, E could swear the darkness had taken on humanoid form, fists pounding at their shield. Allure tensed, a pained expression crossing her features as she chanted more forcefully.

The return to the land of the Mer was a long and arduous one. E feared Allure might run out of energy before they made it. But the delicate Mer was more resilient than E gave her credit for. They passed through the gates, safely into the Mer world. Yet it was all Allure could do to shift the field from around them to plaster against the gates before collapsing. E ignored the writhing black mass that fought against the pearlescent shield of the still open gates, crouching at Allure's side.

"*Allure, are you okay?*" E asked, still grasping one delicate hand. The Mer's eyes popped open, and in that moment every single person around them was held in that same paralyzing stream of thought E had experienced only moments ago. Easton's life flowed through their consciousness in a never-ending stream of images and feelings. This time, E wasn't protected from the full brunt of the emotion. The horrors of her life washed over her, stealing her breath.

The pain and fear... the embarrassing degradations; they were something that were always a part of E, but she had locked them away so deeply in her mind that she'd felt only a dull echo of it through the years. Now, with every memory raw and exposed, sensation lashed through her soul sharper than any knife. E gasped and would have fallen, if the current of Allure's power wasn't holding everyone in utter stillness. Sickness roiled in her stomach as images of her parents' deaths spun into images of every person who had ever hurt her.

The faces flashed through their minds, each of their horrendous crimes in striking contrast to her crystal clear emotions at every moment of those crimes. E felt her cheeks flush with both embarrassment, shame and fury. Nothing of her life was kept private. Not one spec.

E had quite honestly forgotten how many memories there were. It seemed her life was one endless stream of battle and pain. Bare snippets of joy leaked through. Memories of her mother reading to her from the book of hook, the beautiful chime of her laughter as Easton ran about the room swinging a hanger in the air pretending to be Hook himself. The few moments of joy she'd stolen from life with her friends at her side. Mostly it was chaos. Everyone in the room felt the unerring sense of loss, despair, and tense unease that she had moved through her daily life with.

A horrible blackness engulfed them, sucking and draining, wrenching, pulling, filling to bursting. Everyone in that room felt the same sensations E had in traveling through the Rift. What would they think of her traveling to this realm? Would they understand it for what it was? Would they hate her for it, or would it bring understanding? Then, something miraculous happened. Peace and warmth flowed over her, easing the sting of her past. And E knew exactly what part of her memories they had hit. Her life here with Hook and the crew. This was a feeling of home, companionship, loyalty and love.

A collective sigh of relief rustled through the crowd, proving the audience was just as relieved to have the reprieve as E. And then, the relief changed to surprise and horror of their own as E's memories of walking in Pan's presence formed, proving Acquis as the traitor he was. Silence fell. E forced herself to find her voice.

"You see? Avida spoke to me of the pain she has endured, and how it has changed her, helped her mature. And she spoke to me of her brother, Acquis. The Mer that deepens the pain she suffers time and again, because of a selfish need to see her, to lessen his feelings of guilt for having used her as a pawn to bring down the Hooks. And worse yet, to do this all, he has aligned with the Pan!" Shock rippled through the arena.

"It was Acquis who made a pact with Pan, who betrayed all the Hooks! In this pact he agreed to deliver the Hooks to Pan, in return that Avida and Acquis would be under Pan's protection always. Acquis lured Avida into her fears of loss and rejection, and sent her running into Pan's arms for hope. And when

Avida was sent into the Rift, Pan had to change the way he kept his bargain, by bringing Avida through the Rift to meet with Acquis, time and again."

"Lies, and more lies! It's a trick!" Acquis croaked.

"The Fates are not forgiving, Acquis." Easton repeated Avida's words from that night. Acquis swallowed hard, stumbling away another step. *"Each time you pull her to you, her pain is doubled upon her return. She has begged you to leave her be, to accept your part in the destructive game you played, just as she has. But you refuse. She promised to never forgive you if you pull her to you again. And in return you promised to pull her endlessly still. What kind of brother does that? What kind of devotion can you have, when you knowingly put your own sister through such torture? If you are capable of that, surely you are capable of being touched of the Pan due to your own choices, just as Avida was. Unless of course you are going to try to blame that on my influence as well?"* Acquis stared at her in mute shock. Her eyes shot to the Council and crowd alike.

"You sent me into the Rift, to let your own eyes be the judge. I hope what you've seen has shown you the perilous situation we are in. There are so many among you that are following Acquis' lead. Whether you want to be divided in war or not, it's happening. The decision of whose side you are on is coming."

A roar of fury sliced through the air, cutting E's speech short. Time slowed as E watched Acquis run towards them with stark fury painting his features. Ian shouted out a cry of warning, but he couldn't span the distance soon enough. Acquis slammed into Easton, one clawed hand reaching out to yank the protective necklace from Allure's neck in the same moment. Allure cried out in alarm as her hands raised, trying to keep the shield over the still open maw of the Rift as Acquis and Easton crashed through it, eyes wide in horror.

With Allure now out of the picture, the Rift was swallowing them whole. Acquis' lips stretched thin over his sharp teeth as he gripped her throat, dragging her with him toppling wildly into the Rift. The crushing weight and tormenting feelings returned as the Rift devoured them. But the worst of the torment was the sound of Ian's agonizing shouts of loss. Her promise was broken; he was going to lose her forever.

381

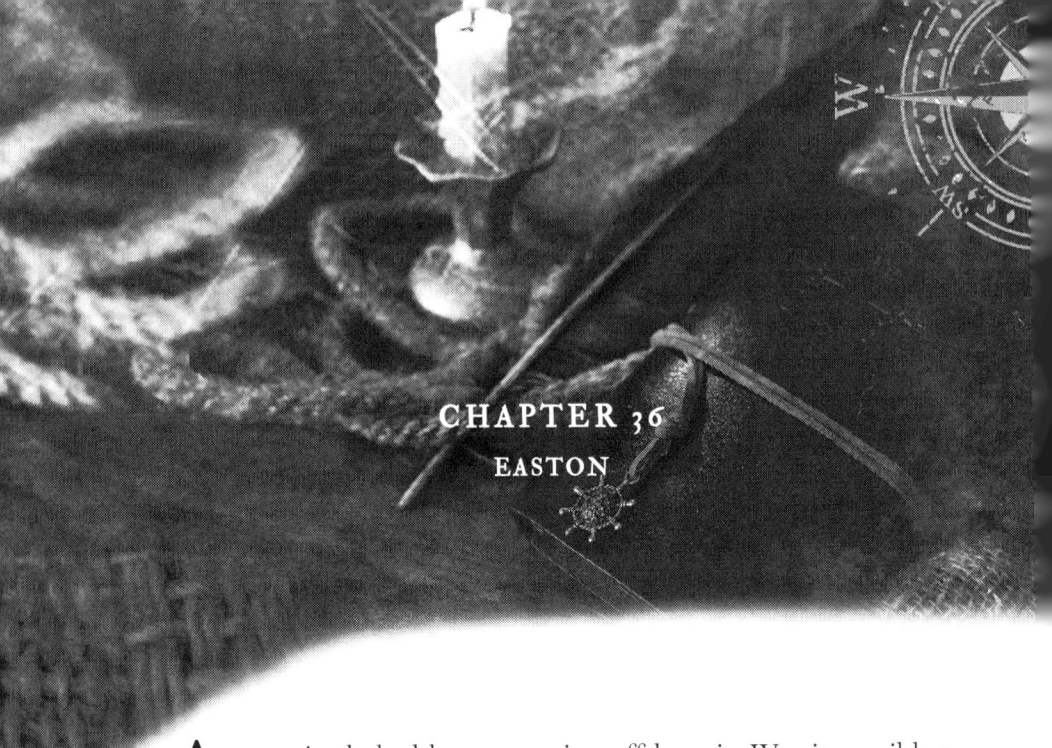

CHAPTER 36
EASTON

Acquis choked her, squeezing off her air. Was it possible to die in the Rift? E kicked out blindly, trying to free herself from Acquis' grip. She knew the crushing sensations had to be tearing him apart inside, too, yet somehow his sole focus seemed to be ending her, rather than worrying about his own physical pain.

Something hard and cold slammed into her side, pulling a ragged scream from her ravaged throat, adding it to the tumult of pained screams of the damned that already echoed in the darkness around them. Allure had told E that they wouldn't be able to talk in the Rift. But apparently, now that E and Acquis had become part of the Rift, that rule no longer applied.

E glanced down, realized Acquis had rammed Allure's sharp metal necklace into her side, his nails also biting through her skin. It burned like fire.

"You! You took everything from me! My respect, my people, you even turned my own sister against me!" Again and again Acquis rammed the metal into her side, the burning growing with each assault. But it lit another fire within Easton, too.

Though logically she knew there was no going back, no escape from the Rift, E's soul wasn't made to quit. It was made of slim chances, impossibilities, and never going down without a fight. It's who she was, and it had gotten her this far when everyone else said she shouldn't have made it. So whether she escaped the Rift or not wasn't the point. She had to fight, because Easton James was a fighter, a survivor. Easton Bendal was no less. She was *more*, because she had so much more to fight for. She had Ian. And if there was any way in this hell that she could escape and get back to him, she was going to find it. She'd made a promise. A cry of fury tore from her chest, words garbled under the strain to fight past the grip on her neck.

"You did all of that to yourself, you sick, demented freak! And you're not going to take me down with you!"

"Too late, little Panling, I already have! I think I shall enjoy tormenting you for eternity!" Acquis twisted the metal into her side once more.

Fighting through the pain, E gripped his hand with hers, stopping his movements. Acquis' movements were fueled by his insanity, but E was fueled by her own brand of crazy. Something Ian often reminded her of. A smile curved her lips. She was going to show Ian just how crazy she could be. Acquis wouldn't bring her down, and neither would the Rift. She would rip it to shreds before she let it have her. Slowly she felt strength grow within, blossom and spread.

E began to push Acquis' hand away from her side. His arm shook as he fought against her. Her smile grew as his turned into panic under her sudden strength. He released her throat, adding his second hand to the first's efforts to fight back. He cried out in pain as, with a sharp twist and downward yank, E broke Acquis' wrist while simultaneously ripping the metal from his now limp hand. She quickly wrapped the chain around her own wrist to make it harder for him to take it back, crouching over, ready for a fight.

And then, a soft red glow began to emanate from her hand. The metal of Allure's necklace had shifted, curved into a hook as it glowed. The red illuminated the impenetrable darkness around them, slowly pushing it back. When it touched Acquis panicked features, E felt a moment of triumph. He was totally freaking out.

The triumph disappeared into E's own freak out mode as the light extended, and illuminated what surrounded them. Rows and rows of hideous creatures hulked over them. Mouths and eyes gaping open, as black and soulless as the Rift itself. E instinctively knew that these ghouls were the souls of the damned sent here by Ian's hook. As though in answer to her thought, a single disembodied word scraped through the air like metal against rock.

"Hook!" Red eyes glowed in the blackness, reflecting the hate in that one word. Locking onto their vengeful track of mind, Acquis' hand shot out, one accusing finger pointed directly at E.

"Behold the bride of Hook, he who imprisoned you here! See how it also burns in her eyes!"

Apparently freaks understand when they have found another freak to be friends with because the Rift ghosts completely ignored Acquis, their empty eyes all shifting toward E. She might as well have had a sign glowing over top of her head shouting, 'Hook's woman, seek revenge here'. The dark shapes loomed toward her, bony shadows of fingers reaching for her, their howls of pain and torment ringing in the darkness. E crouched low, her new hook held out before her. A hook sent them here, a hook could take them out again. She gritted her teeth and waited.

One of the specters separated from the crowd and dashed toward her. Something about the shape made E hesitate, a hesitation that would normally get a person killed on the streets and Neverland alike. But when the specter crashed into a nearby shadow, hurling it away from her rather than attacking her, E smiled. The shadow stood before her, a regal sort of power issuing from its protective stance. The shadows didn't back down, but they didn't continue in their advance either. The face of her protector shifted slightly, revealing the side of a graceful jaw and nose.

"Sister?" Acquis' words came out pained and weak. Though shadowed and gaunt, Avida's features still held a haunting sort of beauty to them. Perhaps it was because she hadn't been here as long as the others, or maybe because some part of her had just refused to completely give up yet, some amount of life still hung to Avida's presence.

"You were once my most beloved brother, Acquis. Now, you quite simply sicken me. I warned you, but you did not listen. Now you are no longer my brother." Acquis stumbled back from Avida's words as though they were a punch in the gut. E grinned. She may have her frustrations with Ian's first wife, but in this, they could agree. Avida turned her attention to the other shadows.

"Leave Hook's bride to me. She is mine to do with as I will."

The shadows hesitated. E could feel their hunger, their need to rip her to shreds. But there was hesitation in their actions as well, as though some sort of twisted code of ethics was at play here, leaving the second wife to the first wife to deal with. E wasn't entirely sure where she stood on the matter. Was Avida still on her side here or, now that E was in the Rift, were the metaphorical gloves off?

Slowly, the shadows moved back one step. It wasn't much space, but it was a pretty big deal to E's pounding heart. The claustrophobia of them breathing down her neck lessened some. Acquis clearly felt anything but relief by their actions.

"Pan will give me justice," Acquis hissed. "He used to bring Avida to me from the Rift, he'll do the same for me when he realizes I'm gone. He'll want to know what happened to me. He's too curious not to! And when he does, I'll tell him everything. Even where your beloved Hook's lair hides. That's right, I know where it lies. I've known for some time, the fool. I should have done it long ago, but my honor bound me to protect that which my people believe to be family. Yet my people no longer hold me to honor. They have betrayed me as surely as the Hook did. I'll have my final revenge on them, you, and the Hook alike. Pan will decimate them all!" E reacted, arm furiously shooting out, the metal slicing across Acquis' face.

"I don't know if you can die in the Rift, but I'll find a way to make it happen before I ever let you hurt Ian and Neverland again!"

Horror shone across Acquis' features as he clasped his clawed hands over the gash she'd opened wide across his high cheekbone. She smirked darkly, letting him know she was going to do a whole lot more than that before letting him take her down. And then, everything began to go wrong, so very wrong. The opening on

Acquis' face kept growing, splitting open like a rotten pumpkin. Red light shone from its depths as the split widened, pushing out from the inside.

E had seen the Rift happen in the past, when she and Ian fought their way back home from the pigmite death trap. This wasn't at all what it should be. The Rift was supposed to suck the person inward. This was doing the opposite. Acquis' insides squished outward in a grotesque display of guts E knew she'd never be able to scrub from her mind again. Nor the feeling of the hot sticky substance that was now splattered all over her skin. He'd exploded. Literally exploded. Silence filled the normally torment-echoing expanse of blackness.

And then, a new sound rose. Utter fury and blood lust rattled from the black soulless around them. Clearly, they didn't like the idea of whatever the crap E had just done, or the fact that she could turn it against them. With a muttered curse, E grabbed Avida's arm and pulled her along, sprinting away in a random direction.

"There is nowhere to run, you ninny! Think you I have not attempted escape in the past? We are trapped within the Rift for eternity!" Avida cried out oh so helpfully.

"Shut up, I'm thinking!" A soulless leapt toward them and E slashed outward. The explosion happened much quicker this time, and a lot less messy, but it was there. New fury added to the cries of the damned, and E pushed her legs to move faster. With each shadow she exploded, the rest seemed to grow angrier, hungrier.

"Where are we going?" Avida gasped.

"That way!"

"Why?"

"Because… because!" E ground out. She wasn't sure where they were going, honestly. She was just following her gut right now, following the pull that drew her toward the darkness and trying to stay alive. If she could still be considered alive. Suddenly, they bounced off the blackness, as though they'd run face first into a brick wall.

"Damn it!" E shouted, hands crawling all over the darkness, searching for something, anything. There had to be more. Just… more. There had to be. She could feel it beckoning to her from beyond the black wall, something pulling her toward it as though grasping her very soul. And yet she couldn't reach it. E clawed at the wall, desperate. This couldn't be the end.

"They're coming." Avida's creepy calm tone had E shuddering.

"You would have made a great actress, you know that?" E glanced over her shoulder. The shadows were pressing in towards them, somehow managing to push the red glow of the hook back, as though suffocating the warmth of it.

"Damn it, this can't be the end! It can't! I made a promise. I made a promise," E whispered, slamming her fists against the black wall, as though they could somehow break it down.

"You fought well, bride of Hook. Octavian would have been proud." E glanced sharply at Avida. Her surprising reaction only fueled Easton's desperation and she pounded harder against the wall. She had to get back to him, she couldn't give up, she couldn't lose him.

With renewed fury, E slammed the hook into the black wall, stabbing away at the blackness as she mentally screamed at it to release them. A small popping sound drew E's gaze, her heart leaping as the metal somehow pierced the black wall, allowing a tiny sliver of light through. E grasped Avida's hand tightly.

"I'm not done yet. I have a promise to keep!" With a wild arc of her arm, E sliced across the black wall.

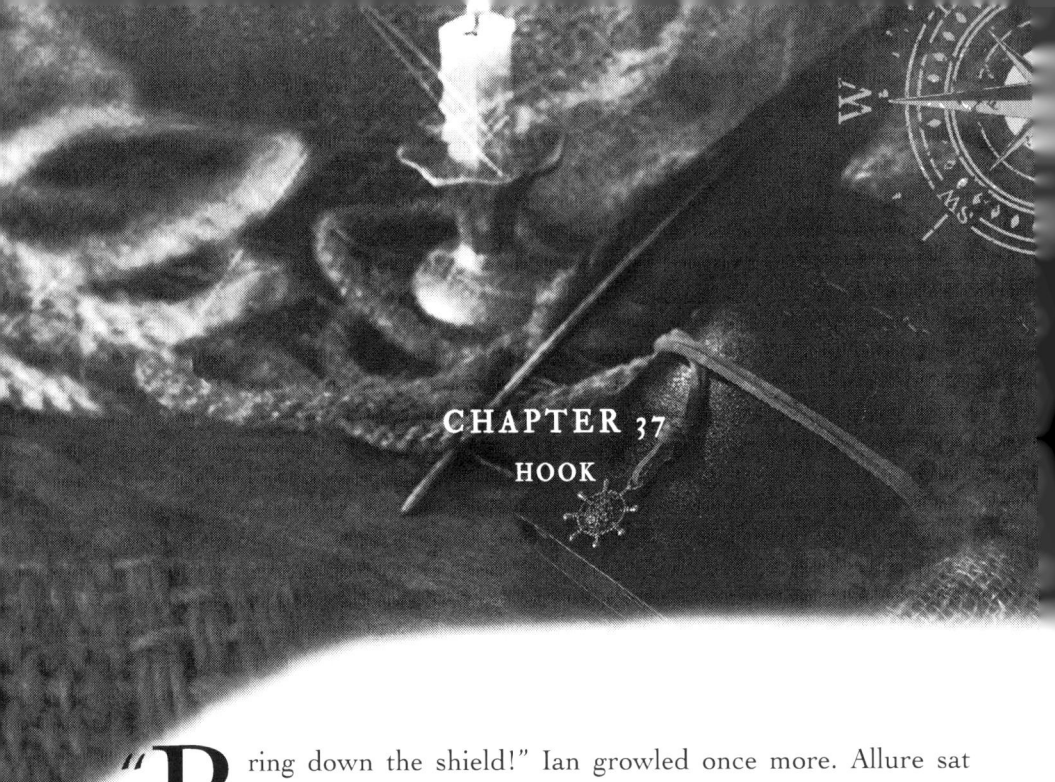

CHAPTER 37
HOOK

"Bring down the shield!" Ian growled once more. Allure sat slumped on the floor, hands upraised as she fought to keep the shield in place. It was now bowing outward, as though pushed from some internal force intent on escape.

"I cannot!" Allure gasped. "It is all I can do to keep the Rift at bay. With my necklace within, the Rift is exposed, the gates will not close. My shield is all that is protecting us!"

"Then let me through!" He gripped his patch-covered eye, cringing. "I can feel her pain, hear her screams." Or, he had. Now there was nothing but silence. His head lifted, jaw clenched in fury. "Acquis got through somehow; I will, too!"

"He has royal Mer blood. Only a royal Mer can pass through the shield of another Royal Mer," Bered intoned, moving to stand beside Ian.

"I don't *care* how he did it! Nothing will stand in my way."

"You would leave Neverland to its fate?" Ian clenched his jaw, refusing to meet Eventide's inquiring gaze. "You are the last guardian of this world, Hook. If you go, there shall be none to save it."

"And none shall save me," he whispered, his head falling against the invisible shield. With Easton gone, Ian felt his soul's salvation gone with her. There was nothing left of him but a shell. Without his heart, he was nothing.

Allure suddenly screamed, jerking everyone's attention her way. Her arms trembled as she fought the shield.

"Does the time draw so near, child? Can you hold it no longer?" Eventide rushed to her side, physically adding her support to Allure's weakening body.

"Something... something is coming through. I cannot stop it!" Allure gasped.

All eyes shot back to the portal. Ian's fingers hovered over the crystal casing on his hook, ready to unsheathe it, ready for what would come through. He wasn't sure if his hook would do any good against something already within the Rift, but it was his greatest weapon. A slash swept across the portal, red glow seeping through it like a beacon of doom. But no, that glow... he knew that glow.

"Wait!" Ian shouted, halting the Mer soldiers that swam up to surround the shield, sharp-bladed tridents at the ready. They paused, eyeing him uncertainly. "Wait," he said once more, eyes glued to the slowly opening slash.

A figure suddenly flopped out of the slash and rolled across the ground. One tightly clasped hand fell through the shield, the rest of the body still inside. The shield was too foggy to see clear details of what was happening inside, though Ian could see the blurry shapes of shadows on the other side. The hand moved back into the shield an inch as the shadows grasped the escapee's foot, trying to drag it back within the slash.

The view was blurry, but all Ian needed to see was that one delicate hand on the outside of the shield, bearing his ring. He quickly grabbed her hand and yanked E through the shield, immediately cradling her in his arms. A rush of hot air riddled the water with bubbles as it flowed over them, sending them all tumbling in the wave. Ian hunched over E's form cocooning her from the force. Allure slumped to the floor in relief as the Rift closed with a dull popping sound, finally allowing her to lower the shield.

Ian rocked E back and forth in his arms, tears freely mingling with the sea water. Scratches covered her body, her once beautiful dress was ragged, bits of green gory mess slowly seeping off her skin into the ebb of water encasing them, her hair a wild mess. Still her beauty rivaled all. His fingers gently brushed along her neck, tracing the graceful opening and closing of her gills, before moving to press over her heart. It thrummed strong and true beneath his touch.

"Bad manners, feeling me up in front of the Mers." Ian's eyes flew to hers, drinking in their warm brown depths.

"Beautiful little butterfly, you have come back to me."

"I promised," she smiled softly.

Pulling her against his chest, Ian sat there with his wife draped over his lap, rocking her, grinning like the besotted fool he was, and not caring a bloody damn who saw.

"But how did you escape, Easton? The Rift alone is impossible to escape, but you also moved through my shield. How is it possible?" Allure questioned, weakly making her way towards them with the aid of Eventide. *"Only royal blood can act as a conduit to pass through the shield."* Ian leaned back enough for Easton to speak. She held up one shaky hand, covered in all kinds of muck.

"I think she may have helped me with that." Her hand opened to reveal a small blue glowing orb. The crowd gasped. With a delicate reverence, Ian picked up the pearl. New tears escaped as warmth flowed through him.

"Keep her safe, Octavian. She has earned you. Let your soul be at peace, as mine now is." Avida's disembodied voice drifted through Ian's mind, issuing from the blue orb in his hand.

"Thank you, Avida." Ian closed his eyes, heart aching in too many ways to discern.

Caol drew a sharp breath. Gingerly lifting the pearl, he cradled it to his chest. Avida must have spoken to him as well, for shimmering tears etched his eyes when they opened.

"You brought her back." The Mer spoke, voice crinkly with emotion. *"You retrieved the soul of my sister."* Seeing her blank stare, Caol explained further.

"When Mer pass on from this world, our bodies cease to exist, but our souls carry on forever within pearls. The pearls are a sacred and beautiful gift to all. We treasure them, protect them in our sanctuaries. Families are able to visit

them, even converse with them at times. It is a great comfort to all. Treasured One, you returned my sister's soul to us." E sighed then gave a single weary nod.

"*Good.*"

"*Good? This is miraculous. I had no idea it was even possible.*" Caol eyed her for a moment longer, curious intensity in his gaze. "*Then again, you are capable of much, aren't you, Easton?*"

"*Is that... okay?*" E's eyes widened in uncertainty. Caol smirked at Ian as he gathered her closer, daring any to argue her safety amongst them.

"*Have no fear, little sister. Your trial went well. No harm will come to you amongst the Mers now.*" He paused, glancing towards the royals, obviously just remembering he wasn't actually the one who determined that fact. Eventide offered a stern expression, though it was softened with a smile.

"*Caol is correct, child. Though he has not yet been crowned to take his brother's place on the Seat of Council, we are in agreement.*" Caol's face paled slightly at that realization of responsibility. "*No one shall harm you here. We pass judgement of innocence upon you.*"

"*What will you do to Avida?*" Ian was slightly surprised to hear the protective edge to Easton's question.

"*Avida committed many wrongs. Yet she has done her best to right these wrongs. No matter her past, we shall honor her final actions. With her aide, you have warned us of dangers that could have destroyed us from within. The Mer shall ever be grateful and indebted to you.*"

"*Does that mean you'll help us fight on land?*" E pressed. Ian tensed. What E asked was much. The Mer fought Pan when he encroached upon their waters. When the Sirens attacked, they fought back. Yet the Mers had not blatantly chosen war outside of their waters in all of history. They protected their own. Eventide's face became shuttered, though troubled shadows remained in her gaze.

"*What became of Acquis?*"

"*He won't be following me.*" E shuddered.

Eventide watched her closely for a moment longer, then answered.

"*You have shown us many troubling things. That Acquis harbored hatred toward the Hook was no secret. But to turn to the Pan so blatantly is against our laws. That his hatred has infected those around him for so long, it is a troubling thought. We do not know how deep his rot has seeped into our people. All borders shall be closed, none shall enter or leave, until we have come to a decision and understanding of our people's hearts. Except for the two of you, of course. We have detained you long enough. When you are well enough to travel, you shall be free to depart."*

Ian recognized dismissal when given. With a smile, Ian helped Easton to her feet. She wavered, slumping against him. His arms immediately wrapped about her, supporting her weight. She cringed, gasping in pain. Covered in all the gore upon exiting, Ian hadn't been able to discern her blood from that of what she'd encountered in the Rift. Teeth gritting, Ian carefully lifted her into his arms, forcing a smile he didn't feel. She'd been through enough, she didn't need to see his panic.

"*Come, little butterfly. You must rest so that we may fly away together.*" Easton nodded against him, then paused.

"*Wait. Allure.*" She held out her other hand. "*Your necklace.*" Allure's hand went to her heart.

"*I am so grateful to you, Easton. Had you not managed to retrieve it, the portal gates would not have closed, and the Rift would have entombed us all.*"

"*Yeah, it's pretty handy. Without it I never would have found a way out of hell.*" She shuddered, holding the necklace farther away from her. Allure's grin melted away into a blank stare as the metal touched her fingertips. Allure gently pressed Easton's hand back to rest on her stomach, not taking the necklace. Ian blinked. Something was wrong.

"*Thank you, Easton.*" Her gaze shifted towards him, colors glimmering like oil in her irises. "*I will come to retrieve the necklace later. Right now your wounds are more important.*" Without another word, Allure turned and swam away. Pushing the troubling sensation of Allure's reaction away, Ian focused on his wife. Carefully clutching his precious treasure, Ian swam toward the healing chambers.

CHAPTER 38
HOOK

Ian carefully watched the rise and fall of Easton's gills as she lay in the healing bed before him. Her body was encased in the glowing blue kelp of the Mer that was the source of her swiftly returning health. Far and wide Neverland had been known for its healing miracles, the kelp highly sought before the war. The Mers had grown quite wealthy from its trade, as none other could grow the material. After the war, the Mer had carefully guarded the material, no longer trading with anyone outside of the Mer.

Ian had never been more grateful for the Mer than he was now. His wife had been in dire condition, her body covered in wounds, though none as grievous as the holes that riddled her side. Without the healing kelp, Ian had little doubt as to whether or not Easton would have survived the ordeal. Ian tensed for a moment as the door at his back opened. A quick glance over his shoulder revealed Queen Allure, and his muscles instantly tightened for new reasons. Easton hadn't relinquished her vice-like grip on the necklace since Allure refused to take it.

"*Queen Allure, what's wrong?*"

"*How does she fair?*" Allure hesitated, floating closer.

"*She's healing.*" He stated simply, knowing all too well that Allure carried news that could be more dangerous to his wife than her current wounds. Allure nodded slowly, then met his gaze.

"Eventide and Bered have secured the city. But I fear there are those who had already fled. I have little doubt that they carry news of your bondmate to the Pan. Sanctuary's whereabouts are not common knowledge to any but the Council. When sharing her memories, I was careful to exclude certain areas of those memories from all but the Council, and you. With Acquis gone, I feel Sanctuary's location is still safe. But Easton's isn't. I feel it likely that once word of events here reaches Pan, he will come for her."

Ian's shoulders drooped under the new exhaustion her words brought.

"It would have come eventually. We will exercise greater caution when we leave. Thank you for protecting Sanctuary. Once we are home, she will be safe there."

"Your wife has Awakened the metal."

"What?" Ian's attention jerked back to Allure. The statement was so preposterous he could find no other words for response.

"I felt...something, when she came through the shield; a memory that made no sense. But I knew for certain the moment the metal touched my skin." She held out the metal necklace. *"Somehow Easton has awoken the calling. The metal answers to her now. She has used it not only to escape the Rift, but also to kill. Octavian, it turned into a hook at her behest."* His brow furrowed. Allure nodded slightly. *"She rent Acquis and others within the Rift, shredding their souls from existence entirely."*

Ian's fingers hesitated over the metal beneath Easton's fingers, mind racing over all of the possibilities this matter presented. Allure would know. She was one with the metal almost more than he was with his hook. She descended directly from the line that created his own hook. She had carried the last known piece of it with her for most of her life. Closing his eyes, Ian pressed a solitary finger to the metal, slipping his skin along the length. A warm tingle echoed in his hook as it greeted a long dormant friend. Easton's metal answered with a timid hello of its own, sending a warm pulse through his fingers. His wife had awoken the metal. He glanced up, carefully gauging Allure's reactions.

"Why are you telling me this now?"

"To be a Pan, to have wielded the Hook's power and lived? Others already know she was able to fight her way free of the Rift. But they don't know how. If they knew of her power to wield the Hook? Pan must not know of her power. He already knows too much. You need to get her back to Sanctuary as quickly as possible."

"Is it only the Fiend that you fear, Allure?"

"If the other Mers knew of Easton's power… that she could twist our most precious metals to do her bidding without having been through the proper cere-monies to bond her, and with the blood of Pan running in her veins? Fear and doubt would return once more and she would become seen as more of a danger to all." She paused, *"You know us to be a people of laws. We honor them most stridently. Our wills are bound to them, our honor and very lives. Our laws and minds have already been stretched enough for you, Octavian. They have stretched more for you than any other in all of our existence. The laws will stretch no further, nor will others' minds. It is best we not tempt fate so soon. Her power must remain secret."*

"Yes," he acknowledged hollowly. There could be no argument that would save them should this come to light.

"I have seen within Easton's heart. I know she is of pure intent. While others saw her memories and felt her emotions, they have not seen within, they do not understand her as I do. I tell you this now because I do not wish harm to come to either of you. I know you are the last hope for Neverland." She paused. *"I feel that she is… needed. Not just for Neverland's survival, but for yours as well. I have enough strength left for this one last gift before you depart."*

She stood straight and held a hand over Easton's where it still clutched the metal. A whispered blessing sifted through their minds as she added the Mer bond atop whatever bond Easton had already managed to form with it.

It began to glow red, the color of a Hook. Easton's eyes sprang wide, a gasp of shock on her lips. The last of the red Hook glow echoing in her normally brown eyes as Allure sealed her blessing. Blinking, Easton settled back into her healing slumber, as though nothing earth-shattering had just occurred. Ian sank heavily into his chair.

"It is done. Should it be discovered that she wields the Hook, at least she

will bear the mark of my approval of bonding. It will be enough to fool most into thinking I am the reason she can use it. Most, but perhaps not all. So care is still needed in protecting her secret, for now." She stroked her finger lovingly over the metal once more, an almost wistful expression on her face. *"It feels odd, no longer being the guardian of it. But my time has ended. Now it will serve her well. With her, your order has been reborn. Protect one another, Octavian. You are Neverland's only hope."*

"I will, till my dying breath. But how did this happen?"

"I cannot say for certain. Perhaps it was her distress in the Rift in the presence of the Shades that caused the metal to awaken and answer her needs. Perhaps it is her very being that caused a change in its makeup, as she did to your hair."

"She is not a danger, she didn't corrupt me," Ian growled.

"Would I be here on her behalf if I thought she had?" She censured. Ian rubbed his eye tiredly. Allure sighed, clearly exhausted herself from the extent of magic she had performed that day.

"I wish that I could give you answers, Octavian. But I have none. Nor can I say how this will affect her soul. Yours was protected by the ritual before the bonding. She holds no protection. That, along with the fact that she comes from the heritage of the Pan…it should be impossible for her to even control it, much less bond it. Her health now could simply be a short reprieve of what is to come. This could have damaged her beyond what we can see on the outside."

Ian felt himself go cold at the words Allure spoke. They too closely mimicked the words that had haunted his mind these long hours he'd watched over her.

"She will be fine. Easton is a master at turning the tides in her favor."

"I truly hope you are right. Time will tell. However, a few things are certain. That metal is now hers as surely as the hook is yours. It has bonded to her, as you can clearly see she has bonded to it. Her use of it goes wholly against our laws, but it has happened. And now that it has, you find yourself in more danger here. You must be on your way as quickly as possible."

"Who says it's against your laws?" Ian jumped at Easton's voice shouting in his head. She offered a small mental wince in apology as she moved to sit upright. *"Sorry. Groggy and volume control don't go well together."* Ian wrapped an arm under her shoulders, assisting her. He sat on the edge of the healing bed, urging her to lean against him.

"*Who says it's against your laws?*" Easton repeated.

"*The ritual hadn't been performed for you to take on the name of a Hook when you wielded it.*" Allure explained calmly.

"*I've always felt like I was a Hook at heart. But when I married Ian, I took his name. He is a Hook, which means I am a Hook. Official enough for me.*"

"*You took on his name alone, not the title of Hook. You have not taken the appropriate oaths to wear that mantle. Not to mention the fact that you are a Pan. A creature this weapon was meant to destroy, not strengthen.*"

"*But by your own laws, any oaths my husband has taken, I take upon myself as well the moment I marry him. Isn't that so? Otherwise I would not be subject to your laws. As you are the ones who set the laws that formed the Brethren of the Hook, you can't deny those laws. You yourself said that you are a people of law. If you deny one, you deny them all, then your whole foundation crumbles and all laws become pointless. Besides, your laws state that the weapon was meant to kill the Pan. It didn't say specifically that it could not be used by someone descended from a Pan.*"

Allure stared at her in awe and a healthy dose of respect. Ian's face bore pride in the wicked little tilt of his lips. E flushed under their attention.

"*I may have been reading up on your laws a bit, before the trial,*" she admitted.

When he'd asked her why she was reading the other night, she'd stated that she knew her rights front and back in her old world; that one had to understand them when you lived on the line between good and bad. Why should this world be any different? Ian pulled her tighter to him and kissed the top of her beautiful vermillion head.

"*You have gained a formidable companion, Hook,*" Allure noted with quiet curiosity.

"*I have come to the same conclusion, many times.*" Ian grinned wickedly down at the woman cradled to him.

"*You like it.*" E wrinkled her nose at him and he wholeheartedly agreed.

"*It is good.*" Allure nodded. "*She will need that in the times to come. But now, you must be on your way as quickly as possible. It would appear she is too stubborn to sleep any longer.*" Allure's lips curled upward on one end as she fought a smile. *"Though that will work to your advantage. No one will expect her to have recovered so quickly. The more time she is here, the more likely suspicion will rise, and the more time the traitors have to share their news with the Fiend. Easton was correct when she said we are divided. There are still those amongst us who will be eager to do her harm, now that they know of her truth."*

"We understand. Thank you, Queen. I am in your debt." Ian bowed his head in deference.

"No debt is necessary. You are most welcome to my help." She paused, speaking to his mind alone. *"Octavian, I know this is a heavy burden for you both. I know that you fear for her safety. But perhaps you can find reason to rejoice in this as well. You will no longer have to fight this battle alone. That is why she was sent here: for you, for Neverland."* With a nod, Allure floated out of the room.

Ian pulled his wife closer to his side, pressing a long kiss to her vermillion hair. Easton *had* been sent to help him. Allure had no idea how true that statement was. But Easton wasn't just here to help him. She was here to save him.

"Are you well enough to travel, my heart?"

"Better than that. I'm well enough to fly." She grinned up at him. *"Let's get out of here before I become permanently pruney."* She paused as she looked down at the metal in her hand, the silent understanding of the burden of it settling on her shoulders despite her earlier bravado. Ian carefully took the metal, removed the broken chain and wrapped the metal in twine from one of the pouches at his belt. With loving gentleness, he slipped it over her head, then placed a kiss on her nose.

"I happen to love prunes."

"You happen to love anything you can put in your mouth." Her mischievous grin faltered as she realized the double innuendo. *"Uh, well, you know... food, I meant."*

"You happen to be right, on all accounts, my dear." He helped her up from the table, once more gluing her to his side as they floated towards the door. *"Though you will be the only woman I ever devour again, until the end of time. This I promise you."*

"And I know how strongly you hold to promises," she whispered in his mind, a gentle caress that warmed him through.

"Then trust me when I promise you that we'll both get through this."

"Together." She made her own promise. And her promises were something he would never doubt again. She'd gone to the ends of the Rift for him, just as she promised she would. He would never doubt her heart.

"Together." With a soul-searing kiss, Ian sealed the promise. When they pulled apart, Easton grinned up at him.

"When this is all over, you and I are going to have some exploring to do with this unique underwater breathing thing."

"Is that so? How?" Ian's brow rose, intrigued.

"Not telling you," she sing-songed.

"Devious wench. I fear I may be in very real danger of falling in love with you," he smirked.

"Too late." She winked, then took his hand, and together they set out on the next leg of their journey.

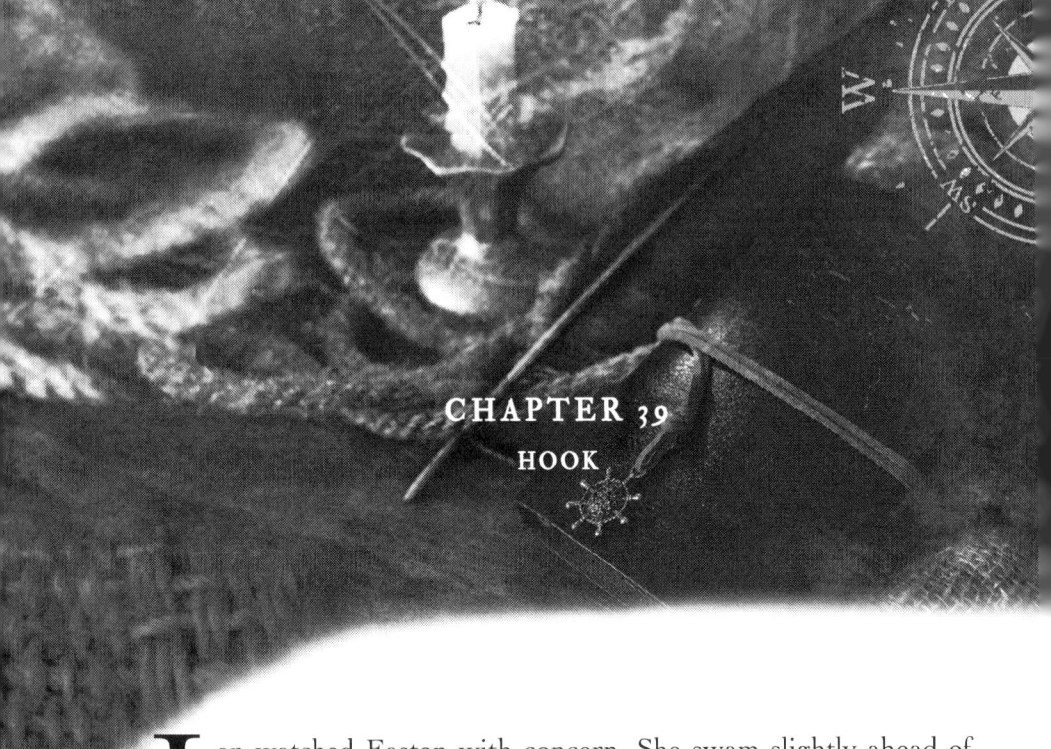

CHAPTER 39
HOOK

Ian watched Easton with concern. She swam slightly ahead of him, her face scrunched the way it always did during thought. From the moment they had left the healing chamber, she'd gone silent. She put all her focus on keeping her mind locked down, protected from those around them. They couldn't risk others learning of her unorthodox induction into the Order of Hook. Ian had taken up the flank to watch her back for any attack as they silently swam for the gateway. It gave him a lovely view, but also allowed him time for his own thoughts to whirl.

"Stop staring at her like she's about to sprout horns. She passed the trial, she's fully healed and she's fine." Caol bumped him with his elbow.

Caol had allowed no argument in escorting them back to Sanctuary. Caol had never been to Sanctuary, though it wasn't for a lack of trust. Ian trusted his brother entirely. They had both agreed it was safer for all involved if he didn't know its exact location in the past. In his line of soldier work, he could be captured by the Pan at any time, and the herbal remedies the people of Sanctuary used to keep Pan out of their heads didn't work on Mers.

But things had changed with this trip to the Mer realm. Caol watched Easton as though she were a treasure amongst men, which she was, of course, but her actions at the trial had obviously put her on a pedestal for Caol. After she'd rescued Avida, Caol had taken it on himself to become one of her faithful protectors.

"Yes. Fine." Hook repeated dully. He couldn't shake the growing gloomy feeling hanging over his head like an albatross forewarning of doom. The gateway was just ahead of them, and no one had looked twice at them. But he was growing twitchy. Every sound in the water, every moment that passed had his stomach in knots. They were far too exposed here.

"Is that the gate? Finally!" E rejoiced.

"Wait. Let Caol or I go first" They both quickly swam to either side of her as they approached the shimmering water that glowed in the distance.

"Fine, fine. But hurry, I'm so waterlogged I feel like a jellyfish. I may never feel dry again!" she moaned pitifully. Caol grinned and nodded for him to go above the surface to check for danger. Ian returned the affirmation and slowly ascended. Water slipped across the top of his scalp as he slowly broke the surface.

The usual sounds of Neverland met his ears, nothing dangerous carrying on the air. Rising further, he gripped the edge of the pool and looked about. His gaze froze as they snagged on a large hunched figure. The man sat on a mossy log, his head in his hands as though in despair. He was covered in grime, clothing torn, shaggy hair wild with twigs. Hook's eyes narrowed as he floated there, debating. Finally, he decided it would be safer to address the situation while still within easy access of the ocean, Easton safely below with Caol.

"Who are you?" he growled.

The man jerked, scuttling off the log and dropping into a tired, unstable crouch. He stared at Hook with wide, light green eyes that spoke of terror and confusion. His lips moved, but he didn't speak a word. A suspicion formed in Ian's mind, and he struggled with what to do about it. He knew every face of the villagers in the land, and every one of the Lost Boy's smoky faces, too. This face, he'd never seen.

"Wiley?" He watched carefully, and got the reaction he expected and somewhat dreaded. The man's eyes widened in recognition quickly followed by fear and determination. One hand flew out to grab up a thick stick nearby, never taking his gaze away from him. Careful steps began carrying him further away. Ian watched him for a moment, indecision warring within. The man carried the wildness of Pan in his appearance, had been in the Fiend's clutches for far too long to be safe. But Easton… he sighed, already knowing what he must do.

"Wait, please." His hand disappeared below the surface and beckoned. The man had paused, but was a startle away from outright running. Wild like the animals of the forest. Easton's head broke the surface dramatically, the water draining from her gills as she coughed a little and sucked in air. The man turned to run.

"Finally!" Easton gasped, pushing the hair from her face. Ian's attention darted to the man who had frozen mid-step. Ever so slowly he turned their direction. "Oh blessed sun!" Easton continued on, floating toward the edge of the pool. "Oh it feels like forever since I…" She stopped talking as she followed Ian's pointed finger, finally noting the man. A gasp tumbled from quivering lips.

"Wi? Wi!" Immediately she struggled to push herself from the water, and Ian helped with a push on her backside. Moving swiftly, he climbed from the water so that he could stay close to her.

"Steady on, Easton…" he cautioned. Her hands reached out to help steady him as his Hook slid against the muddy bank, slowing his exit. As she did, their gazes met, hers letting him know her emotions weren't getting in the way of her instinct of the possible dangers. Though he found himself missing her voice in his mind already, they had grown quite adept at speaking through a glance over their time together. She was brilliant, assured, cautious but so very full of life. How he loved this fiery woman. He couldn't be more proud to call her his wife, and vital addition to his crew.

Caol slid from the water with grace, casually watching their backs as Ian gained his footing on dry land. E turned back to Wiley, taking one step closing, gauging his reaction.

"Wiley? Still with me, buddy?" Wiley stared at her blankly. She took another step, and with it, Ian and Caol moved as well. Wiley tensed. E reached back, fingers finding his.

"Think you're going to have to trust me on this one, Captain," she murmured.

"Vermillion..." Ian tensed, already knowing she planned to go the rest of the distance alone. "Are you certain?"

"Not one hundred percent, but... I'm going for it, anyway. He's still in there, I know he is."

And so, though it went against everything in his core, he kept his feet rooted to the ground as she moved toward danger.

"Wi, talk to me." She took each step with precise shifts, arms out to the side, no sudden movements. "Come on, dude. You haven't gone this quiet on me since that time you nearly killed that kid from Gull team for punching me. I didn't let you pull away from me then, I'm not letting you now, either." Wiley's jaw clenched, but his expression remained vague. E stopped only feet away.

"Okay, so you've seen some deep shiz. I get it." She bit her lip, hand moving toward his before retracting to her side. "But I'm not going to be mad at you just because you're broken in different ways, Wi."

He blinked, bloodshot eyes tracking toward her face. His hands rose upward, and Ian and Caol tensed once more. But instead of attacking, his fingers flicked around in a curious way. Finally, he was talking.

"Yes, it's really me." Easton nodded sadly. His fingers moved more animatedly. "It's a long story, but I've been safe. I'm so sorry you haven't been. But you will be now. I promise." She sighed heavily. "Next time you go hiding, leave me some clues. I've been looking everywhere for you, Wi."

Ian and Caol tensed, watching as the man stood there with numb shock on his face. Ian's grip twitched to the weapon at his side as Wiley's arms lifted, closing around Easton, lifting until she dangled from him like a tiny kitten. Still Easton didn't give the signal, and Ian forced himself to hold firm, even as Wiley's head fell into the crook of her neck and he began to shake. Ian and Caol exchanged a glance as the man silently sobbed into Easton's shoulder.

"Oh, Wiley." Easton crooned sadly, holding him back just as tightly. "I am so sorry we couldn't find you earlier." Silent tears tracked down her cheeks. Ian watched the reunion, wanting to feel happy for his wife, but unable to step away from the feeling of suspicion and concern. Wiley was alive. But was he truly still Wiley? He stepped closer while the man was distracted, Caol mirroring his movements. Immediately they halted when his head jerked upright, fury blazing in those wild green eyes. He took a step backward, gripping Easton tightly, taking her with him. Ian immediately drew his sword.

"Stop."

He tried to keep the panic from his tone, to keep it firm and low. He didn't want to startle the man into doing something that would hurt his wife, but he couldn't let him disappear with her either. E pulled back from the hug, but he didn't release her. She pressed against his chest; he didn't even glance her way. She held up a warning hand Ian's way, stopping him mid-step. She tapped Wiley on the shoulder.

"It's okay, Wi. They're my friends." He didn't reply. "Wi, put me down please." When he still didn't move, her face scrunched with temper, and Ian saw the kick coming before her foot even twitched. The solid attack against his shin finally yanked Wiley from his staring contest with Hook, and he turned wide eyes her way.

"I said put me down, please." Ian nearly smiled at the authoritative sound to her voice. Thoughts skittered across the man's face, and he carefully lowered her to the ground. His face scrunched like a child reprimanded, hands rising to movements so quickly Ian wondered how anyone could read them. E's hands rose to rest atop his, holding them steady.

"Slow down, Wi. It's okay." He nodded, hands shaking as he worked through the motions slower.

"I know you didn't want to do it, Wi. And you didn't. You ran."

His hands lifted, and Easton watched carefully.

"She helped you? Who is she?"

They signed back and forth for a good several minutes, silent but animated. Ian itched under the uncomfortable sensation of the stirrings of jealousy. What was he saying so passionately to her? Why wasn't she translating? Finally E sat back on her heels, looking up toward the sky, thoughts running around in those beautiful brown eyes. The thoughts slowed as she came to a decision.

"I know you didn't want him in your head, Wi. He's good at tricking people, making them do and think things they normally wouldn't. But you're with us now, you're safe." Wiley's head lifted, wide eyes silently pleading as his hands moved again. Easton's brow creased, not liking what she heard.

"No." She stopped his hands as he moved them again. "I said no, Wiley. I just found you; I won't let him have you again." She promised, eyes bright with determination. "I can't risk the danger it might bring to the others in Sanctuary. But we will find you a place…"

Ian stared at his wife's back as she continued brainstorming how to keep her friend safe. She hadn't even considered asking Ian to bring him into Sanctuary, though he could practically feel her fear for her friend. She understood her duties as a Hook, her duty to the innocent people within. Relief and pride alike filled him. No, Easton was nothing like he and Avida had been.

Sanctuary was different than the Hooks' home had been. Sanctuary would live up to its name. It protected all within from the corruption of the Pan. If he could get Wiley inside, it would disconnect the Fiend's power, if not cut it completely. He could only assume Pan's link to Easton's mind was due to his blood connection. Still, if the Pan was deep enough in Wiley's mind that even Sanctuary wouldn't completely block it, they would have to take precautions. The main risk they ran with Wiley now, however, was being out in the open with him.

"You will stay in Sanctuary." Ian stated. Easton turned wide eyes his way.

"…are you sure? Is it safe?"

"It is safe enough, but I have demands that must be met in return. And they must be answered quickly."

"Aye, Captain." She smiled softly up at him. "Name your terms." He pulled his gaze from the warmth in hers, to rest on Wiley's nervous expression.

"You'll be held in confinement until we are certain the Fiend's

influence no longer taints you. And you will be rendered unconscious before we begin the trek there, so that the Fiend will not be
able to use you to lead him to us. You will remain blindfolded and
restrained until the protective drink starts working. Do we have an
accord?"

Wiley lifted his hands. Easton relayed his question to Ian.

"It can protect you from him." Ian agreed. Wiley poked one
finger to his head, eyes wide. Ian needed no translation for that.
"Provided the bond isn't too deep, yes, even your mind. But the
drink will help with that as well."

Without a second thought, Wiley fell to his knees, tears brimming
the lids as he held his hands out to be tied. Ian felt his heart constrict
under the pain and begging in those eyes.

"Caol, if you will."

Caol immediately moved forward, pressing his fingers to Wiley's
head. Wiley's eyes rolled back in his head and he slumped forward,
Caol catching him before he tipped fully.

"You can knock people out just from touching them?" Easton
asked as Hook quickly tied Wiley's hands.

"I don't like to brag." Caol grinned, hefting Wiley onto his shoulder. E's lips parted in surprise.

"Fish have a lot more muscle than I realized."

"I do like to brag about that one," Caol chuckled.

"Quickly." Ian led the way. "The Fiend will no doubt notice the
missing connection, now that he is unconscious."

They rushed for the entrance of Sanctuary, and Ian didn't
breathe a sigh of relief until they were on the other side of the cave.
Caol looked around with interest as he easily carried Wiley to the
holding cells of Sanctuary. Comfortably situated on a cot, hands
untied, they barred the gates behind them.

"How long until he wakes up?" Easton asked Caol.

"Now that I am no longer in contact with him? That will depend
on him. When he wakes will be determined by how much sleep his
body currently requires. Given his previous circumstances, I would
assume he will need much."

"Yes." Easton nodded, words a bare whisper. "He's lost so much weight. It's like he was becoming a ghost." How true that sentiment was, in more ways than physical.

"Caol, feel free to explore at your leisure. The inn will have a place for you when you are ready." Caol rubbed his hands together like a giddy child and took off. Ian shook his head, knowing he had just unleashed havoc on the town.

"Easton. A word?" She hesitated, nibbling her lip uncertainly as she watched over Wiley. "He will be alright. The guards will alert us when he wakes, if you wish it."

He held out his hand, waiting for her decision. She wrapped her hand in his, holding his arm to her as she leaned into him. He pressed a kiss to her head and began walking. They walked some distance, moving to sit atop a grass knoll away from the busy passages of townsfolk. Easton settled between his legs, a heavy sigh escaping as he wrapped his arms around her from behind.

"Are you sure it's safe for him to be here?" She twisted to look up at him. "I could never forgive myself if he brought danger to everyone here... to the children."

"He is far safer here than anywhere else Neverland could offer." He pressed his nose to her hair as he continued. "But I must own that I have misgivings. As happy as I wish to be for you, wife, I must question the situation. Don't you find it suspicious that he came right to us, after all our time searching for him? Especially knowing that the Fiend held him captive."

"I would find it strange...except I think it's my fault."

"Come again?"

"I've felt strange, since the Between. Like it... opened me up, I guess is the only way I can explain it. It feels like I have all these strings pulling me in different directions." Ian frowned, his worry growing. Was this one of the consequences Allure had feared? "I felt one of those strings pulling me to you when I was in the Between. It was what guided me back. I felt something similar pulling me back to Sanctuary. And... I think one of the strings was tied to Wiley." She waved her hands in the air as though it would whisk away her thoughts.

"I know it sounds stupid, and I didn't know I was doing it at the time. I've just been thinking about it and in hindsight I honestly think I did it."

"Slow down, explain," he soothed, running a hand through her hair to calm the nervous energy flying off of her.

"I was trying to keep my mind focused, to keep the Mers from hearing my thoughts. And my mind just kind of kept turning to Wiley. How Avida told me he had escaped and that I needed to find him quickly before Pan got him again. And the more I thought about it, the tighter my chest felt, the more urgently I felt pulled... like I had to swim faster, to get out of the water quicker. Every time I thought about Wiley I felt that tugging on my mind and eventually... I grabbed hold and started pulling back. When I asked him how he found us, he said he felt something similar. Something reeling him in like a fish on a line."

"Why didn't you tell me you were feeling strangely?"

"I didn't want to worry you." She scrunched up her nose on a cute little wince. "So I kind of just ignored it and hoped for the best?"

"You do enjoy playing with fire, my dear," Ian murmured; mind rushing through her words as his fingers slipped through her hair.

"Is there any other way?" she sighed, leaning into his touch.

"Not in Neverland, anyway," Ian acknowledged. He relinquished her silky strands to tilt her chin toward him, holding her gaze. "Now that you are aware of this new... skill set, we must exercise caution. That could have been very dangerous, yes? What if the Fiend were simply using Wiley for bait to catch you?"

"Yes. Although..." She turned weary eyes to him. "Would it have been so bad if he were?" His brow rose in surprise. "I'm tired of running, Ian. Maybe it's time we take the fight to him."

"We were hardly prepared then, my sweet."

"I know, I know." She groaned, turning to press her face to his chest. "It's just... the longer it takes to bring Pan down the more we risk. Look at our battles when I first arrived. He cut a large number of us down then. He picks us off little by little and eventually we will lose the war simply from a loss of manpower."

"Yes, we have suffered many losses. Yet look at our numbers of success since your arrival. We are already taking the fight to him, and we are gaining ground. We've managed to start time again, Easton! That alone is a huge success. You can't imagine how much hope you've given Neverland in that one act you so swiftly achieved. You've turned the tides, Easton. We're wearing him down now. With you at our side we are making the Fiend fear us once more."

"And then we can hope his hold on the land and people disappears with his head when we cut it off." Ian blinked at her in wonder. She shifted her shoulders uncomfortably under his intensity. "What? Too blood-thirsty for you, Captain?"

"You are a marvel, you beautiful, deadly little thing. Together we will heal Neverland and our people one step at a time." Pulling her closer he nestled her below his chin. "But let's walk a bit more carefully, shall we? I'm in no rush to risk you further, my Vermillion. Not today."

"Hmm." He could tell she wasn't thrilled with his answer, but was accepting it for now. He smiled softly, drinking in the comfort of her within his embrace. His eye opened lazily at the clearing of a throat. Easton tensed in his arms. Isen Fermond, once known as Jaguar, stood before them. His head was bowed, his short, shorn hair grown shaggy in his time in Sanctuary. A gray robe of the penitent covered his large form.

"I was hoping I could talk to you for a minute, Easton."

Ian glanced sharply at his wife, waiting for her reply. If she were uncomfortable, he'd send the man away. This was a discussion they both needed in order to move on, but perhaps now wasn't the right time. She sat stiffly in his embrace for a long moment. Then slowly, her shoulders slumped.

"Go for it," she replied stiffly. The man fell to his knees, head still low.

"I saw you all at the jail earlier... did you find Wiley?"

"We did."

"Good." Relief poured from his words in a way that couldn't be false. Ian examined Easton's features, searching out her emotions.

"Isen... was that your name?" She asked. His head jerked

upright at the use of his name. Irony twisted the length of his lips as he shook his head.

"It was, at one time." A pitiful laugh jolted his hunched shoulders. "Figures, I finally get you to use my name and it's the one I've been trying to leave behind all these years. The one I was so ashamed of. I suppose that's fitting."

"Why are names so important to you, anyway?"

"I hated myself for what I did to you. I wanted you to see I was different than the boy who had destroyed my life. It was all in my head, but the guilt wouldn't leave me. Every time I would see the condemnation in your eyes... it was worse because I didn't think you knew what I did, but it was still there. I wanted you to see me as Jag, the guy that was a total screw up, but was trying to make it better the only way I knew how." He shrugged, a helpless sort of gesture of a man lost. Ian had seen the gesture often enough in the mirror to recognize it.

"Names aren't what make us who we are. Actions are," she replied sharply, and his head ducked lower under the verbal lash. Easton sighed, fingers rising to rub at her eyes. "Why are you here?"

"I... I want to try to make things right, in any way I can. I know it's too late. But time here has made me want to change. To be a better man than I have been. And I guess I was hoping you could tell me what to do to fix what I can?"

"I can't tell you how to fix yourself. I won't. It's not my job."

"I know."

"I could hate you. I *have* hated you in many ways at many different times. I have *every* reason to hate you."

"You do."

"But," she looked to Ian, held his gaze. "time here has taught me a thing or two, also. And one of those things is the need for healing. I have a responsibility to help heal this place and its people. And I can't do that when I have a pit of hatred burning inside." Ian smiled gently, pressing her hand to his heart. She took comfort in the support he offered, before turning back to the tormentor and protector of her past.

"So, I'm moving past you, Isen. I'm not going to hate a boy for doing a stupid horrible thing in an effort to win his father's love. And I'm not going to hate the man that hammered a cage into place around me in a screwed up idea of what was right. But hear me now, I am not going to love you for it. And I won't thank you for it, either. You want my advice on how to move on yourself, Isen? Fine, I will give it to you." He lifted his head, eyes red with unshed tears, but hopeful.

"Learn how to be good, and change. Drop the stupid cat name. Accept who you are, and then change it to fit who you want to be. Find a way to take Wiley back home where he will be safe from all the screwed up things Pan did to him. And then fix all the screwed up things you did there, too. Make life safe, in a healthy way, by teaching the rats how to be good, too. Make a new life; help others make new ones as well. And stay out of mine. That is the only healing you and I can have."

"Thank you." The man stood, scrubbing tears from his cheeks. He didn't meet either of their gazes as he bowed low once, then turned and left.

"All right, little butterfly?" Ian pressed a gentle kiss to her ear. She nodded against his lips.

"I will be. Like you said, together we will get this healing thing down." Pulling away, she stood and held out her hand. "And for now, healing means a good long nap in your arms. Take me to bed, Captain."

"With pleasure, wife."

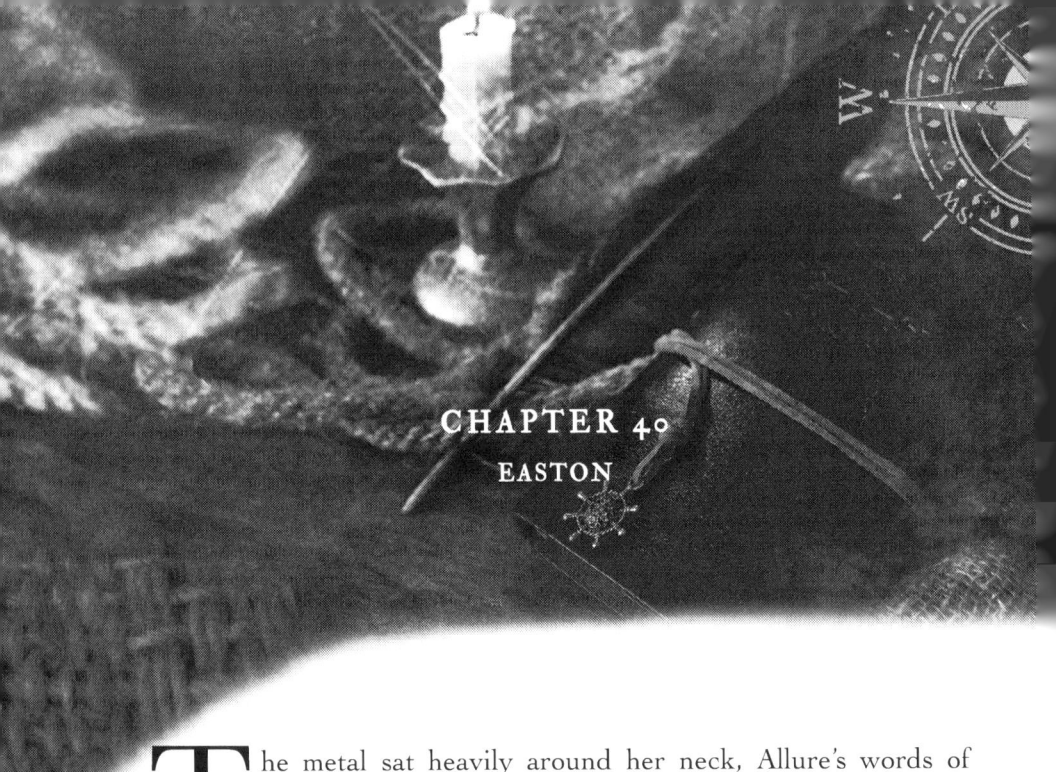

CHAPTER 40
EASTON

The metal sat heavily around her neck, Allure's words of warning echoed in her mind. People were never freer with their speech, than when they thought you couldn't hear them. Wi often used sign language to put people at ease with the false idea that he was deaf, rather than just mute. Thinking he couldn't hear them, they happily talked about all sorts of information that came in handy for a thief down the road.

Allure and Ian had both thought she was asleep, and had freely discussed their fears. Fears she hadn't wanted to make worse for Ian, when she'd given him half-truths about her current situation.

The truth? The truth was, she worried they might be right; that the Between and her bond with the metal had caused her irreparable damage. Her mind was filled with whispers she couldn't quite hear, and her skin crawled with the sensation of the Rift shadows' touch. She'd learned long ago how to put memories of unwanted touch in her past. Yet after Allure and the entire Mer jury had riffled through her mind, her little mental boxes she'd neatly stored things away had been broken open in a way she could no longer close. Now it seemed like all of Neverland was clambering to get inside her head, too.

When she focused, she could feel the tiny strings, hundreds of them. So many thin strings that tied her to all the beings of Neverland. They reverberated, rattling about in her soul like wind chimes. And then, there were some that were thicker, stronger. They were those whom she had built a stronger connection with. She could feel Ian in the distance where he was dueling with Caol to the enjoyment of his crew. She could feel his worry for her, and his valiant efforts to leave her time alone.

She could feel Wiley, who lay motionless on his bed, hands chained to the floor, strange metal blindfold locked in place over his eyes. No emotions stirred within his string, still unconscious. She could feel, though it irked her, Isen as he sat in a quiet room. The ever-present guilt and hope saturated his string. The hope, the will of betterment, was what had pushed her to move beyond her past with him. Though despite her words, she still hadn't found the exact key to getting rid of her angry feelings toward the man. She supposed that would come with time.

Easton closed her eyes and concentrated on the strings. She could feel Bell, her great however-many-times grandmother was out for a stroll. E paused at the next string, loath to go anywhere near it: Pan.

There had always been that connection to him from her ancestry, of course. But she had no doubt that Pan was one of those thicker strands that lay silent now, while within the embrace of Sanctuary. It lay in her mind like a motionless snake, taunting her with its existence, lying in wait for her unguarded moments. It seriously ticked her off.

Who was Fate to toss them about on the waves of time so carelessly? She was tired of being a chess piece on the board. For now, she would give Ian his reprieve, gather her strength. And then she'd hunt down Pan and kill him herself if she had to. This madness had to stop. She was taking her happily ever after, Pan and the Fates be damned.

"Hi, Bell." E cleared a throat gone itchy under the force of her emotions. Bell's approach paused mid-step, before moving to join her.

"Either you have become more adept to your surroundings, or these old bones have gotten too loud in their movements."

"Your bones are fine," E sighed. Bell wordlessly joined her at her vigil outside of Wiley's cell. Soon the silence became too much, and E filled it. "Some stuff went sideways at the Mers place. I came home with a few fun souvenirs. "

"Ah."

"And as soon as Wiley wakes up and I know he's okay... I'm going to use one of those to hunt down Pan and take him out."

"Ah." Bell repeated.

"Yeah. So. There's that."

"You sound as though you could use some tea." Bell motioned to the nearby guard and sent him scuttling off after some tea. Easton couldn't help the small smirk at the way Bell sent people about random errands. The guard was probably thrilled. Though it couldn't be more boring than guarding a sleeping prisoner.

"You carry mine and Peter's blood, child." Bell placed her hand atop E's. "I've the feisty blood of the Tinkers, stoked in the fires of our hearths. And Peter...well, you know about Peter's temperament already."

"As does all of Neverland."

"Sadly, yes." Bell patted her hand and withdrew. "My point, dear one, is the need to ensure you don't fall prey to the same ways as the Pan." E's eyes shot to Bell's, a stirring of petulant annoyance inside that Bell would even compare them. Bell replied with an imperious expression that dared argument. E sighed once more.

"I've always had a temper. And it did tend to get me in trouble when I let it get away with me," she finally conceded.

"It's the vermillion." Bell smiled affectionately, picking a tiny white wildflower that grew in the grass at their feet. "There's nothing wrong with fire girl, just don't let it consume you, is all." Pressing the flower into the hair just above E's ear, she let her withered fingers trail across her cheek to lightly boop the tip of her nose.

"How else am I supposed to take him down?"

"By using what's beneath all that fire, that's how." Bell scoffed and wrapped a slightly less affection knuckle against E's head.

"Ow," E sulked, rubbing at her head. "Okay, okay. I get the point."

E jumped as Wiley suddenly sat up on the cot, the chains on his hands jangling. She hadn't felt the vibration of the string signaling he was awake. Maybe it only vibrated when the person moved? His hands lifted, questioning.

"I'm here, Wi," She answered. His hands lifted again.

"What's that, what's he doing?" Bell replied stiffly, eyeing Wiley carefully.

"He's talking, Bell. He's mute, he speaks with his hands. This is my friend, Wiley."

"I see him, dear. I also see the taint that comes along with every Lost Boy Peter ever consumed. It may be incomplete, but it's there."

"Wiley?" E asked, caution returning. "How are you feeling?" His hands lifted, the motions clumsy in the confining chains, but she got the gist.

"What, what?" Bell piped up, clearly annoyed she couldn't read Wi's mysterious language. E chuckled as the old lady straightened, jabbing her walking stick imperiously at the ground.

"There's that Tinker feistiness." Bell scoffed at her, but her shoulders relaxed. E smiled. "He said he's feeling better. He can feel Pan in the back of his head, like the dull ache left from a headache. But he can't feel him talking to him anymore. He says he's relieved."

"As welcome as the reprieve might be, he'll never be entirely free of the Pan. What was lost can never be regained, even when Peter dies." Wi's hands fell to his lap in resignation and E sent Bell a heated glance of her own.

"It's a good thing the tea is here, you need it more than I do." Standing, E moved toward the guard who was finally returning with two steaming mugs. Thanking him, E motioned Bell to sit on her bucket and handed her the drink.

"I'm sorry, boy, but to lie to you about the gravity of your situation would be far crueler."

"Move aside if you please, ladies. Captain said he needs to start drinking this right away." The guard moved to unlock the cell, placing a large cup in Wi's hands. Wiley immediately began drinking, clearly desperate for its effect to kick in.

"There's nothing else we can do?" E tipped another bucket over and sat.

"Nothing but stop more damage from being done." Bell shook her head sadly.

Wiley's hands lifted, signing more animatedly now. E frowned and rolled her eyes.

"Okay, somebody needs to start explaining who this mysterious woman is before I lose my mind."

"Woman?" Bell sat straighter.

"Avida told me..."

"Avida!" Bell's mouth dropped.

"Ah. I guess Hook didn't tell you that part. So yeah, I kind of met Ian's ex. Oh, and Pan for like a second... but that's a story for another time. Anyway, Avida told me about this mysterious woman that I needed to find, that 'she' would help Wiley escape. And Wiley here just told me I need her, too. Though he has yet to fill me in the details. So spill, Wi."

He took another deep dragging gulp of the drink, wincing at the taste. The herbal concoction was mixed into every meal and drink of the inhabitants of Sanctuary, to help mask their minds from Pan. E had forgotten how gross it had tasted when she first came to Sanctuary. She all but forgot it was even in her daily diet now, honestly.

"*What happened to Jag?*" he signed, empty cup discarded and taken away by the guard.

"He's still around," she answered hesitantly.

"*Good. If Jag had been caught by him...*" He didn't have to finish for her to know what he meant. Jag wouldn't have lasted long in Pan's grip before falling to his darkness, E had no doubts of that.

"*You and the pirate are together?*" He signed.

"We are."

"*He's not forcing you?*"

"Never."

"*And... he is good?*"

"He is good. I'm sure Pan told you things, bad things about him.

But Hook isn't any of those things. He is a great man. He helps people. He protects and cares for his people. He's not like our previous leadership experiences at all."

"And here I thought Jag was such a good leader." His lips cocked to the side. Then, all the joking left his motions. *"Pan was worse. Much worse."*

"Wiley. Tell me about the woman." Wiley relaxed at her question, a smile touching his lips.

"She was like an angel. She came to me in my mind. She spoke to me when he wasn't there. If she hadn't, I would have lost myself a long time ago."

"Did you ever see her in person?"

"No, I only heard her." E and Bell exchanged a glance. *"I'm not crazy, I didn't just imagine her."* Wiley argued when they remained silent.

"I'm not saying you are, Wi. I've seen some crap, too, ya know. I'm just not sure how to find her if she only spoke to you in your head."

"I… I don't know where he keeps her, but I know she's in his lair some-where. That's why she helped me. She is just as much a captive as I was. She told me I needed to escape to find you so that you could save her."

"Do you know the way back?" Wiley went still. He shook his head fiercely.

"No. I can't go back there. I can't leave here. He'll make me do things."

"It's okay, Wi, I don't need you to lead me back. I think I will be able to find him." E turned to Bell, formulating a plan. "We'll gather the men, as many as are able, and we'll march on…" She broke off as Wiley jerked against his chains.

"No! You can't march on him. You'll never find his lair. No one can enter unless brought in by him. She protects it, keeps it hidden. If you want to be able to take him down, you have to get to her first. She's the answer."

"Then I'll have to get him to invite me in, I guess."

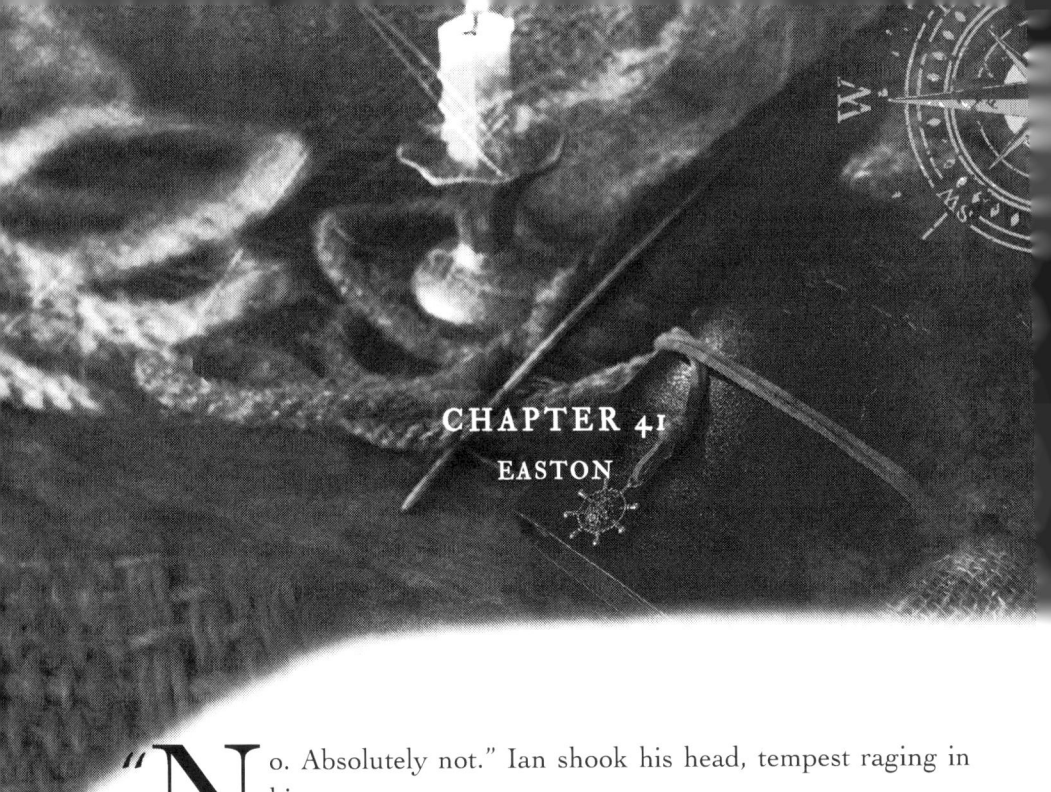

CHAPTER 41
EASTON

"No. Absolutely not." Ian shook his head, tempest raging in his gaze.

"It's the only way…"

"Then it's not worth it!"

"Ian…"

"No!" He cut his hand through the air. "It would be suicide. You'd walk into his lair and never return."

"If I don't do this, we'll never find him. Unless I can get to this woman and get her to take down her shield this war will never end!"

"We'll find another way."

"How long have you been searching for him? How long has he evaded you? We have no choice."

"You can't leave without me guiding you out of the cave."

"Yes. You could keep me from leaving. But I think we both know that would not end well." Her soft spoken words hung heavily in the air.

"I can't do it, Easton. Don't ask it of me, not this," he whispered, turning his back on her, fist clenched at his side. E's rigid stance melted. She moved to wrap her arms around his waist from behind, holding him close. His hand shook as he gripped hers tightly, pressing it to his heart.

"I can't escape the certainty of dread that overshadows my soul. The certainty that once I let go of you, I will lose you forever."

"Ian…"

"How can you ask it of me? To send yet another woman I love running into his grasp? Running to her doom?" E bit her lip, tears rising to match those in his tone. "I could not bear it," he vowed, his voice even gruffer than usual. "I could not bear to lose you now. You hold the last of my soul, Easton. If I lose you, it will turn into a pit of endless night. There will be no saving what is left of the man that is Hook."

"You won't lose me. I won't let him take me from you." He spun in her grasp, roughly pulling her to him. The sea in his eye raged with a typhoon of emotion.

"Swear it! Swear to me that you will be safe. Swear that I am making the right decision."

Pinned in his gaze, her resolve wavered at the uncertainty and fear she saw reflected in his expression. Through all of their struggles, all the dangers they had faced together, Easton had never seen Ian look so afraid, so lost. Gently reaching upward, she ran her palms over his jaw, enjoying the soft scratching of his rugged facial hair against her skin. Putting every ounce of promise she could into her tone, she asked him an honest question.

"Ian, do you trust me?"

"I…" Ian blinked at her, as though taken by surprise with her question. He shook his head, jaw clenching. "It's the Fiend I don't trust."

"I didn't ask that." She ducked her head, forcing him to meet her gaze. "Do you trust *me*, Octavian Ryes Bendal?"

Slowly his tense shoulders dropped, the creases in his brow smoothed. He shook his head, closed his eye and drew a deep breath. When he met her gaze again, there was an unwavering answer, drowning in sorrowful resignation.

"I trust you, wife. With all that I am, I trust you."

"I will never betray that trust, Ian. I am not Avida. I am made of tougher stuff, and I refuse to let him take me from you. I *will* return to you, I swear it on my life." His forehead fell to hers, tone reverent but firm.

"Protect that life always, my butterfly. It is worth far more to me than any other treasure." He pressed her to his chest, his swift heartbeat pounding in her ear.

"Ah, what a great fool am I," he murmured into her hair. "Fate is determined to torment my soul until the day my heart breaks beyond repair."

"Screw Fate. We are a packaged deal, you and I. Nobody and nothing is getting in the way of that. I get what I want," she argued. Ian chuckled in that quiet, crushed velvet way that she loved.

"Such fire in my saucy wench." He pressed a warm kiss to her forehead.

Her hand held tightly in his, he silently led the way to the cave. Exiting, they stared out at the woods. Pressing one last lingering kiss to his soft lips, she backed away. His fingers gripped hers, rebelling in the need to release her. Finally, he pried his clutch free, his whole body shuddering as he released her. Far too soon, the trees cut off her view of him, still lingering at the mouth of the cave, hand clutching his heart.

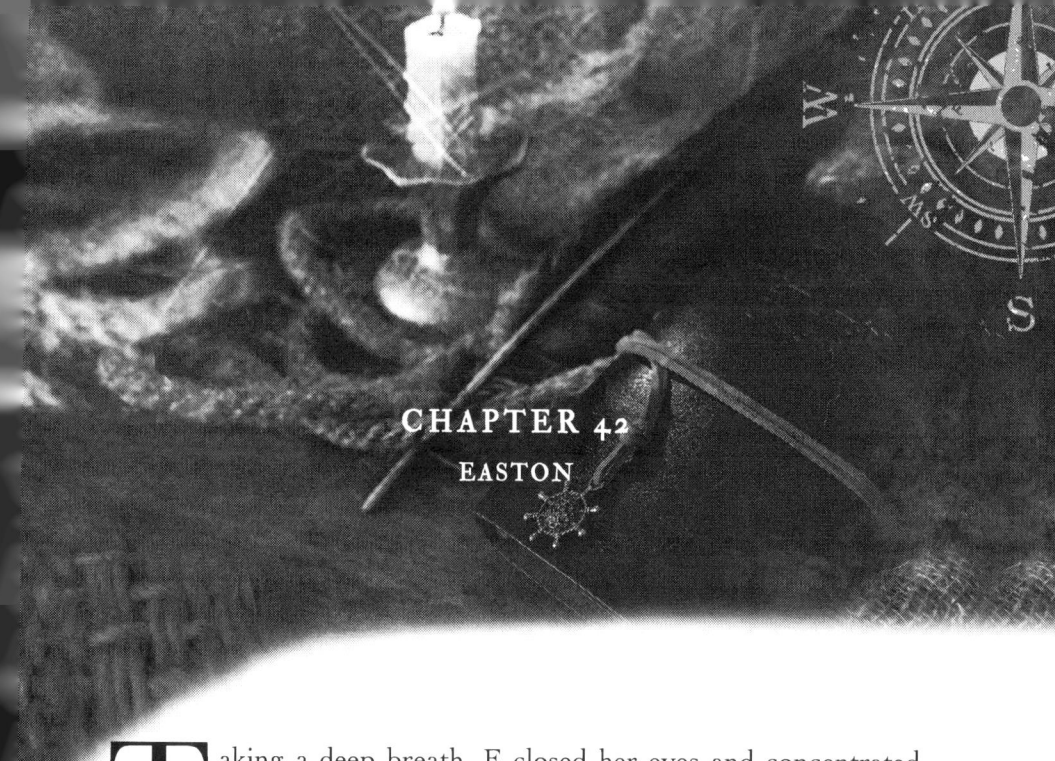

CHAPTER 42
EASTON

Taking a deep breath, E closed her eyes and concentrated. She wouldn't fail. She'd just have to be careful of her thoughts until she managed her escape. In and out, like the thief she'd been raised to be. She would save Ian and all of Neverland. She would not fail. She could not. There was no other way.

Collecting herself, E carefully picked her way through the dangerous leaves and vines. The forest seemed to whisper with her passing, the leaves going out of their way to slide along her arms. It was creepy. She had loved walking through the place once. But without the crew, without Ian at her side, the woods now felt ominous and hateful.

E walked for an hour, determined to put as much distance between herself and Sanctuary as possible. She felt naked without the Hook metal dangling around her neck. She'd had to leave it with Ian when they parted ways. There was no way Pan would let her close to him, no way he'd believe her story if she still wore it. He'd sense the power of the Hook, the danger she posed to him, and kill her before she got close.

Swallowing hard, E forced her feet to stop. If she didn't stop now, she'd keep walking until she talked herself out of it all. Satisfied there was enough space between her and Ian, E sent up a silent prayer. She hoped this stupid plan would work. And she hoped she was strong and smart enough to keep true to her plan. E took the plunge.

"Pan!" The word rang through the trees, quieting the crickets. "Pan!" The birds fell silent, as did the frogs and other strange animals in the forest. "Peter Pan!" She called once more, and the winds picked up, whipping around her, sending her hair flailing about, whipping the sensitive skin of her cheeks. "Peter..."

The final word lodged in her throat as the man himself suddenly appeared before her. E swallowed her leap of fear, shoved it down cold-heartedly. And in its place, she accessed the pain of her past. She dredged up the pain of losing her family. The pain she felt at their deaths, her childlike helplessness felt that night. Tears welled in her eyes, and without further thought, she slipped into the role she and Bell planned.

"We meet again." Pan offered a tilted grin, though shadows lurked in his eyes.

"Father!" She fell to her knees, arms outstretched imploringly. "Please, Father, please take me away, don't leave me here anymore!"

She sobbed, tears dripping to the ground. Pan had called her 'daughter' in her dream. She was going to play on that for all it was worth. For a long, agonizing moment, E thought Pan had seen through her, that her plan had failed already. Then, his stiff body melted, his arms lifting her into a hug.

"My daughter. I will never leave you now that I've found you. You are mine now."

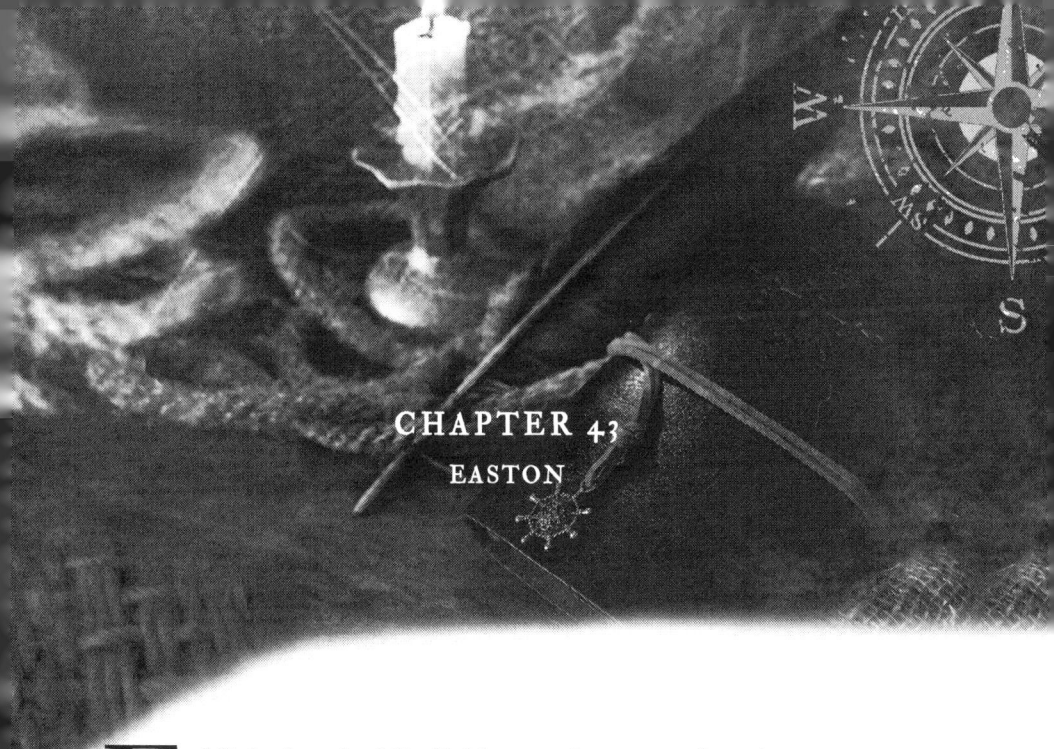

Eblinked as the blindfold was taken away from her eyes. Pan had held her and accepted her readily enough, but he clearly didn't trust her. He'd wrapped the blindfold around her eyes, before lifting her into his arms. After that, E had clung to him even more desperately, flying blindly in his arms. Part of her had hoped he'd taken her bait. The other part wondered if he was just taking her high in the sky to drop her.

He'd laughed at her fear, and dove into a series of loopty-loops and nose dives. It was then she realized he was playing with her. And though it went against the ninety-nine other survival instincts screaming at her, E listened to the single instinct that beckoned quietly. She'd opened her mouth, and laughed right along with him. At first the laugh was a strained little creature. But when his laugh shifted from malicious to playful, her laugh took on a new life of its own. Her arms relaxed about his shoulders, and she simply enjoyed the wild freedom of the ride.

It seemed to be what Pan wanted to see, because not long after that, he paused his cat and mouse game long enough to bring them down to solid ground. E stared up at the Fiend's lair in awe. It was much like she'd always imagined when hearing the story read to her. Only so much more grand.

"Wow," E whispered.

"What do you think, daughter?" A grin split E's face as her eyes fell to Pan's.

"It looks fun!" Pan's answering grin told her it had been the right answer. He held out a hand to her

"Come. Let's play."

E hesitated only a moment before placing her hand in his. Together they ran toward the first tree house, climbing vines to reach the top.

"Last one to the end is a rotten fart!" Pan shouted, scaling the vines with ease.

"I can already smell your stink from here!" E laughed, moving to follow. She refused to lose. Something told her that to fail would mean much worse than losing a game. Her arms shook by the time she reached the top of the two-story-high treehouse. She ignored them and pushed onward. Pan was ahead of her now, climbing to the top of the treehouse and swinging on a vine toward the next house. E grit her teeth and pushed herself harder. By the time she got to the next house, E knew there was no way she was going to beat him following everything he did. With mischief brewing in her gut, E grinned and ran for the next treehouse and jumped.

They were just far enough apart that her toes touched down on the wooden platform, inches from falling. She teetered for a moment, and the whole world seemed to hold its breath. When her balance centered and she still stood on the platform, the Lost Boys cheered, and E felt an exhilaration she'd only known on the thrill of a theft run roaring to life within.

With a carefree giggle, E ran for the next platform. This time, she cleared the distance with much more grace. And the next two as well. Peter crowed at her from the tops of the treehouses, urging her on and taunting her at once. It fueled her determination to win. Two treehouses lay ahead, each farther apart than the last. E pushed her legs harder, the muscles suddenly eager to acquiesce.

Jumping to kick off the side of the hut, E used her momentum to carry her high enough to grasp a hanging vine. The vine swung forward, carrying her swiftly past the first hut, and on toward the second. Then, halfway across the final expanse, the vine snapped. E laughed as she hurtled through the air, adrenaline coursing through her. A distant part of her mind shrieked that she wasn't going to make it. That she was going to fall to her death. That she should scream, not laugh.

E ignored it, stretched her arms wide, closed her eyes and drank in the wind. When she collided with something, it wasn't the ground, but the platform of the last treehouse. The contact knocked the air from her stomach, but E pushed through it, pulling herself onto the landing. Rolling until she pressed against the hut, E sucked in a painful gush of air, finally filling her lungs. She could sense others gathering around her, a tense atmosphere in the air. E rolled to her back, and shoved her fist into the air, a single finger pointed upward at the wide-eyed Pan who dangled above her on a vine.

"I win, you stink!"

The shadowy Lost Boys looked to Pan as one, waiting for his reply. Pan plopped to the ground at her feet, face deadly serious. Reaching down, he grabbed her by the front of her shirt and yanked her to her feet. And for a heart-stopping moment, E feared she'd miscalculated the purpose of the game. Then, Pan grabbed her arm, and shoved it into the air with his own, releasing a crow of victory. The Lost Boys erupted into cries of their own excitement, and the wind whipped around them in its own celebration. E giggled, high on the moment.

"My daughter has come home, Boys!" The shadowy figures whooped and danced about in celebration.

"What shall we call her, father?" one boy asked, the others chiming in with their own versions of the same question.

"We shall call her Moth!" Peter exclaimed proudly. "Because she soars through the air with the grace and daring of one!"

The Boys instantly cheered, all calling out her new name. But E was fighting to keep her smile in place. The wild abandon she'd felt only moments earlier evaporating like water in the desert. *Ian.* Moth was far too similar to Butterfly.

E was horrified by just how quickly she'd lost sight of her goal. She'd been in Pan's presence for less than half an hour, and she'd already nearly lost herself. How could it happen so quickly? Even now the atmosphere called to her, sang in a beautiful promise of never-ending games, laughter and love. Perhaps the blood in her veins held more sway over her than E realized. She was going to have to tread very carefully or she'd lose herself entirely, dooming both Ian and Neverland. Resolve tightened in her stomach. She couldn't fail Ian. She wouldn't. She had a promise to keep.

"Why does she smell of the Hook, father?" one of the Lost Boys asked, shaking her from her reverie, yanking her mind to sharp clarity.

"That is what we are about to find out, Boys. Our Moth has returned, but we need to make sure her wings are pure, and not tainted by the old cod fish Hook. To the Wendy for a story, lads!"

The Lost Boys cheered, leaping from the high treehouses without an ounce of care for their wellbeing. Their shadowy figures effortlessly floated to the ground, then flew away into the trees. Pan wrapped an arm around E's waist and smile down at her. While there was still that loving expression to his face, a malicious gleam in his eyes told her what would happen if Wendy revealed that she was a liar.

"Come daughter, it's time to meet the rest of the family."

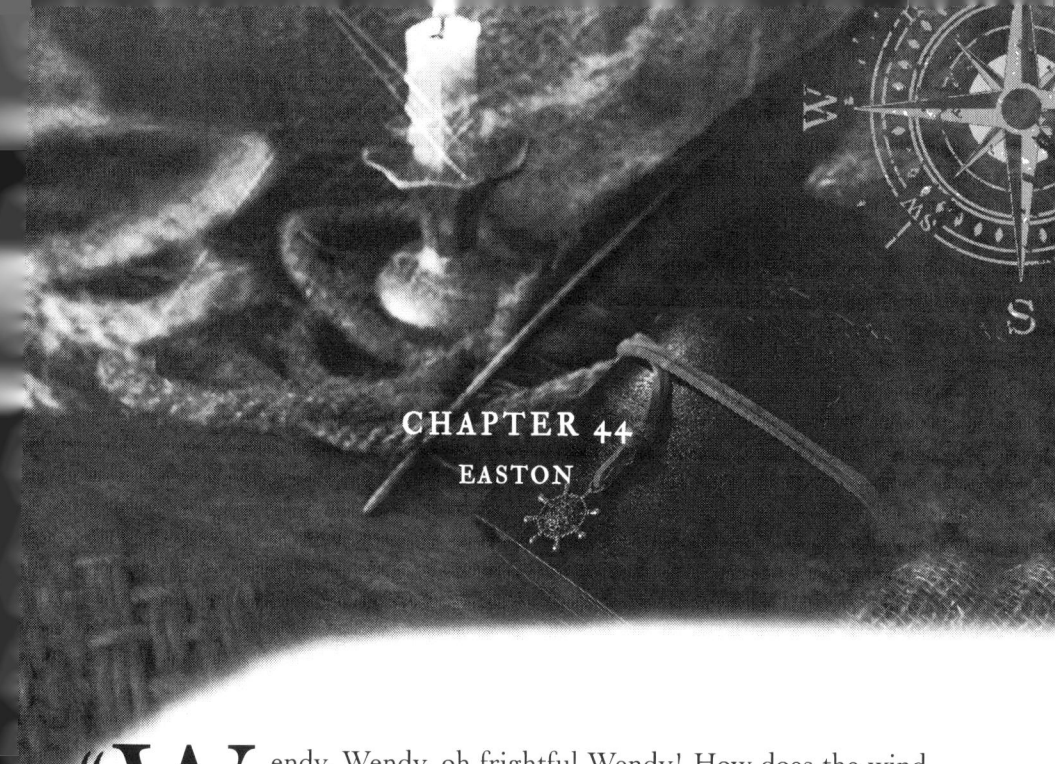

CHAPTER 44
EASTON

"Wendy, Wendy, oh frightful Wendy! How does the wind blow? Be it fair, or be it wary, our ratty-haired beneficiary?"

Pan sang patronizingly, the mischief in his grin nearly blinding as he hopped over the vine-strewn ground. The Lost Boys grinned, bodies nearly translucent as they bobbed up and down in excitement while Pan continued to hop through the vines, singing. The guy was like a flying, beardless, Jack Sparrow. All sorts of crazy rolled up into one hyper bundle.

"Who's Wendy?" Easton asked, shoving down the creepy sensation the freak show was sending down her spine. Pan immediately shushed her, pressing a finger to his lips.

"Hush hush, red thrush. We mustn't frighten poor Wendy away."

Despite his words, the devious grin on his lips said he was anything but worried for the mysterious Wendy's wellbeing. E remained silent, though her mind was reeling. Wendy was the love of Peter Pan in the majority of stories in Easton's world. Here, Bell had taken on that role. So who would the truth reveal Wendy to be? Was this the woman she was searching for?

Suddenly a moan filled the air, sounding as though it came from the very ground at their feet. Pan let out a deep laugh, clapping his hands in delight and dancing around as though he'd won something wonderful. Easton's eyes were drawn downward to the vines that writhed back and forth, undulating to an unheard rhythm. And then a form began to take shape, lifting from the foliage-cluttered ground. The small mound rose, building higher and higher until a form, roughly the same size as E, stood hunched before them. Easton's skin crawled as she stared at the thing, the feeling of something very dark and forbidden hanging in the air.

The vines on the figure shifted, and the moans became reedy, more pitiful than frightening. E took a step back when the face of a young woman appeared in the mass of vines. Her skin was a sickly light green shade. It wasn't the pearlescent green of the Mers' skin, but rather like the color of stomach bile after a long bout of the flu. Not a good look for anyone.

Small vines protruded from various areas of her face, horrifically displayed like some creepy science experiment gone wrong. Her hair color was undeterminable, caked in mud and knotted with vines as it was. Eyes that may have once been beautiful, now stared blankly into the distance, milky and bloodshot to the extreme.

Yet, despite all of the horrors of her appearance, they could not entirely mask the beauty she once held. It floated below her skin, like a diaphanous vision of what could have been. Easton felt her heart clench within her chest, gripped by the air of sorrow that emanated from the being before her. Sympathy rose deep in E's chest, aching for the green lady in a way her soul had rarely felt. Suddenly those milky eyes snapped toward her, jarring Easton's heart with such force she swore it stopped altogether.

"Wendy!" Pan crooned dramatically, stepping close to the mound of vines. Easton breathed a sigh of relief when that haunting gaze finally shifted away from her to focus on the Fiend.

"Pan." The word was broken, cracked and twisted as though it took an intense amount of effort to even speak it.

"Yes, tis me. The most brilliant boy of them all, invincible and immortal, King of all Neverland!"

He crowed again, bounding forward, arms raised triumphantly

for his crowd. The Lost Boys gave a woot, cheering him on. Easton gave a slightly less enthusiastic version of it herself, trying her best to blend appearances despite the queasy nature of her stomach.

"That remains to be seen." Wendy crackled in reply. Pan froze, slowly turning back to the plant lady.

"Now Wendy, don't be rude or you'll have to go back in time out. We have a very special visitor, and we wouldn't want her to think you cruel, now would we?" Wendy's leaves shivered.

"No." Came the fearful whisper.

"Good. Now Wendy is going to tell me all about my little Moth. Every tiny detail." E felt her heart thump clumsily in her chest. Pan grinned deviously, as though he'd heard it. "Wendy knows all. She will know if you are lying to us. You see, Moth," Peter wrapped his arm around E's shoulders companionably. "Wendy is a seer. And a very gifted one at that. She is how I always manage to evade the Hook. She protects this valley from all who would seek to enter it, in order to hurt me. Isn't that so, oh mighty green one?" Pan intoned, grinning at Wendy. Wendy made no reply, other than for the shivering of leaves. Easton fought the urge to fidget under Pan's burning, distrustful gaze.

"She's only disappointed me once. When she lost the Croc and his clock. And she will never disappoint me again, will she?" His grin turned downright evil. Wendy's leaves trembled, rattling like old bones in a basket.

"No, Pan."

"Good girl. Then Wendy, answer my question. Who is this visitor."

"She is your…," Wendy's head cocked to the side as she eyed Easton. A strange crawling sensation swept over E's brain. Pan's stiff arm kept her from shivering against the intrusive feeling. "She is your offspring." Wendy finally intoned.

E frowned inwardly, though her face remained expressionless. Wendy was supposed to be all seeing, according to Pan. She'd just crawled all over inside her head. She had to know that Easton wasn't really Pan's daughter. Pan grinned, feet lifting from the ground, nearly pulling E up with him.

"I knew it, I knew she was my daughter from the moment I laid eyes on her!" he boasted. "But how is it that my daughter has grown beyond a baby? Until recently, time did not flow, no one aged a day." Petulant suspicion returned to his eyes, as though he couldn't quite allow himself to believe.

"The witch's enchantment performed to pull her from Bell's womb worked in strange ways. I see from her mind that somehow she did grow from a baby to as we see her now, all while she was hidden from me."

E noticed how Wendy carefully worded her reply. None of her words were exactly a lie. Yet none of it was exactly the truth, either. She didn't outright say that E was his daughter. Wendy was a clever girl. Could it be that she was on her side?

"Yes." Peter growled menacingly. "Hidden away by the Hook, my worst and most deceitful enemy!" He stalked towards Wendy, an invisible field of fury thundering about him like a mantle. Peter was now in full on Pan mode. "Tell me now and tell me good! Is the girl at my back pure and true? Has she come to be with me as a daughter, or does she come with foul intent? If you fail in your telling, if the Moth betrays, I'll cut you to the quick before the dawning!"

The playful tones Pan typically spoke in all but vanished, devoured by the sudden rise of his temper. The vines shivered around them in reply, a mighty rush of sound filling the air.

"She is pure of intent; she is of your blood! I speak only truth, now and always. That is what you want. That is what you ask of me!"

Wendy's voice crackled, vines trembling so violently that leaves floated down from above like green snow. Pan stared her down, nose mere inches from hers as he glared. One finger rose, flicking a vine at the side of Wendy's face. A wincing moan issued from the girl, drowned out by Pan's merciless laugh.

"See how she trembles!" He flicked the vine once more, broad grin washing his features back to youthful mischief. "Come now, Wendy, I am only being playful." He wrapped an arm about the green girl's shoulders and turned to Easton. "You see daughter, this is why Wendy was the only girl in our midst until you. Girls are whiny and weak." Pan sent a significant look Easton's way. E's mind absorbed the news. Wendy was the only girl, which meant this had to be the girl that Wiley mentioned. E quickly stepped back into her role, lifting her chin.

"Not me! I will be strong like you, Father!"

Easton had seen this bullying tactic a hundred times. Pan was asserting his dominance by making others feel weak. If he thought for one moment that Wendy evoked a sense of loyalty to herself from his followers, he'd just give her a good pummeling. And if Easton was gauging Wending correctly, the girl *was* on her side. To betray emotions of sympathy toward the girl now would mean not only destroying her own chances of blending in here, but she would also be setting Wendy up for more pain.

So, Easton calmly held her ground. Peter watched her closely for a moment longer, before a proud grin burst across his features like the rising sun.

"There is a daughter I can be proud of!" He walked away from Wendy, and the plant girl sighed in relief. It was short-lived. "Now Wendy, let's have a story." Wendy tensed once more. "We want to hear a good one. Out with it. What do you see?"

"Your path has darkened." She intoned stoically, though the vines trembled beneath his stony gaze.

"What's that supposed to mean?" Peter growled, the sound marking the return of his dark temper.

"The portal is lost." E froze. Portal? Could they be talking about the book's portal?

"It can't be lost!" Pan snarled. "I need it to gain entrance to the other world. My family must grow. So many still need me."

"The portal is closing. It has weakened to the point I can barely feel it. There is no hope to attain it now. Should you find it in time, the portal would be a one-way journey. Traveling to the other realm would mean never returning."

"But I need it! I can't go into the next world without it, and I need to go there to save more children, to give them a home where they can be loved." He shoved a finger at E's nose. "But your mother had to go and destroy that for me. She turned to her witchy friends and closed my way off forever!" A slow smile pushed back the frown, though the darkness remained.

"But the Fates found another way. Every once in a great while, they send me a single Lost Boy. I find them and bring them home." He held his arms wide to encompass the shadows around them, at least thirty strong.

"That's a lot of boys." She nodded dutifully, appearing impressed.

" Oh there are so many more than these. They're just shy."

"More? How many more?" E whispered, feeling more than a little creeped out by the idea.

"Hundreds." Peter whispered, a twisted manic sort of pride reflected in his eyes.

"And you save them?"

"Yes. I save them; me, Peter Pan of Neverland, the most benevolent of them all!" He pointed that finger at her again, "Your mother never understood that. She never understood my need to care for and protect our children. She was selfish, and she was proud, just like all the other grownups in the world. But not me. Never me!"

E watched Peter with a new understanding. When listening to Bell's story, E had felt a sense of sympathy for the man. But now she felt that sympathy growing. Peter truly thought he was doing good deeds. No matter how twisted his results, he truly thought that he was saving these boys, protecting them.

"Why do they look the way they do, father?" She asked carefully, artfully adding an air of awe to her tone so as not to appear truly interested, rather than how she really felt when looking at the shadowed figures.

"That is my cloak of invincibility, Moth. So long as I live, no one will ever be able to hurt my Boys." His head cocked to the side. "I would offer to share it with you, but I won't. The cloak of invincibility doesn't work on girls." He nodded toward Wendy. "It didn't work very well last time, you see. And I don't need another seer." Wendy's leaves rustled and quaked.

"That's okay." E forced out. Though the idea of what must have happened to Wendy made her sick to her stomach, she had to feign gratitude and eagerness. "Since I'm your daughter, I will be strong like you without it."

"Yes, maybe, maybe you will." Peter nodded thoughtfully. "You bring up a good point, daughter. Wendy wasn't blessed to have my blood the way you do." His head snapped back toward Wendy. "Is there more?"

"One who can destroy you has entered Neverland through the portal. They are the reason that the portal is closing." E choked on her heart. Had Wendy finally decided to betray her?

"That's not fair!" Peter shouted. "Why would the portal send someone like that? I thought the portal was on my side? I thought it understood?" He began pacing. "Perhaps *he* did something to it, something to make it angry with me." He paused, eyes tracking back to land on E.

"Moth, you and I must talk."

"About what, father?"

"Enough with the 'father' talk for now." Pan waved his hands in the air about his head, as though swatting away pesky insects. "It makes me sound so terribly old when used too often."

"Can I call you Peter?"

"Yes, call me Peter," Pan nodded, chest puffing out like a boastful child.

"What should we talk about, Peter?"

"Let's talk over dinner. I'm starving." E caught sight of Wendy's reaction from the corner of her eye. The wispy plant girl went stiff, frightening eyes wide with fear. But when E looked her way, the girl quickly disappeared back into the ground. E followed Peter, feeling a sense of foreboding hanging over her head.

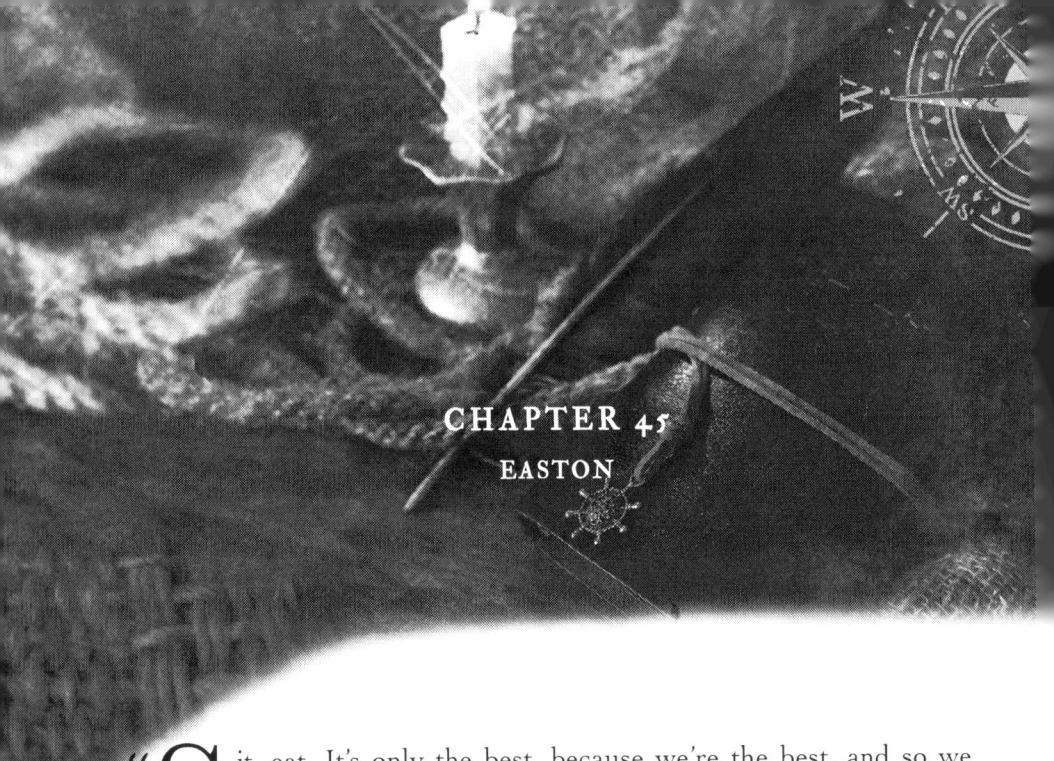

"Sit, eat. It's only the best, because we're the best, and so we must eat the best. Isn't that right, Boys?"

The Lost Boys released a chorus of hollow-sounding whoops, their voices carrying eerily through the darkening air. E reached for the food, a juicy tender drumstick catching her eye.

"Do not eat the food!"

A voice of alarm warned in E's head, stopping her cold. It was the crackling voice of Wendy. E glanced around at everyone else at the table, but like Peter, they were digging into the food with gusto. The food slipped through their shadowy forms, falling to the ground. They paid it no mind, exclaiming it was the best food they'd ever tasted. None of them gave any indication that they had heard the voice. E reached for the food once more.

"Your blood is not pure enough to resist!"

E swallowed, diverting her reach for other items that she could easily conceal the actual motion of eating. Nuts and berries rose to her mouth, but expertly slipped into the recess of her sleeves, only to be carefully discarded under the table while she pretended to chew.

"You are wise, as I hoped. All who eat of the Pan's food see him with

rapture and adoration. They will do whatever he asks. But are you as brave as I hoped? Are you equal to the task, Arrival?"

"Now, tell me." Peter's command made E jump, she'd been listening so carefully to Wendy's warnings. She needed to keep her wits about her, carefully mind her reactions, act as he expected. The food wouldn't affect a Pan the way it would someone with diluted blood. With Bell for a mother it would make her a bit tipsy perhaps, but not as tipsy as it would make someone generations down the Pan bloodline.

"What would you like to know, Peter?"

"What do you think of our little haven?"

"It's amazing. I only wish I'd called to you sooner!"

"Why didn't you?"

His eyes narrowed, holding her hostage with his intensity. Those eyes were very telling. His intellect shone through the crazed sort of haze that so often floated at the surface of that burning gaze. Peter was a dangerous foe. E would need to draw on every ounce of her past life's skills to lie her way out of this one.

"Mother taught me to fear you," she whispered, looking at the table as though ashamed.

"Did she?"

"She said that we must stay far away from you; that the villagers feared you for good reason." Peter leaned forward suddenly, another leg of chicken in his hand.

"I saw you eying this earlier, yet you haven't tried it. Take a bite." E froze.

She opened her mouth to form an excuse, but Pan's eyes hardened, hints of suspicion returning. E fought the panic within. She couldn't deny him without stirring suspicion, yet she couldn't eat so much that the food's effect turned her loyalties.

"You don't mind me taking a bite of yours?" she asked, stalling. Some of his frost warmed, a mocking grin tugging at his lips.

"Your mother hated sharing food, too. I see now that that has made an impact on you." What a lucky coincidence. E hadn't known that, but it certainly was saving her butt now. Peter pressed the meat toward her with new determination. "But *I* care not for such things.

We are family. Family shares everything. Just don't spit on it," he added.

Knowing her stalling was at an end, E leaned forward and took a nibble. At his glare, she took a bigger bite. Peter grinned and drew back, biting into the chicken himself.

"Good, isn't it?" He grinned proudly.

E forced a grin as she chewed. It was good. Really good, actually. But she needed a clear head, and this food wasn't going to help matters. Yet, under Peter's watchful eye, E had no choice but to swallow. The food practically melted down her throat, sitting low in her hungry belly with a warm welcoming that had her craving more. Thankfully for the sake of her resolve, Peter jumped right back into the probing questions.

"Why would you side with my enemy for so long, then come to me? He stole one of my Lost Boys, you know. I was going to let the villagers have him, and Hook stole him instead."

"The villagers? But… wouldn't they kill him?"

"He deserved it. He was a traitor. He ran away. He was rather stupid, that one. Throwing away my generous gifts." He shrugged. "All the more reason he should have died. Now answer the question. Why Hook?"

"I couldn't leave. There is a force field that keeps everyone in, unless Hook personally takes you out." There, that should answer him without giving too much away… or would it? Peter's eyes narrowed and E felt the sharp edges of panic trying to worm their way through the haze formed by the food.

"Why did you run from me when I saw you in your dream?"

"It was instinct. I was raised to fear you. Mother and I were subject to the Hook's will." She stuttered over the words, forcing the falsehoods free.

"You've been living with the Hook all these years, is this true?" Peter finally asked.

"In a way. We live in a special area under his protection, but we live separate from everyone. No one likes me there except for Hook and Mother. It's because of my hair." She swallowed past the warmth in her belly that kept rising, mingling with her thoughts as it tried to confuse her with what was true and not.

"How did you get the Hook to let you out so you could escape to me?"

"I convinced him to take me on an adventure with him and his men. When they weren't looking, I ran."

"If they don't trust you there because of your hair, why would he take you with him?" She flushed, mind reeling through the fog as she tried to find her way. Pan's gaze roved over her features, and a carnivorous grin unfolded.

"He fancies you, does he?" A malicious grin shaped Peter's mouth into a handsome smirk that spoke of mischievous pranks to come. "Well, I've won again, old cod fish. Once again I've been chosen over you!"

E grit her teeth against the knowledge that Peter was reveling in the idea of yet another love of Hook betraying him. It was a good thing that Peter was too busy gloating to himself to notice her reactions. With the warmth of the food that was now spreading to the rest of her body, had E been made to speak in that moment she would have betrayed herself. The words would have come out protectively, rather than that of a girl morose from the attention of a man she found distasteful. Peter sat back for a time, eyes dancing as he reveled in his new victory over a foe as old as time, giving E much-needed time to recover.

"Can you tell us where his hiding place is, then?" Peter watched her expectantly, shrewdness in his eyes. She shook her head no, fighting against the dizzying sensations that were poking at her inhibitions.

"He didn't trust me enough to let me see the way out. He kept me blindfolded from the world around me as we came out so I couldn't see where we lived. He said it was to protect me, but I know the truth. He did it to protect the rest of them. All of them that hate me."

Her words were laced with such bitterness that E even found herself believing it for a moment, before she forced reality back to the surface. Pan sank further into his chair, arms folded over his chest, face a picture of stormy petulance.

"Finish your tale then. Why did you call me? What changed your mind from the poison of your mother's warnings?" Pulling on her years of experience of thieving and lying, E pushed through the warm fog of comfort, and spun more of her story.

"I was taught to fear you. I was taught to fear the others around me, forced to cover my hair each time I stepped foot out of our home, for fear that the villagers might try to kill me." Peter's fists clenched.

"Villagers are all the same, whether under Hook's protection or not, it seems. I'd slaughter them all if they weren't useful to me. Ungrateful gossiping fools, every one of them." He grabbed another leg of chicken and ripped into it. "Keep going." He spoke around the mouthful of food.

"One night, I had a dream. A dream about you."

"The one where you ran from me." He pointed the chicken leg at her accusingly.

"I was scared at first, shrinking away from you in fear as I had always been taught." She paused dramatically, carefully crafting the inflections in her voice, her actions. "But I thought about it often since then. You have the same color of hair as me, and you don't hide it. You do whatever you please, and you don't fear anyone. No one tells you what to do, where to go, how to live your life or who to live it for. You are truly free, as I never have been." She stared down at her hands.

"Mother told me stories about your love for the Lost Boys. I... I hoped I might be able to find a place with you, too." The food whispered to her that she really did want to be accepted by Peter. She shoved it to the side, determined to ignore it. She was no pawn.

Peter stood and floated over the table, landing softly at her side. He was quiet for a long moment, and when she finally looked to his face, E felt an unexpected penetrating stab of guilt. Peter stared down at her with glistening eyes. Without a word, he drew her head to his chest and cradled her close. He hugged her to him as though she were truly his lost child, returned at last.

Despite her hardened years of experience, despite the dangerous man she knew him to be, E felt her resolve waver. Whether it was the food's influence, his blood in her veins that sang to her, or the simple fact of having felt lost and alone for so long after the death of her own father, E let herself imagine if but for only a moment. She threw her arms around his waist and held Peter every bit as tightly as he held her.

"You are home now, daughter," Peter whispered. "I shall never turn you away, nor make you pretend to be anything other than what you are." Thunderous emotions caused an uncomfortable cacophony within her chest. Emotions that were going to make her job that much harder, and emotions that degraded her for doing that job at all. Despite the horrible things he'd done, he really did love the daughter he'd lost.

"I, too, once had an overbearing father." Peter murmured, gently rocking her back and forth. E noticed the table had gone quiet, the shadows watching their display with rapt attention.

"You did?" E sniffed. "What happened to him?"

"I killed him." E's mind tensed in warning, but her body didn't react, remaining in his arms.

"You did?"

"He saved me once, much as I saved those here, now. Stole me away from the squalor of an orphanage, with harsh and abusive caretakers."

E's heart murmured an echo of understanding and kinship with Pan in that moment. She brutally tried to stomp the little ember into smithereens. She only succeeded in its submission, but not its destruction. It would have to do for now.

"He raised me as a father would. We didn't always see eye to eye on matters, he could often be harsh and cold in his own ways. But he loved me and protected me, taught me what I needed to know to survive. I loved him and hated him at once." E's mind flashed back to Jag, her past life in the guild. The little ember grew.

"But in the end, he betrayed me. He grew jealous of the love I showed your mother, and my babe within her belly. The babes I brought over from the other world, too. He tricked me into believing that the villagers would hunt down and kill my wife and children. That I must attack them first, to prevent my own future sorrow. But it wasn't true. The villagers hated me, but they never would have dreamed of rising against me. They feared me too greatly. Still, I was fueled by his lies, and I went into the village, killing many that I should have let live, perhaps. My rage-fueled-slaughtering blinded me to my wife's growing need to leave me. And when I went on a journey to gather more children from the next world, she ran away with our child. You."

"The satyr never once tried to stop her, nor inform me of her plans. When I returned to find them gone, I was broken, split asunder within. The satyr told me it was for the better. He proudly told me of his duplicity, his betrayals. That he had done it for my own good. That is when I turned on my only known father. I was made strong because of the love of my Lost Boys. And the Pan survived only on the love I in turn fed to him. I was far stronger than him. I turned the full force of my hatred on the satyr. And that hatred burned away to the core of the Pan, leaving behind only ashes. Ashes that I then fed to the plants that grow within this valley, ashes that helped make Wendy who she is, when combined with my own magic."

"Where did Wendy come from?"

"Wendy was the child I brought back with me that night. I thought perhaps a girl would make Bell happy, when none of the boys had. I had only brought boys before because I didn't want to feel like I was replacing the daughter we were protecting in Bell's womb. But I put my feelings aside in an effort to make my wife happy. Wendy was blind, no one wanted her. But she had a strong heart and a soul filled with stories that would have made us happy for hours upon hours. I hoped she would douse my sorrow and my hatred, the fires built by the woman I loved more than the whole of the world, and the man who had said he loved me so, too. Fires built by what I did to take them from my life... but Bell had already left me, and taken our child. That was when I went into a rage and slaughtered so many."

Peter shuddered, and E was entranced. This was a far different side of Peter than she understood. He wasn't just the bratty child of her childhood story. He held a pained, tortured side to him, confusion, and yes, even some softness and love, as twisted as it might be.

E tried to force the growing sympathetic confusion down and focused on Peter's continuing story.

"I tried to bring Wendy to my side, to give her the cloak of my protection. But she was terrified, afraid of what she'd heard me do, the anger in my voice. She tried to run from me. Being blind, she didn't make it far. I poured my power into her and pulled on her soul. But instead of becoming as my boys, she became as she is now. She crumpled under my emotionally twisted fury and pain, and I thought her dead. We buried her in the clearing you find her in now, where the ashes of my once-father still lay scattered on the earth. But the earth served as a cocoon of sorts, shaping her into something more than she once was. She lifted from the ground with a new sight. The sight to see things to come. She had formed connections with the plants and things of the earth, gaining that power from the ashes of the satyr. And now, she is as you see her."

"Why are you so mean to her? Is it because she is a girl?" E asked, voice small and questing. "Will you be mean to me?"

"No, Moth." He sighed heavily. "I do not mean to be cruel to her, she is a lost child just as the others. But when I am near, I feel things best left in the past. She brings out emotions that I don't like. Her very existence was brought about by things that gave me only pain." Again E fought with the sympathy she felt for Peter, the ever-growing sense of similarity and understanding.

"I have one more curiosity, Peter."

"Ask it then; curiosity is good for the soul." Mischief twinkled in his eyes.

"Are you and Hook so evenly matched that you will battle one another for all time? How have you not discovered each other's weaknesses after so many years of fighting?"

"Weakness is an ugly word. I am not weak. I refuse to be! Hook's only weakness resides in his love for people that could care less for him." Pan clenched his teeth, fists tightening. "Yet, I can't help but feel a connection to the Hook. The people care nothing for me, either. And I think, in the end, the Hook and I both yearn for the same thing."

"What is that?"

"Peace, and someone to care for us as we care for them. How can I so easily kill a man that only wants what I myself want? How can I not kill him, knowing that I will likely never find that peace, until he is gone?" He frowned. "But what if I kill him and nothing changes? What if I destroy the one man that can challenge me, and give me some fun in his ugly world... and there is nothing left for me?" He shook himself, his distant look of seriousness disappearing as though it never existed.

"Well, I should never have fun again, that is what! And he is so easy to goad into losing his temper. I'd be bored out of my mind if I got rid of him." Peter gave her one more pat on the back, before stepping away from her. The shields of his wild and crazed haze once again descended upon him like a blanket of protection.

"Enough seriousness. I want to play. Moth, you will stay here. The Hook will be looking for you soon. But you're mine now, not his. So you stay here until we can best figure out how to use you in our games!" Peter jumped atop the table, arms held over his head in a grand, attention-grabbing way.

"To arms, Lost Boys! Let us go have some fun!" With that, Peter flew upward, and the Lost Boys eagerly followed. E sat at the table, feeling suddenly very alone and cold. Her muscles shivered, and her teeth clattered.

"Come to me now, Child of Vermillion. Quickly, before he returns." Wendy's voice sounded in Easton's head. E hesitated. Was she allowed to visit Wendy? She frowned in confusion. Wait. Why should she care if Peter would be mad? Wasn't Wendy the whole reason E came to this place?

"Are you pawn, or warrior? Shadow or Hook; now is the time to choose," Wendy spoke softly. E felt her heart tremble. Shadow or Hook? Ian's face swam before her vision, that crooked mischievous grin reminding her that she already knew. She'd stayed too long in this place. She needed to do what had to be done and get out, fast. Shaking off the stupor of confusion, E quickly stood.

She stopped cold when the shadow popped up in front of her. A long sniff issued from the shadow boy, then several more small ones. The shadow drew back, and she could feel his intense dislike of her.

Memories suddenly swirled back to her, of the shadow that sniffed her that night when she saved Wiley in the dreamland.

Was this the same shadow that had sniffed her then? The one who knew her to be a girl, and suggested they offer her to Peter? A sense of smug intention whirled towards her from the shadow boy. Anger and annoyance rose within E. Spine stiffening, E narrowed her eyes.

"Go away," she ordered. The shadow drew back, and she could feel its twisted need to both obey her as a Pan, and dismiss her for a lack of power. E put more force behind her words. "Go away and stay hidden until I am gone."

Sweat broke out across her brow as she fought for dominance over the shadow's will. She may have had Peter's blood, a hint of the power of the Pan, but E wasn't Peter. She didn't have those bonds with the shadows that were built through the strength of magic and soul-eating. Finally, the shadow hissed and flew away. Whether it flew away to tell on her to Peter, or to actually do as she said, E wasn't certain. She thought it more likely it had gone to warn Peter.

Grabbing a sharp knife from the table, she shoved it in the back waistband of her pants. E moved quickly then, in a rush to be far away from here before Pan returned. Part of her ached, knowing he would see her betrayal as cruel as, if not more so, than that of Bell. E shoved the emotions down with a fierce brutality. Peter was no saint. He'd killed so many, stolen the souls and promise of life from so many others. He'd take her life, too, if he knew her intent. And he'd tormented Ian for far too long. That fact alone was enough to steel E's resolve. Soon, E found herself back in the clearing, Wendy waiting expectantly.

"All right, there's no time for games, Wendy. You're on my side, right? So help me out here," E grated, feeling time slip away. Peter would be back soon, she could feel it. She needed to leave, but not without her answers.

"I tried to warn you away when you first walked in the world of dreams, Panling. My plants tried to keep you from wandering into danger, but you fought past them. I tried to show you the fate of your friend, the fate you would share if you continued on your path. Do you not remember this?"

E frowned for a long moment, a distant memory of the terrifying dream she'd had resurfacing. The first dream that had sent Ian bolting for the other side of the room. Her eyes narrowed.

"Yes, I remember. I also remember that Hook felt the presence of Pan in that moment, strong in the air. That doesn't reinforce my optimism of you being on my side. It makes me think it was what it felt like: an attack." Taking a breath, E laid everything out. "I was told you wanted me to save you. I was also told you had answers, that you could help me save Neverland. Is any of that true?"

"I wonder, Child of Vermillion. Do you have the bravery to do what you must in order to get your answers?" Wendy grinned.

"You tell me, you're the seer." E said cautiously, feeling the heavy weight of the knife at her back. Exactly what did this green chick have in mind?

"Only a Pan may slay a Wendy. Whether his child, or his distant descendant, it matters not. You are a powerful weapon." The plant woman smiled, wryly. Translation? She knew Easton was entirely capable of killing her, but she wasn't scared of that fact. Nor was she playing coy with the fact that she knew of Easton's true lineage. E felt her insides harden protectively.

"So I've been told. But how does a Pan kill a Pan?" E challenged boldly.

"There is power within you. You hold destiny, Vermillion Hook." Avida's confusing words from E's dream rang in her ears once more. Wendy was the one that Avida had urged her to find. The woman with the keys to the destiny of the Vermillion Hook.

"You know something important." E challenged. "Please tell me! Help me know what to do." Wendy's grin turned chilly.

"I can give you answers. But in return you must save me."

"How?"

"Destroy me. Destroy me and I shall tell you what you must know to end the Pan as well." The vines around E shifted restlessly. Easton's eyes widened.

"Destroy you? Not 'free you', just 'destroy you'?"

"I grow tired, Child of Vermillion. I shall never know freedom unless I taste it in death. I am a slave, shackled more surely than any other. He commands and my words flow freely, yet their depths cause death and sorrow that I cannot condone nor undo. I was not intended for such things, once upon a time." Her milky eyes stared distantly, a sad smile gracing her cracked lips.

"Once, I was destined to be a solace for the weary of heart. Others could come to me, ask for my guidance, or simply come to me for a lightening of the heart. I was wise beyond my young age, pure of both heart and soul." The leaves quaked, rattling like the tail of a venomous snake.

"Then Pan corrupted the land with the satyr's ashes and his magic's subversion; and with the land, me. I became pliant to his will. My words carry souls to the depths of hell, rather than uplifting to greatness. The rot has seeped deep within my marrow, leaving very little of me untouched. I hold such a small part of my heart alone. And this part has begun to taste the bitterness of defeat. This is why you must slay me."

Her voice rose, deepened in their domineering command. And with the rise of her presence, the rise of the disquieted leaves lifted to a deafening rattle and hiss.

"Destroy me before there is nothing left of my purity. I try to do good, but my efforts so often end in sorrow only. I spoke with Hook's first mate when she came here, tried to urge her towards a different path. When that didn't work, I spoke to her of the future she would lose and you would gain. Her heart was corrupt and she wouldn't listen to me. My words led toward her self-fulfilled destiny of sorrow. Will you follow the same path? Will you only deepen my curse of spreading darkness?" Her milky gaze roved over E, seeing deeper than skin.

"I have faith that you will not. I have defied him much for you; first to save your friend so that his life would bring you strength and hope, and eventually lead you to me. And now I have done so again, to save your life from the Pan himself. But my power is weakening. I am losing my battle against his strength. With my death, you shall take what power I can offer. Power taken from me is power taken from the Pan. Yet worlds beyond this shall fall to Pan's dark destruction if you fail, Child of Vermillion."

"No pressure." E swallowed hard, hands tightening on the dagger hilts at her back. The Wendy's lips stretched into a wry grin.

"I see you understand. Come for me then, descendent of Pan. End my pained existence and I shall give you your answers. But I warn you, no matter what I wish, the land answers to Pan, and I am part of that land. Though I wish for my death, the land will not allow it so easily. You must find a way past my defenses, and you must do it quickly, before Pan answers my distress." E fought the urge to look behind, as though Pan would show up in that moment. "I have held his connection at bay as we spoke. But I can do it no longer. May you have luck, child who would be my salvation."

The vines flew at E without a moment's hesitation. They snapped at her like whips, their thorned lengths lashing her face and body. E slashed at them with her knife, the green appendages dropping to the ground to the serenade of Wendy's pained moans and shrill screams. But where one vine fell, another rose. They snaked around her legs, up her thighs and around her waist. E renewed her efforts, stabbing and slashing anything that came near with the frenzy of a trapped wild animal. The vines began to lessen, shying away from her blade with hisses of fury. Then, the earth shook, and E began to sink, the vines pulling her downward into the soil. If they could not win against her blade, they would win by suffocating her in the dark recesses of earth.

E slashed and stabbed, desperately trying to find purchase in the dirt. Flailing out an entangled leg, her foot broke through a solid wall of dirt. E scrambled, twisting and gasping as she fought to reach the little pocket of air she'd just opened. Only, when she found purchase through the hole, she realized it wasn't just a pocket of air. It was a large underground den, the place of refuge that Wendy sunk to when not needed by Pan. The small cave was lined with thousands of luminescent mushrooms, their blue glow casting the undulating vines in an eerie light.

E gripped the edges of the hole, pulling against the vines still encasing her legs, yelling in pain and anger, E finally pulled her way into the den, far enough that her ankles exited the hole. She used the angle to hack away at the remaining vines that trapped her. They screamed and wriggled away, withdrawing to regain the upper hand another way. E wiped the dirt and sweat from her eyes, thinking quickly. In seconds the vines would return, and with her lagging strength, E wouldn't be able to fight them off again.

Her eyes shifted over the small space, dissecting shadows from dirt and vines. Then she saw it. In the far back of the cave, a stem as thick as Easton's torso, twitched. E shifted towards it, her mind quickly formulating its importance. That vine was Wendy's literal life line. The way it twitched in the shadows betrayed its life-giving efforts. Like a giant straw, it was drawing in all the things that kept her alive. Water, nourishment from the soil, the chlorophyll all plants needed to survive, even in Neverland. Dagger raised, E ran for the stem.

Vines shot out of the darkness, wrapping about her with fierce protectiveness. They both knew what E wanted. The plants were determined to stop her. But the plants clearly didn't know just how stubborn E could be. They yanked her legs out from under her, knocking the air from her lungs as she fell to the ground. The blue mushrooms were crushed beneath her, oozing their luminescent inking onto her skin. It soaked into her, as though trying to poison her. E shouted as the itch of the mushrooms' burrowing blood soaked into the cuts that had been scored into her flesh by the thorny vines.

Still, E refused to give up. Limbs twitching, lower half restrained, E fought to keep her arms free. Slamming the knife into the ground, E pulled herself inch by inch closer to the stem, breaking more mushrooms in her wake. The vines wrapped about her arms and neck, choking her. E pushed the last few inches closer, straining, fighting against time to hit the stem before she passed out. Black spots swam in her vision as she made one valiant slash. The stem hissed in pain, Wendy's muffled scream from above easily heard through the dirt. Green fluid spurted from the stem, Wendy's life-giving plant blood. Then, with the last of her strength, E pushed the knife into the pulsating stem. The force of its suction as it desperately sought to gather more sustenance pulled the blade upward.

With a sickening slurpy thud, the knife found its mark: Wendy's heart. The earth shook, the vines screamed. E pressed upward on shaky limbs as the vines fell away from her. She glanced around, her body now the brightest glowing thing in the cave, she had destroyed so many of the mushrooms.

Panic clawed within E's belly. She was trapped in the dark confining space underground. Fears of being trapped in that smoky hidden room of her parents' house resurfaced; the same fear that had namelessly suffocated her during her first experience with the Truth Light ceremony. E was completely and thoroughly terrified of small dark places, or anything that confined her, held her in place so that she couldn't move.

With a whimper of desperation, E began scratching at the dirt above her head with her fingernails. Several of them ripped, but as she ripped away dirt and roots in her frenzy, dirt showering down on her head as the night sky became visible. E clawed her way free of her would-be grave, flopping to the ground on shaky limbs.

"You have done it, Child of Vermillion. You have slain me." Wendy wheezed happily, green blood leaking from her lips. "I shall finally know peace. Quickly, now come close so that I may speak what you must know. Time is short."

"That descendant sent to earth tethered Pan's life, a piece of his soul; so long as his blood lived in the other realm, no one could harm Pan. But now...with his blood returned from another realm? Things could be different."

"You're saying now that I am here, Hook can kill Pan?"

"I am saying, *you* can kill Peter. You and the Hook, together as prophesied. " E's eyes widened.

"Like the prophecy... how do you know about that?"

"Who do you think spoke to the Hook's soothsayer in his dreams?" Wendy grinned, green blood smearing her teeth, her skin growing ashy. "Your blood is the key. The Hook's weapon alone cannot harm the Pan. But with your blood, order shall be renewed." A cough racked her body, more of that green liquid spilling from her lips. The leaves around the edges of the clearing dried and blew away in the wind, the decay slowly slipping closer. "Closer, Child of Vermillion, my breath is leaving me."

"With my life's blood, I give you gifts. The gift of flight, as the Pan bears, is now yours. It has always been with you, an inheritance of your own blood. Yet it has been dormant, until this moment, only used in your dreams. The power pulses within you." One slender vine swept across the glowing blue lines etched into her skin from the fluorescent mushrooms.

"Once I am gone, place a bit of my ashes upon your tongue. It is the final key to awakening your powers. With my death, it will be a fleeting power. Gone swiftly. But so will be Pan's ability to fly. Flee quickly, as it will be your only hope for escape tonight." Blood gurgled in her throat on a ravaged cough.

"I have one last gift to give. The gift to renew what once was, but now is broken. It is a one-time use, a special gift meant for one close to your heart. It will answer you when the time is right." Wendy convulsed, eyes widening as they stared at the leaves above. "You were born to free the shackles of the soul." Wendy whispered, her words sifting through the air like a breeze.

"My salvation, Hook's salvation, the salvation of worlds you know nothing of. Perhaps, even Pan's salvation. The Vermillion Hook is born!"

The final word stole the last of her breath. Instantly, Wendy, the vines, all her leaves, burst into a cloud of dust. A wind came up blowing the ashes away in a swirl of green dust. The hand that once gripped E's had disintegrated, leaving only a handful of the ashes. Holding her breath, E shoved the ashes into her mouth before she could think better of it.

Cold shot through her veins, sending zings of shock through every inch of her. And then it was gone. In its place rested a weightlessness, a sense of everything being put to right. E felt her birthright burgeoning within. A euphoric answering of her soul to questions she never knew to ask. She could feel everything in the land around her. Neverland spoke to her, through silent words of welcome and hope, awakening to her presence as though flowers shifting to catch rays of the rising sun.

A grin spread across E's face as she tilted her head back and drank in the ever-increasing sensations. And then, the earth shook. E felt the awakening excitement within drain away in fear of the coming darkness. A roar of fury and pain filled the air, lightning split the night. Pan knew, and he was drudging hell up to swallow them all.

CHAPTER 46
HOOK

Ian sensed the Fiend long before he saw him. His whole body shook with the need to attack, the need to destroy the evil that had brought his and Neverland's existence to what it was now. Ian had spent lifetimes adapting steadfast patience and the strength of control over his hook. While he was sorely tested now, he held onto the restraint by a thread. His army needed his head clear and sharp to lead.

He shot a quick glance over the mass amounts of men hidden throughout the forest. Mer faces mingled with those of his men, and Hook felt a swell of pride. He had little doubt that Easton's influence had helped solidify their presence in the coming war. The moment his wife left to fulfill her plan, Ian set his own into action. He'd gathered his army, and sent Caol to call on his. The Mers had arrived not ten minutes too early, and he was grateful for their added numbers.

"I smell an old cod fish!" Pan laughed, setting down in the center of the field that he and his men surrounded in the shadows. Ian could feel his men tensing at his back, ready for a fight. "Come out, come out, wherever you are!"

Pan crowed, eyes staring him down despite the shadows that cloaked them. Moving forward, Hook led the way. Most of his army stayed back in the shadows, biding their time. He stopped ten yards away, silently waiting. Pan grinned, eyes darting from one man to the next. Ian waited for the laugh that would come, could almost guess exactly the amount of time before Pan threw his head back. Twenty five long seconds of his childish staring game, while the Fiend tried to pick at each man's brains.

"Still not going to tell me how you are able to protect your minds?" He chuckled, swiping at the jovial tears gathered from his laughter.

"Still going to ask that question every time we meet?" Ian flashed his clenched white teeth in a grimace of a smile. He was hardly going to give away the secret to the potion mixed into every drink and plate of food served in Sanctuary.

"You're no fun." Pan replied.

"Good." Ian retorted. He carefully pulled the crystal sheath from his Hook, pocketing the little shield. Pan glanced at Ian's weapon and scoffed.

"Always so ready for a fight. I just came to talk, really. No fighting. Just for a few moments, I want peace between us."

"You never stop talking, and peace is something you haven't the taste for," Ian pointed out.

"That's because I'm loads more interesting to listen to than you. And peace can be so boring. But just this once, it won't be." Pan grinned, lifting off the ground a few feet, arms crossed proudly over his chest. Ian resisted the urge to groan in annoyance. Half the battle with the Pan was always getting past the inane talking.

"What, you don't believe me? Where is your trust, cod fish?" Peter chuckled, eyes dancing with unconcealed devilish delight. When Hook made no reply, Pan shrugged. "Fine, be that way. Let's move on to the fun. I come with good news. Would you care to hear my good news?"

"Do I have a choice in the matter?"

"You'll like this one," Pan promised. "But first, I heard rumors that you had a new member of your crew. A girl." The Lost Boys whooshed about, snickering. Ian tensed. The hook burned against his skin, warming his arm, begging for a slash right across that smug face.

"I just thought you might like to know that I have a new member of my own crew." Ian's eyes narrowed slightly, but not enough to give away his cautious concern. Easton would not betray him. She wouldn't.

"No guesses?" Pan asked, floating side to side in pure enjoyment of what he deemed a game. "I'll give you a hint. It's also a girl." The men at Ian's back shifted uncomfortably. Ian held firm. He knew his wife. She wouldn't fall.

"You are not very good at this game," Pan chided, frowning. "Very well, then I will tell you. She has fiery hair, just like mine. She used to be under your so-called protection. Now, she's mine. " A frigid fist clenched Ian's heart. Pan was toying with them, that was all. Easton was okay. She had to be. He remained silent, refusing to play to the Pan's whims.

"Oh fie, you'll never guess so I'll just tell you. It's my daughter!" Ian frowned outwardly this time. He had to trust Easton. He had to play the game.

"You have no daughter."

"But I do. And you've known about her all this time." Peter aggressively challenged, smile slipping into a snarl. "You've kept her from me, hidden her and that traitorous woman away!" The Fiend's eyes burned in a way that left little doubt as to his belief in the matter. "She told me all about how you accepted her into your crew, and took her on your pathetic patrols. You fancied her, but she didn't return your love. She ran to me, rather than be with you for the rest of your eternal doom." Ian swallowed hard. Pan drew near, a devious twist to his lips.

"You do have a terrible sort of luck when it comes to women, don't you? Betrayals left and right. I understand betrayals. Women are full of them. But my little Moth has given me hope." An invisible steel band constricted Ian's lungs. Moth? No, she was no moth, she was a beautiful butterfly. Pan's eyes took on a gleam of maniacal severity.

"She is going to change everything. With her by my side, your escapades are at an end. Neverland will be ours."

"You're wrong. You don't know my wife." Ian growled, prodded into ire so great he could contain it no longer.

"Wife?" Pan blinked, looking surprised. And surprise was something the childish foe never liked. A fire of promised retribution burned in his gaze before the smile returned. "Whether she be your wife or not, it doesn't matter. I knew your first wife. You didn't know of her betrayal. Just as I'd wager you didn't know your current wife is at this very moment within my camp. She came to me, begged me to take her in. Said no one could love her the way her own father could. She begged for freedom."

Freedom, what a crock of lies. Ian's hand trembled. No, she wouldn't find freedom with Pan. She had already found freedom with Hook. And she'd blossomed under it. Just then, a shadow raced to the side of Pan, frantically whispering in his ear. Pan's eyes flew wide.

"What!" Without another word, Pan spun about and flew in the opposite direction. Ian watched him go.

"Please come home, little butterfly," Ian whispered. Suddenly Pan cried out a pained howl, grasping his head. Like an autumn leaf, he plummeted to the ground, bouncing and rolling on impact. Hook's men grew hushed as they watched. Ian tensed, hand moving to his sword. What had happened? Had she somehow found a way to... kill Pan? The Fiend stirred, rolling to his knees, and Ian grit his teeth. Of course not. It couldn't be that simple.

"Wendy!" Pan screamed to the sky.

Neverland answered to Pan's fury, the sky splitting with lightning so terrible Ian feared the world itself would fall apart at the seams. Pan lifted from the ground, though he barely seemed to hover above it, the grass tickling across his bare feet, before he once more sank to the ground. He gave an upward bounce, trying to rise, and once more failed. Black shadows etched his features into sharp contrasts of demonic fury such as Ian had never witnessed.

"You!" The word slithered through the wind, whipping about Ian like a brand. Raising his sword, he ran. Their swords hissed with the scrape of metal across metal as they engaged in battle. Pan slashed at him, his anger giving more force to his attack.

"You sent the serpent into my home! You corrupted my child and turned her against me!" Pan pressed close, the x formation of their crossed swords the only thing separating Ian from his fury. A rich smile spread across Ian's lips, Pan's words lifting his heart with such hope he felt it enlarge.

"Karma always comes full circle," Ian grinned.

Pan screamed, shoving him away. The shadows heeded his scream as though the call to battle and swiftly fell on his men. With shouts of support, Ian's army poured out of the forest to help. Ian ignored the edgy sensations of unease as pigmites and other creatures poured from the forest, brought by Pan's call to arms. His army had arrived, and Ian would simply have to trust his own army to hold against the crashing of its force.

One of his men sent a pigmite flying through the air, bouncing off Pan's shoulder. Ian immediately leapt on the Pan's distraction to slash the Fiend from navel to shoulder with his hook. He grit his teeth in annoyance as the slash sealed back over, leaving only a torn shirt behind as evidence of it ever happening. Pan offered a cruel sneer.

"Still trying and still failing. When will you learn that your hook is useless against me? I've grown too strong to be taken down by your pathetic antique weapon." Ian grunted as Pan got in a lucky swipe across his own chest with his dagger, yet another scar added to the battles recorded across his skin. Pan grinned deviously, pupils enlarged to the point of overtaking the color. A black wind rose, surrounding them in a swirling wall that cut them off from the rest of the battle.

"I have carried our battles out for far too long. I could have ended you long ago, but I wanted to toy with you as a cat with a mouse. I find I have finally grown tired of our little games. I'll kill you tonight and be done with it. And when I return home, I'll bring the games to little Moth." Ian lunged forward, making the Fiend dance backward out of reach of the blade. Pan leapt away, taunting him.

"I'll torment her in more ways than you ever dreamed possible. Endless, everlasting torment, and it will be all your doing." Ian slashed through him once more willing the hook to do its job. "I'm too powerful for you now, old man. Neverland has chosen its rightful king, and I will not be denied!"

The satyr came upon him unexpectedly, appearing from the howling wall of wind to pin Hook to the ground, one knee grinding painfully into his back until Ian was sure the pressure would crush every bone in his torso.

Swiftly yanking Hook upright, it changed tactics, stretching Hook's arms so painfully taut to the sides Ian was certain they would rip free at any moment. Eye sliding closed Ian pictured Easton, the memory of her smiling down at him just yesterday. With a grim smile, Ian clenched his jaw and prepared for the pain.

Yet the satyr sat infuriatingly still, seemingly content to merely hold him in the agonizing position. Excited clapping drew Ian's gaze to Pan, hands behind his back and lips quirked in smug mischief.

"Well done, satyr, you've caught a cod fish!"

"Something you haven't been able to do for a very long time, Panling." Ian mocked. Pan frowned.

"Mock me all you like Hook, but you've lost."

"No. I won so long ago it's pitiful, really."

"Did not," Pan chuckled, arms crossing over his chest.

"Oh, but I have. The people hate you, Pan. Perhaps you'll be able to force them into submission. Perhaps you'll destroy them all. But that still leaves you with nothing. A world that bows to you out of fear, not love. All your life you've fought to be loved, and yet hatred is all you have ever gained. The creatures use your power to their advantage, but the moment you cease to be powerful, they will cease to follow you. Even your Lost Boys can't love you, not really. Perhaps they might have in the beginning. But as they wasted away, so did their adoration. How could they love the creature responsible for destroying their very souls? No," Ian grinned, "no, they are slaves. They serve you out of fear and necessity. Perhaps even they secretly hate you, too."

Pan snarled and gestured to the satyr. The goat creature

wrenched a groan of pain from Ian's clenched teeth as his hooked arm popped from the socket. With another flick of his finger, Pan stilled the creature before the other arm followed. With a low snuffling snort, the creature wrenched Ian's arms down and behind his back. Ian clenched his teeth against the dizzying pain, refusing to give Pan the pleasure of him losing consciousness. His nemesis stepped closer, toe to toe.

"What do you know of love? You've destroyed everything you love as well." Ian grinned against the pain, silently denying that statement. Pan's head ticked to the side in thought.

"No, perhaps not everything. Not yet." Ian's defiant grin slipped as Pan moved to the side, revealing Easton held firmly between two Lost Boys. She couldn't be here, not now, not like this. But she was. His gaze collided with hers.

"Look what my Boys have found: a last meal for the cod fish." Pan released a hearty chuckle. Ian ignored the Fiend, eye firmly locked with hers.

"Are you well, Vermillion?" he asked quietly, an underlying question in the words depths.

"Better than the rest of them will be when we're done with them." She stated boldly, eyes fiery in promise.

His lips quirked in reply. That was his butterfly, ever defiant. That was the woman he was proud to call his wife. She had escaped the Pan whole. A wave of calm flowed over the torment in his soul he'd refused to acknowledge. Though he trusted his wife, steadfastly refused to believe she could be unfaithful to him or Neverland, Ian did fear the Pan's ability to destroy all he touched. Seeing her now, he knew his faith and trust had been well placed. Pan jabbed at Hook's dislocated shoulder with his short sword, just deep enough to draw blood. Hook watched him steadily, defiant.

"Come, Hook! What did you hope to gain by sending her to me? Didn't you learn the lesson with your first wife? Women cannot resist my magnetism."

"Ew," Easton muttered.

"I didn't send her. Easton has no master to guide her about by the lip. She does as she pleases. Nor did I overly worry for her safety. She is strong and capable." Ian shrugged with his good shoulder.

"What words!" Pan crowed, mocking him. "How easily he allows you to play with dangerous things, girl! Perhaps you are nothing more than a toy to him, a tool to be used by his whims."

"Sounds like fun to me," Easton stated with mischief in her eyes. Ian chuckled, love warming his smile.

"Women are a pitiful waste of flesh. What good are they but trouble?" Pan scoffed, grabbing her by the front of the shirt and pulling. The Lost Boys happily dragged her along to their master's lead. Pan yanked her to a stop not a foot away from Ian, whose eye hungrily swept over her body for any signs of harm. Pan grasped her jaw tightly, wrenching her face toward him.

"Now, what have you done to my Wendy."

"I set her free."

Pan's teeth grit together, body shaking under the force of his barely restrained fury. Releasing her chin roughly, he stepped away.

"I must own, Hook, you and I are alike in one aspect: the women in our lives have been very good at betrayal. Though this one was far better at deceiving than your first wife, and much more dangerous, I might add."

As Pan rambled on, Ian's gaze honed in on Easton's. He could see the gears turning. She was formulating a plan in that beautiful head of hers. But what? His brow quirked in challenge to the unspoken question. Her shoulders lifted with the slightest twitch.

"Yes, you chose your tool well. My own flesh and blood!" Pan continued, ignorant to the plans formulating between the lovers' gazes.

"Peter!"

A thin voice called out over the howling winds. Pan stilled, eyes rounding to resemble a lost child as he locked gazes with the old woman fighting to keep her firm stance at the edge of the wall. Pan's shoulders drooped, as though the life had been sucked out of him. The winds died to half their strength. The winds parted, shifted around the woman to bring her inside the eye of the storm.

"Tink?" Pan muttered.

"Aye, Peter, tis me." Bell replied steadily. "Stop this foolishness before you cause more harm. This war must end."

"But," Pan shook his head, ignoring her demands, "you've grown so old." He paused, gaze darting toward Easton, then back once more. "Then it's true what she said? You traded your youth for our child?"

"I did. Then I sent her into another world."

"You sent... our child through the portal?"

"I did. And now Easton has come to right your wrongs." How artfully the woman twisted her worlds, keeping Easton's true identity still a secret. Hook watched in wonder as Pan's eyes misted with tears.

"You hated me that much? Enough that you ripped our child from your womb and tossed her alone and helpless into another world? Were you so eager to be free of all pieces of me?"

"I see time has not lessened your arrogance." Bell sighed, an ironic twist to her lips. "I sacrificed so that our child could have life. You offered the babe nothing but never-ending torment, a prison wrapped in pretty detail. That's all you offered us both." Pan's eyes snapped up, gaze broken, yet angry. His jaw set.

"I tried. I changed, for you! I fought against the only man I knew as father, to be with you!" Bell flinched at his shout, eyes clouding with age old regret and sadness. Pan's nose scrunched with disgust.

"Yet in the end, he was right. You turned against me. You stole away my happiness. You chose retribution against me above all else. I loved you, loved you both. And in return you destroyed the gift of everlasting youth, tossed away our child, and denied the rest of them."

He gestured to the shadows that hissed dark whispers of Pan's anger, their grips on Easton's arms tightening. Ian watched her expression carefully, gauging the pain behind the reassuring smile she offered.

"And as though that weren't enough, you sided with my enemy. All these years you've lived with my enemy while I languished with a broken soul!"

"You forced my hand, Peter! Your crazed behavior would have

destroyed us both had I stayed! I had to save our child. Can't you understand that? Please, let the girl go. End this war before you finally destroy what we should hold most dear," Bell pleaded.

"No! No more!" Pan roared, the wind once more gathering to a wail. Face blank and voice flat, Pan stared down his nose at her. "Go away, Tink. You left me once, but now I shall be the one to banish you!"

"Peter, please!" Bell called out to him again, but her cries were lost to the storm as she was carefully, but firmly shoved to the other side of the storm wall. Once she was completely gone from view, Pan released a sharp sigh, hands behind his back.

"As for you, little Moth," He patted her on the head before withdrawing, "daughter or not, you've lied to and disobeyed your father. You've been a very naughty little girl. You've been playing with the enemy. That is something you must answer for. And one thing all fathers are good at, is discipline." Easton raised a defiant brow but didn't reply. Pan ignored her outward rebellion and began pacing, dictating her crimes.

"You sided with my enemy. You lied to and betrayed me by returning to him, just hours after promising me your devotion. You stole one of my Lost Boys, tricked your way into my home, destroyed my Wendy!"

"Wiley was never yours." E's words dripped with venom, looking to Pan. "And Wendy begged me for release, disgusted with a life of servitude to you!" Pan ignored her.

"All of that makes you a traitor. And do you know what traitors get? Comeuppance."

Hook didn't have a chance to discern the implications behind Pan's glance toward the satyr. Ian's hook lodged into his beloved's ever so soft stomach, his shoulder's recent dislocation offering no resistance to the satyr's forced upward swing of his arm. It happened in the beat of a heart, as if the universe were mocking him with the speed of which it could destroy the remnants of his soul. His pain of movement hadn't even registered before hers began. The chaos of their surroundings fell on ears deaf to every sound but that of his wife's gasp of shock and pain.

"No. No, no, no." Ian choked, dazed, eyes fixated on his hook once again bringing death to one he should have protected.

The shadows released her shoulders, maliciously leaving her to hang atop the hook. Her legs shook as she stood tippy-toed, trying to hold her weight off the weapon, to keep the hole in her torso from opening wider than it already had. Ian couldn't even fight to pull his arm back, the dislocated arm useless to obey his commands, the satyr's grip on it too firm. A tense silence fell over the world, as they all watched, waiting for the Rift to form.

And yet, nothing but brilliant vermillion blood welled from the wound.

"Well! It would seem you are useless against all who share my blood. Not that it matters, you've still doomed her. With a wound that wicked, she'll never survive," Pan cackled loudly.

Ian's body began to tremble, frozen in an inescapable horror. Rift or not, Pan was right; his hook would be responsible for the death of his second wife, and the destruction of his soul would be as immediate as her passing.

"Ian." Easton's gasp tugged his eyes upward from the morbid irony of Fate. She tried to offer a smile, to reassure him around her pain. Ever his brave vermillion butterfly. "Ian, it's okay," E gasped quietly.

"Release me!" Ian screamed, his body's shakes turning so violent he feared worsening her wound. "Devus, release me!"

"It's not Devus you should be begging." Hook stilled at Pan's quiet demand. He clenched his jaw.

"Pan, release me."

"Say *please*." Pan whispered just at the side of his ear. "*Beg* me, Hook." Swallowing, Ian easily spoke the words. For his wife, he would do anything.

"Please." When Pan didn't respond, Ian shouted it to the stormy heavens. "Please release me, Pan, I beg of you!"

Seemingly satisfied at last, Pan flicked a negligent hand toward the satyr. Immediately the creature moved away. Ian dove forward, his good arm wrapping about his beloved's back to support her weight, a sob wrenching from his throat as he carefully dislodged the hook. Together they sank to the ground, her body draped over his leg and arm. His other leg wrapped over top of her body, torso hunching, trying to protect her to the best of his broken ability.

"Ian." She called to him, voice small and weak, yet still so sweet to his ears. Another sob came as his eye rose to hers.

"Easton." Her name fell from his lips like the broken shards of his heart. "I'll fix it. I'll… somehow I'll fix it. I'll…" The words died on a helpless shudder. He couldn't fix it. She offered another gentle smile lined with pain.

"It'll be okay."

"No!" Ian crumbled, voice brimming with sorrow. That useless word kept slipping past his lips, as though it would change anything. "Don't tell me this is okay, Vermillion. Do not believe your life is so meaningless to me!" Forehead resting against hers, he shook his head in denial, unable to meet her gaze when he confessed his inability to save her.

"I'm sorry. I am so sorry, my heart. I can't…" he whispered, tortured to the marrow.

"I know." Easton placed her hand back to his jaw, gently forcing him to move back to look at her. "*You* didn't choose this." He shook his head at her assurances, eyes squeezing shut. "But now isn't the time to grieve. Not yet. We still have a job to do."

His eye snapped open at her words. Determination radiated from her, more fiercely than any sun he'd ever laid eyes on. He flinched as her hand moved to grasp his wrist over the hook, resting it just above her bloodied torso.

"Tell me what you see, Ian."

Unable to refuse her anything, Ian stared at the mortal wound he'd inflicted. And hope bloomed. The wound was a deep, ravaged and ugly thing. Yet the silky skin he'd spent hours worshiping, visible now through torn fabric, was mending. Mending and leaving behind pink freshly healed edges. Ian stared in awe, eyes flicking to hers in question.

"I'm tougher than I look. Child of Vermillion, descendant of Pan. Remember?" She smiled around a pained cough.

She was a descendant of Pan. That meant she could potentially heal like the Pan, too. It was a slow process, slower than Pan's healing, probably because her connection to Neverland was weaker than Pan's. Yet the fact that she was healing at all showed Neverland's timid efforts at treaty. If she could hold on long enough, Neverland just might save her. If he could keep Neverland alive long enough for it to fuel that healing, if he could promise it a new future; if he could kill the Pan. His gaze rose to hers once more, determination rekindling in his ravaged soul, a smile stretching his lips.

"You'll survive. You have his blood."

"And now you have mine." Easton weakly gripped his wrist, drawing his attention back to the hook. "With the Vermillion weapon..." she started.

"Hook shall halt the Fiend's last breath." Ian finished, the words of prophecy that he'd read countless times, gaining new value as he blinked down at the weapon that gleamed with her blood. He was right; his little butterfly had been the key all along.

"I tire of all this whispering." Pan groused. "Speak louder or stop speaking at all."

"End him, Ian! Save Neverland." Easton whispered urgently, ignoring Pan. Ian held her gaze with a promise.

"Save Neverland, save *you.*"

Supporting her weight with his leg, Ian lifted his good arm to remove the chain around his neck. With a solemn devotion, he slipped it over her head. Her fingertips brushed over the metal where it now rested over her breast, a warm smile bringing color to her pallid cheeks.

"I said enough!" Pan shouted. "Easton, be a dear and die for Daddy so he can have some fun."

"I'll deal with you soon enough, imp!" Hook growled. Pan chuckled darkly. Flicking his fingers towards the satyr and shadows, he sent them away.

"Go have some fun with what is left of Hook's crew. The cod fish and I are going to play." The satyr lumbered loyally away, shadows in its wake, leaving Pan to smugly watch the display before him. "Well? Let's have at it. Unless you've lost your will? Though it would be far less fun, I could simply slaughter you where you lie."

"Go. Do what you have to do. I'll be fine." Easton whispered, fingers weakly grasping his shirt in assurance.

"Wait for me then, my love. It won't take long," he promised. Leaning forward, Ian pressed a kiss to Easton's brow before gently shifting out from under her.

"That was quite touching, as your farewells go, Hook. And I have been witness to a great many of your farewells. As soon as the little Moth dies, I'll add her to the long list."

"I'll not lose her; not today, not ever!" Ian growled. With a war cry, Ian slammed his shoulder up against what was left of a stone cottage, forcing the joint back into place with a loud pop. His lips pulled into a scowl as he rotated the arm ensuring its full, if not painful, use.

"Impressive," Pan chuckled. "Though such bravado will be useless soon, as you bleed headless on the ground."

"When this is over, the world will be free of your poison. We will make sure no one even remembers your name," Ian promised. Pan's eyes went wild with fury. A mad sort of chuckle fell from his lips.

"You'll have to do it alone, then." Suddenly a gush of wind rose about them, lifting Easton into the air.

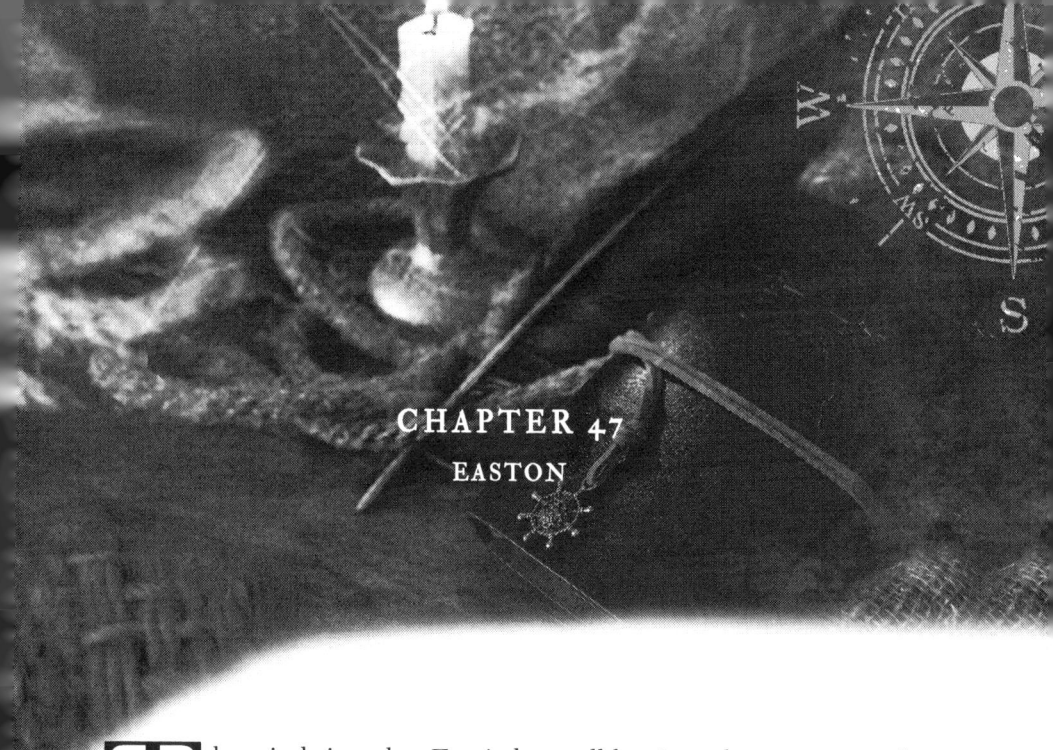

CHAPTER 47
EASTON

T he wind ripped at E, tried to pull her into the outer tornado that still surrounded them. Ian cried out and reached for her. E grabbed hold of his hand, his hooked arm wrapping about a slanting wooden post from a long ago destroyed fence. She cried out as the slowly healing skin in her torso ripped anew. Hook ground his teeth as the wind pulled at them, deepening the pressure on his wounded shoulder, threatening to dislodge it once more. Through it all, Ian still somehow managed to hold onto her, her valiant protector.

E tried desperately to access Wendy's skills of flight. But her magic had depleted during her mad flight from Pan's lair. Wendy's magic was gone, just as she said it would be.

E's eyes shifted to the side as Peter cackled madly, the gleam of death in the wild eyes that fixed on them. The wind swept around him, lifted him from the ground, yet didn't harm its master. E cried out as the wound shifted further along her abdomen, moving up toward her ribs. One arm wrapped about her stomach in an effort to keep her organs in, Easton stared at the gushes of red that flowed past her arm. Her breath caught, stumbling over the fear that lodged in her throat. She was going to die.

"Easton!" Ian cried out, drawing her attention back to him. "Look to me, little butterfly. No fear, now. I'll never leave you to fly alone." He offered a broad reassuring smile. The same smile from the cavern when E thought they were surely about to drown. Only now, his smile was a turbulent mixture of determination and sadness.

It was a smile that told her there was no trick hidden up his sleeve to save them this time. Yet he still would offer her comfort and his strength in their last moments, his words proof to his determination to be pulled into death with her. He would sacrifice everything to protect her until his last breath. Tears rushed over her temples and into her hair, adding to the debris and blood already mingled there. She offered a brilliant, if watery, smile in answer to his.

"It's time for me to spread my wings, Ian." It wasn't too late. Maybe she was going to die. But Neverland didn't have to die with her. Neither did Ian.

"We'll spread them together," he vowed, clutching her hand tighter still.

"What a pitiful final battle this has been." Pan gripped a long wicked dagger in each hand and madness in his eyes as he closed in on his prey. Still Ian held to her, though she knew he must feel death approaching from behind.

"Look to me, butterfly." He murmured assurance, not wanting her to watch their end.

"Not this time," she answered softly. Fighting the force of the wind, E released her stomach and reached toward Ian. Blood slicked his hand as she gripped his fingers, loosening his grasp.

"Easton, don't..." he began, wide eye desperately warning, begging her to not go through with her obvious plan. Yet in his current position, he had no way to stop her.

"Have a little faith in your wife?" she smiled sadly. Then, without another word, without another thought, E yanked against his fingers, releasing her lifeline to him.

"No!" Ian screamed out in horror, his voice rivaling the gales of wind that filled her ears as the tornado ripped her up into its fury.

CHAPTER 48
HOOK

Ian watched in numb shock as his wife was sucked into the devil's wind, her delicate body tumbled about within the debris.

"Everyone you love dies, Hook," Pan snickered, coming to stop at his side.

The Fiend watched with glee as her body was bruised and battered in the debris. With a sideways smirk as his only warning, Pan released the winds. Immediately the storm dissipated, and Easton's body toppled through the sky, falling to the ground like a beautiful bird downed with a well-aimed arrow. Ian's heart plummeted with her.

With an enraged scream, he twisted to the side, wildly slicing the hook's tip through Pan's skin. Ian felt his eyes glow as the weapon of death slid upward through the Pan's flesh, as though it were a hot pudding. Pan's laughing eyes went blank, the glee on his lips wilting into disbelief.

"What...what have you done, cod fish?" Pan choked on blood that bubbled up through his teeth.

"With the Vermillion weapon, Hook shall halt the Fiend's last breath." Ian spoke through clenched teeth, barred in hatred.

The look of shock on his foe's face was replaced with one last defiant sneer of vengeance, his razor sharp daggers slicing through Ian's wrist, severing the hook from his arm. Ian cried out in renewed agony as the Pan sank to the ground. Only seconds passed before the hook, still fully snared by the Pan's body, was sucked into the black hole of the Rift.

Not another word escaped the Fiend, his last breath wheezing out in a wet burbling sound of finality. Silent laughter on his lips the last thing visible before the Pan disappeared into the Rift forever. Ian's mind only distantly registered the completion of his lifelong quest as he spun and stumbled through the destruction of his people.

"Easton! Easton!"

He called over and over, desperately searching the ground for her body, bloodied stump held upward against his chest in an effort to keep the blood loss from ending his efforts to find her.

He wasn't the first to find her. A small crowd of his bedraggled people gathered in a circle. Smee stood in the center, shoulders hunched, dull eyes rising to meet his. The dismal expressions on the crew's faces crushed what was left of Ian's mangled heart.

The crowd parted before he reached them, silently allowing him access to the crumbled form of his beloved. Bell sat at Easton's side, sparkling tears slipping from her cheeks.

"My poor sweet girl," Bell whispered, fingertips lingering at the edges of Easton's hair, as though afraid to touch anything else.

Ian collapsed to his knees, a sob of denial tearing from his throat. Vermillion liquid covered the entire length of her torso now, along with dribbling from her nose and lips. The blood was daunting enough, but it was her still body, the impossible angles of her legs and twisted back that whispered most adamantly of doom to his soul.

Her hair fanned out about her in a macabre beauty, as though an angel dashed upon the rocks at sea. Ian crawled closer across the dirt, the fingers of his remaining hand seeking out the softness of her cheek. Her eyes blinked slowly open at his trembling touch, a shuddering gasp of breath filling her lungs. Absurd hope burst in his chest, even as tears of reality slipped over his cheeks.

"Hold for me, Easton. Hold. You're not meant to fly without me."

"Did…" she coughed a wet terrible sound, "win?"

"The Fiend is dead."

He couldn't bring himself to say they had won. She was dying. What triumph could he find in that? Instead, he grit his teeth, locking her with a deviled gaze.

"I'll not lose you. Not now, not ever." Shifting aside the fabric of her ragged shirt, Ian carefully analyzed the wound across her abdomen. Hating himself for the pain he would inflict, Ian quickly set about straightening her limbs, settling them where Neverland could heal them the correct way. She didn't make a single sound, no groans of pain or protest; simply watched him with dull eyes as he worked, fate already accepted. It made the desperation claw at his insides even more frantically. With nothing left that he could do, Ian sat back on his heels and waited.

"Heal her," He whispered desperately, gaze lifting to the black sky. "*Heal her, damn you!*"

Her fingers twitched in his direction, and he carefully moved his own to touch them. Sniffles of barely contained sobs lifted to the air around them. The magic that protected Sanctuary had clearly been removed, as the people of Sanctuary filed forward to join the crowd of mourning. Ian ignored them all, attention only for the penetrating gaze of the keeper of his soul. Her hand lifted, fingers twitching. He quickly moved closer, granting those questing fingers access to his face.

"Gift… love." Fingertips warm with blood slipped across his cheek. He caught her hand as it fell away, holding it gently to his face.

"Don't leave me." Broken words tumbled from his lips as the life in her eyes dimmed. The right corner of her lips lifted for only a moment.

"I…fly." His blood ran cold as her eyes slowly closed, lips losing the small curve of the smile.

"No," he growled. "Not without me, Easton James Bendal! I need you at my side. The world is set aright, its only adventures for our future now. We're off to hunt down James's treasure, remember?" She gave no indication of having heard him, though her chest still rose in short ragged bursts.

"Neverland! May Devus curse you to the depths of the ocean! The Pan is gone! Grant me this boon and heal her!" Ian shouted to the skies. The people he'd spent his life protecting took slow steps backward, heads bowed in sorrow.

"Don't you give up on her!" He shouted at them, startling some, bringing more tears and murmured apologies from others. Bell still sat on the ground, back bowed, hopeless tears falling as her lips spoke silent prayers. He scowled, turning to his wife. He wouldn't give up on her as easily as they. If he could keep her breathing, just long enough, Neverland would answer.

A sense of utter stillness suddenly filled the air, the winds sifting about them, tugging at him. Flickers of light danced across the ground and over Easton's. The villagers stiffened, staring at something to his back. Ian spun about, fearing the Pan had somehow found a way to return. A blackened, shimmering portal hovered above the ground, eerie in its silence. Despite his fears, no Pan reemerged, nor did any other creature of the Rift.

Low gasps drew his attention back to his wife, where she floated gently in the air, body cocooned in light. A new dread grew. The Rift was calling her home, to her real home in an entirely unreachable realm. A realm without Neverland's magic. Panic clawed up his throat.

"No! You can't take her yet!" He screamed at the portal.

"She was given an allotted time to fulfill her destiny," a disembodied voice floated from the Rift portal.

"Celeste?" Bell blinked from her solemn vigil on the ground, eyes fixed on the portal.

"Bell of the Tinkers." The Rift voice acknowledged. "I am glad the Pan did not destroy you. He is gone and you are whole."

"Yes, Peter is gone." Bell replied with a shallow nod. "But I will only be whole if you allow my granddaughter to stay." Ian quickly looked back to the portal, fixated on its reply. The hesitation was agonizing in its suspense.

"The portal demands balance. She must return. I am sorry."

Immediately Easton's body began to float toward the portal. Ian stumbled alongside her, mind frantically churning, body exhausted from shock and loss of blood. His arms yearned to hold her, pull her to a stop, yet he knew it would only do more damage. The Rift was not going to allow him to stop her progression.

"Take her if you must but please, not yet. I ask only that she be given time to heal. If you take her now, if you remove her so soon from Neverland's power, she will die!" Ian pleaded. Again the Rift paused, considering his words.

"She must return." Came the simple reply.

"Have you so little gratitude? Neverland would be lost if not for her!" No pause, no answer came to his violent accusation. The Rift Keeper was without mercy. Easton's body continued its forward progress, ripping free his heart along with it.

"We have hospitals, medicine. They may be able to help her." Isen emerged from the crowd and moved to stand at Hook's side, gaze fixed forward. Turning, he met Hook with promise in his expression. "I'll look after her."

Ian knew Easton's feelings towards this man, what his family had done to hers. Could he trust her to him now? Did he have any choice? The markings that had covered his body were partially gone now. He'd begun his penance in Neverland's eyes, the judgement magic beginning to lift. It was a start. Ian's fist clutched Isen's shirt, menace rolling off of him in dark waves, though his body was weak.

"If harm befalls her whilst in your hands, no amount of distance nor portals will keep me from you," he promised with a dark growl. Isen nodded.

"I understand. I *will* protect her, until you return for her. And this time, I'll do it right." Ian swallowed hard, turning back to the portal. She was gone. The Rift had swallowed her whole, not even allowing him to say a final goodbye. With a curse, Ian shoved against Isen, pressing him forward.

"Go after her, quickly! Keep true to your word."

"Until you come for her, then." With that final farewell, Isen leapt into the portal. Ian sank to the ground, body finally giving way to his wounds. Isen's words repeated in his mind.

'Until you come for her.'

Clutching the stump of his arm to his chest, Ian wept. Even if he could master the art of opening and closing portals, as James had, it was impossible now. His hook was gone, and Pan's revenge was complete. He would hold onto the hope that she would survive in her distant realm, return to health and live a full life. A life without him, for Ian would never see her again.

"A nd the boy who would not grow up gave a final cry of anger, before disappearing into a fine mist. The ground shook, the earth moaned in a deafening sound of torment and release. It was as though Neverland's very soul was torn between mourning and rejoicing at the loss of Pan."

She listened to the words as they danced through her groggy mind, danced through the dark forest of empty dreams that so long had been her companions. The voice was throaty, but pleasant to listen to. A voice she didn't know, yet found comfort in. A moment of indecision tugged at her, a familiar sensation. She could turn, walk back into the forest and lose herself to it for a time longer. Or she could stay and listen a little longer. Gazing longingly at the trees, she turned back to the voice. Just a little more; she needed to hear just a little more, then she'd go back. As though waiting for her decision, the voice began again.

"And then, Neverland breathed. Wind stirring in eddies around the bodies of the survivors, caressed and flowed about them and into the air. For the first time in far longer than anyone could recount, Neverland took a breath of freedom. A breath it did not know it

473

needed, until it drank it in; the breath of possibilities, now that it's jailor was vanquished. The survivors dared to breath with it, dared to call on hope that so many had long ago forgotten. Slowly the crowd dispersed, long forgotten dreams stirring within their breasts beckoned."

She smiled. That was a good ending. Turning, she moved to rejoin the darkness.

"All except for the Hook."

The words stopped her forward progress, attention snagged by that one sentence. This was important. Wasn't it?

"A broken shell tossed to and fro by the whims of destiny, it seemed as though the life was stolen from him with Neverland's first breath of freedom. Crumpled to his knees, head bowed, hand and bloodied stump alike hung limply at his sides. Tears leaked from his eyes, but they were not tears of joy, nor release."

No. This was wrong. She frowned, turning more fully toward the voice. *You're wrong*, she wanted to shout, but the words wouldn't come.

"Once, he had thought that the death of Pan would be his one solace in life. That the death of Pan would free him just as surely as it would free Neverland. Yet he found no peace."

Her frown deepened. *No! Leave him alone! Let him be happy!* Still no sound came from her mouth. Fists clenched, she walked away from the forest. The reader clearly couldn't hear her. So she would simply have to get closer. She would make them hear, make them give him peace! With painstaking agony, she climbed upward, pushing through the slowly lightening fog. She had to clear the fog, escape its confining depths so that they could hear.

"The battle was won, the land and people within it, freed. Still sorrow clung to him, suffocated him. It wasn't a loss of a hand, nor the loss of glory found in battles, that hung the hero's head in such sorrow. What was the loss of a hand, compared to the loss of a heart, the loss of a soul? He was empty, lost, devoid of the will to continue. The eternity or suffering he'd face at the hands of the Pan was nothing compared to the loss of her. Nothing compared to the horror of countless years that stretched before him, without *her*."

No! She shouted vehemently to the fog. He was so much more than just a shell. He was not at the end of his purpose. She had to make them see that. *Ian!* She screamed. *I'm coming, don't give up!* With one last lunge she pushed free of the fog.

Blinking against the sun's burning light, E felt her heart stutter. That… that was no sun. It was the blinding lights of electricity. The lights, the incessant beeping that grew louder in her eyes every passing breath, the firm mattress beneath her and crisp sheets, they all told her the devastating story she never wanted to hear. She was in a hospital; she was back in her own world. She was never going to see Ian again.

Tears slipped free of her eyes, left cool trails across her skin as they rolled to the pillow below her head. Shudders wracked her body as breath tried to come too fast. The sound of a book gently closing sifted through the air.

"Hush, dear one." The reader's voice returned, this time at her side.

"Is it true?" E rasped, throat dry and misused by whatever methods they had used to keep her alive. Her blurry eyes sought out the owner of the voice, hand weakly rising to search what her eyes could not see. A gentle hand slipped into her own, assuring in its warmth. No matter how she blinked, E's eyes wouldn't clear enough to see more than a fiery blur against the lights.

"Is it true?" she begged once more.

"What do you want to know?"

"Does he suffer?"

"Yes, I am afraid he does." E sobbed at the sadness that clung to her heart.

"I'm never going to see him again." She choked, grasping the hand harder as though it was the only thing keeping her grounded.

"Calm yourself, Easton. All is not lost." E paused, blinking harder, fighting against the hysteria that threatened to erupt within. Cool fingertips caressed her brow, and ever so slowly the blurred image before her began to clear.

"Destiny is nothing but a path that leads us toward purpose. Just because one branch of the path seems to end, it doesn't mean that our original path is lost. I am living proof of this." Brown eyes smiled down at her, freckles dotted porcelain skin, all surrounded by long fiery curls. E gasped, looking at a near mirror image of herself. The reflection's smile softened.

"All is never lost. And that is a mother's promise."

CHAPTER 50
EASTON

"**W**elcome to King of Meaty. Tell us how you like your meat, and we'll ensure you leave with a smile on your face. What may I get you for your ordering pleasure today?"

E droned on from behind the counter. She hated the required greeting of the burger joint she was currently employed with. It sounded corny and more than a bit porny. But it was also the most honest paying job she'd ever owned, and she was determined to do her best. She quickly wrote down the order that ran over the head-set, whilst punching in the order of the customer standing in front of the counter. Everyone was out with some sort of stomach bug, and the last three days had been a hectic mess for the few remaining workers still standing. Unlike the others, E didn't overly mind the chaos. It gave her the perfect opportunity to shut down her mind and simply exist, an opportunity to ignore the matters that pressed heavily on her heart.

It had been exactly one year, two months, five weeks, and three days since E had last looked at her husband. His eye flashed through her mind now, clear and green as the ocean on a summer day. E shook herself and quickly stuffed the random packages of food into bags, handing them off to the customers, and taking more orders. One year, two months, five weeks, and three days was a long time to go without his rakish grin, humor and intensity, without hearing his voice, or feeling his touch. Especially when her last knowledge of him was his suffering.

E and Jag had been missing for two years. Two whole years. Time in Neverland never moved, never passed. It seemed forever, and yet so very short all at once. She wouldn't have believed she was gone longer than a few months in her own world. She'd flat-out called Noah a liar when he'd told her. The doctors, too. They marked it down as part of her extensive brain injuries. It took time for the truth to sink in. And during her recovery she'd had nothing but time to think.

She'd spent a good deal of that time thinking about Ian. What was he doing now? Was he safe? Was he well? Had he healed from his wounds, as she'd intended? Wendy gave her that gift of love to heal... had it worked? Did he go home to his kingdom finally? Did he still miss her? Had her handsome pirate captain moved on without her? Could she really expect him not to?

A new image flashed through her mind; the image of Ian grinning down at a beautiful princess who lovingly caressed a very pregnant belly. A toddler, that looked remarkably like Ian, played at their feet. The plastic lid on the cup currently held in her hand popped off, hurtling through the air from the crushing pressure of her grasp. Sticky orange pop gushed over her hand and splattered across her new, uniform-required, white sneakers. She offered a wincing grin to the short little old lady who still held her hands out expectantly, mouth frozen wide in shock.

"Let me get you a new drink, ma'am," E offered. The little old lady merely blinked owlishly up at her from behind the bottle cap glasses.

"Third drink tonight, girl." Liv, one of E's coworkers chuckled, walking past her.

"Thanks for keeping count."

"Get a grip or you'll be paying the boss to work here." Liv disappeared into the back, and soon more loud laughter joined hers. Obviously Liv was sharing the good news with the cooks.

E sighed and filled another cup, even going so far as to use a large rather than the medium that granny had ordered, as a way of apology. Sending the little pink-haired granny tottering on her way with her arms full of greasy goodness, E grabbed up the mop and started swabbing up the mess. Was someone doing this same chore on Ian's ship right now? Again her mind wandered. So much had happened since she woke up in the hospital that morning.

The hospital staff as a whole considered her a miracle. Isen had apparently given them a story about men kidnapping them in some elaborate slave trading scheme. He told them they'd just barely managed to escape, but that the men had nearly killed her by hitting her with their car. He'd supposedly gathered her up in his arms and ran, losing the men in the crowds and then altogether once inside the hospital.

The staff had flatly refused to give him hope of her survival. And yet, survive she did. Day after day her health improved, her bones knit, the swelling in her brain subsided and her organs healed. It took two surgeries and six months for her to come out of her coma. Something that very nearly didn't have the chance to happen. Two months in there was talk of simply removing the life support, and without familial connection or the money to fulfill the bills, there was nothing Isen, Noah or Sad could do to stop them. That was when Maizy Hook had stepped in.

Swooping in like a summer breeze loaded with money, Easton's birth mother had appeared out of nowhere to literally save her life. She'd provided documents showing her claim to Easton as her legal sister, something none of the hospital staff questioned as the forgeries they were, and covered every single expense. Ageless as she was, and having legally relinquished all claim to Easton the night when she left her at the hospital doors, Maizy took the option of pretending siblingship. E sighed and took the momentary lull in customers as a chance to sit down. Head resting on her arms, E allowed her mind to dig around in all the nitty gritty of her life.

After struggling to wake up, it had taken yet another six months of intense effort for her to relearn to walk. During her year in the hospital, Maizy was there daily for heart-to-hearts with the daughter she'd given up before she had time to truly know her. And during those heart-to-hearts, E found out who her parents really were.

Maizy was none other than Tinkerbell's long lost child, sent through the portal to save her life. A baby who was found in the woods by a childless couple who happened to be hiking the trails when the portal opened. A baby who was raised by a loving family, raised as a normal child but with the knowledge of her unique nature. Her parents never tried to hide the circumstances of her unusual arrival in their lives from her. She grew up around her all boy cousins, sharing wild stories of adventure and a boy who never seemed to want to grow up in her versions.

Enraptured by her stories, her uncle's friend, James, took to pen and paper writing at it like a mad man until the story was done. The story of Peter Pan took off like wildfire, spreading far and wide. Their family joked that the book was imbued with magic that drew people to it. The family prospered well from the book's popularity, and Maizy's life was full and happy.

Until she watched everyone around her grow older, and she remained the same. They grew old and died. Then new people came into her life, and they too grew older and died. A husband, children, grandchildren, all passed eventually. But Maizy? She stayed the same, forever locked in the appearance of a twenty-two year old woman, and no clue why. She went into hiding. She moved from London to the USA, moving from one city to another each time the passage of time and her wandering soul dictated.

Then one day, James the Hook stepped through a portal of his own, and waltzed right into her life. He'd come to her, desperate for help in the battle against the Pan. And finally, Maizy had her answers. She never grew old, never got sick, never felt the sting of death, all because her life was tied to a man and land that never grew old either.

Hook had carefully gotten to know Maizy, observing her heart's weight, earning her trust. And when he'd found her to be untainted by the Pan's hatreds, he revealed all his truths to her. He hoped to convince Maizy to come back to Neverland with him, hoped she would be the key to destroying the Fiend. Yet he found when the time came that he should return, he couldn't do it.

He'd succeeded only in falling madly in love with her, and vice versa. How could he put her in such danger? He couldn't. A decision only further solidified when Easton joined the fun, blooming as nothing more than a promise in Maizy's belly. Yes, James T. Hook was Easton's true father. Something that still blew her mind, no matter how many long months had passed since she found out. Maizy says love has a way of tying people to one another, no matter the distance. That love was what drew her to the story of her heritage.

Love has a funny way of changing things. James grew ever more overwhelmed with fear for the both of them.

No longer could he contemplate the use of Maizy against Pan, no matter the cost to Neverland. But no longer could he deny his own calling. Though time never passed in Neverland, his disappearance could have been a matter of what felt like days to his brethren or perhaps years. He knew he could linger no longer. He was loath to leave his heart behind. Yet he knew the heavy truth of the matter. Staying meant forfeiting Neverland, and endangering his wife and child. If Pan conquered Neverland entirely, it wouldn't be long before the book's power was broken and Pan was able to once again traverse other worlds. Which meant him coming to Maizy and Easton's world.

With soul-breaking sorrow, James said goodbye to Maizy with words of love, a promise to return, but also of warning. 'Protect Easton from Neverland at all costs. Keep her away from the book.'

Maizy held hope that James would return, watched for him every day. But as time passed, James didn't show. Easton was born, and Maizy still held hope. Until the book of Pan tried to pull her newborn child within it. Horrified, Maizy sold the book, and moved to a city far away, Chicago. But still, Maizy couldn't shake the feeling that Neverland called to her babe. Every time they touched, Easton's skin would pale, as though she were disappearing. Celeste's spell meant to protect any descendants of Pan by keeping them separate and more difficult to find, was now tearing a mother from her babe.

Maizy came to the sickening realization that her own connection to Neverland only strengthened Easton's, and therefore the pull of Neverland's effort to return her there. In her gut, Maizy felt that eventually Neverland would win; it would take her baby. But she could perhaps give the baby time to grow, give her time to live. Desperate to protect her, Maizy left her at the hospital with nothing but a blanket lovingly stitched with her name. She kept her distance, though it broke her heart. It wasn't until Easton's recent miraculous story of survival hit the papers that Maizy dared return.

A story that hit papers, thanks to Isen. After placing her in the hospital, the nurses called the police, who in turn spoke with Isen about the men that attacked her. Eight months of undercover record-ings and a string of sting operations later, the entire group of men responsible for the death of Easton's parents were locked behind bars and Easton's record was clean.

She left the hospital able to breathe easier, to walk the streets without hunching, without darting her eyes about her surroundings in constant suspicion. Isen had done it all for her. He'd put his own family and lifelong friends in jail, for her. She knew it was for her and not his own selfish reasons, because a good portion of Never-land's markings disappeared with the act. Even here, the Light's power was strong and decisive.

As part of the bargain made with the police, not only had her record been wiped, but Isen ensured himself the abilities to turn the guild around. He secured government funding that went toward the proper caring of the guild rats. Now, instead of stealing, they worked honest jobs. He helped them find work, and provided a place to live until they got their feet on the ground. Instead of the subway tunnels, they had an above ground apartment complex and access to education.

Isen hadn't exactly told her how he pulled all the strings to make that work. E had a feeling his 'right way' still had a few kinks in the path, but it was a good start. It was hard to move past the guild mentality of 'do what you have to do to get what you want'. But he was actually trying. And so was E, thanks to more of Isen's kinks in the path. E shook her head, wondering at how strange life could be. She had grown to actually consider Isen a friend of sorts now; a delicate strained friendship, but friendship nonetheless.

And as for Maizy, upon Easton's release from the hospital she offered for E to move in with her. It would provide E a safe place to stay, and also give them time to get to know one another. E had hesitantly agreed. And she hadn't regretted it. Maizy hadn't pushed their new relationship dynamic, timidly allowing Easton time to adjust. And E had found herself easily falling into a dear friendship with Maizy, a bond forming surprisingly easily.

The bell dinged over the door, signaling another customer had entered the establishment. E geared up her customer satisfaction smile, pushing away the confusing jumble of thoughts in her head.

"I heard you've been working here."

Easton looked up, heavy heart lifting at the sight of Officer Lee. He watched her from the other side of the counter, a soft smile on his weathered face.

"Lee!" She grinned. "It's so good to see you!" He let out a huff of surprise as she leaned across the counter to give him a quick hug. He eyed her steadily for a moment before patting down his pockets. Pulling out the wallet he made an obvious effort of checking his dollar bills to ensure they were all still there. E rolled her eyes exaggeratedly, but couldn't help the smile that tugged the corners of her mouth.

"I don't do that anymore; if you lost any it's because you're senile and too free with your money."

"I know, just giving you a hard time. I've been keeping tabs on you since you popped back up in town."

"Stalking me now? I thought you weren't on the force anymore, old man?"

"I'm not. Get me a Coke, would ya? Diet. The missus is cracking down on my sugar intake." Easton grinned, moving to do as he asked. When she returned with his drink, he rubbed the back of his neck, looking embarrassed.

"A friend of mine let me know about when you showed up at the hospital. He couldn't give me any details on what happened to you, though." He watched her gaze drop quickly to the cash register. "Was the first time I regretted quitting the force, not being able to help you." Her gaze shot upward to meet his, surprised and touched by his confession.

"I'm all right, Lee. There's nothing you could have done to help me, so don't feel bad. Honestly I was on the straight and narrow by then. It was just… my past catching up to me." She hedged the truth. Her past, her mother's past, and her grandparents' past if you wanted to be precise.

"The past has a way of doing that," he nodded solemnly. Fingers scratching at his white beard, he watched her carefully. "You're ok now though?"

"I'm great." She tried to put as much sunshine behind her smile as she could muster. It wasn't much. "Being on the straight and narrow is rough sometimes. But I'm doing it the best I can. Just like you told me to. Trying to make Dad proud, I guess."

"I have no doubt that he is, him and your mom." Lee smiled. "I am, too. Best retirement gift you could have given me, kiddo." He pulled some money from his pocket and left it on the counter. Lifting the cup at her in salute, he turned for the door. "Keep that new record clean, Howe."

And then he was gone, disappearing into the night. Easton swallowed hard, feeling the foreign sensation of pride in herself. Pride that she could make the man who had been there for her so many years of her life, happy. Glancing down at the counter, E released a frustrated huff. He'd left a hundred dollar bill on the counter, along with the two dollars that would cover his drink. One hundred dollars was an insane tip. Stuffing the two dollars in the register, she grabbed up the hundred and ran out the door, intent on making him take it back.

Her eyes searched the dark parking lot, grumbling when she noted the lack of his old, beat-up junker car. Glancing down at the hundred in her hand, she absently ran a thumb across it. Smiling, she went back inside and went straight to the phone. Ark picked up on the second ring.

"Ark, think you can swing me by the cemetery?"

"Going back to your grave robbing ways, E? I thought we were past that." She smiled at his happy laugh on the other end.

"No. Just making an overdue visit."

"Sorry, no can do. I've got other customers right now, remember?"

Noah was one of the first rats to get a real job. Isen worked him into a position as a cabbie and Noah loved it. He thought it was his true calling in life. The last few weeks he'd been raving about a couple of rich people that came into town and hired him to drive them exclusively. Obviously this is who he was talking about right now. She nodded, happy he was happy in his job.

"Right, totally forgot about your recent obsession with your richies." She teased. "Do they know you are in love with them?"

"Trust me E, if you were here you'd love them, too." Obviously his customers weren't in the cab right now, if he was talking so freely about them.

"Yeah, sure. If I was getting your paycheck, you mean." She rolled her eyes and grinned. "No worries, I'll call another cab."

"Sure. Have a great night, E." She frowned suspiciously at the weird tone in his voice and the speed which he hung up.

The richies must have come back to the car so he had to cut gossip time short fast. After calling for another cab, E stamped her work card and stood outside the door to wait. Stopping by the flower shop on the way to the cemetery, it wasn't too long before she found herself standing outside the iron gates, paying a nervous cabby. Apparently he thought it was weird that she was visiting a cemetery in the middle of the night. She grinned. If he knew half the things she'd seen in this lifetime, he'd understand why she was able to walk in there with a smile while he sped off leaving her alone.

There were a few street lamps strewn throughout the expanse of grass and headstones, the fancy kind that looked like old-time lanterns. They weren't overly bright, but they lent enough light that you weren't tripping over headstones and disrespecting graves.

Finally finding the plots she was looking for, E placed the two roses she'd bought with Lee's money, one bunch in each of the vase holders on either side of the large combined gravestone. Her fingers lightly brushed over the names engraved there: Sabastian and Lacey Howe.

"Hi, Mom, hi, Dad. Been a while, I know. I had to get a few things in my life in order before I came to see you. I got lost and... I don't think you would have liked the person I became for a while. But I'm working on it."

She glanced at the stars twinkling above, wondering if they were looking down on her from up there. Her eyes shifted around the lot. She hoped they were up there, happy and completely oblivious of every stupid thing she'd ever done. Sighing, she stood and went to sit on the small concrete bench nearby. Since no one was around, she felt comfortable sitting at this distance while continuing to talk to them.

"It's funny, I had to get lost in order to find myself. Literally, and in a big way." She laughed softly, thinking of how her mother's eyes would have lit with that soft glow she always got when Easton would spin a big tale. "These stories are actually real, Mom," she insisted. "I got sucked into that book you always read to me. With daring adventures, mischievous imps, and devilishly handsome pirates." She closed her eyes, mentally picturing Ian as he smiled at her from behind the wheel of his ship.

"He truly was devilishly handsome, Mom. You would have swooned over him way more than you ever did the actors in your movies." Easton and her dad loved teasing her mom about her movie crushes. "He was tall, dark and handsome. His smile could melt the coldest of glaciers and his eye... his eye was the window to his soul; his very good and very noble soul." She felt hot tears pooling in her eyes as her voice began to tremble.

"I was right all along, Mom. The pirate captain in Peter Pan was always the good guy. And," she drew a shuddering, wet sob, "and I love him so much. And now he's as far away from me as the both of you are. And I don't know what to do." She leaned forward over her knees, sobbing, letting the tears that had refused to come all this time finally flow free. "He's lost to me and I don't know how my soul will live without him."

"Easton."

The breeze shifted, carrying the voice in a whisper to her ears. Her breath caught, heart suddenly faltering. Her head shot up, searching the darkness. She was alone. No one was here sweetly whispering in her ear. She sobbed again. It had sounded so real, so very much like him. A voice she heard so often in her dreams was now melding with her reality, it seemed. Heaven help her, had she finally lost it?

She paused, awareness shifting about her. No...something was different now. She felt it in the air. Slowly rising to her feet, she cast a wary eye about the dark cemetery, careful to keep her back to the tree. And then she saw it. A clump of shadows in the distance drew her gaze, the grouping too solid and too oddly shaped to be normal. A slight gleam of silver caught her eye then, and her heart ceased as a familiar sense of déjà vu swept over her. She clutched at her chest, fighting to breathe through the palpitations as one shadow detached itself from the group and ever so slowly began heading her way. She was no longer alone.

Her gaze traveled upward, noting the swagger of the gait, the flapping of fabric about the legs. She heard a laugh somewhere in the darkness, a laugh that sounded oddly similar to Noah's. She ignored it, heart pounding faster, breath caught in her throat as she waited. Slowly the man separated completely from the shadows about fifteen feet away, their eyes meeting. A strangled squeak issued from her lips, but nothing else. The left side of his lips shifted to the side in a sensual smirk she knew all too well, sending her heart careening faster down the hill of no return. Easton sunk to her knees in the moist grass, legs unable to hold her any longer.

"Damn, you sent her over the edge, dude." Noah's voice drifted towards them from the darkness once more.

"Are... are you real?" The words fumbled across her lips before she gave them permission, before her mind had caught up to what her heart was begging to know.

"I am if you are."

Her breath caught, eyes drifting closed in sweet torment at the growly soft sound of his deep voice. Oh how she'd missed that sound! Now that her eyes were closed, E was afraid to open them, afraid she'd find herself covered in drool in her bed, dreaming of the one thing she could never have again. The soft sound of footsteps through the grass met her ears.

"Look to me, Vermillion." She squeezed her eyes tighter, tears leaking between them.

"But what if you're just a dream?" She whimpered as warm fingers drifted along the length of her jaw, so soft it truly felt like a dream.

"Have a little faith in your captain."

The words whispered across her heart in the gentle caress of a lover. Gathering her courage, E forced her eyes to open. Open and staring into *two* brilliant seafoam colored eyes that sparked with a passion felt to the depths of her core. Her lips parted wide, heart clambering so hard it hurt.

With a sob, she stood and threw herself into his arms. Ian chuckled, a warm dark sound, holding her close with his good arm, the other still stuffed in the pocket of his jacket. There was so much she wanted to say, so much she wanted to do. And yet only one word managed to squeak past her lips.

"How?" It was the only word she seemed capable of forming. Ian grinned down at her then nodded toward the area of shadows he'd materialized from. The rest of the misshapen shadows detached and moved forward, and soon the street lights revealed recognizable features. E blinked owlishly.

"Noah?" The words lodged halfway out of her throat as her gaze shifted from the rather smug face of one of her oldest friends.

"Walk a ways with me, Easton?" Hook asked in a gentlemanly tone. Noting her dazed nod, Hook looked back to his companion. "We'll return shortly, Mr. Noah." Hook spoke confidently, grasping her hand and motioning for her to walk with him.

"Aye aye, Captain!" Noah gave a jaunty wink and returned to the taxi.

"What..." E stared Noah down. "He knows who you are?"

"Mm," Hook agreed. "He's known for weeks."

Weeks! The sneaky little twerp had been sitting on this huge secret all this time and hadn't even so much as hinted to E that her life wasn't completely over! Oh, that punk had some serious explaining to do. Sending one more scathing glare his way, E turned her attention back to the man that held her soul in his eyes. He slipped her arm through his, mouth dropping to murmur in her ear.

"Come along, little butterfly."

Easton smiled, happily letting him lead her away. She'd deal with Noah later. Ian led her into the center of the cemetery where a small park had been formed. Free of headstones, it was a peaceful plot of grass and trees and small benches. It was a secret garden of sorts where mourners could come to sit away from the eyes of those traveling on the road.

Once in the sheltering embrace of solitude, Ian spun her about. Easton gasped as he pressed her against the bark of an old tree, worshipping her mouth with the most sumptuous of kisses, the kind of mind-blowing kissing only he could bestow.

"How I have longed for your sweet lips, Vermillion," Ian breathed, stealing away her mouth once more before she could respond.

Her head tilted back as his mouth quested down her jaw and into the V of her t-shirt. Glancing about to ensure their privacy, Ian pulled up the hem of her shirt. Goosebumps pebbled across her heated skin as he ran calloused fingertips across her scars. His forehead rested against hers, a long and burdened sigh escaping his lips, hand still lingering beneath the fabric of her shirt.

"I feared the worst," he confided in a low whisper. "Mr. Noah told me of your difficulties with healing."

"I'm tougher than I look." She smiled as he pulled away with a warm, proud grin.

"Aye, that you are. My strong little wench." His wink had her staring in a daze once more. Her fingertips lightly brushed over the jagged scarring that ran the length from his brow, over his eyelid, and down to his cheekbone.

"It worked. Wendy gave me a gift of healing to pass on to someone I loved. But I was so out of it, I wasn't sure it worked." He offered a mischievous grin.

"Aye. You healed the Rift. I am no longer plagued with the screams of the damned." He paused. "You don't overly miss the eyepatch do you? I still have it, if you prefer."

"You were always perfect to me, Ian, and you still are," she vowed, still tracing the lines of his beautiful face. "But how? You being here, how is it possible?"

"After you left, I fell into a month-long drunken stupor. Then Smee nearly drowned me in the river."

"Seems to be a favorite tactic of his," E muttered. Ian chuckled, nodding in agreement.

"Yes, but it works. He told me the time for childish pouting was over, and I needed to take the men out on the ocean before they went mad." He softly grasped a lock of her hair at the side of her brow, twisting it in his fingers. "Your hair has grown so much longer, like it was when you Arrived." He pressed a kiss to it before continuing. "Neverland was truly free. The Fiend's curse was lifted, the Lost Boys' souls given rest, and we were free to sail. But the men refused to leave without their captain."

"Good! Those yellow-bellied slugs had better continue to show loyalty when I'm not around to kick their butts." E grinned, her heart lightening even further. She'd worried, wondering if the curse really had been lifted, if Ian was still trapped in Neverland. She sobered, gnawing on her lip.

"What happened to Wiley? He didn't come back through the portal with us…"

"Wiley is amongst my crew now. After coming so close to being a Lost Boy, it would seem the portal deemed him too much a part of Neverland to send back to your world."

"Thank you for taking care of him. Is he… okay?"

"He is still distant and timid. But as time has passed, and as the crew and I came to learn his language, he has come more out of his shell. He seems to find pleasure in the workings of the ship. He says the sea is good for his soul." Relief washed through her, tension draining from her shoulders.

"I am so relieved to hear that. I've felt so guilty, knowing he was left behind. Again."

"Of course I would care for him." Ian's thumb slipped over her bottom lip, heart in his gaze. "He is my beloved's brother in every way that matters. Which makes him mine, as well. Caol has been helpful in keeping his spirits up. They seem to have bonded in friendship as well. They keep one another out of too much trouble as we hit the different ports. Mostly. "

"So, you left Neverland?"

"Yes."

"And..." she cleared her throat, "It's been a long time."

"Languishingly long." She grinned, loving that he'd felt the distance as strongly as she. "Time that truly felt more torturous than all the time I spent in limbo before your Arrival." He heaved a heavy sigh.

"Did you go home?" She asked hesitantly, almost afraid to hear her earlier daydream had come true, though his behavior now would certainly suggest otherwise. Ian looked in the distance, expression thoughtful.

"After my unceremonious dip in the river, the men and I boarded the Hell-born Hag and set sail. The winds still blow as they always have, though the ocean scent seems sweeter to me now, somehow. We returned the men to their lands to settle their affairs. But I never set foot on soil. I had a task that could not wait. The task of regaining James' treasure." He met and held her gaze. "I found no desire to return to my kingdom without my heart and soul." His hand finally left her scar and pressed his fingertips to her cheek instead. His gaze held her enraptured, her voice diminished to a breathy whisper.

"You didn't?" The passion in those eyes stayed lit, burning her with delicious ferocity.

"No." His eyes narrowed on a wry smirk, "But I think perhaps you feared another answer entirely. Perhaps wondering if I have lain with another in your absence?"

"I... well, it's been a long time." She trailed off at his raised brow.

"Have you lain with another, Butterfly?"

"No!" she practically shouted. Clearing her throat, she replied in a less crazy tone. "No, of course not."

"Easton James Bendal. I take offense to the notion that you would stay true, yet I would not. What kind of rogue do you take me for, wench?"

"I didn't mean... I'm not questioning your honor. I just... it was a long time. And you had no reason to think you would ever see me again. The portal was closed, and your hook..." She shrugged helplessly, unable to finish that sentence.

"I swore to you that there would never be another woman for me. I swore that if there was a way to find you, I would. And when I make a promise, I keep it. I may have lost sight of that for a time in my grief, but Smee's dunk in the river quickly rid me of my melancholy and renewed my vigor to create a way." His stern expression twisted into mischief. "Besides, I certainly wouldn't be here dining on your lips if I had another waiting for me elsewhere. I am a rogue for only one woman." His fingers intertwined with hers, fiddling with the wedding ring still perfectly fit to her finger.

"Oh, thank Devus," she finally said, releasing a breath heavy with relief. "I was going to try to be easy going about it if you had moved on, but I was on the verge of exploding."

"Yes, I could practically feel you vibrating," he teased. Now that that was out of the way, she concentrated on the next important item of business.

"How did you find your way back to me? You mentioned James's treasure? Oh..." She paused, cheeks heating for whatever dumb reason. "I should probably mention that I found Bell and Peter's daughter and she happens to be my mom...and James was my dad."

"Aye. And you also happen to be James's treasure." Ian offered a devilish grin as he pulled her back to him.

"You know?"

"Maizy fully informed me."

"You know my mom, too?"

"Mm. Interestingly enough she was waiting for me the moment I exited the portal. She rather firmly stated that I was late as well."

"That sounds like Maizy all right," E laughed. "I can't believe both of them kept you being here a secret from me, though. So not cool."

"I asked it of them. I wanted to set into motion gathering enough supplies from your land to barter in my realm, to ensure a proper way of caring for you should my inheritance be denied me. Much of the fabrics and materials you have here are not known to my land; they will bring a fair amount of money to our crew. And... I own that I feared you might not want to return with me. In which case I would be staying here with you, and sending the materials back with the crew to provide for them in my absence."

"You would stay here with me, if I wanted to stay?"

"My usefulness to Neverland has passed. Though I love my land, you are where my home will forever reside. If you wish it of me, I will stay." Ian's expression softened in wonder, fingers slipping through her hair. "I can hardly fathom it. Yet there is so much of James's spirit that I can see in you. I always have. I simply never thought it possible that it was from more than your admiration of him in your book."

She grinned up at him. Ian was back, and for the first time in over a year she felt she could breathe. In this moment she almost didn't care if she ever got answers, so long as he stayed at her side. She wrapped her arms around his neck and boldly stole his lips once more.

"My, such fervor you have, my lady. What would others think? Would you steal my good name?"

He pulled away and grinned his naughty grin, teasing her, making her heart skip. His smile was so... carefree now. The previous occasional mischief she'd so loved in his grins in Neverland was now on full brilliant display. He was practically radiant. No other words could describe it.

"Too late, I already did that." She sifted her fingers into his glorious curly hair, pulling free the band that held it back before pressing his sassy face back down to meet hers. Ian gave a chuckle she felt more than heard, pressing his body more fully into hers against the tree. He lifted her hands, pressing them against the trunk above her head, holding them in place whilst he left a feverish trail of kisses down the side of her neck. She moaned as his hand shifted from her hip up to gently squeeze… she paused, eyes flying wide.

"Wait…Ian?"

"Hmm?" Ian murmured against her neck where he was currently nuzzling just below her ear.

"Ian, how are you doing that?"

"Well, I hope," he replied, humor in his tone.

She huffed at him and wiggled. He chuckled as she finally pulled one of her hands free to find the answers he refused to give. Her lips rounded in awe as she gasped his left hand so that she could see. The memory of Pan chopping off Ian's hook, leaving him with nothing but a bleeding stub flashed through her mind. She'd seen it happen with her own eyes, relived the horror of it in her dreams. And yet in front of her eyes in this very moment, she saw a perfectly normal-looking hand.

"Do you like it?" he whispered in her ear. She heard the humor, but also a touch of uncertainty.

"Your hand… did Wendy's magic do that, too?" He smiled at the marvel in her tone.

"No, I'm afraid Wendy's gift had its hands full sealing the Rift over my eye." He smiled softly. "Your world is a marvelous place." He shifted so that he could run the fingers of his new hand along the lines of her nose, cheek and finally lips. "I so often dreamed of being able to hold you this way, as any man should be able to worship the soft curves of his woman. But I knew it would never be a possibility. Yet, here I am, doing just that." He pulled back, no longer leaning into her. Popping free the thick leather cuff over his wrist, he held out his hand between them, let her examine it more fully. "It's what your people call a prosthetic."

"Wow. I never would have guessed. It looks so real." Easton ran her fingers over the barely discernible seam between prosthetic and skin in awe. Ian closed his eyes, face blissful as her exploration smoothed over the rest of the hand.

"It looks and *feels* so real." When his eyes opened they were lit by that burning fire that always sent her lower stomach crazy. "It apparently is filled with something called technology, which allows it to communicate with the nerves in my arms and therefore my brain?" He shrugged with a chagrined smile. "I'm unsure if I explained that correctly. But I believe that is how Maizy described it."

"Maizy again." E felt warmth surrounding her heart, growing ever more grateful to the woman she was slowly growing to know as mother.

"Aye. She helped me to acquire it." He stooped down slightly, gaze taking in her dazed expression. "Does it displease you?" She snapped out of it, realizing quickly that she was giving him the wrong impression. She smiled softly, pulling his hand to press it to her cheek.

"Ian. What did I say to you earlier? You were always perfect, and still are. I love everything about you, and always will no matter the changes that may come." She pressed a loving kiss to the palm of his prosthetic. Her eyes were drawn back to his wrist, the smooth black lines of ink she had seen for only a swift moment when he first revealed the prophecy to her. Ink in the shape of a compass, with an arrow pointing to a single E in solid lines. Her lips parted, fingers tracing over the lines.

"I received that during my Binding upon first entering the Brotherhood." He smiled at her surprised expression. "Yes, we all had to endure the Binding at one point or another." His touch joined her perusal of the ink, their fingertips brushing. "At first, I thought it was reminding me to keep my heart set on home. My kingdom is to the East from Neverland." His fingers shifted to gently grasp her, resting her more crudely drawn compass next to his. His eyes held hers intently.

"Now I can't help but feel the Light was Binding me to you even then. What greater purpose for a compass than to guide a lost man home?" His arm carefully wrapped around her waist pulling her close. "And you, Easton, are most assuredly my home. You are the E." He smiled around the words she had first said when explaining her tattoo to him.

"This brings me back to only one question I have left for you, my love." He pressed her hand to his chest, just over his heart, expression intense. "Will you return to Neverland with me? Will you sail the seas at my side? Or will you at least keep me here at your side?"

"It's about time you asked." She grinned, grabbing his hand to pull him along. "Hurry up, I wanna go home. The Hag is calling my name." Ian laughed, wrapping his arm around her waist and kissing her head.

"As you command."

"So, E, you've been holding out on me." Noah offered a playful glare as they approached where he leaned back against his taxi.

"Apparently I'm not the only one, Ark," she replied innocently.

"Turnabout's fair play, they say. You can keep big secrets, so can I." His smirk turned serious, voice dropped low for privacy. "When you showed up at the hospital nearly dead and missing for two years, you kind of left out the part about pirates, fairies and all that other crazy shiznit." She snorted.

"You would have thought I was still doped up on the hospital drugs."

"Probably," he agreed. "But eventually, I would have come around. Nothing is impossible around you, E. I mean, Jag's a friggin' saint now!" Ian nodded, drawing his thumb down her jaw.

"She is a marvel, isn't she, Mr. Noah?" Noah grinned, clearly enjoying Ian's way of saying his name.

"She's something all right. Though I usually just refer to her as a pain in my butt."

E stuck her tongue out at her dear friend, and Noah returned the childish whim. The taxi's back seat door opened and Maizy climbed out. Smiling, she moved forward and handed E a leather-bound book.

"What's this?" E asked.

"James' journal." A smirk stretched Ian's lips at her confusion. "The journal led me to find things far more valuable than gold."

"What?" Her voice was hushed, eyes wide as she stared up at him. Holding her gaze, he slowly removed something from the inside pocket of his trench coat. E gasped. He held a regal blood red hook. She couldn't help herself, fingers drawn to the metal like a moth to the flame. The metal touched her fingertips, an odd sweeping sensation of warm welcome tingling against her skin. In awe, E met Ian's eyes.

"James' most treasured possession. The key to everything held most dear to him," he confided. "With it he was able to open a portal through the shield of Celeste's power. It led him to your realm, to the woman he would come to love, and the child they would create together."

"And you've grown into every bit of promise James said you would," Maizy smiled softly.

"To think, the daughter of James the Hook, and granddaughter of the Pan," Ian stated solemnly. "It is no wonder Neverland chose you to be it's champion."

"That, or sheer desperation."

"James's journals told their story, along with instructions as to where to find this hook. He hid it away, determined the Pan would never have access to Maizy or his daughter. But he couldn't bring himself to destroy it. He always hoped he would be able to one day return."

"It took me a frustratingly long time to finally understand how to harness its power. All this time I thought James' faith that I could learn to control Rifts was misplaced. Turns out I just needed the proper incentive to learn." He ran his fingers through her hair. "Nothing could keep me from you." Noah coughed, pushing away from the taxi.

"Well, as sweet as this mushy reunion is, I have to get the taxi back before the company decides I stole it." He stepped toward E, a crooked smile in place. "I always knew you were a pirate. The bowlegged swagger and squinty eyes gave it away." He laughed, ducking back as she punched him in the shoulder with a teasing glower. His smile changed to his rare, brotherly care.

"I'm going to assume this is goodbye. You're running away from home, again?" She smiled, pulling him into a hug.

"No. I'm running back to my home."

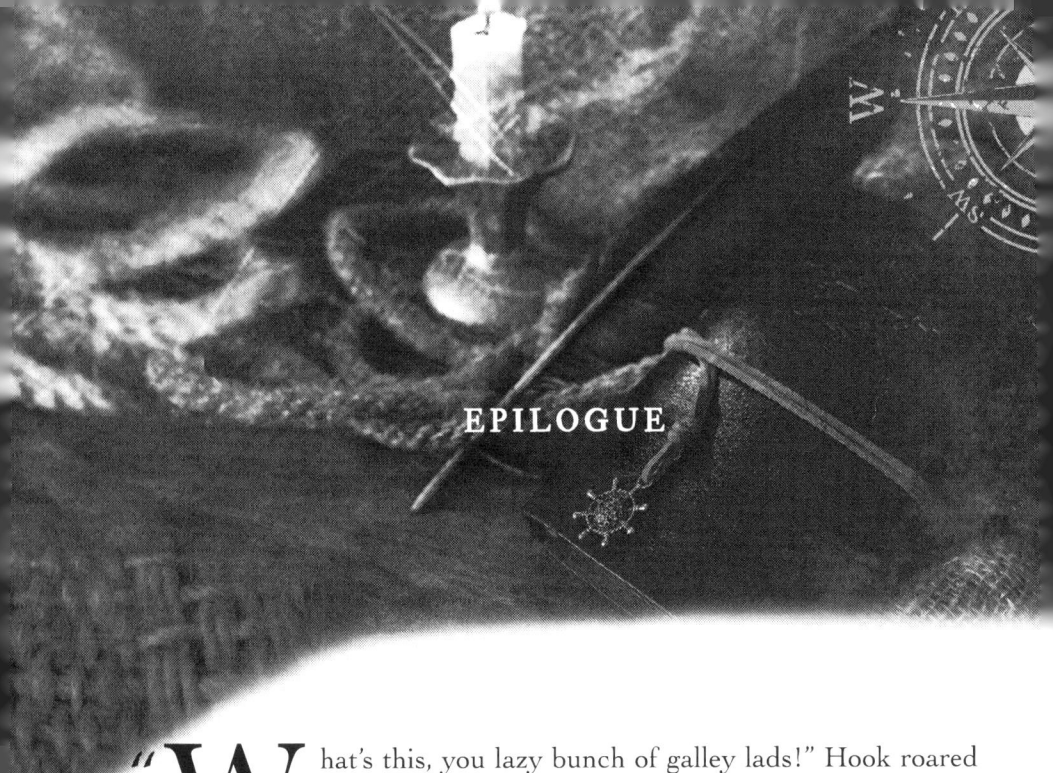

"What's this, you lazy bunch of galley lads!" Hook roared from his perch at the rail. The hook clanked against the metal of his sword, where it hung from his belt. The hook was harmless without intent of use put behind it at his own hand. No longer did he have to fear accidentally sending those he loved into the Between. The men below turned to gaze up at him from the deck.

"We were meant to set to sea before the rise of the sun, yet I see the first glimmers of dawn and here we still sit at anchor!" he clarified.

"Aw, but Capt'n, we had such a long night of work, we're rising a wee bit late is all," Hyrel groaned.

"A long night of work up a few pairs of frilly skirts, and drowning in ale, I'd wager," Ian countered. "To work, the lot of ya!" When more tired grumbles rose, Ian grinned. "I'll just have to see to it my right hand, the Vermillion Lass, gets your lumpy arses moving, then!" The men's eyes rounded, and quiet pleas for mercy replaced tired moans.

"Don't you worry, Captain, I'll get them ship-shape in no time!"

A small voice piped up at his side. A great mop of vermillion hair climbed up onto the railing, leaning over to see the crew below.

"Oiy! I've seen turtles move faster than the lot of you!" Lily shouted, jumping back down. The crew groaned.

Ian caught her before she could go stomping off down the stairs to deal out her punishment. Turning her about Ian carefully straightened her button-up blouse and trousers, clicked the safety line onto her belt, and tied her long mess of hair back with a leather string much like his own. Licking his thumb he wiped away a smear of dirt on her nose. Straight out of bed and she was already dirty. Ian smirked.

"There now. A captain's right hand must always be clean, safe and smart if they're to be taken seriously by the crew, yes?"

"Aye sir, Captain, sir!" Lily saluted him before trying to rush off once more.

"Wait a moment little dervish. What is it a Captain always needs from his right hand for good luck before a journey?" Lily offered a long-suffering sigh that was quickly covered by the giggle and sweet smile he so adored. Leaning in she kissed his cheek.

"Good morning, Daddy." She took a step back, yanking down on her shirt tails with a stiff, down-to-business frown. "Now, I love you, Daddy, but this ship is a sad mess," the little five-year-old stated.

"Very well, go be about your brow-beating, then." Ian watched proudly as his whirlwind of a daughter stomped through the crew, giving out stern orders left and right. The men grumbled and groaned, but he didn't miss their covertly hidden, knowing smiles as they pretended to do just as she ordered. After a tug on his shirt tails, Wiley picked her up to sit atop his shoulders so that she could better dictate orders. Wiley proudly toted her through the crew. The crew would never admit it, but they were just as fond of the devilish angel as Ian was, every one of them.

"She's going to be quite the captain one day. Or a tyrant. I'm not entirely sure which."

Ian turned with a beaming grin as Easton moved to stand at his side. He swept in for a kiss of her sweet lips, before ruffling the curly mass of dark hair on their two-year-old Emerson's head. He blinked up at his father with sleepy eyes from where he perched on Easton's hip, content to merely cuddle up to his mother's bosom. Ian would much rather be there himself. But, as the lad would one day come to learn, a captain is made for these early hours.

"Aye, we'll rule the seas with this brood you're cooking up for us." He grinned, pressing a hand over her firm stomach. "Perhaps we'd best start on making more to better fill out our crew."

"Have you ever heard the story about a Captain who bit off more than he could chew?"

"Aye." Ian pulled her close. "He lived happily ever after." Emerson reached for his father, transferring arms to snuggle into the crook of Ian's neck.

"And where is it we are headed off to this morning, my Captain?" Easton smiled softly up at him. He hesitated a moment, catching her eye.

"I've a matter of conscience to attend."

"Oh?" She watched him carefully for a moment. Carefully, Ian pulled the watch from his pocket. Her eyes fell to the watch, gaze heavy with understanding.

"It's time, then," E stated quietly. Ian nodded, the silver watch sending a small reflected gleam across her skin as he gently ran a finger down her jaw.

"Aye, little butterfly. Maizy and Tink are happily settled in my kingdom. We've filled our pockets best we can with the goods from your land. With them business is prosperous enough to last well beyond our grandchildren's lives. I feel that the time has come to make good on my promise to James." His finger gently lifted her chin to better gage her reaction. "I've ignored the decision for as long as I can. Though I fear the journey will be dangerous."

Lantern light fell across her features, causing the warm brown depths in her gaze to sparkle. Delicate fingers pressed over his, closing his hand over the watch. He knew her answer before the words ever parted her lips.

"Then set sail Captain. Your lucky charms will always be at

your side. We'll conquer the dangers together." He pulled her close, pressing a kiss to the top of her fiery head, his heart full and complete.

"Always and forever."

ABOUT THE AUTHOR

Amy Cook- she's just a small town girl with a penchant for creating wild imaginings in the midst of doing the dishes. Fortunately for her, she is able to turn those wild imaginings into the written word of entertaining proportions. When not up to her arms in soap suds, cleaning up the natural disaster that she and her husband call home, or chasing the four miniature wild savages that live within it, she does have a few hobbies. Gardening, drawing, crafting and insane amounts of procrastination for example.

ALSO BY AMY COOK

Rabids Series

Edge of Instinct

Instinct Ascending

Book 3 Coming soon…

———

Fairy Never After Series

The Book of Hook

.

.

Printed in Great Britain
by Amazon